MEGACOSMIC RIFT

MEGACOSMIC RIFT

RIFT

TORTH BOOK FOUR

ABBY GOLDSMITH

Podium

MEGACOSMIC
RIFT

PART ONE

*"The mind readers stole our land, our liberty, our happiness,
our dignity, our deepest secrets, and our dearest loves.
I will gain it all back, piece by bloody piece."*

—A long-forgotten Yeresunsa who rebelled
against the early Torth Empire

CAVE DWELLERS

Evenjos walked the decks of the starship in the guise of a refugee woman, bundled in rags so that no one would get a good look at her. She had not achieved authenticity as one of the albino people. They were aliens to her, chinless and long-necked.

She kept her misshapen attempt at one of their faces buried in scarves and woolens.

She listened. She searched in vain for familiar customs or familiar languages. Where might she find Yeresunsa who were loyal to her? Where were the royals? The nobles?

Families huddled around lanterns or rubbish heaps lit on fire. They peered forlornly into empty urns that held no water.

Everyone aboard this overcrowded starship was a filthy commoner. Worse—they were foreign. They did not pray to the goddess-empress, as they should. Instead, they whispered prayers to a giant.

Evenjos thought she knew their big savior. Ariock. He had rescued her, as well.

This starship was crude, just an empty shell. It was devoid of furnishings or basic plumbing. It was horrifically overcrowded. If Ariock had made this place, as his worshippers believed, well, he hadn't done a very good job. Unimpressive.

As for the refugees . . . Although they traveled in a vessel capable of delivering them to a new world, their minds held no recognition of that fact. They were nothing but ignorant cave dwellers.

Disgusted, Evenjos dropped her corporeal focus. She disintegrated into a cloud of dust, letting the empty rags drop. The nearest aliens gasped in shock. She didn't care.

She flitted overhead, from room to room, seeking anything familiar. She was nearly desperate enough to revisit that sickly monster-child who called himself Thomas to beg him for advice, but that idea made her shudder, even in her incorporeal state. Thomas was dangerous. He reminded her of Unyat.

Or maybe Unyat's clone. Or his clone's clone?

To Evenjos, the past was a disjointed haze. She feared that her memory might be permanently damaged, atrophied after years of . . .

(don't think of it)

She pushed away the darkness.

Really, she ought to kill Thomas. He was a telepath. He knew that she was scared and alone, and he had the same calculating mind as Unyat, with that creepy, all-consuming curiosity. What was to stop him from tricking all these cave dwellers into serving as his minions?

Thomas could outwit anyone. Even Evenjos herself. That made him an obvious threat. He should be eliminated.

Yet . . .

Evenjos had a disturbing sense that she owed the monster-child an enormous debt of gratitude. He had saved her from that . . .

(no, don't think)

That hellish pit of despair.

Memories kept seeping into her subconsciousness, like sludge filling an ancient well. Hadn't Thomas been trapped inside that terrible prison with her? Hadn't he tried to comfort her in there?

He had.

And he had saved her, after so many others had tried and failed.

So Evenjos would allow the scary boy to live. For now. But if he showed the least sign of becoming like Unyat and masterminding a plot against her . . . well, her generosity and tolerance had limits.

An eerie keening caught her attention. It was followed by another ululating wail, and another.

Albino maidens marched in a procession, eight abreast. They dipped in a choreographed dance, trailing gauzy sleeves while they sang in discordant lamentation.

The bereaved maidens preceded an enormous bier, carried by a formidable troop of nussians. Upon that platform lay Ariock.

Evenjos could not detect life sparks in her disincorporated state. But judging by the grubby-looking albinos who sat cross-legged around Ariock, gazing at him with intense focus—and judging by the concern everyone exhibited for him—she suspected he was gravely ill.

Instead of wearing badges to denote their incarnations and magnitudes, these alien Yeresunsa wore identical purple mantles draped over their shoulders and backs. That made their role hard to guess. Were they healers? If so, why were they failing to complete the job? Or were they telekinetics, struggling to keep Ariock's heart beating and his lungs breathing?

Odd.

The procession included more people. There was the grouchy old man who had been present when Evenjos was rescued. There was the maiden with the peg leg and the auburn hair—the one who had spread herself over Ariock's comatose chest with that possessive look.

As the maiden limped alongside his bier, the fury on her face was plain. Evenjos had trouble reading minds in her disincorporated state, but she could see that the girl's rage was directed inward. She resented this funerary procession.

Did she think it was an unnecessary farce?

Evenjos wondered if the girl was right. After all, Ariock must be alive, or he would not be surrounded by healers or whatever type of Yeresunsa these foreigners were.

What was the cause of his illness? A brain injury? Those were nearly impossible to heal. Was he bleeding internally?

His illness looked like power depletion, but that was unthinkable. A well-bred stormbringer of his magnitude would never be so stupid as to deplete his powers.

Evenjos gathered her various dust particles. For an accurate delving, she would need the focus that only her default body could afford her.

She coalesced amid grief-stricken bystanders. Some of the albinos were tapping the bier with their most venerated family heirlooms: urns, platters, hairbrushes, staffs, and candelabras. That seemed to be their way of honoring the dead.

The procession halted and the keening stopped.

Hundreds of people stared at Evenjos in awe. It was plain that none of them had ever seen a goddess. Or an empress.

Evenjos had been beautiful even in her youth, and with centuries of practice, beauty had become second nature to her. Stylized waves of lavender hair cascaded over her bare shoulders. Wings arced from her back, electric magenta lightened by an opalescent sheen. A shimmering white gown and diadem completed the look.

This was the form she felt most accustomed to, and most comfortable in.

"Oh great one!" The gnarled old man bowed. Unlike everyone else, he alone seemed to recognize her as a sovereign.

Disappointingly, he was not a Yeresunsa. His life spark was common.

Despite his rich cape and trimmed white beard, he wore ornate armor. He had to lean on a staff for support. Not a royal, then. A royal would have been able to afford a healer for his crooked leg. The scars on his creased face bespoke a hard life, confirming that he was merely a commoner.

Evenjos frowned as the old man limped into her range. He was a telepath.

Ugh.

Telepaths were the worst sort of commoner. They worshipped science and Unyat. She prepared to slay him. A bolt of lightning should suffice.

"I am your most humble servant." The old man stooped in an obsequious bow. "If you'll have me." He mentally introduced himself as Garrett Dovanack, and he seemed to have a ludicrously high opinion of himself. "Thank you for gracing us with your royal presence."

Evenjos studied Garrett Dovanack with narrow-eyed suspicion. His mind held a lot of knowledge, but not a godlike amount. He contained the wisdom of one lifetime rather than millions. That was acceptable.

And she felt a strange sense of familiarity with Garrett, as if they had shared a prison cell together. She knew him from . . .

(not worth thinking about)

Somewhere. A time and a place that she did not wish to ponder.

"Rise." Evenjos touched Garrett on the shoulder, signaling that she accepted his servitude. Garrett showed proper respect toward her. That was refreshing. Perhaps he was one of the holdouts who secretly worked against the machinations of Unyat?

Besides . . . although she mistrusted telepaths, she had to admit that telepathy would facilitate communication.

The only reason Evenjos was able to speak the alien tongue of these people was because she was a low-level telepath herself. She kept having to mentally decipher their words. If she wanted to make herself understood, she had to mentally translate, which was a chore. She didn't like it.

"Many thanks, mighty one." Garrett straightened awkwardly. "I hate to beg a favor of you, but I'm afraid we have no choice."

Evenjos rolled her eyes. Of course her new manservant wanted a favor. She couldn't guess much about these people, but she could guess why they'd rescued her. Power. It was always that. Everyone wanted the goddess-empress to grant their wishes.

She sighed.

Garrett chose simple words and spoke slowly, aware that Evenjos needed to translate everything. "This large man over here is on the brink of death. He rescued you, and he also rescued all of us, aboard this ship. We cannot afford to lose him. I beg you." He faced Evenjos with a pleading gaze. "Will you heal him?"

Evenjos strutted past Garrett, pretending that she needed time to decide. She wanted a few moments to study Ariock.

Even unconscious, he was a marvel to behold. His sheer size drew attention. He must have no peers.

He was handsome, in a rugged, oversize sort of way.

He would make an interesting lover.

Evenjos held her hands over his chest, ignoring the possessive, poisonous look from the maiden with the peg leg. What a silly girl. How could someone without powers—a cripple, no less—believe, even for a second, that she was worthy of a majestic stormbringer?

Whatever ailment Ariock had would probably be mendable. These cave dwellers were unimpressive. Evenjos sensed the low strength of their life sparks and figured they just needed a mightier healer . . .

She jerked back.

Ariock had no injuries. His life spark ebbed on the verge of death, curled up tight, beyond any hope of a natural recovery.

He was critically depleted.

"He needs more power than I have right now." Evenjos stepped back, puzzled by the ignorance around her. Did these primitive people not grasp the dangers of power depletion?

And what sort of fool was Ariock? He had not seemed suicidal. Could he really have depleted himself by accident?

"Where is your Yeresunsa Order?" Evenjos demanded. She wanted to calm down, but a darkness inside her rose up, grabbing for answers. Why was everything so alien? What if this was all a delusion? What if she was still screaming in . . .

(stop don't think of that)

In darkness and silence?

"What happened to my world?" she asked, unable to suppress the plaintive note in her voice. "Where are my people?"

"You tore your world apart," the peg-leg maiden said. "Remember?"

Evenjos had destroyed a cesspool of a planet, yes. But not her own beautiful world? No. Surely not. She had torn apart a polluted obscenity crawling with mutant telepaths. The universe did not need a blight such as that.

Why was Garrett studying her with pained pity? It made her feel ashamed. A goddess-empress should never be made to feel this way.

So a few innocent aliens had died in her vengeful destruction. So what? Evenjos always acted with the greater good in mind. She had saved the universe from millions of nasty telepathic abominations. Didn't these commoners trust her judgment?

Didn't they know who she was?

"I want to speak to your powerful Yeresunsa," Evenjos demanded. "Who is in charge among you?"

Garrett coughed in a self-effacing way. "That would be me."

An albino woman spoke at the same time. "I am in charge of all the surviving Yeresunsa. My name is Jinishta."

Jinishta and Garrett gave each other defiant glares.

Both of them lacked an intense life spark. They could not be Yeresunsa. Unless . . .

Had Unyat's inhibitor serum become widespread? Had Unyat mass-produced the cursed stuff, the way he had mass-produced his awful mutation Formula?

This situation just got worse and worse. Evenjos transformed her subcutaneous skin layer to diamond-hard strength. She needed to be careful. She knew, from painful experience, that she was not immune to the inhibitor.

As she surveyed the brutes around her, she concluded that none of them deserved to be in charge. No one here had a drop of noble blood or breeding, except maybe for Ariock.

Just how many years had passed while she suffered in the dark? In that . . .

(bad bad don't think about it)

. . . that hellish pit, sealed away from the universe?

A hundred years? Two hundred?

"How long was I . . ." Evenjos hesitated, because she yearned for reassurance that her world still existed, and that her loyal subjects still supported her, and that everything would be all right.

She forced the question out. "How long was I imprisoned?"

The onlookers blinked as though Evenjos was speaking gibberish. She had painstakingly translated her thoughts into their weird alien language, but perhaps her accent was a problem? Well, she was not a translator. She would not attempt the accents that went with this alien tongue.

Garrett spoke in a soothing tone. "We can discuss that later, Your Highness."

"I need to know." A dreadful guess welled up in her chest, forcing her breath to come in short gasps. "Why is everything so different?"

A thousand generations. That was what Ah Jun had predicted.

No. That was impossible. Ah Jun had been a fraud, a false oracle. A dozen generations might have passed. Evenjos could tolerate that. She could readjust. After all, she had ruled her planet for more than two hundred years, remaining young while her parents and brothers were dead from old age. So what if she had outlived her supporters and loyalists? She would gather new ones.

"It doesn't really matter how long your imprisonment lasted," Garrett said in that soothing tone. "What matters is—"

Her snarl of rage caused electricity to snap around her hair and wings. "HOW LONG?"

Garrett cringed. "Twenty-four millennia, give or take."

Evenjos had to pause and mentally translate his answer into a number she could comprehend.

Except it wasn't merely years. It wasn't even mere centuries. It was so much more.

The shock made her lose bodily cohesion. All the ignorance and alien customs made chilling sense. Eons had passed. The universe had changed beyond recognition. Everyone she knew was dead, crumbled to dust and long forgotten.

Unyat had won the war.

And she had lost.

Her crystal throne was gone. Her world was truly gone.

Evenjos reformed her body, but she was not the same person. The weight of millennia pressed upon her back. She could not stop trembling. That disgusting bald girl, Ah Jun, had been a true oracle, after all. The darkness had come to pass.

And Evenjos had, indeed, suffered a thousand generations without rescue. A thousand generations of lonely, cold, deathly silence.

"I'm sorry." Garrett seemed sincere. "I am truly sorry. I wish you hadn't suffered so much. No one deserves that."

Now Evenjos understood why Garrett's manner was so bold in her presence. She had assumed that he was a rural peasant, clumsy with etiquette. The truth was much worse—Garrett had no idea who she was.

He inhabited a future where people were feeble and impoverished and uneducated. What did he know of etiquette? He was a brute of this era.

Evenjos swallowed, nauseated by how many obstacles she would have to overcome. Maybe she was better off dead.

Except . . . could she die?

Evenjos held up her hand, manipulating molecules until her hand became transparent and glassy. She could disintegrate into dust, or harden herself into titanium, or transform into anything she was capable of drawing or sculpting. Her reconstituted body seemed to come with augmented shapeshifting powers.

Before her imprisonment, Evenjos had been limited in scope, vulnerable to weapons and poisons. That was how they'd trapped her. Elome had made love to her . . . and the next thing she knew . . .

Evenjos shuddered and shoved away that awful memory. She had been a fool. Too trusting.

Now she could eat nuclear bombs while they exploded.

She could transform her strange new body into anything. Anything at all. The price for this power had been far too steep, so she didn't feel particularly grateful, yet the price was paid in full. Not much could threaten her anymore.

"Please." The peg-leg maiden—Evenjos's mind hinted that she had a name, Vy—clasped her hands in desperation. "I'll do anything you want if you help him. Just—please? Help him?"

Evenjos considered the situation. Considered Ariock.

Few weapons could harm her. But after wrecking the planet, Evenjos had felt frightfully weak. She had become so weak, even bodily cogency had been a struggle.

She shuddered to think what might have happened if she had failed to locate this starship. She might have dissipated forever.

Power depletion was a risk for her. She could probably still die that way.

Evenjos pursed her lips. If she donated all her strength to Ariock . . .

The problem was, she was still recovering from her own near depletion. To revive Ariock right now would likely entail depletion for her—and death.

Ariock did seem nice. He had the respect of his people and the love of his friends. But she didn't really know him. The giant might turn into a rival for her throne, or an unruly lover. Evenjos had misjudged men in the past. One such mistake had led directly to . . .

(darkness emptiness loneliness)

To her imprisonment.

"Ariock is worth taking a risk for." Garrett sounded properly subservient, but then he kept talking. "Your Highness, Ariock is a prince among men. We absolutely need him. If you can . . ." He trailed off, because he must have detected her growing fury.

Evenjos took a deep breath and regained her composure.

Time travel was supposed to be impossible, yet here she was, a visitor to the distant future. Maybe she could reestablish herself as the goddess-empress and change things for the better.

She assessed the bystanders. How much of her current weakness did she dare confess in front of strangers?

They seemed harmless. But then, telepaths used to seem harmless to her. It was safer not to trust anyone.

Evenjos contemplated Ariock again. It was true that she owed him a debt of gratitude. That was undeniable. When Ariock had resurrected her . . . when he had held her in his massive arms, with her naked and trembling . . .

She had felt safe.

She wanted to feel that way again.

Evenjos trailed her hand down Ariock's forehead and nose, touching his lips and scruffy chin, and her wings flexed. She did want to get to know this royal messiah stormbringer titan. Ariock did seem interesting. He might be worth talking to.

At least he wasn't a telepath.

"Very well." Evenjos heaved a sigh to show how great a favor these people were asking. No doubt they would pester her with more wheedling requests. That was the nature of commoners. "I will revive him. You have my word."

CHAPTER 2
A FRIGHTENED SNAKE

Vy watched Evenjos, full of hope.

The idea of losing Ariock felt like an amputation, similar to losing her leg, but that was not the only reason she had demanded that the Yeresunsa do all they could to keep his body alive. The starship population needed a hero. Food rations were low. Water was so hard to find; people had resorted to mopping up frost melt. They'd wrung out rags into urns and jugs, but it wasn't enough to quench the thirst of twelve million refugees. People were getting drunk on mushroom ale.

And they were getting angry. They whispered insinuations about anyone who was in charge, looking for someone to blame.

Garrett had not yet recovered his powers. Nor had Jinishta. Ironically, they seemed to feel even more powerless than Vy. They had not protested when the Alashani councilors insisted that Ariock be "honored" with a funerary procession.

Vy had argued.

It was an insult to Ariock, to treat him like he was already dead. He didn't deserve that. But nobody cared what she said.

Thomas, too, remained powerless, a virtual prisoner in the command center. He looked too much like a Torth to risk showing himself in public.

Jinishta kept assuring refugees that everything would be fine, but the haggard anxiety in her eyes told a different story. She understood that her lovely cave cities were gone forever. If Thomas had a destination in mind, he had not announced it. Rumors of being stranded in space were beginning to spread throughout the general population.

So they all needed Ariock to wake up. They needed hope. And sustenance. And safety.

"I require three days," Evenjos said in her exotic accent. "On the third day, I shall revive him. Until then, you must use your powers to keep his body alive."

The exhausted healers looked pained. No doubt they wanted to please Evenjos, their Lady of Sorrow, yet their powers were draining.

Vy could not contain her alarm. "Three days!?"

That was far too long. Yesterday five healers had been necessary. Today it was nine. In three days, Ariock might require twenty or thirty of them in order to keep breathing.

What if one healer needed to take a break? What then?

"Someone like Ariock requires a lot of power in order to overcome depletion." Evenjos sounded cool and unconcerned. "Obviously he may die at any moment. That is a danger." Her tone became disapproving. "He should not have entered this state in the first place."

"Ah, Your Highness." Garrett clasped his hands, wringing them in apparent concern. "Is there any way we can speed up your process? Please tell me what you need. You can ask anything of me. Anything at all."

Vy studied Garrett surreptitiously from the corner of one eye. She had not known him for long, but until now, she had not judged Garrett capable of humility. He reminded her of the maverick surgeon at the hospital where she used to work.

"Do you have some other great Yeresunsa hidden somewhere?" Evenjos asked. "At their full strength?"

Garrett looked frustrated. "I should be at my full strength in another couple of days. I . . ." He muttered, as if ashamed, "I let myself get hit by the inhibitor serum."

Evenjos studied him. "You are a Yeresunsa?" Her gaze became surprised, as if a toy poodle had stood on its hind legs and offered to act as her butler. "A stormbringer?"

"Yep. I'm powerful." Garrett sounded defensive.

The Lady of Sorrow, or whatever she was, shimmered with unearthly light. She could probably help Ariock right now. Couldn't she at least try?

"Ariock saved you from that prison." Vy felt a thrill of fear, but this was too important to let fear stop her from challenging the supposed goddess. "He took huge risks to set you free. Why do you refuse to do the same for him?"

Evenjos stared regally at Vy. They faced each other next to Ariock's gigantic body while the albino healers continued to do their best to keep him alive.

"He built this ship in order to save us," Jinishta said.

Another person spoke up. "He kept healing people. Even when he should have stopped."

"He protected us all."

"We owe our lives to him."

Evenjos seemed troubled by all the critical gazes aimed her way. "Don't the people of your time know anything at all?" Her wings drooped. She seemed defeated. "Every child should know the consequences of depletion. I should not have to explain this. I was an empress, not a schoolteacher."

She fell silent. But Garrett, Jinishta, and everyone else gave her expectant looks of inquiry.

"A weaker Yeresunsa cannot revive a greater," Evenjos said, exasperated. "I am temporarily weakened." She gestured to herself. "I must recover my strength before I dare attempt to revive him. Is that not obvious?"

"Uh." Garrett looked politely servile. "Would you please teach me why, Your Eminence? I am eager to learn."

"Do you not know the effect of combined spheres?" Evenjos made a throat-clearing sound of disgust. "If you truly are a Yeresunsa . . . well, who taught you to use your powers?" She looked ready to hunt down his teacher and give them a lecture.

"I taught myself," Garrett said.

As Evenjos studied him, perhaps reading his mind, her disgust turned to pity. "Oh my." Her wings drooped more. "You are a yerud. An untrained wild thing."

Garrett looked offended. "I do all right."

She stared at him.

"Your Eminence," he added quickly.

"An untrained yerud is a danger to himself and others," Evenjos said. "But I suppose, in this era, it is . . ." She rubbed her finger and thumb together, like a foreigner trying to conjure the right word. ". . . normal." She said it with extreme distaste.

Vy was uncomfortably aware of her own lack of powers. She was not just temporarily disabled, like Garrett and Jinishta. If people dismissed her as an inconsequential nobody, well, it was true.

Even so, Vy could not bring herself to say "Your Grace" or fawn all over Evenjos.

"Help us to understand." Vy put her hands on her hips. "What happens if you try to revive Ariock right now?"

"Well, that depends on how large a sphere Ariock normally has." Evenjos was condescending, as if speaking to a child. "And my own current raw strength, in relation." A new thought seemed to occur to her. "It may help if Ariock has ever had a veracity-crystal reading."

"A what?" Garrett sounded lost.

Evenjos loosened her bodily cohesion. It was just a flicker, as if she was overcome by annoyance. "A veracity crystal," she said, speaking with deliberate slowness. "It measures raw strength in a Yeresunsa."

She held out her hand. A cloud of dust spun off her palm, which then morphed into a simulacrum of a glowing crystal.

"Um." Jinishta sounded hesitant in the presence of her deity. "Pardon, Great Lady, but did you not say that you need to conserve your powers?"

Evenjos rolled her eyes. "I will not respond to every basic question."

Jinishta folded her arms, no-nonsense, and Vy was glad to not be the only person who refused to turn into a cringing mess. "How much raw power does shapeshifting require?"

Evenjos heaved a put-upon sigh. "Shapeshifting is a somatic power. Like telepathy. Or prophecy."

"You mean . . ." Garrett looked fascinated. "It's effortless? You do it automatically?"

"More or less." Evenjos held out a slender arm, admiring her shapely self. "It's a sixth-magnitude ability, so it does require some forethought and planning. But it does not drain me. I can do this forever and feel no ill effects."

Even Jinishta looked interested. The healers around Ariock dared not stop what they were doing, but judging by their frustrated looks, they wanted to eavesdrop.

"What does sixth magnitude mean?" Garrett asked.

Evenjos gave him a look of impatience. "Every schoolchild knows . . ." She seemed to give up. "Let us get back to the question of veracity crystals."

Her fake crystal had drifted into dust. It solidified as Evenjos focused again, and it glowed with white light.

"The nature of a veracity crystal," Evenjos said, "is that it glows when in the presence of a Yeresunsa core. It breaks if it surpasses its limit, which is related to its size and its purity."

The fake crystal flashed brilliant white, then disintegrated into sparkles, which faded away.

"For instance, a tiny crystal"—Evenjos formed a speck above one slender finger, like a diamond—"can measure lesser Yeresunsa. They are said to have a . . ." She searched for the word. ". . . a less than one-ounce capacity."

The fake diamond flashed white, then exploded into sparkles that faded away.

"Such a crystal would break when in my presence," Evenjos explained. "I have a capacity that is measured in tonnage, not ounces."

Vy exchanged looks with Jinishta. They both remembered the humongous power crystal that had broken when Ariock approached it.

"I believe I know what you are talking about," Jinishta said. "Our crystal was larger than two nussians." She threw her arms wide, trying to demonstrate. "And it broke when Ariock was about fifty paces away."

Evenjos gazed at Jinishta with a skeptical expression.

What was her problem? The winged Lady had already seen proof that Ariock was powerful. Why did she need a crystal reading? She had seen Ariock turn into a colossus. She had seen him shield entire cities from nuclear explosions, throw the Stratower, build this starship, and mass-teleport millions of people. Plus, hadn't he reforged Evenjos's body for her?

"What does it mean?" Vy asked.

"Nothing, I'm sure." Evenjos seemed to gather her dust particles and swell with confidence. "Nobody is more powerful than me. That is why I am the goddess-empress. Your crystal reading for Ariock was likely inaccurate."

Now Garrett looked troubled. "Ah, pardon me, Your Eminence. But what if Ariock is more powerful than you?"

Evenjos looked amused.

"What happens if he's more powerful than you and you try to revive him?" Garrett pressed.

Evenjos laughed. Clearly, she thought such a possibility absurd, but she answered with an eye roll. "Then we would both die. And this ship would become nothing more than a floating tomb."

Garrett's face drained of color.

"Do not fear," Evenjos assured him. "I have never met my equal in power."

"What if he is?" Garrett insisted.

"He is not." Evenjos sounded dismissive.

As she observed the worried faces around her, she grew serious. "This is why ultrapowerful Yeresunsa should never overextend themselves. We do not easily recover from depletion. Personally, I never overextend myself, because there is no one powerful enough to revive me." She glanced at Ariock's unconscious form. "The fact that he is in this state does not speak well for his intelligence."

"He's just inexperienced," Garrett said defensively.

"Really." Evenjos sounded unenthused. "So he is another self-taught yerud?"

Garrett ignored that. "Just in case he's more powerful than you expect, are there any precautions we can take to make sure it works and you both survive?"

Evenjos arched one delicate eyebrow.

"Can you use help from other Yeresunsa?" Garrett asked. "Like me?"

"This really isn't necessary," Evenjos said.

"I would like to help." Garrett sounded almost panicky. "In fact, I insist. I think we should bring in as many Yeresunsa as possible."

Evenjos studied him, and Vy did the same. Did Ariock's great-grandfather know something the rest of them did not?

"I'm really afraid that Ariock will be more powerful than you expect." Garrett sounded bashful. "I'm sorry, Your Grace. But I would rather you be safe."

"Very well." Evenjos sounded bored. "If it makes you feel better, I will add other Yeresunsa to my sphere. But we must all be at our full strength. That is vital. Tell anyone who plans to participate that they must refrain from using their powers."

Garrett bowed his head. "Thank you, Your Highness."

Evenjos looked as if she wanted to say more. When she spoke, she seemed less haughty. She almost sounded vulnerable. "Did I destroy a world you cared about?"

Vy did not feel any warmth toward the monster who had slaughtered an entire planet. On the other hand . . . if this monster, or angel, or whatever she was, revived Ariock . . . well, that act would redeem her.

"Why did you resurrect me?" Evenjos asked. "Why do you want me here?"

"There is a war coming," Garrett said.

Vy studied him, wondering if he was stating a fact or not.

"The Torth Empire declared war on us." Garrett flapped his hand dismissively, as if that were no big deal. "And they are your enemies, too, Your Eminence. That's why you're here. We humbly invite you to join us in our fight against them."

On the bier, Ariock lay motionless and pallid. He was in no condition for fighting.

"What is the Torth Empire?" Evenjos asked in her regal manner. She looked from Garrett to Vy, frowning.

She's not a very competent mind reader, Vy realized.

Garrett would not have asked such a basic question. Thomas rarely asked any questions at all. In contrast, Evenjos barely managed to speak the slave tongue. She sounded like a foreigner who was working toward fluency but not quite there yet.

"The Torth are mind readers," Garrett explained. "Telepaths. You don't need to worry about them right now, Your Highness." He gave her an unctuous smile. "It'll be a week or two before they can find us."

"But . . ." Evenjos looked mystified. "I destroyed them."

Garrett's smile lost all traces of good humor.

"I destroyed their world," Evenjos said, as if explaining obvious facts to a child.

Vy studied the unearthly Lady, with her shimmering wings, and wondered just how limited her scope of knowledge was. Did she believe the galactic empire only encompassed one polluted planet?

"No, Your Eminence," Garrett said sadly. "The Torth own everything in the known universe. They inhabit millions of worlds, and they number in the trillions. They are a spreading cancer that gobbles up resources and enslaves the innocent."

Evenjos's eyes went wide with horrified understanding.

"They need to be stopped." Garrett banged his fist into his open palm for emphasis. His subservience was gone all of a sudden, forgotten in his impassioned speech. "That's why you're here," he thundered. "That's why *I'm* here. That's why we need Ariock."

Evenjos lost her regal bearing. Even her hair and wings drained of color.

Garrett was on a roll, oblivious to her reaction. "You helped me defeat some Torth many years ago, when I was suffering in one of their worst prisons. You loaned me your power, and together, we vaporized a thousand Torth." He bowed to Evenjos. "I owe you my life. You're the reason Ariock was able to be born. You saved me and at least a thousand slaves, and you've inspired countless—"

He interrupted himself, seeing that Evenjos was trembling. "I'm sorry, Your Highness." He sounded mortified. "I didn't mean to remind you of that time."

Evenjos backed away, blinking back tears.

"Let's not speak of the past." Garrett spoke as if soothing a frightened little girl. "You're safe here. I promise. I won't let them imprison you again."

"Trillions." Evenjos emitted that word in a frightened squawk. "All Formula freaks? They've taken over the galaxy? I . . . I . . ."

"You are safe," Garrett said. "The Torth can't get to you here."

"They got to me before." A tear ran down Evenjos's colorless cheek.

"You have friends among us," Garrett said kindly. "It will be different this time. I promise."

"I . . ." Evenjos's wings and body collapsed into sparkling powder. "I need to think."

She became dust and rushed away, flying over people in a serpentine motion. She whipped around a corner and was gone.

Vy stared at where the dust had vanished. Evenjos was so powerful she seemed immortal, yet she was afraid to stick around and hold a conversation?

This was the ally that Thomas had pinned all his hopes on. Garrett had spent a lifetime searching for the Lady of Sorrow. Was this all she was—a frightened, self-absorbed snake with the power to destroy worlds?

A gnarled hand clapped Vy on the shoulder.

"Don't judge her too harshly," Garrett said. "She might have a touch of PTSD after suffering twenty-four thousand years of torment. I'm sure she just needs some adjustment time."

Vy looked at Ariock's great-grandfather and wondered, not for the first time, what his story was. Why had he abandoned the Dovanack family when Ariock was just a baby? What had prompted him to reemerge and begin to help Ariock?

Jinishta looked worried. "We need her."

"I know." Garrett sounded patient. "Don't worry. I think she'll help us."

Vy wished she could dive into Garrett's mind just to learn what made him so confident. He seemed to be playing chess with living pawns, and he wasn't letting anyone else in on the game. "How can you be sure?"

"It's not like she has anywhere better to go." Garrett glanced toward the comatose form of Ariock, and he almost looked amused. "Or anyone better to go to."

CHAPTER 3

INCOGNITO

Thomas made one last adjustment to the autopilot interface. "You'll be all right at the helm?" he asked Varktezo.

"Of course!" The adolescent ummin exuded confidence. "I remember everything."

Thomas surveyed the glowing workstations he'd grown so familiar with. In addition to learning how to navigate the control center of a colony-class starship, he had absorbed the life history of every adolescent ummin in this room. He had taught this crew how to read relevant glyphs and how to judge certain sliders and readouts.

Nothing had fallen apart during his naps.

As long as the crew stuck to their respective roles and did not experiment with things they did not understand, he figured they could maintain the ship's life support for many hours.

"We'll be fine, Teacher," Varktezo said. "How long will you be gone, anyway?"

Thomas had no idea what the revival of Ariock would entail. "Probably no longer than a nap. I'll be back as soon as I can."

He floated toward the escort of nussians awaiting him.

Weptolyso was impatient, unfolding an oversize woolen blanket. "This will keep you safe." He proceeded to cover Thomas and the hoverchair completely, obscuring his humanoid shape by bunching and tenting the blanket. The hoverchair was likewise hidden, as the huge blanket cascaded all the way to the floor.

Thomas approved. The blanket could be concealing an exotic alien rather than a boy in a hoverchair. The escort of ten thorny nussians might arouse suspicion, but Thomas was not suicidal enough to risk floating through crowds without bodyguards. He could defend himself . . . but lashing out with pain seizures and wildfire would cause untenable complications. The last thing Thomas wanted was twelve million refugees mobbing up against one lone *rekveh*.

Besides, he was supposed to be at his full strength in order to help Ariock.

All the Yeresunsa warriors aboard the starship were now at their full strength, waiting for Evenjos to tell them what to do. They had spent three days doing practically nothing. They were unhappy about that—everyone was unhappy, thirsty and hungry and angry—but they had dutifully conserved their powers.

"Oh wait!" Varktezo dived behind a workstation and emerged with Thomas's NAI-12 briefcase. "Just in case you're not back in time for your dose."

"Thanks." Thomas's next injection was due in eighty-five minutes. He was impressed that Varktezo remembered. His ummin assistant had plenty of responsibilities weighing on his mind.

Varktezo lifted the blanket and loaded the briefcase into the cargo compartment of the hoverchair.

Privately, sometimes, Thomas wondered if the hassle of NAI-12 was worth the
few extra months of life it granted him. If he died tomorrow instead of three months
from now, would anyone care? Varktezo could muddle through the starship controls, with input from Garrett. Many people would feel safer with one less *rekveh*
aboard the starship.

But there was so much left to learn.

Thomas wanted to soak up Garrett's secrets, as well as everything Evenjos
knew. He wanted to learn the prophecies of Ah Jun. He was going to die young, and
he accepted that. But surely he could find a way to learn just a few more interesting
secrets?

"Ready?" Weptolyso rumbled.

"Ready." Thomas felt absurd, hidden under a blanket like a child playing at
being a ghost.

"Good luck, Teacher!" That was Varktezo's voice. "You can see without using
your eyes, right?"

That was, of course, the case.

Thomas dipped into the minds of nearby nussians and created an accurate spa-
tial map. All he could see with his own eyes was woolly darkness. Peering through
nussian eyes was like wearing strange lenses. Their vantage points were higher than
he was used to. They could see traces of infrared. The trade-off was lower contrast
in terms of light and shadow.

Thomas followed Weptolyso into the corridor, easily avoiding the bodyguards
who flanked him. He slowed when they slowed. He sped up when they did.

"How can the *rekveh* see through that blanket?" one of the nussians rumbled in
a low tone, their version of a whisper.

"He is reading our minds." That came from another unnerved nussian.

"Spooky," another said.

Thomas wasn't sure what made him more nervous: Evenjos or angry mobs. He
sensed that these nussians resented acting as his bodyguards. The only reason they
were here was because they respected Weptolyso.

"Hush." Weptolyso glared at the cohort. "Never mind how he is navigating. He
is an ally. He is going to help bring back the Son of Storms."

The nussians grumbled. None of them really knew the so-called Son of Storms,
but they were all too familiar with the critical shortages of food and water. They
understood that the ship needed a miracle worker. Otherwise riots would break out
and a lot of people would kill each other.

"Keep quiet." Weptolyso loped into an overcrowded thoroughfare. "Try to remember who saved you."

The cohort assumed that Weptolyso was referring to their savior, the Son of Storms.
Only Thomas picked up the truth: it was an oblique reference to Thomas himself.

Weptolyso remembered that Garrett, Evenjos, and even Ariock had seemed ready
to flee the Torth Homeworld and leave millions of people to die. Thomas was the one
who had suggested a planetary evacuation. Thomas was the one who had architected
this starship. Without it, Weptolyso knew, all these refugees would be dead.

And before all that? When Ariock was hanging helpless from a metal cross,

Thomas was the one who had come to his rescue. Thomas had paved the way for Weptolyso, Kessa, and others to escape the dreariness of enslavement.

Weptolyso did not want to feel indebted to a mind reader who used to own slaves. Internally, he had played up Ariock's heroic deeds while downplaying everything Thomas did.

But his loved one, Yuey, was alive thanks to this space ark. Even her parents were alive. So Weptolyso had reevaluated the gratitude he owed. Privately, he found that he respected Thomas even more than he respected the Son of Storms.

That was why he had volunteered to personally escort Thomas through the overcrowded decks.

Thomas withdrew from Weptolyso's mind. He felt a little stunned, almost embarrassed. It was nice to be acknowledged. At the same time, he wasn't sure he wanted fervent gratitude from a former slave. It felt a little too close to worship.

He didn't want to feel as authoritarian as a Torth. Not ever again.

Even the respect from his ummin crew made him wary. What had he done to earn it? The supergenius mutation was just something he'd been born with. Had Kessa been born with such an advantage, people would respect her in the exact same way. Probably even more so.

Thomas wanted to earn respect the way she did.

The nussians trooped across the deck, from one vast sector to the next. Camped-out onlookers blocked every window view of space. Weptolyso led Thomas and his escort past rationing queues and spiritual advisers who offered solace to crowds.

Thomas sensed ambient frustration. He overheard violent thoughts as well as reassurances. Refugees told each other they had heard Kessa the Wise speak. She said they were traveling to a better world.

This starship could have been its own version of a somewhat better world, with leafy boulevards, aquaponic lounges, and privacy pods. Instead, it was a barren, industrial slave zone. There hadn't been enough time to finish it.

Thomas floated past a line of happily chatting aliens. He caught hints of what they were waiting for, and he glided to a stop.

Cherise?

Judging from nearby memories, these aliens were taking lessons from Cherise. She was applying the English alphabet to the slave tongue, giving them literacy.

And it seemed she had a knack for teaching. She made the lessons fun and relevant. She lost her shyness when she realized how much she was improving other people's lives.

Amazing.

Literacy would not quite put nontelepaths on par with the Megacosm. But it was a huge step toward bridging the communication advantage Torth had over slaves. It opened up a lot of possibilities.

Part of him yearned to glimpse Cherise with his own eyes. To speak with her.

Which was ridiculous. On Earth, Cherise's supportive presence—her worship, really—had helped Thomas cope with his abandonment issues. But now he understood how unhealthy their friendship had been. He had been a sage and she had been his sidekick. It had been very similar to the unequal relationship between Torth and slaves.

Why did he still feel like he needed Cherise? Why was he tormented by fruitless wishes for her forgiveness?

Cherise might even feel pressured to forgive him if she saw him. That would only pave the way for her to go back to living in his shadow. Then they would both regress. She would shrivel, returning to her self-hatred, and Thomas would start acting superior and egomaniacal again.

Enough of that.

Cherise was better off with Flen—or, really, with anyone who wasn't a telepath. She needed the freedom to develop her own counsel and wisdom. She had outgrown Thomas. What she needed him to do was to leave her alone.

Weptolyso backtracked to see why the blanketed hoverchair had stopped moving.

Thomas glided forward, woolen corners dragging along the floor.

They floated across a few more decks, up a ramp, and through more crowds. They finally arrived at a formidable wall of nussians.

"It is Weptolyso," several of the nussians told each other.

The central guards shuffled aside, opening an aisle into a large room that was crowded with Yeresunsa. Floor-to-ceiling windows displayed real-time views of outer space.

"Thank you for continuing to stand guard," Weptolyso said, moving past the nussians. His own cohort broke apart. Thomas floated onward alone, following Weptolyso.

A sense of potential thrummed inside him. There was a lot of power in this room. It pinged his Yeresunsa sense.

Thomas expanded his awareness. He could not identify individual life sparks. It was all one throbbing blaze of power.

Hundreds of albinos turned to study the floating blanket. Thomas saw them without seeing them. Their white hair was tightly curled, their shoulders draped in purple. He recognized Orla, Flen, Haz, and many others.

Weptolyso yanked the blanket away. "I have brought Thomas Hill," he announced in his gravelly voice.

Thomas tried to look as harmless as possible. His thin blondish hair was mussed, and that probably helped. He was small and hunched.

Unfortunately, his slight shape allowed everyone to see the garish hoverchair. Its backrest and armrests glittered with metallic red accents. The thing must have belonged to a Crimson Rank, or maybe to a Torth who'd idolized the military ranks. Not a good look.

"Excellent." Garrett approached, his cloak wrapped across his chest and over his shoulders in imitation of a Yeresunsa mantle. "Thank you, Weptolyso. Now we're all assembled."

Ariock lay inert on a raised dais on the far side of the room. He was draped in blankets and surrounded by flickering candelabras. Dozens of Yeresunsa healers frowned around him.

Jinishta stepped away from the dais. "When will the Lady of Sorrow appear? Where is she?"

"I'm sure she will show up soon." Garrett leaned on his silver staff.

Thomas sensed unspoken tension, like an ultraconcentrated version of the tensions throughout the starship's population. Some of these Yeresunsa warriors had a problem with the command to conserve their powers. They would rather heal refugees who obviously needed help instead of waiting for a nebulous shapeshifter who might or might not show up in order to save a messiah who no longer seemed quite so dependably miraculous.

Jinishta and Garrett had persuaded everyone that Ariock, once revived, would magically produce water and food aplenty. According to them, this was not a matter of valuing the needs of one man above the needs of millions. This was about helping everyone.

At least, that was what Garrett—a *rekveh*—said. And Jinishta, who seemed uncommonly tolerant of *rekvehs* these days, supported him.

Thomas grimaced, because he half agreed with the pragmatism on the other side of the argument. Had he been clueless about the larger picture . . . and if Ariock wasn't a friend of his . . . well, then he would also hesitate to favor a comatose warrior over people who were dying from want. Ariock had very little chance of making a full recovery. Yet he was tying up all the Yeresunsa power they had aboard this ship.

Heads turned and gasps resounded throughout the room as a sinuous cloud of glittering dust snaked through the air.

"Ah. Here she is." Garrett sounded as if he'd never doubted that Evenjos would show up.

The dust poured into a feminine shape.

Evenjos, shining and regal, solidified near Garrett. She surveyed the room with purple eyes that matched her purple hair. "These are your most powerful Yeresunsa?"

"Yes, Your Eminence," Garrett said.

"Hmm." Evenjos sounded disappointed.

Thomas stretched his awareness toward Evenjos, curious about her life spark. He detected something like a live wire. The power in the room seemed overwhelming, impossible to differentiate or individualize. Perhaps his sphere of influence was engulfed within hers and others?

Evenjos scrutinized Garrett, and her contempt faded slightly. "You are a stormbringer," she said with mild surprise.

"Yes, Your Eminence." Garrett bowed his head as if bashful.

What a faker. If Evenjos bought his humble act, even for a second, then she must be a very handicapped mind reader indeed.

"Hmm." Evenjos turned a critical gaze toward Thomas. "And his power is not trivial. I suppose . . ." She interrupted herself as Thomas floated forward. "Halt!"

Thomas stopped.

"Do not come near me!" Evenjos commanded him.

Thomas wasn't going to fake subservience, but he showed his empty hands, heart pounding. "I'm on your side. I'm just here to help revive Ariock."

"Stay out of my range." Her voice trembled.

"Yeah, same here." Garrett sounded vindicated. He gave Thomas a stare that echoed the regality of Evenjos. "Stay out of my range."

Thomas tapped his fingers on the armrests. He had sipped a tiny amount of their knowledge, yet he craved so much more. He would shave off the remainder of his short life-span if he could bask in Evenjos's treasure trove of knowledge. He wanted to defy her.

Well, he would figure out a loophole. Or he would persuade her and Garrett. He just needed a bit of time.

He settled back in his hoverchair. "No problem."

Excitement filled the air like exclamation points. Thomas could taste it. He felt some himself. Ariock had been unconscious for four days. Everyone on this starship needed his power for some reason or other.

"Are we ready?" Garrett asked. Now that the moment was nigh, he seemed to have trouble hiding his eagerness.

"Yes." Evenjos stepped onto the dais with swanlike grace.

"What do we do?" Garrett asked.

Evenjos stood behind Ariock's head, serene. "It is simple." She held her hands out to either side, like a mother expecting her children to grab on. "Anyone who wishes to join me will combine their spheres with mine. And then we will combine with Ariock."

CHAPTER 4

TO REKINDLE A STAR

Vy had not been invited into this auditorium-like room, let alone near the dais with Evenjos. Yet no one asked her to leave.

She stood against a view of stars in deep space, arms folded. No one looked at her. The warriors must have gotten used to her ineffectual presence; Vy had hardly left Ariock's side while he lay unconscious.

During the last four days, she had ignored couriers who asked for her help in tending to patients. When some adolescents from Duin had begged her to teach technical skills, she had declined. She was not helping Cherise teach literacy, either.

As a nurse, Vy knew that she could make minor differences for the sick and injured. Instead . . .

Well, she had feared that if she left Ariock's side, the Yeresunsa healers would quit.

They marginally trusted Vy as an alleged "angel from paradise." They grudgingly obeyed Jinishta, but they did not respect anyone else. Certainly not Garrett.

To make matters worse, rumors kept getting exaggerated. People whispered that the messiah had accidentally brought on all the calamities they had suffered. People whispered that they were trapped inside a gigantic slave zone under the control of one sadistic, ultrasmart Torth.

People were homeless and scared, and their messianic prophecies said nothing about any of this.

So Vy stood in the out-of-the-way alcove and waited. She was keen to see Ariock back on his feet and, well, back to being his awesome self.

"Take my hands," Evenjos commanded.

Thomas steered his hoverchair toward her. "How does combining spheres work? It requires touch?"

"It has to be consensual." Evenjos eyed him the way a gazelle might watch an approaching lion. "Come no closer."

Thomas floated to a frustrated stop.

"Let me try this." Evenjos extended one hand toward him, and her arm transformed into glittering dust.

It unfurled like a dust tentacle with a feminine hand on the end. Garrett watched as if intrigued by the possibilities of disembodied fingers.

Evenjos made a frustrated sound. "No." Her ropy arm plumed back to a normal length. "I cannot concentrate properly while I am doing that." She sounded profoundly disappointed.

"I'll try not to scan your mind," Thomas offered. "I just want to help revive Ariock."

Evenjos pouted.

"What about the rest of us, Great Lady?" Jinishta asked. "Shall we join hands?"

"The rest of you will not be needed," Evenjos said to the crowded room. "Your power is too weak to matter."

If that insult had come from anyone else, the warriors would have flown into a violent rage. They only bristled. Jinishta balled her fists and looked helpless. Vy could empathize with that feeling.

"But I want to help!" Orla whined.

"We conserved our power for three days," someone else said angrily. "Was that for nothing?"

"Uh, forgive me, Your Highness, but . . ." Garrett hesitated. "Would you mind giving us a short explanation of how this works?"

"Please?" Thomas added.

Vy stared at him. Thomas rarely used entreaties. That was his version of pleading.

Evenjos looked flustered. "I cannot believe this." She gave Thomas a particularly quizzical look. "Have you never combined your sphere with another's?"

"If you'd rather not explain it," Thomas said, "you could just let me enter your range for a second."

"Stay back, monster!" Her eyes blazed. "When I allow you into my presence, you will not read my mind. You will only be there to rekindle Ariock's sphere. You will not stay within my range a moment longer than it takes."

Thomas watched Evenjos with wary curiosity.

Garrett bowed his head. "We humbly beg you to teach us."

After a moment's consideration, Evenjos held out an empty palm. "Very well. Have one of your serving staff fetch me a drawing implement. This will be easier to explain visually."

Garrett looked flummoxed, searching the room as if hoping to locate a stick of chalk.

"Here." Vy limped to the shrine of gifts people had donated to the messiah. The Alashani used chalk for marking garments and pottery, and she remembered seeing a corkwood box full of colored pieces.

She opened the box for Evenjos.

The winged Lady selected a white piece of chalk without thanking Vy, then turned to the dark wall behind the dais.

"These are people," Evenjos said, drawing random dots. She circled each dot with hasty messiness. "Here are their spheres of influence."

The Alashani warriors moved closer, interested. A few of them were so curious, they even deigned to stand within range of Thomas or Garrett.

"Some Yeresunsa engulf everyone nearby within their sphere of influence." Evenjos drew a gigantic circle around all the other circled dots. "Here is Ariock." She poked a dot in the center. "This is his core body."

Vy guessed the huge circle might be an accurate representation of the size of Ariock's sphere of influence, compared to others'.

"He drained his powers to depletion." Evenjos drew harsh lines, like spokes, that bled from the gigantic circle to the dot of a body. "Power normally regenerates on its own. The problem, in this case, is that he drained himself beyond a healthy point." She scribbled an asterisk over the dot. "Now he is trapped here. He is too weak to recover on his own."

"His power needs to be rekindled?" Garrett said, as if to make sure that he got the terminology right.

Evenjos gave him a barely tolerant look. "Correct." She turned back to the wall drawing. "Let us say that a lesser Yeresunsa is stupid enough to try to rekindle him." She sketched a medium-size circle with a dot at its center, to represent the subject. "All of this"—she waved her arm vigorously at the gigantic circle—"is a crater waiting to be filled. The raw power of the lesser Yeresunsa is insufficient to fill it." She indicated the lesser circle, showing that it was quite a bit smaller than the gigantic circle. "So what happens if he tries?"

Evenjos scrawled power-draining spokes to show the draining of the lesser circle.

"The empty crater of this great Yeresunsa sucks away all of the lesser's power, and more. He is instantly depleted past the point of death." Evenjos hacked chalk *x*'s over both dots. "And since he led the link, he drags his cohort—Ariock, in this case—into death with him."

Vy felt a chill, staring at those crude scribbles. Evenjos spoke casually about a process that could get people killed.

Thomas looked thoughtful. "That's the principle of riven moduli, in a cosmological context."

Evenjos thinned her lips, clearly unwilling to ask for clarification.

"Can you say that in plain language, boy?" Garrett said.

"The energy to create a star needs to be twice as great as its peak potential," Thomas said. "Theoretically due to the counterbalance of dark energy."

"Are you saying we need *twice* his peak power?" Garrett sounded aghast.

"That would be ideal," Evenjos said.

"Not necessarily," Thomas said. "We would need that much for him to wake up at full power, but we should be able to rekindle him with less than that. We just need at least as much power as Ariock has at his peak."

"Oh, that's all?" Garrett was sarcastic, and Vy commiserated. Who knew how strong Ariock was at his peak?

And they had to top that. Anything short would mean his death. And theirs.

"I am sure I have twice his power," Evenjos said reassuringly. "And if I am short, then you will make up the shortfall."

Garrett and Thomas exchanged looks. Vy saw uncertainty there.

"Your Majesty?" Garrett hunched his shoulders defensively. "I would like the Alashani warriors to join in."

"Their power is inconsequential," Evenjos said dismissively. "I am certain that I can rekindle Ariock's sphere on my own. Anything more is probably . . ." She appeared to search for a word, then found it. "Overkill."

Her flippancy reminded Vy, sadly, of Ariock. He had also ignored Garrett's repeated warnings. Now he was at the mercy of whatever risks this revival process entailed.

"Please?" Garrett sounded desperate. "Every scrap may help."

After a moment, Evenjos nodded in allowance. "I can see that you are fearful."

"Thank you, Your Majesty." Garrett bowed.

"Are spheres of influence cumulative when combined?" Thomas asked.

Evenjos gave him a distasteful look. After a pause, she turned to the makeshift chalkboard and drew two concentric circles. "If you add your raw power to my raw power, the total is this." She tapped the outer circle. "Greater than either of us. And if we add his raw power?" She scribbled a tight circle around the first two. "You can see the result. It is less than impressive, because my power is already so great to begin with."

To Vy, it seemed the power was not cumulative.

"I assume there are variables?" Thomas said.

"I do not know the variables." Evenjos tapped the chalk in her open palm like an impatient schoolteacher. "Are there any other questions before we commence?"

"Yes," Thomas said.

Evenjos's chalk tapping became annoyed. She surveyed the crowd, clearly hoping someone would interrupt the supergenius.

"Am I correct in assuming that combined spheres can be used for more than just reviving power-depleted Yeresunsa?" Thomas asked.

"Of course." Evenjos put aside the chalk. "Now—"

"I apologize, Your Majesty," Garrett said. "But I have a question."

She gave him a look of tolerance.

"What happens if we just barely match Ariock's level of peak power?" Garrett asked. "Will that deplete us? I mean, will that entail our deaths?"

It was Thomas who answered.

"That's a dangerous situation," he said, rotating his hoverchair to face Garrett. "The weakest of us would be at risk of death by depletion, for sure. We'd end up in comas. Ariock would be rekindled, but he would still be drained, just barely above depletion. He would have to refrain from using his powers."

The warriors muttered. They had been told that reviving Ariock would solve everyone's problems without creating new ones.

Garrett studied Thomas. "Then what chances would we have for recovery?"

Thomas shrugged, studying Garrett just as intently as the old man had studied him. "It depends on how close to the limit we are. I assume the strongest of us would wake up after a day or two."

"Have no fear," Evenjos said airily. "I have done this before." With her wings, she looked like an angel. She held out her hands invitingly. "Now, let us—"

"Hold on," Garrett said.

Everyone in the room glared at him.

Instead of answering their impatience, Garrett limped toward Vy.

She assumed he must be aiming for someone else—surely not her—and by the time she realized his focus, it was too late to dodge away. She braced herself for whatever he wanted.

"Vy," Garrett said. "On the off chance that we all collapse, you need to prevent Ariock from depleting himself a second time."

Vy could hardly believe this. What sort of power did Garrett mistakenly believe she had?

"This is a life-or-death situation." Garrett stood at eye level with her, nose to nose. "I mean it. You'd better make sure Ariock refrains from using his powers if the rest of us get depleted. Jump on him if you have to. Slap him if that's what it takes."

Vy gave Garrett a look of incredulity. Even if she punched Ariock with all her strength, it wouldn't have any effect. Ariock was stronger than steel. He was unstoppable.

And if he saw people in need? Well, then Ariock would rescue them, or heal them, no matter what anyone else said.

Wasn't that a quality that made him worthy of respect?

"I don't care about your lovey-dovey excuses!" Garrett threw up his hands. "This is important! If you fail, then this ship becomes a floating tomb!"

She swallowed.

"Understand?" Garrett demanded.

Vy didn't want to understand, but there was no avoiding it. If all the Yeresunsa aboard the ship got depleted . . . including Ariock and Evenjos . . . then the twelve million refugees were also doomed. There was no way for ordinary people to magically teleport water and food onboard. Even if the ummin crew could figure out how to ferry people to an uninhabited wilderness planet, the starship population was too large to be sustained by hunting and gathering.

And then the Torth Empire would target their undefended haven.

In fact, the Torth were probably targeting planet Earth right now, daring Ariock to show up. If he died . . .

Vy shut off that line of thought. No one would die. Garrett might be overreacting, fearing a very unlikely worst-case scenario.

Garrett continued to focus on Vy with intensity. "I want you here and paying attention. You'd better do what's necessary. All right?"

Vy gave a hesitant nod. She had no idea how she could possibly get Ariock to listen to reason.

"I'm counting on you. We all are." Garrett gave her one last unnerving stare. "Remember, if you fail, that means death for all of us."

With that, he made his way back toward the dais.

Vy let out a tense breath. The next time Ariock's great-grandfather limped toward her, she would run—or limp—the other way. Why did Garrett keep assuming that she had some sort of power over an ultrapowerful hero?

"We will be fine," Evenjos said in a bored tone. "Now, are we ready to begin?"

Garrett turned toward the Alashani warriors. Jinishta took charge before he could speak.

"We must make contact with one another!" Jinishta bellowed. "Touch the shoulder or hand of your neighbor."

Hundreds of Alashani surged toward the dais, eager to participate. Those up front must be the staunchest warriors, because they moved within the telepathy ranges of Thomas or Garrett.

Jinishta bravely hooked her arm around Garrett's. Her people trailed behind her, forming an interlocked net of albinos. Snow-white hands rested on shoulders. Their determined faces looked carved from soapstone, capped by white hair. They blanketed the room like a bridal train.

Vy had an urge to join in.

She knew that was ridiculous. But hadn't Thomas theorized that humans might have a power-boosting factor?

"You should join, Vy," Thomas said.

Tentative, Vy made her way closer to Evenjos. She doubted that her presence would augment the power in this room. Thomas's theory was far-fetched. Even so, she prepared to reach out.

"You may enter my range," Evenjos told Thomas with reluctance. "Do not read my mind."

That was all the invitation Thomas seemed to need. He floated onto the dais and glided to a stop at Evenjos's left side, opposite Garrett on the right side.

Vy put her hand on Thomas's shoulder. She was part of this.

Evenjos clasped Garrett's hand and Thomas's hand at the same time. She twitched when she made physical contact with them. "Have we linked before?" she asked in a wondering tone.

"You offered your power to me," Thomas said.

"You saved my life with your power." Garrett gripped Evenjos's hand.

Evenjos looked troubled, as if she didn't know what to make of them. "Well." She cleared her throat. "The next step is, you offer your power to me. Yes. Like that."

Vy felt every hair on her skin stand up. The air had an electric tingle, the way it felt before a storm.

"If you want the lesser Yeresunsa to participate," Evenjos said, "they must offer their power to the next link in line, all the way to you, and then to me."

Small items levitated, caught in unseen ripples of power. People's earrings defied gravity. The fringes on their garments bristled as if magnetized. Candles flickered wildly.

Far away, in the doorways, nussians watched with wide-eyed wonder.

Vy felt a shift inside her. Energy seemed to course through her body, channeling down through her hand and into Thomas's thin shoulder.

That had to be her imagination.

"You are all linked to me." Evenjos spoke in a soft tone, audible only because everyone in the room seemed to be holding their breath. "Now," she said, "I will combine with Ariock's sphere."

Due to the electric tingle of power everywhere, Vy expected sparkles, or fireworks, or some version of power made visible. She watched Ariock with eagerness. Any second now, he was going to sit up. He would probably joke about the inconveniences of being in a coma. Vy smiled, thinking about the comments he would likely make about his new clothing and all the worshipful gifts.

The power in the room felt enormous. It must be enough to rekindle a star. Surely it was enough to . . .

Thomas slumped in his seat, limp and unconscious.

Throughout the room, Alashani keeled over. They fell en masse, sprawling insensate on the floor or on top of one another.

Garrett toppled to one side, no longer able to lean on his silver staff. He fainted halfway on top of the unconscious form of Jinishta.

Candelabra flames winked out in lazy exhalations of smoke.

Every subtle sound in the room died. The ship's reactor engines and electrical systems must have had all their power sucked away as well, because the space views vanished. The room went pitch-black.

Just before the light died, Evenjos melted into a pile of inert dust.

Vy stood in an auditorium full of fallen Yeresunsa. A scent of extinguished candles tainted the air. It was so dark she might as well be blind and so silent she might as well be deaf.

She pushed past the hoverchair. She stumbled over one comatose body, then another, until she found the bier with Ariock by touch. In utter darkness, she felt his face, desperately searching for any sign of wakefulness.

CHAPTER 5

GRASPED

Ariock felt drained.

He thought he had won a battle. Had he?

If so, it must have been a long battle. He remembered shielding people from hydrogen bombs.

He hoped he had killed a lot of Torth. No one else could do the things he could do. He needed to force the Torth Empire to let their slaves go free and to leave innocent people in peace. Only he could . . .

Who was crying?

It sounded like Vy.

Ariock became aware that he could feel her, soft and small—everyone except nussians was small to him—weeping against his chest. What was wrong?

He gently wrapped her in his arms.

Vy's quiet weeping stopped. She sniffled, then stared at him in wide-eyed wonderment, as if she couldn't believe her eyes. Strands of her hair hung around her face, lush and auburn in the flickering candlelight. Beyond the lanterns set on the floor, Ariock saw dead wall screens set in crude metal walls.

He began to remember the rush of building this colony starship.

Had it worked? Had they escaped the Torth armada?

Other people showed up next to Vy, peering at Ariock as if he might be a figment of their imaginations. Weptolyso. Kessa. Pung. Even Cherise, with her black hair held back with a headscarf, shani style.

"Ariock," Kessa said with warmth. "I am so glad to see you awake."

"How are you feeling?" Vy rubbed the tears from her face. She sounded like she could barely contain joy.

Was she faking happiness? She ought to be relaxed enough around Ariock by now to be genuine. She was beautiful, especially when she was genuine.

Ariock began to sit up. A wave of dizziness forced him back down.

He felt . . . well, awful. Terribly thirsty. Terribly hungry. His body was leaden and hollow at the same time, and his head throbbed with a miserable headache. Why did he feel so weak?

He began to say that he was fine. But they were all studying him, and Vy was a nurse. She would not appreciate being lied to.

Ariock figured there was no harm in being honest. "Like I got hit with one too many nuclear bombs," he said.

He began to force himself into a sitting position. Had he fallen in battle? If so, other people must be hurting a lot worse than he was. Who had he been protecting?

As Ariock struggled to remember, the whole apocalypse came to him. "The Alashani."

He jerked upright, not willing to lounge around while people must be dying on the Torth Homeworld. "I have to save the Alashani!"

Vy shoved herself against his chest, as if trying to knock him back down. It didn't work. Her mass was too light to push him off balance and she only ended up on his lap, gripping his massive shoulders.

"No!" she shouted.

Ariock blinked at his bizarre surroundings. Albino people lay everywhere, blanketing the floor. Each had a makeshift pillow, and they were draped in blankets, as if this was a slumber party for a thousand people. Lanterns flickered between them.

And . . . oh no.

Thomas never looked healthy even at the best of times, but now he was deathly pale. He lolled in the red hoverchair, which was parked on the ground. Someone had propped his head up with rolled towels. His closed eyes looked sunken.

Was he asleep?

Or dead?

Ariock reached out with his awareness. Thomas's life spark was barely an ember. He was dying.

The albinos were near death as well. Hundreds of them.

Ariock shifted. He needed to heal Thomas, then all the albinos in this room. This was an emergency. His own exhausted, weakened state was inconsequential.

"Stop!" Vy was desperately shouting at him for some unfathomable reason.

Weptolyso also had something to say, his deep voice a forbidding rumble. Even Pung was yelling for him to stop and rest. So was Kessa. And Cherise.

Why were they so worked up about his health status?

Ariock figured he would worry about their crisis later. They were healthy. They could wait.

Matters were even worse than Ariock thought, because Garrett lay amid the unconscious figures. His great-grandfather looked more geriatric than he ever had before, with his mouth hanging open, displaying nicotine-stained teeth. Near death.

Ariock wasn't ready to lose the closest thing he had to a father.

"STOP!" Vy shrieked at him. "If you use your powers, we'll all die!"

What was she talking about? Ariock couldn't think of any scenario where that made sense.

Oh no, was that Jinishta on the floor? The premier of Hufti was laid out next to Garrett, also unconscious and near death. What sort of disaster had occurred here?

Thomas could probably explain what had happened and what to do about it. Ariock sidled closer to the parked hoverchair. He lifted his hands, eager to begin reviving people, starting with Thomas. Once he had inundated the boy with a torrent of healing power, then maybe he could afford a bit of time to try and understand whatever problem Vy and the others were babbling about.

He plunged his awareness into Thomas, connecting with his ember of a life spark.

Someone grabbed Ariock. And not his hand or his arm.

The firm yet feminine hand was farther down. Vy had a handful of his . . . well.

Ariock's extended awareness collapsed. He was fully in his own body and very fully aware of Vy touching him in a place that was not publicly appropriate.

She pressed her full lips against his lips, sensuous and insistent. She kissed him like he had never been kissed before. Tingles ran over Ariock's body.

Why was she doing this?

Ariock focused on that question, desperate to remain cognizant of his goals. Vy was sexy and soft and everything he had fantasized about.

But seriously, he couldn't afford to be distracted right now. He needed to—

"Do I have your attention?" Vy demanded.

Ariock swallowed. Now her ivory-carved prosthetic was pressed against the area where her hand had squeezed. It was a dainty appendage, but he would rather have her hand there.

"Listen to me." Her breath was soft on his face. "Or everyone on this ship is going to die. I don't want to die. Are you actually listening to me?"

"Um." Ariock realized he had never given Vy his complete attention. Not like this. In fact, he doubted he had ever given so much attention to one person.

"Yes," he said.

"We're going to die if you use your powers," Vy said, relentless. "Even a little bit. All the Yeresunsa gathered here pooled their powers together to revive you from death. It took everything they had to rekindle your life spark, or your sphere of influence, or whatever. It took all of their power to bring you back."

That explained the thousand unconscious Yeresunsa. Ariock had drained them. It made him want to crawl under the blankets and hide in shame.

"And we didn't even know whether it had worked," Vy said. "You wouldn't wake up."

"It's been hours," Cherise said.

"We feared you were still depleted and dying," Weptolyso rumbled.

Maybe that explained why Vy had been weeping.

"It's been five days since you saved everybody from the destruction of the Torth Homeworld," Vy said.

Had he slept that whole time? That explained why he felt weak.

"Your Yeresunsa powers are depleted," Weptolyso said. "It will take several days for you to recover."

"You collapsed while saving people," Kessa said.

"The planet got destroyed," Cherise said. "We saw it explode. But the Alashani survived, mostly, thanks to you."

"Everyone on this ship owes their survival to you," Pung added.

"They had a funeral for you, Ariock." Vy looked at him, her eyes glistening with unshed tears. "Everyone was ready to write you off as dead."

As Ariock processed all that information, he saw the strain his friends must have been under for the last week. They would have needed to reassure millions of refugees, including their loved ones, while privately fearing that they were stranded aboard this starship without any defenses. They hadn't known whether Ariock would ever wake up.

They still didn't know if Thomas or the other Yeresunsa would wake up.

"Evenjos knew how to revive you," Vy said. "But Thomas mentioned that it might drain everyone of power. Garrett warned me that if that happened—if everyone collapsed—then it means you're all depleted. Including you."

If Evenjos was able to make helpful suggestions and have rational conversations . . . if she had come aboard this starship and specifically offered to revive Ariock . . . well, that was wonderful. She would make for a powerful ally.

"Where is Evenjos?" Ariock twisted around, curious to see if the winged Lady lay unconscious among the depleted warriors.

"I think she'll be okay." Vy sounded dubious. She pointed to a pile of dust. "I guess that's what she looks like when she's, uh, not taking any form."

Kessa eyed the flaky pile with fascinated disgust. Like Ariock, she had visited the underground prison at the end of the hallway of prophecies. Ariock had reconstituted the mummified remains of Evenjos using a lot of raw power and his own blood.

He hoped he wouldn't have to do that all again.

The barest hint of a life spark glowed in that pile of dust. All he could do was hope Evenjos would recover on her own.

"So this is what depletion feels like." Ariock supposed the headache was to be expected. He had felt the same sharp pain while healing people, after all those frantic and messy mass-teleportations.

"Right." Vy pushed him, trying in vain to get him to lie back down. "You should rest. Your powers will come back, but you need to give it a day or two."

Rest?

Ariock felt ridiculous, lounging on a makeshift bed amid woolen blankets while a thousand Yeresunsa lay in critical depletion comas. It wasn't right.

"Who's at the helm?" Ariock asked. "I mean, who's piloting the ship?"

"There's a crew of ummins." Vy made that sound perfectly normal. "I think Thomas put Varktezo in charge."

"Hmm." Ariock wondered what he could volunteer to do to make himself useful.

Without powers.

The idea of being a normal person seemed utterly impossible. Ariock remembered life without powers. He used to watch TV. Pace around. He used to shave with a razor instead of using his powers to manifest a blade. He used to build furniture. With his hands, instead of with powers.

But during those years of powerlessness, his mother had been silently dying from cancer. He hadn't even noticed.

He had been unable to save his father from acrid smoke in the plane crash that killed him.

That was what being powerless meant. It meant being useless.

What good was he without powers? Was he going to just . . . what?

Sit around?

"Pardon." An Alashani poked her head into the room. "Kessa the Wise? The mob on deck one is becoming violent. They . . ." The albino woman faltered as she noticed Ariock sitting up. "Oh, *Aonswa!*" That was the Alashani word for "messiah." The albino woman prostrated herself on the floor. "Thank all that is holy! We are in desperate need of water! And food! And warmth! We humbly beg—"

"Out," Vy said.

Weptolyso made a gesture, and nussian guards closed in toward the woman.

Ariock wanted to tell them to back off. This was cruel. The visitor was an innocent person with innocent requests. Sure, he knew better than to attempt teleporting supplies onto the ship right now—that throbbing headache warned him not to—but he must be able to do . . .

Well, something.

He began to stand up. At the very least, he could reassure innocent people that he was alive and recovering. Maybe that would quell the riot.

"No." Vy shoved him, trying to force him to sit back down. "I told you, you need to rest."

Ariock stood at his full height, ignoring the dizziness. He towered over Vy and everyone else. The nussian sentries had already hustled the albino woman away, but now more nussians crowded the entryways. They watched him with respectful red gazes.

Ariock knew they would obey any orders he gave. They were no longer slaves, but they were messiah worshippers.

Suddenly Vy's hand was grasping that not-public-appropriate place. She couldn't reach his face, but she could reach elsewhere.

"You're being an idiot!" she said fiercely, glaring up at him. "There are twelve million people aboard this ship, and not all of them are friendly. Some people blame you for the loss of their world. Are you really going to make us try and protect you from angry mobs while you go on a fun little adventure?"

She spoke as if Ariock was an untrustworthy child. Was that what she thought of him?

"We can't protect you." Her grip was firm and unmistakable. "And if you use your powers, guess what? No one can revive you."

At least Vy's body hid what she was doing from everyone else. She looked beautiful even when she was furious.

"Do you get what I'm saying?" Her gaze heated up, in a way that was sexy and not sexy at the same time. She squeezed just a little bit.

"Yes." Ariock cleared his throat, trying to get rid of the thick feeling there.

As he gazed down at her, he saw a caring look beneath her fury. She was watching out for his well-being—because she figured he would not. She did not trust him to make wise decisions.

Was she right?

As Ariock thought about the risks he'd taken in the time Vy had known him, he realized that he had not given her much cause to trust him.

"Ariock." Vy took a deep breath, which did interesting things to her woolen shirt.

Ariock forced himself to listen. She appeared to have something important to say.

"I know it's easy for you to ignore people," Vy said. "You do it by accident. You might not even hear a person shouting at you when you're in the middle of trying to save a world."

Ariock thought he did remember glimpsing Vy in a crowd aboard the starship, striving to get his attention, while he was teleporting people away from the apocalypse.

"I begged you to stop." Vy bit her lip and looked away. "So did Garrett, and other people who are your friends. I just wish . . ." Judging by the set of her shoulders, she was waiting for a blow. This was a hard thing for her to say. "I wish you had tried to hear us. Or see us."

Ariock realized that she was right.

He had ignored her. He had deprioritized his friends while he was busy saving a planet.

Kessa looked like she had not slept in days. Cherise knelt next to the inert body of Flen. She gently fed him water from a canteen, careful not to spill any or cause him to choke. While Ariock slept in a coma, his friends had grappled with the possibility of dehydration and starvation.

"I will never ignore you again," Ariock said.

Vy gave him a searching look. She clearly didn't trust him.

"I promise," Ariock said. He didn't care if people thought him a careless idiot—he was—but he had a bad track record of accidentally killing or hurting people. If he kept doing that, the only people who dared get close to him would be fanatics.

He didn't want to drive away his friends, especially not one who cared about him as much as Vy. If he kept treating Vy like a random worshipper and ignoring her . . . then he would lose her.

Even an idiot could see that.

"I should have listened to you," Ariock said. "I'll make that a priority from now on."

She looked amazed and disbelieving.

Ariock sat down, putting himself at eye level instead of towering over Vy. Part of him wanted to jump back up. It felt absurd to sit on comfy blankets while refugees cried for help and while Thomas and Garrett were deathly pale and unable to wake up. His headache wasn't that bad, really. He could function. It felt like pretending to be feeble in order to escape from responsibilities.

But Vy had told him to rest.

And she needed to be able to trust him. Otherwise she would give up on him.

"It may be hard for me," Ariock admitted. "Like you said, I don't always hear people. But I need to do better."

She gave him a tentative smile.

He almost invited her to grab his attention whenever she felt like it. She certainly had an effective way. Ariock swallowed as he remembered the sensuality of her lips. And her hand.

He restrained himself from even hinting about that. Trust would take time. They were on shaky ground.

Vy's smile broadened. Her gaze roved over his body, as if she was studying him, imagining him in different situations.

She situated herself in his lap, nestling there, making herself comfortable.

"Maybe I can help you find things to do that, you know, don't require powers," she said.

CHAPTER 6

DROPOUT

The child known as the Colossal Failure had never anticipated that adult society would take notice of him.

He was an underdeveloped, pimply preadolescent with horrifically misaligned teeth and bedsores. Although he was a fully ripened supergenius—old enough to be on par with the Twins and the Death Architect—he had never contributed to society. He had never risen in rank nor even graduated from his baby farm on the planet Yoft.

He had never left his bed. He had never bothered to use a hoverchair.

If only he had quit paying attention to the Megacosm.

He hadn't cared when a hybrid supergenius was discovered on a primitive planet. Nor had he particularly paid attention when that supergenius went renegade and wreaked havoc. So what? The news was the news. It was irrelevant to his short, miserable, pointless, loathsome life. The Colossal Failure tuned out the galaxy, because the galaxy surely did not care about him.

He had barely noticed when the Torth Homeworld was blown to smithereens. It was just another boring day to him. He'd eaten a cookie and been bathed by his slaves.

And when the Upward Governess got elected to be a sort of nominal interim leader of the galaxy? So what. Good for her. Some supergeniuses found fulfillment in serving the Majority, as if bending over backward to please people was somehow noble.

But then . . .

The Majority wanted to locate the Betrayer's rebel starship. They sent probes throughout the galaxy, and a few Servants of All had revealed yet another secret power they had been hiding.

Clairvoyance.

The Colossal Failure should have suppressed his initial reaction. He should have pretended to have zero knowledge of ghosting, or floating around disembodied.

But he had accidentally leaked surprise. That news stunned him. He had never guessed that other Torth could do that magic trick. He had been so certain that he was the only one.

You're a Yeresunsa?!

One little accidental emotional spurt on his end, and suddenly, the galaxy found him worthy of interest.

Yeresunsa supergenius. The news about what he was leaped from mind to mind, hooking more and more Torth, until the hubbub reeled in a whale. The eldest supergenius pinned him with her vast attention.

We need to be competitive with Our enemies, the Upward Governess thought. *We need you in military service.*

As if he needed a lecture.

The Upward Governess went on, relentless, and she had the Majority to back her up. Her audience was as near infinite as a galactic disk. They orbited the blazing thunderhead that was her mind, and the Colossal Failure could not help but feel flattened and humbled beneath them all, no matter how much he wished to ignore them.

It behooves Us to erase any gap where Our enemies can outmaneuver Us, the Upward Governess thought. *A supergenius Yeresunsa on Our side pits Us evenly against the Betrayer.*

The Colossal Failure sneered. He didn't care how many trillions of Torth endured his unsavory emotional reaction. What were they going to do, kill him?

He should have been killed years ago. He should have been killed as a fetus. In fact, he spent every test session taunting his testers, daring them to extinguish his useless life. He ignored exams. He spat nonsense instead of caving in and giving the testers what they wanted.

Any child with a normal mind would have been murdered and carved up as an organ donor. But he got to keep living. The idiotic adults cut him slack no matter how often he failed, because he had so, so, so very much potential.

How he hated them.

Well, he wasn't going to cooperate with the Upward Governess, either. He had no interest in appeasing the Majority or being a good, dutiful little supergenius. He had not chosen this life. He would rather have been born a slave.

Annoyance snapped off the mind of the Upward Governess in crackling waves. *The Torth Empire has given you a lot of care. Think of all the resources (slaves, food, luxuries, and all the order that comes with civilization) that go into your daily upkeep. Don't you owe the Majority a bit of gratitude?*

The Colossal Failure considered disconnecting from the Megacosm. Really. Was he supposed to be grateful for an existence devoid of pleasure or wonder? Did a nectar milkshake make up for being bedridden and dying and the utter lack of meaning in his existence?

Idiots. This wasn't living.

Slaves are alive, he thought. *We (Torth) are nothing but useless leeches.*

Ghosting was the only thing that made his existence bearable. Whenever the Colossal Failure dared to go into a clairvoyant trance and leave his body—while he pretended to be asleep—he visited slaves in their homes. He lingered, unseen and unheard, near his favorite slaves. After years of practice, he could do it for up to ten minutes before the tug of his body snapped him back.

He lived vicariously through people who could laugh and cry freely. Slaves were magical creatures to him. Yes, they were filthy and ignorant, but they were also wonderful, if one took the time to learn their names and their interpersonal dramas. They knew what love was.

That was how the Colossal Failure got through each day. If he could have erased his life and been born over again as a slave, he would have done so.

Pathetic! the Majority shrilled.

Trillions of Torth reeled away from his repulsively emotional mind, or else they studied him with fascinated disgust. Quite a few thought the Colossal Failure ought to be killed.

He is an asset. The Upward Governess seemed to be trying to convince herself of that as much as her audience.

Emotions, the Twins chimed in, *are tied with Yeresunsa powers.*

Also, clairvoyance—

—is probably a prerequisite—

—for teleportation.

That grabbed everyone's attention.

Even the Colossal Failure wanted to learn a bit more about his power. Could he actually teleport?

Wow.

Ghosting seemed like a mostly useless ability. Unlike a visit to the Megacosm, ghosting left him feeling weak and drained. Its sole benefit was that he could visit places that were not in the Megacosm. But what if . . . ?

What if he could permanently escape his all-too-familiar bedroom suite, with its black drapes and black granite decor?

What if he could teleport himself into a slave farm?

What if he could hide there for the rest of his life?

The Majority attached themselves to his mind, harmonious and inescapable. The Colossal Failure understood that he could not brush them off the way he did with the testing committee. A mob of billions would not cut him any slack.

We forgive you for all your past failures, billions of minds sang.

But now you must cooperate.

It is the duty of every Torth,

no matter how great or small,

to vanquish the enemies of civilization.

The pressure of their attention became sharp, almost painful.

If you refuse—

—if you choose to waste the gifts you were born with—

then you are choosing to ally yourself with the Betrayer.

Their expectations blazed like a supernova. *DO NOT FAIL US.*

For the first time in his life, the Colossal Failure understood the pressures high ranks must endure. He was a speck of dust caught in a maelstrom. If he dropped out of the Megacosm, as he wished to do right now, adults would burst into his bedchamber in a matter of minutes. They would sit near him and force him to listen to the Majority through their minds.

And if he ghosted? What if he went into a clairvoyant trance to escape them?

The Colossal Failure did not have to imagine the consequences. Everyone knew what happened to renegades and traitors and uncooperative kids—they wound up tortured to death in the Isolatorium. It didn't matter that the Isolatorium was now gone. The galaxy was full of prisons, and there were plenty of ways to inflict pain.

Deep down, the Colossal Failure had anticipated that a day like this would come.

He had prepared for it.

He beckoned to his most loyal slave, and he spoke, requesting the secret poison he had concocted years earlier. It was stored in a random vial amid his various painkillers and other drugs. The custom-tailored poison was designed to make his throat and lungs swell up and simultaneously drop his blood pressure so that his cerebral circulation would stop. He should be brain-dead within a minute and fully dead not long after.

STOP HIM, the Majority roared, even more stridently than the Upward Governess.

Adults raced into the baby farm, determined to please the Majority. They sprinted through the singular gate, one after the other. From there they crowded into the elevator, or they jumped onto slides, using children's routes in their haste to get to his level.

Even the local children picked up on the frenzy. They raced toward his bedchamber, eager to please the adults who served the Majority.

"Fetch me my blaster glove," the Colossal Failure instructed his slave. "Then block the door as best you can."

As the slave obeyed, the Colossal Failure swallowed his custom-tailored poison in one gulp. The effects were almost immediate. He began to wheeze.

He tugged his blaster glove onto his hand and aimed it at his own face.

STOP!!! The Majority was a furnace in orbit around his mind.

Traitor!

Renegade!

Yet even now, many still wanted to use the valuable asset that was his brain.

The Colossal Failure could no longer breathe. His chest cramped, but he smiled like a slave. He invited the Majority into his dying mind.

You think I'm a Colossal Failure? he thought. *You think I'm the only worthless dud among your treasured military assets? Idiots. You ought to be suspicious of anyone smart enough to influence you.* He gurgled, choking. *Take another look at your revered Upward Governess. Take a closer look at the Twins, and the Death Architect, and the rest of them.*

The Majority slithered like a nest of snakes. He felt their unease.

All his fellow supergeniuses spewed reassurances to their huge audiences, trying to undo the damage he had caused with his dying thoughts.

Good.

His vision was going black, and he was slipping from the Megacosm. The Colossal Failure forced himself to cling to consciousness for a moment longer.

He sent one last thought for the Majority to chew on.

She (the Upward Governess) is in love with the Betrayer, you idiots. You cannot trust her.

CHAPTER 7

DECISIVE

"This reminds me of snowstorms," Vy said.

She lay in Ariock's embrace, his arms covering much of her body. The windows displayed nothing but frost blisters. The walls were also veined with frost, despite the warmth of many flickering candles.

"Did you have power outages at your house?" she asked. "I guess you must have, up in the mountains."

"All the time," Ariock said.

Vy snuggled closer. She liked the deepness of his voice, the way it made her whole body vibrate.

"Did you have kerosene heaters?" she asked. "I don't remember seeing a fireplace in your sky room."

"I would sit in the library," Ariock said. "There was a huge fireplace there. But it needed firewood. When I was younger, I would go out and chop wood—but only after dark." He sounded ashamed of his fear of being seen. "What about your home?" he asked. "Did you have fireplaces?"

Vy figured he would be shocked by the decrepit Hollander home, with its rickety staircase and peeling wallpaper. In his imagination, it was probably a neat and cheerful TV home, where every kid had their own private bedroom.

"We had a stove," Vy said. "But our main problem with losing electricity was the kids' medical equipment. Two kids needed nebulizers for emergencies. And some of our foster kids used wheelchairs, and those need to be recharged. Plus, with so many kids, we really needed running water."

"Hmm." Ariock hugged her. "So what did you do?"

Vy laughed sadly. "Mostly, we freaked out. Until Thomas came to live with us. He knew how to manage an investment portfolio, so he bailed us out of debt. That was when we bought a backup generator."

She glanced toward the unconscious form of Thomas. He lay on the dais, wrapped in blankets, alongside Garrett and a bowl containing Evenjos's pile of dust. Without hospital equipment, the easiest way for Vy to monitor Thomas's condition was to watch for faint puffs of vapor in the cold air. That proved he was breathing.

A team of ummins worked on his hoverchair nearby. They had found containers of black and purple pigments and enough oil and turpentine to mix them with. They were repainting the crimson hoverchair. Red symbolized Torth military ranks, but black and purple were associated with Alashani warriors.

Those colors now symbolized the resistance against the Torth.

Kessa had suggested the black-and-purple rebranding. She was taking measures to insulate Thomas and Garrett against *rekveh* hatred. She had also made sure that the two mind readers were reclothed in plain woolens. They must not be seen wearing anything Torth-like.

A few of the nussians guarding one of the entryways jostled aside, allowing Weptolyso to enter. He carefully picked a path between unconscious Alashani warriors, all of them heaped with blankets. "Ariock? Vy?"

Vy switched to the slave tongue. "What is it, Weptolyso?"

She wished for more privacy. Ariock had, in fact, wanted to leave this big room full of activity, where chambermaids tended to comatose Yeresunsa. But Vy had seen the dangers of leaving a well-guarded zone. This starship was chock-full of desperate refugees seeking help from the messiah. Some would do anything to make Ariock hear their prayers. There was no privacy.

Therefore—although the memory of Ariock's big hands running over her body made her feel tingly—Vy told him to calm down. She would not allow Ariock to look like a hedonist while everyone else was thirsty, scared, and starving.

It seemed he was serious about listening to her. He had settled for spooning with her.

That was nice, too. Whenever Vy was next to Ariock, the scale of everything shifted. She felt cute and dainty rather than ungainly and oversize. He made her feel . . . well, adorable. Desirable.

It was a feeling she wanted to get used to.

"I apologize for disturbing you." Weptolyso sounded ashamed. "I have merely come to ask, is there any chance you can tell me when the Son of Storms will be able to perform a feat of magic?" His small red eyes shifted toward Ariock. "I fear the engines are a critical problem. They must be restarted."

Vy scrutinized Weptolyso's broad face. She did not think he would ask unless there was some kind of dire emergency.

"I can take a look," Ariock offered. "If it's a matter of electricity, I might have enough power to—"

"Shush!" Vy gave him an exasperated look.

At least he wasn't flying into hero mode. She shifted her ire toward Weptolyso. "Can I speak with you alone for a minute?"

Judging by Weptolyso's grim expression, he knew the ramifications of what he was asking. Vy stood and urged him to step aside, away from Ariock.

When they were far enough to avoid being overheard, Vy whispered, "What happened?"

Weptolyso settled into a nussian crouch and bent down, putting himself close to her level. "Varktezo sent a message that we are all going to freeze to death unless the engines get restarted. And," he added, as if that wasn't enough, "there was a riot on deck one. Eighteen people are dead by violence, that I know of."

Vy bit her lower lip. The starship's population could not be expected to endure oppressive hardships with infinite patience.

"It will soon get much, much worse," Weptolyso said. "You rely on nussians to control the violence. Well, my people require more food than what is available. We do not succumb to thirst as fast as you do, but we are not built for this much hunger or cold. Kessa is doing her best to keep everyone calm, but—"

"I get it." Vy barely remembered the endless slog through the dead city, but she knew that Kessa and Weptolyso had pulled everyone through it.

Except this time, instead of a hundred and fifty refugees, they were burdened with a flock of twelve million.

Vy assessed Ariock from a distance. They had spent a day together, cuddling and talking and catching up on sleep. Maybe Ariock was well rested by now?

Could she trust him to be honest about his condition?

She knew one thing for certain: if Ariock depleted himself while all the other Yeresunsa were drained to the point of being comatose, there would be no third chances. There would be no hope.

Vy led the way back to Ariock. "How's your headache?"

He sat up. "It's more or less gone."

Weptolyso gave Vy a patient look. So did Ariock.

Of course, they were not the only people awaiting her decision. Vy felt all the lives depending on her choice.

She had to look away from their expectations. Life-or-death decisions were more difficult than she'd imagined. People didn't give Ariock or Thomas enough credit.

"I want to visit the command center." Vy limped toward the exit. "Let's find out exactly what needs to be done."

Ariock followed her. He looked pleased to have the burden of decision-making off-loaded to someone else.

CHAPTER 8

AT THE HELM

Thousands of people watched them as they crossed multiple decks.

Vy did not see much from behind the barricade of nussians. The guards crouched elbow to elbow, forming an aisle that held back the masses. Only Ariock was tall enough to be seen over their spinal ridges.

Judging by his shamed expression, the onlookers were not praising him.

"They're right to blame me," Ariock said.

Vy wanted to remind him that he had done everything humanly possible, and more, to save people. She wanted to hold his hand. But the messiah could not afford to look weak or uncertain.

"If they want to throw blame around," Vy said, "they should think about the Lady of Sorrow. She's the one who destroyed their planet."

Ariock still looked guilty. "I set her free. I insisted on leaving the Alashani, and that set off a chain of events that led to here." He was apparently determined to shoulder all the blame. "They're right to hate me."

It must be startling, Vy thought, to go from being powerless to having godlike powers and then back again. At least as a nurse, she'd had some prior experiences with high-stakes dilemmas.

She supposed she agreed with Ariock's reasoning, somewhat. Yet . . .

"I worked in a trauma center," Vy reminded him. "Some patients got worse instead of better. Sometimes there was a reason, but I accepted that everyone around me was doing their best and working their hardest. Because that was the truth. And I definitely see that in you."

"Every time I save people," Ariock said, "I end up getting other people killed."

They walked between square pillars, through a corridor where Ariock had to bow his head to avoid the ceiling. Vy refrained from touching him. That would make the nussians gossip.

"You literally didn't know your own strength," Vy said. "But now you do. This kind of thing doesn't have to happen more than once."

Ariock looked dubious.

"I see you fighting smarter each time," Vy said. "You learn from your mistakes. I'm not sure anyone else learns as quickly as you, except for Thomas. And you know what? Everyone makes mistakes. I could say that I should never have screamed on that tower top after we crash-landed. My scream distracted you at a critical time. Because of me, ummins died. And I lost my leg."

"That was my fault." Ariock sounded certain. "I should have—"

Vy cut him off before he could get any further with that line of thought. "It *wasn't* your fault," she emphasized. "It wasn't my fault, either. I was in pain. You were in battle mode. And if you really think it's important to assign blame, let's say it was half and half."

The nussian barricade led them to a side tunnel, almost too narrow for Ariock and Vy together. They entered the command center.

As soon as they were alone, Vy reached up to tug Ariock. "Come here."

He knelt with a wary, questioning look.

Vy seized his scruffy cheeks. "Stop hating on yourself."

He looked abashed, clearly determined to prove how horrible he was.

"You're strong," Vy said. "So everything you do is outsize, and it has outsize effects. But that's true for the good as well as the bad! You've done true miracles, Ariock. Those twelve million people out there?" She pointed. "They would be dead if not for you."

He looked slightly less guilty.

"Everyone knows it," Vy said. "Otherwise you wouldn't have an aisle of nussians determined to protect you."

He had no argument for that.

Vy let go. She tugged his arm, leading him farther into the corridor. "We'll make it a priority to learn the scope of your powers so you won't make huge mistakes. But Ariock?" She gave him a look full of affection. "Please remember, you do more good than harm. You've saved a lot of lives." She entered the room at the end of the hall. "Including mine."

As her eyes adjusted to the dim light of holographs, she became aware of frenzied ummins dashing from one workstation to another. They wore brocaded outfits and embroidered head covers, like wealthy merchants, but Vy recognized them as adolescents from Duin.

"Bringer of Hope!" said one.

"Vy!" said another.

A planet loomed in the window views, blue, marbled with white clouds. It reminded Vy painfully of Earth. The most obvious difference was that it lacked signs of civilization. There were no roads, no satellites, no cities.

A reject planet.

Vy tried not to speculate why Thomas had chosen this destination, or why the Torth had never colonized it. Swarms of flesh-eating bugs? Hundred-ton predators? Intensely heavy gravity?

Nope, it wasn't worth thinking about.

She found Varktezo leaning over a workstation, waving his fingers across a geometric display. His gray eyes looked glazed. He jumped when Vy said, "How are you doing, Varktezo?"

"Where is Thomas?" Varktezo peered around anxiously, as if he expected to find a hoverchair floating behind Ariock.

Vy hesitated, unwilling to mention Thomas's comatose condition out loud.

Varktezo suddenly seemed to notice that Ariock was a living person instead of a random pillar. "Bringer of Hope! Are you here to deliver us to the new world?" Varktezo flung himself at Ariock's feet. "Oh, thank you, thank you, thank you!"

Vy spoke quickly, before Ariock could make any promises. "Varktezo, we heard there's a problem with the engines?"

He seized Vy by her woolen wrap. "When will the Teacher come back?"

She tried to think of an answer.

"I have not slept in three wake cycles," Varktezo said. "I took herbs to stay alert, but I cannot monitor everything, and this ship is missing all kinds of parts, and I'm going to fall over at some point, and then I can't predict if something will break down permanently and cause all the air to freeze, or the gravity to stop, or something like that!"

"Hold on." Vy gave herself a tone of smooth authority. That usually calmed panicky people in the trauma center. "It looks like your workstations have power."

"Because the Teacher told us where to find the backup ignition switches!" Varktezo made a sound of despair. "He said he would only be gone for a pendulum tick. It has been twelve! When will he come back? I think I figured out how the fusion capacitor works, but I don't know what this blinking white light means, only that it's an emergency. He taught us the mathematical symbols, but not enough about their interactions. I am reasonably certain that this"—he indicated an icon—"describes a frozen carbine. But I don't know where it is. And if we have to fix it—"

"Slow down." Vy spoke with authority.

Varktezo took a breath.

"Can you show us which engines need power?" Vy asked.

"All of them!" Varktezo leaped to an adjacent workstation and motioned through the holographic menu. It zoomed out to show a diagram of the starship, with multiple areas glowing red.

"I got the internal reactors working again. Otherwise we'd all be icicles." Varktezo laughed as if to dismiss such a ridiculous fate. "But they're running at a fractional capacity, and I cannot figure out how to balance their hydrogen lines without creating a radon leak, which I think would kill everyone."

Vy realized, with chagrin, that everyone onboard the ship—including Ariock and herself—probably owed their lives to Varktezo. Would they even have life support if he hadn't taken herbs to stay awake?

"I can't access the antivortex siphon," Varktezo said. "Or the oxygenators or the lithosphere reactors. That is why we need Thomas. And you can see that the core reactors are crippled." Varktezo jabbed each glowing area. "Here, here, here, here, here, here, and also here, here, and—"

Vy interrupted him. "Thanks, Varktezo. I think you and your crew have saved all our lives."

His owlish eyes bugged out at that praise.

"Can you explain what needs to be done?" Vy asked. "In simple terms?"

She didn't expect Varktezo would be able to supply an answer, but he pulled up a fresh holograph before she'd finished speaking.

"This is the ice core," Varktezo said. "The outer layer, here, is supposed to be liquefied. But the water taps are all frozen, which means the whole layer is frozen, due to the dead abaxial reactors. Here and here." He gave Ariock an anxious look. "Is there any way you can restart them?"

Vy considered Ariock. He didn't look exhausted, but he might be faking that.

"If you can just unfreeze the outer core," Varktezo said, "I think I can handle the rest."

"What happens if we don't?" Vy asked.

"Then the internal reactors will also freeze," Varktezo said. "Within a few pendulum ticks. And that would be very bad."

"Why?" Vy prompted.

"Our life support would end." Varktezo did not even hesitate. "We would all freeze and suffocate to death."

Vy took Ariock's hand. Even if that reject planet was as close as it appeared, she had explored the starship enough to know that it lacked shuttles. And she would not ask Ariock to mass-teleport everyone to the planet's surface. That would drain him for sure.

Varktezo fiddled with a holograph, and a path lit up in the diagram of the starship. It snaked from one deck to a lower deck. "This shows you how to get to the tank," he said.

"Thanks," Vy said.

The last thing she wanted to do was ask Ariock to tax his powers while in his depleted state. Was this suicidal folly?

When she had been a slave, death had been a constant worry gnawing at the back of her mind. The nuclear cube had nearly destroyed her. Really, she should be used to life-threatening situations by now.

"Are you sure you feel up to doing this?" She bit at her lip, wondering why she expected a massively powerful Yeresunsa to be candid with her.

Although . . . well, she had managed to persuade Ariock to do a few things.

"Please be honest with me," she said.

Ariock knelt to eye level so he could meet her gaze. "I don't know," he said. "That's the truth."

Vy wiped at her face. She felt like crying, but maybe she was too dehydrated for tears.

Ariock put his huge hand around her shoulder, gentle. That was his version of a hug. "I need to do something to restore people's trust. And lightning comes naturally to me. Anything weather-related should be relatively easy."

That was probably the most reassurance she would get.

Vy wished they could put this experiment off for another day. Instead, she gave a reluctant nod. "All right," she said in a small voice.

They both studied the map. Before leaving, Vy squeezed Varktezo's shoulder. "You've been really helpful."

He hardly seemed to notice. He was frantically tapping holographic icons.

"You shouldn't work until you drop," Ariock said. "Take it from me."

Vy felt unqualified to add her own advice, especially since Varktezo was the functional equivalent of a starship captain. What could she say in the face of that much expertise?

"Maybe after this," she said, "you can get some sleep."

"Sleep?" Varktezo gawked as if she had suggested that he walk out an airlock. "If I just go off and sleep"—he laughed at that ridiculousness—"the life support systems will break." He stretched up to whisper to Vy. "I'm not sure the rest of these ummins paid attention to everything Thomas said."

CHAPTER 9

FLURRIES

Ariock walked past the icy gazes of albinos, nussians, and others.

Kessa watched him with warmth and trust, but she seemed to be the only one besides Vy. Several thousand people filled the spigot room. They surrounded handcarts piled high with urns, jugs, and empty canteens. They sat upon frozen fountains.

This was only a tiny sliver of the shipboard population—but these were the elders, the councilors, and the gang bosses. Ariock must be the youngest person in this crowd.

He felt like a fraud, not a messiah. He couldn't blame these people if they spoke of his failures more than his successes.

Frost blistered the tank wall. Ariock placed one hand against its numbingly cold surface and offered Vy a nod of reassurance. Even that felt deceptive. He wished he had paid closer attention to Jinishta's lessons about power depletion when she had been teaching him.

Well, something had to be done, or else people would fight to the death over a drop of water.

"I will do what I can," Ariock announced to the crowded room.

Tentatively, he spread his awareness through the wall and into the core of the ship.

He had a vague recollection of how it was constructed. Thomas had explained everything, but Ariock barely understood reactors and superionic ice. This starship was more of an unpolished cave than a technological marvel. It was embarrassing.

Ariock inhabited the outer tank, cubic mile by cubic mile. This tank comprised the bulk of the megastructure that was the ship.

This part was supposed to be liquid water, according to Varktezo. It was almost entirely glaciated.

And Ariock lacked a wildfire ability. He could not generate heat the way Thomas could. If he threw lightning superbolts into the tank, he might damage the reactors. Ice was likely to rebuff his electricity instead of conducting it.

Finally, deep down, he detected slush. It wasn't much liquid, but it should be enough.

Ariock centered his awareness in that mineralized slush. He pulsed energy into it.

Electricity forked the ice. Water seeped into newly formed cracks.

There was not much gravity at the ship's core. Since the core rotated, it generated some centrifugal force, and the liquid spewed outward, farther into the ice. Its force cracked more ice. And more.

Ariock helped it along. He electrified the water again. And again.

Miles of ice cracked. With every surge of power, the ice broke apart exponentially more, changing to slush and finally to liquid.

Excess lightning scrawled away from Ariock. The crowd leaped back. Water erupted from the spigots, spraying across handcarts and head covers.

People waded through the overflow, laughing with relief, eager to fill their jugs. Ariock sensed a distant reactor firing up. Then another. The machinery of this starship was finally getting restarted, no doubt due to Varktezo.

"Stop!" That was Vy, her voice distant.

Ariock withdrew his awareness and slammed wholly into his body.

The headache was immediate and sharp. Pain surged through his skull. It felt manageable, but it kept intensifying. Ariock sagged against the cold wall.

He became aware of cheering cries and joyful splashing. The tensions had evaporated, everyone was laughing and talking, and Ariock realized that he must have been oblivious to a lot of subtext.

These leaders had made promises. What had they said? Probably *The messiah will bless us with water.* And if they had been wrong? They would have faced a lot of rage. Their people might have torn them apart.

But everything was fine.

Vy pranced in a circle, gazing at the snowflakes that sifted down. Her woolens and hair were damp and clinging to her body. That was a sight. Ariock admired her rosy-cheeked beauty and tried not to stare.

A happy nussian brought them each mugs of ice-cold water. "A drink to life!" she shouted.

Once they had quenched their thirst, Vy grabbed Ariock's hand. "Come on!"

He allowed Vy to lead him through the celebrating crowd. He winced with every step because his head hurt so much.

Why was it snowing?

Ariock supposed he must have caused some flurries, thanks to condensation and excess ionization in the air. He seemed unable to avoid unintended consequences.

Vy tugged him down a side corridor. They wove past excited people bearing messages or hauling rickshaws laden with water jugs. Vy's footprints in the snow were dainty. A foot and a dot.

She pressed him into a secluded maze of rooms. They passed aliens who offered respectful murmurs and left the vicinity. Vy asked a couple of nussians to give Ariock privacy. The nussians lumbered away, leaving behind a flickering lantern.

"Now then." Vy had a mischievous look. "You need to rest and recover." She pulled folded blankets off a shelf and spread them. Supply crates offered a wall of semiprivacy.

Snowflakes tingled on Ariock's skin. Despite his headache, he was curious as to what Vy had in mind.

"Lie down," she said.

Ariock lay on the blankets.

"Stay there." Vy straddled his lower body. "You're not using your powers again today. All you're going to do"—she snuggled closer, lying completely on top of him—"is warm me up."

He wanted to touch the warmth of her bare skin. She was so bundled up in woolens, so cozy-looking.

Her hair formed a tangled privacy curtain around their faces. "I take it," she said, snuggling even closer, "that you're in too much pain to—"

Ariock wrapped his arms around her.

It was an impulsive move, but Vy snuggled close and kissed him. One of her dainty hands grasped his neck.

She was a bundle of gorgeous invitation. She adjusted her position on Ariock, and he became aware of every curve of her body. A section of his own woolen outfit was growing too tight. He dared to hold her not so gently, to make sure she wouldn't easily slide—

"Ariock Dovanack," an icy voice said with a foreign accent.

That wasn't Vy.

Ariock jerked upright, causing Vy to yelp. Crackles of electricity jagged off him until he reined in his awareness.

Evenjos stood there.

She was colorless, her lips and eyes whiter than a corpse, the ends of her long hair coiling as fog. Her extremities—wings and feet—were barely a hint, just vapor. Most of her body seemed to be composed of ice granules.

"You drained me," Evenjos said. "You nearly killed me."

Ariock studied the frozen Lady and tried to figure out if she was alive or undead. Could she breathe? Did she have a heartbeat?

"You are stronger than anyone I have ever heard of," Evenjos said, each word a throaty caress. "You depleted me. You depleted your friends, and this ship."

Ariock guessed she must be fishing for an apology. He sighed. Evenjos deserved his gratitude, but really, she had chosen the wrong moment to materialize.

He just wanted her to go away. Nothing short of Armageddon was worth interrupting his private time with Vy. He had yearned for intimacy all his life. He had a lifetime of loneliness to make up for.

"Your strength," Evenjos said, "can build worlds."

"Please come back later," Ariock said.

"Yeah." Vy clung to Ariock. "No offense, but the two of you are depleted. You should both take some downtime and get some rest."

The ice-sculpture version of Evenjos stared down at Vy, as if taken aback that such a person would dare to speak in her presence. Her cohesion faltered, and her body loosened into a simulation of a woman-shaped blizzard.

She tightened into a solid state again and pointedly ignored Vy. "Are you a self-taught yerud?" she asked Ariock.

"I . . ." Ariock considered polite ways to ask Evenjos to leave. He didn't want to get drawn into an academic conversation right now.

"I am flexible." Evenjos demonstrated, making her body as narrow as a ribbon. Then she filled out into a boldly voluptuous shape. "I can stretch myself to any shape or size."

She grew taller, and Ariock felt his face redden. Had Evenjos delved into his fears?

He had begun to have secret—but major—worries about sex. If he could resize himself, that would solve the potential problem.

Vy looked pained. Had the same worry crossed her mind?

"A little education about your powers will go a long way." Evenjos smiled and extended a tendril of vapor. Her moisture caressed the back of Ariock's neck.

"Perhaps you can resize yourself. How are we to know?" Her voice softened, full of innuendos. "Unless we experiment?"

Her tendril withdrew just before Ariock could wave his hand to dissipate it.

He inwardly admitted that he wanted to learn whatever tricks Evenjos could teach him. She had apparently ruled a planet. She exhibited total control over her powers. She must know more about being a Yeresunsa than anyone alive today.

And since the Torth Empire had declared war, Ariock would need all the help he could get.

But. Even so.

He needed to figure out how to tell Evenjos to schedule an appointment. He just had to do it without angering her beyond reason.

"Ariock can't use his powers right now," Vy said. "He'll let you know when he's ready to take a lesson." She glared.

Evenjos looked icier and more chiseled. "Send away your service girl," she told Ariock. "It is inappropriate—"

"Vy is not a servant." Ariock's own voice was hard, but he didn't care. "The people on this ship call her an angel. I'd rather you do the same." He wasn't going to tolerate insults aimed at someone he cared about.

Both Vy and Evenjos looked taken aback.

"I am too weak for this argument." Evenjos collapsed into a dusty, granular fog. Vy looked pleased.

A second later, Evenjos solidified again. "Ariock Dovanack? A Yeresunsa with raw power such as yours cannot afford to make mistakes out of ignorance. You will get people killed that way."

Ariock did not need the reminder. Sadly, he had already gotten people killed.

"Not all the Yeresunsa who joined our link survived," Evenjos said.

Was she talking about the room full of unconscious Yeresunsa?

Ariock studied her colorless visage, trying to figure out if she was lying in order to grab his attention. Surely he would have noticed dead bodies being carted away?

Then he saw Vy's mournful lack of surprise.

"Three of the warriors stopped breathing," Vy confirmed when she saw Ariock's look. "They were taken away before you woke up." She touched his shoulder. "Ariock, we don't know if they died from depletion. It could be they were already weakened for some other reason. Maybe they were just sick."

But Ariock knew. It was his fault.

"They were warned not to use their powers beforehand," Evenjos said. "But they were just untrained yerud. Ignorance got them killed." She lost cohesion, becoming a cloud of snowy dust. "Seek me when you are willing to learn," she said, disembodied.

Her dust ribboned away, snaking into the darkness. She vanished.

Ariock was left feeling cold. He curled his arm around Vy, but their moment of passion was gone. Vy's mind was clearly elsewhere.

And Ariock felt much the same way. He really did need to learn how to stop making stupid, deadly mistakes. If Evenjos could teach him to fight smarter, to resize himself . . . to get passionate without the risk of hurting Vy . . . well, he needed her lessons.

CHAPTER 10

THE FULLNESS OF TIME

Had anyone in history ever had such a lasting mega-audience before?

Hundreds of billions, and sometimes trillions, orbited the mind of the Upward Governess whenever she rose in the Megacosm. The Majority paid attention to her every whim. They relayed her smallest thoughts across the galaxy, from the bustling hub planets to the sparse populations of the outer fringes.

She was famous beyond compare.

Servants of All bowed in her local presence, respectfully aware of the enormous audience that now watched their every move. One of them offered a hover-tray, exquisitely molded from brushed palladium. He opened the lid to reveal vials full of a pale-green serum.

NAI-13.

The Upward Governess quivered with unrestrained eagerness. The proffered medicine was not quite everlasting life, but it was a start. A good start. The best start she'd ever had.

NAI-13 was an improvement upon NAI-12. Instead of necessitating an injection every six hours, it only had to be injected once per day.

An oblivious team of human "scientists" on Earth had developed this refined version. The Upward Governess was certain that she could improve it even more, given half a chance.

NO. Her massive audience coiled around her.

You work for Us.

Against the enemies.

You will get another supply of NAI-13 when—

—if—

—your schemes lead to the destruction of the Betrayer.

Or the Giant.

DO NOT FAIL US.

Their harmony was inescapable. The Torth Majority was as ubiquitous and necessary to her survival as the air she breathed.

Of course. The Upward Governess wanted to defeat the enemies as much as anyone. She assured the Majority that she would obey and serve. She was trustworthy. She was the opposite of a mad renegade, like the Betrayer.

Now (don't just stand there), she thought. *Give Me a dose!*

A beautifully engineered injection pen, embossed with curlicues and embedded with diamonds, lay next to the medicine. One of the Servants of All reached out with his awareness, showing off his telekinetic power.

He was clumsy with it. The Majority chastised him, and soon the other Servant took over, using his hands.

This Servant was one of the fools who wore an inhibitor patch. Did he think he could erase the fact that he had powers? The cabal of Yeresunsa could not be stuffed back into secrecy. Most Servants of All were smart enough to resign themselves to their new fate—they were criminals who also happened to be living weapons.

Sort of like supergeniuses.

And they were doomed, too. Just like supergeniuses. As soon as the enemies were destroyed, the Servants of All would be executed. That was justice.

The Upward Governess could not help but feel some kinship with their ilk.

But Servants of All were more fortunate than she was. She tried not to resent the fact that they could go wherever they wished as long as the Majority approved of it.

She already missed her indoor lake. Her bountiful gardens. She missed the stellar observatory atop her palatial suite.

But she had to stay hidden.

The Betrayer had two friends who could teleport. If he was determined to win this war—and all signs indicated that he was, indeed, fully renegade—he would hunt down and assassinate every supergenius in the Torth Empire. The Upward Governess had no doubt about that.

So she dared not reveal her new location. The Imposter and the Betrayer were all too capable of scanning the Megacosm.

The other supergeniuses seemed to welcome their shiny new laboratories and their private armies and their secret lairs. Most of them viewed it as a promotion. The lesser supergeniuses were either children or low ranks. Many lived on baby farms. They were unused to owning more than three slaves and a handful of private rooms.

Now they were coddled as never before. The Spin Overture seemed to overflow with her own self-importance these days. The Geodesic Flux was proud to be valued as a crucial military asset. They trusted the Torth Majority to reward them with ever greater gifts.

The Upward Governess rotated her well-cushioned hoverchair, surveilling the shiny countertops and workstations of her newly constructed underground laboratory. An adjacent room was already full of slaves in cages, ready to be experimented upon. Construction overseers had installed specialized equipment, such as enantiomeric scaffolds and chiral adsorption surfaces, to her specifications.

She had no valid reason to complain.

But did she really need Servants of All standing guard full-time inside her underground fortress?

Did she really need an army of Red Ranks nearby, ready to run to her aid if she mentally cried for help?

In private, behind her mental screen of trivial data, the Upward Governess suspected that she was not the only supergenius who found this arrangement to be . . . well, ominous. She was sure that in secret, the Twins, at least, lusted for the same thing she longed for.

Freedom.

They yearned to delve into the forbidden sciences: artificial intelligence, superluminal travel, gene therapy. They wanted life without barriers. Like her, they were sick of the constraints that polite society shackled them with.

The one who had killed himself—the Colossal Failure—had been open about his deviant, illegal yearnings, in his own sick way. He just hadn't been crafty enough to bide his time and play smart with the Majority.

What a pathetic creature. His mind had stunk like a billion depressed slaves.

Even so, his death was a loss.

The Servant of All dabbed the Upward Governess's fleshy arm, preparing the injection site. He emanated such a potent mix of emotions, his mood was like that of a slave. Many Servants of All seemed to have suppressed kinks.

They were capable of hiding quite a lot.

Might one of them hide a sinister power? Could this one brainwash people?

The Upward Governess did not like having a Servant so close to her, within low telepathy range. After all, she had calculated the statistical probabilities. The Betrayer was almost certainly not the only telepath in existence who could twist minds.

His power might even be common.

Nevertheless, the Upward Governess screened her unease behind a cascade of trivial calculations, and she welcomed the injection. She would not let paranoia rule her life.

She envisioned the runaway cellular deaths in her spine halting, giving her a real chance to live to adulthood. It was glorious. She relished the injection. This supply of NAI-13 belonged to her alone, and it would last for three whole months.

Please Us, the Majority sang.

Please Us, and We will reward you with MORE.

Well. The Upward Governess supposed she ought to get back to work.

Before dropping out of the Megacosm, she scooped up the latest news and updates. Nuclear engineers were hard at work. They were mass-producing warheads to protect every major hub of civilization. Chemical factories were outputting lots and lots of inhibitor serum. Factories were manufacturing rail guns and entropy bombs by the thousands.

The Torth Majority wanted military innovations and munitions. No one could guess what *enough* might look like.

The Death Architect had requested humans for her secret experiments. She claimed to be working on a surprise.

People speculated wildly on what that might be, but they had no hints to go on. Military scientists were careful not to leak schematics or anything that might imply what they were innovating.

The Twins had their own secret project. Although they had not given away any hints about it, the Upward Governess had drawn her own private conclusions based on the chiral derivatizing agents that they had ordered for their respective laboratories. They must be researching neurotransmitters. In all likelihood, they were making improvements to the inhibitor serum.

As for the Upward Governess herself . . .

Well, she felt confident that her project would save civilization. It was simply brilliant.

She assigned one of her less important experiments to the Spin Overture, and she gave calculations to the Stemmer Linguist, who was only six years old. The youngest supergeniuses were not privy to what the empire's top minds were working on, but they were eager to help out.

Her audience spun and danced, singing praises throughout the Megacosm.

The Upward Governess is so perfect!

So cunning!

So promising!

Bitterness wafted from the usual corners. *Scientific frippery is not enough to defeat the Giant,* the Former Commander thought. *We must have Yeresunsa who can outmatch him in battle.*

The Former Commander barely held a fraction of the audience she used to command. She had once been the most powerful being in the known universe, commanding all living things by dint of her popular influence and the authority the Majority had vested in her.

Now she was something else.

A military general? A wayward champion of civilization?

Even while the Megacosm had reeled during the destruction of the Torth Homeworld, many Torth had begun to theorize about the Giant's heretofore-unknown powers. How might they gain powers like his?

Now that the Torth Empire was at war, the Majority was urging every citizen to remove their inhibitor patches. Torth were encouraged to experiment, to find out if they had dormant abilities.

And there were, indeed, dormant powers among low-ranked Torth.

Many were Yellow Ranks. Some were even pubescent teenagers, fresh off baby farms. They were too timid, too flabby, too frail, or too physically disabled to join the military. Many had psychological blocks. In normal times, these unfit people would have been rejected from the upper ranks. They never would have risen into the highest ranks, the Servants of All.

But now? The Torth Empire was at war.

These new additions to the military were almost as numerous as Red Ranks, although they lacked discipline and combat training. Until a few days ago, they had been ordinary citizens. Now they were fledgling Yeresunsa.

The Majority had voted to give them pink-colored irises. Neither red nor white, they were Rosy Recruits.

And they were powerful.

Clairvoyance—otherwise known as astral projection, or ghosting—was likely the key to teleportation. But it was a draining power, and the few Rosy Recruits who were able to do it could only ghost for less than a minute. Then exhaustion overtook them, and they suffered a dangerous warning headache, which could lead to a coma and death.

The Former Commander believed that they would improve. The Rosy Recruits had only been experimenting with their powers for a few days. They were like newly hatched moths, flexing their wings for the very first time.

I agree. The Upward Governess adjusted one of her refactoring experiments. Teleportation was an enormous advantage. The Torth Empire could not afford to lag behind. Let the Rosy Recruits continue to exercise their new powers.

The enemies will not teleport any time soon, she predicted. *The fact that they are fleeing rather than attacking implies that the Giant is depleted.*

Her audience silently trumpeted her opinion, sharing it with everyone. The entire Torth Majority pulsed with pride.

Find the enemies.
KILL THEM.
Find the enemies.
KILL THEM.
Find the enemies.
KILL THEM.

The motivational drumbeat filled the background of everybody's mind. Whosoever appeased the Majority would be showered with rewards.

The Upward Governess did not need the reminder. She would save civilization.

Anyhow, the Torth Empire was the mightiest civilization in history. Their specialty was innovation. She would learn everything the enemies knew and improve upon it. She could not help but be victorious.

The Upward Governess smothered a strange sense of disappointment at that thought. She was naturally entitled to victory. Of course she was.

Yet, deep down, she secretly hoped the Betrayer would throw another unexpected challenge at her, if only to make life more interesting. If only . . .

If only he had stayed with Me.

The Upward Governess hid that borderline-illegal thought.

But she could not quite hide her own yearning from herself. She wanted to visit the Betrayer one last time, if only to find out why he'd betrayed her and the rest of the Torth Empire. Was that so wrong?

He had a certain boldness. A daring ambition. He was exceptional.

That was why she had vouched for him when he was merely a primitive. That was why she had insisted on welcoming Yellow Thomas as her one and only pupil.

And now her handpicked pupil was somehow flourishing, although he was surrounded by mere runaways and primitives. It was mysterious. And frustrating.

His death would be a major loss to the universe. A necessary loss, but still. A major loss.

The Upward Governess forced her thoughts toward science. She was not going to dwell on meager matters.

Find them.
KILL THEM.
Find them.
KILL THEM.

The drumbeat went on in its strident loop, promising to end only once the enemies were dead.

CHAPTER 11

AGAINST A GODDESS

Vy knew that Ariock used words like *bumbling* and *monster* to describe himself. She remembered the way his mother had spoken about him, like he was fragile. She remembered that Ariock had spent years hiding, concealing himself from the world, thinking of himself as a freak.

But that was not reality.

In reality, Ariock looked like someone who was capable of throwing the Stratower. Add a beard, and he might pass for a classical god, like Zeus or Thor or Shiva. Was she crazy to think so?

Unfortunately, Evenjos saw it, too. And she was busy making him aware of it.

"You have immense power." Evenjos twined around Ariock. "You could reignite all the engines at once, and it would not dent your prodigious strength. You are a god."

Ariock, predictably, looked uncomfortable.

He stood in the command center, facing a detailed holograph that Varktezo had conjured at a workstation. The starship's reactors needed power. Thomas probably could have figured out a way to get them restarted, but Thomas was still unconscious, along with all the other Yeresunsa.

People were worried. They had water but not much else.

And people kept asking about their loved ones among the warriors. Cherise kept checking in on Flen. Chaniyelem and other councilors seemed concerned about Jinishta. Vy had also revisited the room, not only to check on Thomas and Garrett, but also to make sure that Thomas was receiving his regular six-hour dose of NAI-12.

She had not told Ariock yet, but she worried that if some of the warriors were not revived soon, they might stop breathing. They seemed so weak.

"What do you think?" Ariock looked questioningly toward Vy. "I could try to reignite the reactors. Or should I try to revive Thomas instead?"

"You can do whatever you wish," Evenjos said in a purring tone, completely ignoring Vy, as if she didn't exist. "Wait another day, and you should have enough power to do both."

Ariock kept disentangling himself from Evenjos's grasping arms and wings, but she kept sidling up to him again. Apparently she could not take a hint.

"How fast does power replenish?" Ariock asked her.

Evenjos pouted. "There is an equation to determine the exact replenishment rate, but I do not remember it."

When Ariock looked disillusioned, she hurriedly went on.

"There are two variables. I remember that. Health is one, and the other depends on how fast the Yeresunsa drained his power." She regained her teasing mood. "But if you would like to conserve your powers . . ." She trailed a finger across his chest. "I can think of pleasurable ways to pass the time."

Ariock began to protest.

Evenjos said, "Would you not wish to learn whether or not you are a sixth-magnitude healer?"

"A . . ." Ariock trailed off, looking annoyed by his own ignorance. "What's that?"

Although Ariock was clearly just tolerating Evenjos, Vy felt dangerously angry. She wasn't even entirely sure why.

Maybe it was fear. Evenjos seemed capable of lurking anywhere—in the air vents, in snowflakes, anywhere—and Vy didn't like feeling so vulnerable. The winged Lady might act harmless, but everyone knew that she could destroy a planet.

"I am a sixth-magnitude healer." Evenjos snaked her body, loosening her cohesion as if to demonstrate her power. Then she resolidified. "That is what enables me to shift forms."

Vy wished Ariock would tell Evenjos to go away. Instead, he looked intrigued.

"I was famed for my healing power," Evenjos said. "Many Yeresunsa—at least, in my time—were third-magnitude healers. Some were even fourth. But fifth was very, very rare. And sixth? Unheard-of."

She gave Ariock a playful tap on his chest. She seemed unable to quit touching him.

"I have overheard stories among your people," she said. "It is said that you are a very powerful healer. Perhaps you are fifth magnitude?"

"What does fifth entail?" Ariock seemed entirely absorbed in what Evenjos was teaching.

Or maybe he just enjoyed looking at her.

It was impossible to deny that Evenjos was attractive, in her default form. Her slinky gown emphasized a slender waist complemented by cartoonishly proportioned breasts. Her wings shone like blades. Although her face was too long, and her eyes too wide-set and big, Vy figured that most men would see her as young and innocent.

Her skin might as well be airbrushed. She glowed with an ethereal light that made everything about her sparkle.

"At fifth," Evenjos said in her sultry voice, "one can cause plants to grow or die. A powerful fifth-magnitude healer could cause a forest to grow dense underbrush or manipulate roots to form barricades, all very quickly."

Ariock gazed at Evenjos as if she was the most fascinating person he had ever met. "And you can do that?"

"Of course." Evenjos waggled her hips. "I told you, I am sixth. That means I have all of the lesser magnitudes."

"And those are . . . ?" Ariock asked.

As Evenjos filled him in on the various magnitudes of the healing power, Vy wondered why she was bothering to sit nearby and watch the two of them chit-chat. She had nothing worthwhile to contribute to a conversation about Yeresunsa powers.

And if Ariock was going to rest—as Vy herself had recommended—then he might as well spend that time learning.

Vy understood that. Or she tried to.

"It sounds as if you are at least a fourth-magnitude healer." Evenjos pressed even closer to Ariock, touching him in too many places. "Would you like to learn if you can control your physiology?"

"How does it work?" Ariock was no longer trying to escape her fake-accidental touches.

"So eager to learn." Evenjos laughed teasingly. "It is an art form. It is much like sculpting. Every form I take, I have studied and perfected over many years."

She made her "art" sound beautiful and creative, like Cherise's drawings. But Vy was sure it was all vanity. Evenjos might as well be a porn star, bragging about all the plastic surgery she'd had done.

Ariock glanced at Vy, as if seeking her permission for some unknown thing.

Vy didn't know how to react. But when Ariock returned his attention to Evenjos, Vy stood. She was not going to watch Ariock take sexiness lessons from an ancient crone passing herself off as a gorgeous angel. If that was what he wanted, well, fine. But she had better things to do than watch.

Ariock pulled away from Evenjos.

"Ariock Dovanack." Evenjos had a stroking, caressing tone. "You think so little of yourself. I cannot understand it. You and I, we are not ordinary people." She ran her arms over his. "In my time, people worshipped Yeresunsa like us as gods."

Your time failed, Vy wanted to say. But she did not quite dare.

Evenjos looked Ariock up and down. "Do you really wish to shrink your size? I like you as you are."

Vy wished for a giant vacuum cleaner so she could clear away the dust.

But wishful thinking would not put her on equal footing with someone as powerful as Evenjos. Vy limped toward the exit. Even the ummins were too busy to pay attention to her.

"Hold on," Ariock said. "Vy?"

She turned.

"I can take a lesson later." Ariock went to her and put his big hands on her shoulders. "I don't want to ignore you or shut you out."

Vy searched his gaze. She expected buried annoyance, but Ariock only looked concerned and gentle.

"I just . . ." His gaze became earnest. "I may need help."

Vy met his stare. This was the first time Ariock had admitted that he was not invincible.

And why not? His near-death coma must have shaken him. He had met the limit of his strength. The Torth Empire would never quit hunting him and his friends, and he must fear that he would not be strong enough to fend off their next attack.

And there was a matter of size.

Vy liked the size difference between herself and Ariock, yet at the same time, she was aware of how gentle he was with her. There was an awkwardness between them, a barrier to intimacy, and it was as much her fault as his.

Because, inwardly, Vy was unsure how intimacy with Ariock would work. He was majestic but also . . . well. Intimidating.

Maybe his reasons for wanting to change his size had nothing to do with Evenjos and everything to do with Vy.

She gripped Ariock fiercely to let him know that she cared and that she considered him hers. "Take your lesson."

He gave her a questioning look.

Vy nodded. "I want to check on Thomas, anyway."

As she considered the full day she had spent with Ariock, she realized that she had ignored a lot of messengers and unspoken requests. Perhaps it would be a good idea to engage with the ship's population instead of ignoring them.

"I'll check on Kessa, too," Vy said.

Ariock smiled gratefully. "I'll be glad to know how she's doing."

"I'll let you know." Vy offered her own smile, letting Ariock know that she trusted him.

She exited the command center. As she limped away, she heard Evenjos's silken tone, full of admiration, telling Ariock what power magnitudes meant. Vy dropped her smile. It had begun to feel as artificial as Evenjos's ridiculously proportioned body.

Plenty of people wanted Vy's attention. Well, she supposed they actually wanted Ariock's attention, but they were willing to settle for his girlfriend, or whatever she was to him. They begged for her opinion on judicial matters and all sorts of other topics. Vy made promises as she walked through the starship.

The unconscious Yeresunsa all remained in a persistent vegetative state. At least their friends were attentive to their needs.

Garrett's eyelids twitched in REM sleep. His color had warmed to that of a living person instead of a fresh corpse, and Vy figured that he, at least, was likely to recover without outside help.

Thomas looked like he was on the verge of death. But Weptolyso swore that bedside medics were taking care of his needs, albeit resentfully, and he did look clean and well cared for.

After Vy had given Thomas his scheduled dose of NAI-12, she went to acquaint herself with the starship's population.

She visited an impromptu bazaar. She checked out a makeshift tavern. After asking around, she found the room where Cherise was teaching alphabet basics to aliens.

Vy sat in during the last part of the class, trying to be unobtrusive. She never could have imagined her foster sister being so . . . well, talkative.

This was a Cherise Vy had never seen. Confident. Outgoing. Beautiful.

Cherise still hunched her shoulders sometimes, and she would get embarrassed if anyone addressed her in a challenging tone. But then some of her most engaged students would defend her. They truly wanted to learn, and their needs seemed to open up a well of helpfulness inside Cherise.

After the class, Vy and Cherise found a makeshift tea vendor where they could sit on crates and chat.

"Is Flen okay?" Cherise asked.

"I think so. He has plenty of care."

"And Thomas?" Cherise lowered her voice. "He's well cared for, right?"

Vy nodded, studying Cherise. "Have you given any thought to how you're going to handle them once they wake up?"

Cherise looked quizzical. It was clear that she saw no conflict of interest in having a close relationship with a Yeresunsa who hated the guts of her ex–best friend, who also happened to be a Yeresunsa.

Well, maybe she was right. Maybe Flen and Thomas were mature enough to let bygones be bygones and live and let live.

Vy shrugged the matter away. "I mean," she said, shifting away from her original question, "are you going to keep teaching? I hope so. You're making a world of difference."

Cherise's face relaxed in a self-conscious grin. Somehow, that smile looked more natural on her than her typical solemn expression.

"I just wanted to show Flen that we still have a future," she said. "And we can do something other than sit around and mourn for the dead."

Flen was grieving for his parents and sister, lost in the flood and Torth invasion.

"Does Flen want to teach, also?" Vy asked. The Alashani had their own form of writing, with a lot of loops and curlicues, but only lawmen and clerks practiced it. Warriors such as Flen had no use for reading tax documents or merchant's bookkeeping, so they never learned literacy. "What would he teach?"

"Alashani values," Cherise said promptly. She gestured at the aliens around them. "You know, an introduction to freedom."

Vy inwardly wondered if Alashani values might be problematic. The Alashani considered themselves superior to all other species. They had lived in freedom, so therefore, as far as they were concerned, they were better than all the species who had been conquered and enslaved by the Torth.

But that would be a heavy discussion, and probably best left for some other time.

"Well," Vy told Cherise, "what you're doing is above and beyond. Everyone really appreciates it."

They chatted a bit longer. Soon Cherise needed to teach another class, and Vy was free to explore the starship.

The more she explored, the more impressed she was by the ideas springing out of the mix of cultures. Former slaves might not need lessons about how to navigate freedom. They were teaching themselves, encountering philosophy and a system of justice for the first time.

Meanwhile, homeless Alashani were gaining respect for street-savvy aliens who knew how to hustle, as well as those who knew how to survive without stealing from fellow refugees.

Everywhere Vy went, she overheard excited people swapping stories or educating each other about a craft, a merchant practice, spiritual beliefs, or whatever they considered to be alien and interesting.

She was in a garment gallery, where aliens were adding their own flair to Alashani fashion, when a nussian showed up and made an announcement.

"Tomorrow," the nussian rumbled in a jovial voice, "Ariock Dovanack and Jonathan Stead will hold a war council."

That news quieted everyone in the room.

"They will hold it in the biggest gallery," the nussian went on. "Obviously, room for attendance is limited. Kessa the Wise will send a rotating queue of messengers to every deck to repeat what is said so that everyone may hear. None of you will be left out."

The crowd began to buzz with conversations, and Vy found herself glum and left out. Had Garrett woken up and learned that the Torth Empire was doing something ominous? Or had Ariock learned something incredible from Evenjos and decided to make it a big public announcement?

Someone tugged Vy's cardigan. She turned and blinked in surprise. She hadn't seen Pung in a while.

"Garrett sent me to find you," Pung said before Vy could speak. "There is a seat reserved for you at the war council. He wants you to be there."

Vy felt mollified, but she had questions. "Garrett's awake?"

"Yes." Pung made a face. "He is weak and sickly, and he says it will take another three days for him to recover his powers. But that does not stop him from giving orders like he's a premier Yeresunsa."

Vy could imagine the cantankerous old man offending everyone, aliens and albinos alike. He would need to invoke authority—that of Ariock—to get things done.

Which explained . . .

"This war council is Garrett's idea," Vy guessed. "Isn't it?"

Pung nodded.

"Does Ariock even know about it?" Vy asked.

"Weptolyso is telling him right now," Pung replied. "Garrett asked that Ariock and Evenjos attend. He also wants as many elders and councilors as we can fit in the room. He says he has very important things to tell us all."

Vy folded her arms. She was glad that Ariock's great-grandfather was awake, and she was grateful that he had remembered to include her, even sending her a personal invitation. Yet at the same time, her level of unease jumped by several notches. Garrett Dovanack, aka Jonathan Stead, had a way of roping her into actions that went way beyond her comfort level.

She suspected he was going to start doing the same to Ariock.

CHAPTER 12

A THOUSAND TIMES A THOUSAND

A sense of disquiet was growing inside Evenjos.

Ariock was a pinnacle Yeresunsa, an immensely strong stormbringer, yet he refused to acknowledge her advances. Didn't he understand that she was . . . well . . . perfect?

He and she were peers. Royals.

Surely they ought to get married?

Evenjos could not carry a pregnancy, so they could not have royal children, but even so. All the ancient laws and customs dictated that royals belonged with other royals, just as commoners belonged with other commoners.

But Ariock was making his preference for commoners quite plain.

When Ariock had received a message from one of his inferiors, he had quit Evenjos's lessons without a second thought. He seemed utterly unaware of how insulting that was. Garrett was just a steward or a minister, or something like that. Yet Ariock hurried to him like he was not the superior Yeresunsa.

Evenjos trailed after Ariock in the form of dust. She lurked in a ventilation shaft, unseen.

So she overheard when Garrett brushed Ariock off.

"You'll have to find out what this is about tomorrow, along with everyone else," the old man said in a booming voice that bore no trace of servility. "Sorry. I only have the energy to say it once."

Instead of rebuking the old man, Ariock retreated like a chastised child.

Evenjos could not understand that. Which one of them was in charge? Shouldn't it be the most powerful Yeresunsa? Ariock was clearly the superior, yet he didn't act like it.

Evenjos followed him again, waiting breathlessly for their lessons to resume. All Ariock would need to do was say her name.

Instead, he sought the crippled serving wench.

Evenjos spied on Ariock with incredulity. She had assumed that the wench was just a casual pleasure giver, a toy. Commoners existed to please royals. Evenjos used to bed her own household servants. She had never considered any of them worth sharing secrets with.

But Ariock was clearly not using the commoner girl, Vy, as a sex toy. He conversed with the wench. At one point, he asked a merchant to gift Vy with an embroidered hair ribbon, which the merchant eagerly wove into her hair.

The people of this ship were treating that crippled wench like a queen.

It was ludicrous, and horrifically insulting, but everyone acted as if Vy—and not Evenjos—was a powerful Yeresunsa worthy of being the equal of Ariock.

They were wrong. So wrong. Yet they didn't even seem aware of it.

Evenjos lurked closer to Ariock and Vy, listening to them converse about things that seemed incomprehensible. What were "slaves"? And what was "Earth"? The two of them seemed to originate from a place Evenjos had never heard of.

If Evenjos understood their conversation correctly, Ariock used to be powerless.

That might explain why Ariock had no basic comprehension about the fundamentals of powers. He didn't know the difference between magnitudes and incarnations. He couldn't even recite his own stats.

The more he spoke, the more uneasy Evenjos became. Ariock considered himself to be some type of commoner, like Vy. They were "human," whatever that meant.

Evenjos had always been aware, in a vague way, that the line between royals and commoners was blurry. A royal family could lose its status if it went six generations without producing a Yeresunsa heir. At that point, the family would lose its hereditary lands and titles and become mere nobility. They could fall even further if they failed to adequately serve their betters as clerks, tax collectors, and so forth.

Likewise, a commoner peasant might miraculously be born with Yeresunsa powers. If it was not a royal bastard—if it had no provable royal lineage—then it was a genuine miracle. Such a blessed child would then elevate his or her entire family to royal status.

That used to be every commoner's dream.

Then Unyat's Formula had created a whole generation of . . .

Evenjos shivered, although she had no corporeal body. The past was dangerous to think about. She wasn't going to.

She watched in silence, unseen, as Ariock ate a light dinner of mushroom paste with Vy. They joked with each other in teasing tones.

And then, later, Ariock slept with Vy curled in his arms.

Disgusting. They had no concept of peerage.

When they awoke, Evenjos followed them into the gallery of Yeresunsa. Ariock visited each comatose person and revived them, starting with that dangerous monster known as Thomas.

If not for these cave dwellers, Evenjos supposed she might be dead from depletion. She owed them her strength, at least a little bit. She ought to join Ariock and help revive every one of them.

Instead, she watched from the shadows near the ceiling, unseen and undetected, while Ariock worked. Her own weakness made her feel . . . well, unusually vulnerable.

Anyhow, Ariock had more than enough power to spare. He was not yet at his full strength, but he was still strong enough to pull a thousand weak Yeresunsa back from the brink of death. He was magnificent.

Presently, all the Yeresunsa were awake, if groggy.

The dangerous one floated away in his newly repainted hoverchair. He was needed in the command center, and Evenjos was relieved to see him go. Although she existed as a loose collection of dust particles, she still had a consciousness, with thoughts and emotions. Any telepath in the room could read her mind.

The gallery became busier. Half the ship's population wanted to mingle with these low-level Yeresunsa.

The old man, Garrett, limped through the crowd. "Weptolyso," he called to a nussian. "Would you mind having someone haul a wagon up there, onto the dais?"

The nussian looked resentful.

"I'll need to be up high," Garrett added. "So everyone can hear what I have to say."

Weptolyso obeyed, but only after he received a covert nod from the elderly female ummin who seemed to be a top chieftain.

Evenjos had trouble understanding the interpersonal dynamics between these people. She used to receive diplomats from Nuss and from Umdalkdul, as well as from other alien civilizations. But where were the famed merchants of Jodinak? Or the gnomes of Yoft, for that matter? She had not seen a single jodinak or yoftian aboard this starship.

And since when did nussians and ummins get along so well?

How was it that such a wide variety of aliens shared a common language? It made no sense.

"I'll need you up on the dais," Garrett told Ariock. "Sit by my side." He patted an embroidered rug next to the parked wagon. "And can someone go find Evenjos? She needs to hear this as well."

Wasn't Garrett aware that Evenjos was present and listening? As a mind reader, he should know.

Well. Evenjos decided that she would visit Garrett later, in private, and gain a summary of whatever public announcement he wanted to make. It was probably something boring. She disliked raucous crowds.

"Evenjos will definitely be interested." Garrett glanced over the heads of ummins and govki, as if searching for her. "I'm going to explain why it was so important to rescue her. She will want to hear every detail of what I have to say."

Sneaky. Garrett must know that she was lurking in the air, but he was tactful enough to not let anyone else know.

That was a gesture of respect.

He had piqued her curiosity.

Evenjos gathered her particles and materialized just outside the gallery, in an opening between nussians. She swept into the room as if she had just arrived right now, by coincidence. Her hair flowed. Her wings gave her enough space for grandeur. She glided past row upon row of cave dwellers, ignoring their awed stares.

Lady of Sorrow. Their minds were full of that title, and they meant it for her.

Evenjos had no desire to be their Lady of Sorrow. What did these alien people expect of her?

She supposed Garrett would explain.

She forced herself to nod toward the lesser Yeresunsa as if she cared about them. They were clearly loyal to Ariock. She might need their loyalty, so it was prudent to treat them with a modicum of respect.

The aliens in the room were elders or chieftains. Evenjos gave them nods of respect, although the scars on their necks were very disquieting. Those scars meant something horrible, something Evenjos had no desire to learn about.

Garrett perched upon the wagon. "Your Majesty." He gave Evenjos a winsome smile. "I'm so glad to see you. Will you please have a seat next to Ariock?"

Evenjos looked at the rug with disdain. There was no throne, not even a chair. These people were barbaric.

To make matters worse, Vy sat cuddled next to Ariock, looking content.

"Shouldn't Thomas be here?" Ariock sounded concerned. "Maybe we can hold off until he's able to get away from piloting the ship?"

"Nah." Garrett waved dismissively. "He'll suck up everything by osmosis."

Evenjos tried to ignore the fact that the untrained old yerud was apparently in charge. Garrett had summoned everyone in this room. It was surreal.

His explanations had better be worthwhile.

Evenjos arranged herself on the crude rug next to Ariock and Vy. She was aware of several dignitaries seated on this dais as well. There was that elder ummin, Kessa, and also the lead albino warrior, Jinishta.

They seemed comfortable with each other.

But Evenjos was a stranger to these people. Nobody here would be willing to starve to death in order to protect her, the way the last of her loyalists had. Evenjos had never felt so . . . inconsequential.

It was awkward. She didn't like it.

"It looks like a few representatives are still trickling in." Garrett eyed the crowded doorways. "But I'm going to get started."

He clambered to his feet, using his silver staff as a crutch. The wagon gave him height.

The whole audience must be able to see his white beard and hair, as well as his tattered cloak. Garrett looked similar to the albino people, really, except he was larger.

And his boots and armor were well engineered. His clothes were not made of wool or leather, but more durable materials.

Evenjos found herself reassessing Garrett. Whoever he was, he was not one of these lesser Yeresunsa. Nor was he one of the refugees. He was something else.

"Alashani!" Garrett said, loud enough to be heard across the vast room. "Nussians! Ummins! Govki! All of you!"

He had the powerful voice of an orator. His servility was gone.

"My name is Garrett Dovanack. Most of you know me by another name: Jonathan Stead."

That sent ripples of awe through the assembly.

"We are here," Garrett said, "because the Torth destroyed your world and everything you care about."

Evenjos did not contradict him, although she supposed that technically, she had been the one to destroy their world.

"They enslaved you," Garrett went on. "They forced you into hiding. They've ruined your lives. And they stole everything from you."

The crowd murmured with agreement.

"This is my grandson." Garrett gestured. "Ariock Dovanack. Like many of you, he was a slave. The Torth used him for their own sick entertainment. They had no idea that he is destined—by ancient prophecy—to lead you to glory. And to destroy the Torth Empire!"

A cheer went up. Aliens shouted and pumped their fists. The albino people seemed less enthused, but even the most solemn of them were listening.

Evenjos sensed Ariock's extreme unease. He had not expected this blunt announcement.

"It is time to reclaim your lost cities!" Garrett shouted. "And your dignity!"

"YES!" Fists pumped in the air.

Once the assembly quieted, Garrett went on. "I know what I look like." He made a helpless gesture to himself. "You can call me a *rekveh*, because it's true." His voice lowered with shame. "I am a mind reader."

The murmurs darkened.

"But I will fight anyone who calls me a Torth!" Garrett said in his orator voice.

He began pacing the tight space atop the wagon, as if too full of energy to stand still. "I killed my first Torth when I was six years old. This face"—Garrett indicated his own grizzled, bearded visage—"I inherited from my Torth father. But my heart, and my soul, come to me from my Alashani mother." He stopped pacing and stared at the vast audience. "I am an Alashani. My mother was Eidelwen, premier Yeresunsa of Hufti. My father was a Torth, and he murdered her. And I killed him when I was six years old."

Ariock stared at Garrett as if he'd never seen him before.

Evenjos had the sinking realization that she had misjudged Garrett. She knew this type of man. He could shift crowds as easily as she shifted her corporeal form.

Her first lover—the only one she had ever fallen in love with—had been a talented orator like this. He had been a mere commoner, yet he had swayed the entire Yeresunsa Order to open up trade with the Jodinak Empire.

"Though I am a mind reader," Garrett admitted, "I never considered myself to be a Torth. I recognize the Torth for the vile, evil monsters that they are. And I have devoted my life to destroying them!"

The crowd roared with approval.

While late arrivals found places to stand, others hushed them. Everyone wanted to hear what plan Garrett might propose. All gazes fixed on him.

"We are at war," Garrett said. "The Torth will hunt us no matter where we go. We have no choice but to fight them!"

Ariock emanated unease. He did not want to be pressured into acting as a weapon of mass destruction, and Evenjos did not blame him. She hid her own bitterness. She had killed countless millions of those nasty Torth, and yet there were still more of them.

How many more?

It seemed the Formula freaks—those telepaths spawned by Unyat's Formula—had spread throughout the galaxy. Had the Torth conquered all the great civilizations? Was that why so many alien refugees lived in squalor aboard this starship?

Garrett resumed his pacing, drawing the crowd's attention to him.

"One hundred years ago," Garrett said, "the Alashani saved my life. They gave me shelter and succor when I otherwise would have died. I remember your mercy. I absorbed memories of my Alashani mother, and though she was killed on the night of my birth, I love her still. Though I grew old, I never forgot my debt to you."

The albino on the dais, Jinishta, looked gratified and proud.

"Many years ago," Garrett said, "when Ariock was just a babe, I decided to risk my life to repay that debt." He planted himself on the wagon and focused on the assembly. "I joined the Torth in order to learn how to destroy them."

The crowd murmured with shocked curiosity.

"Outwardly," Garrett said, "I was a Blue Rank of the Torth Empire. But in secret? I killed as many Torth as possible."

They listened, rapt.

"While pretending to be a Torth," Garrett went on, "I came across a relic that my telepathic compatriots did not value, but which I recognized as something my Alashani kin would value very much. It was a collection of ancient prophecies, copies of paintings that were yet more ancient. Imagine my surprise when I opened that book . . ." He paused for dramatic effect. ". . . and recognized myself in an illustration."

Ariock wore a wary look. Evenjos sympathized. She wanted no part in prophecies, either, not ever again.

Garrett was oblivious to their reactions, caught up in telling his story. "I saw a painting of Jonathan Stead," he proclaimed, "freeing slaves from the Isolatorium!" He clenched his fist, illustrating how important that painting had seemed. "I saw the lightning I had loosed! The transports falling from the sky! The horde of freed prisoners! And there was the Isolatorium, in the background! It was all accurate, painted by some unfathomably ancient hand!"

He paced.

"For the next several years, I worked hard at translating that book. I learned that the original paintings had existed since before the Torth Empire arose. The painter had predicted the Torth rise to power. And . . ." He paused dramatically. "She predicted their downfall."

The audience murmured with eager curiosity, but Evenjos felt more disquieted than ever.

She recalled an eyeless little girl named Ah Jun. That child—a painter—had been hailed as the most powerful oracle to have ever lived.

Hadn't she painted prophecies like what Garrett was talking about?

"If you ignore my warnings," Ah Jun had told Evenjos, bowing her bald, eyeless head, *"then I see only darkness for a thousand generations. Your cities will crumble and rot. Your people will grow feeble and hide in caves. If you ignore me, Your Grace, you will suffer the torment of a thousand times a thousand lifetimes."*

Evenjos blinked, forcing her mind back to the present. Ah Jun was long dead. The Crystal Hall was long gone. The many lifetimes of torment were over. It was all done with.

"I saw striking similarities between the book's predictions and the Alashani messiah prophecy," Garrett went on. "I realized they were one and the same. Your messiah prophecy is a fragment from that book. Ariock"—he indicated— "is your messiah, but he is also one of four Yeresunsa predicted to come together to destroy the Torth Empire. All four are necessary. Should any of the four fail, then the Torth Empire will continue to thrive."

Silence. Everyone was listening.

"I am one of those four." Garrett's voice carried to the far ends of the gallery. "The book of prophecies defines each of us by a dominant trait. Ariock is Strength. I am Will. The others are Transformation—" He indicated Evenjos. "And Wisdom, who is . . ."

Evenjos reeled, losing track of the words. She recalled words spoken in another era, often repeated by the cult of Ah Jun, even after the girl had hanged herself.

"There is but one glimmer of hope. You will recognize Strength by his great height and the wound on his shoulder. He will come to you in darkness. He will come to you

in need, but he will leave with an army at his heels. Mind readers shall grovel for his mercy, save the one who has earned it. He will be your salvation. Only he can lead you into light and restore you to your former glory. Follow him or perish. Write my words down. Remember, remember, or the darkness will stretch to eternity."

". . . I know you're all tempted to kill our Wisdom," Garrett was saying, "but please, I beg you to keep him alive. He is vital to fulfilling the messiah prophecy. We are going to need him."

Evenjos stood. Ah Jun's prophecies could not be happening now. The oracle was long dead and crumbled to dust.

She backed away from Garrett. "I am no part of that prophecy."

"Yes, you are." Garrett looked at her. "You're the Transformation. We need your help or else the Torth will win for the rest of eternity."

"No." Evenjos backed away farther. It was a sick joke, as if the blind oracle was reaching across the eons to slap her.

Did these people intend to use Evenjos as their weapon? She should have known. Why else would anyone want her around? That was all anyone ever wanted from her—power.

They would be disappointed.

She was not going to fight someone else's war. She had no intention of getting anywhere near the inhibitor serum.

"Let me prove it to you." Garrett flourished, and a huge tome appeared out of the air, dropping heavily onto the wagon. Dust puffed out from its yellowed pages.

Garrett coughed and dropped to his knees, leaning over.

Ariock reached out a steadying hand. "Are you all right?"

". . . more drained . . . than I thought," Garrett said, hacking and wheezing.

Ariock waved dust away. "You shouldn't use your powers while you're recuperating."

That ancient tome filled Evenjos with dread. "I have seen those paintings," she said, trying to make these people understand. "I will not participate again."

"You were in a prophecy?" Garrett's gaze burned with curiosity. "What was it? What happened?"

"IT FAILED." Evenjos emphasized each word. "I was there when Ah Jun . . ." She stopped, because the memory was too painful to explain.

Ah Jun had stood before the crystal throne and warned of a war that would end all wars. And Evenjos . . . she had laughed at the little doomsayer. Told her to go away. After all, Ah Jun was just a Formula freak, a jumped-up commoner, and a child on top of that. What royal would listen to such a wretched little creature?

Evenjos wished now, a thousand times a thousand, that she had listened.

"You met Ah Jun in person?" Garrett jumped off the wagon and approached her, his eyes ablaze with intense curiosity. He clearly wanted to read her mind.

Suck up her past.

Taunt her.

Use her as a weapon.

Trap her in a prison.

Evenjos gathered her sense of body. She hardened her skin, condensing in midair. "I am not your chosen one," she snarled. "Choose somebody else!"

She tore herself apart into glittering dust and flew over astonished faces. She fled out the doorway, down the corridor, and through a series of ventilation shafts until she found a crack so deeply hidden that no one on the ship would find her.

Her dust particles settled in the dark silence. She did not dare shift to a corporeal form.

Although she wanted someone to reassure her that everything would be all right, she knew that would never happen again. No one here loved her. No one here knew her. She was alone.

Dust could not cry. Although she lacked tears and voice, she wept.

CHAPTER 13

OVER A BOOK

Ariock frowned at the exit through which Evenjos had vanished. He had written her off as shallow, but she had just learned that her rescuers wanted to use her as a weapon. Didn't she have every right to be upset about that?

Maybe Ariock ought to try to reassure her.

"So." Garrett clapped him on the back. "Ya ready to slay a few trillion Torth?"

Ariock did not grin. He wanted some reassurances himself.

War might be necessary, but it was definitely not something to be jocular about. The Torth had endless weapons and an endless amount of slaves. They owned just about everything in the galaxy. If Evenjos was terrified . . . well, she had good reason.

Ariock gave his great-grandfather a stony look. "I thought our goal was to escape the Torth."

"That's impossible," Garrett said. "They've got clairvoyants. They can't ghost beyond their own spheres of influence yet, but I'm afraid it's only a matter of time before they figure it out. And once they do? There is the possibility that some of them will learn how to teleport."

Ariock was startled. That had not occurred to him.

Although he supposed it should have. The Torth had conquered the known universe by stealing knowledge and improving upon it. Now that they knew teleportation was possible, their supergeniuses must be scrambling to figure out how to emulate what Ariock could do.

"And don't forget," Garrett went on, "they own the temporal stream network. They've already updated their station probes to detect unusual activity going from one temporal stream to another. So they'll know if we travel conventionally."

Jinishta was staring at the exit. "The Lady of Sorrow . . ."

"I know. Touchy, isn't she?" Garrett jumped back atop the wagon, causing it to rock alarmingly. "Friends!" he shouted. "Our Lady of Sorrow has begged for time to adjust, but do not worry. She will fight for us!"

The murmurs quieted. People glanced at each other, reassured.

"Kessa?" Garrett aimed a warm look her way and made an inviting gesture. "Would you mind taking center stage?"

Kessa looked taken aback.

"We're going to have a new home," Garrett said. "With plenty of food, and new materials and supplies. It would be wonderful if you can keep people organized and busy."

Kessa made her way toward the wagon, looking uncertain.

Garrett hopped back down to the dais. "You," he told Jinishta, "should take control of the Yeresunsa warriors. We'll need them ready for war. See if you can get someone to hammer out some armor that's stronger than leather? And maybe you can ask Pung to train them in the use of blaster gloves."

Jinishta gave him an incredulous look.

"Make sure they're ready to fight at Ariock's command," Garrett said.

Jinishta planted her fists on her hips. Her flush of anger turned her skin pink. "Who gave you the privilege to order me around?"

"Uh . . ." Garrett appeared to be at a loss for words.

Ariock had to smile. Premiers, such as Jinishta, won their appointments due to a mix of factors. Sheer raw power was not the greatest of those factors. Compassion mattered. So did the quality of their family. And their relationships with other Yeresunsa.

Garrett might be able to teleport, but he did not have the qualities it took to win over the warriors.

"I don't care who is in charge," Garrett said. "This war is not something Ariock can handle entirely on his own. We need Alashani warriors to help out."

"By the laws of my people," Jinishta said, "you should be taking orders from me." She was right.

Ariock began wondering how he might quell this argument. Jinishta had agreed to obey Ariock as her leader aboveground, but she had made no such promises to Garrett.

The room was full of people. Anyone could overhear. A petty argument over who was in charge seemed like a bad idea right now, especially while Jinishta and Garrett were still recovering from near depletion.

"I am sorry, Jinishta." Garrett visibly forced his shoulders to loosen. "My concerns were all for my great-grandson. I wasn't thinking clearly, or treating you with the respect you deserve."

Jinishta softened. Family loyalty was the most important value to her people, and Ariock realized that Garrett had said the perfect thing to mollify her.

"I will speak with the other premiers." Jinishta swept away. She began to gather the distinguished-looking albinos with purple mantles.

Garrett gestured to a distant corner of the enormous room. He picked up the dusty book of prophecies and headed in that direction.

Ariock tried to be unobtrusive as he stepped off the dais, along with Vy. That book must contain vital clues about how to defeat the Torth without harming any slaves. He needed to look at those ancient pages.

Kessa temporarily stopped speaking as the assembly got distracted watching Ariock leave. He drew attention even when he was being sneaky.

Nussians set up a perimeter, giving them a semiprivate alcove. One of the tall, window-like monitors displayed a view of space. A picturesque planet floated within the field of view.

Garrett set the book on a ledge. "We have a few days at most," he said in a lowered voice. "Before the Torth find us."

Ariock had hoped for more time than that.

"How do you know?" Vy asked.

"The Megacosm," Garrett said gruffly. "I spy on the Torth Majority several times per day. They haven't located us yet, but they are putting together a massive armada. They're stationing battleships and swarmships near every temporal stream."

"Swarmships?" Vy asked warily.

"Like aircraft carriers used in planetary conquests." Garrett waved away her question. "They're even sending unmanned probes. When they find us, they will go after us in force."

The solution seemed simple to Ariock. "Can't we just go through another temporal stream?"

Garrett turned to him. "Is that what you want to keep doing? You want to keep running away? They'll keep finding us again and again. Is that the existence you want?"

Ariock inwardly admitted that he was sick of hiding. When he had made Torth flee from him instead of the other way around . . . that felt right.

That felt like justice.

"I know it sounds simple to run and hide," Garrett said in a tolerant tone. "But you forget, the Torth have sixteen supergeniuses on their side of this war. Well, fifteen now, since one committed suicide." He said that with a callous lack of sympathy. "I should have gone around assassinating them when I had the chance."

Ariock stared down at his great-grandfather. Garrett sounded casual about murdering disabled children.

"They're not disabled children," Garrett said. "Or not *just* disabled kids, anyway. You're not just a warrior, and I'm not just an old man. The Torth know what they have. They've secured their supergeniuses in hidden lairs, kept secret from the Majority. I cannot find them."

Vy gave him a critical look. "Didn't you say we're predestined to win?" She gestured to the book. "Isn't everything all laid out?"

"It's laid out," Garrett said, "but that doesn't mean we can sit back with our feet up. We have to *make* it happen."

He made that sound difficult.

"Look," Garrett said in a tone of admission. "I may not know exactly how prophecies work. They're very difficult to interpret. But I've found the paintings to be a useful guideline."

Ariock tried to get a look at the book. If he could leaf through the prophecies, he would gain a better idea of how useful they were.

"The future is volatile." Garrett sidled to one side, blocking the ledge where the book rested. "It can be dangerous to know the exact details. Sometimes, in trying to make something happen, you might do the opposite. It's better not to know."

That sounded nonsensical to Ariock. What good were prophecies if they had nothing to do with causation?

"Trust me," Garrett said. "They work, but in roundabout ways. For instance, the Alashani would have decapitated me—and you, for that matter—if not for the messiah prophecy." He gestured grandly to himself. "The fact that they mistook me for their messiah is the reason that I was able to live long enough to get back to Earth and establish my family there. That is the reason you were born. It was Ah Jun's prophecy."

The implications gave Ariock pause. The messiah prophecy had predicted his arrival, and it had also caused him to exist in the first place?

He wanted Thomas's advice.

"Nothing is guaranteed," Garrett was saying. "But I've seen enough to know that the chance is there. We can destroy the Torth."

"So what do we do?" Ariock demanded.

"Step one is obvious," Garrett said. "We need an army. We'll arm the refugees. We'll free more slaves and arm them, too. The more people we gain, the bigger our army will be."

"Not everyone is suited to fight," Vy pointed out.

"An army needs medics and pilots and so forth," Garrett said. "Those jobs are just as important as the soldiers. Besides, we . . ."

He trailed off as the assembly grew hushed. Kessa had been speaking to various elders, and Jinishta had been talking with the premiers. Everyone fell silent when Thomas entered.

People recoiled from his hoverchair. Thomas floated in a bubble of his own personal space while people whispered and cast wary glances over their shoulders at him.

At least no one attacked the *rekveh*. Ariock stayed wary, knowing that Thomas must have had a hefty escort of nussian guards just to get here. His powers were still drained. He looked sick, with dark bags under his eyes.

"Is the piloting crew all squared away?" Garrett asked.

"They're fine." Thomas glided to a stop.

Ariock began to say that he was glad, and he hoped Thomas was feeling all right. But the boy went on, acerbic.

"You know, when discussing tactics for a protracted war, you might want to include your tactician." Thomas indicated himself. "You're making a few blind assumptions."

Unlike Evenjos, it seemed Thomas was volunteering to help. Ariock hid his relief. He had been worried that Thomas would keep avoiding his own potential, trying to escape responsibilities. He was glad to be wrong.

"Did you, um, hear everything?" Vy asked.

Thomas smiled thinly. "I sucked it up by osmosis."

"We'll discuss tactics later," Garrett said, dismissive. "What we need from you is innovation." He sized up Thomas, looking as if he disapproved. "The Torth supergeniuses are hard at work inventing new weapons. We need you to do the same."

Thomas gave Garrett a bland look. "Weapons aren't my forte."

"You don't have a choice." Garrett's tone grew hard. "Something that makes us impervious to the inhibitor serum would be welcome. Make Ariock invincible in battle."

That did sound nice. Ariock inwardly approved of that idea.

"You're proposing a weapons race," Thomas said. "Me against the Torth? That's a guaranteed fail. Their eldest supergeniuses are light-years ahead of me in terms of pure knowledge. They spend every waking second of their lives in the Megacosm. I don't have that advantage."

Garrett made a growling sound. "Then—"

"Use me as your tactician," Thomas cut in. "I'll invent tech boosts when I can, but I'm not the Death Architect. I don't spend all my time imagining ways to kill."

"That's—" Garrett began.

"And on an engineering level," Thomas went on, "the Upward Governess and the Twins can outthink me ten different ways. A few of the lesser supergeniuses are up there as well." He paused just long enough to let that sink in. "The best way to use me is to play to my strengths, the same way you lean on Ariock's talents as a warrior. Let me plan our battles."

Ariock thought that sounded sensible. With Thomas in charge of planning, he would feel a lot more confident going to war.

"We need you to drive the ship and to invent things." Garrett remained obstinate. "Believe it or not, I'm not half-bad at tactics. I outwitted the Torth Empire. Twice!"

"So did I." Thomas looked unimpressed. "Except I did it without any sort of aid or guideline." His gaze slid toward the book.

Garrett moved to block his line of sight.

"Imagine what strategies I could come up with," Thomas said, "if I had knowledge of the future. The way you do."

Garrett met his challenging stare with defiance. "Stay where you are."

"That's how you knew where to find us," Thomas said. "And *when* to find us."

"Obviously," Garrett muttered.

Ariock remembered when the old man had surprised them on the border of the dead city. Did the book of prophecies include maps and timelines? Was that how he had known?

"The book doesn't spell anything out," Garrett said sourly. "I had a vague idea of which prophecies had already happened, and which had yet to happen. The next painting showed the Will—that's me—saving the Wisdom. That's all. There's never any hint about how or where or anything like that."

"So how did you figure it out?" Vy asked.

"Deduction," Garrett said. "I knew the so-called Wisdom was in trouble, or dying. I knew that he was with Ariock, otherwise known as the Strength. Which meant the Strength could not save him."

The stress came back to Ariock. He had repeatedly tried, and failed, to heal Thomas.

It was hard to believe that Garrett had saved Thomas's life, but he had. The boy had been in awe.

"Judging from news in the Megacosm," Garrett went on, "you had crash-landed in the dead city and vanished there. I figured you must be in the Alashani underground, as per the prophecies. So I moved nearby, to Stratower City. Then, on a daily basis, I ghosted, clairvoyantly, underground. When I detected a messianic army marching along the River of Tears, with you at their head, I got ready. I judged your direction so I knew where you would emerge. And I went and stood on the border wall around the right place and time."

Ariock figured he needed to learn more about clairvoyant searches. It might be a useful skill.

"The book told you to heal me," Thomas said accusingly.

"Yup." Garrett sounded unsympathetic.

"You said you did it to prove your goodwill," Thomas said.

"I lied."

Ariock turned a disbelieving stare on Garrett. Had he only pretended to be concerned and grandfatherly when he'd magically appeared?

Apparently so.

He had revived Thomas, but not out of kindness. He had done it to enact an ancient painting. It was part of the step-by-step guide for destroying the Torth Empire.

"I need to see that book," Thomas said.

"No." Garrett blocked it.

"Either that, or I'll soak it up from your mind." Thomas glided forward.

Garrett raised his hands in a warding-off gesture. He was backed against the ledge. "Do not get within my range."

Thomas circled toward him.

"I'm warning you, boy," Garrett said. "Don't start a fight you can't win. We're both depleted right now, but you know who's the stronger once we recover our powers."

Ariock could hardly believe the threats. What made Garrett think this level of cruelty was acceptable? He prepared to forcibly move Garrett—and then he saw fear in the old man's eyes.

Fear.

"I will make this book disappear!" Garrett blustered. "My powers are drained, but I will teleport it away even if it kills me!"

That was quite a threat.

Thomas glided to a frustrated stop. Ariock stopped as well.

What was Garrett so terrified of? Was there some calamity at the end of the book? Something bad that had not yet occurred? The old man clearly believed that if Thomas learned the future, there would be a major failure of some sort.

Ariock exchanged a glance with Thomas. Maybe they would lose the war?

His friend looked thoughtful, perhaps plagued by the same concern.

Garrett slid the book to the far side of the ledge and stood guard over it, glaring fiercely. "No one opens this except me."

CHAPTER 14

PIVOTAL MOMENTS

"I'm sorry." Garrett slumped, his tone begging Ariock to understand. "It's just . . . there are things you aren't meant to know."

"For my own good?" Ariock sounded more bitter than he meant to. Maybe Garrett assumed that his great-grandson was too immature, or too stupid, to handle whatever was in the book of prophecies.

And maybe he was right. Even so, it hurt to be dismissed that way. As a mind reader, Garrett ought to know him pretty well.

"Ariock, it's not that." Garrett sounded pained. "At all. You deserve to know everything. I . . ." He tightened his grip on the book. "Let me try to explain. The prophet Ah Jun predicted pivotal moments that are crucial to our victory. But they have to happen in the right way, and in the right order, or else the end result won't happen. And I've found them to be extremely unclear before they happen. They're very easy to misinterpret and very easy to screw up."

Thomas spoke in a mocking tone. "But you're smart enough to interpret them correctly?"

"You have a certain myopia when it comes to ethical matters." Garrett gave him a challenging look. "And, if you must know, I've seen a few things about your future that make me strongly doubt the wisdom of giving you access to the bigger picture."

Thomas's yellow eyes blazed with anger and hurt. Ariock wanted to intervene on his behalf—but he could see the conviction in Garrett. Something about the future was making him secretive.

"How about this?" Garrett opened the ancient book. "I'll give you an example of one that's already happened."

Ariock was tall enough to peer into the alcove, but the old man hunched over the pages like a vulture. His loose sleeves hid it from sight.

After a moment, he showed them a two-page spread. "Here."

The paper was decayed, the ink faded, but Ariock still recognized the metal cross beneath the three moons of Umdalkdul. The limp figure chained to the cross must be himself.

There was a hovercart parked in the foreground of the painting, with passengers. A boy in yellow robes was reaching toward the chained figure with a gloved hand. Above them, nighttime clouds formed the bearded face of an old man, also reaching toward the chained figure.

"'Wisdom and Will Free Strength,'" Garrett said. "That's the title of this painting."

"You were there." Vy sucked in her breath. "You helped protect Ariock when he was crucified."

"Yes." Garrett gave her a grouchy look. "At the time, I only understood this prophetic pivot when the boy sentenced Ariock to death by crucifixion. That's when it all clicked into place. Until then, I had to wait for the right conditions, watching helplessly from afar."

Ariock felt rather stunned that his recent life had been mapped out in an ancient book by a long-dead prophet. He wanted time to think about it.

"They're all like that." Garrett gently closed the book. "They all have cryptic titles, like 'Will Saves Wisdom.' 'Wisdom and Strength Free Transformation.' They're vague until you're in the moment."

"You're making my case for me," Thomas said. "What's the harm in letting me look at the next one on our timeline? I'm sure I'd figure it out long before you're able to."

Garrett looked threatening. But then he seemed to think about it, and his expression melted into good humor. "Well," he said, "I suppose it might be interesting to get your take on the next one."

He transferred the book to the ledge, hunching over it with his cloak spread, so no one could see him turning pages.

After a moment, he showed them another two-page spread.

Dread crept through Ariock as he studied the reproduced painting. He recognized all four figures: Thomas, Garrett, Evenjos, and himself.

But why was Thomas contorted, naked and apparently screaming?

Why did the rest of them look so calm, so smug, surrounding Thomas as if they didn't care about his suffering? Evenjos, especially, looked triumphant. In the painting, she wore a simple white gown. Her purple hair was tied in a casual ponytail, without any tiara or royal crown.

"Any insights?" Garrett said, sardonic.

Thomas was pale as he studied the pages, and no wonder. The painting seemed to depict him as a victim.

"It's titled 'The Transformation of Wisdom,'" Garrett said.

Ariock exchanged glances with Vy, but she did not seem to have any clues, either.

"Well . . ." Thomas floated backward a few inches, indicating that he was done studying the prophecy. "At least I know it's nothing to worry about until I see Evenjos put her hair in a ponytail."

Garrett snorted.

"Is every page like that?" Vy asked.

Ariock thought that was an excellent question. Judging by the thickness of the book, it must contain hundreds of prophecies.

"No." Garrett flipped toward the beginning of the book and showed them pages filled with indecipherable, archaic writing. "There's a lot of commentary by her disciples." He showed them a small, crudely painted panel. "And uncertain guesswork between the prophetic pivots. I get the sense that Ah Jun saw things in a dreamlike way. Some of these panels show dead ends, or they're inaccurate. They're branching possibilities." He closed the book and stroked its leather-bound cover. "It's like a symphony. There are overlapping and repeating notes and then a final concerto."

Ariock wondered how he might coax the book out of Garrett's hands.

"But the main ones are painted large?" Thomas asked.

"Yes," Garrett said. "Those are the pivots. They're the crucial events that propel us toward the goal we want: victory over the Torth Empire."

"I'm better suited to deciphering that book than you are," Thomas said.

Garrett glared. "Shouldn't you get back to piloting the ship?"

"We're docked in orbit," Thomas said. "No piloting necessary."

"Oh." Garrett glanced at the window view, where a blue-and-white sphere floated in space. The planet looked similar to Earth, except for its lack of city lights.

"What planet is that?" Garrett asked. "I assume it's somewhere without Torth?"

"Yup," Thomas said.

Garrett raised an eyebrow. "I don't have all six-thousand-plus reject planets memorized, boy. Is this the one with the water buffalo chimera problem?"

"This one should be ideal," Thomas said. "The Torth rejected it for colonization due to its proximity to an unstable white dwarf star."

"So this whole solar system could be wiped out in a supernova?" Garrett asked.

"Maybe." Thomas looked unconcerned. "It could happen now, or centuries from now. No one can predict supernovae." He studied Garrett. "At least, as far as I know."

Ariock studied the uninhabited planet, admiring its Earth-like glow.

"Reject-81 suits us," Thomas said, "in terms of climate and terrain. There are no sapient beings. Lots of animals."

"I suppose it will do." Garrett sounded grudging.

Vy wrapped her arm around Ariock's hand. "You're not going to ask Ariock to teleport everyone down there, are you?" Judging by her tight grip, she was concerned. "He just revived a thousand Yeresunsa from death comas. He needs more rest."

"We can wait another day," Garrett said agreeably.

"He's stronger than you give him credit for," Thomas told Vy. "When he mass-teleported everyone off the Torth Homeworld, he was already drained from resurrecting Evenjos and fending off nuclear bombs and a ton of other things. He hadn't slept properly in three days. It will be a different matter when he's well rested and not battered from fending off an army."

Ariock was glad to hear that.

"But we shouldn't need teleportation to off-load our population," Thomas said. "I've mentally architected a latticework descent ramp that can reach the ground from low orbit. Ariock can construct it from recycled components of our starship. That will be less intensive than mass-teleportation."

Vy and Garrett looked approving, and Ariock was relieved.

"Excellent." Garrett tucked the book of prophecies under his arm. "Let's get that underway tomorrow."

"We'll get it underway when I recover my powers," Thomas said. "You'll need me to project holographic schematics."

Garrett looked like he wanted to argue, and Ariock took a deep breath, prepared to intervene. He was beginning to feel like a referee at a sparring match.

Come to think of it, perhaps a structured sparring match would resolve some of the tension between Thomas and Garrett? Sparring, with fair rules and a referee, seemed to work for Alashani warriors and also for nussians.

"I do need to get back to the control center," Thomas admitted. "Varktezo is catching up on sleep. He kept us all alive, you know. I don't think anyone else would have done as well."

"We should think of a way to reward him," Garrett said.

Thomas offered a thin smile in reply. No doubt he wanted to escape the old man. He gave Ariock a nod of respect, then floated away.

"While we're all waiting for your powers to recover," Garrett called, "aim your gargantuan mind toward something useful. Brainstorm superweapons for us!"

Thomas did not deign to turn around or reply.

Ariock considered going after Thomas. He did want to discuss strategies for waging war against the Torth.

But that could wait. He also had reasons to converse with Kessa and Jinishta and Weptolyso. And perhaps he ought to seek out Evenjos, to make sure she was feeling all right. But first . . .

"Do you have to be so disrespectful to Thomas?" Ariock asked. "He's the only reason we're still alive."

Garrett slumped. "I might be being too hard on him."

At least he was able to admit it.

"I have trust issues," Garrett said. "And, to be honest, I don't like what he did to you. When he had you crucified."

Ariock supposed that had been a low point for Thomas.

But then Thomas had returned to save him. Unlike Garrett, Thomas had been right there with Ariock, helping him escape from the Torth Empire.

Where had Garrett been during that time? Getting foot rubs from slaves and sipping nectar smoothies?

"It wasn't as easy as you think, to be a Torth," Garrett said dryly. "It doesn't come naturally to me." He began to limp away. "I need somewhere to stow this book. At least until I regain enough strength to teleport it back into my personal cache."

Ariock wondered if Garrett's personal cache was on some random planet, in an underground treasure chest or something like that. He knew it would be useless to ask. Garrett kept so many secrets. Would he ever trust anybody?

The old man was half Alashani, half Torth. What did family mean to him? Why had Garrett abandoned his family when they needed him most?

Why had Garrett allowed Ariock to grow up without any grandfather or great-grandfather? Why had he let Ariock's dad perish in a terrible accident?

"We need to talk," Ariock called.

He expected a dismissive reply. Garrett had a way of barreling past problems he didn't want to deal with. Ariock figured he would need to ask again and again. He would confront Garrett repeatedly until finally the old man could not ignore . . .

Garrett stopped. Judging by the defensive stoop of his shoulders, he wanted to refuse.

Instead, he nodded toward a supply room, packed with crates and wagons and devoid of people. "You're right," he said. "I owe you a lot of explanations. Let's do some catching up."

CHAPTER 15

HELPLESSLY POWERFUL

Garrett led the way to a secluded corner of the supply room. He climbed onto a wagon and patted the bench, inviting Ariock to sit with him. But he gave Vy a contemplative look.

"You know," he told her, "some of those revived warriors will have complications from being in a depletion coma. They could use a nurse to check up on them."

"Oh." Vy looked like she was hiding a feeling of being rejected. "Right." She began to leave.

"No." Ariock gently put a hand on her shoulder. "Stay."

It was increasingly hard for him to like Garrett. The old man was manipulative, sometimes cruel, and Ariock did not want to keep letting that behavior go unchecked. Perhaps Garrett needed more adjustment time to go from being a Torth to being a human. But if he was going to be part of Ariock's crew, or his team, or whatever this was, then he would need some basic human compassion.

Garrett raised his palms, as if showing himself to be defenseless. "All right, all right. We're going to talk about private family stuff, but if you don't mind Vy being a part of the discussion? That's your call."

Ariock ignored the unspoken warning and gave Vy an encouraging nod.

She looked uneasy. "I could go."

"I'd rather you stay." Ariock realized that he might have said that too firmly, as if it was an ultimatum. He softened his tone. "If you want to. I would like you here, but I'll understand if you'd rather not be around for this." He could not predict where a conversation with Garrett might lead.

Vy seemed to understand that Ariock might want a second opinion. She smiled and perched on the bench seat.

Like most Alashani furniture, the wagon was made of flimsy mushroom corkwood. Ariock expanded his awareness to reinforce the axles and underlying structure. Then he gingerly sat on the flatbed.

The wagon creaked and sank. Ariock tested his reinforcements, then carefully withdrew his awareness.

He didn't want to see Garrett's reaction. Maybe the old man's reasons for abandoning his family had something to do with Ariock's growth disorder? Did he assume that his gigantic great-grandson was nothing but a freak?

"No." Garrett gave Ariock a raw look of suffering. "I never thought poorly of you. There's some heavy G adaptation in my lineage. My Torth father was a borderline giant, and I believe you got a runaway mutation, in the same way your Yeresunsa powers were augmented." He waved dismissively. "It was never my intention to abandon you. Or your parents. I want you to understand that."

Ariock waited for an explanation.

"I believed that you were safe." Garrett seemed to plead for understanding. "Yes, I knew the Torth were out there, but I had carried that fear all my life." He made a fist over his heart. "A fear of being discovered. Every day. For a century."

Ariock tried to empathize. Garrett's fear of the Torth must have been lifelong and crippling. Maybe he had felt a desperate need to escape it, or to confront it?

A shadow of paranoia creased Garrett's weathered face. "I was worn down. When I left, I assumed—well, I had every reason to believe—that you were safe. I felt sure the Torth would never learn of your existence."

"You were wrong." Ariock stated it flatly.

"I know." Garrett fell silent, apparently gathering his thoughts.

Ariock had time to remember the fiery deaths of his father and the pilot. Ariock had nearly asphyxiated from smoke inhalation, unaware of his dormant Yeresunsa powers at the time, helpless to save anyone. He had been nine years old.

There had been other mysterious deaths leading up to that one. His grandmother, dead in a car crash. Her husband, a suicide. His uncles, his cousins, even household staff members and former friends of Garrett Dovanack. One by one, they had died in freak accidents.

Garrett looked away. "My fears came true," he admitted. "And I could only watch from afar while that Torth agent murdered the people I loved."

"Why?" Ariock asked.

"Couldn't you have teleported to Earth?" Vy spoke gently.

"I . . ." Garrett spoke with a pained hitch in his voice. "Agh. There's so much to explain. You need to understand the circumstances."

Ariock studied his great-grandfather, searching for signs of the Torth within.

"When I was about ninety years old," Garrett said, "I was dying in a nursing home. I had lived a good life. But throughout it all, fears had weighed heavily on my soul. And there was the debt I owed to the Alashani. I wanted to be their messiah. I kept wondering if it was supposed to be me, and if I had run away like a coward."

Ariock could relate to that.

"So I figured I had a choice," Garrett said. "I could spend my final days eating sweet potato puree and watching reruns of *Jeopardy!* Or . . ." He paused, giving his words a dramatic effect. "I could take a risk and finally use my abilities to search for a way to aid the Alashani and stop the Torth Empire."

He had made the moral choice. Ariock could not fault him for that.

"I didn't yet know what the Torth were, really," Garrett went on. "I assumed they were evil aliens, but I had only the faintest idea that the Megacosm existed. I had never used it myself. I had only heard echoes of it in the minds of my enemies: my father, and the Torth who tortured me in the Isolatorium."

It was difficult to imagine Garrett being so ignorant.

"All I knew for certain," Garrett said, "was that I could access spaces that were inaccessible to slaves and Alashani. I had a gift. And perhaps I should use it to help people."

"So you joined the Megacosm," Vy said.

"I joined the Torth," Garrett corrected. "I faked my death—for a second time— and I traveled to a Torth-ruled planet. Incidentally, that is how I've managed to live as long as I have." He patted his chest. "Longevity pills. The average Torth lives to be about one hundred and seventy, thanks to those pills."

"They slow the process of aging?" Vy sounded interested, perhaps due to her training as a nurse.

"Yep," Garrett said. "The Torth have laws against gene therapy, but some super-genius found a partial workaround. She was immortalized in the Megacosm for her invention of longevity pills."

Ariock thought of his mother. She might have benefited from such pills. Why hadn't Garrett returned to share the longevity pills with humans?

"I left my family a huge inheritance," Garrett said. "I figured you would all move on and live happy lives."

For a few years, they had.

"But then the Torth discovered us," Ariock said. "Where were you?"

Such a simple question. Ariock felt energized, sure that the answer would unravel a huge knot of mysteries that had haunted him all his life.

Garrett clasped his gnarled hands and stared down at them. "I was in a crowded trading forum at the time. When that news—about my family—whirled through the Megacosm, I had to pretend it meant nothing."

Ariock stared.

"If I dared drop out of the Megacosm," Garrett said, "I would face an instant death sentence. I could not allow myself to react. I could not show any hint of being upset."

How could a loving father calmly accept news that his daughter and her family were slated for murder?

Ariock could not imagine stomping down his own feelings to that degree. Surely the surrounding Torth must have picked up some emotion from the old man?

Garrett closed his eyes. "Right now," he said, "I am sitting here talking to you, and I cannot describe what a miracle it is." He wore a blissful expression. "I waited twenty years for this. To be human again."

He looked human. He had married a human. But Ariock remembered that Garrett had not a drop of human blood.

"When you are pretending to be a Torth," Garrett said, "you have to put your emotions in a box. You hide your humanity in a corner of your mind and . . ." His voice grew small. "You forget it's there. I only dared to take out that box and dust it off during my bedtime. I couldn't react otherwise."

Excuses.

But Vy looked thoughtful, and Ariock wondered if he was judging the old man too harshly. Hadn't Thomas said something similar about existing in the Megacosm?

And Thomas, no matter what anyone else said, was a hero.

"I was rigid with my self-imposed rules." Garrett's voice had a raw edge, as if he was desperate to make Ariock understand. "I had to be. If I threw away my identity among the Torth, I would lose all the inroads I'd made in deciphering the prophecies. I would have to give up my goal of destroying the Torth Empire. Forever."

"What do you mean, give it up?" Ariock wondered if Garrett was being melodramatic.

"The only reason my act worked was because the Torth never suspected they could be fooled," Garrett said. "They had never encountered an imposter before, a renegade mind reader who took the risks I took." He shook his head. "Now that they know? What I did will never work again. The whole Torth Empire is on high alert for imposters and secret renegades."

Ariock raised a suspicious eyebrow. He knew that Garrett could spy in the Megacosm, seemingly whenever he felt like it.

"Oh, sure, I can get away with it for a couple of seconds." Garrett rolled his eyes. "I'm so practiced at thinking like a Torth, I can casually fake a random identity and maintain it for a few seconds. I have a whole queue of fake titles and ranks and backgrounds, all of them ready for a onetime, throwaway use."

He made it sound easy.

"Easy?" Garrett made a sour face. "Let me tell you about the first time I tried to fake being a Torth. First, I teleported to a Torth-ruled planet and camped out in the wilderness, spying, until I understood Torth culture. Then—"

"Wait a minute," Ariock said. "What do you mean? You physically watched them?"

"Sort of," Garrett said. "I ghosted into their city." He walked his fingers. "I astrally projected. It's much easier to do it within one's own sphere of influence. Ghosting to different planets is a whole other level of expertise and power drainage."

Ariock stored that information away.

"And," Garett said, "I began to spy in the Megacosm for the first time. I wasn't yet sophisticated about it, so I found it easier to camouflage myself as a Torth out camping rather than trying to disguise my life on Earth. I needed to work myself into a peer group in that local city. You see, all Torth have a network of close associates. I had to duplicate that in a way that might stand up to casual scrutiny." He grimaced at a memory. "I spent five months building my first identity, and it lasted for less than a day. I was terribly depressed afterward. I almost quit then."

Ariock stared at Garrett. It sounded even more dangerous and complicated than he'd imagined.

"It was a massive ordeal every time," Garrett said. "Gradually, I learned what fooled the Torth and what did not work. My next identity lasted a week before too many Torth became suspicious. I learned to move around a lot so I could cite distant peer groups as references. I would go through stages of that until I appeared as if I had earned my title and rank and whatnot."

Vy studied him with fresh appraisal, and Ariock felt the same way. Garrett did have a valuable skill.

"I am the only person you'll ever meet who can spy on Torth." Garrett gestured grandly to himself. "And I am one of a kind. Your supergenius friend can't do what I do. His freak show of a mind stands out in the Megacosm. He's instantly recognizable. He can't blend in, even if he tries."

Ariock empathized with Thomas.

And he supposed that Evenjos, too, would have trouble disguising her mind among the Torth. She seemed completely ignorant of the Megacosm.

"Evenjos cannot ascend into the Megacosm," Garrett said. "She's, ah, somewhat handicapped in the mind-reading department."

That meant Garrett's information-gathering skills might prove vital in the war against the Torth Empire.

Ariock had questions. "How long can you spy in the Megacosm?" he asked. "Can you do it indefinitely?"

"Oh, no," Garrett said. "I usually manage to go undetected for a few seconds. But that's long enough to glean whatever news I want." He shrugged. "If I stick around longer than that, my false identity tends to implode. Then a horde of Torth vote to kill me."

That sounded deadly.

"It was deadly when I lived among the Torth," Garrett corrected. "Here? I don't need to worry about random Torth neighbors coming to shoot me in my sleep." He gave Ariock a winsome grin. "I have you for protection."

Ariock marveled at Garrett's jauntiness. Did he view his great-grandson as just a big guard? A useful tool for destroying enemies?

What did family mean to him?

Ariock understood the difficulty of life-or-death choices. He tried to empathize with the choice Garrett had made, to stand idle while his family on a faraway planet got slaughtered. Garrett had chosen to pretend that his loved ones were merely dangerous primitives whom he had never met.

Meanwhile, nine-year-old Ariock had been screaming. He had desperately tried to pull his father out of burning wreckage.

Garrett lost all his good humor. "I heard about the sabotaged plane at the same time every Torth in the empire heard about it. You and your father were already going down in flames. If I had teleported to you? That very likely would have entailed a death sentence for everyone on the planet Earth."

"What do you mean?" Ariock figured that had to be a lie, or a gross exaggeration.

"Earth is a controversial topic in the Megacosm," Garrett explained. "Even before my father used Earth as a hideout, there were other Torth Servants of All who did the same. Humans and Torth look too much alike. It's too easy for a renegade Torth to go there and disappear among the crowds of humankind."

Vy looked sick with worry. She and Ariock had discussed this topic before, and they both feared that the Torth Empire might already be invading Earth.

"A large minority of Torth keep voting to conquer and enslave Earth," Garrett said. "The internet exacerbated that."

"The internet?" Ariock wondered if he had misheard.

"Right," Garrett said. "The Torth consider social media to be something like a primitive precursor to the invention of a Megacosm. So those votes have gained steam in recent years."

"Oh." Ariock had a sinking feeling that Earth would need protection.

"If I had shown up in person to save my family?" Garrett gestured to himself. "I'm Jonathan Stead. I'm an enemy of the Torth Empire. If I showed up in all my power, I have no doubt that would have pushed the minority of voters over the edge into becoming a Majority. It would have doomed Earth."

Ariock tried to respect Garrett's logic. Perhaps he was right. Perhaps if he had appeared to protect his family, that would have given the Torth Majority all the excuse they wanted to invade Earth.

But still.

How could he have been so calculating about letting his loved ones die?

Or . . . had he?

Ariock, after all, had survived that plane crash.

His mother had attributed his survival to a miracle, but now Ariock suspected that a Yeresunsa must have shielded him from the impact, and the flames, and smoke. He hadn't even suffered any broken bones. Just a few bruises and scrapes.

Someone had intervened. Someone had saved him.

But why just Ariock? Why not his father as well?

The answer occurred to Ariock in a flash of bitter realization: Garrett cared about those damned prophecies more than anything. He must have recognized Ariock as being the Strength. He had been saving a future messiah, not a family member.

"Ariock." Garrett gave him a pained look. "I didn't know you were in Ah Jun's prophecies at the time. You were just a gangly kid. I mean, you were tall, but you had yet to hit your major growth spurt."

"Oh." Ariock reconsidered.

"It wasn't me." Garrett's tone was gentle. "I'm telling you, I wasn't there. If I had jaunted off to Earth, I would have gained experiences saturated with human emotion, and that sort of thing is impossible to hide in the Megacosm. It would have ruined my efforts to study the prophecies. And it would have doomed Earth."

Ariock searched his gaze.

"I didn't rescue you," Garrett confirmed.

But someone had.

A new suspicion formed in Ariock's head. He had a strange memory of the trauma. He had tried to save his father, but a force had pulled him away.

Or shoved him away.

A force had shoved him out of the burning wreckage, away from the smoke and into fresh air.

Ariock tried to shake away his weird idea. Surely his father had not had Yeresunsa powers? Surely it would have been obvious?

"I think it was Will, too," Garrett said.

CHAPTER 16

MORE VALUABLE THAN ANYTHING

Ariock remembered his father as . . . well, ordinary. Wholesome.

His dad had liked to work on cars in the Dovanack mansion's garage. He had taken Ariock on camping trips. He had taught Ariock how to ski, how to build a campfire, and how to navigate using a compass. He'd had a telescope, and he had shown Ariock the planets and how to read the sky during each season.

But there had been no hints of magic. No superpowers.

"I knew Will was powerful," Garrett said. "He had a ridiculously vibrant life spark. So I tried to give him the easiest life possible. I did my best to ensure that his powers stayed dormant and never got triggered."

Ariock wished he could see his mother's reaction to this news. "Did my parents even know powers existed?"

"They weren't mind readers," Garrett said in a pained voice. "They wouldn't have known if they were being spied on by Torth agents. So no. I never told them. I couldn't risk having them think about secret powers all the time. A secret like that would be nearly impossible to keep, especially with Torth around, pretending to be humans, scanning crowds of people in search of outlaws."

Ariock tried to see it that way. Pragmatic.

"You're saying it's possible for powers to be dormant throughout someone's life?" Vy asked.

"Exactly so," Garrett said. "Yeresunsa powers only manifest with trauma, or with a rite-of-passage ritual that involves trauma. That's how Servants of All and Alashani warriors awaken their powers."

Ariock thought the plane crash should have been enough trauma to awaken anyone's powers. Why had he remained oblivious?

Or had he?

He used to catch his mother looking at him askance sometimes. But maybe that was just her own way of dealing with his weirdnesses. As far as Ariock knew, his powers had remained dormant while he grew from a child to an overgrown adult, watching TV and reading books in the sky room.

The first time Ariock remembered using his powers, he had been trapped in a dungeon cell, chained up, between gladiator fights. The sight of his own hateful reflection had triggered something within him.

"That explains how the Torth Servants of All kept their powers secret for so many generations," Vy said in a tone of realization. "None of them have any idea beforehand, do they? Their powers are dormant until they get inducted."

"Exactly," Garrett said. "Until now, the Torth Majority never questioned the mysterious 'special training' their honored Servants of All undergo. It was illegal for a lower rank to probe the mind of a higher rank. But I've pieced together the basics. First, a bunch of elite Servants of All vote on new candidates. They choose someone—usually an Indigo-Blue engineer or a Crimson-Red captain—to join them. Approved candidates get an invitation to the Stratower. From there, they get sent into the dead city with limited supplies. In other words, they are put into a traumatic life-or-death survival situation."

Ariock realized that the Alashani warriors who hunted aboveground had, unwittingly, been helping to awaken the powers of newly appointed Servants of All.

"Those who make it out alive come out with their Yeresunsa awareness activated," Garrett said. "From there, they get trained in wildfire or ice, depending on their raw power and proclivities."

Ariock tried not to wonder what trauma had triggered Garrett's powers. *I killed my first Torth when I was six,* he had said.

"And that is how they detect others like themselves," Garrett went on. "They get taught how to widen their Yeresunsa awareness."

Thomas had alluded to "special methods" that the Servants of All used to detect Yeresunsa. DNA tests. Global electromagnetic fluctuation analysis. Wind pattern analysis, and an amalgam of other sciences.

But that was misleading.

In reality, the Servants of All simply widened their Yeresunsa awareness. That was how they knew.

And no lower-ranked Torth ever dared to probe their minds or ask too many questions about their special Yeresunsa-hunting techniques.

"How many Torth have Yeresunsa powers, do you think?" Vy asked. "What percentage of their population?"

"An awful lot," Garrett said darkly. "You can sense their life sparks," he told Ariock, "and in any given neighborhood, there are a few who blaze brighter than they should."

Ariock had a sinking feeling. Torth Servants of All already outnumbered his small fighting force of Alashani warriors. How many average Torth civilians had dormant powers? How many Red Ranks were actually Yeresunsa?

How many Yellow Ranks?

Even children on baby farms?

"The Alashani rate is one percent of their population," Garrett said. "I suspect the Torth have at least that. It seems to be even greater, maybe three or four percent."

"There are thirty-eight trillion Torth." Ariock tried to calculate one percent of that. Definitely more than a million.

More than a billion?

Whatever the number was, he didn't like it.

"We only have about twelve hundred Yeresunsa," Vy pointed out.

Garrett nodded gravely. "Which is why we need our supergenius to do whatever he can with weapons and defenses. We are badly outmatched. There's no getting around that fact. The Torth have more of everything: more Yeresunsa, more supergeniuses, more planets, and whatever else. We need to whittle them down and steal as much from them as we can."

Ariock eyed the book. Why was Garrett so casual about engaging in a war against an extremely powerful galactic empire? Just how predestined was their victory?

"Your grandmother had powers as well," Garrett said. "And hers weren't dormant."

"Grandma Rose?" Ariock barely remembered his grandmother, other than the fact that she'd owned too many cats, and she had seemed cranky. He had never liked visiting her.

"She figured her powers were satanic," Garrett said dryly. "I don't blame her for falling into those beliefs, really. What was she supposed to think, when I kept warning her not to use her powers?" He hunched his shoulders. "Torth agents can imitate human beings. I used to find them. Hunt them. And kill them. Rose got curious about my trips. And I . . . well, I had to keep an eye on my daughter. I needed to keep her safe."

He sounded ashamed.

Ariock imagined his great-grandfather ghosting around, spying on Rose.

Now he understood why she had detested her father and her family. She might have seen Garrett slay a Torth or two and had drawn the wrong conclusion. Grandma Rose had thought her father was an unrepentant murderer. With superpowers.

And no one would want a father who could secretly spy on them and read minds.

"I gave her privacy as much as I could," Garrett said defensively. "But she might have accidentally attracted Torth attention by causing an earthquake or something. I couldn't allow her to just run off and do whatever she wanted."

"What did you do to her?" Ariock dreaded the answer. Had Garrett stuck an inhibitor patch on his daughter?

"I scared her." Garrett looked depressed. "I insinuated that Torth were demons, out to get good people like her. I made it clear that extremely bad things would happen if the public ever learned about the powers we had."

That explained some of the Dovanack family dysfunction, Ariock thought.

"She ended up being a disaster of a mother," Garrett said. "She wasn't fit to care for a child. When her husband committed suicide and she descended into alcoholism, I took custody of Will. And I was determined not to repeat the mistakes I'd made when I raised her. So I gave Will the most peaceful, idyllic existence possible. I didn't scare him with threats about the Torth. I just let him enjoy life. I gave him everything he could want."

And he had told Will nothing of importance.

That matched what Ariock knew about his family. His parents used to describe Garrett as a generous and benevolent grandfather, somewhat mysterious, with a twinkle of humor in his eyes. Even so . . . that supposedly wonderful patriarch had not lifted a finger to save Will from burning to death in airplane wreckage.

And he could have.

It might have led to the doom of Earth, but Garrett could have saved everybody aboard that plane. He could teleport. He had the power to heal fatal injuries.

Garrett hung his head. "I am the Will in the prophecies. Will means determination. It means having faith and unwavering resolution. I made a choice to trust in the book. If I had left the Torth to interfere with your young life? The four heroes of prophecy would never arise. Our chance to destroy the Torth Empire would never occur."

Ariock tried to understand. He supposed that Garrett had made a noble decision, in a cruelly calculating way. Garrett had chosen to sacrifice everything—even his compassion and his beloved family—for a chance to destroy the Torth Empire and free all the slaves in the galaxy.

That was admirable. Not a choice that Ariock could relate to, but he tried to respect it.

"I regret that decision every day," Garrett said, his tone full of heartache. "Every day."

Ariock regretted it, too, in some ways. His teenage years had been lonely and awkward, especially without a father.

"Why didn't the Torth invade Earth after Ariock survived?" Vy asked. "They must have guessed that a Yeresunsa protected him, even if it wasn't you."

"All they had were theories and uncertainties," Garrett said. "Some of them assumed that Ariock saved himself. Others guessed that it was his father. Still others theorized that I was secretly alive and at large. But you see, that uncertainty was exactly why they backed off and decided to study Ariock from afar. They became very wary."

And that wariness was what had enabled Ariock to grow up.

"Torth hate uncertainty," Garrett explained.

While the Torth Empire had studied Ariock from afar . . . hadn't Garrett been doing the same?

He said that he had kept watch. He had spied on his remaining family.

And what had he seen? A lonely kid with excruciating shame? A freakish giant? A future messiah? Or a waste of skin?

"Your suffering," Garrett said, "was the hardest thing I ever watched." He traced the suicide-attempt scar on Ariock's forearm. "I was doing stupid Torth things when this happened. I missed it. But I would have wanted to be there."

Whether he had missed seeing Ariock slice open his arm or not, he must have witnessed the aftermath. Ariock's mother crying. Ariock himself, staring blankly at television shows for months and years, uninvolved with life. Garrett must have had better things to pay attention to.

What about the months when Ariock was forced to fight alien beasts in a gladiatorial arena?

"I visited you as often as I could," Garrett said gruffly. "But it was an indescribable effort. Clairvoyance is the most draining power there is, and when we're talking interstellar distances—tens of thousands of light-years—it's no simple matter. I had to move my core self across the galaxy each time. That meant I had to ensure that I would be safe and unobserved. I was lucky if I could manage a few minutes every few days."

"Is that why you didn't show up for us on Umdalkdul?" Vy asked. "What were you doing while we were slaves?"

Her tone was light, not accusatory. But Ariock knew that she had suffered at the hands of the Torth as much as he had. Ariock's mother had nearly died as a slave. Couldn't Garrett have helped them?

"When that happened . . ." Garrett looked ashamed. "I was in the middle of something I thought was vitally important."

"What?" Ariock wanted to know.

"It doesn't matter now." Garrett waved away the question. "It turned out to be . . . Never mind. I'm sorry. All I have are poor excuses. I did watch over you, but by then, I'll admit, I recognized you as the Strength in the prophecies. I surmised that your supergenius companion must be the Wisdom. And I trusted in the book. I trusted that Wisdom and Will would rescue Strength."

So that was it. Garrett seemed single-minded about the prophecies.

"Look, I want you to know something." Garrett put his hand on Ariock's arm. "The prophecies mean a lot to me, but you're family. You come first in my mind. I've watched over you all your life. And I will always watch over you. No matter what. I am here for you."

He sounded sincere.

Ariock studied his great-grandfather again, remembering that storm in the desert. So many things could have gone wrong that night. But lightning, sand, and wind had never touched him. Garrett had intervened in an absentee way, like a guardian angel who smoked cigarettes and cursed.

Maybe he wasn't such a bad guy.

"Thank you," Ariock said. He was still grateful to Thomas and his other friends, yet he also owed his life to Garrett.

Garrett swatted away the gratitude. "I'll always protect you, Ariock. As much as I can. I could say it's because of the prophecies. Or I could say it's because I failed to protect your parents and my daughter. Or I could say it's because you're my heir, and the only family I have left. But it's really more than any of those reasons." His eyes shone with admiration. "You're better than I am. You're the person I wish I could be."

Ariock wasn't sure what that meant.

"My biggest flaw is that I'm a mind reader." Garrett tapped his head. "This power corrupts everyone who has it. I'm glad you didn't inherit this."

Perhaps that was part of the reason why Garrett had such a problem with Thomas.

"I needed those visits to you on Earth," Garrett said, "in a way I'm not sure you can imagine. I needed to remember who I was, even if it was only for a short time every so often. I had to remind myself that I had a name. That I came from Earth. That I had loved ones."

His voice trembled.

Ariock had barely survived the loneliness of his teenage years. He could not imagine surviving the way Garrett described.

Thomas, too, had described being a Torth as grueling.

"Those visits to you were the highlight of my existence as a Torth," Garrett said. "I cannot describe what it's like to be cut off from human contact for years and years. I had absolutely no one to talk to. I felt trapped and so alone . . ."

He looked at Ariock, and at the same time, they both seemed to realize the irony.

"It sounds like we're not so different," Ariock admitted.

Garrett offered a lopsided grin. "You mean everything to me. That's no exaggeration. Forget the prophecies. You're the person I care about most. I want to be there for you whenever you need help, or just advice."

He sounded like a father.

Ariock had to look away, overcome by the notion. In all his imaginings, it had never occurred to him that he would find someone who felt legitimately proud of him. Someone who cared about him without conditions or strings attached.

His actual father probably would have felt disappointment upon seeing Ariock, or upon learning all the failings his son had.

"No," Garrett said. "Will was proud to be your father. He would have liked who you are. I have no doubt about that whatsoever."

Could that be true?

Ariock saw sincerity in Garrett.

And he remembered Vy's surety when she had insisted that Ariock always did more good than harm.

Was it possible that the way Garrett looked at him—with admiration—was an echo of how Will would have felt?

It seemed unbelievable. Yet Ariock felt as if he had set down a huge burden he hadn't even known he had been carrying.

"We're family." Garrett clasped Ariock's hand. "And I'm Alashani, so family is more valuable to me than anything."

CHAPTER 17

CONTRITE TRANSFORMATION

Evenjos felt drained from hours of hating herself. She was dust in a black crack, but she felt even lower than dust.

She had failed. Looking back, it was all clear to her. She had failed her people, her world, her civilization. Her poor judgment had doomed them to eons of misery. Because of her, everyone on her world had become enfeebled, reduced to ignorant cave dwellers.

She had been "blinded by the glow of treasures and deafened by the laughter of merriment," as her critics had put it.

She could run from the truth again . . . or she could join this band of rebels and attempt to rectify all the wrongs she had inadvertently caused.

Ariock and his friends didn't know it, but they were entitled to her help by every standard of law, culture, and morality. The irony was that she no longer trusted herself to right her wrongs. How could anyone trust her judgment? Least of all Evenjos herself.

She had believed a liar. She had dismissed a truth teller.

These meager rebels didn't stand a chance against trillions of coordinated mind readers. Defeating the Torth Empire would likely be impossible, especially if the Torth leaders were supergeniuses like Unyat.

Yet she owed it to the rebels to try.

Reluctant, Evenjos swirled out of the crack. She wormed through the ventilation shafts and emerged into a corridor, where she took her default form.

She did not add shimmer. Instead of a pearled gown, she wore a woolen peasant dress, befitting this feeble era. Her wings and her royal crown should be enough to remind people—well, to remind herself, at least—of who she was.

The minds of passersby indicated where she might find the leadership team. Everyone aboard this starship was cognizant of who their leaders were, and Ariock was the leader of their leaders.

It seemed he was cloistered with some people whom he must consider to be his advisers. A nussian. Why? That one-legged girl. What a poor choice. An ummin. Did Kessa the Wise have more wisdom than the other ragged refugees aboard this starship? One of those albino warriors. And that old mind reader, Garrett.

Evenjos disapproved, especially, of the mind reader. First- and second-magnitude telepaths were relatively harmless, but Garrett was at least third-magnitude. He was likely to stab someone in the back.

That was what high-magnitude mind readers did. They pretended to be loving and loyal, and then they sprinkled inhibitor serum into one's tea. And plunged a knife coated with inhibitor serum into one's back.

Evenjos shivered. At least the really dangerous one—Thomas—seemed to be elsewhere.

She bypassed the nussian sentries at the door by transforming into dust. The chamber beyond was crowded with stacks of supplies. Evenjos concealed herself between stacked crates, allowing herself to rematerialize so she could focus on eavesdropping rather than lurking. She wanted to get the gist of the conversation.

". . . if you need slaves to rebel," the ummin was saying, "I have interviewed some who are willing to go undercover. They will spread whatever message needs to be spread."

"That is very brave." Ariock sounded reluctant, almost horrified, by whatever suggestion Kessa had expressed. "But I can't ask them to do that. I don't want any of our people to get reenslaved."

There was that word, so frequently mentioned. *Slave.* Evenjos wondered what it meant.

"They want to help," Kessa assured Ariock. "These are exceptional people, willing to take the risk."

Ariock sat cross-legged on a blanket. Seated on the floor, he was at eye level with everyone who perched on crates. They faced him in a semicircle. Only the nussian sat on the floor like Ariock, squatting in the repose position of his species.

"We may need undercover agents in slave populations," Garrett said to Ariock. "They could be useful when we're conquering cities."

Ariock looked troubled.

"We need to take as much as we can from the Torth," Garrett said. "Sure, it will be difficult and dangerous. At first. But once we get rolling, I'll bet we hit a critical mass and it will be all downhill from there."

Ariock responded to that optimism with a skeptically raised eyebrow. "Even if we manage to take over multiple planets," he said, "I can't be everywhere at once. How am I supposed to protect billions of people spread out over different planets?"

"We'll cross that bridge when we come to it," Garrett said, as if it was a simple matter.

"Shouldn't Thomas be here?" the one-legged girl, Vy, asked.

Garrett rolled his eyes. "Eh, he's better suited for engineering problems."

"I don't see why we're having a strategy meeting without him." Ariock folded his massive arms and gave Garrett an obstinate look. "You make space battles sound simple, but they really aren't, because there are innocent slaves aboard the warships. Even on land—"

He went on, expressing his worries about kamikaze slaves, whatever those were. Evenjos had heard enough. She walked into view.

Ariock trailed off into silence as she approached, showing off her subtle poise and elegant shape.

"I will help," she announced.

They all looked surprised, except for Garrett, who merely looked pleased.

Ariock gave her such a grateful look, she nearly blushed like a young maiden. "You'll help us fight the Torth Empire?"

It was nice to see him look at her that way—not with disgust, but with admiration.

"Yes," Evenjos agreed. "I will help."

They all looked at her with such high expectations, she felt a need to clarify. "I do not think we will win."

Garrett tried to reassure everyone. "The prophecies give us a clear path toward victory."

Evenjos doubted that Garrett knew the difference between a seer, a prophet, and an oracle. He was an ignorant cave dweller of this era, pretending to have expertise on prophecies. She supposed it was up to her to enlighten these untrained children.

"You rely on the paintings of Ah Jun?" She indicated the dusty book Garrett kept beside him.

He gave a wary nod.

"Ah Jun was an oracle." Evenjos took a seat on one of the crude crate benches, between the fierce-looking albino woman and the one-legged maiden. "A *prophet*" —she emphasized the difference—"will see a person's future by touching them. But an oracle sees many, many possibilities, all branching off each other. An oracle can foresee the likely rise or fall of civilizations."

Garrett looked impressed.

"And so," Evenjos concluded, "we have no guarantee of following the path she chose for us."

Garrett frowned, clearly trying to puzzle out what she meant.

Ariock simply asked. "What do you mean?"

"The power of an oracle," Evenjos explained, "is to influence the future. Ah Jun chose what to paint. She emphasized the branch that pleased her most, and that is what she painted. She invented chants to go with that desired outcome. And she sent out her zealots, all in hope that her chosen branch would be remembered, so that future people would help to make it happen."

They stared at her, expressions ranging from dumbfounded to disappointed.

"But a lot of her prophecies have already come true!" Garrett sounded defensive. "We've passed the fourth pivotal event. We only have a few more to go!"

"Ah Jun warned that there is 'only one hope.'" Evenjos felt rather sorry for Garrett, disillusioning him. "That means only one branch offers the victory we seek. One branch, out of countless possibilities, leads to us winning this war. All the rest offer failures." She saw their lack of understanding and clarified. "That means we cannot make even a tiny mistake. If we veer from the path she laid out for us, even a little bit, we are guaranteed to fail."

The news did not seem to affect Ariock or most of the others. Garrett, however, turned red and blustery.

"Then we won't fail." He folded his arms. "Even if you think our chances are iffy, I say we have a moral obligation to try."

"I agree," Evenjos said simply. "I will help."

Garrett looked mollified.

Evenjos assessed the other advisers, mystified by their determination. "What about you? Why are you willing to fight?"

The nussian, the ummin, and the albino all exchanged glances.

"My people have lost their world," the albino, Jinishta, said. "They are vulnerable, and I do not want them to become slaves to the Torth."

Evenjos internally tried to translate the word *slave*, but it had no equivalent in her language. It seemed to mean something like a serf.

"My people are slaves," Weptolyso, the nussian, said. "They need to be set free."

"And mine." The ummin, Kessa, touched her neck. "Slavery is not living. It is just survival. And often, it is death."

Evenjos scrutinized the ummin's neck scar. As a low-magnitude telepath, she could not delve into Kessa's mind. She needed a summarized version of the word. "What is a slave?"

They all exchanged looks, as if her ignorance made them uncomfortable.

"I do not know this word," Evenjos admitted.

Only Kessa seemed brave enough to explain. "Slaves are property, without any rights. The Torth do whatever they wish to slaves. When they owned me, I had to wear a choke collar, which forced me to wake up and eat on a schedule. If I displeased a Torth, they would torture me. I lived in constant fear."

Evenjos had heard of animals being abused with such brutality, but never a sapient being. "That is horrible." She scanned Kessa's thoughts and shuddered, because she detected truth there. "I am sorry." Even so . . . it was hard to believe that such abuse was widespread. "Do the Torth abuse all slaves this way?"

"More or less," Vy said.

Now Evenjos understood why so many aliens on this ship looked unhealthy and downtrodden. They were slaves, or they had been.

She remembered Suro Delvakan, the ummin ambassador from the Desert Empire, who had been so genial and refined. She hoped he had not lived to see his people treated worse than animals.

Nussians. Ummins. Who else? Evenjos had seen other species among the refugees, yet a few were notably absent.

"Where are the jodinak people?" she asked.

"Jodinak?" Ariock looked uncomprehending. "What's that?"

The jodinak were so civilized, their empire so powerful, Evenjos could not imagine them becoming grubby slaves. Perhaps they had held out against the Torth Empire? They had had their own starships and their own Yeresunsa.

"The maned people." Evenjos reshaped her upper body, trying to imitate the classic willowy frame and flat face of a jodinak, surrounded by a woolly mane.

It was imperfect. She had never properly studied or sculpted an individual of that species, and her imitation was embarrassing, more mockery than art. But it should be close enough for a clue.

"You know," she said. "They look like this."

Her audience looked mystified. A few looked disgusted at what her body had become, and she quickly morphed back.

Except for Garrett Dovanack. He nodded with understanding and offered an answer. "The Torth destroyed that civilization."

Evenjos slid abruptly to the floor, struggling to comprehend the scale of such an enormous loss. She could not wrap her mind around the horror. "That's impossible," she whispered. "The jodinak had a Yeresunsa Order. They had thousands of warships. Hundreds of planets."

"Really?" Ariock looked impressed. "They had Yeresunsa?"

Their surprised reactions only confirmed what Garrett had said. It seemed the brutes of this era had never heard even a remnant of a myth about the mighty Jodinak civilization.

Evenjos used to be painfully aware of how primitive her own planet was in terms of technology. Her people were always scrambling to keep up with the latest innovations and trends from Jodinak. She tried to explain. "Our empire was a tiny backwater compared to theirs."

"The jodinak must have really put up a fight," Garrett said, "because the Torth systematically destroyed every relic left by the maned people. They tried to erase them from history entirely. But I'm a collector of relics. I ran across enough tantalizing hints to know that the maned people must have been powerful. They probably defied the Torth in a way that no one else did. That's what got them wiped out."

Evenjos began to sob. Something as great and powerful as the Jodinak Empire was far, far too much to lose. It staggered her.

Garrett sat next to her and hooked an arm around her shoulders. "I'm sorry."

Evenjos sensed his sympathy. She leaned against the old mind reader, grateful that one other person understood the loss, if only in a dim way.

If the Jodinak Empire had failed to defeat the Torth, well, then what chance did this band of ignorant refugees have? Ah Jun must have been grasping at a very slim branch.

"The Torth want to enslave my people," Vy said. "The humans of Earth."

"They're my people as well," Ariock told Evenjos.

"They enslave or destroy everything they touch," Garrett said. "That is why they need to be stopped." He gently wiped away one of Evenjos's tears with a gnarled finger. "We've inundated you with enough bad news. Maybe we can stop talking about our enemies for a while? I'd love to hear about your time."

Evenjos sniffled. Maybe he was right. There was a certain comfort in looking back at her life as the goddess-empress.

"Would you feel like talking about it?" Garrett asked gently.

Ariock looked interested. Evenjos wanted to believe that his curiosity was playful and sweet, but she was enough of a mind reader to scan his surface thoughts, so she knew the truth. Ariock wanted clues that might help him defeat the Torth.

And so did Garrett.

Of course. They all did. They didn't care about Evenjos's background so much as gaining an edge over their enemies.

Well. She owed them that. These people were unaware of how much blame lay on her shoulders for the rise of the Torth Empire, but she felt the great weight of guilt.

And if her memories crossed into traumatic territory? Well, Evenjos reminded herself that it was nothing but dead history. The most terrifying monsters of her era—men such as Elome, Audavian, and Unyat—were crumbled to dust and forgotten. They could not hurt her, or anyone, anymore.

"All right," she agreed.

CHAPTER 18

BEWARE THE FIFTH

"In my time," Evenjos began, "the ability to read minds used to be a rare gift. Like prophecy."

Her audience leaned forward, eager to hear more. It seemed they had waited a long time to learn about the origins of the Torth Empire. She had their complete attention.

"Telepaths used to be respected members of the Yeresunsa Order," Evenjos went on. "People sought their help for intervention in political matters. Or judicial matters." She had to pause, seeking the correct words in the alien slave tongue. "And also for solving maladies of the mind."

Garrett nodded in a knowing way. "They were the psychologists of your world. And the detectives."

"Makes sense," Vy said.

"Telepaths were very rare," Evenjos reminded her listeners. "Only the wealthy could afford their services." She paused, because it felt strange to explain things that she still thought of as common knowledge. "When kings or queens had a dispute, they hired a telepath."

"Did you hire them yourself?" Garrett looked fascinated. At least he was conscientious enough to refrain from probing her memories.

"I am a telepath," Evenjos admitted. As a member of the House of Telepathy, she had had easy access to all the telepaths in the Yeresunsa Order.

Jinishta recoiled. Ariock and the others looked embarrassed on her behalf.

"I am only second magnitude," Evenjos assured everyone. "That means I can detect truth from falsehood, but I cannot reach deeply into somebody's memories. I cannot delve into your secrets." She indicated Garrett. "He is a third-magnitude telepath. He is the one who would have been in high demand." *The one whom you should fear*, she nearly added.

But despite her wary mistrust of Garrett, she inwardly admitted that the old man seemed . . . well, kind.

And he clearly wasn't one of Unyat's creatures. Now that Evenjos could detect his sheer, raw power, she figured he must be royalty, or whatever the equivalent was in this era. Like herself. Surely that meant he was a finer class of person than the average brutes aboard this starship?

"Go on," Garrett said.

"How many magnitudes are there?" Ariock asked. "Three?"

"There are seven." Evenjos was saddened that she had to explain such basics about Yeresunsa powers. "But the seventh is theoretical. No one has ever met a seventh-magnitude prophet, for instance."

She chuckled at the thought. Her childhood tutor used to scare her with such tales, theorizing that a seventh-magnitude prophet could travel backward and forward through the medium of time itself. Such a being would wreak havoc by accident, just by existing.

"So you're a second-magnitude telepath." Garrett looked as if he was trying to solve a tough calculation problem. "But I assume that you're a higher-magnitude shapeshifter?"

"There is no such thing as a shapeshifting power," Evenjos corrected him. "It is the healing power. But yes. I am a sixth-magnitude healer."

She reshaped some of her dust, trying to project an illusion of the classic power chart. Unfortunately, it proved too complexly academic for her to recreate. She gave up.

"There are eight powers," she explained. "Four intracorporeal, four extracorporeal." She saw their confusion and simplified. "Four internal. Four external."

"I guess telepathy is internal?" Garrett said.

"Yes," Evenjos said. "So is healing. And prophecy, as well as clairvoyance. Those are the four internal powers."

"Electricity," Jinishta guessed, "is external?"

"Right," Evenjos said. "Although it is not electricity, but light and energy manipulation. Heat manipulation is another. Gaseous and liquid states of matter is another. And the fourth is solid matter."

Ariock looked as if he was grasping an important concept for the first time. He leaned forward, eager to learn. "You're talking about air, fire, water, and earth. Right?"

Evenjos had to roll her eyes at that gross oversimplification. "If you wish to reduce it so. Yes."

Garrett exchanged excited looks with his great-grandson. Evenjos had the feeling that she had just handed them keys with which to unlock a dangerous vehicle.

"So if I'm understanding correctly," Garrett said, "a Yeresunsa can have any or all of those eight powers, but each one has a different magnitude—or limit? That's what you mean by magnitude?"

"Correct," Evenjos said.

"And you can boost magnitude by linking?" Garrett seemed to be imagining all sorts of magical possibilities. He spoke in an excited rush. "I'm a third-magnitude telepath. You're a second magnitude. If I link my powers with yours . . . do you then become a third-magnitude telepath?"

His ignorance was painful.

"No," Evenjos informed him. "That is not how it works."

Garrett looked as if she'd crushed his dreams of gifting Ariock with new and interesting powers.

"Magnitude is fixed." Evenjos held her hands steady, to illustrate. "It is different for every individual, but nothing can enhance the limits you were born with."

"Ah." Garrett was clearly struggling not to show his disappointment.

"However . . ." Evenjos hesitated, wondering if her lessons about Yeresunsa powers might be weaponized in new and horrible ways in this brutal era.

But weren't the basics harmless?

And Ariock looked so interested. Evenjos wanted to hold his attention, to please him, and so she decided to go on.

"Raw strength and magnitude are separate," she said. "It is possible for strength to far exceed magnitude, but it can also fall short. That is when linking is useful. In my time, as now, there were Yeresunsa with puny spheres of influence. Some of them barely had enough raw strength to light a candle. But they could link with someone of far greater strength—me, for instance—and thereby generate enough heat to power a star."

Ariock and Garrett looked stunned. They exchanged looks, no doubt seeing new possibilities. Even Jinishta looked excited.

"So," Garrett said, all but squirming in his excitement, "are you saying it's possible that Jinishta over there might be a sixth-magnitude healer? Or a sixth-magnitude telekinetic? And all she needs is a boost—a link—to realize her potential?"

Evenjos eyed the albino warrior with skepticism. "It is possible," she admitted. "But very, very unlikely."

"So I might be a sixth-magnitude earthshaker?" Garrett said with a twinkle of mischief in his eyes. "Or a sixth-magnitude clairvoyant?"

He was like a child learning the basics for the first time, allowing his imagination to run wild. Evenjos hid a smile. "Sixth magnitude is exceedingly rare. Almost no one has that magnitude. Seventh is unheard-of, except in ancient legends. And," she added gently, "someone with your raw strength can reach the higher magnitudes without needing to link with a greater Yeresunsa. By now, after a lifetime of practicing your powers, you must know your true limits."

Garrett looked slightly disappointed. But only slightly. He eyed Jinishta with new speculation and respect.

Ariock seemed to be weighing darker possibilities. "So the Torth," he said, "are all third-magnitude telepaths?"

"Correct," Evenjos said.

"Then they're Yeresunsa," Ariock concluded. "All of them. That's what you're saying."

Evenjos sensed the worries around her. "They would have been," she admitted, "long ago. But things changed during my reign. Telepaths became very numerous and troublesome. So we voted to remove them from the Yeresunsa Order."

Garrett raised his eyebrows at that.

"They were stripped of their lands, their titles, and their wealth," Evenjos explained. "They were reduced to being ordinary commoners, no longer Yeresunsa."

That was when the real troubles had begun. It was easy to see that now, in hindsight.

Garrett leaned forward, emanating so much intense curiosity and interest, he glowed to her senses. "I would like to hear about that."

But Ariock wanted to pursue a different line of questioning. "Are there higher magnitudes for telepathy?" he asked. "Like fourth and fifth and sixth?"

The others seemed to hold their breath. They dreaded the idea of common Torth wielding malevolent powers.

Evenjos doubted that the Torth had any high-magnitude telepaths. Otherwise, why bother with choke collars? They would simply brainwash their slaves.

She shuddered, remembering Audavian, with his fifth-magnitude pin.

"Yes," she admitted. "A fourth-magnitude telepath can influence or change other people's minds. He can stir emotions and manipulate intentions." She forced herself to go on, giving no hint of the manipulations she had undergone. "Fifth magnitude is even worse."

Her audience exchanged anxious looks.

"I doubt it's something we'll have to worry about." Garrett spoke to the others, although mainly to Ariock. "The Torth tightly control their genetic variation through baby farms. If they had a ton of brainwashers among them, I'm sure that's something that would have entered into common knowledge."

He had such a comforting, grandfatherly tone, most of the others looked reassured. Except for Ariock.

And herself.

Evenjos focused on her hands, her wings. No one in this era could have a power like Audavian's. Such evil would be obvious. She must be safe.

"Fifth magnitude is exceedingly rare, of course," Evenjos said in a steady voice. "Someone with fifth-magnitude telepathy can gain complete control over other people. He will ruin their minds and turn them into his proxies, or puppets. They become mere extensions of his will."

A grim certainty emanated from Ariock, from Vy, and also from Weptolyso, Kessa, Jinishta, and even from Garrett.

"It was illegal," Evenjos clarified. "Even before my reign, it was considered an evil power. If victims were discovered, then telepaths would trace the crimes to their source. The brainwasher would then be doomed to lifelong imprisonment in the undersea penitentiary."

Her explanation had little effect.

Evenjos began to realize that their grim certainty came from personal experience. They had witnessed mind control firsthand.

They knew a fifth-magnitude telepath.

"Who is it?" Evenjos sat straighter, on high alert. She must defend herself.

Ariock and Vy exchanged glances. No one seemed willing to reply.

It was a friend of theirs. An ally. Or so they thought. They believed in their friend's goodness the way children believed in fairy tales. The fools. If it wasn't Garrett . . .

There was only one other telepath aboard this starship.

"The boy?!" Evenjos lost bodily cohesion for a moment, sick with terror.

Their minds confirmed it.

"He has a flawless memory *and* he's a fifth-magnitude telepath?" Evenjos gaped at Ariock, then Garrett. She could hardly believe that these powerhouses were willing to tolerate such a sinister, freakish, dangerous creature in their midst.

The little monster might creep into their rooms and destroy their free will. He could turn them into mindless weapons. It would be easy for one with his intelligence.

"Surely you know that is a devastating combination." Evenjos gawked from Garrett to Ariock and back, unable to comprehend how they could trust a monster. "That is the worst combination possible!"

Garrett made an equivocating hand motion. "It's actually the best," he said, "since he's on our side."

Ariock squared his shoulders. "Thomas has earned my respect. He's my friend."

"Indeed," Weptolyso rumbled.

"He is on our side." Jinishta met Evenjos's gaze. "He has proven it."

Vy had the temerity to mutter, "Someone here destroyed a planet, and it wasn't him."

Garrett shot her a glare, and she fell silent.

Evenjos stared from one to the other. These leaders might as well be bumbling children who had adopted a venomous snake as a pet. "He might have forced you to trust him," she pointed out. "He could have brainwashed you all."

"Nah," Garrett said.

"If he had done that," Vy said, "then everything we've been through would have to be false. We wouldn't be here if not for the things we've all been through together. With Thomas."

"I keep him at a distance," Garrett told Evenjos. "Just don't let him into your range, and you'll be fine."

Evenjos stared at the old man, wondering if he was overconfident to the point of lunacy. Did he actually believe it was possible to outthink and outmaneuver a monster with a supergenius brain?

A monster like Unyat.

A monster like Audavian.

Each man had been terrifying in his own right. And now a monster existed who embodied both of their qualities, combined into a single person. It was beyond frightening.

"We need the boy." Garrett stated it flatly. "The prophecies depict him as one of the four heroes, beyond the shadow of doubt."

"Leave Thomas alone," Ariock said with a hint of threat in his voice. "He's under my protection."

Evenjos blinked at him. Ariock had more raw strength than anyone she had ever known, and he was a leader, yet he seemed heartbreakingly naive. Really, he was an overgrown child ruled by idealistic hopes.

Somehow, Evenjos would need to educate him. She would help Ariock see the danger in his midst.

If only someone in the Crystal Court had loved her enough to do that.

If only someone—a credible person, not a stranger like Ah Jun—had warned her in time. She should have recognized the danger posed by Audavian and his loyalists. And she never should have fallen in love with Elome.

"Will you please tell us what happened in your time?" Garrett asked in a gently begging tone. "Why did you kick all the telepaths out of the Yeresunsa Order? You said it used to be an uncommon power. But suddenly it was common? Why? What happened?"

Evenjos realized that her new allies needed to understand the dangers Thomas posed. They had to understand how and why the Torth were created. And why they had won.

Why they kept winning.

She braced herself for a painful review of her reign. Maybe, if Ariock and his advisers were lucky and smart, they might somehow learn from her mistakes.

CHAPTER 19

UPLIFT EPIDEMIC

"The telepath problem started with Unyat." Evenjos watched Ariock and his friends for any reaction to that name, but it seemed Unyat was neither feared nor revered in this era. He was entirely forgotten.

There was justice in that.

"He was a commoner," Evenjos went on. "Powerless. He was the ninth child of a wool merchant."

Ariock and Vy exchanged a glance, as if sharing an unspoken judgment. Did they have a problem with Evenjos's tone? Why?

"He became a hedge doctor," Evenjos went on. "One of those poor medics who travels through villages, offering rudimentary herbs and potions for whatever small fee the peasants can pay."

"He wasn't a telepath?" Ariock asked, for clarity.

"No."

Evenjos had visited the squalid villages where Unyat had spent much of his life. No one could have guessed that such a weak, meek, unassuming peasant would be capable of ruining civilization. Without a doubt, Unyat should have lived and died without leaving a mark on the world. Except . . .

"My world was undergoing a lot of changes," Evenjos explained. "The Jodinak civilization made contact with us for the first time during the reign of my predecessor. Their alien presence, and their advanced technology, rattled everyone. We were made aware that other civilized planets existed. And that we were not at all alone in the universe."

Garrett frowned. "What sort of technology did they bring?"

"Bioengineering," Evenjos said. "And genetic science. That came from the sagacious people of Mer Nerct. I was wary of the nerct, since they were a fast-expanding civilization. But many of my royal peers were more interested in trading with the two ummin empires. The ummins built the fastest starships, and no one else had solved artificial gravity quite as well as they had."

Kessa shifted forward on her seat, blinking with interest.

"The ummins came to you?" Vy sounded astonished. "For . . . trading purposes?"

"Yes," Evenjos said. "They all came after the jodinak. They traded with every empire, of course, great or small. And I, as the goddess-empress, understood that my people should not remain ignorant and excluded. We had to join the intergalactic alliance, or else we would be torn apart by more powerful, multiworld civilizations."

"The others were multiworld?" Garrett asked.

"They were," Evenjos said. "The Jodinak Empire straddled hundreds of planets. They were the oldest and most powerful empire in existence."

"Are you saying your world was a backwater?" Ariock studied her.

Evenjos sighed, feeling a remnant of the hopelessness and shame that used to grip her. She had been the almighty goddess-empress to her people, yet to the jodi-nak, she had been quaint. Provincial. Not quite on their level.

"When I ascended the throne," she explained, "the royal families of my planet were desperately making deals with aliens, trying to gain spaceships and territories beyond our world. We lacked technology, you see. We had nothing to offer for trade—except our Yeresunsa. So we sent some of our best Yeresunsa to perform works on foreign planets. In exchange, we received technological gifts."

She paused, wondering if she ought to describe the overcrowded slums and the horrific pandemics that had resulted from the improvements wrought by alien technologies. Some of her royal peers had, unfortunately, herded their commoners into tenements, forcing them to work extralong shifts in factories.

But that wasn't really a part of the story, she figured.

"Your world," Garrett said in a guessing tone, "had very little science, I take it? Before alien contact?"

Evenjos nodded in confirmation.

"You weren't spacefaring," Garrett guessed. "Did you have electrical power?"

"No," Evenjos admitted. "We had never needed much. Yeresunsa ruled. And we provided for our people. We made rain for the crops. We healed the sick."

"Until aliens came along and handed you some new toys," Garrett said.

Evenjos was not going to apologize for accepting improvements for her world. "Yes," she said. "Instead of relying on tamed beasts of burden, commoners began to rely on hovercarts and transports. Instead of treating ailments with herbs, commoners could buy alien remedies. There were vast improvements. Our world population grew quite a lot."

"And Unyat?" Garrett prompted her. "Did he peddle alien remedies?"

"He did." Evenjos stopped short of explaining Unyat's reputation as an outstandingly good doctor. So what if he had cured a few hundred children? He had still been just a peasant. Lowborn. Unworthy of attention.

"Unyat gained a meager patronage," Evenjos said. "He was popular among commoners, and that patronage afforded him whatever educational materials he wished to get his hands on. A man of his lowborn class should not have been able to obtain recordings of geneticist lectures from Mer Nerct. But I suppose he obtained them illegally."

If only someone had stopped Unyat then.

"Unfortunately," Evenjos said, "Unyat was interested in doing more than curing diseases. He wanted to prevent them. He believed that every peasant, no matter how crude, should have the health and leisure time of any royal."

"Hmm," Ariock said.

Evenjos sensed that—incredibly!—her audience felt sympathy and respect for Unyat. Although she had not spoken of slums, they judged Unyat and other commoners to be oppressed.

They were familiar with the gulf between extreme power and its opposite. They used to be slaves. Their friends had been slaves.

Well. There was more to Unyat's story.

"Unyat began to run experiments in secret," Evenjos said. "First on animals. Mostly rats. But his aim was to induce Yeresunsa powers in people, and for that, he needed test subjects. So he invited pregnant women to visit his office. He gave them variations of a secret formula he was developing."

Jinishta looked uneasy. "Did he pay those women?"

"I do not know," Evenjos said. "But Unyat was known to be generous and kind, so I suppose many peasants trusted him. Perhaps they owed him favors for curing a sick child or such."

She wished she could conjure an image of the so-called good doctor so that her audience could see his flowing gray hair and his genial, weathered face. So many people used to trust or fear that face.

But Evenjos could not mimic a face unless she had studied it in depth, and she had never met the good doctor in person. She only knew him from newscasts and spy reports.

"Did it work?" Ariock looked fascinated. "Did they give birth to Yeresunsa?"

"Not at first."

Her audience was attentive and wide-eyed.

"But he kept at it," Evenjos said. "He worked in secret for years. And he began to see some success when he was an old man."

Jinishta and Vy wore the exact same gawky expression of wonderment.

"Telepath babies?" Ariock guessed.

"They were barely empaths." Evenjos recalled newscasters chatting about an epidemic of deformed, first-magnitude Yeresunsa born in a certain slum. She had hardly paid attention at the time. "The earliest generation of Formula children were afflicted with mental and physical disabilities. Fewer than half were Yeresunsa. And of those? They were all very low magnitude. That means they were empaths. Seers. Low-level dream walkers. They couldn't do much."

"What's a seer?" Ariock asked.

Evenjos tried not to show her disdain, just in case one of her listeners had that low-grade ability. "A seer can sense when something very bad or very good is about to happen."

"And an empath?" Vy asked. "You mean they can pick up emotions. But not thoughts?"

"Correct," Evenjos said. "An empath senses moods."

"Super lame," Garrett remarked.

"What happened to those babies?" Ariock sounded on guard, as if he expected pain.

"They gained fabulous wealth and status." Evenjos shrugged. "That was the law, at the time."

Ariock looked stunned.

Evenjos laughed at his reaction. "Did you think someone like me would feel threatened by weak babies? No. I welcomed them into the Yeresunsa Order, as did my royal peers. There were good reasons to do so. Even a first-magnitude Yeresunsa has innate advantages over ordinary people. A seer can leverage their sense of luck in a gambling situation. An empath will find it easy to become—how do you say it?—a trickster? A con artist."

Garrett looked pensive. "So you took them off the streets. But what happened to their families? I mean, their mothers?"

Evenjos chuckled at the misconceptions Ariock and Garrett seemed to assume. "Their families had to become royalty. That was the law." Her good humor faded.

"But it did cause some upheaval. Established royals were not eager to welcome a lot of uplifted commoners. We could not grant huge tracts of land to all the new royal families. Instead of living in country palaces, they had to make do with palatial apartments in cities."

Her listeners exchanged looks.

"So all of a sudden," Garrett said, "you had a whole new aristocracy? And they were pissed off at the old royals? And vice versa?"

Evenjos nodded. "It was a bad situation," she admitted. "It caused quite a lot of rancor. And a few petty wars."

Garrett stroked his beard.

"There were no good alternatives," Evenjos said, defensive. "If we welcomed the children while forcing their mothers and families to remain in peasant slums . . . well, imagine how much resentment there would be once those children grew up?"

"Indeed." Garrett sounded as if he understood.

"It was unthinkable," Evenjos said. "So we gave them what we could."

"And . . ." Garrett leaned forward, hands clasped. "I'm guessing hordes of commoners demanded that Formula invented by Unyat?"

"Yes," Evenjos affirmed with bitterness. "Millions of pregnant commoners flocked to Unyat. They would have sold their elder children for one injection of Unyat's Formula. But he gave it away for free."

How she wished she had paid more attention to domestic news. The threats posed by powerful alien empires had seemed so much more dire, so much more important, than any number of territorial disputes and troubling reports coming from her own backwater slums.

"All Unyat asked in return for his Formula," Evenjos said, "was the right to run further experiments on pregnant women."

"But . . ." Ariock looked uneasy. "You said the Formula entailed disabilities, and it didn't work every time. What if they gave birth to a baby with no powers and a lot of special needs?"

Evenjos stared at Ariock, wondering if he had ever seen a peasant family. They left infants to die in sewage gutters—especially ones with special needs. How else could they afford to feed the rest of their children?

"It must have been worth the risk to them," Vy said.

"Yes," Evenjos said. "Before Unyat, a fluke Yeresunsa born to commoners only happened once every few generations. It was almost unheard-of. If such a miracle happened, that peasant and her family would never have to work again. They were raised to royalty."

Garrett leaned back against a supply stack. "So," he said. "Your Yeresunsa Order got flooded with deformed children. The supposedly 'worthy' royal Yeresunsa resented them. And the commoners must have hated them, too, because they were sick with envy." He laced his hands together and settled into comfortable repose, as if prepared for a good story. "I would love to know what happened next."

Evenjos blushed, as if the ensuing problems had been her fault.

But she had been concerned with appeasing alien empires at the time. As the goddess-empress, she had been busy with interstellar diplomacy, convincing the jodinak that her little civilization was powerful enough to defend its own interests.

The sudden influx of new Yeresunsa had sounded like good news to her.

Anyway, how could she be held responsible for envious mobs of peasants? Those minor complaints should have worked themselves out.

"Unyat improved his Formula," Evenjos said. "The next wave of Formula children were more likely to be born with powers and less likely to be crippled by mutations. They were mostly telepaths. Some second magnitude. Some third."

"I imagine you had larger worries." Garrett studied her with a probing gaze.

"I did." Evenjos shifted away slightly, unwilling to let the old man delve into her memories. "But Unyat was becoming a concern for me, yes. I outlawed his Formula. I offered an enormous reward for his capture, dead or alive."

"He evaded capture?" Garrett sounded impressed.

"He had friends among the newly raised royals." Evenjos knew that now, in hindsight. It should have been obvious, even then. "There was even a well-established one, the king of Yonce, who sponsored Unyat in secret. That king was in danger of losing his titles and lands due to his lack of Yeresunsa heirs. He was newly wedded at the time, and he would do anything, pay any price, for a perfected version of Unyat's Formula to give to his pregnant wife."

She guessed, now, that Unyat must have hidden in remote bunkers provided by the king of Yonce. Unyat would have used the king's money to grab whatever resources he wanted, legal or not.

"Did Unyat create a perfected version of his Formula?" Garrett asked.

"No." Evenjos wished she could feel more smug about Unyat's failure. "He improved the Formula, but he was unable to make it a one hundred percent guarantee. Sometimes the babies were born with fatal mutations. Some lacked powers. Unyat kept trying, and according to a book he published illegally, he learned that there is a natural tie between raw power and emotions."

Ariock and Garrett looked rapt. It seemed they might have suspected that natural tie.

"So he altered his experiments." Evenjos swallowed. "The third wave became a pack of feral freaks. They were abominations."

"Telepaths?" Garrett asked.

"Every single one of them," Evenjos answered. "None were crippled. None lacked power. They were all Yeresunsa . . . but they lacked emotional inhibition. Their intellect was missing. They might as well have been animals."

CHAPTER 20

FORMULA FREAKS

Evenjos shivered, recalling newscasts about feral, apelike children who attacked in packs, feeding on anything or anyone they found.

"The cannibals," Jinishta breathed.

"The wild zoved?" Vy said in a guessing tone.

Newscasts used to label the insane children *zoved*, which meant "cannibals" in the language of Evenjos's time. She looked sharply at the two women and scooted closer to Vy. "Show me."

Vy raised a questioning eyebrow.

"In your mind," Evenjos clarified, although she thought her meaning should have been obvious. "Imagine, for me, what you are talking about."

Vy and Jinishta emanated nervous fear.

Ariock, however, leaned closer to Evenjos. "I saw the cannibals, too," he said.

He envisioned a horde of apelike creatures, with knobby spines and enormous jaws, snapping at him amid the sludge-covered ruins of skyscrapers.

Evenjos nearly flinched away. The last thing she wanted was a reminder of the obscenely twisted version of her planet, all toxic and dreary. The cannibals Ariock had encountered were hardly recognizable. They were beasts, not people at all. Not really.

And yet . . .

"Yes," she admitted. "I think you encountered the descendants of Unyat's failure. They behaved like beasts. They murdered and devoured untold millions of peasants."

"Didn't you have an army?" Vy scrutinized her. "Couldn't you have, uh, gotten rid of them?"

Evenjos met the girl's criticism with a cool stare. She was not about to allow a commoner to judge her leadership capabilities.

"Armies were sent to deal with the problem. Of course. When the armies were hunted to death and devoured, I sent Yeresunsa into that region. But do not forget, we are talking about telepaths. The wild zoved proved terribly good at cooperating and hiding in rubble. My Yeresunsa were unable to root them all out. In the end, that area was declared a quarantine death zone. Huge walls were erected to keep the wild zoved at bay. And there they stayed, prowling the night and preying upon each other."

Her audience seemed less than impressed. Even the ummin looked judgmental.

"And copulating with each other," Garrett said in a sardonic tone.

"Did Unyat keep doing experiments?" Ariock asked.

His tone was polite, but Evenjos blushed as if she'd been accused of gross misconduct. It was obvious that she should have gone to greater lengths to root out Unyat, no matter how many kings protected him. The wild zoved calamity was more than enough justification to have Unyat executed.

"We assumed the problem would die out on its own," she admitted.

"Your Yeresunsa Order had bigger fish to fry," Garrett said. "You were dealing with subtle threats from alien empires with a lot of power."

Evenjos wondered if he was mocking her. But when she studied the old man, she detected sympathy.

"And," Garrett went on, "I assume the newly raised royal families put an enormous strain on your worldwide resources? There must have been minor wars spinning up all over the place. On top of that, you had to appease ancient royal families, as well as powerful Yeresunsa who must have felt threatened by the massive influx of Formula children. I'm guessing your Houses of Telepathy, Prophecy, and Clairvoyance felt like they'd been reduced to working as babysitters for unhealthy peasant children." He gently touched her hand. "You had an awful lot to deal with."

"Yes." Evenjos felt grateful that one of her listeners was not quite as ignorant as the rest. "Yes. It was a stressful time." Garrett was a telepath, but even so, it was nice to have one person give her sympathy instead of a judgmental stare.

"Well," Vy muttered, "I guess the wild zoved are gone now."

Evenjos had destroyed all the cannibals without even realizing it. But was that a travesty? No one should mourn those dangerous apes.

A nussian entered the room, making efforts to be quiet. Weptolyso intercepted the nussian and they spoke in rumbling whispers.

Ariock did not interrupt the aliens, but his respectful attention cued the rest of them. Evenjos waited until the nussian assistant had received instructions and loped away. Then, at a signal of interest from Ariock, she continued her story.

"Unyat began to lose his health. He was elderly. He feared that he would die without perfecting his Formula. That was his greatest fear. And so he began a new secret project."

Ariock looked interested. "He tried to invent immortality?"

"What?" Evenjos blinked at that offhand guess. "No. In my time, prestigious people could live extended lives due to Yeresunsa healing, and I suppose that Unyat may have had access to that sort of care. I do not know. But he wanted to continue his life in a more certain way. He paid peasant women to give birth to clones of himself."

Her audience looked shocked and fascinated.

"Unyat made his surrogate mothers take his Formula," Evenjos said. "And he bioengineered the genetics of each of his clones, optimizing them. He wanted the next version of himself to be superior in every way. Particularly in intelligence."

Ariock and Vy were open-mouthed with astonishment. The others looked fascinated, as well.

"The next version?" Garrett said. "Don't you mean the next versions? How many clone children did Unyat make?"

"He only allowed one to grow beyond infancy," Evenjos clarified. "Unyat feared that each of his wealthy patrons would want to hire an Unyat clone, and in that case, the clones would make war upon each other. He had a competitive nature. He feared that many clones of himself would tear each other apart in a struggle to claim all of the patrons, or all of the inheritance possible, and in that war, his precious Formula would be put aside and forgotten. So, in order to ensure that his clone would carry on his work of improving the Formula, he chose only one. The smartest one. And he groomed that one to be his sole heir."

Her listeners were rapt, processing that.

"And the supersmart one he chose was a telepath?" Garrett said, guessing.

Evenjos nodded. "The second Unyat was a Formula baby. Even as a child, he gained a cultlike reputation among his peers for being preternaturally smart. He gained membership in the House of Telepathy, and his father dumped a lifetime of knowledge into the boy before he even went through puberty."

"I see." Garrett seemed to be reevaluating his own knowledge.

"It's confusing that they were both called Unyat," Vy commented.

Evenjos shrugged. Commoners were enough alike as to be interchangeable. As far as she was concerned, all versions of Unyat were the same person. They were continuations of the original.

"And the second Unyat wanted to work on the Formula as well?" Garrett asked.

"Yes." Evenjos swallowed, burdened by memories of overwhelmed, overcrowded Yeresunsa chapter houses. "He honed the Formula. The new version all but guaranteed a telepathic baby."

She recalled endless arguments about where to draw the line, what pretext was needed to get rid of the masses of ugly, maladjusted, unwanted babies, children, and teenagers who barely had enough ability to qualify as Yeresunsa. The top sorcerers of the Yeresunsa Order had threatened to quit—to start a new organization—unless the Formula freaks were banished.

"The accompanying mutation rate was high," she said. "Many of the Formula . . ." She stopped herself from calling them freaks. "The children had congenital disabilities. But they were telepaths."

Ariock wore a frown. "Torth?"

"They weren't slave owners," Garrett said, studying Evenjos as though seeking confirmation. "I assume they were as varied as individuals everywhere. Some were kind, some were cruel."

Evenjos nodded. "But there were millions of them. Far, far too many. The Yeresunsa Order began to feel a strain we had never experienced before. Our treasury emptied as we paid pensions to their families. We did not have enough teachers for them. Or housing."

"Where did Yeresunsa normally live?" Garrett asked. "In palaces?"

"You might call them that." Evenjos recalled the glorious chapter houses dominating every city, great and small. She supposed they no longer existed. "Every Yeresunsa resided in a palatial suite, with chambermaids to serve them. But the House of Telepathy grew too numerous, and eventually, they had to ask their members to rent apartments, as if they were mere commoners."

Ariock looked unimpressed. "That's why they rebelled?" he asked in a bland tone. "They figured they were too good for apartment living, so they enslaved the galaxy?"

Garrett shot his great-grandson an annoyed look. "Let's hear the rest of the story."

"No one was aware that the telepaths were discontented." Evenjos reviewed her memories, trying to puzzle out if there had been any hints. But she had been occupied with summit meetings with alien dignitaries and the usual royal balls and banquets to seal truces and treaties. "We did sever the House of Telepathy from the rest of the Yeresunsa Order," she said. "We had to. There was no choice."

She supposed she must sound defensive. But she wanted her audience to understand the pressures the Formula freaks had foisted upon her.

"We needed to establish new chapter houses on alien worlds," she explained. "If we kept on stealing wealth from our royal families and redistributing it to every peasant who happened to have a Formula relative . . . well, we would lose all our income. We needed the royals."

"And they were your families," Garrett said gently. "Weren't they?"

"Of course," Evenjos said. "Almost all Yeresunsa were royal born. The natural ones, I mean. Not the Formula children."

"Did the telepaths . . . integrate . . . into commoner life?" Ariock sounded skeptical, and Jinishta made a noise of doubt.

"Yes," Evenjos said, although she was no longer entirely certain of the facts. She had trusted Elome's reports. "Many became judges, detectives, and psychologists. They were well respected among commoners. And do not forget, the House of Telepathy remained cordially tied to the Yeresunsa Order. There were people who were full-fledged members in both organizations."

Audavian had been one of those. Evenjos remembered honoring some promising young Yeresunsa with their new magnitude pins, and there he had stood, a gangly but proud adolescent with a deformed jaw.

Ugly, Evenjos had thought.

But otherwise, she had not judged him poorly. Had she? No. She had been gracious.

After all, Audavian and other rarities like him—Formula freaks with uncommon raw power—had every right to compete with the royal born. No one had denied them their right to become Yeresunsa. They must have studied hard in order to attain the same aptitude as naturally born Yeresunsa, but they had acted just as polite, just as well reared.

"There must have been resentment simmering beneath the surface," Garrett said. "You're saying the telepaths essentially became second-class citizens."

Evenjos regarded Garrett with exasperation. "Beneath the changes wrought by the Formula," she reminded her listeners, "they were peasants."

Ariock looked unmoved. Everyone faced Evenjos with a judgmental expression.

Was it possible . . . did these leaders actually sympathize with the Formula freaks and their families?

It was ludicrous. Telepaths were their enemies. And the Formula freaks had never been oppressed! Not really. Not like slaves. Evenjos had never hurt them! The telepaths of her era had enjoyed respectable jobs, even if they were just commoners with weird mutations. They had no longer needed to grub in the dirt like their ancestors. That should have been enough.

"So," Garrett said, "the new version of Unyat improved the Formula. Did the original Unyat die?"

"I am sure he did," Evenjos said, "but the new version stepped into his legendary name. And he, too, believed the universe would be better off if everyone was born with an equal amount of power and wealth."

She said that with the scorn it deserved. Even now, she wondered how such a clever scientist could be so . . . well . . . stupid.

Some stars burned more brightly than others. Some planets were fairer. And some people were simply more powerful. That was nature. Mass equality was the sort of perverse, unnatural obscenity that only a dull peasant could obsess over.

"His goal never wavered," Evenjos said. "Perfecting his Formula was all he cared about. He truly believed he could give equality to everyone. He honestly believed that uplifting every commoner was a righteous and noble idea."

Ariock and Vy looked troubled. Surely they could not feel sympathy for Unyat's goal? How was that possible?

Evenjos went on, determined to make them understand. "No one noticed when he began to befriend clerks who were in charge of food and beverage manufacturers. I do not think anyone guessed his true aim."

The attention of her audience perked up.

Garrett sounded disbelieving. "You're not saying . . . did he put the Formula into beverages?"

Evenjos nodded. "He created a new version that was liquid. It no longer had to be taken as an injection. And he stealthily took control of the manufacturing of beverages, worldwide."

Her audience was silent, absorbing the ramifications.

"He put it into rivers," she said. "And into wells. He manipulated beverage companies, and they gave out free sodas and coffees, full of the Formula."

They were finally beginning to understand. Their eyes went wide.

"You mean he had everyone in the world drinking it?" Vy asked in disbelief. "Without their consent?"

"Everyone." Evenjos was filled with more regrets than she could voice. The ensuing wave of Formula children had been a flood, an unstoppable tsunami. "For a few terrifying years, every baby born was a third-magnitude telepath."

Even Ariock looked stunned. Perhaps he understood now that Unyat was the root cause of all the troubles in the galaxy, past and present. It could all be traced to his shortsighted focus on equality.

"He wanted everyone indebted to him." Vy sounded as if Unyat had personally offended her. "He had total control of distribution. He wanted to rule an empire."

"No." Evenjos corrected that misconception. "Unyat never claimed power for himself, as far as anyone knew. He believed he was doing a good thing, without personal gain. And peasants actually loved him for it." She could not keep the disgust out of her tone. "They saw him as a folk hero."

The ties that held civilization together had begun to fray and break, unable to bend toward that impossible goal of equality for all.

"Telepaths vote on everything," Evenjos went on. "Most of them got swept up in his idealistic, romantic visions of equal powers at birth. During that time—a worldwide pandemic of telepath babies—the House of Telepathy elected a new head."

She paused, steeling herself.

Then she forced herself to admit to yet another failing. "Many people, including me, welcomed Audavian as a perfect bridge between the old and the new. He was comfortable with common telepaths as well as top sorcerers. He was a Formula freak . . . I mean, a Formula child . . . but he had enough raw strength to qualify as a full-fledged Yeresunsa. His friends included kings and queens. In summary, he was popular. He was everybody's favorite choice."

Garrett seemed to brace himself for a tirade. He must have sensed her long-pent-up rage against Audavian.

"And with him in charge of the House of Telepathy," Evenjos said, "the dark times truly began."

CHAPTER 21

BACKSTABBED

Evenjos took a moment to reflect on how much, exactly, she should share with the people of this current brutal era. Perhaps she should tell them about her lover, Prince Elome of Narranth? His quick wit. His graceful, well-bred handsomeness. His tender way of speaking to her deepest hopes and fears.

His lies.

Evenjos's fingernails grew into claws, which dug painfully into the skin of her palms. No. Ariock would lose respect for her and would have trouble trusting her if he learned any hint of her most embarrassing mistake. It was best to leave Elome out of her tale. Best to pretend that he had never existed.

Good riddance to that viper.

She retracted her claws and forced her hands back to normal, healing her skin. "I believe that Audavian and Unyat secretly teamed up," she said.

Her listeners made themselves more comfortable, nestling into folded blankets. Vy leaned her head against Ariock, as if she belonged there. Ariock wrapped an arm around her.

Evenjos tried not to notice how comfortable they were with each other. She would need to teach Ariock his own value. There were so many reasons why someone with his raw power ought not settle for a common wench.

Garrett cleared his throat. For a second, Evenjos feared that he would inquire about her thoughts and mention her long-dead lover.

But he must have noble etiquette, because he did not bring up Elome.

"I would think," Garrett said, "an alliance between Unyat and Audavian could not be kept a secret. They were both members of the House of Telepathy, weren't they?"

Curiosity emanated from the listeners. They thought Garrett had a valid point.

Clearly, these people had no concept of the political situation in her time.

"Unyat was a criminal," Evenjos reminded them. "The House of Telepathy had to publicly reject him. They were a respectable organization, albeit no longer part of the Yeresunsa Order. To stay respectable, they could not openly welcome the mastermind behind the massive distribution of a black-market drug. Not if they wished to remain on good terms with the Yeresunsa Order."

"I see." Garrett looked curious. "So Audavian never spoke to Unyat in public, or vice versa?"

"Or in private," Evenjos clarified. "They never met. There was never any proof that they were allied in any way. My spies said nothing. No one suspected. It was only later, when I was . . ." She faltered. *Imprisoned* was far too mild a word for the millennia of torment she had endured. There were no adequate words.

"When you were imprisoned," Garrett said gently, helping her. "That's when you pieced together the fact that Unyat and Audavian must have been working together?"

She swallowed. "Yes."

Garrett looked more fascinated than ever. "So Unyat was a known criminal. But Audavian . . . I guess he seemed respectable?"

"He charmed everyone." Evenjos could not help but blush, furious at the way he had manipulated royals, even her. "He was a member of three power Houses," she explained. "And he was fifth magnitude in one of those. None could deny that he belonged among the most powerful and elite. And he was the very model of correct behavior."

And he had been an imposing block of a man. He would have been handsome, if not for his deformed jaw.

Evenjos blinked back sudden tears. Why had she not seen through his act? If only she had bothered to ask a few pointed questions about Audavian's origins in the slums of Woth Caith.

But really, who would think to be curious about the meager lives of commoners? They were all bland. If only . . .

Well, the world had eventually learned of the cruel way Audavian had destroyed his own roots.

"His first terrible act," she said, "was to murder his own family when he was a child. He was so ashamed of his peasant mother and brother that he used his powers to force them to kill themselves."

Vy looked pained. "Why?"

"Yeresunsa mostly come from good families," Evenjos explained. "Or they used to. Very few were from . . . well, the sort of people Audavian was from. He did not want any chance of his royal peers and teachers accidentally meeting his Formula whore of a mother, or his money-obsessed brother."

Vy looked as if Evenjos had said something rude. Even Ariock looked as if the story had taken an impolite turn.

"You say he brainwashed them into suicide," Garrett said. "But I thought brainwashing was illegal in your time?"

"Very much so," Evenjos agreed. "No one knew until much later, when he was investigated for worse crimes."

"No one reported their suicides as being strange?" Garrett said. "A strange coincidence, I mean?"

"No one important." Evenjos masked her impatience, wondering why she needed to explain things that ought to be self-evident. "A few commoners may have raised the question, I suppose. But in my era, commoners tended to exaggerate. Besides, low-class people often cheat each other or get into trouble from drug addictions or gambling. Their deaths would not have been attributed to anything as outlandish as illegal Yeresunsa activity."

She vaguely remembered that a telepath or two had investigated the suicides. But, of course, those telepaths would have been under the influence of Audavian. And who else would bother to dig into what seemed to be an inconsequential matter?

"What else did he do?" Garrett asked. "You mentioned that Audavian was investigated for worse crimes?"

"The House of Telepathy amassed an obscene amount of wealth." Evenjos flattened her tone, unwilling to share how bitter she had felt upon realizing that Audavian had somehow gained more wealth than she herself. "At the time, royal families were mysteriously losing their assets. The Yeresunsa Order was on the verge of financial collapse. Meanwhile, the House of Telepathy began to construct opulent branch offices in alien cities. Audavian erected a pleasure palace for his own amusement."

"Sounds like a Torth," Ariock stated.

"He was stealing it?" Garrett asked.

Evenjos gave Garrett a nod of acknowledgment. "He hid his thieving for years. More than a decade. His conspiracy was eventually uncovered by a jodinak cargo merchant whose corporation was plagued by embezzlement. The merchant kept hiring telepaths to investigate the corruption, and they kept feeding him believable answers, but after a while he grew suspicious of the telepaths themselves. He caught one in the illegal act of brainwashing his employee."

There was a story there, but Evenjos did not know it. She only remembered the feverish newscast headlines about corruption in the House of Telepathy.

"That opened up a lot of suspicion," she went on. "If one telepath was illegally using mind control in order to steal from a major corporation, might there be others?"

Rooting them out had been a hellish project that consumed multiple years and all the remaining resources of the Yeresunsa Order. Who could hide secrets better than a mind controller? And if telepaths could not be trusted to tell the truth—as they were legally obligated to do—then who was trustworthy?

Evenjos had placed her trust in Elome. After all, he was royal born, not a Formula freak. He was a natural telepath. And a far more salient fact was that he was a Yeresunsa prince. His loyalties were clear. He loved Evenjos and the Yeresunsa Order. He disdained Formula freaks.

So he'd always insisted. So he'd told everyone.

"Audavian was sent to the undersea penitentiary," Evenjos told her listeners. "It was a specially fortified compound built to hold criminal Yeresunsa. We intended for him to spend the rest of his life in isolation there. He was supposed to die there."

Elome himself had sentenced Audavian. Elome had assured Evenjos—and everyone—that the worst rumors about the House of Telepathy were absolutely false. Telepaths could not communicate across vast distances. How ludicrous! The fringe conspiracy theories about Audavian secretly communicating with Unyat and other telepaths . . . well, those were nothing but paranoid fantasies. Ridiculous!

Evenjos had allowed herself to be reassured.

"I concentrated on rooting out corruption in the House of Telepathy," she said. "I shut down contaminated beverage factories as much as I could. But a lot of telepaths worked against me."

That was an understatement.

"They had allies everywhere," Evenjos went on. "Even among aliens. Young people believed that Unyat was a progressive man of science. I was supposedly nothing but a backward-looking icon from an obsolete time."

She recalled satires making fun of her incompetence. She had felt the bitter sting of humiliation for the first time in her long life. As the goddess-empress who sat upon the crystal throne, she should have had total control over her own propaganda. Instead . . .

Well.

Looking back, she should have taken the criticisms of her reign as a troubling warning sign. Instead, she had assumed that she was invulnerable. People ridiculed her behind her back, but she had thought ridicule was as far as it would ever go. Surely no one would, or could, unseat Evenjos—the most powerful Yeresunsa in existence. She was Glory.

"There are always doomsayers," Evenjos said, trying to make the others understand. "In every decade, in every age, there are doomsayers. Ah Jun came to my attention. But she was just a child." A Formula freak, but Evenjos forced herself to be tactful and say, "A disabled child. Just another result of the Formula."

"You mean . . ." Jinishta looked as if she dreaded the answer. "The oracle Ah Jun was a telepath?"

Evenjos recalled the girl's eyeless deformity of a head. "She was low magnitude in telepathy, like me. But telepathy was just about the only way she could communicate. She was born without eyes or ears. Someone rescued her from a slum, where she lived, feral, among rats and dogs. She barely knew how to speak."

Vy looked pained.

"Is that why she painted so much?" Garrett asked.

"I suppose so." Evenjos had never given the matter much thought. At the time, all she had seen was a pathetic rabble surrounding a sadly freakish child. She had assumed that the child's handlers were trying to win fame by pretending that the eyeless girl could accurately predict the far future.

Third-magnitude prophecy was extraordinarily rare. Fourth made for legends. Fifth was unheard-of. To claim that a common street rat—a feral child without eyes or ears, no less—had such a valuable, once-in-a-millennium type of power . . . that claim was simply too implausible to be believed.

Garrett looked fascinated. "Couldn't you tell that she was powerful?"

"No. Prophecy is somatic," Evenjos explained. "Like telepathy, even the high magnitudes have a low strength threshold. One can be a far-seeing oracle and still be as weak as a commoner."

Garrett seemed to be recalculating his knowledge.

"But," Evenjos said, "that means one cannot detect a prophet except by their deeds. Ah Jun was never inducted into the Yeresunsa Order. Because she grew up without parents or caretakers, she did not know she was Yeresunsa until she was seven or eight years old. She barely even knew that she was a person rather than a dog."

Vy looked as if she wanted to save the eyeless girl herself. "Whoever rescued her must have been someone special."

Evenjos did not want to admit that Vy might be right. The telepath who had rescued the eyeless child must have taught her how to speak and how to paint.

"Did the telepaths try to silence Ah Jun?" Ariock sounded like he dreaded the answer. "She was going around warning anyone who would listen that the Torth Empire was going to be a thing."

"Most telepaths ridiculed her." Evenjos could not quite hide her own guilt. She had laughed right along with Elome when he had joked about Ah Jun and her doomsday cult. After all, the notion of telepathic supremacy gave common mind readers an excuse to play at being important. "People saw her predictions as over-wrought and impossible."

"Even though you had a pandemic of telepaths being born?" Garrett asked.

"They were commoners." Evenjos wondered if the brutes of this era even knew what commoners were. She tried to explain. "They were unimportant. Powerless. Unyat thought he was transforming peasants into powerful individuals, but the third version of him finally realized the folly of it. A glut of telepaths meant that telepathy was no longer special at all. It became . . ." She shrugged to show an easy dismissal. "Mundane. Just about everyone was a telepath."

"And none of them talked about the Megacosm?" Garrett asked with sympa-thetic caution. "No one mentioned that a mental language was evolving, where tele-paths could talk to each other in secret?"

Evenjos gazed down at her hands, ashamed. "The followers of Ah Jun spoke of it. A few others spread those rumors as well. But most telepaths denied it."

"Of course they did," Ariock muttered.

"Ah Jun hanged herself," Evenjos said. "When she was twelve."

Her listeners absorbed that in mournful silence, as if to acknowledge the death of a friend.

"She must have felt frustrated," Vy said. "No one with power would believe her."

Evenjos recalled the frantic-looking brushstrokes of the girl's paintings. Frustration was, indeed, probably why she had committed suicide.

"What happened to her followers?" Garrett asked. "And how did you react? What were you doing at the time?"

He spoke with gentleness and sympathy, but Evenjos could not help but cringe in shame. "I do not know what happened to her followers," she admitted. No one important had been paying attention. "I suppose they dispersed. Perhaps they made preparations to survive the doom she predicted."

They might have squirreled away relics underground. They must have prepared bomb shelters. As for herself . . . well, what had she been doing?

She had been enjoying herself.

Banquets and ballroom dances. She had felt safe.

Underground parodies making fun of the goddess-empress were easy to shut down. Subversive writers and artists were easy for her law enforcers to ar-rest. Evenjos remembered warm nights in Elome's arms between merry days full of music. Despite Ah Jun's predictions, she had not seen so much as a hint of im-pending rebellion. She had not guessed at the intense rage simmering in most Formula freaks—a bitter envy toward the naturally powerful Yeresunsa and their royal families.

Perhaps there were a lot of little incidents. Perhaps they had all added up, like storm clouds gathering for a deluge.

Worst of all: she had not suspected Elome.

She had never guessed that such a charming, regal prince could be a brain-washed pawn of Audavian. But she knew, now, that Audavian had applied his mind control power liberally. Even imprisoned beneath an ocean, the former head of the House of Telepathy had maintained a telepathic connection with his minions.

How much of Elome's lighthearted personality had been genuine? How much was a ruse? She could not guess.

"I would like to know how the telepaths came out on top," Garrett said. "You had a government with entrenched power. Audavian and Unyat were both confined, limited in what they could achieve. They were forced to work in secret. So how did they knock down the top sorcerers?"

That was a difficult question.

"I can give you many answers." Evenjos ached for her long-dead people. "One factor was the third version of Unyat. He groomed another cloned replacement for himself—but this time, he modified its brain so that it could absorb knowledge faster than any living being."

"A supergenius version." Garrett looked concerned.

"I suppose so," Evenjos said. "Unyat believed that he might achieve his goal of universal equality only through greater brainpower. So that is what he gave his next self."

"What did the supergenius version of Unyat do?" Garrett asked.

Evenjos tried to suppress her chills. Her story was leading, inevitably, to the traumatic end. "I cannot guess all of it. I was not around to . . . to see what happened to him."

She hesitated. It was difficult to speak of her defeat.

"But I know one thing," she went on. "The third version of Unyat finally acknowledged that granting powers to every peasant did not entail equality. Because there were always exceptions. There was Ah Jun. And Audavian. And others of their ilk."

"Unyat was no longer an average joe himself," Garrett pointed out. "He was a cloned supergenius telepath. Did he really want equality?"

"I think he did." Evenjos wondered if Unyat had even been aware of his own hypocrisy. His recorded speeches had always sounded high-minded and noble. "In his warped, idealized vision of society, there would be no commoners or royalty. No inheritances. Everyone would be born with the same abilities and the same status." Her tone soured. "I suppose he thought that a supergenius like himself could achieve that impossibility."

"But he did achieve it," Kessa said in a musing tone.

Ariock gave her a questioning look.

"The Torth," Kessa said, "are equal to each other. They are all born equal."

Evenjos considered what she had learned about the Torth Empire, and she inwardly realized that the elderly ummin was right. Torth were, ostensibly, born equal.

"I wonder," Kessa said, "if Unyat would have extended his equality to everyone? Would he have granted telepathy to ummins?"

That sounded like boring academic pondering to Evenjos. Who cared what Unyat's exact philosophy on equality had been?

"So he gave up on the Formula," Garrett prompted. "But he still wanted universal equality. How would he achieve that?"

Evenjos shivered. "He invented a hideous brew, something that could disable the powers of any Yeresunsa. Even one as powerful as me."

"The inhibitor," Ariock said in a tone of realization.

Evenjos wondered how many years the second and third versions of Unyat had worked together, in secret, on that abominable serum. "Yes. The new version of Unyat decided that the best path toward equality was to destroy Yeresunsa powers entirely. If commoners could not all attain royalty, then he would turn all royals into commoners."

Her listeners had inward-facing looks, perhaps pondering the implications.

"He was working toward a drinkable version." Evenjos surveyed her listeners. "But I suppose he never finished it?"

She was afraid that someone might contradict her and tell her that a drinkable inhibitor existed. That was cause for terror.

To her relief, no one spoke of such a poison. Ariock looked unnerved by the idea.

Garrett remarked, "Audavian could not have been thrilled about the inhibitor project. He didn't want universal equality, did he?"

"Audavian wanted power," Evenjos confirmed. "That was all he ever cared about. More authority, more money, more followers, more and more. And he did not get picky about how he got things. He was nothing but a common thug."

If only she had seen that from the start. Audavian had fit in with kings and princes. He had hidden his greed under courtly restraint. But underneath his polished demeanor . . . well.

"I later learned that Audavian secretly disparaged Unyat's goal," Evenjos said. "He called it a joke. But the inhibitor opened up a possibility for him to depose me, so he praised it publicly. He called Unyat a hero for wanting to destroy the unfair advantage that royals and sorcerers were born with."

"Wait a minute," Vy said. "Why would the public care what Audavian thought? I thought he was locked in an undersea prison?"

"He was. But commoners—especially telepaths—still loved him, even in his absence." Evenjos was embarrassed to admit how severely she had underestimated Audavian's popularity. "Many people mistook his thieving for a form of justice. They believed he stood up for poor telepaths and their commoner families."

Vy looked introspective. "He was Robin Hood."

Ariock seemed to understand the reference. Perhaps it was from a folk tale.

"So he engendered a quasi-religious movement?" Garrett asked.

Evenjos gave a hesitant nod. Zealotry fit the mobs who had wanted to tear her down. "Perhaps he telepathically brainwashed a few key leaders from afar. Those would have encouraged the rest."

"And Unyat had his own groupies." Garrett rested his bearded chin on one hand. "And they all wanted to get rid of people like you."

It sounded painfully obvious now. Evenjos wondered if her friends and staff members had expected a coup. Had everyone anticipated it?

Everyone except for her.

"Wouldn't Unyat rather partner with an insider in your royal circles?" Vy asked. "He must have known that Audavian wasn't entirely trustworthy."

Evenjos thought of Prince Elome.

But she refused to talk about her most shameful blindness. Instead, she explained, "I believe that Unyat saw Audavian as a means to an end. He used him. They used each other. One was the muscle, so to speak. The other was the brain."

Ariock looked as if something she had said made him uncomfortable.

Good. Maybe he was finally beginning to see the danger posed by his friend Thomas.

"So," Garrett said, "Audavian and Unyat gave each other bonus minions. Maybe they secretly unified the House of Telepathy against you?"

Evenjos nodded.

"And Unyat gave the telepaths a plan to depose you," Garrett went on, guessing. "Plus the inhibitor?"

"Yes." Evenjos felt cold, remembering that day. That awful day. Looking back on it now, she realized how coordinated the coup had been. How well planned. It must have been strategized by Unyat.

"What happened?" Garrett asked gently. "Did Audavian escape that prison?"

"There were telepaths among the guards." Evenjos felt like a fool admitting that. "They smuggled him out."

If only she had been forewarned.

She focused on Ariock. She needed to make him understand how blindsided she had been, how innocent.

"It had been years," she said, "since anyone important spoke of Audavian. He was buried and forgotten. No one went within telepathy range of him, inside that undersea facility, surrounded by lava and military weapons. Of course, we did not know there was a secret mental language for telepaths."

"Your, um, friends did not tell you?" Garrett asked with courteous diffidence. "You were a member of the House of Telepathy yourself. No one ever told you?"

"No one." Evenjos spread her hands. "I am a second-magnitude telepath. Only third magnitude and higher can access that mind language. I was never told."

Garrett looked sympathetic.

Evenjos leaned against a crate, steeling herself for the final leg of her tale. "At a mental signal from Unyat or Audavian—I don't know which one was really in charge, even now—the telepaths poisoned their Yeresunsa friends and superiors. Our water supplies were monitored, of course. But they procured sleeping aids and put them in our food. And when we were sleepy or unconscious? They stabbed us."

Elome must be long dead, rotted to dust, but even so, fury rose in Evenjos and threatened to choke her.

She had trusted him. She would have trusted him with her life.

And what had he really thought of her?

He had mixed a strong drug into her tea, and then, after she took a few sips, he had playfully embraced her. Kissed her. Nuzzled her, as if to charm her into bed.

He had stabbed her in the back with a syringe.

"I'm sorry," he had said, as if surprised by his own cruelty.

And Evenjos, rendered powerless for the first time in her long life, had detected that he was lying. Telepathy required no raw power. Even reduced to nothing, she could still read minds.

That was when she had learned that his third-magnitude pin was a lie.

Elome was fourth magnitude. He could pass as third only because he lacked the raw power to telepathically brainwash anyone.

Except when he stole power from his lover.

In their most intimate moments, while Evenjos was consenting and oblivious, Elome had linked spheres with her. He was a tender and attentive lover. And no wonder. When he put her into ecstasy, he boosted his own raw power by linking to hers. And then he secretly proceeded to adjust her thoughts. He erased her worries. Put her at ease. Made her feel safe. Made her feel good.

What a prince.

Evenjos had launched herself at him, screaming, trying to gouge out his eyes or his throat. But she became frail and ghastly, reduced to her true form—an aged hag. Elome had shoved her away as if she weighed nothing.

"*I'm sorry,*" Elome had said. "*I have to do what Audavian wants. That's how it is with power. If it means anything, you're a better master. I prefer you.*"

He preferred Evenjos. Yet he helped her enemies depose her.

So what was their entire fifty-year relationship? It was as meaningless as dust. Prince Elome was a liar who had never loved her.

Oh, perhaps he had felt some affection for Evenjos. But his main loyalty was to the head of the House of Telepathy. Whether or not he worshipped Audavian, he had been under that freak's control.

CHAPTER 22

DISEMPOWERED AND DISEMBODIED

Evenjos did not want to remember her humiliating defeat, but she forced herself to keep talking. Her new allies needed to understand how dangerous telepathic super-geniuses and mind controllers were. They needed to be forewarned and prepared, the way she never was.

"Audavian had me tied up." She was careful not to mention her former lover. "He sealed me inside a mockery of my throne room. The outer hall was lined with the paintings of Ah Jun. You see, the telepaths had secretly rejoiced in their future victories all along. They believed the oracle. In public, they had mocked Ah Jun . . . but in private?" She slumped, remembering her humiliation. "It was yet another way to mock me."

Ariock looked slightly sympathetic.

"You would not have guessed," Evenjos said, "that Audavian, locked in that undersea penitentiary, could pose a threat. But the House of Telepathy was full of traitors who had been plotting against me—and against the Yeresunsa Order—for decades. They were our clerks. Our subordinates. In a few cases, they were even our friends." She wished she could forget her traitorous prince consort. "They must have been communicating in secret for a long time. And they agreed upon a day on which to overthrow all those in power and replace all royalty with themselves."

Garrett looked skeptical. "There were no whistleblowers?" he asked. "All it would take would be one. Just one telepath who lost the nerve. Or one Yeresunsa who figured it all out."

Evenjos gazed at her hands on her lap. She supposed there must have been whistleblowers and traitors to Unyat's cause. But who had heard them? Who had listened?

Not her.

"There were Yeresunsa who were sent off your planet," Kessa pointed out. "You said they were on Jodinak and other worlds. Were they not safe?"

Evenjos nodded an acknowledgment. "Yes. Some Yeresunsa escaped. Some were notable, such as the stormbringer Iriade. I can only guess at what happened to them, since I was not around to . . . I did not see . . ." She took a breath, smoothing her inner turmoil and shame. "I was not around to see how things ended."

"Understood," Garrett said kindly. "So, um, how did they imprison you in those mirrors, exactly?"

Evenjos went wary.

Yet she noticed how attentive Ariock was, how curious. She sensed no malevolence from any of her listeners. It seemed Garrett and the others merely wished to learn from her.

Evenjos took a breath. There could not be much harm in telling them, since . . . "I do not believe it would have worked on anyone else," she explained. "I think it was unintentional. It was an effect of imprisoning me: a sixth-magnitude healer."

Ariock looked more curious than ever.

Evenjos touched her wrists, where the long-ago shackles had bitten into her skin. "I am very tough to kill. I can survive torment that would destroy anyone else."

Audavian's visits had been brutal. He used to start with scathing criticisms of her regime. He had called her stupid. Frivolous. Decadent. Stuck in the past. Oblivious to the suffering of peasants.

And then . . .

Evenjos refused to share the unspeakable indignities Audavian had subjected her to.

Instead of reliving the rapes, the torture sessions, and the various humiliations, she merely said, "He chained me to the mockery of my throne. He gave me no food and no water. He kept me on the inhibitor so that I was too weak to help anyone. I could not even help myself."

"I'm sorry," Garrett said quietly. He emanated sympathy, and Evenjos remembered that he, too, had suffered as a prisoner. They shared a certain resonance.

"I cannot guess how long that went on," Evenjos said. It had seemed like a year. "But he began to seal other prisoners in with me. They were royals. Other Yeresunsa, robbed of power. Inhibited. I knew that Audavian must be insecure on the throne he had stolen from me."

If only she had assessed him more truly. She could have prevented the Torth Empire from arising.

"He was mad with power," Evenjos said. "And always hungry for more. He took over the minds of as many Yeresunsa as possible. No one was allowed to challenge him. He had each Yeresunsa dragged to him in chains. Then he would seize their free will. He gave them a mental twist, and they would become mindless puppets, ready to do his bidding. They would die for him."

Ariock's eyes widened.

Good. Let him think about how easy it would be to fall victim to his young friend in the hoverchair.

"And they did die," Evenjos said. "By the thousands. Audavian would use each of his victims for a day, maybe two, until they died from whatever rigors he put them through. Then he would seize another. He ran through victims until he mind-controlled the very people who had helped him seize the throne."

"Why didn't he use you that way?" Garrett asked.

Evenjos acknowledged the wisdom of his question with a nod. She was—or she had been—the most powerful Yeresunsa in existence. Audavian could have transformed her into an exceptional weapon.

"He kept me in reserve," she explained. "Like a snack in his cellar. The high form of mind control is fatal. Victims never live for more than a few days. Even I would have collapsed."

"I see." Garrett nodded his understanding. "Audavian didn't want to waste you too soon. His victims were onetime-use-only deals."

"Exactly." Evenjos was glad that she did not have to overexplain such matters. Garrett had a sharper mind than his scarred, brutish face suggested.

"Not everyone welcomed Audavian as their god-emperor," she went on. "A few Yeresunsa managed to hide from him, either underground or on alien planets. I caught hints that the jodinak sent a fleet of warships to destroy Audavian. But in the end . . ." She wished she could feel some satisfaction about the death of her worst tormentor. "It was not the jodinak, or the surviving Yeresunsa in exile, who tore him apart."

Garrett raised his bushy eyebrows, questioning.

"It was his own worshippers," Evenjos said.

"That," Garrett said, "is a very Torth thing to do."

Evenjos did not know much about the Torth, but she supposed it made sense. "The telepaths finally recognized him as a tyrant. He brainwashed anyone who displeased him, and at last, they turned against him. They outlawed high magnitudes entirely. They made his raw strength of power illegal."

Evenjos had wept with joyful relief when she had heard that news. She had assumed it meant the reign of the rogue House of Telepathy was over. She had expected a rescue.

"I suppose everyone expected the House of Telepathy to be reasonable after that," she said. "But no one actually knew what the telepaths wanted, because they no longer spoke out loud. I cannot say whom they elected as the new leader of the House of Telepathy, or if they even had a leader. But . . ."

Evenjos tried to wrench herself out of the long-ago time, unwilling to relive her worst trauma.

"It turned out they were in no mood to free me," she admitted. "Instead of rescuing me, they sealed me in that underground chamber, with my starving loyalists and royals. They buried us alive."

Ariock looked tormented by sympathy. "Didn't the inhibitor wear off? Couldn't you recover your powers?"

"I was starved, beaten, and chained," Evenjos reminded him. "And I was sealed inside a mirror chamber. My valet was trapped inside the false throne room with me, but he was too weakened from starvation to crack the mirrors. As was I. Audavian had kept me in a near-death, depleted condition."

Ariock looked quizzical. "What do you mean? Do mirrors keep you depleted somehow?"

Evenjos looked from him to Garrett. Didn't the brutes of this era understand what mirror containment entailed? They knew so little about Yeresunsa, they might as well be peasants.

"Reflective surfaces block clairvoyance," Evenjos said, explaining a basic principle. "That is why Audavian kept me imprisoned in a place of mirrors. No one could project into my prison to find me. And I could not project outside. None of my starving loyalists, within or without, were strong enough to break the mirrors. Audavian saw to that. He had the surfaces reinforced, and he double-checked them every day."

Garrett looked fascinated. "Yet . . . I guess you figured a way out?"

Evenjos held up her hand and demonstrated her shapeshifting power by dissolving it into dust particles. "I could not transform into molecules, as I can now.

But I could alter my shape." She healed her dust particles back into a living hand. "I found ways to pour myself into the tiniest of cracks between mirrors. It was barely enough. But it gave me enough room to project."

Only Garrett seemed cognizant of the hardship. He looked more sympathetic than ever. "That must have been very draining."

"It was all I could do." Evenjos faltered, ashamed of how helpless she had been. "My poor loyalists were dead. They had no water, no food, and they ran out of fresh air."

All she had done was watch, disembodied, as her clerks and serving people died, clawing toward the sealed exit. Queens and kings, as well. And lesser royals. They had all died in that underground mockery of her palace.

"That's why you were so drained," Garrett realized. He turned to his great-grandson and explained, "Health and sphere of influence are tied together. In her condition, starved and near depletion . . . she wouldn't have had much opportunity to recover her powers."

"Correct." Evenjos supposed that she might have recuperated some strength by licking condensation from the false throne. By the time Audavian was killed, her companions in the darkness were all rotting skeletons. But perhaps she could have eaten bugs?

Instead . . .

"I refused to believe that I was forgotten," she confessed. "I felt sure that some of my loyalists and allies must be alive aboveground. They would surely rescue me."

Even now, Evenjos had trouble believing that her most powerful allies had failed. What had become of the stormbringers of her era? What about the empress of the Jodinak Empire?

"Clairvoyant projection can damage the mind," Evenjos explained, for Ariock's edification. "If one uses it too often. Yet I found it tempting. I was alone, an empress of the dead. I was a living skeleton. And I felt sure that I could be restored to my crystal throne—if only someone knew where I was and how to find me."

"So you used clairvoyance to locate hypothetical rescuers?" Garrett asked with his uncanny way of guessing her motives.

"Yes." Evenjos clasped her hands together. "The mirrors were a terrible barrier. I had to filter between the cracks, and I suppose . . . well . . . I suppose more and more of myself became bound up inside them."

That was a side effect no one could have foreseen. Well, perhaps Ah Jun had foreseen it, but no one else. Even Unyat would have been shocked by her strange form of survival.

As long as her body had remained alive, the umbilical tether had kept tugging her home.

But then her body had died . . . and instead of dying herself, the mirrors had become her tether.

"An ember of my life spark must have remained nested in those mirrors," Evenjos said, "even after my body wasted away."

"What did you see?" Garrett asked. "What was it like?"

He radiated curiosity, yet Evenjos had no satisfying answers. What had she seen? War. Pestilence. Starvation. Death.

"Nothing good," she said. "And the more I parted from my body, the less coherent my thoughts became."

Eventually, the only thing that could sharpen her mind toward any semblance of consciousness had been a resonance with someone in a similar plight. Other prisoners. Dying. In sorrow. In pain. And despair. Only those sorts of moods had attracted her scattered consciousness.

And only if they were within a feasible range.

She had not quite been dead, but without a living body, unable to breathe or wake up, she had lacked the strength to roam far from the mirrors she was tethered to. She could never have escaped. She could not have resurrected herself. All she had been able to do was exist in a hellish twilight between life and death.

"I tried to hold on to my sense of self," she said. "But if you are clairvoyant, then you know what it is like. It feels like dreaming."

The last solid memory she had was a scene of despair. Peasants hiding underground. Evenjos could not guess whether they were true peasants, or former nobles, or even Yeresunsa. They'd been ragged.

And their enemies? Coordinated armies of telepaths patrolled the city above, armed with alien technology. Somehow, the telepaths had obtained military transports from one of the ummin empires.

"As years passed," Evenjos said, "I lost my ability to hold thoughts. All I could do was wait."

She fell silent. Her rescue had come, and here they were. She had waited a thousand generations for Thomas and Ariock.

"I cannot tell you much more." Evenjos hid the tremor in her voice. "I cannot guess how the telepaths defeated the remnants of the broken Yeresunsa Order. I suppose they stole technology from the jodinak and the ummins and other spacefaring civilizations. They gained all the knowledge of every enemy they defeated."

She looked down at her familiar hands, sculpted from years of practice. She wanted to stay young and beautiful. She was not a mere ghost of glory. Not a defeated empress. She needed to shed that identity and move on.

"That," a soft voice said, "was enlightening."

A boy's voice.

Him.

Evenjos leaped out of his range and hardened her skin to impenetrable diamond toughness. Thomas's freakish mind should be impossible to overlook. The only reason she had failed to notice his thunderous mental presence was because she'd been so wrapped up in telling her tale. That and, as a second-magnitude telepath, she was unable to fully experience another person's mind. She could only sense his layers of knowledge in a dim way.

Still, he was a galaxy rather than a speck of dust. His complexity was frightening.

And he had lurked behind stacks of supplies, eavesdropping. Absorbing her life.

Had he brainwashed her?

Evenjos prepared to slay the monster with sheets of lightning. She owed these allies her help, but if they failed to recognize Thomas as a tyrant waiting to happen, well, then, she had to take charge.

Ariock extended his arm, and Evenjos sensed the air hardening along that trajectory. He created a shield between her and the monster.

"Don't hurt him," Ariock commanded.

Were these leaders already brainwashed?

Some telepaths, like Elome, could alter emotions with subtle delicacy. They subverted people's moods rather than hijacking their free will outright. Evenjos would never guess if that was the case. She would just fall victim . . . and be imprisoned again . . . and tortured . . .

"I'm not a monster." Thomas faced her, his yellow eyes iridescent. What an unnatural color. "I'm sorry about what you went through."

He sounded empathetic.

But of course he did. Telepaths were experts at fakery.

"He's on our side." There was a threat in Ariock's deep voice.

Evenjos hesitated, aware that Ariock was nearing his full power. He was formidable. The last thing she wanted to do was fight him.

But she was trying to help him win!

The boy was a sinister combination of the powers of Unyat and Audavian. Only a moron would tolerate him!

Garrett made a growling sound at the monster. "Why aren't you in the control room?"

The monster floated with childlike innocence. "I thought I might offer input on war strategies."

"Well, certain members of this council are not interested in your ideas." Garrett slid an uneasy glance toward Evenjos, as if she was the most dangerous person in the room. Then he shifted his gaze back to the boy. "Let's get together later, all right? We can discuss strategy when we're all a bit more settled."

The monster gave a thin, unfriendly smile. "You might be surprised at what insights I can provide."

Garrett seemed about to argue, but the monster went on.

"For instance, thanks to Evenjos's tale, we now know that isolated pockets of telepaths can keep secrets independently from one another. Audavian had a faction and Unyat had a faction. Each kept their own secrets, and when they joined up, their secrets merged."

"So what?" Garrett looked annoyed.

"So that's a danger to watch out for," the monster said, "if we ever manage to fracture the Megacosm and reduce it to isolated pockets."

Evenjos lowered her arms. Inwardly, she admitted that the monster had an interesting hypothesis. Perhaps there was some merit in listening to his advice.

If such a creature could be trusted.

"I am not your enemy." Thomas spoke fluidly in Evenjos's forgotten language, words meant only for her. "I am not like the ones who imprisoned you."

Even if that was true, he was clearly a freak. And in this lawless, demented era, he could enslave the universe. All he had to do was lull powerful people such as Evenjos and Ariock into a false sense of security.

"The Torth are my enemies, just as they are yours," Thomas said in that soothing tone. "I agree that they've had a long enough reign. It's time for it to end. I want to help end them."

He sounded so reasonable.

For a moment, Evenjos considered turning to dust and flitting away, into space, to find an empty planet to inhabit. Thomas was terrifying. She would rather be alone than team up with . . .

Well, no.

She did not want to be alone ever again. Not at any price.

"I promise," Thomas said, switching back to the common slave tongue. "I would never hurt anyone on our side."

Reassuring everyone.

Because they knew, now, that telepaths like Thomas were descendants of Formula freaks.

Oh, perhaps Thomas had other genetics mixed in, as he and his friends seemed to believe. Perhaps he truly was a renegade. That didn't matter. At his root, Thomas was descended from long-ago commoners like Unyat. Like all Torth, he came from peasants who had willingly mutated themselves. In their misguided frenzy to gain equality, they had devolved into selfish tyrants.

His roots were mud.

How could anyone respect an adviser—or a supposed friend—whose heritage was excrement?

The boy looked hurt. Ariock watched Evenjos with expectancy. They were all so protective of this monster. So naive.

And yet . . .

Ariock was someone worth knowing. Evenjos sensed kindness and strength beneath his readiness for battle.

She wanted his trust.

And Thomas had rescued Evenjos, as much as Ariock. They had worked together to free her.

"All right." Evenjos faced Thomas and pretended to relax. "I will let you live."

But if she was going to help these allies, she needed to feel safe among them. She could not remain in a state of hypervigilance at all times.

She was not going to tolerate a creep who lingered, unseen, in adjacent aisles, imbibing her secrets.

"On one condition," she said.

They all tensed.

"The monster will never enter my range again." Evenjos stared at Thomas, making sure her seriousness was plain. She had boundaries. And he had better respect those boundaries.

"I have given fair warning in front of witnesses," she said. "If he enters my range without my permission? Then I have the right to kill him."

PART TWO

"Outside of stars and planets, the universe is dark, cold, and empty. Life is rare. It is a treasure. And it exists in isolated biomes. Mind readers fall into the dark, cold gaps. We stretch and contort to brush life with our fingertips."

—Unyat clone

SWIFT CHANGE OF PLANS

The Swift Killer picked up an alien meal called a "hot dog" from a street vendor in the human metropolis known as New York City.

She paid for it using a digital wallet. She was familiar with the ludicrously complex barter systems that humans used, thanks to her secret training in the Stratower, plus several stints on Earth.

But she had skipped the conventional rules this time. Instead of using a ready-made false identity from a database in the Stratower—which was now gone—she had simply broken into an apartment and stolen a phone from the terrified occupant. She had tormented the young woman with pain seizures until the human had permanently unlocked the device.

Also, instead of docking her jumper shuttle in a designated remote location, as Torth law required, she had simply parked it atop a random skyscraper.

Why not?

Like any stealth vehicle, her shuttle was cloaked in adaptive cells, rendering it effectively invisible. What were the chances that a human would bumble against one of its spindly legs? Only a Torth with the proper key could unlock its door and cause the ascension ramp to unfurl.

Sure, the ramp would be visible. But the Swift Killer had taken care to land in a derelict part of the city, where few security cameras were likely to capture the sight of anything odd. And anyhow . . .

Human civilization was not going to last much longer.

The Swift Killer strolled down the sidewalk, enjoying the exotic taste of the hot dog. Grubby indigenous minds streamed past her.

Human beings were always frustrated by each other, unable to quite figure out each other's minds. They suppressed their emotions while working off stress in gymnasiums or recreational parks. Really, they were a lot more like children than like slaves.

Perhaps that was why scientists typically advocated for leaving Earth alone. New York City was like an enormous baby farm. The people here were so obsessed with rising to the top of their petty social bubbles, they were oblivious to the Swift Killer's geometrically patterned robes. She had not even bothered to wear human garb.

Well, except for her sunglasses. She had stolen those from the woman in the apartment, along with the phone. Her blaster glove went unnoticed—humans mistook it for a fingerless sports glove—but her empty white eyeballs were a different matter. She had to cover those or else draw a lot of unwanted attention.

Whatever.

I want to govern Egypt, the Swift Killer silently announced to her inner audience.

Her popularity surged at the outrageous statement. Many of her orbiters wanted to learn what Egypt was. Others wished to find out whether the Swift Killer was a viable contender to win governance over a newly conquered province. Such honors were usually reserved for champions of a conquest.

I will be a champion, she assured her inner audience. The Serendipitous Day would probably lead the invasion, and she magnanimously told him, *You can have New York*. She aimed another comment toward the Former Commander. *And you can have Tokyo. I want Cairo.*

She would remake the Great Pyramid into a gymnasium for her daily workouts. What an honor for humanity's most famous neolithic monument!

Perhaps humankind would forget their own ancient history in less than a generation? The challenge would be fun.

Oooh. Some of her admirers approved.

The Swift Killer had gained more regular orbiters during the annihilation of the Torth Homeworld. Amid that cataclysm, she had commandeered one of the last available jumper shuttles. From there, she had boarded an overcrowded dreadnought. Now here she was, a week later, on Earth.

She had gotten lucky. Even so, many Torth admired how handily she had escaped death.

Yet she also had plenty of detractors. *The conquest of Earth may not be as easy as you imagine*, her critics sang.

Her inner audience used to be a lot less condescending.

The problem with being a Yeresunsa, these days, was a lack of respect. No one aspired to her rank anymore. The Majority seemed to think she was just a lowly part of the military, like a Red Rank, only more expendable.

How are you going to combat the Giant? many Torth chorused condescendingly.

If he can teleport to Earth—

—then you will find yourself badly outmatched—

—against the Betrayer's forces.

The Swift Killer ate the last bite of hot dog. She crumpled the wrapper and dropped it to the pavement for some human to clean up. Personally, she thought the Betrayer would act stupidly if his human foster mother was threatened. Never mind his supergenius mutation. He was far more human than the Majority was willing to believe.

All one had to do was threaten Elaine Hollander.

Then the one-legged girl would tense up, and the Giant would go on alert. The Betrayer would likely cave in to any demand the Torth made.

"Might makes right" is axiomatic, the Swift Killer thought, uncaring that her opinion was appalling to the lowly masses. *It's a law of nature. It's as immutable as a law of physics.*

She was mighty. That fact trumped all laws.

Deep down, everyone knew it. Even the Rosy Recruits were awakening to their own superiority over common Torth. In normal times, only the best individuals— the fittest bodies, the sharpest minds—had been cultivated for repeated promotions. Those became Blue Ranks and Red Ranks. And then, only those with secret powers could hope to attain the rank of Servant of All.

The rest . . . ? Well, they would have lived their lives unaware of what they truly were.

Now things were different.

Power detection had never been an exact science, yet even so, the Majority seemed shocked by how many of their neighbors had escaped detection. The number of Rosy Recruits was increasing every day.

The Swift Killer took it in stride.

And she was thankful. For most of her life, she had only dared to relax her mental constraints in lonely, isolated places. Never in cities. Never among other Torth. Never, never in the Megacosm. To do so would have meant exile and execution.

She used to practice telekinesis only in remote wildernesses. She used to throw fireballs only in the Stratower, when that building had still existed, in secret combat with other Servants of All. She had not even known how to put herself into a clairvoyant trance.

Until this week.

Now? She was learning how to ghost.

She felt reborn. For all she knew, she might be able to teleport, but first she had to ghost more often, to build up her endurance.

What other dormant powers might she have?

Everything was different, and in her opinion, the newly upset galaxy was better than the old version. Even animals were sensible enough to obey the law of might makes right. Lesser Torth ought to stop listening to feeble little supergeniuses and instead obey powerhouses such as herself.

By your (faulty) reasoning, the Giant should reign supreme over everyone.

A gargantuan mind bulked into the Swift Killer's awareness. Many of the Swift Killer's listeners bobbed and switched orbits, like ionized electrons.

Like all supergeniuses, the Death Architect was a disabled child. Countless millions of Torth minds orbited her vast consciousness, for she was a titan as well as an undersize girl with scoliosis.

She wore her hair in pigtails. Tied with ribbons. How jarringly incongruent.

The Giant is certainly more powerful than you (Swift Killer), the Death Architect thought. *Should you then cringe before him?*

What an offensive insinuation!

Or perhaps you want to cringe before the Betrayer? The Death Architect seemed to be idly pondering an academic matter. *He can (very likely) use mind control on the Giant. So he is potentially the most powerful person in the galaxy.*

The Swift Killer wished she could visit the smug little Death Architect in person and punch her tiny, dimpled face into a bloody pulp.

Or perhaps, the Death Architect went on, *you have his same power. Such traits are heritable.*

If only.

The Swift Killer ground her teeth. Mind control ought to be hers by dint of genetic legacy. She was the biological aunt of a boy who was capable of threatening all of galactic civilization. That was power. Surely her pedigree meant she was superior to all her peers?

So she had secretly attempted to dominate the free will of slaves. She had tried it on humans. She had tried everything imaginable.

Why? Why! Why did she lack his power to brainwash people?

It wasn't fair!

She forced herself to breathe in, breathe out. It was best to not drive away her mental audience with a rage-induced tornado. The Majority needed to keep what little respect they had for her.

One of the native New Yorkers saw her grimacing and did a double take. His mind filled with primitive sexual fantasies.

Ugh. She was definitely going to retrain their kind.

Ah well. The Death Architect seemed to be in a conversant mood. *You (Swift Killer) cannot brainwash, but you are clairvoyant. Have you figured out how to teleport yet?*

The Swift Killer did not want to admit how hard she had been trying. And failing. But a supergenius had asked her a direct question, which meant everyone was now curious. Millions clawed at her mind, demanding an answer.

???

She had to give details about her power practice to put a stop to wild speculation. So she reluctantly revealed her efforts. Yes, she could ghost, but only for a minute and a half. Then she would snap back to her body. If she did that ten times in a row, she would suffer a warning headache.

Ten times in a row is impressive, the Death Architect responded. *Few Servants or Rosies have that much stamina. Most suffer the warning headache after four or five attempts.*

The Swift Killer felt encouraged.

You will likely be able to teleport, the Death Architect thought. *If not your whole body, you should at least be able to teleport items (like bombs) with small mass. Keep practicing.*

The Swift Killer tightened her lips. She was not a Rosy Recruit, to be ordered around. The Death Architect was a Turquoise-Blue Rank. Impressive for a little girl, but not a top rank. She wasn't even the eldest supergenius. She ought to mind her own business! Didn't she have weapons to invent?

I have a request for you, Swift Killer, the Death Architect thought.

A request? Ha. Even a fool could guess what the Death Architect and her mental peers craved. An extra supply of NAI-13 was located on this primitive planet. The Upward Governess had already been rewarded with a supply, apparently just because she was the eldest. Who deserved the next reward?

I am not a delivery pilot, the Swift Killer thought. *Someone else will fetch NAI-13 for you—when you have earned it.*

The Death Architect emitted a pulse of muted curiosity. *That is not My request.* She reacted as if the medicine had been the furthest thing from her mind. *No. Medicine would be a pleasant gift, but My life is but a pittance against the needs of Our great and glorious Empire.*

She was a difficult one to read.

Ooh. Orbiters buzzed with admiration for the little girl's altruism.

Even the Swift Killer inwardly admitted that the Death Architect had leadership potential. At least she wasn't unapologetically greedy. Really, the Upward Governess should not be put in charge of anything more important than a banquet.

You are All too generous and kind. The Death Architect responded to the praise with breezy politeness. *I would not wrest leadership from My esteemed colleague (the*

Upward Governess). She has earned Her elevation. I am merely exploring additional strategies that might ensure triumph for Our Empire.

Her immense focus swung away from her orbiters and wholly onto the Swift Killer. That was unnerving.

I calculate that you (Swift Killer) would best serve the Empire by stationing yourself on Umdalkdul, the Death Architect thought. *Go there.*

The Swift Killer blinked with annoyed disbelief. Umdalkdul? Why? Was she supposed to act as a backup guardian for the spoiled Upward Governess?

No. She had better things to do. Like scout out the pyramids of Egypt in preparation to enslave humankind.

It is merely a suggestion, the Death Architect thought serenely. *Rare Moonrise MetroHub could use your presence.*

The "suggestion" was laced with unspoken threats. Images of Torth corpses leaked from the Death Architect's hyperrealistic imagination. She was hinting that she knew what was best for the future of the galactic empire.

As if she was more than pipsqueak.

She was nothing but a prepubescent child!

The Swift Killer nearly punched a human, just to release her frustration. She might have done so if fewer Torth were orbiting her mind. Instead, she began to stride faster than the humans around her. She wished she could find the Death Architect's lair, if only to roast her alive in wildfire. That would teach her and her ilk to stop giving orders!

Emotional diarrhea. The Death Architect seemed to mentally hold her nose. *The Swift Killer is as mentally unstable as her disgraced (deceased) clone sister.*

Orbiters peeled away from the Swift Killer's mind. They did not wish to associate with someone who was slavishly emotional.

Other listeners pried into her thoughts, searching for any hint of malfeasance or secrets. Was she going renegade? Was she planning to go rogue on Earth the way her clone sister had done?

The Swift Killer stopped walking. She leaned against a brick wall, trying to placate her inner audience. *I am loyal to the Torth Empire.* She forced herself to send out reassurances. *I am but a weapon for the Torth Majority to use. That is Me.*

Her orbiters assured her that she was expendable. She was a mere military rank, one of many thousands, who could be easily replaced.

Prove your loyalty, the Death Architect suggested. *Leave Earth. Be ready to serve the Empire on Umdalkdul.*

Well.

The Swift Killer realized her glower was drawing stares from more natives, but she didn't care. Rare Moonrise MetroHub was in the same region as New GoodLife WaterGarden City. Wasn't the Upward Governess safely hidden somewhere in that desert?

The Swift Killer growled. The fat Indigo-Blue Rank could not be such an imperiled, crucial target. Like all supergeniuses, she was protected by secrecy, traps, and specially chosen guardians, each of whom possessed an encrypted map to the lair. No one was allowed to ask them location-specific questions or probe their minds. The Majority had agreed. Disobedience meant execution.

Why? the Swift Killer demanded. *Why do you want Me near the Upward Governess?*

The Death Architect did not deign to clarify. She thought it would be foolish to leak war secrets into the Megacosm. The Imposter was known to suck up Torth news on a regular basis.

I am in SweetNectar City on Verdantia. That came from the Glory Snatcher.

I am in Lambent City on Tenth Ocean. That was the Clement Serpent.

Other Servants of All chimed in. They were in major hub cities, on major hub planets: Firmament, Nuss, Vagary, Parity, Mer Nerct, and other populated worlds.

It seemed the Death Architect had been busy making suggestions. The clairvoyant Servants waited for . . .

Something.

They practiced combat moves, or they explored their powers, or they shopped for new weapons. Some were asleep in places where it was the dead hours of the morning.

The Death Architect did not even seem to appreciate their cooperative obedience. She was simply going around, making offhand remarks, as if her oblique suggestions would save civilization.

The Swift Killer's orbiters chorused a reminder. *She is a supergenius.*

  She must have a solid plan.

    Besides—

      —We need a clear picture of the enemies' strengths and weaknesses.

      Before We pick a fight on Earth.

      Earth should be deprioritized right now.

Perhaps that was wise.

The Swift Killer gazed up at skyscrapers that looked flimsy and square when compared with Torth structures. Even so, they did have a crude sort of majesty.

She gazed at the herds of humans, so oblivious to extrasolar threats. Yet despite their ignorance and filth and rudeness . . . well, the Swift Killer rather liked masquerading as a human.

The Death Architect had better have a stellar reason for taking Me off Earth, she thought. *Otherwise . . .*

She stopped herself. Threats were overkill. If the little girl was giving random nonsense advice, well, the Torth Majority would tolerate that for only so long.

Too many people trusted supergeniuses. Bad advice from one of their ilk would be tantamount to treason.

The Swift Killer smiled. If the Death Architect turned out to be a traitor, she hoped the Majority would entrust her with the special honor of carrying out the girl's execution.

For now, the Swift Killer tossed aside her stately robes, revealing a sleek bodysuit that did not look out of place amid New Yorkers. She jogged back toward the building where she had parked her cloaked jumper shuttle.

With her enhanced musculoskeletal structure, plus a daily workout, she could jog for miles at a steady pace without tiring. She could handle just about any crisis in a battle. Although she hated being manipulated . . .

Well. Perhaps she would find a noble purpose waiting for her on Umdalkdul.

CHAPTER 2

TOUCHING PARADISE

Perhaps all habitable planets looked like beautiful blue marbles floating in space.

Unlike Earth, or any other terrestrial planet Ariock had seen, planet Reject-81 had no artificial satellites. No roads. No cities. No cultivated farmlands. No dams, or mines, or anything industrial.

It had everything else. And a lot more of it.

The planet's continents and oceans sparkled to Ariock's extended awareness, teeming with uncounted life sparks. Its glitter was more alluring than any jeweled grotto. Ariock sensed alien jungles. Forests. Herds and flocks of animals in the land, water, and air.

He felt like a grubby thug as he prepared to ground his gigantic colony-class starship.

Reject-81 was healthy in the most pristine ways possible. Its primeval wildernesses were endlessly bountiful. And he was going to scar a mountain valley with millions of refugees plus several metric gigatons of steel.

He had already nullified the reactors with help from Thomas. Together, they had stabilized the superionic core of the ship, and soon they would deactivate the artificial gravity blanketing every deck.

"I promise you," Garrett was saying, "we are better off dismantling the whole ship. If we leave it in orbit, that's like a big sign saying, 'Here we are!'"

Thomas answered in a pedantic tone. "It's a virtual guarantee that they'll find us, ship or no ship. Even if we hide in caves, we'd have less than a zero point zero zero one percent chance of—"

"Give me a break," Garrett interrupted. "You're paranoid. The Torth hardly have any surveillance tech! They never invested much in cameras, thanks to their overreliance on the Megacosm."

Thomas answered between gritted teeth. "You're failing to take into account Ariock's sphere of influence."

Ariock had given up on feeling guilty about his inability to hide. His life spark was an ominous glow to the senses of other Yeresunsa who came within his influence, which encompassed a solar system. But he didn't have to stay with his friends. Now that he could teleport, he could probably—

"So they'll find us," Garrett said with a roll of his eyes. "In a few weeks. And then? Pshaw. You and Ariock can reconstruct this ship in a heartbeat."

"Contrary to popular belief," Thomas said icily, "this ship isn't a miracle from heaven." He tended to sound emotionless and neutral with most people, but he was clearly frustrated by Garrett. "A colony-class starship isn't something we can slapdab together. Have you forgotten how close we came to having an incomplete life support system?"

Ariock gazed through the wraparound windows at the continents below. The reject planet was definitely a better habitat than the one he had crudely made.

Garrett gave him a comforting pat on the back. "You did fine." He turned to Thomas. "Look. The ship is of no consequence. If the Torth have us cornered? Well, then, Ariock will teleport us—and our entire population—elsewhere. No biggie. I'm planning to teach him to ghost to other solar systems."

Ariock beamed. He was really looking forward to those promised lessons. Once he mastered far-distance clairvoyance, he would be able to teleport across the galaxy. The Torth wouldn't be able to corner him.

"And," Garrett went on, "Ariock is going to conduct a daily clairvoyant sweep of our solar system. Anything large, such as a Torth dreadnought, will be obvious. If the Torth are going to attack, he'll see them coming from literally a parsec away."

Ariock nodded.

"Uh-huh," Thomas said dryly. "Until we start raiding Torth cities on other planets, and our population is left defenseless while Ariock is off elsewhere."

Garrett had an immediate answer. "We have Evenjos."

Ariock wished Evenjos would help him ground this massive starship. He did not sense her potent life spark anywhere nearby, and he figured she must have already disembarked. Was she lounging on some fluffy clouds? Enjoying fresh air, away from people? It must be nice.

"And I'm a powerhouse," Garrett went on grandly. "I can defeat a Torth armada all by myself if it comes down to it."

Thomas's tone became chilled. "You're not thinking it through. Ariock is the only one of us who can mass-teleport our entire population. If he has to bring us to another solar system, all at once—twelve million people—that is likely to drive him to depletion."

Ariock didn't like that.

"And you want to grow our population," Thomas added in an acidic tone. "Plus, you are severely underestimating the Torth. They can ghost. What's to stop them from finding us? Again and again?"

"They haven't found us yet," Garrett pointed out. "Their clairvoyants can't ghost very far. They're weak."

"Give them time," Thomas said tersely. "They have multiple supergeniuses and top scientists working on the problem. I would bet on them finding us sooner rather than later." He paused, then delivered his conclusion. "Our chances of survival are forty-five percent higher if we maintain our colony starship in a ready-to-go state."

Ariock figured that Thomas had good points. However, Garrett had a valid point as well. They were running low on food. They would absolutely need to steal from the Torth Empire. And really, if they meant to free slaves, then they had to fight. That was the whole point.

Why flee?

Why hide?

When Garrett had insisted that they needed a planetary base, Ariock had nodded fervently. He was done with claustrophobic limitations. He was done with darkness and mildew. Thomas wanted to keep traveling into deep space, but Ariock was willing to fight for an extra scrap of freedom.

Garrett thought they ought to set up on a tropical island. It was gorgeous but totally impractical in terms of defense. Ariock had no desire to watch miles of open coastline.

Meanwhile, Thomas suggested hollowing out a mountain range. Caves again.

In the end, Ariock had chosen ground that he felt was a compromise. He could see his ideal landscape through the windows. Down there, his refugee population, camped along a forked river, would have access to fresh water. A mountainous perimeter would make it difficult for Torth to sneak up on them from ground level. And if Ariock had to dig out caves in which to hide? Well, the mountains were limestone, easy to carve.

And after some grumbling, both Garrett and Thomas had agreed that it was ideal.

"I'm ready," Ariock said. "Let's ground this ship." That ought to put a pause on the argument.

Thomas projected an illustrative holograph with a region of topography lit up in red. "Ease it down in the area I've highlighted," Thomas said. "Remember, ships of this size were never designed to be grounded. So be extra gentle and careful."

Ariock steeled himself for a feat of massive strength. "Got it."

This crow's nest was cramped enough that Ariock could spread his arms and lean on opposite walls. He planted his feet, minimizing focus on his core body. He did not want any distractions in terms of balance or breathing.

Then he embraced the entire miles-long length of the ship within his awareness.

His core self was its central underside. He lowered himself toward the continent and soon felt the intense pull of gravity.

He defied gravity.

They were not going to smash into the surface like a meteorite. They would not crash or burn. Instead, this enormous starship, which was the size of a mountain range, would settle upon the ground as gently as a leaf.

"We don't have any shuttles or escape pods?" That faraway voice came from Vy. Ariock was glad to have her nearby, although he wished she would dare interrupt Garrett and Thomas once in a while.

"Nope." That was Thomas. "We didn't have time for bells and whistles when we were in construction mode."

Ariock fully inhabited the starship's frame. Gently, he lowered himself through ozone, ignoring the scratchiness of lightning along his hulls. His lower self sank past wispy clouds. The strain increased, yet he remained aware of every part, careful not to crush anything or cause damage.

The ship's underbelly touched soft soil, covered by green vegetation.

Ariock supposed that he could have extruded some legs in an effort to prevent the ship from resting on the uneven ground, thereby ruining its structural integrity.

Yet legs would have bitten deep into layers of virgin soil and bedrock. What he was doing felt sacrilegious.

"It looks like paradise." Vy gazed at steep, snow-capped mountains that gleamed sharply against a cerulean sky. Alien grass fuzzed undulating hills, broken only by the snaking bends of the river. It might as well be a scene from a fantasy novel.

The ship groaned as it settled, parts of it strained or broken. Ariock reinforced structural weak points. He fixed tears and stopped leaks.

Garrett stuck a cigarette in one corner of his mouth. Soon he was puffing on carcinogenic smoke. "Hard to believe this is a reject planet. It's a nice one."

That could be read as a compliment to Thomas. Perhaps the old man was letting go of some of his anger?

Ariock gently withdrew his awareness. He dared not snap back. Recklessness could cause major damage or get people killed.

"We need ramps down to the surface," Thomas said. "Let's give people multiple options for disembarking. I've designed the basic structural components." He projected a holograph of complexity. "These struts ought to be pulled from a cargo bed, here . . ."

Ariock got to work.

Millions of life sparks moved through his extended awareness, and he was careful to work around them. He stripped the starship to scrounge construction materials. Following Thomas's instructions, he put together cables and ramps, connecting portholes to the hilly ground beyond.

"I'm going to make a science lab," Garrett told Thomas. "Whatever you need in order to invent immunity to the inhibitor serum, you should let me know. Give me a list."

Thomas did not mock Garrett or say that it was impossible. He merely shrugged and said "thanks," then went on instructing Ariock in the fine art of frictionless cable anchors.

A cure for the inhibitor?

Ariock surreptitiously studied Thomas, wondering what was possible. Armor and helmets were one thing, but immunity . . . ? That would make Ariock invincible. He would be unstoppable in battle.

He completed one ramp, then began to extrude another. Maybe he should turn them into slides, to move cargo and people down faster.

"I'm taking the hulls apart," Garrett stated cheerfully. "We could use protective walls and roofs around our makeshift city." He spread his hands like a sorcerer casting a spell.

Thomas sighed raggedly. But it seemed he had given up on arguing about keeping the ship intact.

Ariock sensed a shift in the structure. The floor trembled as gigantic outer plates of tungsten polymer loosened themselves. He gave Garrett a look of exasperation.

In truth, however, it was nice that someone else had titanic strength like his own.

From now on, Ariock would not need to fight every battle alone. He would not be the sole person everyone relied on for protection. Maybe, if he was lucky, the Alashani would start calling Garrett or Evenjos their messiah and quit praying for Ariock to solve every little problem they had.

Garrett ripped away one curved hull piece. Then another. Each piece was larger than a row of skyscrapers, enormous shapes that could fend off stray meteorites.

One after another, they sailed across the sky and embedded themselves in the foothills. Garrett's cloak floated, caught in the excess of his concentration.

"Very impressive."

Evenjos made no sound as she breezed into the crow's nest with them, other than her seductive voice. Her accent was unmistakable. So was her perfumed scent.

Ariock saw Vy tense up.

He attempted to ignore Evenjos. He had work to do. The ramps were not going to build themselves. He focused on girders and eyebars and . . .

"Have you not worked long enough?" Evenjos swished in front of him.

She seemed to have made herself taller.

Not quite as tall as his nine feet, six inches, but she was definitely in his size range. Eight feet tall? She was a towering presence in comparison to Vy or Garrett, yet she remained willowy and feminine, a female titan he could embrace without needing to be extra cautious and gentle.

Her hair billowed out in silvery-purple ribbons. Her wings gave her an otherworldly look—and also blocked the view so that Ariock could not comfortably focus anywhere except on her.

"So serious all the time." Evenjos reached up to caress his chin. She could reach his face easily, unlike Vy or anyone else. "Do you not ever smile?"

Ariock cleared his throat in a businesslike way. "I'm busy, Evenjos."

He hoped she would take the hint and leave. Either that or do some actual work. It would be wonderful if she would take over half of the ramps under construction.

"I can take over the ramps," Garrett offered.

Evenjos smiled as if she had won a game. "Let the old man do this work," she said in that disturbingly seductive tone. "Allow me to show you better uses for your power?"

Ariock began to refuse.

Before he could speak, a foreign presence joined the pillars he was building, taking control. Struts settled into new configurations.

"I've always wanted to work on major construction projects like this," Garrett said proudly.

It would be dangerous and foolish to wrestle for control over the ramps and slides. Hundreds of life sparks were already moving down them.

Ariock withdrew his own awareness with caution, watching Garrett for any sign of weakness or refusal. It felt strange to entrust someone else with an effort on which lives depended.

"This is no sweat for me," Garrett said with a happy grin. "Seriously, I got this. You kids go have fun."

The last thing Ariock wanted was for Vy to get the wrong idea. "I'd rather—"

Before he could finish his refusal, Evenjos held out a feminine hand, and the window-wall tore away in a gust of wind.

It went flying, revealing the true view outside.

They were at least a quarter of a mile above the ground. Ariock squinted against the frigid wind. Thomas backed away from the wind tunnel with a whimper of fear.

Beyond the steel remnants of walls, there was an untarnished landscape.

Ariock figured he should probably repair the wall before someone got hurt.

"Let's play a game," Evenjos said in a teasing voice.

She blasted Ariock with force.

Before he could even register the attack, he was falling, unsupported, out of the starship. He flailed with instinctive terror. He would hit the ground in a matter of seconds.

But . . .

Annoyance took over his terror. He could fly.

Ariock connected with the air around himself, pressurizing it into gel. That stopped his free fall.

"Catch me!" Evenjos yelled from above. Laughing, she plunged out of the starship, transforming into a purple-and-gold bird as she fell.

Even her avian form was otherworldly. She was a bird of paradise, a phoenix with shimmering plumage.

Grinding his teeth, Ariock catapulted himself toward her. They needed to have a serious talk about respecting boundaries.

The Evenjos bird darted away at the last second, leaving him with nothing but a single feather.

Ariock had no intention of playing her stupid game. He drifted in midair, wondering what she would do if he returned to the crow's nest and went back to work. Would she interrupt him again? Would she bother him relentlessly? Until . . . well, until what?

Until he snapped?

They simply needed to have a conversation about mutual respect. It didn't have to be a big deal.

He growled with frustration as the Evenjos bird twirled nearby. Did she think this was funny? Did she have so little respect for their population of refugees that she was happy to play in full view of them rather than work on their behalf? How could she be so self-absorbed?

Ariock darted toward her with lightning speed, determined to seize her for long enough to open up a conversation.

When he grabbed her, however, the Evenjos bird morphed into an Evenjos snake. She slid out of his grasp and fell, ropelike, hissing with laughter. Her metallic scales gleamed in the sunlight.

Ariock hesitated again. He really should return to his duties. And Vy.

He glanced up at the crude, unwieldy starship, which was already partially dismantled.

Then he glanced at the gorgeous vista spread around him.

There were no enemies here. Nothing on this paradise of a world could hurt him. It might as well be a playground, even more benign than his mansion.

And a planet was big enough for him to experiment with his powers.

He finally had some time for learning, too. He might gain a real sense of his limitations and prepare for his next battle.

Was it possible? . . . Did Evenjos actually have something to teach him?

Ariock figured he would return to the ship if he was wrong or if this turned out to be a waste of time.

Vy would understand. That was what was so amazing about her. She had a knack for understanding what he meant and what he needed.

Anyway, Garrett could take care of construction projects. Ariock ought to get used to relying on someone other than himself. Maybe he should . . . well, dare he . . . ?

Enjoy himself?

Ariock plunged toward the mountains, where Evenjos had transformed into a beautiful bird again. She winged toward fluffy white clouds.

Ariock chased her. Although he wanted a serious conversation, despite his determination, a smile began to form on his face.

CHAPTER 3

MENDING MORTALS

Anyone sensible would back away from the broken wall.

Frigid wind whipped Vy's hair. Would Ariock even notice if she fell? Anyone could see how much fun he was having now that he had fewer concerns to hold him back.

"Your urban planning is suboptimal." Thomas spoke past her, to Garrett. "If you arrange the shelters with Ariock's bungalow at the center, you'll paint a bull's-eye on him. You should bury our command center along one of the spoke boulevards. Keep it under the same roofs as everything else. That way—"

"Yeah, yeah, I got it, kid." Garrett stood braced in a position akin to how Ariock had stood, no doubt supporting gigatons of steel. "Look, I need to focus. Can you go make yourself useful elsewhere? Maybe find Weptolyso and micromanage his cargo brigades."

Vy could see them in the sky. Why had she ever believed that she was adequate for a hero with godlike powers? How could she have deluded herself so thoroughly?

They were a god and a goddess.

Laughing.

Chasing each other through gigantic, impossibly beautiful clouds.

Garrett chuckled in a wistful way, watching them. "Ah, the joys of youth."

His wistfulness was fond, not bitter. Not jealous at all. He only wanted what was best for Ariock.

That was the way Vy was supposed to feel, wasn't it? That was love.

Garrett must sense the anguish twisting through her heart. Either he was hinting at how she ought to feel, or he was politely pretending not to notice.

How kind.

Vy stepped closer to the edge. She didn't care what Garrett thought. If she walked off, would she splatter into a bone-liquefying mess? Would anyone bother to catch her?

Probably not.

She was just a footnote in Ariock's life, an easily discarded accoutrement.

"Vy," Thomas said urgently.

Vy heard the concern in her foster brother's voice. What was his problem?

"Vy." Thomas sounded insistent. "Let's go. Will you come with me?" His voice softened. "Please?"

How unusual.

Thomas would not beg unless he desperately needed something. Vy could not imagine what he needed from a mundanity like herself.

Well. She supposed she had better find out.

Vy trudged after his hoverchair, out of the crow's nest and into a corridor that was choked with fast-moving foot traffic. Harried albinos swerved wide around them. Nussians and other aliens gave them space, perhaps momentarily scared into thinking that they were a couple of Torth.

Judging by their looks of loathing, the aliens understood that Vy didn't belong here, among heroes, having galactic adventures.

She ought to ask Ariock to teleport her home, to Earth.

Forget him. Forget the rest of the galaxy and this insane war.

Although . . .

Vy was unsure if she could resume her regular life as if none of her adventures had happened. Could she return to her weekend lessons at the airport? She used to dream of sitting in a cockpit and soaring above the world. What did it matter now?

Could she return to hospital work, knowing that Earth might be invaded by Torth at any moment? Earth would not even be a livable planet if Ariock and Evenjos brought their version of war there.

"No one has ill will toward you," Thomas said, floating next to her. "Trust me. It's all aimed at me."

Now that he had pointed it out, Vy realized that the hateful glares were, indeed, aimed at her foster brother.

It hardly mattered that his hoverchair had been repainted to a friendly purple hue or that he wore low-key woolens. He still had those iridescent-yellow eyes.

"My eyes will require surgery," Thomas said, "if I want to restore their natural hue. The Torth implanted artificial lenses. They do that to all citizens."

The problem, Vy thought, was not really his eye color. It was his whole vibe.

He was a renegade Torth. Everyone knew it. People acted as if he had a deadly contagion, and why not? Vy did not particularly want her foster brother soaking up her feelings of worthlessness.

She quickened her limping pace. Why had she thought that Thomas, the super-genius, needed her help with anything? He had caretakers among the ummins. She was nothing special. Who was she kidding?

"He loves you," Thomas said with certainty. "Not her."

Vy teetered to a stop.

Coming from anyone else, she would have assumed those words were empty platitudes. But Thomas told truths. He would never speak a direct lie.

Would he?

What if he was trying to soothe Vy into sticking around? Vy had seen him do things like that before. He would say just the right thing and time it for just the right moment, thereby tricking a kid into sticking around long enough for someone else to pop back into the room and apologize or do something else that Thomas must have silently predicted. He had socially engineered the Hollander home to suit himself.

"Ariock does need to learn a few things from Evenjos. But his heart is with you." Thomas sounded more certain than usual. "He would never discard you."

Vy stood in the thoroughfare and studied Thomas.

Oh, how she wanted to believe him. She burned with the desire to believe him.

But she had seen Ariock playing in the sky with that magical dust bunny. Any halfwit could see how much fun they were having.

"He's socially inexperienced," Thomas said. "And socially inept. You know this. He doesn't have a clue what he looks like with her. But trust me. He loves you."

The rage and fear Vy had been holding drained away. She had not realized just how wrecked she had felt. How discarded and broken. It was almost like losing her leg all over again. And with a few short words . . .

Her shoulders relaxed.

But she didn't quite trust that relief. She studied Thomas again, wondering how he could predict that Ariock would never, ever want to upgrade to a more powerful girlfriend. What if Ariock was falling in love with Evenjos right now? After all, Thomas could not read minds from a distance.

"I guess . . ." It was painful for Vy to admit, but she forced herself to go on. "I guess Evenjos is a closer match to him than I am."

Vy stopped herself before she could confess her intimate fears. She had tried to joke with Ariock about their size difference a couple of times. Despite her jokes, he seemed nervous about it as well. Their difference in size was . . . well. Intimidating.

And Evenjos could resize and reshape herself at will.

Thomas appraised Vy with sharp yellow eyes. "I think Ariock will have more of a problem with age differential than size differential."

That was encouraging.

Vy blushed, embarrassed by whatever Thomas had soaked up from her mind. But she felt more like her usual self again, less shaky. Thomas was giving her fuel to dynamite the last of her doubts.

"And," Thomas said, "Ariock likes you better. That's just a fact."

Vy smiled. She wasn't quite sure if she believed Thomas, but she wanted to. The fact was nice to hear.

She had nearly forgotten what it was like to truly have Thomas on her side.

Thomas looked sheepish. "I actually did want to ask you for a favor."

Vy considered the possibilities. There were a limited number of favors that someone like Thomas would want from a mundane person. As she considered the situation, she realized that someone must have propped Thomas's head up on a neck pillow. Someone was changing his clothes and helping him to use toilet facilities. Someone was taking care of his fragile body.

Not Cherise, she guessed.

It was probably Naglitay or one of the other ummins. And as former slaves turned caretakers, they must feel uncomfortable overtones of the relationship between masters and slaves. Vy still had nightmares about displeasing Torth.

"I wasn't going to ask for physical help." Thomas sounded almost appalled. "I completely understand why you'd rather not."

He hesitated, leaving Vy to imagine other possibilities.

Surely he couldn't want her advice. Unless it was about . . .

"Oh!" Vy beamed. "Cherise?"

It was long past time. Not only did Vy want Cherise to be welcome in the makeshift leadership group—Ariock, Thomas, and their friends—but she also thought Thomas could use some positive word of mouth. Cherise was well loved as a teacher. She could encourage people to trust Thomas as an exceptional *rekveh* instead of hating him.

"Okay," Vy said in a receptive tone, her imagination already leaping ahead. Healing the frosty silence between Cherise and Thomas would be a challenge. Really, Thomas should start with an apology. That was the only way—

"No," Thomas said.

Vy looked at him with consternation.

"I'm not interested in . . ." Thomas took a deep breath and began again. "I didn't approach you for advice. I just want some, uh, company getting down to the base camp."

Vy reassessed him. Thomas rarely sought company. Was he working up the courage to ask for something else?

Well. Vy figured she would give him some of her time. Why not? Maybe, somehow, she could encourage him to apologize to Cherise.

"All right. Come on." She patted the backrest of his hoverchair.

Thomas steered without moving anything but a finger. To someone unfamiliar with his neuromuscular illness, he looked lazy. But Vy knew that Thomas strived to move. The fact that he required a pillow to prop up his head . . . that was a bad sign.

"I'm just living the best life I can." His dark tone was full of resignation.

Vy noticed his case of NAI-12 tucked next to him. "You're taking your medicine regularly, right?"

"Yeah." Thomas's shrug was weak, the barest hint of a movement. "It's not enough. I am no longer in the running for long-term survival."

He expected to die soon. Vy saw his resignation, and it made her ill. He used to fight so hard against death.

"It's okay, Vy." Thomas gave her a look of reassurance. "My energy is best spent on goals that are achievable. Making me healthy is not achievable."

If that was supposed to make her feel better, it didn't work. Vy swallowed a lump of guilt in her throat. Because . . . well . . . hadn't she and Ariock failed to rescue Thomas from that cold, damp, filthy Alashani dungeon pit?

That never should have been allowed to go on for as long as it had.

"I'm sorry," Vy said. That imprisonment was likely the reason Thomas was so weakened. He was going to die because of her failure as a foster sister and as a friend.

Thomas looked like he was struggling with something internal.

"You don't deserve even a fraction of the hatred you're getting from everyone." Vy gave him a curious glance. "Who's been helping you with personal hygiene and stuff?"

"Mainly Naglitay and Gosmaga." Thomas sounded ashamed. He must feel humiliated and awkward whenever he begged for care from people who used to suffer as slaves.

And that was fair enough.

"I can take over their duties," Vy offered. It seemed the least she could do after allowing Thomas to suffer. And it wasn't like she had a busy schedule—especially if Ariock meant to spend his time with that winged piece of lint.

"I'm sorry, too," Thomas blurted.

Vy assumed that he meant he regretted his shortened life expectancy. But he went on, his tone full of remorse.

"I'm sorry for what I did to you. And to Delia. And . . . you know. To Cherise. I mistreated you when I had power." He looked ashamed, an awkward and unusual look on his normally emotionless face. "I keep finding ways to excuse myself. I truly believed that everything I did would protect you. I still believe that. But that doesn't change the fact that what I did was damaging and traumatic."

Tentatively, Vy reached out and took the hand of her foster brother.

Thomas had given a pain seizure to a girl who trusted and loved him. But he had also risked his life to save millions of refugees who despised him.

Thomas was the person who had invented a treatment for spinal muscular atrophy. He had saved Vy's life, along with Cherise, Kessa, Ariock, and others. He might even free countless slaves across the galaxy from bondage.

Thomas was doing a lot of good in his life, no matter how unfairly short that life was.

It took courage to admit to being wrong. That probably went double for a supergenius. But Thomas sounded as if he had bottled up his apology for a very long time, just waiting for a chance to release it.

Waiting for a chance.

No one had given him that chance, until now.

"We're family." Vy gently hugged him, then touched his hand. "Always. I won't abandon you ever again. You're better than everyone believes."

Thomas squeezed her hand in his weak grip. "Same back at you."

CHAPTER 4

DOUBLE RAINBOW

A breeze riffled Vy's hair. It smelled faintly of crushed pine.

She was tall enough to see over most heads, and she saw daylight. Aliens gawped at distant snowcapped peaks. A few cringed away from her and Thomas, cursing about *rekvehs*, but many failed to see the hoverchair since they were busy pointing at verdant hills and fluffy clouds.

"It's so bright!" Albinos squinted and shielded their eyes.

Others whispered in tones of awe. "How can we see with so much light?"

Thomas stared morosely at the one-way traffic. "I can't go down without help," he said. "My hoverchair has to go on a separate cargo conveyor belt. Will you hold me, on the slide?"

"What do you mean?" Vy asked, perplexed. "What slide?"

It was soon apparent what Thomas was talking about. People funneled toward a ramp that looked impossibly long and far too steep. Instead of guardrails, it was a simple groove, like a half-pipe. People careened down the center on mats, one at a time, all the way to the distant base camp.

Vy bit back a curse. Was this Ariock's goofy idea of how to off-load a starship?

"I regret that I left the ramp designs up to him." Thomas seemed increasingly nervous.

Nussians were assisting people, sorting out cargo, and making sure each passenger was secured on a mat before sending them down the slide. Vy wondered if Weptolyso was responsible for the orderliness. The nussian attendants were all quite polite and solicitous.

Even so, as people shot fearful glares toward Thomas, Vy began to worry. What if the nussians mistook Thomas for a threat? What if they got violent?

"We're safe," Thomas told her in a quiet voice. "I think the nussians have been told who I am. I'll warn you if there's a problem."

"Okay." Vy breathed deeply. If Thomas ended up having to use wildfire or mind control against a crowd of refugees . . . well, she did not want to imagine the aftermath.

Fortunately, the nussians did seem to recognize Thomas. One attendant pointed out the cargo pallets.

Thomas parked his purple hoverchair on an appropriately sized pallet. Once he powered it down, Vy lifted him, aware of his fragility. She limped to the slide entrance. A nussian attendant helped her to sit on a mat with Thomas in front of her.

"Give us a moment, please," Vy begged the attendant. "I've got to get us arranged."

The attendant grunted in annoyance.

Vy took her time, wrapping Thomas with her arms and legs. His head had to remain propped up. His weak spine needed cushioning. She added rolled cloths for additional strategic support and glared at the nussian every time he made a threatening move.

"I really hate high places." Thomas rolled his head to one side, trying to bury his face against her cloak.

Was this what he had been working up the courage to ask for?

Vy realized that it was. He was afraid of a slide.

Freed slaves treated Thomas as if he was the bogeyman. The galactic empire was whipping up space armadas against their Betrayer. Evenjos quaked in fear whenever Thomas showed up, and Garrett's gruff avoidance of "the boy" suggested that he, too, was afraid.

And Thomas was afraid of a slide.

"I've got you." Vy double-checked to make sure they were secure on the mat.

The world spread out below them, so distant that even forested canyons looked flat. From Vy's perspective, this chute was a steep and narrow strip of metal that looked like it might sway in the wind.

Garrett's power had better hold it in place.

"Ready?" the attendant demanded.

Vy braced herself. "Ready."

The nussian shoved her.

The mat gained speed. They were hurtling downward, one of many people on various slides.

The speed gave Vy a thrill. She resisted her inclination to lean forward, to go faster. Thomas's teeth were bared in a grimace of fear.

"I don't want Cherise to forgive me," he said.

Vy realized that he was making a confession, in part to distract himself from his own terror.

"I don't deserve forgiveness," Thomas went on. "And we can't go back to the way things were. It would be an unequal relationship, and I promised myself I would never do that again. Not to her."

Vy tried to think of reassurances.

But she could not deny that Cherise was vibrant without Thomas. These days Cherise wore embroidered garments, with gold and gemstones holding back her hair. Admiring students surrounded her. Flen was not the only albino who gazed at her with lustful longing.

More importantly: Cherise was not pining for her old life. She had never once mentioned the Hollander home. Or Thomas.

"She's better off without me." Thomas sounded certain. "Anyway, I'm almost dead. It doesn't make sense for a dying slice of her old life to show up and throw a wrench into her momentum." He sounded like he was trying to convince himself. "She doesn't need me."

Vy wondered if Thomas was correct. Might he be misjudging Cherise? Underestimating what she was capable of dealing with?

No. He was a mind reader, with the power to peer into other people's souls.

"I respect that." Vy hugged him gently. "But if you ever want to reconsider talking to her, I'll be happy to open things up for you two. She might want to see who you've become. Because you're different than you were a few months ago."

Refugees were frolicking in the river below. Meanwhile, a massive piece from the starship floated over grassy hills, levitated by Garrett.

Much of the encampment was already set up. Huge shards from the starship formed dark, silvery roofs that jutted across miles of gently rolling terrain. More refugees were busy subdividing those long shelters. They hung curtains or stacked crates and barrels. Outside, people set up cooking fires and tables in the alleyways of trampled grass.

"If you ever want to talk," Vy said to Thomas, "about anything, I'm here. I'm on your side."

He gave a slight nod, no doubt battling his fear of heights. "Thanks."

A distant crowd made delighted sounds. Vy followed their pointing fingers and saw a phoenix bird sail across larger-than-life clouds.

A double rainbow arced across the sky.

The dropping sensation in Vy's stomach had nothing to do with their speed.

"So." She searched for a topic that would absorb her focus so she wouldn't feel tempted to stare upward at the all-too-happy day. "I guess Garrett wants you to have a lab? Do you have any ideas for superweapons?"

"Garrett's an idiot," Thomas said.

Vy looked down at the top of his head. "Does that mean you don't want to invent weapons?"

"It would be exceedingly stupid to start an arms race against the Torth," Thomas said. "Their supergeniuses have a lot more general knowledge than I have, and some of them specialize in weapons. I don't. We won't win if we prioritize that endeavor."

"Oh." Vy wondered if Thomas had a winning plan.

"I have ideas," Thomas said.

At the end of the slide, their mat slid parallel to the ground and they shed their momentum.

"The first thing to do," Thomas said, "is bolster our localized defense. If the Torth show up here, I need to be able to drop out of sight on short notice. Same for you. And Kessa. And also Cherise. Anyone who is a potential military target should have a secret bolt-hole dug out, with a disguised trapdoor on top."

Vy scanned the idyllic encampment. "You think we'll be attacked here?"

"I can't rule it out," Thomas said. "Garrett and Ariock should be scanning the solar system for threats. Instead? They've decided it's playtime."

Vy thought Ariock had done plenty and he deserved a little downtime. Also, Ariock was quite savvy when it came to protection and military matters. Of course he would take their defense seriously! How dare Thomas suggest otherwise?

Except . . .

The rainbow was now a triple beauty. People interrupted each other's work to point out the vibrant colors against the dramatic sky.

Ariock seemed extra distracted right now, cavorting with that self-absorbed dust bunny.

He had promised to listen to Vy.

She had better have a chat with him.

As Vy swung her legs over the edge of the slide, preparing to stand on her good leg, a nussian attendant lumbered over. "Wait here." The nussian sounded female, even with the rumbling voice of her species. "I will bring his chair."

"Thank you." Thomas sounded grateful. "There's a white button on the right-hand armrest. If you press and hold that button for a few seconds, the chair will power up and float."

Strangers bustled everywhere, and Vy realized that the attendant was offering protection. Otherwise Vy would have to limp through a potentially hostile mob of people with Thomas in her arms.

"Weptolyso made protecting me a priority." Thomas smiled weakly. "I owe him a favor."

Vy rearranged herself, still seated, with Thomas propped against her hip. "Would bolt-holes really be protection? I mean, can't the Torth just read minds and figure out where we are?"

"We should not make our locations common knowledge throughout the encampment," Thomas said.

"Okay." Vy thought that Kessa might be able to blend in with crowds, but humans stood out. As for Thomas? He owned the only hovervehicle on the planet, and it was big and purple.

"I don't plan on leaving my lab once it's set up in a nondescript tent," Thomas explained. "As for clairvoyance . . . that's the purpose of bolt-holes. The Torth clairvoyants won't think to scan underground."

"What about your life spark?" Vy recalled Ariock saying that Yeresunsa glowed to his senses. Ariock could easily home in on a Yeresunsa, even if they were among a crowd of millions, even if they hid underground. That was how he had detected the Commander of All Living Things and her elite Servants when they had believed that they were safely hidden.

"That's strictly an Ariock thing," Thomas said.

"Really?"

Thomas seemed to brace himself to give a lecture. "All Yeresunsa can detect life sparks within their sphere of influence. But if their sphere is encompassed by a greater Yeresunsa, they can't. It's like trying to see a flame inside the sun. With a greater Yeresunsa nearby, everything gets eclipsed, or washed out."

Vy recalled that Thomas had described his own sphere of influence as a flame in comparison to the burning sun that was Ariock.

"So . . ." Vy studied him. "You're unable to sense life sparks because Ariock is nearby?"

"Correct," Thomas said. "To my senses, Ariock is a dazzling titan of power. He eclipses everything else. I can't even sense his exact location. He's just, like, an overwhelming force. Like a storm. And that's how the Servants of All will feel once they're on the same planet as him. They won't be able to detect me or anyone else."

Vy wondered how the Alashani warriors had reacted when Ariock had crash-landed on their planet. Had they suddenly felt overwhelmed? Unable to sense life sparks? No wonder they had predicted a doomsday.

"Well, the Alashani were never able to detect life sparks in the first place," Thomas said. "Because there were always Servants of All in the vicinity. Or perhaps because of the ghostly presence of Evenjos."

That explained why Jinishta had never offered Ariock any lessons about life sparks.

"Ariock is never near anyone of greater power than himself." Thomas spread his fingers, too weak to lift his hands. "So he can always sense life sparks, no matter how weak or powerful they are. But the rest of us can't. Not unless we're very far away from him—like, on another planet."

"Good." Vy saw the nussian approach, pushing the floating hoverchair. She was relieved that no one had stolen Thomas's medicine case.

"You'll tell me when you're due for an injection, right?" she asked.

"In an hour," Thomas said.

Some nussian refugees must have caught river critters, such as alien fish or crayfish, because an aroma of stir-fry wafted over. Whatever they were cooking, it smelled a lot more appetizing than mushroom paste—which was all Vy and her friends had eaten for the last week.

The attendant seemed to notice Vy's look of longing. "Would you like to join them for a meal? I can introduce you."

"Please." Vy did not hide her gratitude. "If they have extra food, we would really appreciate that."

The attendant seemed unperturbed. "For you, good human? They will have extra." She included Thomas in her gaze. "Also for the renegade."

"Thanks," Thomas said.

As Vy arranged Thomas in his hoverchair, she wondered what else he planned to do besides begging people to dig bolt-holes. Was hiding really the best strategy he could come up with?

"So." She propped up his body with the malleable cushions. "Superweapons aside, do you have some idea on how we can fight the Torth?"

"Maybe." Thomas rotated his hoverchair, ready to follow the attendant.

Vy sighed. If only Thomas would feel comfortable opening up to someone. Anyone. It didn't have to be her.

Thomas gave her a frustrated, defensive look. "I'm not trying to be secretive. I just don't feel comfortable sharing certain ideas in progress with Garrett. And Evenjos."

Of course. The mind readers would have trouble keeping secrets from each other, especially if they confided in nontelepaths.

Vy limped next to his hoverchair, wishing they could all simply trust one another. Why was that so difficult?

"I want to talk things over with Ariock first." Thomas offered a thin smile. "My military strategy will be a little, uh . . ." He hesitated. "Controversial."

That crafty look was exactly what Vy had hoped to see. Whatever was going through Thomas's head, it was almost certain to give the Torth Empire grief.

CHAPTER 5

POWERS THAT BE

For the first time in his life, Ariock was not trapped, hiding, or in a crisis.

He tried not to enjoy himself too much. But this world, without enemies, meant unfettered freedom. He could fall for a mile and survive. He could uproot trees with a thought. Evenjos plunged through a grove of alien trees and he pursued her, faster than a speeding bullet.

Every time Ariock drew near, she swerved.

He interwove branches into a net designed to trap her.

Evenjos transformed into dust, only to coalesce farther away. She skimmed the sparkling blue surface of a tropical ocean.

Ariock created water funnels, designed to throw her toward him.

Evenjos elongated into a leviathan and plunged into translucent blue waves.

Ariock had a human respiratory system, and he lacked fish fins, so for a moment, he thought he'd lost the game.

But he had so much power at his disposal.

Ariock spread his awareness, trawling the oceanic depths. Beneath the waves, he sensed alien whales and eel-sharks that crackled with electric energy. Which one was Evenjos? Probably the most powerful leviathan.

Even if he guessed wrong, he supposed it didn't matter. He would figure it out by process of elimination.

Ariock encased his body in pressurized air and slammed downward. He displaced water so fast he created a temporary vortex. Air bubbles raced upward. Sea creatures squirted out of his way.

He tunneled through tons of water until light faded, until he was in a cold abyss as black as a cave. He maintained an air pocket that kept him breathing, defying the ocean.

His target, a powerful leviathan, swam recklessly toward him.

She swerved.

That action was too intelligent for a beast. Ariock expanded his electrified air pocket.

The leviathan thrashed, caught halfway in his air bubble.

Her surprise only lasted a second, but that was enough time for both of them to know that Ariock had won the game. He leaped at the gigantic sea monster and seized her, and the force of her monstrous thrashing sent them both speeding downward.

Ariock sensed the rocky floor an instant before they slammed into it.

He had just enough time to infuse his body with extra strength and agility. He absorbed the shock of the high-impact landing for both of them, then straightened, simultaneously defying the crushing oceanic pressure. They were at a depth that would kill most vertebrates.

Evenjos morphed back to her default form, the winged woman. Ariock placed her on the rocky ground inside his large air pocket.

Laughing softly, Evenjos pranced up to him and pressed her warm body against his.

Her outfit appeared to be made from kelp. It barely clung to her bouncy chest. Her purple eyes sparkled with mischief. Strands of silver and sea flowers held back her purple hair, emphasizing her exaggerated, plastic beauty.

Ariock reminded himself that it was all artifice.

"Are we done?" He pushed Evenjos away, losing his feeling of triumph. What was he doing down here with the so-called Lady of Sorrow? He had duties and responsibilities he needed to get back to. An encampment full of refugees awaited him. Vy must be waiting for him, too.

"Your duties can wait." Evenjos tugged him, pouting. "Come. I have much to teach you."

"People are waiting." Ariock wondered why he was defying this alien ocean by holding up thousands of metric tons of water and still breathing with ease. Did he have something to prove? Why was he wasting strength on a frivolous game?

This was stupid. People needed him.

"People worship you." Evenjos trailed an opalescent fingernail down his chest. The way she did it, slow and lingering, seemed to emphasize his solid immensity. "They want a god. They do not want a man with flaws and failures."

Her tone held a note of sincerity, not like her usual coquettishness. Ariock saw that she understood the pressure to be perfect.

Perhaps she used to endure a similar pressure? As a goddess-empress—a world ruler—she had not been allowed to fail.

Until she had broken. Her failure had devastated the universe.

So perhaps she understood exactly what pitfalls he needed to avoid. She might warn him of any weaknesses he had so he could strengthen himself into an invincible warrior and truly become the hero everyone expected him to be.

He needed a trainer of high caliber. Garrett was self-taught. Jinishta had already given him most of her knowledge. But Evenjos . . .

Her slender hand closed over his. "I was the leader of Yeresunsa, in a time when the Yeresunsa Order was more powerful than they have ever been, before or since. I was the pinnacle. I know incarnations. I know degrees of magnitude." Her tone became intimate, as if she was stroking him with her voice. "I know what linking can accomplish."

Ariock pulled away. Why did she keep trying to seduce him? Couldn't she read his mind and figure out how much effort he was putting into resisting her ridiculous game of flattery?

It was all fake. Nonstop teasing.

And she had a dangerous contempt for "commoners" such as Vy. What would she have thought of Ariock's human mother? Nothing good. She showed no remorse for all the innocent people who had died when she'd wrecked the Torth Homeworld.

"Are you hungry?" Evenjos asked.

Ariock evaluated her innocent question, suspicious. As a mind reader, she knew that he was hungry. Not that it was hard to guess. Thanks to his growth disorder, he had the appetite of a teenage boy.

"Come." Evenjos backed away, hips swaying. "Either one of us can kill a beast, rip off its hide, and roast it on a turning spit. We can have a . . . what is the colloquialism from your world? . . . a barbecue. We will use our powers to gather rock salt and wild herbs and fruits. Let us share a meal. We will discuss power. And if you are not impressed? We will rejoin your friends."

Ariock wanted to turn down her invitation. He ought to remind Evenjos that he was not at her beck and call.

But he was also maddeningly curious about what she might teach him. Evenjos could give him an edge that would enable him to win battles. She did not have to say that.

Also? He was sick of eating mushroom paste. Rations aboard the starship had gotten so scarce, even Thomas had not protested when Ariock insisted on setting up camp in a bountiful land, full of edible vegetation and animals that could be hunted.

"Power," Evenjos said, "is not just a weapon for fighting battles. In my time, power was a way of life."

She began to show him what she meant.

They flitted across the ocean floor like it was their own private mansion, dappled with sunlight and walled by coral. When they emerged, they shed water in diamond sparkles.

They discovered a tropical lagoon. They used a big seashell as a basket and collected alien limes and other plants that Evenjos deemed edible. They added cactus fruits from a canyon that glowed red under a setting sun. Then they swerved back toward the sunny afternoon, soaring past a range of jagged black mountains and a distant crater.

"Our main course?" Evenjos suggested, slowing above a herd of grazing creatures.

Ariock thought the animals looked like strange, long-necked wildebeests. They had stripes and manes.

"We will not find premade burgers here," Evenjos said with gentle good humor. "Or domesticated animals. And I cannot teach you to ghost to other worlds to obtain goods there. That is a lesson Garrett will have to take charge of."

"No problem." Ariock sized up the herd of animals. Combat was one thing, but he would not enjoy killing peaceful, innocent creatures.

"The physiology of these animals will render them tasty," Evenjos stated. "As a sixth-magnitude healer, I am an expert in physiology, beyond anyone else you will ever meet." She casually pointed to one of the alien wildebeests. "How about that one?"

Ariock had no protest.

The animal fell. Evenjos must have used her powers to cut off circulation to its brain or something.

"Powerful Yeresunsa have natural resistance against invasive attacks like that," Evenjos said, laughing at his unnerved reaction. "You are competent enough as a healer that my first attempt would not kill you. Furthermore, you would instinctively track the source of the attempt, and you could easily break my focus with a counterattack, or simply by doing something unexpected."

Ariock supposed he had learned such lessons from sparring with Jinishta and other Alashani warriors.

While the herd stampeded, Evenjos gracefully pointed to a distant plateau. "Our picnic table?" she suggested.

"Sure."

Every experience was pleasant and easy. Ariock began to feel at peace in a way he never had before.

When he was among ordinary people, there was always a tension in his chest and back, a fear that someone would stare at him or expect a miracle.

Most people wanted an acknowledgment of some kind. Ariock had felt that even before people started worshipping him. His mother used to give him that sad, burdened look. She had been full of unspoken expectations. She had wanted a normal son whom she could introduce to friends. Someone who could visit her in a hospital.

As Ariock watched the seasoned meat roast over a cook fire he had created with a snap of lightning, he knew that this experience was not like sharing a meal with friends. Nor was it like eating alone.

Evenjos sat cross-legged, adorned in metallic lacework. It was a dress for a fancy club, not a campfire, yet she looked completely at ease. Glamour was as natural to Evenjos as being oversize was to him.

And Ariock found that he preferred to embrace their weirdnesses rather than struggle to minimize himself.

Evenjos made him feel all right about being . . . well, who he was.

In her company, he did not have to mask the fact that he was extremely powerful. He did not need to be gentle or inoffensive or constrained.

He waved his hand, and the meat rotated in midair. It emitted a mouthwatering aroma.

The sky was a clear blue, touched by wispy cirrus clouds. It was an extension of his mood. And there was no shame in that.

"You were hurt." Evenjos gestured to the jagged iron barbs that stuck out of each of Ariock's forearms.

"Yes." Ariock had reshaped the hooks to suit himself, but he remembered the agony when the Torth had hammered the iron loops into his bones. The Torth had wanted a way to easily chain him up between arena fights.

At the time, he had not even dreamed of wielding power. Or perhaps he had, but it was only the meager power of winning physical fights against monsters. To crush their spines. To rip their limbs out of their sockets.

"We have that in common." Evenjos flexed her wings slightly. The wind played with her purple-silver hair. "Physiology is my primary power. I cannot be permanently damaged in a physical way. But make no mistake, I have scars."

Ariock believed her.

"I want us to become a force the Torth cannot defeat," Evenjos said.

"I want that, very much," Ariock said.

"What is your primary power?" Evenjos asked. "Is it energy manipulation? Or solid matter? You are a stormbringer, but there is always a dominant power. It is usually the power you first discovered."

Ariock thought back to the first time he had knowingly used his powers. "I dented a mirrored wall," he said. "So . . ." The second time, he had moved sand. "Telekinesis, I guess?"

"It sounds like solid matter manipulation," Evenjos said. "Geokinesis, you might call it."

She went on, teaching Ariock what powers he might still have undiscovered and which he clearly lacked. It seemed he was utterly deficient in thermokinesis and telepathy, two powers that were common among the Torth.

There were higher magnitudes of clairvoyance, healing, and energy manipulation, which he might have yet to discover.

As they devoured their meal, Evenjos explained her own powers. She utterly lacked prophecy, and she was weak in clairvoyance and telepathy. Her strengths, in addition to physiokinesis, were telekinesis and hydrokinesis, or energy manipulation and phases of matter.

"With our raw strength," she explained, "we can be certain of our magnitudes. A lesser Yeresunsa would not be so certain."

When Evenjos asked about Garrett's powers, she expressed surprise upon hearing the various things that the old man had done—or claimed to be able to do.

"Really?" Evenjos looked stunned. "That is remarkable. It is rare for a Yeresunsa to possess all eight powers. And especially one with the strength of a storm-bringer . . ." Her look turned considering. "Garrett is going to be very useful."

Thomas was another matter. When Evenjos heard Ariock's analysis of the boy's powers, she sounded skeptical. "He only has telepathy and thermokinesis? Are you sure?"

"Is that a bad thing?" Ariock asked.

"It is just strange." Evenjos used her powers to strip meat off a bone and chewed thoughtfully. "If he is one of four heroes of prophecy, I would think he would have greater power."

"He can also project holographic illusions," Ariock pointed out.

Evenjos waved dismissively. "That is just low-magnitude hydrokinesis, combined with his supergenius ability to imagine things."

Ariock held a steak, enjoying its rich taste. He privately thought that Thomas's supergenius mind was like having several superpowers. Thomas had a flawless memory, ultrafast processing speed, a superhuman ability to multitask, and probably a whole lot of other things that Ariock wasn't aware of.

"Why do all these stats matter?" he asked.

Evenjos looked surprised. "For training, of course." She gestured to herself. "I would not have even known I could shapeshift without such analysis. And then I studied hard in order to master my power. I learned from the best sculptors of my day and also from anatomical illustrators. And theater performers."

Ariock reappraised her. He had not expected so much artistry in her background.

"I should have spent more time with artists outside the Crystal Spire," Evenjos said, "rather than within it." Her cheeks pinkened, as if with shame. "But one thing you should understand about power, Ariock Dovanack—" Her voice caressed his name. "Any fool can throw a tantrum and smash or kill. But to truly master a power? That is an art." She picked up another strip of steak. "In my time, there were a few dozen stormbringers. Only one, Iriade, was renowned. She would divert rivers to irrigate crops, which ended famines. So it was her name that commoners prayed to. Iriade could stand upon a raft and make water carry her faster than a breath. So people whispered that she could teleport. When trouble came? It was her that other Yeresunsa rallied to. She was the one who led linked circles, not the other stormbringers. She was not the strongest among us. But she was the most skilled. You understand?"

Ariock had no trouble understanding that. When he had fallen in the dead city, it was Kessa who ensured that everyone carried on. And he had heard about Kessa's organizational competence aboard the starship.

Competence was often more important than raw strength or power. Ariock might be a hero, but he felt sure that he lacked the experience necessary to be a leader. He was only twenty-three years old. He had barely left his mansion until less than a year ago.

Garrett and other people needed to stop insinuating that this was Ariock's war. It seemed obvious to him that someone with real competence ought to be in charge. Like Kessa. Or Thomas.

He was mostly silent while Evenjos continued to educate him.

She spoke of her favorite forms and how each had entailed years of careful study and practice. In order to become a bird, for instance, Evenjos had sketched wings and feathers, and she had dissected avian musculoskeletal structures. If she wished to become a different type of bird, such as a raptor or a swan, she would need to start all over again.

"What about the monster?" Ariock asked, remembering her as a city-wrecking beast. "Was that something you studied and practiced?"

"Oh." Evenjos looked ashamed. "No. That was a thoughtless form. I am sure you could tell."

She was right, Ariock realized. The Evenjos monster had kept morphing, its details vague and never quite solid. It had been rage personified.

"Let us speak of limitations," Evenjos said. "There is a limit of strength, of course. But there is also a limit of focus. And there are limits of complexity. Structural complexity, for instance. Have you encountered this limit?"

"I think so." Ariock had tried to manifest things from thin air. The problem was complexity. A piece of stone, for instance, was made up of various sediments and alloys and crystal structures, which were made up of molecules, which were made of atomic elements. Each layer had its own flow, or its own arrangement, and each arrangement interacted with the whole in various ways, like a symphony. And that was just for something as simple as a pebble.

Ariock could copy things. He could move things and rearrange things. But if he wanted to manifest a new creation? He supposed he would need to possess the mind of a supergenius.

"Exactly." Evenjos looked at him with respect. "That is a limit of structural complexity. There are also limits in terms of energy balance and dynamic systems complexities. For instance . . ." She hesitated. Then she seemed to force herself to go on, as if confessing a secret shame. "My sphere of influence is one of my hard limits. I cannot scatter myself. If I am ever torn apart and distributed to different planets, my consciousness will break apart, and I fear it will never recover."

She was admitting to a vulnerability. Ariock wanted to reassure her. "Then we'll make sure you don't get broken apart and scattered."

Evenjos looked grateful, but perhaps the topic made her uncomfortable. "Before we begin in-depth lessons," she said, "we ought to discuss therapy. Are you aware of the necessity of psychological therapy?"

"Um . . ." Ariock wondered if she was mistranslating something from her archaic language.

"In my time," she said, "it was a vital requirement for being a member of the Yeresunsa Order."

She explained that young royals and adolescent Yeresunsa required a deep understanding of their own psyches. They needed to study emotions in depth. They were not allowed to self-medicate or use recreational drugs unless a master telepath recommended it as the best therapy for controlling a specific and ongoing emotional imbalance.

"I think that makes sense," Ariock said. Normal people could afford to get drunk or stoned or to allow a mental problem to go unchecked. But someone like him? Someone with the power to destroy worlds?

No. He had to be self-disciplined.

That was part of why Ariock was enjoying himself right now. Normal people were nowhere in the vicinity.

They finished their meal and chatted until the sun sank low. Ariock knew that he ought to return to the camp of refugees. But when Evenjos suggested a lesson about linking and spheres of influence, he agreed.

Her talk of the Yeresunsa academy, with its mandatory classes for every Yeresunsa from the age of toddlers through adulthood, hinted that he still had a lot to learn. Perhaps Thomas and Garrett would benefit from these lessons as well?

But when Ariock suggested that, Evenjos laughed. "They will learn through you," she said, caressing his cheek in a too-fond way. "They are mind readers."

Only when the last trace of sunset faded did Ariock insist on adjourning the lesson. He kept thinking of Vy. Was she keeping busy? Or was she worried about his absence?

"The stars are out," Ariock said. "People will wonder where we are."

Evenjos danced in the starlight, adorned with a crown of icicles. "Let them wait."

But Ariock felt duty weighing on him. "We'll continue this another time," he told Evenjos firmly.

He half anticipated a bad reaction. Evenjos might flit away in a ribbon of dust or whirl into a terrifying rage. She could probably use a few of the mental health sessions the Yeresunsa of her day used to deem mandatory.

Well, Ariock felt rested and able to argue. He had shared his true self with Evenjos, and he would continue to do so. If she could not handle the fact that he prioritized different things than she did . . . well. Then they would have to part ways.

Evenjos clung to his arm. "I will go wherever you go."

Ariock tugged out of her clinging grasp. He could not figure out why she wanted to fake an obsession over an oaf who barely understood his own powers. She must be pretending to like Ariock. After all, he had no experience with royalty. He was nothing like Evenjos. They came from different worlds, from different times.

"Come on." Ariock had been ready to teleport to the encampment. Instead, he flew.

Evenjos trailed after him.

CHAPTER 6

TO MASTER THE COSMOS

Ariock soared above miles of long metal rooftops that had not been there this morning. The grounded starship was stripped to a skeleton of its former magnificence, no longer recognizable as a spacefaring vessel.

Apparently, his great-grandfather had been busy. The makeshift city had gained a perimeter wall. Huge, armored plates overlapped each other, shielding the habitats from wind and rockslides, creating a sense of protection and peace. People strolled hilly pathways with lanterns in hand.

Ariock widened his awareness. Life sparks blazed through him, as ever-shifting and innumerable as moonlight sparkling on waves. If he really tried, he could even detect bugs and blades of grass, but small life forms were a lot dimmer.

Evenjos was different. Her spark was a thrum so bright that it completely washed out several neighborhoods' worth of life sparks.

Only when Ariock distanced himself from Evenjos was he able to discern another unusual blaze. That must be Garrett, standing out like a beacon.

Ariock dropped from the sky.

His great-grandfather reclined next to a large campfire, ensconced in a chair carved from logs. "Ah. There you are."

Garrett seemed utterly unsurprised by the sudden arrival. Had he been scanning the continent, looking for Ariock?

"Are you hungry?" Garrett was smoking a pipe, and he used it to point to several lidded pots. "There's beef stroganoff. Buffalo quiche. And my favorite over there, a local fish that tastes quite a bit like Alaskan salmon."

Ariock hid his surprise. Beef stroganoff did sound good, but he wanted to find Vy. In hindsight, the way he had flown away from her, without a backward glance, seemed rude. He ought to apologize.

"No, thanks," he said. "Uh, where's Vy?"

Evenjos chose that moment to alight next to him. She had a graceful way of landing, folding her wings as silently as an owl.

"Sit, sit, you two." Garrett made a lazy gesture, and two rustic stools dragged themselves to the edge of the campfire. "Name any dessert you'd like. Or can I get you a drink?" He raised a large, beautifully carved mug off his armrest. "Hot apple cider with scotch?"

"I would like to try that." Evenjos sounded genuinely curious.

Ariock hesitated. He did not want to be rude. After all, his great-grandfather had clearly spent the day working while Ariock had gone off to entertain himself and learn from Evenjos. Garrett was probably exhausted.

Evenjos sat with willing graciousness. She held out her hands, and Garrett placed a full mug in her grasp.

She arched a purple eyebrow at Ariock, hinting that he ought to sit.

"Sorry I left so much work for you," Ariock said guiltily. Perhaps he did owe a few minutes to his great-grandfather.

"Oh, don't feel bad about that." Garrett waved dismissively. "You deserved some rest and relaxation. It's important to have a healthy work-life balance."

Ariock took a seat on the rustic stool, which was uncomfortably short for him. His knees ended up high, so the only natural position was to lean on his thighs.

Well, he wouldn't stay for long. "Is there anything you need me to do?" he asked, hoping to escape quickly.

"Now that you mention it," Garrett said, "I did make a list."

Ariock had a sinking feeling. "How long a list?"

"Most of it can wait until tomorrow." Garrett fished in a breast pocket of his cloak and pulled out a crumpled sheet of paper. He smoothed it and cleared his throat.

"You'll need to import ten thousand metric tons of rice and other grains. That should tide our people over for a few days, in addition to whatever they hunt and scavenge. We'll want at least a hundred thousand hovercarts. And twelve million blaster gloves. That should—"

"Hold on," Ariock interrupted.

Garrett looked up.

Ariock thought back to the magical day he had just shared with Evenjos and wondered if he would ever feel unfettered again. "Can Evenjos help with importing supplies?"

"I cannot teleport." Evenjos offered Ariock a smoky, seductive look. "What you can do is quite unique."

Garrett added a respectful nod. "She's right. I am unfortunately limited in the scope of what I can teleport. My limit is about half my own body weight, plus myself." He gestured. "And I get worn out after a few trips."

Ariock resigned himself to a lot of heavy lifting. It seemed he would have to become a one-person import operation.

"We'll need hoverchairs," Garrett went on. "That will help the elderly and injured veterans among our populace. We'll need to consult the boy on what he needs for his lab. He went to bed, so we'll talk with him tomorrow. Also, I estimated quantities for high-priority items. Pharmaceuticals. We obviously need those. Detergents. Textiles, such as bolts of cloth, adhesives, papers, rubbers, plastics. Batteries and tools. Sunblock for our albino friends. We ought to consider data tablets and tutorial programs, if the boy can figure out how to reprogram—"

"That's enough for me to get started," Ariock said.

"Great." Garrett folded the paper and tucked it away. "I've been waiting for you to show up so I can teach you how to ghost across the galaxy. It's a lot trickier than you would think."

Ariock clasped his hands, ashamed that he wanted to put off such an important duty. "I'm sorry. But can we do this tomorrow?"

Garrett gave him a stern look. "Your human friend went to sleep already, if that's your concern. She's perfectly at ease. There's no reason to apologize to her."

"Vy?" Ariock wanted to make sure there was no misunderstanding.

"Yup," Garrett said. "And I'm sure she would want you to help other people."

That was likely true.

"Intergalactic teleportation is complicated," Garrett said emphatically, although he still sounded jovial. Maybe he was relieved to share the burden of this power with someone else. "I just want to show you the bare outline of how it works."

Ariock braced himself for yet another power lesson. Would he ever become a master instead of a student?

"First of all . . ." Garrett grabbed his staff and clambered to his feet. "Let's go over the practice of fetching objects without actually teleporting your body to the location. That's a key skill, because bodily teleportation is a lot more costly in terms of raw strength."

Ariock had seen Garrett make items appear out of thin air. He knew it would be a useful skill. And ever since his near death from depletion, he understood the importance of power conservation.

"Show me how," he said.

"I'll explain the mechanics," Garrett said. "I've already done quite a lot today, and I'm near depletion."

"Sorry," Ariock said.

"Just pay attention," Garrett said. "The first step is ghosting. You need to know exactly where the thing is. That entails scouting the area clairvoyantly. In other words, ghosting is the basis for all of this."

Ariock felt like an amateur. He had ghosted and teleported during a crisis, to transport millions of people off a dying world. Could he do it again? Should he make a habit of it?

"Then," Garrett went on, "once you've located the thing you want to import, you need to establish a physical presence there so you can encompass it in your awareness."

Ariock nodded, trying to follow the lesson.

"A physical presence does not have to be your entire body," Garrett said. "It can be the edge of your fingernail." He held out a hand, demonstrating. "Or a hair."

Ariock raised an eyebrow as Garrett went on. He was grateful for Evenjos's lesson on limitations, because teleportation had every limit imaginable.

One of the main constraints, as Garrett explained it, was focus. Ghosting was such a severe mental strain that one could not maintain it for more than a few minutes at a time. That meant every act of teleportation had a hard time limit.

"It's easy to ghost from here to there." Garrett pointed to a mountain range, silhouetted against the starry night. "But when we're talking about the distances between stars? It becomes exponentially harder."

"I did not even know it was possible," Evenjos admitted after a dainty sip from her mug. "No one attempted such a thing in my time."

That was surprising. Ariock looked from Evenjos to Garrett. He had assumed that the Yeresunsa of the ancient past had superior knowledge in every way. It seemed his great-grandfather had pioneered an entirely new ability.

"You have maybe five minutes before you snap back to your body," Garrett said. "Maybe ten if you practice ghosting every day, and if you do it correctly, without enfeebling yourself."

Ariock made a mental note not to enfeeble himself.

Garrett went on, firelight flickering on his white-bearded face. "The reason the ancients never tried to skate across solar systems is because they didn't know where to go, and five minutes is insufficient for exploring the galaxy. Especially since we are limited by our spheres of influence." He made a circle with his arms. "It's possible for someone with clairvoyant talent to stretch the sphere. But even with stretching, no one has a sphere that encompasses more than a parsec. Not even you."

"What's a parsec?" Ariock asked.

Garrett looked annoyed and waved dismissively. "It involves trigonometry and astronomical units. Never mind. All you need to know is that it's more than three light-years and less than four."

Ariock wondered if temporal streams were involved. Would he need to make intense mathematical calculations, like a starship computer? Or a supergenius?

"We don't need mathematical precision." Garrett tapped his pipe, and ashes fell. "This isn't science. I don't even know what a temporal stream is."

Ariock considered that. "Okay. So . . ."

"Here's what I do." Garrett blew, and smoky vapor rose off his pipe. The vapor took a curling shape, like a nebula. Embers glowed like stars. Garrett blew, and another nebula formed.

"I study and memorize star maps," Garrett said.

Ariock searched the old man's face, trying to figure out if he was joking.

"I am serious. And no, it isn't easy." Garrett spoke dryly, as if from arduous experience. "That's for sure."

Ariock gazed at the dissipating mock-up of a star map. "Are you saying you stretch across a parsec, then object-teleport there, without moving your body, and then stretch again? Along a route you've memorized?"

Garrett nodded.

"Like . . ." Ariock could not believe it. "A route of a million light-years?"

"Yup, pretty much," Garrett said. "Although, unlike you, I cannot encompass an entire parsec. My sphere of influence is smaller than an Earth-like planet. I just inch across the galaxy." He demonstrated with a quick, jerky motion of his fingers. "And I have to do it within a few minutes, or else I'm sick and reeling from ghosting for too long."

Ariock attempted to hide his dismay. How could anyone with an ordinary memory learn every mile of a journey across a million light-years? It sounded like it required a supergenius mind.

"There are distinctive stars and other astronomical objects you can use as landmarks," Garrett said. "You'll learn to recognize certain globular clusters, hypergiant stars, and so forth. You'll become an expert in nebulae."

Ariock had a feeling he would struggle with these lessons.

"It's not impossible," Garrett said reassuringly. "There are only a few routes you'll have to memorize. When I lived on Tenth Ocean, I ghosted to the Dovanack mansion almost every night, so I learned that route really well. It will be the same for you."

"How did you learn the route in the first place?" Ariock asked with dread. He imagined years of trial and error.

"Oh, I happen to own a stolen cache of galactic maps." Garrett sounded smug about it. "It's a great study guide." He clapped Ariock on the back. "Don't worry. We'll start you off easy. Relatively easy, I mean. Omophia Prime is a journey of less than forty light-years from here. It has a few Torth-ruled urban outposts. They don't have the greatest defenses, and if you randomly show up, they won't be able to stop you from taking a bunch of their stuff."

Ariock wasn't sure how he felt about stealing supplies and weapons from the Torth Empire. In theory, it was appealing. His refugees would welcome a refresh of supplies.

But in practice? Wouldn't the Torth retaliate somehow?

Even if they couldn't find Ariock in the vastness of the galaxy, they might respond by depriving their own slaves of food. Torth certainly wouldn't endure hardships unless their slaves suffered first.

"You're powerful enough to teleport people." Garrett rubbed his hands together, as if excited. "That means you could feasibly import slaves as well as supplies. Steal them from the Torth and bring them to our side. You could surprise-attack random cities and slaughter all the Torth there." He grinned, as if slaughter was a delicious dessert. "That part goes without saying."

Ariock peered into the encampment, wondering where he might find Thomas. He wanted to discuss these ideas before he began to zoom around the galaxy, slaughtering Torth and raiding warehouses and slave zones.

How many billions or trillions of freed slaves could he protect before he failed?

How many before he could no longer afford to sleep?

"Sleep," Garrett said, "is an excellent idea." He limped a few steps and used his staff to point down one of the wide boulevards. "I set up a cushy suite for you and Evenjos. You'll find a couple of worshipful chambermaids waiting over by that kiosk, and—"

"Wait." Ariock stared at his great-grandfather. "Stop." He nearly got up, but then he would tower over everyone. He wanted to remain at eye level. "Evenjos and I are not sleeping together."

Garrett gave him a pitying look of inquiry. He seemed to be implying that Ariock must be a fool if he was turning down a night with Evenjos.

"I am happy to share a bedchamber with you, Ariock Dovanack." Evenjos's exotic accent made every word a lingering caress.

Garrett's hinting look was impossible to miss. He bounced his eyebrows.

"No." Ariock stood, no longer caring that he towered over them. "I would rather share a bedchamber with Vy." He looked down the many alleyways, frustrated that he didn't see Vy or anyone who might know where to find her.

"You have millions of refugees depending on you to import goods tomorrow," Garrett said. "Please, use the bedchamber I set up for you. I put a lot of thought into it. Health is vital for us to do our jobs. You shouldn't shirk on a good night's sleep."

Ariock shot a wary look at Evenjos.

She looked away, as if ashamed. "I will leave you alone, Ariock, if you truly wish it."

He wasn't sure he could trust her.

"I do not require sleep, anyway," Evenjos mumbled. She sounded dejected.

As Ariock and Garrett watched, her body crumbled to dust, like ashes from the campfire. The ashes broke apart and blew away in the nighttime breeze.

That seemed like an overly dramatic exit. Ariock wondered if she was truly gone. Might she be lingering in the air, spying on him?

"You're not giving her a fair chance." Garrett leaned on his staff and craned his head back to give Ariock a judgmental look. "She's a goddess. She's perfect in every way. What's not to like?"

Ariock opened his mouth, but he wasn't sure how to explain all the problems.

Sure, people believed that Evenjos was a goddess. That fed her ego. She believed her own hype. She had ironclad beliefs, and she seemed unwilling to reexamine anything that she believed.

That made her brittle. She might snap under pressure instead of bending and springing back into action.

Ariock was concerned about how she would handle life-or-death combat situations. He wanted her lessons, but even more than that, he wanted her to be a force that the Torth would have to reckon with. That was why he needed Evenjos.

Otherwise?

"I'm with Vy," he told Garrett sternly.

Ariock left the old man standing by the campfire. He strolled away, determined, imagining ways to show Vy that she was important to him.

CHAPTER 7

INHERENTLY WRONG

"Place the metal shavings on top of the capacitor array," Thomas instructed. "A little farther up."

Varktezo worked with the aid of a magnifying lamp. The tech crew had gone on a lunch break, but Varktezo tended to get absorbed in whatever he was doing. He had spent the past two days and nights aiding Thomas in everything while also absorbing Thomas's lessons about linear time-invariant systems and differential equations.

"Would you please move back?" Thomas asked.

Varktezo backed away, eyeing the two dime-size devices on the makeshift table. "Why? What will they do?"

"It's more about what I'm going to do." Thomas floated closer.

As soon as Varktezo was at a safe distance, Thomas spread his awareness into one of the metal shavings, heating it up. A wisp of smoke curled off the metal. The air sharpened with the scent of ionization.

"I'm joining the array in parallel, using a process called soldering," Thomas explained as he worked. "We could heat this scrap metal with a flame, but that would take longer."

Varktezo seemed fascinated. "And the fused metal completes a circuit?"

"Correct." Thomas backed away from the devices, letting them cool off. "Let's test them out. Will you hand me one, please? Put it within reach of my hand."

Most former slaves feared Thomas and his mysterious powers, but Varktezo was too curious to be afraid. He placed one transistor device beneath Thomas's finger.

Thomas pressed the button. "Hear this?"

A tinny echo of his words came out of the other device.

Varktezo hopped back and stared at the device, beak open in amazement. He had learned quite a lot about radio transmissions and broadcast engineering, but the concepts were still new to him. He had no idea how crudely makeshift this operation was.

"Let's try it from a distance," Thomas said. "The signal should carry across Encampment City."

Varktezo understood the need for experimentation. "Yes, Teacher!" He snatched up the small device and scampered through the curtain flap, into the bustling alleyway and out of sight.

Thomas remained in the shadows of his makeshift workshop, amid disemboweled electronics and half-working monitors on top of supply crates. Not everyone in Encampment City trusted a yellow-eyed *rekveh*. Perhaps he should have begged Vy to find some nussians to stand guard.

Nah.

He figured nobody was likely to invade his workshop or steal his supplies. Besides, thanks to the labor of friendly nussians, Thomas had had a secret trapdoor installed beneath the clutter, a place to hide in case of an emergency.

"Teacher?" The device under Thomas's finger vibrated with Varktezo's tinny voice.

Thomas pressed the button. "I hear you."

Varktezo's voice chortled. "Oh, wow. This is like having the power of Torth!"

Thomas thought they had a long way to go. But this was a worthwhile start to creating a specialized internet protocol that could handle the disjointed, mixed-mode effects of temporal latency.

"People are staring at me." Varktezo's voice was amused. "They don't know who I am talking to!" To him, being stared at was a fun and novel experience.

"Try it from farther away," Thomas urged. "Maybe go past the mud zone and through that garment district?"

"Okay, will do!" Varktezo sounded exuberant.

While Thomas waited for the next ping, he picked up one of the charcoal sticks on his armrest. Every movement was an agonizing effort. He was too weak to write for more than half a minute, yet he forced himself to etch an impedance formula onto a stretched canvas.

His representational mathematics leaned against various crates and supply boxes. After all, he needed to teach his ummin crew about ortho-mode transducers, eigenfunction properties, and so much more.

"Teacher, can you hear me?" Varktezo's voice came.

Thomas toggled his speech button. "Loud and clear."

"Good. I'm at a stir-fry stand. Would you like me to pick up lunch for you?"

Thomas hesitated. Would a simple "Yes, thank you" seem trite and dismissive?

He wanted to acknowledge Varktezo as a peer, even a friend, rather than just an interchangeable student. The adolescent ummin came from a ruined backwater where he had been born into slavery, yet his scientific curiosity was formidable. His mnemonic capacity and deductive prowess were greater than that of any scientist Thomas had ever worked with—human or Torth—with the exception of super-geniuses. Varktezo craved knowledge in the same hungry, never-satisfied way as the Upward Governess.

"Only if you get food for yourself, also," Thomas said. "Let's both take a little break to celebrate."

"Will do!"

Thomas's weak hand trembled on the canvas, and he had to give up on writing. He allowed his uncooperative body a rest. All he could do was wait.

It was unusual for him to be alone, without a caretaker or assistant. His unoccupied mind leaped to problems on a larger scale than mathematical equations.

Such as the future of the galaxy.

The future of slaves.

And of Torth.

He would need to lay out each point of his overarching military strategy with delicate care. It would be as dangerous as mixing volatile chemicals. One misstep and he would encounter hostility or outright refusal. Getting other people onboard would be a trial of nerves.

If only he could handle that as easily as he solved mathematical formulas.

He needed to gather enough courage to present his plan to Ariock. People respected the big guy. Warriors and everyone else would follow where Ariock led.

And then, if he persuaded Ariock? This war would kick into high gear.

A lot of slaves would gain freedom.

A lot of Torth would die.

Thomas gazed at the mathematics in front of him while his imagination wove visions of dead and defeated Torth. He smelled blood.

He smelled genocide.

He tried to blink away those disturbing visions, but it did no good. His most optimistic scenarios just did not feel like victory. Every time he imagined winning, he froze.

And he put off his plan for another minute. And another minute.

His mother had sacrificed everything, including her sanity and her life, to give her son a chance to live. Thomas contained that memory. He remembered his mother, though she had been nameless and voiceless.

She had also been selfless.

The Torth were his mother's people. Weren't some of them salvageable?

What would become of his former mentor, the Upward Governess? She was a teenage girl who liked sweet things and fuzzy animals. What future did she deserve?

A lot of Torth had secret quirks and mental aberrations. Lots and lots of them. Thomas used to be one. The Majority tolerated strangeness, so long as every citizen obeyed the laws.

He tried to force his thoughts back to smaller matters.

He was still trying when someone pushed aside his stall curtain. A large figure blocked the daylight, and Thomas rotated his hoverchair to welcome Ariock. He braced himself for the conversation that needed to happen.

At least Ariock valued mercy. Ariock also felt the corrosive guilt that came from killing one's own kin. He would understand the hesitancies Thomas had. Ariock was, by far, the best person—the only person—with whom Thomas would feel comfortable discussing war strategy.

But it was not Ariock who ducked into his stall.

"What are you working on, boy?" Garrett limped into the dimness, leaning on his staff. The curtain fell shut behind him. He had to keep his head tilted to avoid the low ceiling.

"Communications," Thomas said.

Garrett stared around at the clutter and mathematical formulas with distaste. "Elaborate."

It was a command.

Thomas decided to humor him. "Our weakest vector is communications. I'm using what meager materials I could collect in order to begin strengthening our weakness."

"Bah! You're reinventing the wheel." Garrett growled in disgust. "If we need walkie-talkies, we can just have Ariock steal some from Earth."

"We need to do better than walkie-talkies." Thomas wondered why the obvious benefits were so hard for Garrett to grasp. "We need to match the Megacosm. Or come as close as possible, anyway, using technology."

Garrett studied him, uncomprehending.

"If you want a galaxy-spanning empire," Thomas said, trying to be patient, "then you need to be able to communicate across the stars."

"We're not in a building-it-up phase," Garrett said dismissively. "We are tearing it down."

"Either way, we need to rival the Torth." Thomas indicated one of his eigenfunction formulas. "The empire outlawed superluminal research. They had a variety of reasons, not least of which is that their needs are already filled by the Megacosm. But we are not beholden to Torth laws. We can explore avenues of research that—"

"This is unimportant!" Garrett threw up his hands. "This is a sidetrack, boy, and you know it." He jabbed his finger at Thomas. "I specifically asked you to work on immunity to the inhibitor serum."

Thomas had no desire to argue with a fool. Nevertheless, he made an attempt. "An antidote to the inhibitor will require years of research, plus enormous resources. We're better off focusing on an improvement that is swiftly attainable. Something that will boost our army right away, to give us an actual chance in hell of beating a comparable Torth force."

Garrett narrowed his eyes. Clearly, he wanted to argue, but he lacked valid counterpoints.

"I'm going to cut to the chase," Garrett said. "The Torth found out where we are."

"That's news you could have announced sooner." Thomas made rapid recalculations in his head. According to Garrett's spying in the Megacosm, the Torth Majority had elected the Upward Governess to guide their military forces, which made her a commander. Their next wave of attacks would have supergenius cunning. The Torth Empire might devastate Encampment City. Or even Earth.

Unless Ariock accepted a radical shift in strategy.

Thomas hid those thoughts beneath a screen of random trivial data. He wasn't going to mention radical ideas while he was alone with Garrett. He wanted protection.

"They're maneuvering a fleet into position outside Reject-81," Garrett said. "Before I alert Ariock, I want to make sure you're on board with my plan."

"Your plan?" Thomas did not like the direction of this conversation. He felt as if he needed armor whenever he dealt with the old man.

"Yup." Garrett took a limping step closer. Then he seemed to remember that Thomas could absorb his life history, and he stepped back, out of range. "I want you to use your zombification power."

They stared at each other.

"Either in battle, or afterward," Garrett said. "I can grab a few prisoners."

Thomas floated back a step. He felt like a kid facing a schoolyard bully.

"What's your problem?" Garrett sounded genuinely curious.

"It's a bad idea," Thomas managed to say.

"Why?"

Thomas struggled to figure out where to begin. An image of fiery destruction surfaced in his memory, the prophetic vision he had absorbed from Migyatel as she died. He wanted nothing to do with that vision.

"It's wrong," Thomas said. "Morally, ethically, and strategically, it's wrong."

Garrett's mouth became a thin line. "Your feelings about it are irrelevant. It has to happen."

That suggested that Garrett believed it was inevitable. He might believe it was foretold.

Had he glimpsed something like Migyatel's vision in the ancient book of paintings by the oracle Ah Jun?

Well, Thomas didn't care if a thousand prophets had painted him acting like a tyrant. He wasn't going to become that monster. Not as long as he had free will.

He tried to use reason. "Zombified victims die fast. They wouldn't be much use to us."

A sharp wind cut through the stall curtain, causing debris to overturn. Garrett's gaze became dangerous.

"You and I," Garrett said, "bear the stain of Torth sin. We are the direct descendants of murderers and slave owners. Never forget that."

As if Thomas could forget.

"We have a moral obligation to set things right." A fierce intensity lit Garrett's eyes. "We must follow the prophecies of Ah Jun." He took a threatening step closer, and Thomas floated backward. "Destroy a bunch of Torth," Garrett said, "and you will go a long way toward counteracting the sins of your mother. Just as I am working to counteract the sins of my father."

Thomas hovered backward until he hit the stall divider. Canvases and debris fell over.

Garrett seemed so focused on sins, he was probably oblivious to the fact that his religious fervor was an Alashani trait. That was not something he had inherited from his "evil" Torth side.

Yes, they were mind readers. But that did not make them inherently bad or evil. Did it?

Thomas wanted to assert that he was a good person. He valued free will. Surely that made him good?

He lacked enough conviction to say it out loud.

After all, Thomas had fooled himself before. When he had agreed to become a Yellow Rank, he had believed he was doing the right thing.

"You know what's at stake," Garrett said. "We cannot afford to lose. We can't even lose a single battle. We're too weak." His tone hardened. He thumped one fist in his open palm for emphasis. "So you need to get over your prissy little fear and zombify our enemies!"

Maybe Garrett was right.

Maybe Thomas should cast aside his inner convictions, or his "prissy little fear," as Garrett called it, and reexamine the possibility that he might be wrong.

Like Unyat.

Twenty-four thousand years ago, if Unyat had reexamined his convictions, the Torth Empire never would have arisen. Instead, Unyat had believed, at every step of his multigenerational life-span, that he was doing the right thing.

Thomas forced himself to remember the most awful things that the Upward Governess had done. And his birth mother. They were villains. They were Torth.

Maybe all Torth deserved death.

Except . . . well, hadn't they had done those things under pressure from the Majority?

Just like Garrett was pressuring Thomas right now.

"No." Thomas tried to sound tough, but his voice came out in a small squeak.

The air gained an electric charge. The wind blew, stirring tapestries.

"What's your problem?" Garrett didn't seem to realize that his mood was influencing the weather. "Do you think any of them are worth saving?"

Thomas dared not answer that.

"Then deep down," Garrett said scathingly, "where it matters, you're still a Torth."

"You want to wipe out a brilliant civilization." Thomas choked the words out. "You want genocide. And you think *I'm* the evil one?"

He regretted that retort as soon as he spoke it. He could not win a fight against Garrett by brute force, and he should have tried to de-escalate the argument rather than stoke their mutual outrage.

"A brilliant civilization." Garrett's tone dripped with scorn. "Really. Does their supposed brilliance justify all the slaves they torture to death?"

"No, of course not." Thomas tried to sound placating. He edged around Garrett, toward the flapping curtain, trying to get to open air. "I want to stop the Torth. I'm just not convinced that genocide is the answer."

"It's the only answer." Garrett stalked after him. "They're a blight on this universe. Consider all the people your birth mother murdered."

When Thomas remembered his birth mother, all he could think of was the horror he had absorbed during his Adulthood Exam. Her eyes clawed out. Her throat torn open.

"Do you really believe a piece of scum like that should be forgiven?" Garrett demanded.

She had never had a name. Or a voice.

She had died in the Isolatorium. She had been a hideous wreck by the time the Torth Empire was finished with her. She had suffered worse than Garrett, worse than Ariock, and throughout her ordeal, she had poured heroic effort into forgetting that her son existed. She had done that solely to give him a chance to live.

Tears stung Thomas's eyes. He paused in the doorway, yelling over the wind. "She paid for her sins!"

"She killed my daughter!" Electricity snapped around Garrett's staff, uncontrolled. "She murdered my family! You don't end payment on a debt like that!"

As if Garrett's conscience was clean.

"You abandoned your family!" Thomas snapped. "Not to mention your slaves!"

Garrett whipped a blue-white bolt of lightning at Thomas. Alashani tended to get violent if anyone insulted their devotion to family, and Thomas realized, too late, that he should have been more sensitive.

The lightning missed his head by inches. It leaped across the street, punched through a curtain, and probably struck a divider wall. People screamed in surprise. A few ducked or ran, assuming a Torth attack.

"I did what I had to do," Garrett snarled, stomping after Thomas, "in order to work toward defeating the Torth Empire. That is what I will always do. Because I have principles!"

Thomas struggled to form an ice shield. Snowflakes formed in the wind around him.

"You had better do what's right, boy," Garrett said, "whether you agree or not. You will zombify any prisoners I bring in. Otherwise? I swear, I'll drop you from a mile aboveground, over and over, until you—"

An unseen force yanked Garrett back a few paces. He froze in midair, dangling by his upper body, his legs kicking.

Thomas's hoverchair suddenly flew up, out of his control. He toggled the button, but it was useless. His hoverchair might as well be stuck in unseen gel, in midair.

"What is going on here?" Ariock's deep voice rumbled in the silence.

The sky looked ready to storm.

CHAPTER 8

BETWEEN WILL AND WISDOM

Ariock felt a bit guilty about having picked up his friends, holding them apart and helpless in midair. It was rude. These were his allies.

But people in Encampment City had enough to worry about without adding renegade mind readers dueling each other to that list. Refugees peeked out from between curtains. Snide comments were bad enough, but lightning and ice crystals? That was inexcusable.

"What is this about?" Ariock said.

Thomas looked ashamed.

Garrett, predictably, looked the opposite of Thomas. "We can't trust the boy," he said with airy confidence. "He's made it clear that he has Torth sympathies."

"That's a lie!" Thomas shot back.

Ariock sighed, trying to ease the tension in his shoulders. He had been enjoying a relaxed morning with Vy. They'd had had a rare moment of privacy, snuggling in blankets. Ariock wanted nothing more than to return to her.

The clouds were ominously dark. The sky reflected his mood. Or maybe it was Garrett's mood.

Cautiously, Ariock set the two mind readers down. He could not plan on holding his allies apart indefinitely. All he could do was ask, or beg, them to be reasonable.

"Thomas is on our side," Ariock said firmly. He withdrew his awareness, but he watched Garrett for any signs of violence. "I want you to show him some respect. You can stop calling him 'the boy.' He has a name."

Garrett defiantly adjusted his leather armor. "People have names. Torth do not. I'll call him 'the boy' until he proves that he's committed to fighting for our side."

The insinuation was plain.

And plainly ridiculous. Ariock glared at the old man. After all the things Thomas had done to escape the Torth, why would he ever go back? That was nonsensical. Anyway, the Torth Empire would never trust their Betrayer again.

Garrett seemed to read Ariock's ire, even from a distance, and he spoke in a more reasonable tone. "I know I sound paranoid. But the boy has issues, and the prophecies paint his role as . . ." Garrett seemed to rethink what he had been about to say. "Ambiguous."

Was that supposed to sow doubt?

Ariock didn't believe there was any painting that depicted Thomas as dangerous or threatening to his side of the war. He wanted to have a look at the prophecies. Whatever Garrett had seen, he must have misinterpreted it.

"Ariock." Thomas spoke in a measured tone. "Garrett said the Torth have found us. We need to discuss strategy."

One glance at Garrett confirmed it.

Ariock did not explode in rage. Instead, he gave Garrett a look.

This had to be a result of the old man's incautious nature. Garrett had taught Ariock a cosmic route to one other planet, a sparsely populated outpost with a semitoxic atmosphere. Ariock practiced every day, encompassing warehouse items within his awareness. He was beginning to get the hang of ghosting and teleporting. The cargo he stole was enough to keep the residents of Encampment City stocked with the minimal supplies they needed.

But how many habitable reject planets were within the cosmic neighborhood of Omophia Prime? Probably only one: Reject-81.

That was undoubtedly how the Torth had figured out where to find him.

"What?" Garrett looked self-righteous. "We needed supplies. Anyway, trust me, we could not have stayed hidden. The Torth sent probes and survey ships everywhere."

Ariock glanced at Thomas for a fact check.

Thomas gave a reluctant nod.

"Then we have important things to discuss." Ariock stepped back, implying that he did not want to mediate. "Can I trust you two to stop fighting for a while?"

"Gladly," Thomas said with stiff dignity.

Garrett squinted up at the brooding sky.

Ariock braced himself for yet another petty argument. He was losing patience with the old man's stubborn defiance. This was ridiculous. The encampment could not afford to endure Ariock wrestling his great-grandfather. A fight over leadership would only distract from real problems, such as how to defeat the Torth.

"Garrett?" Ariock prompted.

"Crap." Garrett lifted his staff in both gnarled hands. "They got here sooner than I expected."

Ariock suspected that Garrett might be making an effort to skate away from responsibility. How childish.

Unless . . .

Had Ariock remembered to sweep his awareness through space this morning?

He was supposed to check for life sparks in the void beyond the outer atmosphere of Reject-81 on a daily basis. He might have gotten distracted, kissing Vy and making her giggle about lines from movies they both liked. It seemed he had a thousand duties to remember.

"Everyone, run!" Garrett shouted.

He thrust his staff upward, and a shock wave expanded into the sky, following the trajectory of his thrust. The clouds got sucked upward.

Several things exploded up there, hidden by clouds.

The ground shook with the force of those distant explosions. Shrapnel began to rain down.

People fled in all directions. Many dived under the shelters. Those who owned blaster gloves donned them. Others grabbed trays or other items to use as shields.

"Well." Thomas directed his seething, acid tone at Garrett. "At least we know whose strategies we shouldn't trust."

"I don't see you countering them!" Garrett retorted. "You're the supergenius. How about if you come up with something brilliant?"

"A little forewarning would have gone a long way." Thomas gave Garrett a disparaging look. "Combat isn't my department."

With that, he sped toward his workshop.

There was a camouflaged trapdoor in there, Ariock knew. The bolt-hole should keep Thomas safely hidden if Encampment City got invaded.

The Torth had better not invade.

Ariock loosened his awareness, intending to gain an overview of the threat. He arrowed his perceptions skyward. Soon he spanned thousands of miles of empty air.

Odd little life sparks zoomed through him in chaotic directions. It felt as if the sky had people in it.

Beyond the atmosphere and the tug of gravity, Ariock sensed a breathable habitat that thrummed with living things. He could not estimate the number of living beings aboard the ship, but there were a lot. At least a thousand. Maybe ten thousand?

The problem: some of those might be slaves.

"They've already deployed the swarm." Garrett yanked blaster gloves onto each of his hands. "You won't gain much by shoving away the swarmship. Let's concentrate on the threat at hand."

"Swarmship?" Ariock sensed chaos overhead, approaching at a rapid pace.

"Yeah. It's basically an aircraft carrier." Garrett faced the opposite direction from Ariock, scanning the skies. "It carries a whole lot of military shuttles, and when they reach a planetary target, they swarm, like hornets."

Ariock swore. It was hard for him to track complexity. He could easily shove things in one direction, but those life sparks in the sky were moving in erratic chaos, without any discernible pattern. That made them impossible to group together.

"I'm sorry." Garrett sounded truly guilty. "The only way they got here so fast was with a supergenius taking remote control of their navigation. Maybe she boosted their thrusters as well." He held out his arms, and scraps of metal molded themselves around the parts of his body that were not armored. "I didn't expect this. I should have let you know ASAP."

"I'm sorry, too." Ariock inwardly vowed to keep better watch. He should have taken a few minutes this morning to ghost through space or expand his awareness. He might have detected the swarmship.

"You're getting the hang of things," Garrett said. "Don't feel too bad about it."

Ariock sensed hundreds of shuttles coming at him from multiple directions. And there were heavy, ominous objects falling toward Encampment City. Bombs.

He dared not deter them simultaneously. Such a task would absorb all his focus, leaving no room for self-protection or situational awareness—unless he stopped caring about collateral damage. And he wasn't going to do that.

Ariock swept an enormous, wrenchingly fast tidal wave of air overhead, causing static electricity to crackle across the sky.

Bombs exploded and lit the clouds with golden fire. Shuttles tumbled in insane directions.

Instead of withdrawing his awareness, Ariock encompassed the whole city in a towering dome.

He could not maintain a solid surface over such a vast area, so he made it a net. Crisscrossed bars of electricity glowed against the gloom. The fierce glow reflected off metal rooftops.

"Perfect," Garrett said with warm approval. "Uh, how long do you think you can hold a citywide shield in place?"

Ariock tried to estimate things. Thinking was tough when he was spread over several miles.

"Never mind." Garrett gave him a friendly pat on the back. "I'll make you some armor, and then we'll get this party started."

Before he had finished speaking, pieces of reinforced, pliable plastic and scraps of metal cartwheeled toward Ariock. The scraps assembled themselves over Ariock's woolen clothes. They melted and melded together, forming overlapped plates.

Torso shields. Abdominal and pelvic segments. Leg pieces, gauntlets, shoulder caps, boots, gloves, and a helm.

The mismatched armor made Ariock even more titanic. But he had no time for body shame right now, and anyway, he knew the value of armor. Woolens would not protect him from microdarts of the inhibitor serum.

"You're doing great," Garrett called. Wind whipped his beard. He made a throwing motion with his staff, and a white-hot bar of lightning leaped off the silver metal. It struck an individual shuttle, causing that shuttle to explode and fall apart.

"Will they send drones?" Ariock asked. If any of the incoming shuttles lacked a telltale life spark, they would be difficult to detect, and therefore much harder for him to stop. "I mean, do they have robotically operated shuttles, without pilots?"

"The Torth Empire never bothered much with robots or drones," Garrett hollered over the wind. "So I doubt it."

Explosions tickled Ariock's surface. The violent heat touched him in a remote way, like pinpricks on his skin. Life sparks winked out of existence as pilots slammed into his barrier and died. They fell like dead embers.

"But I don't know if we can expect a normal battle," Garrett said. "I'm afraid they're being choreographed by a supergenius."

The sky was chaos. Ariock gritted his teeth. He needed to stay colossal, covering his city, because he was the only shield between his people and utter ruination.

CHAPTER 9

OUTSIDE ROUTINE

The Upward Governess rode the perceptions of several hundred military ranks simultaneously.

She helped them pilot their swarmshuttles. She attempted to dodge the lightning bars of the Giant's dome shield, although that was difficult. Death screams reverberated through the Megacosm, giving a disturbing backdrop to the many ongoing commentaries.

Billions of Torth were focused on this battle. Only a few thousand made the mistake of vicariously experiencing death. No one wanted to experience shock, panic, or pain, and most people in orbit around a dying mind spun away.

The Upward Governess guided military pilots toward foothills. There, out of sight from the encampment city, Torth landed and stepped outside. They activated the camouflage on their armor, which mimicked environmental data and made them almost invisible at a distance. They crept toward the city.

But they were scared. Pumped with adrenaline.

Why attack prematurely? That was an undercurrent in the Megacosm, instigated by Red Ranks.

Our military is not equipped to fight the Giant with a single swarmship.
Can't We wait—
—until We have a superior force?
—or until We have a newly invented superweapon?

Frustration pooled, creating spiky terrain across the Megacosm. Her approval ratings were plummeting.

As if every Red Rank mattered.

The Upward Governess struggled to hide her disdain. This was a galactic war. Casualties were inevitable. Where were the protests when supergeniuses grew fatally ill or died? Why did the Majority care so much more for military drudges than top scientists?

She reminded her listeners, *The Torth Empire has never faced a threat like this before (a renegade supergenius controlling rogue Yeresunsa). It is imperative that We (Your leaders) test the enemies for weaknesses and shortcomings.*

Reaction chains rippled with criticism.

We have surprised them, the Upward Governess elaborated. *The element of surprise gives Us a tactical advantage. At best, We will capture (destroy) the Betrayer. At worst? We will kill enemy warriors and give the enemies more to fear.*

The Majority offered tacit support. Many Torth sat in their hoverchairs or spas or beds, or they shopped in forums or enjoyed exercise or travel, and they waited for results. The smart ones realized that this military test strike was barely a fraction of a fraction of the individuals whose lives had been extinguished when the enemies destroyed the Torth Homeworld. This was barely a skirmish.

Whatever the outcome, win or lose, it was worth it. The enemies would be weakened.

A cake entered her workshop.

The Upward Governess withdrew her attention from the battle, momentarily distracted by the confectionary treat.

A gift! the Majority thundered.

From Us—

—to You!

But of course! Today the Upward Governess was officially the eldest supergenius in the history of the known universe.

Daily doses of NAI-13 had significantly improved her health. The medicine was not a cure, but it was more effective than NAI-12 at halting her physical deterioration. She no longer needed a ventilator.

Would any other supergenius live long enough to get this far into puberty? Doubtful.

The Upward Governess was a phenomenon. She was unstoppable. The Betrayer was a footnote in history, compared with her. He had made the biggest mistake of his life when he had given up on her. And left her.

For the sake of a slave.

The cake was shaped like a kneeling and collared human girl. Expert dabs of frosting depicted cascading black hair. Glass lenses obscured the slave girl's eyes. There was even an indication of tears on her cheeks, in the form of sugar beads.

The Upward Governess took her first nibble of the syrupy garnish around the cake. She wiggled her toes in delight.

The confectioner, a fat Green Rank in her audience, mentally bowed. Everyone knew that creativity was obscene. Still, no one made a big deal out of it. Personality quirks and talents were acceptable—even welcomed—so long as creatives were savvy enough to avoid having strong emotions in public.

The Upward Governess returned her mind to the distant battleground on Reject-81, where Red Ranks were finding sneaky ways into the dome shield.

The Giant could not pay close attention to every foot of a miles-long perimeter. Most of his attention was aimed upward and outward. He protected his city against bombs and swarmshuttles. He failed to notice life sparks at his very edges, where solidified air met ground. There were gaps. Torth combatants sneaked through those gaps.

Find the Betrayer, the Upward Governess reminded her troops. *Neutralize his powers. Collar him. Bring him to Me alive.*

If any overzealous Torth made the mistake of killing the Betrayer, she would be displeased. Any such incompetent combatant would suffer a terrible death.

Also, the Upward Governess decided, *if you see either of the human runaways, capture them alive.* She added, as an afterthought, *And that ummin.*

It seemed ridiculous to prioritize the capture of an elderly runaway ummin. But a few freshly collared slaves had begun to spread a tale about a certain "Kessa the Wise," an ummin who ordered Torth about. Kessa's public execution should help squelch those stories.

Her military ranks fanned out. They spread into the city like viruses invading a host's bloodstream.

"Where is your supergenius?" a Red Rank demanded in a loud voice.

"Where is Thomas?" another demanded.

They did not have an easy time. Albino warriors stalked them and threw lightning at them. Former slaves shot at them with blaster gloves. One enterprising nussian managed to kill several Red Ranks simply by smashing their heads with rocks.

The Upward Governess sent more and more military ranks into the city of refugees. Her mind extended like tentacles, watching and nudging and invading. She pieced together a mental map. She explored the squalid encampment.

The Betrayer had given up everything for the sake of a meager teenage girl from Earth. Cherise Chavez was so mundane as to be absurd. What sort of supergenius would go for one such as her?

A failure. That was what sort.

The Betrayer was probably cowering. Hiding.

"Where is he?" Torth combatants rasped as they grabbed refugees, probing their minds. "Where is the supergenius?"

In the Megacosm, somebody reimagined the enemies as a grotesque leviathan, and other Torth built upon that mental image. The Giant was the trunk of the monster. But the Betrayer? He was its head.

The Majority formed a motivational background chorus. *The Betrayer heads Our enemies.*

Lop off their head!

The Upward Governess savored another bite of her celebration cake.

Really, she deserved a tasty treat, simply to get away from neuroplasticity readouts and toxicology analytics. It seemed all she ever did these days was work.

Her secret lair was specially outfitted just for her. Even so, she missed her observatory deck, her indoor lake, and the bountiful blooms of her private gardens. There was nothing marvelous to gaze upon in this underground industrial complex.

She would be able to resume her luxurious life as soon as the enemies were vanquished.

Things were getting interesting on Reject-81. Rosy Recruits entered the fray, and they ran through the grassy streets, pumped with adrenaline, laying waste to every albino they encountered. They flickered in and out of the Megacosm as they used their powers.

The Giant had proven to be formidable in terms of strength . . . yet it seemed he was quite limited in terms of attention. He could not maintain a solid perimeter on his dome shield. He was so occupied with keeping the swarm out, he could not hunt down the individual Torth who sneaked inside his dome.

And the Shapeshifter wasn't doing anything at all.

True, she might masquerade as an ordinary ummin or nussian. The possibilities made everyone uneasy. Yet if she lurked in this battle, she was not going out of her way to be terrifying. No one had knowingly encountered her.

So neither the Giant nor the Shapeshifter was being particularly dangerous. It seemed they dared not go into berserker mode near their own people.

The Imposter, however, was extra vicious.

He could fly. He could leap in superhuman bounds. He kept showing up where he was least expected, and one by one, he took Rosy Recruits and Red Ranks by surprise. He seemed to anticipate every attack. He acted fast, roasting people in their armor or slamming them down so hard their bones liquefied. He was a nonstop murder machine.

The Imposter will kill Us all! one of the Rosy Recruits reported as she hid behind a handcart.

A second later, an unseen force yanked her off her feet. She was smashed to death before she could even figure out which direction her attacker was coming from.

Hm. The Upward Governess ate more cake. The Imposter was, indeed, quite effective at stalking and murdering individual Torth. He moved in a blur of speed.

His combat strategy in this battle implies a weakness, the Upward Governess thought, elaborating for her audience. *Note that he avoids teleportation.*

Her orbiters chorused with admiration. *The Imposter fears depletion in this battle?*

Teleportation must be high cost for him.

This is good to know.

The battle went on. Refugees died. Red Ranks screamed as they got blasted into gory pieces.

All the while, there were no humans in the chaos. No scientific lab. No hint of the Betrayer.

A Servant of All began complaining. *You (Upward Governess) claim that any outcome is a victory for Us, yet the Giant can easily replace his losses.*

Other military ranks clamored in agreement. *The Giant can grab slaves, weapons, whatever he wants.*

He can do that any time he feels like it.

The Upward Governess acknowledged the growing concerns. True enough, the Giant had made several forays on Omophia Prime. No one could predict when he would show up. No one could stop him.

When she judged her audience to be at peak receptivity, she answered the critics. *I have absorbed psychoanalyses of human nature.* She had gained that from the Betrayer himself before he had betrayed her. *Slaves, even runaways, are poor allies. All We must do is remind them of how worthless they are. Many of these supposedly brave runaways will throw down their weapons if We offer them a semblance of safety. They don't want to fight. They want routine and peaceful living. They will beg Us to snap collars around their necks.*

The Torth Majority hummed with speculation. They knew that slaves tended to be uncertain and timid.

A loss will devastate them, she predicted. *Even a small loss. And the Giant will blame himself. He, too, will feel devastated by even a handful of deaths on his side.*

The Torth Majority sang in anticipation of the Giant's devastation.

And, the Upward Governess reminded them, *We are going to pile a lot more pressure upon him. This is only the beginning.*

The Torth Majority roared its approval. They had, after all, mobilized the largest armada in known history.

Every military ship in the galaxy was being activated and maximally armed. Slow travel was still a factor. The armada positioned to invade Earth, for example, would require a couple of days to surround its target.

The Majority sang with anticipated triumphs. The ancient wildlife preserve of Earth was finally going to be civilized and divvied up! There would be new cities to govern.

Upper ranks surged, each one contending for a larger audience, striving to prove that they deserved a province. The Majority would assign land masses to deserving individuals, who would then construct industrial complexes, slave factories, and slave-breeding farms.

We are Torth!

No one will defeat Us!

The Majority imagined all sorts of victories, sharing and resharing the most popular scenarios. Earth was a ripe fruit. It was more than ready to be plucked and devoured by the Torth Empire.

Exactly. The Upward Governess chewed cake with a borderline-illegal grin. The Torth military would soon be geared to deploy to any planet or space station in the galaxy. The enemies would have nowhere to hide.

The Death Architect surfaced in the Megacosm. She tended to emerge just long enough to gather news and then slipped back down and out of sight, back to mental privacy. This time, however, she chimed in.

There is no need to worry, the Death Architect thought to the Majority. *No need at all. Even if Our military somehow proves insufficient . . . well, We supergeniuses will unveil a few innovations, in terms of weapons.*

The Upward Governess eyed her workstation holographs. None of it conveyed the direction of her research. Her work needed to remain top secret, since the Imposter tended to lurk in the Megacosm, undetected.

Only somebody who was intimately familiar with this type of science would realize that her primary focus had switched from structural engineering to thalamocortical resonance. The major shift in academic interest was extreme, for her, and it was only made possible because she had absorbed so much of the Betrayer's expertise.

Our innovations, the Death Architect went on, *are guaranteed to defeat Our enemies.*

That was a bold claim.

The Upward Governess did not dispute it, although she wondered what her younger colleague was working on, exactly. The Death Architect's work involved human test subjects. Captive Alashani and humans were shipped to her secret lab on a regular basis.

They did not last long.

The Death Architect always wanted more, claiming that her test subjects were dead, and dead again.

No one dared ask questions, though. That would be treason. Top-secret projects had to remain top secret.

I trust that Our Greatest Mind (the Upward Governess) will come up with something that will win the war, the Death Architect assured the Majority. *She is, after all, the eldest supergenius in history. On top of that, She had the opportunity to absorb everything in the Betrayer's mind.*

That was quite flattering.

The Upward Governess knew that she ought to be grateful for the publicity boost. And she was pioneering something truly innovative. It was something to be proud of. Even so . . .

She blotted out her misgivings beneath a storm of trivial data.

The instant she had the Betrayer under her power, she intended to sabotage her own research and wipe out her weapon in progress. A dark-energy distortion zone such as this should only be used as a last resort. If it began to exist beyond limited military use—if it ever gained widespread use—the enemies might not matter anymore.

The Upward Governess hoped that her colleagues were working on safer projects.

She shifted her attention away from the dangerous topic of superweapons. How inappropriate! The Megacosm was a social space.

She fixed her focus on the Death Architect, pinning her in place with an enormous galactic audience. She had a question for her younger colleague.

Is there any particular reason, she asked, *why you (Death Architect) have stationed Servants of All on My homeworld?*

The direct question was rude. Torth could not deceive each other, so asking a question like this was tantamount to making a mild accusation. The Upward Governess did not care. Now that she was effectively the ruler of the galaxy, she was impatient with the constraints of etiquette.

Oh. The Death Architect remained serene, apparently oblivious to the rudeness. *I have stationed powerful Yeresunsa on every hub planet. It seems a wise (strategic) precaution, considering the fact that Our enemies can teleport.*

Indeed. That was a sensible answer.

The placement of the Swift Killer seemed deliberate to the Upward Governess. Everyone knew that she had a history of thorny relations with that particular Servant of All.

But really, what other answer could there be?

The Upward Governess devoured another bite of human-slave cake. She was probably being paranoid, seeing patterns that meant nothing. It just seemed an odd coincidence.

And why were all the Servants of All stationed on Umdalkdul powerful clairvoyants? Was that by design?

It must be just a random coincidence. The Upward Governess gave a mental nod to her younger colleague, aware that she ought to trust her peer. The Death Architect sank out of her orbit.

It was strange how she kept feeling a very vague, irrational suspicion about the Death Architect. The younger girl was just difficult to read, that was all. Her smoothness was enough to trouble anyone who relied on the rough complexities and subtextual hints of moods.

!!!!!!!!

Hide in the hills!

Wait for reinforcements to arrive?

Run!

Nightmarish deaths rattled the Megacosm. The Giant had finally let go of his dome shield, and he was emulating the Imposter. Learning from him. Together, the two monsters were decimating the swarm. Rosy Recruits desperately sought routes out of the enemy camp.

The Upward Governess allowed her troops to fend for themselves. She hated to give up on the Betrayer today, but there would be future battles. Bigger, better battles.

He was probably cowering in one of the refugee stalls.

Let him cower. He had nothing but substandard minds on his side, plus a few stolen scraps from the mightiest civilization in history.

She was sure that she was smarter. More innovative. More creative. She owned all the resources, all the planets, all the ships and weapons and troops.

The Upward Governess bit into the head of her cake. She would win. She was the ruler of the galaxy, not him.

BRUTAL PROTEST

Dawn reflected off collapsed roofs. It touched smoldering heaps of rubble with a bleak, foggy glow. The rising sun had yet to burn off the ground mist.

The bleakness matched Ariock's mood.

He sat on a boulder by the river, resting his forehead in his hands. He had spent last evening and all of last night hunting and killing people.

Torth. Not people. They screamed like people. They ran and they fought like people, even though they wore creepy camouflage armor that made them blend in with rocks and grass. The life sparks of Red Ranks were indistinguishable from the life sparks of ummins and nussians.

He had to try and forget that when he smashed them to bloody pulp or when he snapped their spines.

No one else seemed to have a problem with separating friends from enemies. Jinishta and her warriors bragged about how many Torth they'd killed. Garrett boasted right along with them, loudest of all.

But Ariock felt no joy whenever he used his powers to squelch another life. It was ridiculously easy for him to find combat. The night had glowed with wildfire, blaster explosions, and lightning. Wherever intense life sparks clashed—Alashani warriors versus Torth Rosy Recruits—Ariock had sensed them as hot spots.

So he had gone around putting out fires. And ending lives.

Yet he did not feel righteous or exhilarated tracking down random life sparks in the foothills and striking them with deadly bolts of lightning. He had unfair advantages. How could anyone brag about that?

Toward the end of the night, he had gone titanic again in order to shove away the Torth ships approaching his refugee planet. He'd cleared the space around Reject-81. Encampment City should be safe for another three days.

Yet he did not feel victorious.

The river ran dark with debris and ashes. Its rushing sound did not quite mask the sounds of lamentation in nearby neighborhoods.

Ariock had healed everyone who was barely clinging to life. During the battle, he'd paid special attention to the warriors, since they were protecting everyone else. Jinishta had asked Ariock where her people would be most useful. He had told her.

Despite their best efforts, there was a death toll.

More than thirty warriors had died.

More than a hundred refugees were gone.

A dozen more were maimed, having lost limbs. Supplies had been blasted and burned. And of course, the cozy illusion of safety was destroyed.

Perhaps forever.

The deaths were unacceptable, especially in a city that was supposedly protected by the messiah. All the surviving warriors were now healed and healthy and aiding refugees in piecing their lives back together. But if they no longer believed in the messiah . . . Well, Ariock would not blame them.

He was right there with them.

What was my plan? Ariock asked himself for the hundredth time.

The answer was disgusting. He hadn't planned at all. He had even forgotten to scan the space around his appropriated planet.

He supposed he had been relying on Thomas, and Garrett, to do all the thinking for him.

And Evenjos?

He could not rely on her at all. Evenjos could probably eat bombs, but instead, her powerful life spark had lurked in quiet neighborhoods on the outskirts of the city. She had avoided combat altogether. For all Ariock knew, she had transformed into an innocuous pile of dust during the battle.

At least Garrett had been brave enough to fight. At least Thomas had insisted on setting up blaster glove practice facilities. If not for the two of them, the death toll would have been much higher.

Ariock inwardly hardened his resolve to never trust Evenjos. If she considered the job of protecting innocent people to be beneath her dignity, then she was near worthless as far as he was concerned.

"Ah," called a gruff, incongruously cheerful voice. "There you are."

Ariock did not feel ready to converse with anyone, let alone his great-grandfather.

He had not even spoken with Vy beyond a few words to make sure she was okay. He could not handle the way Vy looked at him. It wasn't like he deserved sympathy. Or rest. Sure, it had been a long night, but he didn't deserve anything like a reward after that disaster.

"We didn't do too badly," Garrett said, limping downhill toward Ariock. "All things considered."

"What?" Ariock stared at Garrett with mistrustful disbelief. Did the old man have to exaggerate everything? Now was the wrong time for tasteless levity. Now was a time for mourning.

And guilt. And reassessment. They needed to do better.

"The Torth were going through the streets, searching for the boy." Garrett still wore his mismatched armor, which was dented and battered, splashed with blood. "They didn't find him. They didn't find Kessa or any of their targets. So, like I said, we did pretty well."

"Right." Ariock slumped.

Maybe Garrett would get bored and go away. Ariock just wanted to sit by these waters. He needed to reflect on the terrible costs that innocent people paid whenever he failed.

One of his worst flaws, he thought, was to misjudge his own capabilities. It turned out he could not seal ten square miles with complete perfection. Maybe he could manage it for a few minutes at a time, but his attention span was . . . well, human. Limited. He had found it impossible to be unflaggingly attentive to every square yard of that shield, especially as the battle wore on and he grew concerned for his friends.

"Seriously," Garrett said. "You protected the entirety of Encampment City all night. You shoved away the rest of the Torth fleet. That's no easy feat. You've protected us for the next few days, and you kept the deaths to a minimum."

Did Garrett actually sound proud?

Ariock stared in disbelief. Hundreds of people were mourning friends and family members. They were crying. Couldn't Garrett hear them?

"Win some, lose some," Garrett said. "We'll handle the next battle better." He gestured uphill. "Come, I have something to show you. I think it will cheer you up."

That sounded improbable. Ariock gave his great-grandfather a reproachful look. Cheeriness seemed obscene in the aftermath of a slaughter. They both ought to brood over their own incompetence.

"Look." Garrett sighed heavily. "People see you sitting here. You're impossible to miss." He made a gesture that indicated mass. "And they see your mood." He used his staff to gesture at the struggling red disk of the sun. "It would be nice if you quit demoralizing everyone."

Ariock narrowed his eyes. "So I should fake being happy?"

Garrett gave him a no-nonsense look. They were at eye level, with Ariock hunched over and seated and Garrett leaning on his staff. "Ariock, you successfully protected twelve million people." He made that sound like a miracle. "A few died, okay, but give yourself a break!" Garrett's tone turned to something like a plea. "You are not omniscient. You and I did everything possible."

Did Garrett honestly believe that "a few" lives lost was excusable?

Ariock looked away, unable to hide his disgust. Maybe extended life-spans transformed certain people into callous, egocentric jerks. Garrett and Evenjos had probably forgotten what it felt like to be vulnerable. To be human.

"Please?" Garrett backed away and indicated that Ariock should follow him. "Life goes on. I need you to have a look at something. We can turn a Pyrrhic victory into a solid one. Our next battle doesn't have to go this badly."

Ariock could not ignore a lure like that.

He stood with a sigh of resignation. As he followed Garrett over grassy hills, past people mending their wares, he was inwardly glad that he remembered how it felt to be vulnerable. Maybe that was why he cared about the damage and the lives lost.

Privately, he vowed to always remember how it felt. He needed to hang on to his human memories of pacing the sky room, and quiet moments of chatting with his mother, and fighting for his life and sanity in a prison cell.

Human perspective was vital. Otherwise, how could Ariock be sure he was one of the good guys?

The encampment did not look as devastated as Ariock felt. Most people seemed to be going about their normal lives. They had replaced broken crates and torn-down curtains.

On the other hand, Ariock suspected that people went into best-behavior mode when they caught sight of him. They murmured grateful words. He overheard "the messiah" and "protected us" a few times. Some people even genuflected.

That only made him feel more guilty. They must have such meager, low expectations, to call his failure a success. They deserved better.

Garrett led him to a gulch that was crowded with battle leaders, elders, and councilors.

Ariock nearly turned back. He didn't have the fortitude to face Jinishta or Weptolyso yet.

Or Kessa. Or Thomas and Vy. They were here, too.

Ugh, and Evenjos.

She looked proud of herself, standing apart from everyone else with her head held high and her wings arced behind her. Why did she feel the need to wear an imperious dress? And, of course, it was provocative, with skin peeking out in strategic places. What a surprise. Even after a complete disaster, she wanted to show off.

Did this assembly expect an invigorating speech from the messiah?

Ariock wasn't feeling it. He began to leave.

"You're not here to give a speech," Garrett assured him, giving his arm a friendly tug. "I gathered everyone here, including you, because we have prisoners."

Prisoners?

Ariock peered over the heads of the crowd—that was easy for him to do—and saw a narrow cage at the focal point of the assembly. The cage's bars were slashed together in a haphazard way. Garrett had probably created it using his powers.

Two Torth stood in the closely confined space. In their bulky red armor, there was not enough room for them to sit.

Their helmets and gloves were missing. No doubt Garrett had taken those. The Torth peered out at the assembled battle leaders with eerie, fluorescent-pink eyes. One looked like a stout male. The other was a wiry female.

"Rosies?" Ariock went on alert.

"Don't worry," Garrett said. "I disabled their powers. They're on the inhibitor."

Garrett limped toward the cage, looking pleased with himself, cloak trailing him like a cape. People moved aside, giving him an aisle to walk down. Their looks encouraged Ariock, so he followed Garrett, albeit with reluctance.

"Behold!" Garrett announced as he strode down the grassy aisle. "We have our first prisoners of war."

The Rosies grasped the bars with their bare hands, staring in the expressionless way of their species. Their fluorescent eyes might as well be surveillance cameras. They must be conveying everything they saw to the Torth Empire.

"Why do we have prisoners?" Ariock stopped, unwilling to get within telepathy range of the Rosies in the cage.

"Why do you think?" Garrett turned to Ariock with mischievous glee. "Do you see the possibilities?"

Ariock folded his arms. He expected a reasonable explanation, and he was not going to beg for it.

The audience sounded restless. They whispered about "Torth with powers" and "should just kill them." It seemed they agreed with Ariock. They had been waiting for Garrett to show up and explain the prisoners in the cage.

Garrett milked the anticipation. Finally, he pointed at the Rosies. "We have two vessels there."

The prisoners looked uneasy. The facial expressions made them look a lot more human.

"And . . ." Garrett pointed toward Thomas. "We have the means to turn them into zombified bio-robots who will do whatever we tell them to do."

Thomas sat in his purple hoverchair, withered and physically helpless. The glare he aimed toward Garrett was defiant.

"No." Thomas said that very emphatically.

Garrett turned to Ariock, as if the boy's refusal was insignificant. "You need to understand the scope of the problem we face. We can't afford to ignore a weapon. The Torth Empire is poised to invade Earth."

"What?" Ariock went on alert all over again.

"Exactly," Garrett said. "We're safe here for a few days, thanks to you. But Earth is in danger. We can't fight the whole Torth Empire unless we're willing to use every weapon in our arsenal."

Did he really believe that Thomas was a weapon?

Earth.

Ariock glanced at Vy and saw an echo of his own concerns in her face. Except she must be far more worried. Her mother and foster siblings lived in the Hollander home. That might be the first place the Torth invaded.

Ariock supposed he should have guessed that the Torth Empire would extend a tentacle in that direction. The Torth could afford to throw away ships and soldiers, just as a means to distract Ariock. They could do whatever they wanted. They owned everything in the galaxy, except for whatever scraps Ariock managed to steal from them.

"Two zombies isn't much," Garrett said in a tone of admission. "But it's a proof of concept. We ought to see whether the boy can zombify two at a time."

"I can't," Thomas said, seething. "And there are better ways to fight the Torth."

"We should see if zombies retain their combat reflexes," Garrett said. "And when the inhibitor wears off? I'm really curious as to whether they can access their Yeresunsa powers when they're brain damaged."

The assembly stirred with unease.

"The Torth need to fear us." Garrett rubbed his hands together in gleeful anticipation. "There's no question at all. We need to do this."

But Thomas was not alone in his refusal. Everyone in the assembly looked hesitant or outright dismayed. Voices raised in protest.

Before anyone could raise a coherent objection, however, they were distracted by a violent, wet thud from the direction of the cage.

Ariock gawked in disbelief. Had one of the prisoners just slammed the other's skull against the bars?

The injured woman slumped, insensate. Blood poured from a wound in her forehead. Her head looked dented.

She did not fight or move while the male prisoner used a small metal stick to puncture her neck. Twice. He worked with businesslike efficiency. Her blood spurted out.

"No!" Garrett rushed toward the cage, but he seemed to remember they were Torth, and he skidded to a halt before he could enter their ranges of telepathy. It would be foolish to allow them to soak up secrets.

While the female Rosy lay dying, the male wasted no time in puncturing his own throat in the exact same way. The metal piece jutted out of his throat. He left it there.

His defiant glare faded into a dull, unseeing glaze.

Ariock saw that the male's chest plate hung loose. There was a missing buckle. That must be the weapon the male Rosy had used to stab his partner and then himself.

"Crap." Garrett sounded as if he was watching an innocent boxing match rather than a violent murder-suicide.

Thomas spoke into the silence. "They knew better than to let me twist their minds."

Ariock stared from the prisoners to Thomas. Was he serious?

Maybe there was time to save the life of the male prisoner. The female was dead. Ariock sensed her lack of life spark. But the male's was guttering, and if Ariock acted fast . . .

Instead, he stood immobile.

Alashani warriors carried poison pills. If captured, they would kill themselves as an alternative to allowing a Torth to scan their minds and learn where their families lived. Were these brazen deaths a Torth equivalent of the Warrior's Pact?

That was what it looked like.

It seemed impossible. Torth did not feel joy or love. They lacked families. They drugged themselves with tranquility meshes. Surely the Torth did not care deeply about anything?

The male's life spark died.

"They took the quickest path to brain death," Thomas explained, perhaps in answer to someone's unspoken question. "The Majority might have guided them, but they agreed to die. They preferred death to zombification."

He made that sound reasonable.

Perhaps it was.

Ariock gazed at the corpses, each one slumped and sightless, glistening with drying blood. Torth were trained from birth to obey the Majority. If the Majority had pressured these Rosies to die, then of course the Rosies would obey. They had probably obeyed without a hint of protest.

They had done it as a protest against losing their free will.

How ironic.

Ariock turned toward Garrett and Thomas. If either of them had brilliant ideas about how to defeat the Torth Empire, then he was interested. But it seemed a horde of zombified minions was unfeasible.

He thought that was probably a good thing.

After all, wasn't his side of the war fighting against the injustice of slavery? Ariock wanted to win battles by using his powers to smash armies. Somehow, that seemed more noble than asking his friend to warp Torth prisoners into mindless minions.

On the other hand . . .

How else was he supposed to defeat a galactic empire with countless worlds and trillions of slave masters?

"We need to discuss things," Ariock said, facing the mind readers on his side.

CHAPTER 11

DESPERATE MEASURES

"There's nothing to discuss." Garrett used his powers to make a lit cigarette appear between his fingers. "We'll grab more Torth prisoners. Things will go differently in the next battle."

Fortunately, Thomas had a challenging look. "What you're suggesting is wrong."

Ariock nodded.

He was dismayed to see how many albinos and other leaders looked toward Garrett with respect. They liked the idea of zombified Torth minions. Well. Perhaps they simply appreciated the idea of having a plan, no matter how flawed and shaky it was?

"The boy is right." Evenjos sounded regal. "His power is evil."

Everyone stared at her.

She looked self-righteous, arms folded as if she had accomplished something. Everyone knew she had abandoned the city during its hour of need. How dare she show her face to an assembly of battle leaders?

"Look," Garrett snapped, "desperate times call for desperate measures. We can't stick to some idealized notion of good and evil when the Torth won't restrain themselves." He gestured at the corpses in the cage. "That was totally my bad. I should have prevented them from reaching for things. Next time, we'll make sure our prisoners don't self-destruct before we can—"

"Have you learned nothing from my tale?" Evenjos said. "Audavian was a monster." She pointed toward Thomas. "Set him to rampage, and he will make this universe worse than it already is."

That was quite an insult. Ariock braced himself to stop a fight.

Oddly, though, it was not Thomas who looked offended, but Garrett. The old man's face clouded over. The sky darkened, clouds thickening to hide the sun.

"She's right." Thomas gave Evenjos a look of respect. "Zombifying Torth is no better than what they do to slaves. It's worse."

"It is prophecy." Garrett sounded stony and definite.

Exasperated, Ariock turned to his great-grandfather. Was he really trying to follow Ah Jun's prophecies? Or was he merely irritating everyone?

"This is a war," Garrett said in a holy tone. "If you want to have an attack of consciousness, that's fine, but it won't last. Prophecies cannot be denied."

He smoked, apparently untroubled by the prospect of removing people's free will.

"All I'm suggesting," Garrett said, "is the surest path toward winning this war." He gave Ariock a look of forced patience. "We are the heroes of prophecy. Think about it. Each of us has a unique skill that the Torth have trouble countering. You can mass-teleport. No one else can do that."

Ariock eyed Garrett with wariness, unsure what point he was building up to.

"Evenjos can shapeshift," Garrett went on. "I can spy in the Megacosm. And the boy?" He pointed. "That boy can twist minds to do his bidding. That is valuable. It is not something we should let go to waste."

"Thomas is not a weapon." Ariock didn't care if he sounded brutal. He didn't care that even the whispered conversations fell silent. Why was it so hard for his friends to give each other mutual respect?

"If Thomas says no," Ariock said, his shadow covering Garrett, "then you will respect that."

Garrett gawked up at him for a second. Then he closed his mouth, thwarted.

But surely the old man must understand that no one in Encampment City was an interchangeable weapon or tool? Thomas was not expendable. He was not property. Ariock was no longer a chained-up gladiator, and he would not let Thomas be mistreated that way, either.

"You know what?" Thomas spoke from behind Ariock. "It's fine. Garrett has perfectly valid concerns."

Ariock turned, trying to read Thomas's face.

"I do need to address how we're going to fight the Torth." Thomas gave a tight-lipped smile. "Will you assemble a war council? Tomorrow morning. Over on that hilltop." He gestured with his chin. "We'll talk strategy."

Vy touched Thomas's small hand. "You sure?" She sounded concerned. "I thought you wanted to talk with Ariock one-on-one first."

Ariock remembered Vy mentioning that to him.

"I've changed my mind." Thomas eyed Garrett in a defiant way, as if sizing up an opponent for a duel.

"Are you sure?" Ariock knelt in front of the hoverchair, putting himself near eye level with Thomas. He didn't want to loom. He searched for words, wanting to apologize on behalf of the Dovanack family. Garrett was difficult to wrangle.

No. He was worse than difficult. He was abusive, and Ariock would not tolerate abuse aimed at a disabled child.

"Garrett will back off," Ariock said firmly. "No one will force you to do what you don't want to do. I promise."

Thomas's expression softened. "I appreciate that." He hesitated. "I like working behind the scenes, but I think I need to get out of my comfort zone. Let's discuss my ideas in public." He gave Ariock a look of significance. "Take today to rebuild and regroup."

They could use a day for funerary processions. The Alashani wanted to honor their dead warriors.

"Tomorrow morning," Thomas said, "gather the leaders and meet me. I have a plan."

Ariock straightened. He wanted to demand answers right now, but Thomas was already floating away. It would be rude to chase after him.

And perhaps imprudent?

Thomas had a plan. That was good enough, for a day.

The assemblage chatted and whispered, glancing at the gruesome corpses of the two prisoners. A few turned away in horror. Premiers tapped Jinishta on her purple-mantled shoulders, hinting that they wanted her to take charge, but she brushed them off.

The only people who had taken this scene into stride were, unsurprisingly, the mind readers.

Garrett tapped ashes off his cigarette. "We'll see who gives better advice at this so-called war council."

"Will you just . . ." Ariock forced himself to soften his tone. "Leave Thomas alone?"

"For one day? I can manage that." Garrett tossed away his cigarette. "If you want to listen to him, that's your prerogative. But he's trying to weasel out of doing the work we need from him. Sooner or later, that will become clear, even to you. We can't avoid prophecy."

Prophecy, prophecy, prophecy. Ariock wanted to snap, but he figured they could both use time to cool down. He glared. Garrett got the hint and stalked away.

Good.

Ariock knew that they ought to learn better ways of respecting each other. He reminded himself that Garrett had schemed to bring down the Torth Empire since before the rest of them were born. The old man had spent a lifetime in pursuit of that goal. Was it any wonder that he had developed unshakable opinions on how it should be done?

If only he would be less . . . well . . . stormy.

The assembly broke apart, with people going off in various directions. Vy lingered, waiting for Ariock. Evenjos also seemed to be waiting for him.

Ariock looked from Evenjos to Vy. Could he get in a quick word with Evenjos before he found refuge with Vy? He wanted to learn what would make the former empress a reliable partner in combat. He had no desire to shame her publicly, but he did need to understand why she had failed to fight.

If only he could sneak through the dissipating crowd. Too bad he was sized like a nussian, not an ummin.

Evenjos made the decision for him. She approached with a look of shame.

"I fled," she admitted. "I am sorry."

Ariock had not expected Evenjos to admit fault so readily. He tried to guess her motives.

"It is just . . ." Evenjos cringed, as if filled with guilt. "I have never willingly gone into battle. I am unused to it."

Ariock tried to work up some sympathy, but her excuse just wasn't good enough. Evenjos had enough power to destroy enemies with a thought. Did she think battles were a joke? Was life just a series of playful games to her?

Ariock remembered what it felt like to be powerless. He had been terrified the first time the Torth pitted him against enraged alien beasts. That zoo-like stench still haunted his nightmares, along with that horrible silent audience, their eyes tracking his every move.

That first time, when an alien beast had pawed the ground and lowered its massive head, Ariock had felt sure he would die a violent death. He had seen madness in its bloodshot eyes. He had lacked weapons, unless one counted the iron hooks in his forearms. And his size.

"I am afraid of the inhibitor." Evenjos spoke as though a confession had been ripped out of her.

Ariock didn't believe her. After all, Evenjos could harden her skin to diamond armor if she felt like it.

"I am dust," Evenjos whispered. "This body you have gifted me with"—she gestured to herself—"is sustained only by my power. It is my sixth-magnitude power. Somatic, yes, but it still requires a trickle of power."

She wrapped her arms around herself. She was trembling.

A chill ran down Ariock's spine. If he understood what Evenjos was implying . . . well. The inhibitor was dangerous to any Yeresunsa, but for Evenjos, it was dangerous on a different level. If she lost her powers, then for her, death would be instantaneous and total.

"Your mind can't be preserved?" Ariock asked.

She shook her head.

Ariock now regretted his thoughtless assumption that Evenjos could take the same risks he took. She was a being of sheer willpower. Was it any wonder she was frightened? Could she even afford to lose consciousness?

"I have not required sleep since you resurrected me," Evenjos confirmed. "I dream while I am awake. And I fear that losing consciousness means death."

She was fragile. Exceedingly powerful, yet exceedingly delicate.

"I understand," Ariock said.

He would need to do better. Evenjos was a person, not a cog or a weapon. If he wanted her to become a warrior, then he had to respect her limits and her needs. Every warrior deserved that much respect.

"I assume your life as an empress didn't include combat training?" Ariock guessed.

Evenjos looked shy. "No," she admitted. "The first time I ever fought was after you resurrected me."

That explained a lot. Her life had been dancing, banquets, and imprisonment.

But that last part was important. Evenjos was a victim of the Torth as much as anyone in their camp. She had suffered for unimaginable eons. Of all people, she deserved kindness and patience, perhaps more than anyone else.

Evenjos sidled closer to Ariock. She clung to his arm and whispered, "I would be grateful for any tutelage you can give me."

"I'm not qualified to teach." Ariock stepped away.

He had much to learn himself. Garrett seemed quite effective in the Torth-killing department. Perhaps both he and Evenjos could use lessons from the old man?

He became aware of Vy's wistful expression.

She stood alone, at a respectful distance, waiting. But her expression . . . that looked like how Ariock used to feel when he had watched perfect people acting out perfect lives on TV.

Did he want his friends to respect each other? Well, then, maybe he ought to stop being such an inconsiderate oaf.

Ariock pulled free from Evenjos's grasp and went to Vy without a backward glance.

CHAPTER 12

A LEG TO STAND ON

Alien salamanders crooned in the grass beneath a huge sky streaked with purple clouds. The open plains probably looked desolate to people who had spent their entire lives in slave tunnels or urbanized caves.

But to Vy? It was freedom.

She inhaled mountain air. She used to feel claustrophobic in New Hampshire, where dense forests blocked almost any view. Maybe that was why she had been so obsessed with pilot training, with big skies, and with the weather.

"You've probably already heard," she said to Cherise. "But there's going to be a war council tomorrow morning."

She took care not to mention Thomas. She figured Cherise would refuse to come if she heard that her ex–best friend had summoned all the battle leaders. It was best to make it sound as if Ariock was in charge of everything.

"Ariock invited you," she said.

In actuality, Ariock was busy attending funeral processions and helping people rebuild shelters. Pung had volunteered to arrange tomorrow's meeting. But Vy felt sure that Ariock would have invited Cherise if he were to handle the invitations.

"Mmm." Cherise sounded uninterested. She made a mark on the slate in her lap. Her black hair was tied back in elaborate braids, and she looked stylish in a tunic that bared her shoulders.

A heap of slates awaited Cherise's attention, each one etched with alphabet letters. It looked like she was doing the equivalent of grading papers.

The two of them used crates as makeshift chairs beneath an open sky. Cherise's school had no walls, no desks, no textbooks. When class was in session, the students—aliens, of course—sat on blankets spread over grass, with a view of alpine slopes abloom with yellow wildflowers.

"How come I never see Alashani students here?" Vy asked, trying to open up a conversation that might engage her foster sister.

She regretted her question as soon as she saw Cherise's pained look.

"Sorry," Vy said. "I didn't mean to be offensive."

"No, it's okay." Cherise sighed, then seemed to choose her words with care. "They just don't consider literacy to be worthwhile. The only Alashani who read and write are clerks and tax collectors. That's it." She looked ashamed. "And those would want to learn their own alphabet. Not mine."

"Ah." Vy recalled that Cherise was dating an illiterate Alashani warrior, and she didn't want to make any comments that might accidentally sound judgmental. She searched for a change of subject.

It felt good to sit. She rubbed the amputated part of her thigh. It ached and chafed where it met the peg leg, no matter how much padding she used, no matter what straps she secured it with.

"Anyway," Vy said, "can you get someone to substitute teach your morning class? I think they might discuss Earth at the war council. We should both be there."

"No, thanks." Cherise sounded wistful.

Vy studied her, wondering why she was refusing. "Why not?"

Cherise adjusted her glasses. "I don't think it's my place. I'm not a battle leader."

Vy was taken aback. "You're a leader, though. More than I am."

"Am I?"

"Well, yeah!" Vy wondered why she had to explain. "I guarantee, you'd be welcome there. And if anyone gives us crap? Ariock will give them a look, and they'll stop."

She waited for her foster sister to cave in. Cherise must be curious, at least, about what the next battle might entail. Everyone in Encampment City felt unsettled and eager to find out what was going to come next.

"Well . . ." Cherise hesitated, her tone apologetic. "I mean, Flen told me he isn't welcome at the war council."

"It's not that he isn't welcome," Vy said. "It's just, we can't invite the entire city." She made her tone gentle, but she wanted to offer a clear explanation. "I think Jinishta doesn't want to show favoritism to one of her warriors above all the others, based solely on who he's friends with. I mean, who he's dating."

There were more than a thousand warriors. That was a thin slice of the refugee population, but it was still too many to crowd upon that hilltop and expect to hear what was being said. Besides, the rank-and-file warriors had duties around the city. They were needed.

"If he can't go," Cherise said, "I would rather not go."

Perhaps Cherise was acting admirably, showing solidarity in support of her man? But Vy saw a hint of regret in her eyes.

"Did he ask you not to go?" Vy said it teasingly, because the idea was ridiculous. People spoke highly of Flen. He was always nuzzling Cherise and buying gifts for her. If he was the type who would throw a fit just because his girlfriend got a perceived privilege that he lacked . . .

"No." Cherise laughed, as if to dismiss the idea. But it sounded forced.

Vy searched her gaze.

Cherise grew serious. "Vy, he's going through a lot right now. He's mourning the loss of his family. And his world. Plus, he's adjusting to the whole idea of . . ." She gestured at the mountains, their snow-capped peaks stark white in the sunset. "This."

Alashani were terrified and awestruck by even the mildest of weather. They exclaimed over breezes. They screamed and ran around in circles if there was a light misting drizzle. Alashani scholars spent hours debating the nature of clouds.

"I don't need to be there." Cherise picked up another slate from the pile of student work. "I'm not sure I want to be a deciding factor in the fate of Earth, anyway, if that's what they're going to talk about. Why should I get to speak for seven billion people?" She etched a grade and picked up the next slate. "Just tell me what gets decided. Okay?"

"Okay." Vy stood and offered Cherise a warm smile and a hug. "I'll let you know how it goes."

Cherise hugged Vy back, not self-conscious at all. "I just hope we don't get flooded with human refugees on top of everyone else."

That was too upsetting to contemplate.

"By the way," Cherise said with a sparkle in her eyes, "Flen is learning to stir-fry. He said you and Ariock are welcome to come by for a meal, any time."

Vy smiled at a mental image of moody Flen prancing around a rustic cook fire. "Thanks. Maybe we will." She just hoped Flen didn't use mushroom flavoring. She doubted Ariock would eat anything cooked by an Alashani, at least not any time soon.

After a round of goodbyes, Vy hiked into the city proper, through winding, chaotic, overcrowded grass-and-mud streets. Lanterns at the openings of stalls added a glow. Children darted between shelters, screaming in delight as they chased each other around lumbering nussians and rickshaws.

Everyone knew that Vy was dating Ariock. People gave her warm smiles. Some of them even bowed, as if she was a princess.

She had the equivalent of an open line of credit at any bazaar or merchant's stall. But Vy didn't want to shop. She had no permanent home, no place to hang clothes, no walls to decorate.

She tried not to miss the Hollander home.

And her mom.

The prospect of visiting Earth was a real possibility, now that Ariock could teleport across the galaxy. Unlike Garrett, Ariock could bring passengers. He could bring an entire army if he wanted to.

But visiting Earth came with a horde of dangers. For instance, what if the Torth decided to use Vy's mom as bait for some scheme?

Or . . . what if Vy decided that she loved home too much to ever leave it again?

She was sorely tempted to get a real prosthetic to replace her ivory peg leg. Walking on grass and mud was painful, especially after a few hours. But if she got one, she would be tempted to visit her mom. And her friends. And her foster siblings. What if she could not resist warning the people she loved about the risk of alien invasion?

What if her warnings actually triggered the Torth to invade?

Vy forced her worries aside. She refused to let her mind gnaw on the future or the past, or anything she could not affect. She reminded herself to stay grounded in the present.

She limped toward the elite stalls.

Not that she and Ariock actually slept together. Vy blushed. On the starship, she had overheard a couple of albino maidens tittering about how—or if—the messiah had sex. There had been a lot of giggly insinuations and sneaky glances toward Vy.

Half of those insinuations were too embarrassing to speak out loud, let alone to Ariock. The other half . . . well, hmm.

Maybe his size wouldn't be the big problem she was worried it would be?

"Vy?"

She turned, and there was Ariock, ducking beneath a rope of laundry.

Vy grinned. "I didn't expect to see you this early." She had figured Ariock would be busy elsewhere, reviewing cargo shortages with Councilor Deschuba or practicing combat with Garrett. He had a million things on his agenda.

"Nope." He sounded almost mischievous. "I have a surprise gift for you."

"Oh, really?" That was so unusual, Vy studied his face. She had to crane her head back. Normally, she made a point of not noticing his size, but when he was standing this close? He was a wall encased in woolens. He blotted out the sky.

"Do you have fifteen minutes?" he asked.

"Uh . . ." Vy said, uncertain, as he gently clasped her shoulders. "Sure?"

Her ears popped. She smelled ozone. She felt dizzy for a moment, and only the huge hands around her back and shoulders kept her from stumbling.

The sounds of Encampment City were gone.

The light was different. It was daytime. Alien songbirds warbled in trees.

They stood in a primordial cloud forest.

Vy pushed away from Ariock and limped in a circle. Brightly colored little beasts, like reptilian hummingbirds, flitted amid ferns and tropical flowers. A distant waterfall misted a rocky gorge.

"Where are we?" Sometimes Vy wasn't sure whether to feel awestruck or afraid of the things Ariock could do.

"Just a different continent. I wanted us to have privacy." Ariock cupped his hands and focused on his palms, brow furrowed.

A feminine leg appeared in his open hands.

"I made a leg for you," he said proudly.

Vy gaped at the prosthetic. It looked like it was fabricated from some sort of high-tech polymer. The thigh cap might fit comfortably around her amputated limb.

"Well, okay, Thomas engineered it," Ariock amended. "I would never figure out something this elegant on my own. But I asked him for the help."

Vy could not stop staring at the well-crafted prosthetic. This must have taken Thomas and Ariock a while to make. Thomas would have had to project holographic blueprints. He would have described the materials and articulated every mechanical aspect of the prosthetic. Then Ariock would have needed to locate those materials and teleport them. Then assemble them. Altogether, they had probably spent at least twenty minutes hyperfocused on this task.

She was so stunned, she couldn't think of what to say.

"The joints work really well." Ariock demonstrated, bending the leg's knee. It bent naturally and stayed in place. He unscrewed the top part of the prosthetic and offered it to Vy. "Want to try it?"

Vy cradled the section. It was hollow, which made it lightweight.

"Garrett taught me how to teleport things without transferring my whole body," Ariock explained. "So I can import things to wherever I am."

He nodded to the ground behind Vy, and she turned. There was a cushioned stool that looked handcrafted by some Alashani merchant.

Vy did not question it. She sat.

Ariock showed her how to attach the new prosthetic, with adjustable bands designed for comfort. While Vy unstrapped her old peg leg, Ariock said, "Thomas already wants to redesign it. He said he can make a prosthetic that integrates with your neuromuscular system, but we don't have the resources here. This was the best we could do. For now."

Vy stretched out her thigh, allowing Ariock to tighten the prosthetic into place. This new leg was beyond price. Even if Thomas did invent a better one, she would treasure this gift that Ariock and Thomas had built together.

"Stand up?" Ariock made that an invitation.

Vy stood.

The joints were definitely designed by a supergenius. The prosthetic had springiness in the knee and ankle joints, bending and straightening in a natural, intuitive way.

She wanted to test it by walking, but Ariock knelt and rolled up her woolen legging. "I need to adjust its fit. I'm going to mirror the dimensions of your natural leg."

He focused on her lower body. Vy felt her stance become more natural and even, her weight better distributed, as Ariock custom-fitted the prosthetic to her.

"This is incredible," she said softly.

"Do you want it to be the color of your skin?" Ariock indicated the prosthetic, which was an artificial white. "I can do that. Thomas gave me a pigmentation tutorial. The lighting here should help me make it look natural."

Vy felt overwhelmed, unsure how she could thank him. "I guess? . . . Sure."

"You can change your mind later if you want." Ariock was already at work, altering the color of the prosthetic. Vy watched her new leg take on the hue of living flesh.

"And . . ." Ariock held out his hand, and a pair of ornate boots appeared. "New boots."

Vy didn't know how to express what she was feeling. Ariock didn't even seem to know how amazing he was. "You're a miracle."

"I had these commissioned." Ariock helped her tug on each boot. "I hope you were ready for new footwear."

"This is more than a gift. This is life-changing." Vy leaned forward. Since Ariock was kneeling, she was able to dart in and kiss him on the lips. "Thank you."

Ariock looked startled.

Vy kissed him again. This time she lingered, her skin tingling where it touched his.

After a moment, though, Vy began to think about how unrestrained Ariock could get.

His extreme care around her was visible. It was a wariness in his eyes, a tension in the way he moved. In battle, though . . .

Vy had seen Ariock carelessly pick up huge men—Torth Red Ranks in heavy armor—and literally throw them. Or smash their skulls. Or step on them and grind them beneath his feet.

When Ariock leaned into the kiss, she pulled away.

"You're amazing." She gave him an apologetic look that felt both feeble and inadequate.

But.

Vy knew that her tingly feeling was in peril. She wanted greater intimacy, but she wasn't ready to test her own limits. Sex had always been a far-off potential in her life. She didn't want it to be a casual game, fraught with worries and risks.

That was why she had never gone there. Her boyfriends in college and high school had been experimental flings, not deep romances, and the idea of close and sweaty intimacy with them had not been enticing.

Ariock, she thought, was more than just a casual boyfriend. They tended to stay up all night talking to each other, filling each other in on books the other would like, or movies they wished they could watch together, or personal tidbits. Ariock missed the same TV shows and music she did. They were both fascinated by each other's weirdnesses.

But the risk factor was . . . well. It was large.

Probably enormous.

"I'm going to test out my leg!" Vy jumped away before Ariock could kiss her again.

He looked chagrined. But it was a gentle chagrin, since he was as restrained as ever. Soon they were both laughing as Vy got used to her new prosthetic.

CHAPTER 13

TITANIC RESOLVE

"Where is Thomas?" Ariock asked.

The war council seemed fully assembled. There were a lot of albinos. They stood in groupings, their wide-brimmed hats and bonnets giving them a mushroomlike appearance. Thirteen premier warriors stood apart from all the councilors, quivers full of spears slung over their Yeresunsa mantles. Perhaps they anticipated sudden violence in the midst of a civil meeting?

The nussians also looked ready for anything. As battle captains, they were also overrepresented.

Ariock supposed he could not fault the leaders for their wariness. Garrett and Evenjos stood on the rocky dome of the hilltop. Everyone else encircled them, which meant Garrett was probably running this meeting.

"Come on up here, Ariock!" Garrett said in his booming voice. He beckoned with both hands. "I want to discuss a few things before the boy shows up."

As if Thomas was just a nuisance.

Next to Ariock, Vy squeezed his hand and then let go. That was a vote of confidence.

It seemed all Ariock ever got were unearned votes of confidence. Chieftains, elders, and premiers watched him lumber toward the hill's crown. How many of them believed that they were following an actual messiah? Did any of them believe it?

Ariock felt like a fraud. He could not even wrap his head around the astronomical number of slaves who needed to be set free throughout the galaxy. Quadrillions. The number was so huge as to be nonsensical. His idea of his own limits was sketchy, but he knew that this war was likely to turn into a bloodbath—with his side the losers.

But what did he know, really?

He was only twenty-three. Perhaps this war council would enlighten him.

"We need to decide what our next steps should be." Garrett spoke like an orator. "You're all a part of this." He bowed, turning in a circle in order to acknowledge every battle leader. "This is your future as much as ours. We're not going to make any decisions that go against your needs."

He was definitely playing to the assemblage.

Ariock could not object to the sentiment, though. He agreed. These refugees had lost their homes, their loved ones, and their sense of control over their own destinies. They should reclaim some of that. They needed to feel as if they had at least some control.

Ariock could see their stony expressions grow more open and accepting. Garrett sounded like an Alashani. He signaled, in all kinds of subtle and obvious ways, that he had emotions. That he wasn't a heartless *rekveh*. That he was on their side.

"The Torth had a goal when they attacked us," Garrett said. "And they'll have the same goal again. Specifically, they want the boy."

Ariock tensed. If this was going to turn into an angry rally against Thomas, he meant to stop it before it got started.

"The boy is the weakest of the four of us"—Garrett's gesture included Ariock and Evenjos, as well as himself—"and the Torth consider him the most dangerous. Therefore? We need to keep him hidden. The Torth are concealing their supergeniuses. We ought to do the same."

Ariock supposed that made sense.

"Why can't we just flee?" someone shouted.

Murmurs of agreement.

Evenjos suddenly grew taller. She attained the colors of a storm, which effectively drew everyone's attention. "That is wise," she said in a grand tone. "We should flee to another galaxy."

Garrett looked at her sideways.

"This universe is bigger than anyone knows," Evenjos said, majestic. "The Torth are limited to one galaxy, but we are not. Ariock has the unprecedented power to mass-teleport. He can take us somewhere unknown to the Torth Empire. Someplace they cannot reach."

She had a point.

The Torth leaped from solar system to solar system by using a poorly understood network of space wormholes known as temporal streams. According to Thomas, the streams had been created by an extinct alien civilization. Perhaps the Jodinak Empire? In any case, the Torth Empire forbade research into temporal streams and faster-than-light travel, so they lacked the knowledge to create new ones. They had never discovered any that led to another galaxy.

Garrett glared at Evenjos from beneath bushy eyebrows. "Ariock cannot mass-teleport quadrillions of slaves off hundreds of millions of planets. It's too much."

That sounded like nightmare material. Ariock could evacuate planets, but each time, he would be drained and depleted and helpless. How many times? He would need decades. Centuries.

"Even if he could," Garrett went on, "how could he find enough uninhabited worlds to support that population? He would need to explore an entire new galaxy. Oh, and large populations require infrastructure and agriculture. If Ariock just drops them off, they'll be doomed to a slow death by starvation." He paused, then spoke in a tone of conclusion. "What you're suggesting is unfeasible."

Evenjos remained proud and unmoved. Ariock hoped the rest of the assembly would drop the idea, but instead, they began discussing ways to make it work.

One of the warriors said, "Why are you speaking of rescuing slaves, Jonathan Stead?"

Another said, "We do not owe quadrillions of slaves a rescue."

"The Lady of Sorrow speaks wisdom."

"She wants to protect us."

Dozens of albinos murmured in agreement.

No one else looked happy, though. Nussian captains snorted. The former slaves in the assembly were relatively few in number, but they all looked dismayed.

Vy sat next to Kessa, sharing the same boulder as a seat, and she wore the same burdened look.

Ariock could guess why. The entirety of the human race was slated for enslavement.

If Cherise were at this meeting—and why wasn't she?—then she, too, would have a problem. So would Thomas. None of them would be okay with abandoning Earth to an awful fate.

The wind picked up, cold and cutting, carrying an alpine scent. Ariock feared that he might be losing his serenity without realizing it.

Then he saw Garrett's stormy face.

"If hiding is what you want," Garrett growled, glaring at the leaders, "then I won't stop you." The breeze rippled his cloak. "But I'm done letting the Torth win without so much as a fight. I'm not quitting. For me, this is a fight to the death."

Ariock had been prepared to argue against Garrett. Instead, he found himself inwardly agreeing with the old man. This war was not about surviving anymore. Not for him.

It was about stopping the Torth.

It was about causing the Torth to lose, no matter what it took.

"I sacrificed a lot to get this far," Garrett went on, stabbing the ground with his staff. "So have you. I saw my wife and daughter buried. You've all seen loved ones die because of the aggressions of the Torth."

There were nods of agreement and fierce looks. Jinishta looked chagrined. The warriors watched Garrett with fresh respect. Empathy was a two-way street, and they felt it.

"I've wanted to give up plenty of times," Garrett acknowledged. "Death is easy. You crunch a pill between your teeth, or you scream defiance at a Torth, and then it's over." He pointed toward Encampment City. "But the fight is worth it because of *them*. They have loved ones, too. And do you know why they exist? Why any of us exist? I'll tell you. It's because countless generations have worked to protect and preserve each other against the depravities of the Torth."

Ariock felt keenly aware of those generations. Before he had existed, his father had grown up in an idyllic mansion on Earth. Garrett Dovanack had protected three generations of his family. He had sheltered Yeresunsa whom the Torth Empire would otherwise have murdered.

And before Garrett? There had been a brave Alashani warrior named Eidelwen, who had defied her own culture to protect her baby.

There had also been a renegade Torth, but Ariock preferred not to think about his Torth ancestor. That ancestor—a rapist and murderer who had once been an overseer of the Isolatorium—did not count. Torth were the enemies. That was not what this was about.

What about the generations before Eidelwen?

The Alashani people were albino because they had hidden underground for twenty-four thousand years, suffering through an Age of Chaos, an Age of Starvation, and several genetic bottlenecks. They must have come close to total extinction several times. The ones who existed now were all descended from the hardiest survivors.

A thousand generations of Alashani had lived and died to ensure that exceptional survivors like Eidelwen lived long enough to bear children of their own and protect those children.

The same was true for everyone in this assembly.

Kessa existed because her ancestors had survived a thousand generations of dangerous, degrading slavery. They were the smart ones, the savvy ones, the lucky ones—and also the ones who protected their loved ones and who were, in turn, protected.

"Selfless dedication to your families, and to people who matter," Garrett said, "is what allows people like you and me to exist." His gesture included Ariock. "We all owe our existence to people who cared about the fates of their children and their parents and their siblings. People who were willing to put themselves in danger to protect those they loved."

The albinos in the assembly were clearly reevaluating their goals. Family was a big cornerstone of Alashani cultural values. They understood that some heroes were quiet and unknown, yet heroic nonetheless.

Even Evenjos looked like she was reconsidering her suggestion to flee to an unknown galaxy.

"The slaves of the Torth Empire matter," Garrett said. "They're no less brave and no less worthy than any of us. They've suffered long enough. I owe my life to runaway slaves who were brave enough to flee the Isolatorium with me." He nodded toward Ariock. "Your messiah would not be here if not for that. And he was helped by runaway slaves when he fled the Torth. I will not ignore that. I swore an oath to free everyone oppressed by Torth, and as far as I'm concerned, I've barely begun to fulfill that oath."

Ariock stood straighter. There was a nobility to Garrett that he had not seen until now. His great-grandfather might have faults, but in this moment, Ariock was proud to be related to him.

"What do you think, Ariock?" Garrett looked toward him. "Are you willing to fight for justice and freedom for this galaxy? Is it worth it to you?"

"It's worth it." Ariock walked a few steps to stand next to his own warrior ancestor. His formidable size drew attention, but right now, that was what he wanted. Let everyone see that he agreed with Garrett. This war had a purpose.

If any of these so-called battle leaders wanted to quit, then let them do so. But Ariock would not work for cowards who valued their own safety more than what was right and just. He was done hiding. If he could save people like Kessa, and Weptolyso, and people like his own defiant ancestors, such as Eidelwen . . . then it was not a tough choice for him. A thousand generations had lived and died to ensure he would survive long enough to become a warrior. He would carry on that tradition.

Evenjos gave a thoughtful nod. The breeze shifted her curls against her bare shoulders. "You are right. I stand with you." She stepped closer to Ariock. "I fight with you."

There was a moment of silence while the battle leaders looked stunned. Perhaps they had not had enough time to examine their own core beliefs and values.

But then they came to a collective decision.

They pumped fists in the air, stomped their feet, and their determination was fierce and unanimous. "WE FIGHT!"

"We fight." Ariock felt grim satisfaction now that there was no question of fleeing.

All he needed was a better idea of how to slaughter the Torth while protecting his own population of refugees. He searched the assembly for any sign of Thomas. He recognized Thomas's primary assistant, Varktezo. Was the boy delayed for a reason? Had Garrett said something nasty to him beforehand?

"We need to fight," Garrett said gruffly. "However, I don't see us winning battles unless we are willing to commit all our resources toward victory."

Resources.

Garrett considered Thomas to be a weapon to be used or else discarded as useless. Ariock was careful to keep a tight rein on his temper. But if Garrett insisted on beating this drum, he wasn't going to get any support.

It was too bad that the albinos seemed to consider Garrett to be one of them, despite his mind-reading power. He acted like one of them. He was family.

"Then you counsel retreat, for now?" Evenjos sounded almost hopeful.

All eyes were on Garrett.

"We can steal resources," the old man said. "Slaves. Weapons. Armor. We can make ourselves stronger."

Ariock wondered if adding to his ragtag population would really entail more strength. He didn't think so.

"I see little choice," Garrett said. "Until we gain invulnerability to the inhibitor serum, or some other new weapon, we are at a disadvantage. But we can certainly bolster our forces. And maybe we can exhaust the Torth by harrying their outposts and stealing from them. We will eventually become a force to be reckoned with."

Eventually.

Ariock gazed at the mountain peaks fringed with clouds. Thomas had chosen a magnificent paradise to serve as their base of operations.

"Okay." Ariock tried to force the decision to feel good. He supposed he would need to get used to transferring loads of cargo and large populations from one planet to another. The amount of work was daunting. It seemed inelegant. But it was a start.

"What about Earth?" Vy asked in a soft voice.

Ariock tried to imagine mass-teleporting all humans to safety. Billions of fresh refugees. They wouldn't all mesh well or get along together.

Battle leaders murmured with similar concerns. Ariock overheard a premier warrior say, "There are a limited number of us. How can we protect an ever-growing population?"

Dozens of warriors had died since Ariock showed up. Could the survivors be expected to protect an endless number of shanty towns? Could they heal everyday injuries for a billion refugees? Or trillions? Ariock did not think so.

"I don't like it, either," Garrett said. "But I don't see what choice we have. The boy isn't being cooperative."

A ripple of unease went through the assembly.

Nussians lumbered apart, forming a wide aisle. The rest of the crowd jerked away from Thomas's hoverchair as he glided up toward the rock dome at the center. No one wanted to be within his telepathy range.

"I'm the Wisdom in the prophecies." Thomas's yellow eyes blazed in the sunlight. "So maybe that means you should listen to my wisdom."

He glided to a stop and faced the whole assembly. Ariock was relieved that he remained a respectful distance from Garrett, beyond telepathy range.

"His idea of grabbing more and more stuff," Thomas said, indicating Garrett, "is shortsighted. It's unsustainable. And it means guaranteed death for us."

The clouds overhead thickened, covering up a patch of blue sky. Garrett's mood had clearly darkened.

But Ariock felt secret relief, because Thomas had voiced his exact concerns. He just hadn't trusted himself enough to question Garrett.

"We won't win that way," Thomas said in a tone of finality.

"Do you have a better idea, boy?" Garrett seemed to expect evasion for an answer.

"Yup," Thomas said.

Ariock felt lighter, as if a burden was lifting off his shoulders. He grinned.

Thomas rotated to face him. "Do you think you can keep people quiet until I'm done explaining? Interruptions will be a problem."

Ariock hoped he wouldn't need to gag Garrett. He gave a nod of encouragement. "Go on."

CHAPTER 14

IN FAVOR OF REDEMPTION

After suggestions from Garrett and Evenjos, Ariock felt ready for something different. They probably shouldn't have even started this war council without Thomas.

"Okay." Thomas looked grim, like he meant to weather a hurricane. "Every Torth endures an Adulthood Exam before they're allowed to become a full-fledged Torth. It's a rite of passage, designed to weed out emotions and other supposed flaws. I propose that we offer the Torth a reverse Adulthood Exam."

A few people in the assembly made intolerant murmurs.

"Like theirs," Thomas said, "our exam would select for Torth who have a full range of hidden emotions. But instead of killing them, we'd welcome them."

Ariock wasn't sure he understood.

"We need Torth on our side." Thomas sounded definite. "I'm proposing that we lure them with benefits they can't get on their side. We'll use them for menial labor. And they should be soldiers for us, too. But we'll also offer them a way to rise out of the prison labor system."

Garrett cut in. "What the heck are you talking about, boy?"

Ariock privately had a million questions, as well. Torth wouldn't want to join his side as menial laborers or soldiers. Why would they?

"We'll offer them everything they can't have as Torth." Thomas raised his weak fingers, ticking off items. "Emotions. Friendships. They'll have the freedom to feel joy. To be creative. To pursue happiness. To have sex. To be something other than a Torth." He let his fingers fall. "All that before they even have the possibility of earning their way out of our prison labor system."

His proposal struck the assembled battle leaders like a detonation. There was a heartbeat of dead silence at the impact.

Then a shock wave ripped through the crowd. Everyone spoke at once, shouting to be heard, gesticulating and arguing.

"Torth on our side?"

"That's what he said."

"They'd act as slaves?"

"How is that even possible?"

Garrett wheezed. He seemed to be having a fit of incredulity.

Vy looked excited. She seemed to be considering new possibilities. Kessa frowned in thought.

Ariock remembered thousands of silent Torth watching him in the prison arena, their cold faces as far from human as it was possible for sapient beings to be. Did Thomas honestly believe there were secret renegades in a population like that?

"Are you kidding, boy?" Garrett choked out. "Torth don't care about emotions!"

Thomas gave him a level look. "I believe you've met a few who secretly have a full range of emotions. And . . ." He looked innocent. "Aren't you one?"

Garrett turned purple with rage. If any insinuation could make him go nuclear, it was the accusation of being a Torth. The air pressure dropped. Grass rippled, and thunder rolled. Lightning sparked along Garrett's arms and staff.

"Calm down." Ariock held out a hand, ready to solidify air into a shield for his friends.

Garrett gripped his staff, visibly channeling his anger along its length and into the ground. "You can't trust that boy. Don't you think the Torth know how to cheat on exams? If you give them a way to join us . . . oh, they will! They'll send spies and assassins! This is insanity. We can't let the enemy into our camp."

Ariock inwardly shared that concern. Some Torth specialized in faking being human. The one who had murdered his father—Thomas's nameless mother—had blended in with the human population for months. She must have been good at it.

One of the premier warriors stamped a spear down for attention. "The only good Torth," he said, "is a dead Torth."

Angry mutters of agreement rippled through the crowd.

"Some of them will fake it," Thomas acknowledged. "It's a risk. But we'll mitigate that risk by keeping our enslaved Torth far apart from any assassination targets. They won't be privy to our leadership meetings. If they break our trust in any way—if they attack a former slave, for instance—they'll die. And we'll relegate them to menial labor. They'll support us by cleaning our latrines."

That sounded almost as unbelievable as Torth fighting on Ariock's side of the war.

"Torth serving us?" someone whispered in awe.

"This is pure fantasy." Garrett sounded disparaging. "It's well and good to imagine happy Torth helpers"—he rolled his eyes—"but let's be real here. There aren't more than two renegades in the whole Torth Empire."

Ariock figured that was probably accurate. Non-Torth genetics accounted for Garrett and Thomas going renegade. As for other renegades . . . Thomas's nameless mother, Garrett's nameless father? Torth like those had to be extreme rarities.

"I think you're wrong," Thomas said. "I'm guessing a lot of Torth want to go renegade."

Garrett puffed up. If he were a nussian, he would have been bristling with spikes. "I'm not *wrong*." He made that word a savage mockery. "I've lived undercover as a Torth for twenty years, boy. I know what they are. If Torth had human emotions, they wouldn't vote to torture people to death. They wouldn't own slaves."

Ariock nodded in agreement. Surely Garrett was right about all that.

"Humans have owned slaves," Thomas said pointedly. "Humans have tortured people to death."

"That's different and you know it," Garrett snapped. "Humans know it's wrong!"

"That's debatable," Thomas said. "Anyway, you've owned slaves."

Garrett flushed red with anger. "Gah! I had no choice. Same as you! Every monster story about the Torth is true." He turned to Ariock, pleading for understanding. "They are spineless, soulless, heartless leeches, bent on perverting every good thing that was ever—"

"What about that renegade boy you sent to the Isolatorium?" Thomas broke in.

Garrett sputtered. His eyes bulged.

Ariock frowned, wondering if Garrett was choking on rage or pride. What had Thomas just accused him of doing?

When Garrett found his voice again, he sounded hoarse, as if he'd been smacked in the throat. "How the devil do you know about that? I haven't let you into my range long enough to soak up my recent life!"

"I'm capable of putting two and two together," Thomas said coolly. "Every daily news story during my time as a Yellow Rank is stuck in my mind. There was one particular incident that occurred in NobleShade City on Athpinar. You happened to mention, while we were searching the Isolatorium, that you were on Athpinar when I sentenced Ariock to death."

Garrett swallowed. Clearly, he had not expected anyone to mention the "incident," whatever it was, much less in front of an assembly.

"What happened?" Ariock asked.

"Nothing," Garrett snapped. "It has nothing to do with this discussion. It's not important."

"You're normally a much better liar than that," Thomas said in a sardonic tone, similar to how Garrett normally addressed him.

Garrett could not escape all the speculative stares aimed his way. He plucked a cigarette out of thin air. The end flared, and he inhaled smoke that must be soothing to him.

"All right, so I met one renegade Torth," Garrett told Thomas. "One. So what? Big deal. Flukes happen. I don't see the relevance."

"Humor us," Thomas said in a patronizing tone. "Why don't you explain that incident to Ariock? And to everyone else here?"

Garrett shot Thomas a hate-filled glare.

But he was hiding something, and Ariock felt curious. His great-grandfather kept so many secrets. What was this one about? Something that made him ashamed?

"I'd like to hear it," Ariock said.

"It's completely irrelevant." Garrett's shoulders slumped in defeat, seeing Ariock's hard stare of determination.

Ariock waited.

"Fine." Garrett inhaled smoke from his cigarette. "I lived in NobleShade City for a couple of years. During my time there, a boy from the local baby farm went missing. The whole city went on high alert, searching for him."

"I thought the Torth don't care about their children?" Vy said.

Ariock had the same question. To the Torth, children were just as disposable as slaves. They were not considered people. Torth produced babies through artificial means, and their infants and children were tended in isolated facilities known as baby farms.

Well, perhaps Torth children got some guidance via the Megacosm. But they had no families. They did not feel loved. A Torth child had to pass a battery of mental and emotional tests in order to graduate to personhood, and anyone who failed became an involuntary organ donor.

"They're assets," Garrett corrected. "And in this case, the boy was scheduled to have his Adulthood Exam that week, so a lot of local Torth were preparing to welcome him as a Yellow Rank."

A child so close to adulthood probably seemed somewhat valuable. By that age, he would have proven himself to be mentally robust and emotionally stable, without any of the long list of "flaws" that rendered a Torth child disposable.

"Baby farms are sealed facilities," Garrett went on. "They're just about impossible to break into or escape from. So it's highly unusual for Torth children to disappear. It was a big mystery, and it dragged on for weeks."

"I take it you had nothing to do with it?" Ariock asked.

"Of course not." Garrett looked ancient and sad as he puffed on his cigarette. "I was just as mystified as everyone else. But I wasn't paying much attention. I had other things on my mind."

Such as the book of prophecies. And watching over Ariock.

"Maybe he teleported?" Vy guessed.

"No," Garrett said. "Yeresunsa powers were illegal at that time, remember. Dormant powers that went undetected would have been fine. But a child who exhibited the faintest hint of powers—like clairvoyance, the prerequisite for teleportation—would have been executed right away with no debate."

Unless they happened to be a supergenius with a valuable medical invention. Ariock still marveled that the Torth had welcomed Thomas.

Of course, the upper echelons of Torth society were all secret Yeresunsa, and there must be others. Quite a lot of Torth had dormant powers.

"I was pressured into leading the investigation." Garrett sounded more ashamed than ever. "After all, I was a high rank—a Blue, which is an intellectual rank. I couldn't refuse, you understand. And I thought it would be harmless. I had no idea that the boy was . . . well."

"Go on," Ariock prompted.

"A team of searchers found him in a nearby slave farm," Garrett said. "It turned out the slaves there were hiding and protecting the boy. He'd gone rogue."

"He had emotions?" Ariock guessed.

Garrett gave a curt nod, as if admitting a sordid fact he would rather not acknowledge. "Apparently, the boy believed that he was an Athpinari native in Torth skin. That happens sometimes, you know. Torth children are raised by slaves. Sometimes they develop an affinity for them and imprint on them, substituting the slave caretaker for a mother figure."

Ariock didn't want to feel sorry for Torth. And yet . . . children like that had to be innocent. How many were like that?

"Obviously," Garrett went on, "the childhood tests are designed to weed children like that out of the gene pool. Most of them are killed before they hit puberty. But this particular adolescent was good at hiding his secret emotions. He knew how to fake being a Torth, in other words."

Kessa scrutinized Garrett. "But he was a Torth," she stated. "There is no faking it."

"Well, I suppose." Garrett sounded blustery, like he didn't want to continue the conversation. "Anyway, adolescents like that are rare. They tend to go rogue, hiding or attempting to join underground slave movements."

When Ariock had first escaped the Torth, a village full of ummin slaves had taken risks to keep him hidden. He owed his life to the villagers of Duin. They should have rejected him—and Thomas—as monsters, but instead, the ummins had given them food and shelter. They had gone to great lengths to empty their minds whenever Torth showed up in their area.

And Ariock had repaid them by flying away. They could only cram about one hundred and fifty ummins into the stolen transport, leaving most of the villagers to suffer whatever punishment the Torth Empire deemed fit.

That renegade adolescent Torth must have found a similar village.

With a similar outcome?

"The whole village kept him hidden?" Vy asked. "For weeks?"

Garrett nodded. "They really liked him. It seemed his personal slave had smuggled him out of the baby farm through a garbage chute. Before the boy went into his self-imposed exile from the Megacosm, he absorbed enough info to find his way through the toxic vapor desert—that's a feature of the landscape on Athpinar—to the home village of his favorite slave. There, he was able to talk his way into hiding. The Athpinari slaves put him in a cramped closet. They did their best to keep him safe."

Ariock hoped the kindhearted slaves had not suffered any punishments for showing mercy to a renegade. They must have been brave, to shelter a mind reader. And curious, or else they would not have taken such risks.

He did not even know what an Athpinari slave looked like.

"What happened?" Vy sounded as reluctant as Ariock felt.

"Well." Garrett tapped ashes off his cigarette. "What you would expect."

That wasn't much of an answer. Whatever had happened, Garrett clearly did not want to talk about it.

"You were there," Thomas said. "Weren't you?"

Ariock studied his great-grandfather anew. He saw the way Garrett avoided eye contact with everyone and the way he began to say something defensive, then closed his mouth.

"Why didn't you rescue that renegade?" Thomas asked. "Or any of the slaves?"

Garrett looked like he was struggling with something internal.

"You were right there," Thomas went on, taunting. "You said the Torth Majority elected you to be in charge of the situation. Couldn't you have stopped them from torching that village full of innocent slaves?"

Ariock felt pained. He wanted to ask Garrett if it was true. Had the Torth destroyed the village—had they murdered those slaves—for showing mercy to a renegade?

The answer was plain on Garrett's guilty face.

He really was an awful coward.

"It wasn't possible to save them." Garrett spoke to Ariock, pleading for him to understand. "I wanted to. But a lot of attention was on me, in the Megacosm. I was standing in a spotlight, so to speak. I couldn't show mercy without being obvious about it. And mercy would not be acceptable to the Torth Majority! They would have killed me and torched the village anyway!"

Ariock thought of Duin. At least he had managed to rescue most of the adolescents. He had saved more than a hundred of them.

"You're a powerful Yeresunsa." Thomas leaned forward, watching Garrett with condemnation in his yellow eyes. "You could have smuggled out a few slaves. And you could have saved that renegade Torth boy. You could have waited until he was en route to the Isolatorium and then used your powers to knock down the prison guards. You could have done *something*."

Thomas was right.

And Thomas, of all people, should know. He had done something heroic when he was a Yellow Rank, even when he was on the inhibitor. He had rescued Ariock's mother, Vy, Cherise, Kessa, Weptolyso, Pung, and Ariock himself.

Garrett struggled to look composed but winced as he accidentally burned his finger on the cigarette. "I get your point," he snapped at Thomas. "It's not easy to stand up to the Torth Majority. Fine. Point taken."

That answer did not satisfy Ariock. "Why didn't you do anything?" he asked.

"Let's say I rescued that renegade child," Garrett said. "Then what? Was he supposed to live in my closet for the rest of his life?"

"You could have brought him to Earth," Vy said.

"The kid was a mind reader." Garrett sounded defensive. "How was he supposed to blend in among humans after being raised on a baby farm?"

"He would have given it his best shot," Thomas answered. "He would have done anything to escape dying in the Isolatorium."

A tear trembled in the corner of Garrett's eye.

"You got to grow up on Earth," Thomas said. "Your monster of a Torth father gave you that chance. But you denied it to that renegade child. He's dead now. Because you failed to save him."

Ariock felt sick with disappointment. He wanted his great-grandfather to be a hero, noble and just. Instead . . .

Well. Apparently Torth society corrupted everything and everyone it touched.

Garrett looked broken. "I planned to rescue him."

"That's a lie," Thomas said, merciless. "You were busy acting like a Blue Rank. Hundreds of slaves died in that village, screaming. You went back to your luxury suite like none of it had happened."

The assembly was shocked into silence. They stared at Garrett with unspoken accusations.

But Ariock remembered Garrett saying very similar things about Thomas. Hadn't he? Garrett had accused Thomas of abandoning his friends to slavery and death in order to enjoy his cushy life as a Yellow Rank.

And Thomas had not denied it. He had wept.

Garrett clenched and unclenched his fists, looking helpless and defensive. "You are grossly misrepresenting my role. I would have saved that village. Of course I would have. But the Majority—"

"—makes the rules." Thomas spoke in exact unison with Garrett.

"Everyone else—" Garrett began, and Thomas finished with him, in perfect sync.

"—has to follow."

Only mind readers could achieve such spontaneous unity. The effect caused the assembly to back away, murmuring with unease. They knew that Thomas and Garrett were *rekvehs*, but they did not like such a blatant display of that vileness.

Garrett's shoulders hunched with shame. He hung his head, unwilling to meet anyone's gaze.

"You could have saved them, Yeresunsa," Thomas said.

Thomas had taken over the war council. He had everyone's attention. He was directing their focus, like a maestro conducting a symphony. When he floated to face Ariock, everyone shifted their attention with him.

CHAPTER 15

MILLIONS AND MORE

"You forgave me for the crimes I committed when I was a Torth," Thomas said.

Ariock did not deny it.

"You know it was difficult for me to defy the Majority," Thomas said. "I found it nearly impossible. Now you know the same was true for Garrett."

And that was the whole point.

Ariock could not avoid it. Thomas had publicly humiliated Garrett, but he had done it to make a point. Thomas and Garrett were among the most clever, strong-willed, and stubborn people Ariock knew. If even they could be pressured into cruel obedience by the Torth Majority . . .

Couldn't anyone?

Maybe there were other good people among the Torth.

They might torture slaves, they might torch villages, they might murder people, but some Torth must feel as if they had absolutely no choice but to go along with what the Majority wanted. Those individuals might secretly long for escape. They might grasp at straws, willing to do anything—even clean latrines—for a chance to live apart from the Torth collective and make their own decisions.

"Bah!" Garrett said. "The boy and I are exceptions because we're hybrids. We're not really Torth!"

Ariock thought there was undeniable logic to that argument. Thomas was half human. Garrett was half Alashani. Each had plenty of good reasons to rebel against their mind-reader brethren.

In contrast, real Torth were raised in the uncaring womb of the Megacosm. The few who had the fortitude to rebel and go renegade must be a truly rare phenomenon.

Garrett regarded Thomas with contempt. "We grew up in an emotional society, steeped in the traditions and values of Earth. You can't expect the average Torth to be like us."

"I do expect that," Thomas said. "Look how hard each Torth struggles to be emotionless. They wear tranquility meshes. They are in a state of constant escapism, through the Megacosm, where they travel to exotic places or imagined scenarios. And even with all that effort? A lot of them are edge cases. The Swift Killer can barely hold her emotions in check. The Upward Governess has all kinds of slave-like urges and addictions, which she disguises. And they're not the only ones."

Ariock thought of the silent audiences in the prison arena and wondered. What had really been going on behind those masklike faces?

"Plenty of Torth get pressured into doing horrible things they'd rather not do." Thomas included Garrett in his gesture. "We both did. The Majority of Torth just go with the flow. They follow an influential leader, but their leaders are almost always sociopaths, because their societal devaluing of emotions paves the way for socio-paths to rise to the top."

Ariock had never quite considered Torth society in those terms. Thomas made them sound human.

"Most Torth," Thomas said, "are just struggling to survive. They take pains to avoid thoughts that make them seem too emotional or empathetic. They suppress their humanity."

Garrett threw up his hands. "They're not human!"

Ariock looked from Garrett to Thomas. They, of all people, ought to have an accurate measure of what the Torth were like. Both had lived among Torth. Both were mind readers, clever and astute. How could they disagree about something so basic?

"The Torth deserve a chance for redemption." Thomas floated to his maximum height off the ground, striving to face Ariock. "I'm not saying they shouldn't pay for their crimes. They should. Just as we should. But there should be an end to the payment at some point."

The assembly was full of derisive murmuring, but Ariock tuned them out, wanting to think.

He was paying a debt of guilt himself. His own poor decisions had entailed people's deaths. Vy had had her leg amputated because of him. In leaving Duin, and the Alashani underground, he had upset the scales of justice. He was trying to right that wrong by saving more people than he got killed.

It seemed Garrett was trying to do the same.

And Thomas.

"If you plan to forgive Garrett for his failures," Thomas said, "the way you forgave me . . . I'm begging you to give other Torth that chance."

A chance to be rehabilitated. A chance for redemption. Ariock nodded slowly.

One of the nussian captains rumbled with disgust. "Torth do not offer slaves anything like forgiveness. Why should we be so kind to them?"

Hundreds of leaders aimed accusatory stares toward Thomas, and a furious outpouring began.

"Right? Why should we give them leniency instead of the deaths they deserve?"

"They're Torth!"

"I'll never welcome those vile *rekvehs!*"

"They don't deserve forgiveness!"

A premier warrior jabbed an accusatory finger at Thomas. "He's manipulative scum!"

Inwardly, Ariock knew that it might be impossible for his refugee population to trust millions of random mind readers. It seemed too much to ask.

And was it even worth doing?

He would be infuriating his own army and alienating his own people, not to mention inviting spies and potential assassins into his camp. What for? A handful of extra mind readers on his side?

"Exactly." Garrett looked grimly righteous. "It's not worth it. Everyone in our camp would have to be on guard all the time, terrified of getting their minds read. You want them to live in fear? Why? So we can rescue a bare handful of fluke children?"

"It won't be a handful," Thomas said. "It will be millions."

"Millions?" Garrett gasped. "You have got to be joking."

"Perhaps billions," Thomas said. "And we need to win them over, if we mean to win this war."

He sounded deadly serious.

Several of the battle leaders sputtered with outrage. Eyes bugged out in disbelief. They probably assumed that Thomas was grossly exaggerating, trying to win clemency for people who did not deserve it.

But Thomas never lied. He believed every word he said. Ariock could see it in his eyes.

"They won't join us," Garrett said, obstinate. "Not willingly. Even if a few of them want to, they'd see it as too dangerous."

"Unless," Thomas said, "we offer them protection. And make our side attractive to them."

"Why should we?" someone shouted.

"You want them to clean our latrines," Jinishta stated, skeptical. "How is that attractive?"

The assembly murmured in angry solidarity.

"Look." Thomas's tone became one of concession. "They won't join us now. That's true. But we need to make this offer as soon as possible and give it time to sink into the Megacosm. It should work its way into every Torth's subconscious. And we have to mean it. After we win a few battles, maybe a Torth or two will dare to join us voluntarily. And then a few more. Once the benefits become obvious, a lot more Torth will flock to our side. They'll join us in droves."

Garrett gave him a look of disgusted skepticism. "You're insane."

Droves.

Ariock found himself getting excited about the idea, despite his own skepticism. He had long suspected that some Torth must secretly chafe under all the restrictions of their culture.

Evenjos's quiet voice drew attention. "Do you truly believe that many Torth can be rehabilitated?" She addressed Thomas directly, speaking to him as if he was an ally rather than a frightful monster. "From what I have learned about them, they are beyond salvation."

Thomas rotated his hoverchair to face her. "They are not Formula freaks, Evenjos. At least, they're not the freaks you remember. Yeresunsa powers require a full range of emotions."

Evenjos looked deeply thoughtful.

Ariock, too, had to consider the implications of that statement. Yeresunsa powers did require a nuanced understanding of one's own moods. Ariock felt a sense of stature whenever he widened his awareness. Intense emotions, such as anger or joy, could distort his intentions and push his awareness into a violent storm or a sudden rainbow.

If moods were tied to Yeresunsa powers . . . didn't that imply that quite a lot of Torth were capable of experiencing moods?

"The Torth Majority pressures the Servants of All into suppressing their emotions," Thomas said, "and that hampers their powers. They'll need to get in touch with their emotions if they want to be more effective in battle. That's the case for all those new Rosy Recruits, as well."

Jinishta looked contemplative. So did a number of warriors. They understood the implications.

"Imagine how free they'll feel," Thomas said, "if they don't have to suppress any of that."

Perhaps the Torth would have some incentive for wanting to switch sides.

Ariock found the idea both exhilarating and terrifying. He had a certain level of trust with Thomas and Garrett. He couldn't imagine feeling even remotely friendly toward a Servant of All. The idea was akin to unsealing the lamplit cities of the Alashani underground and allowing sludge serpents and cannibals to mix with good people.

"We'll have rules for them to follow," Thomas said. "The enslaved Torth will not be permitted to enter the Megacosm. Obviously, they won't be allowed to harm anyone. They won't have access to weapons or sensitive information. They must agree to obey and serve any refugee."

Ariock envisioned work crews of Torth, overseen by free aliens who used to wear slave collars.

It was justice.

It might actually work.

A few of the nussian captains grumbled in a positive way. They liked the idea of Torth Servants of All scrubbing their floors and cleaning their latrines. Everyone else, however, remained skeptical.

"Who is going to enforce these laws?" Garrett said, belligerent. "You?"

"Nope," Thomas said. "You."

Garrett looked affronted. He puffed up, bristling with outrage.

Thomas spoke in a placating tone. "You spy in the Megacosm on a regular basis. It will be a cinch for you to detect any info that leaks out of our camp into the Megacosm. We can work together to track down the moles."

"As if that will be easy!" Garrett said, full of spiteful sarcasm. "There will be spies and assassins everywhere. Loads of Torth are willing to sacrifice themselves in service to the empire!"

That was true. Ariock knew it.

But Thomas said, "They'll be working in fields and factories. If they want to fight alongside us, that's a privilege they'll have to earn. Same thing if they want to get close enough to probe anyone's mind. The number of enslaved Torth who get that far will be limited, because earning our trust won't be easy."

Kessa asked the question that was on Ariock's mind. "How will they earn our trust?" She stood on a boulder to be better heard and seen. "I like the idea of Torth serving as slaves," she said cautiously. "But I do not understand how we can ever trust them."

The assembly quieted. A lot of people had the same concern.

Ariock, too, could not imagine allowing mind readers close enough to polish his boots. They could disable him with a pain seizure and stab him. They might soak up his thoughts and then broadcast his secrets all over the Megacosm.

He wasn't going to have Torth slaves.

"I earned your trust," Thomas said to Kessa. "At least a little, I think."

Kessa gave a hesitant nod. "But," she said cautiously, "the circumstances that led to me trusting you were exceptional. You are not an average Torth."

Ariock strongly agreed.

"We cannot extrapolate those circumstances to a widespread exam," Kessa pointed out gently.

Thomas nodded, accepting her criticism. Then he said, "Our exam should take months or years to complete. It should be as close to foolproof as possible, unlike the Torth Adulthood Exam. I figure each penitent Torth will be judged by former slaves."

"Penitent Torth." Kessa tested the phrase and seemed to find it dissatisfying, perhaps unrealistic. "How will they be judged? On what criteria? On what merits?"

Thomas gave her a respectful look. "I'd like to leave that up to you."

Kessa took a quick step back, stunned.

"I respect your judgment, Kessa," Thomas said. "And I trust you to come up with a fair set of criteria for judging whether or not an individual Torth is rehabilitated."

Ariock felt warm with approval. Kessa was an excellent choice. People would trust her judgment of mind readers, whereas they would be very suspicious if Thomas went around pronouncing random Torth as rehabilitated and safe to be near. As a lifelong slave, Kessa was unlikely to let any Torth "graduate" to trustworthy status—unless they proved to be as human as Thomas.

"I do not think I am suited for this." Kessa clicked her fingers nervously. "Please, pick someone else."

"I can think of no one better." Thomas looked at her with sympathy. "I suppose we could nominate candidates, but I know I'm not the only one who thinks Kessa the Wise is the best choice for managing enslaved Torth." He glanced at Ariock, as if seeking approval.

Ariock nodded.

Other battle leaders nodded in favor of Kessa. Weptolyso said, "It should be her."

"Torth stole my child from me," a nussian rumbled. "They murdered her right before my eyes." He stared hard at Kessa, challenging her. "Do you really think they deserve mercy?"

"I have no goodwill for Torth." Kessa shrank away from all the scrutiny aimed her way. "Torth killed the person I loved most. They ripped me away from my family. I nearly died a slave, many times over." She indicated the collar scar around her neck. "What if I decide the Torth must repay their debt by working until they die from exhaustion?"

The grumbling nussian said, "Now that would be justice."

Several premiers stamped their spears in approval. Nussians snorted with agreement. Even the sour people looked more respectful of Kessa.

Thomas faced the assembly with a look of pained empathy. "The Torth should pay for their crimes," he said, acknowledging the point. "And they will. Justice is important. It has to matter. But we can't win Torth to our side if we're just murdering them." He shifted his gaze to Kessa. "There needs to be an end to their enslavement at some point. There must be a goal they can work toward. This will be part slavery and part rehabilitation program."

Kessa wore a considering look.

"Exactly," Thomas said, replying to something Kessa had not said out loud. "Allow them to have a hope of redemption. Set a debt for them to pay, and a way to work off their debt, so they have a goal. Give them that, and allow them to feel emotions. When you're through with them, the Torth will no longer be Torth."

To Ariock, it sounded amazing. Hope coursed through him.

Yet it also sounded ludicrous. He could hardly imagine powerful Servants of All scrubbing floors and harvesting wheat.

Thomas gave a nod. He seemed to be confirming that enslaved renegade Servants of All were, indeed, plausible.

"If we combat the Torth Empire as it exists right now," Thomas said, "in all its galactic strength, that's a guaranteed fail for us. We need to fracture their cohesion. Split them." He hammered a weak fist on his armrest. "Frankly, anything else won't work."

Ariock suspected that Thomas was right about the need to fracture Torth unity. Even Kessa had a light in her eyes, as if she had new ideas.

"The Torth cannot be allowed to continue as they are," Thomas said. "I agree with Garrett on that point." He gave the old man a nod of acknowledgment. "Their society needs to undergo a complete and permanent transformation."

Everyone in the assembly looked as if they agreed on that.

"You're wise, and I trust you to be fair." Thomas bowed his head to Kessa. "Please think on it. If you're willing to take this on, your endeavor will be a big part of shaping a new galactic civilization."

Kessa seemed overwhelmed. "You cannot be serious."

"I never lie," Thomas said.

Torth amnesty. It had been utterly unthinkable an hour ago. Ariock turned the concept over in his mind, searching for hidden flaws. He still couldn't imagine Torth being willing to join his side. Certainly not in droves. It was improbable.

Yet . . . wasn't it worth a try?

They could be killed if they broke any rules. And there was a lot of justice in enslaving the slavers.

Ariock wished he could have rescued the boy Garrett had failed to save. Renegades like that deserved a refuge. In his camp, perhaps they would thrive.

"Okay." Ariock assessed the battle leaders, looking for agreement. "I think this is a good idea."

Vy broke into a wide grin.

"Are we in agreement?" Ariock asked.

"No!" Garrett said.

But no one valued Garrett's opinion on this. Rows of aliens nodded, no doubt eager to dash away and spread news to the rest of the camp. Evenjos also gave a hesitant nod, although she looked as if she was reviewing some part of her ancient past.

"The drawbacks are minimal." Jinishta stamped her spear for attention. "If it fails, we will have enslaved Torth serving our needs. And if it actually works?" She smiled thoughtfully. "Then it is worth it, a thousand times over."

"Yes," Weptolyso said. "I wish to see Torth slaves. I am in favor of this."

Garrett drew himself up, cloak flapping in the wind. He glared at the assembly with consternation. "You're all so focused on this nonsense," he said, "you're forgetting the minor fact that we're about to get walloped by a Torth armada."

Ariock inwardly hated to admit it, but Garrett was pragmatic. The flood of Torth renegades joining his side were a long way away—if that was ever going to happen. The strategy of offering Torth amnesty would do nothing to help his side survive the next battle.

"How can any Torth take our meager little offer seriously?" Garrett said. "We can't protect them."

Not easily. Ariock had enough trouble protecting their current population of refugees.

"Let's say a few of them do secretly wish to join us," Garrett said. "Well, they'd have to be suicidal to outwardly admit it. If they're with us, their brethren will murder them as soon as our backs are turned."

Thomas nodded, the grave look on his face confirming that Garrett's concerns were valid. "We do need to win battles. It's imperative that we smash the Torth, conquer a few hub cities, and send the Majority into a panic."

That sounded amazing.

"We need to be stronger," Thomas went on. "Not only to protect our enslaved penitent Torth, but obviously to keep our freed slaves and our own armed forces safe."

"I don't see us winning any battles," Garrett said. "Not unless you get to work." He jabbed an accusatory finger at Thomas. "Invent some superweapons! And zombify some Torth for us!"

Thomas leveled a disparaging stare toward Garrett. "I'm not just an inventor. I'm an expert tactician. Let me strategize our next few battles, and I guarantee we will win."

A guarantee? That sounded too good to be true.

Garrett looked taken aback.

Ariock leaned forward, eager for genius advice. If he defeated the Torth a few times in a row? Well, that could really change things.

"Now the *rekveh* is our battle commander?" one of the premier warriors said.

"He wants to make every important decision for us," another said, sarcastic. "How noble."

"You know what?" Thomas addressed the crowd. "I have no desire to make the big decisions. That should be left to people better than me." He nodded toward Ariock, then Kessa. "But I'm here to destroy the Torth Empire." His voice went stone-cold. "I won't be part of a losing effort. We do it my way." His yellow gaze flicked over the assembly, particularly everyone who had expressed uncertainty. "Or I'm out."

"Is that a threat?" Garrett sounded strangled. "Is he making a threat?"

"I think it's an ultimatum," Ariock said.

Whether by accident or by design, Thomas had seized control of this assembly with unassailable authority. None of the battle leaders had wiggle room for disagreement.

"I want some respect." Thomas shifted his gaze to Ariock. "Enforced by you."

Ariock had not expected to be called out or to have any demands made of him. But he nodded. If Thomas guaranteed that they could protect planets like Earth, and devastate the Torth, while keeping their own losses to a minimum? Then Thomas deserved all the respect these leaders could give.

"Our next battle will be an overwhelming victory over the Torth," Thomas said, "if you let me plan it. We will have Torth prisoners who will become our slaves and hopefully begin their journey to redemption. They will become penitents."

That was a big enough promise to silence even the Alashani.

Garrett slumped, defeated. "Penitent Torth?" he muttered. "You're dreaming. We're not going to get any takers."

"We'll get millions," Thomas said. "And more."

PART THREE

"Power takes the nicest person and transforms that individual into a tyrant. No one wants to be a tyrant. But everyone, even nice people, want power."

—Unyat clone

TO BRING DOWN GODS

Kessa stared at the unblinking little device Thomas called a camera. It was perched on the armrest of his hoverchair.

The thing was supposed to be devoid of consciousness or sapience. Even so, she felt a sense of many gazes peering at her through its singular eye.

"Release your slaves." Kessa tried to sound certain, but her voice quavered. "I am here to tell you that your reign is at an end. If you harm a slave? You will be killed."

She could not imagine any Torth actually listening to her, much less obeying her. It was absurd. The rich, embroidered garments she wore only emphasized the scar around her neck. Anyone could see that she was just a disobedient slave.

"You need to be more self-assured," Thomas said, popping out from behind the camera. "Stand up straight and make them believe it. This is the only warning they're going to get."

That almost seemed unfair.

"The ones who ignore you will regret it," Thomas said. "And their mental orbiters will learn a lesson. And then the next time you speak in public, Torth will listen."

"You want me to do this more than once?" Kessa trembled. She'd assumed that Thomas had chosen her as the spokesperson only because he planned to invade New GoodLife WaterGarden City. There, Kessa used to be a respected elder in the slave Tunnels. She had left behind many friends. The local elders would not trust Thomas, or even Ariock or Vy, but they would welcome Kessa home. They would likely trust her.

This war still seemed like a dubious fantasy. "Surely you can find someone else," Kessa said. "If there is a next time."

"I'd like you to be the face of our war," Thomas said. "That's an ongoing position. Freed slaves won't trust leaders who look like Torth."

Ah. So Thomas wanted to hide behind her face. Her words.

He wanted to put Kessa out in front, where everyone in the known universe could see her. And somehow, she was supposed to shield everyone—including giants such as Ariock and Weptolyso—with her tiny, frail ummin body?

"Do you want to try again?" Thomas invited.

Unanswered questions needled Kessa's mind. Even if Thomas deigned to answer her, though, she guessed that a few extra crumbs of information would only sharpen her curiosity in frustrating ways. Thomas must have plans within plans, multilayered and interlocked, reliant upon information that Torth grew up with but that slaves did not. It would take years for him to fully enlighten a nontelepath.

Thomas probably had no idea how it felt to yearn for answers the way a starving person wanted food. He knew almost everything without any effort.

Kessa hopped off the rock she had been standing on. "Why New GoodLife WaterGarden City?" she asked.

"Why not?" Thomas said. "We have to start somewhere."

That was evasive.

If Kessa was going to be a mascot for freedom—a flimsy living shield—then she wanted to know if the risks were worth it. She wanted more than vague promises.

"You could take control of Earth," Kessa pointed out. "You could gain seven billion human allies." Not to mention all the mysterious technologies of paradise. "Why not preemptively send our forces there?"

Thomas looked uncomfortable. "I'd rather not bring seven billion people into a galactic war they otherwise might be able to avoid," he said. "That's a major decision. They deserve to make it for themselves rather than have me make it for them."

Kessa supposed that was an acceptable answer. She clicked her beak, but she was not satisfied.

"Why not a city full of nussians?" she asked. "If you take New GoodLife WaterGarden City—assuming you are successful—you will gain a few million ummins. But aren't there cities with fewer ummins and millions of nussians?"

"You're assuming nussian allies are more desirable than ummin allies," Thomas said dryly.

"They are." Kessa felt no shame in admitting a truth. "In terms of fighting," Nussians tended to charge into battle at full speed, whereas ummins were often more thoughtful and timid. Most nussians seemed to enjoy throwing their weight around, whereas Kessa knew plenty of ummins who would rather hide. "You will find a lot more warriors among nussians than among ummins," she said.

Thomas conceded that point with a tight nod. His head rested on a neck brace since he was too weak to hold it up.

"So." He floated closer and glided to a stop just outside a range in which he might overhear her thoughts. "You'd rather liberate some other city?"

Kessa reassessed Thomas. He had shifted the focus of conversation away from his secret goals. Was he trying to sidetrack her?

It seemed he did not respect Kessa enough to trust her.

In the slave Tunnels, someone who hoarded secrets would fall prey to gangs. A closed and secretive attitude usually meant few friends and a premature death. If Thomas wanted to transform the Torth . . . well, perhaps he should start by taking a more critical look at himself.

"Friends respect each other," Kessa dared to say.

Her point seemed to rattle Thomas.

After a moment, he gestured next to her with his gaze. "May I? Would you mind if I got a little bit closer?"

So. He was afraid to be friendly with Kessa unless he could be certain of her inner thoughts and moods? Interesting. His immense knowledge endowed him with all sorts of conversational advantages, yet he was afraid of someone whose mind was a cipher. Either that, or he wanted to assert his superiority.

He might not admit it, even to himself, but he was unwilling to put himself on equal footing with a nontelepath.

Kessa beckoned. "I have no secrets."

She switched to a different mental topic before he got close enough to read her mind, although she was unsure how effective switching focus would be.

Thomas said nothing for a few seconds. They sat in silence together, listening to creatures chirp in the alpine forest. The thoroughfares of Encampment City were far away.

"I have a particular hope." Thomas sounded hesitant.

Kessa focused on him.

"There is a certain Torth who is overly invested in New GoodLife WaterGarden City," Thomas said. "When we attack it, we will grab her undivided attention."

It was easy to guess which Torth he was referring to. The Upward Governess was the elected chief of the entire Torth Empire. If Thomas disrupted that chief's attention, perhaps he would disrupt her executive plans? That might force the Torth to postpone their invasion of Earth.

Kessa supposed that was an admirable goal.

"She wasn't my friend," Thomas said quietly. "But in another life . . . if we had both been raised on Earth . . . I think things would have been different."

Kessa needed a moment to figure out why he sounded wistful.

It seemed impossible that warmth could develop between people who suppressed their emotions. Surely Thomas did not have friendly or romantic feelings for that chief of all Torth?

"You . . ." Kessa hesitated, uncertain of her guess. "You want her on our side?"

Thomas appeared to struggle with an inner dilemma. Kessa considered going to him, to hold his hand and offer comfort. But perhaps she was misreading his face?

Finally, Thomas wrested out a few words of explanation. "She saved my life."

That was not something Kessa would have guessed. The Upward Governess was the epitome of Torth power, selfishness, greed, and corruption.

"The Majority wanted to execute me," Thomas said. "I was a hybrid, an abomination raised by primitives. But she vouched for me. She helped persuade the Majority, and then afterward, she helped me survive among Torth when I had no idea what I was doing."

Thomas cared about her. The truth was on his face.

If he said the Upward Governess had saved his life, then she must have done so. He never lied.

"You believe she will join our side?" Kessa did not bother to hide her skeptical tone. She had seen the Upward Governess, who was as bloated as an inflated balloon. Hundreds of personal slaves catered to her every whim. That girl was severely disabled, and she would never fetch and carry, or scrub floors, or serve as a menial laborer.

Then again, if any Torth was likely to have a mental breakdown due to deprivation, it would be that one.

"She wants to be human," Thomas said. "I think she might go to some lengths for that goal."

"Hmm." Kessa gazed up at the puffy white clouds and pondered the idea of a god who wished to give up godhood. Or—as the Alashani saw things—the Upward Governess must seem like a fat demon who yearned to transform into an angel of paradise. It was hard to believe.

"We could really use her help," Thomas said, his voice low with confidentiality. "Not just because of her abilities, although she is a formidable supergenius. But her status and influence are even more important."

Kessa looked at him quizzically.

"If she joins us," Thomas said, "I think half the empire would follow."

He said it casually, but Kessa could tell that he truly believed it.

She forgot to breathe for a moment. Half the Torth Empire? That would be trillions of Torth.

Such a momentous victory would flip the war in their favor. They might actually win. If things worked out the way Thomas wanted, they could free all the slaves in the known universe.

Kessa stared at him, searching for any hint that he had hidden reservations.

"It's a gamble," Thomas admitted. "There are a lot of factors in play, and I can't predict what will happen. I don't know what she'll do."

Kessa realized that Thomas was sharing his fears. Uncertainties and risks must seem frightening to a mind like his.

"It's a huge gamble," Thomas amended. "Perhaps the biggest I've ever taken in my life."

Hyperbole? Kessa did not think Thomas was prone to hyperbole or exaggeration.

"If it fails," Thomas said, "we shouldn't be worse off than we are now. She'll continue to be our enemy. But if we can get her on our side . . ."

He paused. For a split second, Kessa saw hope on his face.

Then Thomas looked grim, his hope suppressed. "Our problems wouldn't end there," he said brusquely. "She would be a major target for assassination."

It took Kessa a moment to figure out what Thomas was worried about.

Then her beak fell open. Of course the Upward Governess would not, could not, settle into life as part of a chain gang of slaves, or a day laborer. She had value. Her influence in the Megacosm was likely to induce other Torth to contemplate switching sides. So if she went renegade . . . of course the Torth leadership would want to silence her. They would try to kill her much as they tried to kill Thomas.

"Exactly." Thomas offered Kessa a thin smile, reading her thoughts.

Kessa considered the problem. "We would need to protect her."

But that defeated the point of turning an overprivileged Torth into an underprivileged slave. If the Upward Governess was treated like a treasure, protected by an army and shielded inside a fortress, the refugees would complain. They would assume she was privileged because she was a Torth. Certain albino warriors, and perhaps even nussians or govki, would likely try to murder her.

And yet if she was treated poorly, she would go unprotected. Which meant she was likely to be killed in a sneak attack by Torth. That would defeat the point of gaining her as an ally.

"And I thought I had problems," Thomas said with levity.

Now Kessa understood the gamble that Thomas wanted to take. If he won the Upward Governess to his side, her presence could win the war. Or devastate his plans.

She might draw half the Torth Empire to his side.

Or she might get assassinated, and that would possibly deter half the Torth Empire from joining his side.

Either way, if the Upward Governess defected, refugees and former slaves would despise her and also grow more suspicious of Thomas's loyalties. Thomas was risking the hatred of everyone for the sake of gaining one gigantic potential advantage.

"It's worth it," Thomas said. "I calculated the risk-to-reward ratio, and I accept it. I can stand hatred aimed at me. It's nothing new." He floated away. "So now you know." He indicated the camera with his gaze. "Will you give your ultimatum speech another shot?"

Kessa swallowed, aware that Thomas must be juggling a lot of knives in his mind. "Just a moment." She wanted time to process his gamble. "Have you confided this to Ariock? Or anyone else?"

"No."

"Wouldn't it be best if—"

"No." Thomas was brusque. "If the Torth Empire catches even a hint of what I want, they'll secure the Upward Governess. Or—more likely—they'd murder her. That would preclude any possibility of her switching sides."

Kessa closed her beak. If the de facto leader of the Torth Empire was not the ultimate, highest authority in the known universe . . . well, she supposed it made sense. No matter how many privileges the Upward Governess enjoyed, she was just another Torth. She was vulnerable to the Torth Majority.

So Thomas's gamble had to remain a secret. Otherwise, any random Red Rank or Rosy Recruit might soak up the inner thoughts of Ariock, or Jinishta, or Weptolyso, during battle, and the Torth Majority would take action. A mind reader could absorb secrets even while they were getting smashed or blasted to death.

The Torth Empire could leach information so easily. That was one of their core advantages.

"I see." Kessa gave Thomas a nod of respect. "Thank you for trusting me with this."

His expression softened. "Thanks for not laughing in derision."

Kessa understood why he had worried about that. To a former slave, an extremely pampered individual was an object of contempt. The Upward Governess was a visual representation of the imbalance between slaves and their masters.

And since the Upward Governess was manipulative enough—even sociopathic enough—to climb to the top of Torth society, she might well fake being a renegade. Not even Thomas could delve into her deepest thoughts to pull out the truth.

That explained why Thomas had not suggested luring all the Torth supergeniuses to his side with promises of unlimited NAI-12 or whatever else they craved. The Upward Governess might prove perfectly obedient. She might behave exactly like a trustworthy friend or a slave. Yet it would be nearly impossible to trust her. Everyone would have lingering suspicions. Kessa would. Ariock would.

And Thomas would, as well.

"I don't mean to rush you," Thomas said, "but our biggest advantage right now is that the Torth think we're scrambling in self-defense mode. I want to hit them before they have a chance to score a victory against us. We need to plant fears and doubts in the psyche of the average Torth."

He made that sound simple and easy.

Kessa wished to be caught up in his enthusiasm, but she was all too aware that the Torth owned almost everything in the galaxy. They had an ever-growing army of Yeresunsa soldiers: the Rosy Recruits. Even if Thomas turned one battle into a victory . . . could that really make a difference?

After all, Ariock had limits. His attention span was human. He could only protect one location at a time. He could not watch his own back every second of every day. He had to sleep like a normal person.

"Your doubts," Thomas said, "are precisely what many Torth believe. That's why they're so overconfident." He smiled grimly. "They assume we can't possibly defend a major metropolis in the middle of a Torth-owned hub planet, and, therefore, we won't bother to try."

"But . . ." Kessa studied the determined gleam in his eyes. "Is that not the case?"

"They're somewhat right." Thomas floated back toward the clearing. "But the Torth Empire has a bad habit of overestimating itself." He rotated, pointing the camera toward her. "We'll see what happens when the Megacosm loses some of its harmonious cohesion."

Kessa wanted to interrogate him. She wanted every detail of his plan and its aftermath. But perhaps that would squander crucial time?

While Kessa spent time with Thomas, she knew Ariock was mass-producing earpieces Thomas had architected. Those would enable the battle leaders to stay in communication even while they fought enemies.

Everyone was rushing about, making preparations. Varktezo was overseeing a so-called advance team. Weptolyso supervised the volunteer army, training them to stand in formation so they could be quickly teleported from one planet to another. Garrett would make sure the soldiers were equipped with armor and weapons. Jinishta and her premier warriors had to learn how to use the earpiece communicators.

Thomas wanted to hurt the Torth Empire. Kessa did not doubt it.

She hopped onto the rock and faced the pitiless camera.

She was just an ummin. She felt ridiculous. If the entirety of the Torth Empire saw this recording, they would judge her harshly and demand her death.

Yet . . .

A renegade supergenius had entrusted Kessa with his confidential secrets.

Not only that, but Thomas was willing to put a major cause that he cared about—a person—into Kessa's care. He trusted Kessa to rehabilitate the current leader of the Torth. That was a monumental task. If that obese supergenius could be transformed from an enemy into an ally, she might bring about the destruction of the Torth Empire.

Thomas had not asked Ariock, or Vy, or Cherise, or anyone else to do it. He had asked Kessa.

"Will you let me rerecord your speech?" Thomas tapped the remote control under his finger.

Kessa squared her shoulders. If her life continued on this path, if she wasn't careful, she would become as puffed up and entitled as the current leader of the Torth Empire.

"Surrender your slaves," she commanded. "I am Kessatovtalun of Umdalkdul, known to all as Kessa the Wise. I command the Torth of this city to release all slaves unharmed. You now belong to us. Obey us. Or die."

Thomas ended the recording and grinned at her. "That was perfect."

CHAPTER 2

NAVIGATING NEBULAE

Ariock wasn't a starship computer. He could not calculate relative velocity and mass on the fly. He had to load cosmic coordinates the old-fashioned way: through study and memorization.

What a headache.

He stared at the holographic galaxy that glowed in midair, impressively bright against the backdrop of verdant grass.

"Okay," Thomas said. "So, once again, here's where we are: Reject-81."

A magenta dot appeared within the spiraled density of stars.

Garrett elbowed Ariock in a friendly way. "Can you name that structure between us and Omophia Prime?"

Ariock had already familiarized himself with the local galactic neighborhood, having made a few raids on the nearest inhabited planet. "The Sagittarius Star Cloud."

"Very good." Garrett stuck his cigarette back in his mouth and puffed on it.

A cerulean dot glowed inside a divot along another galactic arm. "So here's Umdalkdul," Thomas said.

Was that on the Perseus Arm? Ariock hoped he'd gotten that right.

Learning celestial sectors was more challenging than anything he had ever set his mind to. The sheer number of nebulae was overwhelming. What, exactly, was a supershell? What was an open cluster of stars, and how did it differ from a globular cluster? Did any relevant planets exist inside the high-velocity gas clouds that scooted along the galactic halo? Ariock wished he could take a class on astronavigation.

But there wasn't time for that.

"I'll go over it with you until you've got it," Thomas said in a reassuring tone. As he spoke, a magenta thread lit up, illuminating a path from Reject-81 to Umdalkdul. "Here's your route."

The path was minuscule in comparison to the whole map. The holograph zoomed in, then rotated.

Ariock squinted at the sprawling mess of stars. This up-close examination looked every bit as complex as the macro view. Each segment of the route included a large and relatively stable feature. Here, he was supposed to skirt that cluster. There, he would hook past that particular nebula.

"Ready?" Thomas asked.

He proceeded to walk Ariock through each parsec of the interstellar journey—again—from Reject-81 to Umdalkdul.

They went through it again, and then again, for good measure.

Ariock would pass a luminous double star. Beyond that, there was a nebula that vaguely resembled a swung hammer, with motion streaks behind it. A meteor field. An industrial space station with three gyroscopic rings. And on and on.

Space was not quite empty when one could traverse parsecs at the speed of thought.

"Okay," Thomas said, once he seemed satisfied with Ariock's memorization. "Now go there. In ghost form."

They all watched. Not just Thomas and Garrett, but farther away, there was Weptolyso, standing in front of a mass of troops. There was Jinishta, with her premier warriors. A group of ten ummins waited to one side, attired in rags and fake slave collars. That was the advance team.

Ariock tried to relax. He was going to navigate the galaxy by dead reckoning. And he would have to do it while temporarily disembodied and in the time crunch of a clairvoyant trance.

What fun.

He exhaled. He had mastered the basics. Someday, in a more peaceful time, he might be able to revisit Earth. With Vy. She would like that.

He locked his body in place, then went still.

To call interstellar teleportation difficult was an understatement. The first step was to put himself into a clairvoyant trance. Ariock could only do it if he tuned out everything else. He hated how vulnerable that rendered him. He was unable to protect anyone, including himself, while outside his body.

Disembodied, Ariock floated above himself. He ghosted above the refugee encampment of makeshift shelters and dirt avenues.

Ariock stretched his awareness across a nothingness so vast as to be inconceivable to his human brain.

While in this terrible trance, he needed to ghost beyond his utmost limit. And while doing that, he had to drag his elongated sphere of influence along with his core awareness.

He had less than five minutes before the strain caused him to snap back to his body. In order to maximize that short window of time, he needed to run through every step of the route he had just memorized.

So he rocketed away.

Disembodied, Ariock zipped through space in utter silence, insensate, using the complex set of visual landmarks as a guide. His distant body roared a demand that he quit. He should quit right now.

Instead, every time he steered off course, he backtracked and found his way again.

He found the right solar system. He jaunted leftward, seeking Umdalkdul in its current orbit. There was the yellowish-green marble of a planet. Ariock zoomed closer, excited to recognize the iconic moons and orbital factories.

Now he had to find the right continent. And the right city.

Metropolitan areas webbed vast stretches of desert and marshland. But Ariock had already studied a global map, so he knew where to go. He floated through New GoodLife WaterGarden City in the time it might take to blink an eye.

Torth strolled on terraced balconies or lounged in airborne traffic. Slaves trudged in despair. It was an ordinary day.

Ariock snapped back to his body on Reject-81.

He opened his eyes.

Thomas and Garrett watched him with expectant gazes. Ariock had not done anything that they could see, and yet . . .

New things were possible.

According to Evenjos, mass-teleportation was a sixth-magnitude ability, the sort of power that was mythical. No one else had ever been able to do this, to her knowledge. Teleportation across the galaxy was a level up. It was cosmic power. Galactic power.

"They have no idea," Ariock said. "It looks like a sunny day in New GoodLife WaterGarden City."

Garrett grinned. Weptolyso and Jinishta exchanged happy looks. Ariock and his allies were no longer bound to a single planet or constrained to one location.

And soon, the Torth Empire would no longer feel secure.

"All right. Let's get down to business." Thomas turned toward the advance team.

"Hold on." Garrett puffed on his cigarette. "I have concerns about what happens after our invasion. Whether we win or lose, we can't stay in that city. Umdalkdul is a hub planet. It's chock-full of enemies."

"I'll teleport everyone back here." Ariock swept a gesture. Reject-81 would have to be their safe harbor. After all, he didn't expect his forces to sleep in their armor. Even if they won, they could not expect to hang out and enjoy the place.

"We'll see," Thomas said.

Garrett stared at him. "What is that supposed to mean?"

"It means we'll discuss it later." Thomas fixed the old man with a merciless gaze. "I don't want any chance of my ideas leaking into the Torth Empire. Let's keep our long-term strategizing to a minimum. At least until after we win. Focus on this conquest."

As Ariock thought about it, he realized Thomas's point—any battle against Torth entailed a leakage of information. Torth combatants would read the minds of Alashani and nussians, and they would share whatever they learned with their audiences in the Megacosm.

"Got it," Ariock said.

"I suppose there are no real safe harbors," Garrett grumbled, his voice pitched low so none of the troops would overhear. "Especially once the Torth gain the ability to teleport."

He made that sound like an alarming certainty.

Ariock tried not to let his worries show, but he didn't like the idea of Torth popping into his camp without warning. His people had held funeral processions to mourn the dead. How would they cope if there was absolutely no downtime between battles?

"They haven't figured it out yet," Thomas said. "Have they?" His sharp yellow gaze flicked toward Garrett.

"No. Not publicly, at least." Garrett inhaled smoke, as if for comfort. "But they've been experimenting."

"Right." Thomas sounded dismissive. "Well, if they do figure out teleportation, that will necessitate a change to my strategy, so please keep me informed. Report any major changes in the Megacosm to me."

"Yes, sir." Garrett sounded sarcastic. No doubt he was bitter about being subordinate to a child.

"The threat of Torth gaining new powers is part of the reason I want to expedite this battle," Thomas said. "We're going to strike them hard and fast, before they have time to gain new abilities or to even think about what we're doing."

Ariock liked the sound of that. Even Garrett looked cautiously optimistic.

Thomas had outlined the battle plan, and everyone had admitted that it sounded clever. They were going to surprise the Torth and choke off their escape routes.

"On that note," Thomas said, "let's set this plan into motion. Is the advance team ready?"

The ten ummins elbowed each other with encouragement. Their counterfeit slave collars glowed in an on-duty way.

"Yes, Teacher." One of the ummins stepped forward, speaking for the rest. Ariock recognized her as an adolescent from Duin. Like the other ummins, she wore rags, purposely dressed to blend in with a slave population.

These ummins had volunteered for a dangerous, critical task. They would need to avoid notice while jury-rigging hidden speakers in strategic places throughout the city. They would also reprogram the electronic hubs that controlled view screens.

"You have to avoid Torth," Garrett told them gruffly. "Remember, if one Torth probes your mind, then it's all over. They'll evacuate the city and probably murder a lot of slaves. And we might not be able to rescue you."

One of the ummins saluted Garrett. "We understand, Elder."

"We will get everything done," another piped up. "You can count on us."

Ariock understood why Garrett was concerned. These ummins seemed too plucky to pass as ordinary slaves. They carried electronic equipment hidden inside their undergarments and head covers. A few of them had the harsh accents of the Torth Homeworld. That would definitely draw attention if they happened to speak to any local slaves.

Freedom had altered their attitudes. What if they failed to look downtrodden enough?

"These ummins are smart." Thomas said it with confidence. "They know how to blend in with the locals. And they know exactly how critical their task is. They can be counted on."

"We will prepare the city," one of the adolescent ummins said, "for a storm of freedom." He saluted Ariock, and the rest followed suit.

A storm of freedom. Ariock liked that.

Thomas rotated to face Ariock. "Transport the advance team in pairs, please. Drop them off in the control rooms, as illustrated here."

He projected a ghostly holograph of New GoodLife WaterGarden City. Five rooms were highlighted, distributed throughout the sprawl of interconnected buildings. Ariock doubted he would remember all five locations in that hellishly complex warren.

"You have enough power for multiple trips," Thomas assured him. "I'll walk you through these one trip at a time."

Ariock saw that the ummins were placing all their trust in him. If he failed, then they might end up stranded forever as slaves.

So they would do everything possible to ensure his victory. A win for him was a win for them.

"Freedom." Ariock pumped his fist.

"Freedom," the ummins responded fervently.

A feeling of anticipation thrummed in Ariock. This was what he used to feel in the prison arena, before a fight. It was bloodlust.

"Weptolyso," Thomas said, without bothering to turn and look at the former hall guard. "Ready the troops."

Ariock knew what that meant. Every volunteer soldier was already armed, their earpieces tested. They just had to organize into cohorts.

"I'll get my armor on." Garrett tossed away his cigarette. "And Ariock? You'd better make some armor for yourself. The inhibitor is always a danger."

For once, Ariock was not ashamed or afraid of what he could do in battle. He wanted to see Torth kneel before liberated slaves. He wanted the owners on their knees, with collars around their necks. Or dead. This was an unjust universe. Ariock and his people meant to right a few wrongs.

The Torth Empire had invited a storm.

CHAPTER 3

WARRIOR MENTALITY

"You'll deploy at these choke points." Thomas projected dozens of bottleneck routes on his holographic version of the city's layout.

The battle leaders paid close attention. Once the conquest began, their role was mostly to make sure their troops followed the objective—enslave Torth and liberate slaves—and did not go overboard with killing and maiming. Each troop consisted of one Alashani warrior, plus ten to twelve volunteer soldiers, including at least two nussians.

Thomas lit up more areas on his projected map. "Extra soldiers will arrive in the slave Tunnels, to disseminate arms and information and begin liberating slaves."

The leaders had earpieces, so they would be able to report injuries to Evenjos, who was effectively their medic unit. If they ran into problems? Garrett and Ariock were also listening on that command channel.

"You can expect an initial rush toward the spaceport," Thomas went on. He illuminated the relevant routes. "But it won't last. Ariock will sever central power, then destroy any launchpads that are still working."

Behind the battle leaders, volunteer soldiers strained to listen, but they looked somewhat sullen. The Alashani attitude was infectious. They might hate the fact that a *rekveh* was their tactician.

And an apparent coward.

The troops knew that Thomas had Yeresunsa powers. And they knew that he meant to stay behind in the refugee camp, along with children, elders, and other noncombatants. Instead of blasting Torth with his thermodynamic power, he was going to . . .

Well, they probably assumed he was going to lounge around and eat snacks while they fought vicious Red Ranks.

Thomas tried not to be bothered by what they thought. Why should it matter? The refugees and common troops had no frame of reference for what he meant to do in the Megacosm. The most crucial tactic of this battle would take place on a different plane of existence from the physical realm.

"Jinishta will use her powers to obstruct and close this docking bay, here," Thomas said, illuminating a spot on the holographic map. "Guradjur will destroy this one, and Efvaltel will take down this one. That's all in the initial attack. Your goal is to prevent Torth from escaping."

Thomas let his holograph fade away. All eyes shifted to him.

"And then it's just a matter of taking collars off slaves and putting them on Torth," Thomas said.

Weptolyso grinned. The battle leaders exchanged determined glances, and Thomas did not need to be within range to sense their excitement.

"Remember," Thomas said, "any Torth who kneel ought to be shown mercy, as long as they obey."

A few soldiers grumbled.

"There won't be many of those," someone said.

"We'll see." Thomas offered a thin smile, trying to imply that enslaved Torth was the likely outcome.

In truth, he feared he might be overconfident. A lot of alien civilizations throughout history had failed to destroy the Torth Empire. History was littered with the corpses of revolutionaries and renegades. He believed his plan would lead to a win. But what if the Upward Governess somehow anticipated what he was about to do?

Dealing with people-oriented variables was a messy business. It wasn't as predictable as most forms of mathematics.

Vy walked toward him from behind. Thomas saw her approach through the perceptions of nearby people, Weptolyso and Jinishta. Her limp was gone. Her new prosthetic allowed her to walk with natural ease.

She would remain safe on Reject-81 until the battle was over. Thomas didn't want her presence in a war zone to distract Ariock.

How dangerous will it be for Ariock? she asked in her mind.

Thomas rotated his hoverchair to face her. "I would bet on him winning."

Vy studied his face. She seemed to want extra reassurance.

"He'll have Garrett looking out for him," Thomas said. "And Evenjos will be watching from orbit."

The former Lady of Sorrow claimed she did not feel battle-ready. However, she would use her powers to shove away any orbital threats, and she would also heal any soldier or warrior who fell in battle.

Her presence alone should boost morale. Everyone knew she was a formidable backup for Ariock.

"Plus," Thomas said, "you haven't seen his new armor."

Vy raised an eyebrow. Thomas sensed her wondering when the two of them had found time to design armor, between mass-producing earpieces for the troops and laying out the military tactics.

"He designed it on his own," Thomas elaborated. "But I saw the gist in his mind. He's . . . Ah." Thomas cut himself off, seeing the troops on the hills getting excited. Ariock must be approaching.

"Ariock!" More than two thousand nussians rumbled his name.

Huge spikes jagged above Ariock's immense shoulder plates. Cruel barbs spiked his biceps, elbows, shoulder blades, and thighs. His collar and gauntlets were grooved to channel fluids off and away. His new suit of armor was purple-black titanium alloy rather than pebbly gold, but it was clearly inspired by the body style of nussians.

Vy's eyes widened with admiration. Even Thomas could not resist staring. Ariock looked formidable even when dressed in plain woolens, but now . . .

"ARIOCK!" Nussians bellowed his name in their gravelly voices, and the rest of the troops joined in.

They pumped their fists. Even the aloof Yeresunsa warriors looked fierce with pride.

"DOVANACK!" Nussians appreciated long names, and they reveled in the syllables.

"ARIOCK! DOVANACK!"

Ariock joined Thomas on the windswept promontory overlooking the troops. Up close, he blotted out the sky. He seemed oblivious to how much that armor added to his already-massive stature.

"I'm ready." His gaze was distant, brooding with violence. "Are you going to be all right?"

"Of course," Thomas said.

Vy gazed silently up at Ariock, her eyes full of unspoken love and concern. In her airy sundress, she looked so delicate in comparison to Ariock as to be absurd.

Neither of them cared about how they looked together. Ariock scooped her into his arms, and they kissed like they might never see each other again.

Thomas was close enough to overhear their minds. He sensed their hidden fears and reservations, their lust and their love. He wished he had moved farther away.

Cherise was probably aiding the camp leaders with infrastructural duties. She must be worried, too . . . but not about Thomas.

All her concerns would be for Flen.

A thousand Alashani were going into battle today, and they mostly lacked the advantages that Ariock had been born with. Any random Torth might kill Flen with a lucky shot. Cherise must be ill with worry if she loved her warrior even a quarter as much as Vy and Ariock loved each other.

Flen is a better man than I am, Thomas reminded himself.

It was embarrassing to need a reminder. His memory was flawless. He just needed to settle into this reality and accept the fact that Cherise had made her choice.

He hoped she was happy.

Vy looked prim as Ariock set her down. "You be careful," she told him.

"Remember to come get us as soon as the city is secure," Thomas said.

Ariock nodded to them both. "I'll be back as soon as I can."

Thomas sensed traces of insecurity buried beneath Ariock's demeanor. The big guy was plagued by self-doubts. He wondered why people were so willing to respect him.

At least he understood that now was not the time to exhibit any of that uncertainty. Now was not the time for shyness.

Ariock strode to the edge of the promontory. When he pumped one huge, armored fist, he deliberately caused electricity to span his dark bulk in brilliant purple arcs. The clouds thickened, growling with thunder.

"Gather together." Ariock's masculine voice was as loud as the thunder, amplified by his power. "Everyone who isn't coming, please move away. Otherwise I'll take you by accident."

"Form up!" Weptolyso roared.

The troops straightened into hundreds of orderly squares. Every square consisted of a Yeresunsa warrior, garbed in black, surrounded by immense nussians, with a few smaller sapients thrown into the mix. Extra soldiers waited toward the back, in their own squares. Hundreds of govki. Thousands of ummins.

Every soldier should be able to hear their unit's captain. Nussians could convey information to Weptolyso, and vice versa. Premier warriors could hear tinny-voiced commands from Jinishta if she had something to say. All those leaders would hear Ariock if he spoke—his deep voice would override anyone else's.

It was not exactly a sophisticated communications system. It was crude. Pathetic, really, especially in comparison with the Megacosm.

But that was all right.

The Upward Governess and other Torth supergeniuses would expect Thomas to perfect a battle communications system before sending his troops into danger. Torth engineers were used to perfection themselves. They were careful. They ran experiments before releasing any new product. They could estimate how long such a system would take to set up, and they knew their enemies needed more than a handful of days to militarize their assets.

So they would not expect a vicious attack for at least another week.

The last thing they expected Thomas to do was strike a major hub city when his troops were supposedly demoralized, low on supplies, and weak on communications and other technology. They expected Thomas to spend at least three to five days perfecting his plans, setting up a lab, and establishing his dominance over the inferior species, with their uppity notions of freedom.

The Torth had no idea what they were dealing with yet.

This was not going to be another failed rebellion or another defeated alien civilization throwing up a last gasp of defiance. The Torth had never dealt with anyone like Ariock. And they had never dealt with a renegade supergenius—until now.

"Show no mercy to Torth who defy you," Ariock boomed. "Kill them."

He fitted his massive helmet onto his head. With his skin sealed away, he was all but invincible.

The troops screamed in rapture. "ARIOCK! DOVANACK!" They stamped so hard the ground trembled. Pebbles rolled.

Some of the nussians wielded clubs, or even battle-axes. Soldiers adjusted blaster gloves. A few of the Alashani pulled helmets onto their own armored suits. They readied spears. They sparked with electric power.

Ariock's mind vanished in a clairvoyant trance. It was eerie, how clairvoyants could do that. Ariock must be traversing the galaxy while his body remained behind.

The troops began to disappear.

Evenjos and Garrett vanished together. Jinishta and her peripheral guard went next. More troops followed, each square vanishing, a few at a time, as Ariock placed them in docking bays, forums, or on strategic causeways.

They would wreak havoc. The spaceport at the center of New GoodLife WaterGarden City would soon get shut down, and a mass panic would sweep through the locals.

That panic would saturate the Megacosm.

Ariock had no idea how scary he was to a mind reader. He could do quite a lot while Thomas was completely blind to him, unable to read his intentions or even his mood.

Ariock himself vanished with the last of the troops.

A soft breeze blew. The sky seemed more relaxed without the presence of either Dovanack.

Encampment City looked almost idyllic in the waning daylight. People went about their business. Some glanced toward the big, empty plain where the troops had stood. Otherwise, they lit lanterns, tended cook fires, and hung or folded laundry.

"How long are you going to wait?" Vy asked.

"Three minutes." Thomas had started a countdown in his head the moment Ariock disappeared.

Vy watched him, as if she expected to see something.

Thomas sensed her anxiety. He knew that she felt even more blind than he did. She wanted Thomas to give her a window into the battle, a glimpse of how Ariock was faring.

"I'll tell you," Thomas said. "But first, I'll need a solid few minutes in the Megacosm. No interruptions."

"I won't interrupt," Vy assured him.

"Do you mind stepping out of my range?" He wanted minimal distractions.

She looked surprised. She was used to Thomas wanting to absorb everything he could learn.

After a moment, she saw that he was serious. She went to a grassy hillock and sat there, hands locked around her knees. She gazed at the ever-bustling camp of refugees.

Thomas parked his hoverchair and faced in a different direction. The river and plains beyond offered a peaceful vista.

He valued the respite.

He took a second to cherish the lull. The silence of the dungeon pit had been awful, because it went on for days and weeks, but this? This was a welcome moment in which to figuratively catch his breath.

He was about to become a god. At least for a few minutes.

Thomas steeled himself for the awe and judgment of 38.2 trillion Torth.

CHAPTER 4
GIGANTIC

The first time Ariock destroyed a spaceport, he had accidentally killed his mother.

He was far more in control this time. When he raised his arms, metal twisted, meshing the gates shut.

With his awareness spread, he sensed other launchpads beyond what he could see. This spaceport had lobes. It was a complicated flower. Ariock meant to crumple its petals one at a time. He could probably crush this entire planet into oblivion, but he was no longer a blundering titan, oblivious to his own strength.

Ariock wrenched his arms down. He was steel, he was iron, he was a storm of electricity.

Thousands of launchpads collapsed. Shuttles slammed into each other. Life sparks died, and Ariock hoped those were all Torth, Torth who had stupidly ignored the video of Kessa that played throughout the city.

Damage didn't matter. Whether he won or lost today, Torth would have to repair the wreckage.

Ariock stepped over a riven part of the floor. Nothing could launch from this zone. He stalked across the vast bottom of the spaceport.

Torth fled from him. Most shoved each other in their haste to get away, although some dived behind debris. Ariock remained alert and shielded.

"Surrender your slaves," the recording of Kessa commanded.

As Ariock worked, destroying lobes of the spaceport, her recorded image appeared on wall screens and holographic displays. He did not hear her. Torth did not utilize sound systems, and the jury-rigged speakers planted by his advance team were few and far apart. It didn't matter. If even one Torth heard the recording, the whole Torth Empire would tune in.

They must be listening right now.

It was gratifying to see Torth in postures of submission. They knelt, quivering, no doubt hoping Ariock would leave them alone.

Garrett's voice sounded in Ariock's earpiece. "I've destroyed the docking bay. Going after a few Rosies."

Ariock gave his own update. "The spaceport is shut down."

Judging by the distant screams that filtered through his helmet's audio, something was happening at one of the traffic arteries leading into the city. Ariock headed in that direction.

A nussian paraded through a mess of carnage, waving a piece of gore. An arm. It looked as if the nussian had torn his former masters from limb to limb.

"Don't try to stop newly freed slaves from seeking vengeance," Thomas had advised Ariock and the army. *"They've had to obey unjust authorities all their lives,*

and they won't trust new authorities right away. Don't insult their free will by seizing control of their personal justice. Let Kessa and her lieutenants help ease them into freedom. Your only job is to secure the city as fast as possible."

Fair enough.

The triumphant nussian snorted a challenge toward Ariock, but he seemed to sense danger, and he did not come closer.

Ariock forced himself to walk onward. "A nussian here at the southwestern gate may need some oversight," he said, knowing his earpiece would transmit his voice through the command channel. Weptolyso would likely send the nearest nussian troops to restrain the berserker or calm him down.

Ariock felt grateful to have troops. He had never expected so many refugees would take risks along with him.

He ducked out of the spaceport and stepped over corpses in the wide boulevard. As an afterthought, he used his powers to rip a hidden energy generator through a stone wall.

Electricity rippled across the generator as it died. Ariock crammed the twisted metal of its remains into the enormous gateway behind him. Let it be clear that the spaceport was closed. Torth might try to climb over the struts, but they would risk being electrocuted.

They had nowhere to go. And there was a bigger risk: defying Ariock.

Gangs of aliens roved distant alleyways or on balconies. Ariock caught sight of a few liberated slaves threatening to shoot a couple of Torth women. The women clung to each other, unarmed and wearing slave collars.

Up close, however, liberated slaves darted away. Nussians cringed in bristling balls of terror.

Their fear was painful to see. Ariock wanted to pull off his helmet and assure the liberated slaves that he was on their side. He was a friend of Kessa. They must have seen the recording that played in every window display.

But Ariock knew what he looked like. Reassurances would have to come directly from Kessa.

Dead Torth lay sprawled in garden lounges, in pools of blood. Some corpses floated in hoverchairs.

But it was not quite a massacre. Plenty of Torth remained alive. The survivors knelt and touched their foreheads to the floor. Ariock wondered if he could trust their obsequiousness.

"Once they realize they've been conquered," Thomas had warned, *"some Torth might go into murder mode. The Majority will urge them to be martyrs, to do anything to prevent people from joining us. You'll need to put a stop to that."*

One Torth man wore a voluminous robe that might hide weapons. Ariock stripped that away.

He yanked off blaster gloves and shredded those to make them unusable. He crumpled the remains of weapons and tossed them up high, onto decorative cornices or entablatures above windows, where no one could easily reach them.

Ariock expanded his awareness into a light meshwork across the whole city. He didn't need to mess with puny Yellow Ranks. His troops could handle minor annoyances. He wanted to find some real combat. Where were the military ranks?

He sensed millions of life sparks.

That extraordinarily energetic one was probably Garrett. There were a few others in that league, although none quite as strong. And . . .

There.

There were a handful of superpowered life sparks causing other lives to wink out. Either some Alashani warriors had gone berserk, or these were Servants of All on a rampage, mass-murdering innocent slaves.

Ariock took off in that direction.

His boots cracked the stone tiles. He ran as fast as wind. He considered teleporting, but he wasn't sure he could manage a clairvoyant trance while running. That seemed like something that would require practice. Nor did he want to leave his body vulnerable, even for a second.

For a distance as small as a few hundred city blocks, he could get there as fast as it would take for him to drop into a clairvoyant trance and think himself to the place.

Ariock knocked walls out of his way. He leaped hundreds of feet to make the distance go faster. Soon he arrived.

He crashed through a roof and into a slaughterhouse.

The dead lay everywhere, heaps of meat that used to be ummins or govki. Chandeliers and plush couches betrayed the original purpose of this chamber. It was not meant to be a place of butchery. There were alcoves designed for nussians and battlebeasts to stand guard. Chains implied that the murdered victims were here against their will. This had been a slave auction forum.

Ariock slammed to the marble floor amid broken and swirling debris. Ugly sounds filtered through his helmet. Blasts. Squelching body parts.

Three figures, other than Ariock himself, moved fearlessly. The three wore white armor with short capes, splashed with blood. They must have donned battle gear the instant Ariock arrived in their city.

Slaves writhed in agony. They weren't all dead.

"Do not let any Torth get away with murder or torture." Thomas had emphasized that, giving Ariock an intense look. *"They need to learn that defying Kessa's edict has consequences. That's the point."*

The Torth seemed to have their own orders. They rushed at Ariock, shooting blasts and hurling fireballs.

Ariock had survived nuclear detonations. Torth armies were somewhat formidable. But just three Servants of All?

They didn't stand a chance.

Ariock raised an arm, using that bodily trajectory to speed his awareness into all three attackers. He sent them flipping end over end.

At the same time, he whipped chandeliers off the ceiling and stuffed them into exits. These butchers had not offered their chained-up victims so much as a sporting chance to escape, so Ariock would treat them the same way. He made sure all escape routes were blocked.

One of his opponents slammed against a wall with enough impact to crack his armor, thanks to Ariock's telekinetic force. The Servant slid down the wall, a broken mess.

A couple of ummins surreptitiously sneaked toward one of the blocked exits. They must be terrified. Ummins should not need to be so afraid.

Ariock sensed velocity toward his back.

He fortified his personal shield of pressurized air, and a blast exploded harmlessly against his armor. He didn't even feel it.

He casually turned around.

The attacker tried to run. Ariock used his powers to lift the man off the floor. He took a moment to examine the terrified idiot. What sort of hubris led a Torth to attack the Giant?

Their kind could not seem to stop picking fights.

They were nothing more than brutes. That disabled girl? She owned hundreds of slaves and ruled planets, yet she hunted Thomas because he had offended her. That Former Commander? She ordered torture and crucifixion on a whim.

Ariock could keep shouldering the blame for the way Vy had lost her leg. He could hate himself for the death of his mother.

Or maybe he could acknowledge the role the Torth had played.

That was more honest, wasn't it? If the Torth were not so dead set on murdering him, then he would not need to defend himself. If they had never enslaved people he loved, then he would have left the Torth in peace.

They were the aggressors. Not him.

There could be no mercy for the disobedient.

Ariock used air to crush the Servant of All into a crumpled ruin of blood-soaked gristle.

He dropped the unrecognizable pulp.

The remaining Servant, an athletic man, used telekinesis to hurl chains at Ariock. He was trying to crack Ariock's helmet, or trip him, or choke him. It was futile. Overlapped plates of titanium alloy made Ariock a nearly indestructible colossus. Microdarts could not touch him. Beneath the armor, he wore layers of fire-proofed padding.

So he was able to let his guard down a little bit. He could blink. He had time to brace himself and to shield himself.

That made all the difference.

The Servant of All ran up a pillar and used it for leverage to somersault in midair, evading Ariock's telekinetic hammer blow. He shot blasts at Ariock's head.

That cursed blaster glove had been used to murder dozens of chained-up, innocent people. This Servant of All had probably devoted his entire existence to harming and terrorizing slaves.

Like Kessa. Like Weptolyso. Like Vy.

Like Ariock's mother.

Smug, elite Torth like this were the leaders and enforcers in their deranged civilization. They tore children away from mothers. They were the root cause of unfathomable suffering.

Ariock used his powers to tear the blaster glove off the Servant's hand.

His opponent flared with wildfire, a pathetic version of a shield. And then an icy blast. Was he trying to freeze Ariock to death?

Ariock wrapped his opponent in telekinetic force and yanked him upward, holding him off the ground by his neck. The opponent kicked helplessly, unable to bend or loosen Ariock's armored fingers, no matter how much strength he put into the effort.

A pain seizure shredded Ariock's victory.

He nearly dropped the Servant of All.

Instead, he tightened his grip. Lightning crackled around his massive fist as a manifestation of months of pent-up rage. Torth like this used to wield power over him. Not just power, but their own terrible values.

He had obeyed them in that prison arena. Why? Because of pain like this.

Now he knew whom to blame for every innocent beast he had been forced to murder in combat. The Torth believed they were worthy to rule the universe? They were the least deserving. They wanted to believe themselves gods? Their cruelty proved they were unfit for power.

Ariock slammed his fist into the nearest marble wall, uncaring that the Servant was still trapped and choking in his grasp.

His fist cratered the polished stone. Chunks of wall tumbled down.

The pain seizure ended.

The Servant of All was no longer a threat.

Ariock dropped the corpse and wiped blood off his armored hand.

He almost hoped that the man's final death perceptions were shared in the Megacosm. Let other Torth replay the scene. Let the Torth Empire know who they were dealing with. There had to be limits to their sadistic cruelty, and if they wanted to test those limits . . .

Through his waning anger, Ariock understood that Thomas had given him a gift.

The gift of vengeance.

This was for his mother, and for Vy's amputated leg, and for the missing family Kessa had been torn away from. This was for a thousand generations who had had to dwell in caves. This was for alien civilizations that had ended too abruptly.

But this was also an enablement of Ariock's bloodlust.

In battle, he was allowed to be as destructive as the worst Torth. He did not have to pretend to be gentle. He did not have to struggle to be restrained, or kind. He had the freedom to be as violent as his nature demanded.

No one who mattered saw him. No one judged him for it.

Ariock wasn't entirely sure that was a good thing.

CHAPTER 5

MEGACOSMIC QUAKE

The civilized universe should marvel at what the Upward Governess had engineered in just a few short days.

Instead, she floated in boring isolation, beneath the Megacosm. It was unnatural. She had to do all her work alone, in a secret underground habitat, without any audiences to praise her awe-inspiring intellect.

She missed her gushing fans. She missed them so much.

Was this unbearable loneliness the lifestyle the Betrayer had consigned himself to? A mental giant with only oneself for company?

How sad.

The Upward Governess struggled to banish her curiosity about the Betrayer and his inexplicable lifestyle choices. Such thoughts were just useless distractions.

She had a superweapon to perfect.

The trio of slaves scrubbing the adjacent laboratory had no idea that they were test subjects. A couple of desorption pumps, hidden high up on shelves, spread an odorless, invisible dark-energy matrix throughout that room. The distorted encephalographic zone should not bother Torth at all. Indeed, the Upward Governess had finished her second breakfast while sitting within the outer distortion zone, and her perceptions were no different than usual. The gas had no effect on her.

On nontelepaths, however . . .

The Upward Governess licked crumbs off her teeth and surreptitiously watched her slaves from a calculated distance. If they were going to have a reaction, it would be very soon. And it would be quite fascinating to watch.

She kept her finger ready to twitch the door button. She didn't want the test subjects getting too close to her, under the influence of that gas. She would seal them behind glass if they made any violent moves.

One of the slaves—the one nearest to a desorption pump, a male ummin—began to blink rapidly. He dropped the sponge he had been using to clean the floor.

The Upward Governess leaned forward.

She was well beyond telepathy range, so she could not scan the thoughts running through the ummin's mind. But she was close enough.

Another slave dropped its janitorial mop. It was the govki, and it gawked at the ummin. The ummin gaped back. Wonderful. If these slaves were armed runaways rather than docile property, they would falter in battle. They would cease to be any sort of threat.

This was history in the making.

It was monstrously unfair that such a momentous event had to be kept a secret. Without validation from firsthand witnesses, wouldn't the news—when the gas was finally used in battle—lose some of its impact?

The Upward Governess wished she dared invite someone to witness this land-mark moment.

Sure, other supergeniuses might pick up contextual hints from the encrypted notes they all shared with one another. They were smart enough to keep their inferences and deductions a secret. She just wished for one colleague nearby, within her telepathy range, to bask in her brilliance.

Just one *(like Yellow Thomas)*.

Perhaps she should have adopted a new pupil to mentor. Maybe the boy Twin? Or the Geodesic Flux?

Meh. Neither was outstandingly ambitious. They lacked the creative spark that had shone in the mind of *(no, don't think about him)* her former mentee.

Really, nobody met her standards. The only reason she was even considering the boy Twin was because his curious nature reminded her a tiny bit of *(not worth thinking about)* her former mentee, and he was nearly of an age with *(don't think about)* . . .

Argh.

Why was she bothering to guard her thoughts so assiduously? Without the Megacosm, she had obscene amounts of privacy. She could reminisce about Yellow Thomas if she wanted to.

And she wanted to.

The Upward Governess allowed feelings to seep into the bottom of her mind. She liked to replay memories of Yellow Thomas, or memories that she had soaked up from him.

She didn't quite understand why she missed Yellow Thomas so much. Those irrational feelings of loss, and regret, and grief, and jealousy, and anger . . . they felt volatile. Emotions were far more dangerous than the encephalographic distortion zone in the adjacent laboratory.

But there were truths mixed in with those feelings. Alone like this, she inwardly admitted that she missed his way of seeing the universe.

She didn't understand why she missed him so much, but she did. No matter how she tried to—

The extrawide door to her breakfast room whooshed open.

The Upward Governess was so startled, she jerked. Her plate toppled off the armrest and shattered. Crumbs and shards of porcelain marred the clean floor.

She glared at the intruder. What fool dared to disturb her top-secret work?

It was the veteran Servant of All who was in charge of keeping her safe. He guarded her underground complex of laboratories. And just now, he had nearly caught her thinking illegal *(no) (suppress it) (feel nothing)* . . . He had caught her taking a very brief break from work.

It was a good thing he was beyond her range of telepathy.

The Upward Governess adjusted her position in her hoverchair, trying to flush out the dirty flood of feelings caught inside her mind. Cold facts always helped her to regain her dignity and her composure. She wanted to wrest an explanation from this Servant of All. She wanted that right now.

The guardian approached. Servants of All were usually the epitome of self-control, but this one looked concerned.

The Upward Governess shoved down all thoughts of her experiment. She read subtle cues in his face that something was wrong. Was her laboratory under threat? She ascended into the Megacosm, ready to learn the details . . .

!!!!!!!!!!!!!!!!!!!!!!!!!!!!!!!

Facts slapped her. These facts were gigantic, like curling breakers where there should be only lapping waves.

The enemies had invaded New GoodLife WaterGarden City.

The Betrayer had the temerity to invade *her* city.

And her neighbors? Her colleagues? They knelt on dirty floors, stripped of their weapons. They had been taken captive by . . .

Runaway slaves?!

It seemed so unlikely as to be absurd. But the slave tongue dominated posh boulevards and forums, and the recorded voice belonged to that elderly runaway, the one known as Kessa the Wise. The enemies must have hijacked advertisement broadcasts.

How?

They must have rigged a speaker system throughout the city. Had the Betrayer actually trained ummins to rewire electronics?

What else had he trained them to do?

I will escort You to safety, Great One. The Servant of All walked briskly into her immediate range. *Your lair is dangerously close to (the war zone) New GoodLife WaterGarden City.*

He emanated opprobrium. As far as he was concerned, a supergenius such as herself should have predicted this invasion, or at least factored it into her calculations.

Back up Your work, the Servant of All commanded her. *Then hand Me the data marble. I will keep Your research safe.*

The Upward Governess began the process of backing up her latest research. Eddies of blame swirled toward her. The Majority was in shock, but once they began to recover, there would be blame. They trusted their eldest supergenius to protect the empire. And she had failed.

Again.

As if anyone could possibly predict every move the Betrayer would make. He was a mastermind.

She finalized the data marble, aware that the Servant of All would guard her research more assiduously than he would guard her. She did not want to be dragged from one secret lair to another. Did she have no say in the matter? Was she as passive as luggage?

New GoodLife WaterGarden City was hers to govern.

She had given it new skyscrapers, new aquifers. It was her home. It was her protectorate.

This devastating invasion was a personal insult. It was a message from the Betrayer, specifically to her.

He was taunting her.

If she failed to answer the taunt in kind, she would look weak and ineffectual.

Anyhow, what was the point of collecting rare flowers and beautiful animals if she lost them? It seemed fruitless to own things if those things could just be removed without a Majority vote. The loss made her painfully aware that everything she currently owned—including her research—belonged to the Majority.

That had never bothered her before. But now . . . ?

She needed to face the Betrayer.

!!

A towering mental presence thundered into the Megacosm with the force of a supernova.

Him.

He sat far away, on the planet Reject-81. He peered at grassy plains rippling beneath a peaceful twilight sky.

Why would he show up where any random Torth could peer through his eyes and figure out his exact location? What could be worth such a risk?

Billions of Torth flocked to his orbit. The Upward Governess went with them, helplessly curious.

Every one of his orbiters vied to be the first winner to dig out a useful fact. They clawed into his gargantuan mind. Just how numerous were the enemy soldiers? What weapons did they favor? What was their communication system like?

Any sane renegade would have reeled away from all that relentless digging. The Betrayer ought to drop out of the Megacosm.

Instead, he did the most unexpected thing imaginable.

Join Me. The Betrayer loosened his outer cascades of data, inviting his audience closer.

????????????

A roar of confusion scrawled its way across the Megacosm. What was this nonsense? Why would anyone want to leave civilization and join a bunch of runaway slaves? Why would a bunch of runaways welcome Torth into their midst?

The Upward Governess gaped, heedless of the Servant of All who watched her in reality. Lies were impossible in the Megacosm. What sort of insanity was this?

The *???* reactions drove more traffic, more curiosity, toward the Betrayer's towering mind.

I offer a better life, the Betrayer thought to his billions of listeners. *You can feel happiness. Friendships. You can have children and families and loving relationships.*

Two pilots, on different planets, accidentally crashed their transports.

Torth dropped drinks, fell out of bed, or lost control of various situations while they tuned out reality and frantically scanned the Megacosm for any sign of reassurance. Babies on baby farms gnashed their teeth, screaming for comfort.

Throughout the galaxy, billions of Torth reeled out of his orbit, appalled and then ashamed of their uncouth feelings. They struggled to suppress the intensity of their questions.

Why do happiness and love matter?

What is a loving relationship?

Why would anyone want a family?

The Betrayer's sincerity shone like a desert sun. Instead of suppressing his emotions, he allowed everyone in his inner audience to know how much he cared.

I want to save You. He extended imaginary arms throughout the Megacosm, large enough to embrace all the Torth in the universe. *All You need to do is join Me.*

!!!

!!!!!!!!

!!!!!!!!!!!!!!!!!!

!!!

Several Torth on different worlds burst into tears. Raw displays of emotions were a sign of insanity, especially in these troubling times, and so their audiences fled.

Their neighbors felt no compunction in shooting them with blaster gloves, urged by their own concerned inner audiences.

Join Me, the Betrayer repeated, relentless. *You can research taboo sciences if You join Me. Allow Me to show You what mercy is.*

The Upward Governess could not bear another thought. The Betrayer's nerviness knocked all the breath out of her lungs. She feared that she might have a catastrophic illegal reaction herself if she continued to orbit his inviting mind.

She ripped herself out of the Megacosm.

Nearly a hundred Torth citizens throughout the galaxy had died, just now, from shocked reactions to the Betrayer's reckless message.

It was insane.

Anyone with intelligence should be able to reason out the ridiculousness of his offer. Who would agree to become a slave, just so they could experience unknown, mysterious friendships? And forbidden pleasures? And . . .

Well.

Hm.

The Betrayer's gumption stirred unseemly feelings inside the Upward Governess. She suppressed a giggle. He never quit trying to turn society upside down, did he? This was exactly the sort of bold move that she had always suspected him to be capable of, despite his lackluster performance under her mentorship.

No one else in the universe had the ability to surprise her quite like Yellow Thomas.

The Servant of All studied the Upward Governess, his gaze veiled by his milk-white ocular enhancements. A dark judgment radiated from him.

CHAPTER 6

HUBRIS

I want to save You. Please let Me save You All.

With those parting thoughts, Thomas wrenched himself out of the Megacosm.

It was awful to fall back into his mortal limitations. In the Megacosm, Thomas had no limits. He had embraced his mother's people with an infinite number of unraveling arms, entering space stations, palaces, cities, starships, and so much more.

He loved the Megacosm. Without guilt or shame, he loved it, despite its constituents.

But he resisted his urge to absorb the final wave of *!!!!!* reactions. It hurt to abstain from the cosmos of moods and imaginations and glorious knowledge, but he dropped out, leaving a calamitous vacuum as violent as a black hole.

The billions of Torth who had been in orbit around him would have to cling to each other and struggle, in the private depths of their individual minds, to process the benefits he offered.

Thomas inhaled the night wind, with its scents of campfires and wildflowers and distant snow. He opened his eyes.

"How did it go?" Vy asked.

Thomas still felt vaguely godlike from all the galactic attention. But he didn't want Vy to think he was acting superior, so he forced his triumph into a small, constrained grin. "It went well."

Then again . . . hadn't he just delivered a massive blow to the mightiest galactic empire in known history? Perhaps it was all right to bask in his own glory, just once. Vy might not judge him to be a hopeless egomaniac.

Thomas permitted himself an obscenely huge smile.

Vy was so anxious, she didn't even notice his wolfish glee. She was busy standing, still getting used to her new prosthetic. She had no inkling that hundreds of Torth had just died in accidents throughout the galaxy.

"What about Ariock?" she asked. "Is he all right?"

"He's fine." Thomas toned down his smile. "We're winning."

It was probably a good thing that Vy could not absorb other people's perceptions or scan minds. Glimpses of the Giant and his brutality were being shared and reshared throughout the Megacosm. Thomas was unsure how Vy would react to visions of Ariock storming through the city like a god of war, his armor dented and spattered with blood, his eyes alert and aglow.

The tension in Vy's shoulders relaxed. "So," she said in a light tone, "are the Torth falling over themselves to join us?"

"Not just yet." Thomas wondered what his future allies were doing right now. Cowering in their spas? Hiding under their covers with tranquility meshes dialed up to maximum settings?

He suspected that many Torth would join him . . . but only after the first one broke. Someone would have to be the first Torth to go renegade.

The first one besides himself, that was. Thomas figured he didn't really count.

He knew whom he hoped it would be. The Upward Governess had absorbed his message. Switching sides would require the ultimate in courage and sacrifice. She certainly had the courage—the relentless ambition, anyway—but Thomas wasn't entirely sure she would be willing to sacrifice her popularity, her wealth, and her authority.

Those would be hard things to give up. She had a lot to lose.

So maybe the first would not be her. Maybe it would be someone else.

A random Yellow Rank?

No. Thomas wanted the first Torth deserter to be someone popular, someone influential. Anyone of lesser status would simply be shrugged off by the Torth Majority. After all, they had shrugged him off, relabeling him "the Betrayer."

The first renegade ought to be someone popular.

Thomas mentally recounted the most popular Torth in the city. Aside from the Upward Governess, the city boasted one Crimson-Red and several Cobalt-Blue Ranks. He would gather them somewhere public. And he would invite each one, in person, to go renegade and join him. If one refused, he would ask the next. And the next.

He would continue to invite lesser Torth, too, of course. He didn't want to give the impression that his offer was only open to popular Torth with fan followings. He would rescue any Torth who was ready to sacrifice their lifestyle and risk a new beginning.

But popular or not, penitent Torth would have to approach him in chains. They would pass through a gauntlet of his troops. They must be checked for hidden weapons and given an extra dose of inhibitor. His troops would kill any who made a threatening move.

That should ensure that any Torth supplicants who approached him would have a somewhat large audience of witnesses in the Megacosm. They should be risk-takers. If one walked in chains through a gauntlet of enemies with the fierce hope of being accepted as a renegade . . . ? Well, then everyone in their inner audience would know it.

And feel it.

One successful convert to his side might be enough to influence other Torth to join him of their own free will.

"Should we go join Kessa?" Vy asked hesitantly. "And prepare to leave?"

She looked around wistfully. In the starlight, the snow-capped mountains were barely visible, yet she was clearly reluctant to leave this planet's natural beauty. Thomas felt it, too. Reject-81 was not urbanized. That gave it an especially rugged, unrestrained wildness.

One could walk away from duty and expectations in a place like this. One could live apart from people.

Provided, of course, that one could walk.

Thomas hovered in the direction of the lamplit refugee city, angling toward Kessa's headquarters. He would need a dose of NAI-12 soon, as well as a bathroom break and dinner. He couldn't do any of that without help. He floated slowly and allowed time for Vy to catch up and walk beside him.

"What will happen to Earth?" Vy asked.

Thomas sensed her tension. Vy kept trying to suppress her worries, but she was inwardly braced for terrible news. She missed her mother. She missed her foster siblings. And she knew that the Torth must be poised to enslave the people she loved.

The Torth would keep the Hollander home under intense surveillance. At any moment, on a whim, they might casually abduct Mrs. Hollander and use her to bait Thomas or Ariock.

"Today's battle," Thomas said, "hits the pause button on the enslavement of Earth. At least for a while."

"Really?" Vy studied him, hardly daring to hope.

"We have nearly a million Torth prisoners right now." Thomas had caught news flashes of events in the conquered city. Defeated Torth were being collared. Shackled. Chained together. Stripped of weapons. Every single Torth was put on the inhibitor serum, regardless of what eye color they exhibited.

His troops were collecting collars from freed slaves and fitting them onto Torth necks.

The defeated Torth would be corralled into slave zones and temporary holding cells. His troops would command them not to harm anyone. Disobedience was grounds for death.

"They're going to silently plead to be rescued," Thomas said, "in the Megacosm. The whole Torth Empire will have to listen to that. For hours. For days and weeks and maybe years."

Vy looked thoughtful.

"It's possible that an influential Torth or two will order them to shut up, or kill themselves," Thomas said, answering her unformed question. "But I doubt it. That would be bad for morale. Either way, Torth leadership will be extra cautious about driving their military into a situation where they're likely to get hammered and captured."

Vy looked at him with new respect. She had not considered all the ramifications of winning this battle.

"Don't get too confident," Thomas warned her. "The Torth have fifteen supergeniuses, and we have one. It's a matter of time before they outcompete us. But for now, we have an advantage they lack—teleportation—and I want us to milk it. The Torth won't touch Earth unless they're sure of victory there. They can't afford to keep taking devastating losses. The Torth Empire is built on hubris. If losing becomes a pattern for them, then their whole voter base—the Torth Majority—will lose confidence in their elected leaders again. And at that point? I think the whole empire is likely to fall apart like a house of cards."

Vy's eyes sparkled with determination. "Then we should make them lose again."

Thomas smiled. "Oh. We will."

CHAPTER 7

JOIN OR DIE

Move out of My range, the Upward Governess commanded the Servant of All.

He was rudely close. She overheard his inner audience, even though she was below the Megacosm, and they swarmed with suspicion. They wondered if anyone could trust her.

The Upward Governess tried to smooth her own mood. Of course she had no intention of letting herself get captured and enslaved. That would be ridiculous. She was perfectly loyal to the Torth Empire.

Although a part of her could not stop wondering: How would it feel to belong entirely to someone else?

To belong to the Betrayer?

The Upward Governess scanned her laboratory for things she wanted to bring. The Servant of All watched her every move, like she was a nussian that might lose its temper and go berserk. That was fine. Let him watch. Her thoughts whipped into high speed, too fast and too multilayered for an ordinary mind to pry into.

She extrapolated future scenarios. Thomas would never force her to do physical labor or anything menial. Would he?

Of course not. He knew her value, and he would want her at her sharpest. His minions would undoubtedly grant her whatever she required to stay focused on her work instead of on discomforts.

But she would be forbidden from the Megacosm.

Such a loss was painful even to contemplate. She would miss her admirers. The Upward Governess figured that she could survive without her indoor lake, her gardens, her observatory, her relaxing rooms, her spas, and her beautiful collections of seashells and jewels and fossils and so forth. Perhaps she could even go without a weekly gourmet banquet. Perhaps she could stand to eat sweets only on special occasions. Perhaps. As long as those sensory distractions were replaced by something sweeter and better.

But to lose the Megacosm?

That was cruel deprivation. She wasn't sure how the Betrayer managed to survive every day without it, but she wasn't so hardy.

On the other hand . . .

His side didn't have restrictive laws.

She would be able to act out long-repressed fantasies. Might that be almost as wondrous as the Megacosm?

Perhaps she and Thomas could invent medicines and technologies that would empower them to grow to adulthood. Might they invent a way to become immortal? Together, might they pioneer an improved civilization, better than either of theirs? Could they do it side by side, like a queen and king from some human fairy tale?

Maybe this was what Thomas wanted. Was this his aim, all along?

Perhaps that much freedom was worth giving up other freedoms.

What is wrong with Your slaves? the Servant of All inquired.

Her test subjects were on their knees, chores forgotten. Two of them sobbed. The third was silent, apparently overwhelmed by something unseen.

They are test subjects, the Upward Governess warned. *Do not approach them. This should not (become common knowledge) be investigated.*

He studied the affected slaves with an aura of deep misgiving.

The Upward Governess waggled her backup data marble.

Be careful with it, she reminded the Servant as he took it. *Do not let it fall into the hands of enemies. Or idiots. Remember, My work is top secret.*

The Servant of All raised his gloved hand.

She half expected an assassination attempt. Such an attempt would be illegal, and wrongful, but fools sometimes tried to murder that which they failed to comprehend. She mistrusted this Servant as much as he mistrusted her.

The Upward Governess let one of her pudgy fingers rest atop a repurposed button on her armrest. No one suspected the modifications she had made, in secret, to her hoverchair.

My work is vital, she reminded her protector. *If you wish the Torth Empire to triumph, then you need to protect Me.*

The Servant of All casually aimed at one of the weeping slaves and thumbed the trigger.

He murdered all three slaves in quick succession. For him, it was as easy as breathing. The slaves did not, and could not, fight back. They were having enough trouble just processing the effects from the distortion zone.

The Upward Governess flinched at each abrupt, unfair death. By the time the third slave lay in a puddle of gore, she could no longer suppress an acidic boil of rage.

This Servant had no right to end her experiment without her permission. These slaves had been helpless test subjects, not runaways. He had no right to destroy her property.

He had no right to make major decisions for her. To suggest that she flee to yet another hiding place? This was her life!

The Servant strode past her. He was so disgusted by her childish outrage, he failed to respect her rank. *You can restart your experiment with fresh test subjects once you are safely tucked away in another hiding place. Let's not leave hints for anyone to find and piece together what you were working on. I will ensure that your lab is blown up (destroyed).*

The Upward Governess floated after him, noting that the Servant had not removed his blaster glove. The Majority had given him clear orders—they wanted her safe and under guard. All her experiments and property here, including her favorite slaves, would be blown up.

For the good of the empire.

Without her permission.

The Majority had a valid rationale, yet it still seemed monstrously unfair. In her own domain, shouldn't she be in charge?

Fury coursed through her.

The Upward Governess opened a compartment in her hoverchair and used it to lever a candy into her mouth. The flavor helped soothe her, the same way a tranquility mesh might have done.

Once she felt civilized and adult, she ascended into the Megacosm.

The Betrayer was gone. The Megacosm still surged and crackled in his wake, rife with unseemly emotions and illicit ideas.

NEVER SURRENDER!

NEVER CAPITULATE!

Despite those cries of defiance, a discord of counterresistance ran through the Majority. Roughly a million Torth were being forced to bow to the conquering enemies. They didn't want to die. Many of them agreed that they would never surrender in their hearts . . . but they might attempt to survive. Was that all right?

And there were odd, quiet corners of the Megacosm.

No one dared suggest joining the Betrayer, of course. No one wanted to look insane or traitorous. And yet . . . there were quiet corners where there should be defiant proclamations.

I have an idea, the Upward Governess thought.

Billions of Torth instantly latched onto her mind.

Her inner audience swelled, growing to more than nine hundred billion. They wanted someone smart to answer the Betrayer's challenge. Who better than his former mentor? Hadn't the Upward Governess taught the Betrayer much of what he knew? Surely she had a superior mind?

The Betrayer wants a powerful alliance. He wants Me. The Upward Governess felt vulnerable admitting that fact to the masses. But anyone with a modicum of curiosity would wonder why the Betrayer had targeted New GoodLife WaterGarden City. The Majority would figure it out soon enough.

The Upward Governess gave the masses time to process what the Betrayer wanted, and why. Then she rolled out her idea.

Not even the enemies know what I've been working on. She flashed a mental image of herself approaching the Betrayer. *Let Us give him what he wants: Me. But he will get Me with a deadly secret weapon.*

The Megacosm writhed.

Half the Majority feared that she was going renegade. The other half voted that she was brilliant and trustworthy.

The Servant of All turned to face her. Regardless of what his inner audience thought—and their opinions were varied and split—he suspected that she might become a traitor to the empire. His instincts warred against the Majority's indecision.

The Upward Governess is a valuable asset, many minds sang.

She is untrustworthy, others sang. *Too emotional.*

She has never acted against the best interests of civilization, others chorused.

Protect her.

Kill her.

Protect her.

Kill her.

The Servant of All raised his blaster glove and aimed at the Upward Governess's face.

She sensed that he was no longer entirely sure if he trusted the Majority to make good decisions. They had voted to kill everyone of his rank, after all. That might still happen once the war ended and the Torth no longer needed Yeresunsa on their side.

He thumbed the trigger.

The Upward Governess pressed the jammer button on her armrest a split second before the Servant finished aiming at her face. She had retrofitted her hover-chair with a secret wave generator. It emitted a directional signal. It had a short range, but it should be enough to disrupt blaster gloves and other antimatter generators within its invisible penumbra.

While the Servant of All gaped at his gloved hand, shocked that it had failed to fire, the Upward Governess tapped a microdart button on her armrest.

While the Servant processed the fact that he was bereft of powers, and that his weapon was malfunctioning . . .

She had enough time to wiggle her thumb and forefinger into her own customized blaster weapon. Since it was behind the jammer, it was unaffected.

She aimed at his chest and thumbed the trigger.

His confused mind died in ropy sprays of blood and gray matter.

The Upward Governess flinched. This was the first time she had ever inflicted violence, except for pain seizures to chastise disobedient slaves. She truly disliked experiencing pain and death, even vicariously.

The ruined corpse dropped. Blood sprayed across the otherwise spotless floor, and a few droplets stained the pristine robes covering her stomach.

Ugh. Death was so unappealing.

The Upward Governess tapped her weapon into safety mode and sped toward the transport bay. *Allow Me to get close to the Betrayer*, she urged her listeners. *Allow Me to surprise him.*

The Megacosm blared with alarm. *!!!!!!!!!!!!!*

Servants of All rushed toward transports, hoping to intercept her before she could escape her lair and fly toward the conquered city she technically still governed. They would not allow their elected leader to put her own life and freedom in jeopardy. Not even if she had a secret weapon. Not even if it was for the greater good.

Dissenters swirled around those Servants, slowing them down and making them hesitate. *Let Her go.*

Let Us see whether She serves the Empire.

Or not.

The Upward Governess pushed her hoverchair to top speed. She was going to New GoodLife WaterGarden City. She dropped out of the Megacosm as a protective measure. It was best to be sneaky. Her approach ought to be a surprise.

She was going to confront the Betrayer and figure out *(if he would welcome her)* how best to kill him.

Let no one stand in her way.

CHAPTER 8

OLD FRIENDS AND NEW

Freed slaves were beginning to celebrate.

They feasted on gourmet foods and sampled nectar drinks. They splashed in lush bathhouses or in private spas. They exchanged rags for soft, pleasant garments and took joyrides on hoverchairs or hovercarts or hoverbikes. They experimented with the equipment in gymnasiums and pleasure lounges. A few cataleptic dreamers wandered aimlessly, but some former slaves had kindly taken it upon themselves to usher those individuals into recovery suites, where they would receive care.

Ariock soared over the city, buoyed on currents of air that he manipulated. The jubilation below him was almost palpable. Voices rang out everywhere.

He could not guess what tomorrow might bring, but right now? He could hardly contain his pride. He had liberated this city from millennia of harsh oppression. With help from his troops, and from Thomas, he had accomplished something no one had believed possible.

Ariock landed on one of the sandstone balconies that wrapped the largest forum in the city. Aliens taking in the fresh air hurried away, frightened by his menacing size and Torth-like appearance. Perhaps they noticed the splashes of blood on his armor, as well.

Glass partitions separated outside from within. All the doors were jammed wide-open, freely letting in the desert air, defying Torth customs.

Ariock ducked inside.

Under Torth rule, this forum would have been dead silent even during peak traffic hours. Now many thousands of voices echoed off the walls. It seemed the Torth had not taken acoustics into account when they engineered open floor plans.

Ariock spotted Garrett standing on one of the balconies, along with Jinishta and Weptolyso. Garrett was particularly easy to notice. He stood out amid aliens, despite his best efforts to downplay his uncanny resemblance to the conquered people.

Like Ariock, he wore bulky armor with spikes. Torth military ranks preferred formfitting body armor—all the better to slink around in. They did not stomp. They did not speak out loud or smoke cigars. And a Torth would be ashamed to wear such lowly colors as black or purple. That was why Ariock and his troops used those colors.

"Ah, there he is!" Garrett boomed. He waved Ariock over.

Aliens scurried out of Ariock's way as he strode toward his friends. Even the nussians eyed him with fearful respect. They probably assumed that a bigger version of a Torth had conquered their city. Ariock had already removed his helmet, and he tried to look as friendly as possible.

"Peace," he greeted people in the slave tongue. "Peace."

His gentle vocalizations did reassure some of the aliens. Ariock overheard a whispered mention that he was "the prisoner who escaped." At least some of these people remembered him.

An ummin squealed with joy. "It's the Bringer of Hope!"

Ariock recognized her Duin accent. He stopped in his tracks and stared with disbelief and happiness. "Utavlug Hano?"

He remembered the village herbalist. She had helped him recover after being crucified. She had helped his mother, as well.

"Yes!" Utavlug was more ragged and scrawnier than Ariock remembered. "See? I told you!" She turned to a few ummins in the crowd, presumably her friends. "I was not lying about the miracles on my slave farm!" She pointed at Ariock. "That is the Bringer of Hope!"

Aliens stared in amazement as Ariock knelt so he could properly greet Utavlug with a gentle hand-only hug.

"Are you well?" Utavlug asked. Before he could reply, she peppered him with more exuberant questions. "I saw Kessa in the window displays! We all did! Where is she? And Naglitay, my apprentice. Where is she? How about Pung? And Weptolyso? Oh, and Delia? And Vy? And Cherise? What about Thomas?"

Ariock chuckled, despite the pain of having to recount the death of his mother. Quite a few adolescents from Duin had also died on the slog through the dead city. They'd been devoured by telepathic cannibalistic apes. How was he going to explain that?

Instead, he answered her questions simply. "They're well. Mostly well. They'll be here soon."

The surrounding crowd of ummins clicked and squealed with giddy joy. Most of their chatter seemed to be about Kessa the Wise. They couldn't wait to meet her! They would be glad just to see her from afar! They could hardly believe she was a real person and not a myth!

"What about you?" Ariock asked, before Utavlug could begin to ask about the fate of the adolescents from Duin. "I was afraid the Torth would destroy you." Guilt washed over him. "I'm so sorry I wasn't able to—"

"It is all right." Utavlug pressed her tiny gray hands against his armored one, as if to absolve him. "You saved many of us. We understand that you did all you could."

We. That implied other survivors.

Ariock braced himself for news. "What happened to Molyt Dazel?" She was the head chief of Duin. "Did she survive?"

"No." Utavlug closed her eyes as a gesture of mourning. "She died bravely." Perhaps Utavlug did not wish to delve into details, because she hastened to add more. "The Torth did not murder all of us, as we thought they would. They destroyed our village. Some of us died, but they merely collared the rest of us. Now we are city slaves."

That much mercy was uncharacteristic of the Torth Empire. Ariock wondered if some high-ranked Blue or Servant of All had decided not to waste hundreds of able-bodied slaves and had somehow persuaded the Majority.

Or perhaps there was more to it?

At the time, the Torth Majority had been preoccupied with chasing Ariock and his friends. Maybe an especially insightful Torth had lobbied to preserve the Duin survivors, just in case they might be used as hostages, as a means to bait or pressure Ariock and his friends into compliance.

That sort of contingency plan would require premeditation. It seemed like something a supergenius would think of.

Was that why Thomas had targeted this city for liberation?

The more Ariock thought about it, the more sense it made. Thomas's lab assistants were all Duin refugees. He wouldn't feel comfortable working with people whose close relatives and friends were under Torth control.

By liberating Utavlug Hano and other Duin survivors, Thomas had ensured that the Torth could not hold a figurative knife to their throats. The Torth could not demand Kessa's cooperation, or Varktezo's, or anyone else's.

Thomas must have juggled that, plus a million other factors, when he'd planned this battle.

This conquest.

Even Jinishta looked proud as she strode over to join Ariock and Utavlug. Garrett came with her, as well as Weptolyso. They were joined by a hulking nussian, burnt red in color.

Ariock's friends had a few dents and scrapes on their armor. He briefly expanded his awareness to feel their life sparks.

Strong. No one was injured. Ariock relaxed, retracting his awareness.

"Weptolyso?" Utavlug looked overjoyed to see the orange nussian.

"Utavlug Hano?" Weptolyso broke into a huge grin.

While they stepped aside to catch up—Utavlug demanded to hear all about their adventures, and Weptolyso loved storytelling—Ariock straightened to his full height. He would be closer to eye level with Jinishta if he remained on one knee, but kneeling felt awkward with nussians around.

Ariock wanted to hear whether his troops had encountered any unexpected complications. And what about casualties? Even in a victory, some soldiers on his side must have gotten killed. There would be funerary processions even amid the celebrations. Ariock wanted to know the numbers of dead before he faced the general troops and the refugee camp.

"Nice armor," the humongous nussian rumbled to Ariock.

"Thanks." Ariock guessed the compliment was for his shoulder spikes and thorny joints. He had the size of a nussian; he figured he might as well embrace the iconic aliens as a way to help distance himself from what Torth heritage he had. If he was going to attempt something as insane as liberating the whole galaxy, he wanted to consider the people he was liberating to be his family in spirit.

Of all species, Ariock felt a kinship with the nussians. Sometimes he thought of Weptolyso as his brother.

"I am Nethroko." The huge nussian swept his head in a gesture of greeting.

Ariock had learned the basics of nussian etiquette from Weptolyso, as well as in the wrestling pits of the Alashani underground. He swept his head down and up in a greeting.

Inwardly, he wondered why Nethroko looked so familiar. Was the hulking red nussian a captain under Weptolyso's command? If so, shouldn't he be guarding Torth prisoners? Or helping to keep the peace among newly freed slaves?

Nethroko looked hesitant. His spinal ridge matched Ariock's height, yet he looked shy.

Weptolyso seemed to hear the awkward pause. He interrupted his own storytelling and shuffled over. "Nethroko is a friend of Vy and Cherise," Weptolyso said. "He was also a friend of your mother."

Ariock reassessed the enormous nussian. Now he realized why Nethroko looked familiar. He had been among the prison guards. Hadn't Nethroko led the team of guards who had dragged Ariock to be publicly crucified?

"He is honored to meet you," Weptolyso said.

"I am honored." Nethroko bowed his head.

Well, Ariock knew that nussians were as much slaves as any nontelepath species. As guards, they had been at the top of the slave hierarchy, but the Torth would still torture or murder nussians for disobedience. Nethroko could not be blamed for what he had been forced to do.

And if he had befriended Ariock's mother and friends? That meant he must have brought them news about Ariock's condition in the gladiatorial arena.

Kessa would have tried to shelter them. But nussians believed that truths, no matter how dangerous or devastating, must be told to those who asked. It was a moral obligation. *Knowledge*, they said, *is worth pain.*

"I am honored as well." Ariock bowed in return, with sincere respect. Nethroko had probably given Vy, Cherise, and Delia enough hope to fight through another day, another week, another month of slavery. Perhaps the nussian news network had given them courage to flee in the night when such an opportunity came.

"I will be honored to serve in your army," Nethroko rumbled.

"I believe Nethroko will make a good captain," Weptolyso hastened to add.

"Of course," Ariock said. Were they seeking his approval? "I trust your judgment, Weptolyso. And Nethroko, I know you are a top-notch fighter." He smiled to show that he held no grudge. "I'm glad to have you with us. The bigger and better our army, the better our chances of smashing the Torth Empire."

That seemed to be just the right thing to say. Nethroko and Weptolyso snorted in fierce approval.

Garrett walked over and clapped Ariock's gauntleted arm. He looked proud. "You fought well today."

Ariock couldn't help but feel a warm glow of pride. He and Garrett had their differences, and the old man wasn't his father—yet in a way, he was. Garrett had been looking out for Ariock all his life, from afar. He seemed to be trying, in his own way, to apologize for failing to protect the rest of their family.

"I assume you killed a few Torth yourself," Ariock said.

Garrett smiled. "A few hundred."

"With help from me and other warriors," Jinishta put in, unsmiling. "We had to kill many Torth who refused to kneel."

Ariock accepted that. He had not encountered much defiance in the conquered Torth, but then, he might be somewhat more intimidating than everyone else.

The local Torth would have attacked easier prey. They would have gone after the ummin and govki troops. Those brave volunteer soldiers would be crippled by blaster gloves, or dead. Albino warriors might have gotten sprayed with microdarts of the inhibitor and likewise killed.

Ariock braced himself for the downside of fighting for freedom. "How many of our people are dead?"

"None!" Garrett said cheerfully.

Ariock had no patience for tasteless jokes. He gave his great-grandfather a look.

"None of my warriors have gotten killed," Jinishta reported, as humorless as always.

"Zero for real," Garrett said. "Some of our nussians almost got killed. And a govki. They got hit with blasts. But Evenjos healed them."

Ariock stared from one leader to the next. This had to be a joke. Hundreds of Red Ranks were garrisoned in every Torth city, along with an equal number of Rosy Recruits. Many of those military ranks would have fought to the death.

"They were unprepared for us." Jinishta's bearing was regal. For her, that meant she was unusually proud.

Ariock could hardly believe it. He had lost friends and allies in smaller battles. In Duin, and in the rotten dead city, and in the hit on Reject-81 . . . he had lost people.

In a metropolitan area with millions of inhabitants? His side could not have won unscathed. Some of his people must be maimed, even if they were alive?

"Every one of our soldiers is well." That was Evenjos, her sweet voice exotically accented.

She coalesced and took shape, clad in a skimpy dress that made her look barbaric, with her breasts half bared, along with her mass of curly purple hair and her huge, metallic wings.

"I have healed everyone who needed it," Evenjos said with satisfaction. "No one on our side is crippled."

Power exuded off her in sparkling, glistening points of light. No doubt she was straining to be as sexy as possible, but for once, Ariock did not resent her for it. Not today. Evenjos was a miracle worker. Let her have whatever personality flaws she wanted to have.

"I am a sixth-magnitude healer," Evenjos reminded them all.

Ariock was a powerful healer himself, and so was Garrett, but it had not occurred to either of them to interrupt their fighting to track down wounded soldiers and heal them. Evenjos had given his side extra cause for celebration and high morale.

Perhaps she was more valuable as a battlefield healer than as a heavy-hitting warrior. Was that possible?

"We have . . ." Ariock dared to voice the incredible news. "No one hurt. No one dead. A total victory?"

He could easily face Vy, Kessa, and the millions of refugees with a report like this. They would be amazed.

Garrett shared the joy with a grin of his own. "The Torth, on the other hand, took quite a beating. We destroyed hundreds of Red Ranks and Rosy Recruits." Judging by his self-satisfaction, he had slaughtered a lot of those military ranks himself.

"It's time to bring Kessa and everyone else here." Ariock bounced on his toes, too happy to stand still. "Let's move on with turning Torth into slaves."

He put himself in a clairvoyant trance and sped across countless parsecs of space toward Reject-81.

CHAPTER 9

NOT QUITE HEROES

For Pung, the return to his home city felt unreal. Everything familiar was different.

Instead of stately Torth strolling through garden lounges, ummins zipped past on hoverbikes, laughing and whooping to each other. There was trash on the floor. Trash on the bushes. The Torth prisoners had not yet been entrusted with cleaning tasks in the upper city.

Pung imagined the local mind readers as they must be right now, trapped in the dank Tunnels. They would be holding their noses while raw sewage soaked into their slippers. Moldy filth would drip into their powdered hair. Would they squabble over lower-bunk privileges?

Kessa's former owner was probably down there. She would get no special treatment, of course. She was just another Torth. Interchangeable. That was how Torth viewed their slaves, after all.

Meanwhile? Pedestrians moved wherever they pleased, instead of being harried. There were no screams. The grand boulevards, with their mirror floors, were boisterous. Warriors and soldiers sat in lounges, gambling or chatting. They were armed with electric prods, blaster gloves, or Yeresunsa powers. They kept watch over the Tunnel mouths, which they had blocked with heaps of furniture and other items. A few volunteer ummins were down there as well, with radios. They would contact Jinishta in case of an emergency.

No one anticipated any emergency. Not today, at least. The imprisoned Torth had been stripped of weapons and shot full of inhibitor serum.

Although everything familiar was different, a few of those differences had become familiar to Pung. He had known freedom. So he attempted to introduce it to former slaves.

"But why would I have to have a *job*?" a huge mer nerctan boomed. "Free people don't need to work. That's the whole point of freedom, isn't it? Are you telling me we're still slaves?"

Pung stepped back. Mer nerctans had frighteningly large and bony heads, and they could swing those heads using their triple-jointed necks. Most members of that species were introverted, but Hajir was a gang boss. He threw his weight around like he was a nussian.

"No one will force you to work." Pung tried to sound reassuring. "There are no punishments for lazing around. Don't worry about that. But you must understand, Hajir, there are many thousands of cities like this one, and we have not conquered them all. We only have this one. If we fail to defend the territory we have gained, then we will lose our freedom again."

Pung indicated the scar around his neck. Hajir had one, too, and his was a lot fresher.

"You all seem to be doing just fine without me," Hajir grumbled. "What if I don't want to help you fight, or make weapons, or whatever it is your owners are demanding of me and my gang?"

Pung could not help but click his beak in annoyance. Had he ever been this ignorant?

Gralet stepped forward, although Pung tried to hold him back with one arm.

"We have no owners," Gralet said with stiff pride. "And I, for one, have never been a slave."

Pung sighed. Gralet was the eldest son of High Councilor Deschuba. He was of an age with Pung, but he had not grown up doing manual labor—he'd had chamber-maids—and he had no concept of what slavery was really like. He seemed to think it would be fun to personally introduce freedom to former slaves.

Everyone respected the Alashani, since they had Yeresunsa warriors. That meant Alashani councilors also clung to their status as well-respected authority figures. That was why Pung had allowed Gralet to tag along with him.

Maybe that was a mistake.

Hajir stared at Gralet as if he was a garbage-eater that had just bypassed all the security measures around its trash hatch and escaped.

Pung gently pushed Gralet back, trying to signal that the gang boss could be dangerous. "Every one of us is free." He maintained eye contact with Hajir. "But freedom does not mean that we act like Torth."

Hajir cocked his enormous, bony head. "You say we are not slaves anymore, yet you insist that we work? And under the command of someone appointed by your leaders?" He made a rattling sound, a mer nerctan version of disgust. "Then we are not free. You are a liar."

Among slaves, that was an intense accusation.

Gralet began to retort, but Pung squeezed his arm to silence him.

He turned his glare on Hajir. Really, he did not have time to stand here and argue with every single person he found lounging around or gorging on food. A few gang members had simply walked away the instant Pung implied that someone, somewhere, wanted help with some kind of work.

Perhaps it was time for Pung to end this argument just as rudely.

"Do as you wish, Hajir," Pung said. "Either you will help us, or you will act like a Torth and leech off us while we work." He turned away, urging Gralet to come with him. "But do not expect sympathy in exchange for behaving like the lazy gas bugs we have conquered. They were weak. Weak people are never leaders."

As they walked away, Gralet turned to look over his shoulder to see Hajir's reaction.

Pung did not bother. He used to smuggle items for gangs in the Tunnels, but he had never particularly liked Hajir.

"You said the right thing." Gralet looked at Pung, impressed. "That mer nerctan and his friends are going toward the registry clerk."

So it had actually worked! Pung hid his proud feeling and made himself sound nonchalant. "It is a skill that takes practice, to insult a gang boss in just the right manner without incurring violence."

Gralet looked even more impressed.

Pung continued to approach former slaves who looked like leaders. He un-derstood what horrors they feared—endless work shifts full of repetitive, menial tasks—and he tried to address their fears. "This is voluntary," he emphasized, over and over. "Your shift will last from one mealtime to the next. No more."

The registry clerks connected each volunteer worker with a task that might suit their temperament and energy levels. Some volunteers would assist chefs in the kitchens. Others would tailor clothes to fit non-Torth bodies, or make deliveries on hovercarts, or serve as lookouts on the city wall. They could chat with each other and even sing.

If they failed to do what was requested? The only punishment was a small degree of personal shame, because someone else would be asked to fill in for them.

The clerks ensured that everyone had off-duty periods. That was important. People were free to stroll around and celebrate and to eat and sleep as needed. As far as Pung was concerned, volunteer work had nothing in common with slave labor.

He hummed a jaunty Alashani tune as he headed down the boulevard. He was making things happen. It actually, oddly, felt fulfilling. It gave him the same feelings he used to get from smuggling food to unowned slaves who needed it. He was finding niches in the societal fabric that needed tightening, and tightening them.

"How is it going, Nror?" he asked a govki with tawny-yellow fur.

Nror used to work for the same owner as Pung. They used to chat together in the slave zone during work breaks. Although Nror had never met Kessa, the govki recalled that his former coworker used to speak highly of her. That was what had led him to make inquiries until he found Pung.

"Fifty-two napkin rings, so far." Nror held up one of the ornate rings, then let it clack back atop a tower of them. "One hundred and fifty-nine data marbles." He showed one, inlaid with golden filigree. "Five hundred and sixty-six glassware—"

"That is good," Pung interrupted. "No need to tell me the tallies."

Small items with perceived value were spread over a buffet table. Nror sat on a bench lounge, his furry six-limbed body bent at an awkward angle in order to fit on the Torth furniture. Other newly freed slaves sat in ergonomic chairs around the table. Most were ummins.

"Later, Pung." Gralet squeezed his shoulder and went on his way.

Tallying items for use in barter held no interest for the councilor's son. He seemed clueless about their possible uses as gambling chips.

Pung took a seat, joining the others. Once each group of items was tallied, they used tape to mark the number of pieces, using Alashani numerical script.

Exceptional volunteer workers would get rewarded with tokens. Pung had doubts that such a system would work as intended—it seemed too easy to exploit or cheat—but he felt sure the valuables would find their way into use anyway. Everyone, no matter what species, valued items that were well crafted and hard to come by.

It was a good idea to memorize the tallies. And then he would watch who tried to control each supply.

As Pung worked, he glanced out the big windows from time to time. Kessa was supposed to give a broadcast speech later. Her image would appear in windows, and those who wished to hear her words in person would go to the Victory Forum at the center of the city.

Kessa used to reject Pung's attempts to nuzzle her. She was too old, she'd said. She'd had a mate, she'd said. It seemed her heart remained loyal to her deceased mate.

But perhaps, with so many things changed . . . perhaps Kessa would change her mind?

Pung had always admired her. Now that he had seen proof of her good judgment—in the friends she chose, in the words she selected—he admired her more than ever.

"Pardon," someone said. "I was told that Pung is here. May I meet him?"

The new arrival was a pale govki with blue speckles in its fur. Pung made an inviting gesture. There was enough empty space around the table for extra help. "I am Pung," he said. "We are sorting valuables, to hand out later as rewards. Come, join us."

"I am Dyoot." The blue-speckled govki had a vocal range that implied a male gender identity. He settled on his haunches, forgoing a chair.

"You can take over these," an ummin offered Dyoot, showing him an ornate syrup ladle.

As Dyoot set to work, he glanced at Pung. "I heard that you know Garrett Dovanack?" he said.

Most people sought Pung because they wanted to hear about his adventures as a runaway slave. They wanted to hear about Kessa the Wise. Few even knew who Garrett was.

"Is he really Jonathan Stead?" Dyoot asked.

At that name, heads turned. Every slave had heard some version of the legend of Jonathan Stead.

"He is." Pung clacked another napkin ring onto the tally. "I do not think he is quite as impressive as the legend implies. But yes, he is the same hero."

Dyoot looked troubled.

"Why do you ask?" Pung said.

"He was my owner," Dyoot said. "For a much longer time than I have known freedom."

Gasps sounded around the table as former slaves grappled with the notion of a legendary hero who not only looked like a Torth but who had actually *been* a Torth.

A supposed hero who had owned someone they were sitting at a table with. They stared at Dyoot with newfound fascination.

"Did he treat you well?" Pung asked.

He found himself truly curious. Garrett had confessed to masquerading as a Torth, but here was a chance to question one of his slaves and perhaps gain a different perspective on the matter.

"He was a lenient owner," Dyoot said without inflection. "But if you are asking whether he acted like a hero? No." The govki seemed sad. "As a Torth, Jonathan Stead never showed any hint of being different. And I served him for as long as it takes for a govki baby to grow to an adult."

Everyone at the table was silent and thoughtful, processing that.

Dyoot pushed jeweled ladles together, his face pained with memories. "He punished me for work poorly done. He never spoke. He was simply an owner. A Torth."

Pung suspected he knew why Dyoot had sought him out.

"I have heard that you were owned by the one they call Thomas," Dyoot said.

Pung clicked napkin rings together. He should have known these questions would come as soon as people learned the whole story. Liberated slaves were intensely curious about their liberators.

Nror looked like he was suppressing a storm of questions. His gaze was intense. The govki had not questioned Pung much about his adventures, but now it looked like he regretted his own politeness.

"Yes," Pung admitted.

There was no use denying it. Nror remembered the human slaves and their claims about the Yellow Rank, the one they called Thomas. Pung, Kessa, the humans, Weptolyso, Ariock, and that Yellow Rank had all escaped at the same time. Everyone in the city remembered that night.

"Well?" Dyoot studied Pung. "What do you think of Thomas? Is he different now, compared to when he owned you as his property?"

This was a subject Pung tried to avoid thinking about. It felt sore, like an open wound.

Now, as he examined his feelings on the matter, he began to understand why he felt so conflicted whenever someone mentioned Thomas, whether it was in praise or in judgment.

"I have seen him do great deeds." Pung gazed at the pretty items on the table, a spread of wealth that a slave never would have been permitted to examine at leisure before. "He helped save a world full of innocent people. I owe my freedom to him, as much as I owe it to the heroic deeds of Kessa and Weptolyso and Ariock."

And yet.

"He does not speak to you." Dyoot stated it as a fact, with more assurance than a guess. "He never bothered to apologize for the way he treated you when you were his slave."

That was the truth.

"I suppose he must want to distance himself from his time as a Torth," Pung said.

Then he wondered why he was making excuses for his former owner. Why defend Thomas? Pung was not sure Thomas would do the same for him if their roles were switched.

"Garrett has not spoken to me, either." Dyoot gazed out the window, at the distant figures of sentries standing on balconies, watching the skies. "I hear that he is a great hero. A legend. People say he slew a thousand Torth."

Pung understood how disconcerting it was to hear such high praise for someone who used to be a distant, unsmiling, and rather terrifying figure. He still remembered when Thomas had punished him with a pain seizure. And worse: Pung had blamed himself for that pain, for causing trouble for his owner.

He had not dared blame his owner. He had not dared despise Yellow Thomas, because Yellow Thomas was a mind reader with the power of life and death over his slaves.

Pung would always have kind words to say about Kessa and Weptolyso. Ariock, as well. But it was much harder for him to say anything charitable about Thomas. If he tried, a conflicted feeling arose in him.

Surely he did not need an apology from Thomas?

It seemed like such a petty thing to want.

Pung didn't want to be petty, so he sought a way to end the uncomfortable conversation. "We are free now. That is what matters."

Dyoot made a sound of agreement and continued sorting items. "Are you certain these heroes who have liberated us are not just a new breed of Torth?"

Pung made a dismissive sound.

He tried to dismiss the idea entirely. He worked on sorting napkin rings and data marbles. But no matter how many times he reassured himself that Kessa had good judgment, he knew that other liberated slaves must have the same concern as Dyoot.

There was a vast gulf between imprisoned Torth and liberated slaves. Pung wasn't sure if the chasm could ever be bridged, but he suspected that an apology from former owners might go a long way.

CHAPTER 10

RARITY OF RENEGADES

Thomas floated down a mirrored boulevard, accompanied by Nethroko, plus seven other hulking, battle-scarred nussians.

People looked at him with distrust. It didn't matter that his chair was black and purple or that he wore plain woolens. In a city cleansed of Torth, Thomas looked very much like a Torth in a floating hoverchair.

At least he appeared to be under guard.

He kept his eyes downcast, trying to hide his iridescent-yellow gaze. He really needed an hour of downtime to reprogram his artificial irises to be black, or perhaps a low-key shade of brown. Ideally, he would remove the implants altogether and reestablish his natural eye color—but that would require specialist surgery, plus days of recovery time. Something to do on another day.

He had rejected the idea of wearing a fake slave collar. Although it would set people's minds at ease, Thomas felt uncomfortable with that level of deception. It was too close to telling a lie.

As he floated around a bend in the boulevard, he surreptitiously checked the stolen data tablet he had hacked. It lay on the seat beside him, cradled and hidden by a careful arrangement of his lap blanket. Vy had done that. The glowing screen should not be visible to anyone who casually glanced his way. If he had to tap or scroll, he could do so without much effort, and without looking too obvious about it.

"Any update?" Nethroko rumbled.

"Nope." Thomas tapped through different views of the city's outskirts.

He saw peaceful sandstone buildings. Figures stood on causeways, keeping watch. Most of them were eagle-eyed ummins, but there were Alashani warriors present as well. Just in case.

A lone military transport had soared into the city less than an hour ago. That set Thomas on edge. He'd investigated the transport soon after it docked, of course, using sensor drones via his tablet's governance utilities. He hadn't found any threats. No trace of a bomb.

The retracted pilot's seat hinted at a hoverchair user.

Thomas hoped. He really hoped. If it was the Upward Governess, then she had shown up alone. That was a sign of goodwill.

The city was secured on several levels. Besides the sentries keeping watch, there was Garrett. The old man scanned the Megacosm every few minutes. All the news he reported was good—spaceports in every major hub city were ultrabusy, with streamships and shuttles launching every two seconds. The Torth Empire was in a full-blown panic.

And why not? The apocalyptic destruction of the Torth Homeworld was still a fresh wound. The Torth military had not had to defend territory for more than twenty millennia. Their most heavily populated planets—such as Umdalkdul—tendedto be vacation zones or bountiful breadbaskets, with scant military armaments.

The Torth Majority feared that the Betrayer might send the Giant anywhere next. He might invade United MetroHub on Verdantia, or StayYoung City on Bountiful. They couldn't predict what he planned. So metropolises throughout the galaxy were emptying out.

All that evacuation activity implied that the Torth would likely hold off on a major counterstrike. At least for a few days. They were busy.

As an extra precaution, though, Thomas had asked Ariock to spike out his awareness every hour or so.

Ariock was spending the day drinking toasts to warriors, taking reports, feasting, and spending quality time with Vy. But he could be trusted to catch missiles or other unexpected threats. He understood the potential dangers of holding a million Torth hostage.

As for Evenjos . . . well, Thomas was not sure what she was up to. Maybe she was pretending to be a nussian? Or floating in the sky as a cloud?

He figured the less he kept tabs on her, the better. She was perceptive, sneaky, and dangerously paranoid about him.

Thomas glided across a sunny intersection that was devoid of crowds except for albino warriors and armed troops. They recognized Thomas and allowed him to pass, although they did not look happy about it. Each warrior was armed with spears. Soldiers stood with loops of chain, ready to shackle any Torth supplicant who might approach.

Thomas passed through that receiving gauntlet. From there, he entered the most secured place in the city.

The recently renamed Victory Forum used to be a last-minute bargain outlet for Torth travelers. It was adjacent to the spaceport. Delicate-looking bridges spanned the vertical space, connecting tiers of curved steel-and-glasswork balconies. Fountains and gardens decorated the ground floor.

Overall, the forum was larger than several football stadiums. And it was packed with aliens.

Kessa was scheduled to give a speech here soon. Half the city wanted to see her in person.

Thomas hoped she would be able to face this enormous crowd without losing her elegant bearing. She had spoken to refugees before, but never to a crowd so large. This forum must contain upward of two hundred thousand individuals. On top of that, Thomas had arranged camera drones in obtrusive places on the promontory where Kessa would speak, so her image could be live streamed throughout the city.

Gauntlets of warriors and soldiers blocked access to every entrance. But they were not the main reason the place was secure.

Thomas felt extra safe with the Dovanacks present.

Garrett lounged on a comfy chair, smoking a pipe. He wore leatherwork armor and a black cape and mantle. Although he did look out of place, Weptolyso crouched near him. Jinishta, Utavlug Hano, Councilor Deschuba, Vy, and several more people of various species sat in guest-of-honor seats on the mezzanine.

Ariock leaned, arms folded, against a marble door frame that led to an offset gallery. The doorway was oversize, built for nussians and hovercarts, but Ariock still had to slouch.

He had changed his armor. This new set was polished onyx with glimmering inlaid designs, like constellations. A good choice. It was classy and understated, and not spattered with blood. It wouldn't draw too much attention away from Kessa. Ariock seemed to have a knack for optics.

Thomas peeked into the offset gallery.

Forty Torth awaited him in there, shackled, chained, and looking miserable. Three times as many albino warriors sat on marble bench seats around the room. They guarded the Torth with alert gazes.

A premier warrior stood to meet Thomas. "The prisoners are ready for you."

Thomas raised his eyebrow at the number of shackled Torth. He had asked for top ranks—Torth with white, red, or especially blue eyes—but he hadn't guessed there would be so many. All the Servants and Rosies had died in battle. So had a lot of Red Ranks.

"Are these the prisoners you wanted?" The premier sounded skeptical.

"You did well. Thank you." Thomas hid his disappointment. If the Upward Governess had landed in the city, then she hadn't made her way here.

Yet.

He could have projected a holograph of the Indigo-Blue Rank prisoner he most wanted to see, but he didn't want to make it obvious. It was best if the Torth Majority remained uncertain as to whether Thomas meant to kill or embrace his former mentor. He would not make it easy for Torth prisoners to decide to martyr themselves in an assassination attempt.

He probably should have distributed sketches to sentries so they would recognize the Upward Governess and usher her this way. He could have recruited Cherise for the sketch work.

Right. As if she would work for Thomas.

He forced his mind away from that impossible idea. Cherise was probably canoodling with Flen right now.

Not my concern, Thomas had to remind himself. *None of my business.*

Even so, he couldn't help knowing the things he knew. He had absorbed a lot of schedules. So he knew that Flen was off-duty, and so was Cherise.

They were probably picking out a bedroom suite together. Ugh.

The huge crowd quieted. On the far end of the mezzanine, Kessa approached the jutting promontory.

Thomas shifted his focus to things that mattered.

Kessa hopped onto a floating step, which boosted her high enough to be seen over the mezzanine railing. She had chosen a tunic and head cover of simple white elegance. The outfit was understated, with touches of gold and silver, yet it wasn't heavily ornate. Not Torth. Not Alashani, either. If anything, it evoked ancient Egypt.

Kessa might be pleased to know that she looked like an ummin from before the conquest of her world, judging by preserved historical memories in the Megacosm. Thomas made a mental note to tell her.

"Our city," Kessa said, "is free from Torth rulers."

Her voice filled the vast space, crisp and clear, amplified by Yeresunsa-manipulated flows of air. Everyone heard her.

Volunteer workers would relay her speech to other forums. Thomas wanted to set up a citywide speaker system. For the next conquest, he wanted Kessa's message to include unavoidable audio as well as visuals. His system would need to be quick to install and difficult to break.

Her live image was broadcast beyond the glassy walls. She dominated window displays throughout the city. During the chaotic invasion, the Torth had tried and failed to destroy Thomas's overrides to their governance controls. He had embedded false trails and misleading encryption keys, confounding anyone who tried to disable the broadcast. A supergenius could have hacked past the problems he'd set up—but the empire's supergeniuses had been too shocked, or too busy, to work on a relatively minor issue.

Now that Thomas controlled the city, he wasn't allowing any Torth prisoners near technology.

"Some of you remember me," Kessa said, "from when I was a slave in this city."

She recounted her neighborhood in the Tunnels. As she pointed to her friends among the local population, aliens throughout the Victory Forum relaxed a bit. If any had doubted that she was a runaway slave, their doubts eased.

Kessa gestured behind her. "I understand that it is hard to trust the faces of my friends. But I have journeyed with them, and they have earned my trust."

Thomas backed away. He understood that Kessa would likely introduce him to this huge audience of freed slaves, but he privately hoped that she would skip him. Vy and Ariock deserved her praise. He wasn't sure that his good deeds balanced out the things he had done as a Torth.

"This is Vy," Kessa said, tugging Vy upright. "She was a slave alongside me."

Kessa spoke of the human slaves. She explained that Delia had tragically died and that Cherise was elsewhere in the city.

That led her to introduce Weptolyso. The former hall guard grinned and waved to the crowd, earning bellows of approval from hundreds of nussians.

"And this is the Son of Storms, the Bringer of Hope, and the savior of the Alashani," Kessa said, beckoning for Ariock to step more into view. "He is my friend, the Torth-slayer Ariock Dovanack."

The onlookers had quite a reaction to Ariock. Whether it was his size, his armor, his titles, or the things they had seen him do, the aliens cheered or shouted to be heard.

Ariock gave a hesitant wave, and they cheered even louder. Thomas heard a roar of individual voices demanding to hear whether the giant could read minds and how he had earned his titles.

So Kessa told them.

At some point during the tale, she introduced Thomas. The cheering died away completely as people learned that Thomas could read minds. That he was a renegade Torth. That he used to own slaves.

Thomas tried to harden his heart. So what if the aliens judged him harshly? He was used to unspoken criticism.

It didn't matter what they thought of him. It didn't change anything.

They remained silent as Kessa explained that Thomas had helped her escape this city. And how he had aided the slaves of Duin in slaughtering Torth. Utavlug and Varktezo both stood up during that point in the tale, and they helped defend Thomas.

Kessa emphasized the fact that Thomas was half human and that he had been raised by humans. Then there was the fact that Thomas had piloted the stolen streamship to another world. And his quest to free the Lady of Sorrow. His success.

Kessa made him sound absurdly like a hero in a legend.

When she introduced Jinishta and the Alashani underworld, the focus finally shifted off Thomas. The listeners were rapt as Kessa described the freedom of the Alashani. She introduced Jonathan Stead, now known as Garrett, and the aliens were amazed. She described Evenjos's terrible power.

Thomas left the mezzanine, glad to be out of the spotlight. While Kessa spoke to the freed aliens, he had his own, very different, audience to address.

"Nethroko," he said. "Will you bring me one of the prisoners? Please make it that one. The one with blue eyes."

Two enormous prison guards dragged forth a timid-looking bearded man. Not the Upward Governess, but the next best thing: her right-hand underling. She had personally appointed this Blue Rank to take over in her stead. She had entrusted him with her city, with all her favorite gardens and places.

Knowing the way she thought, Thomas suspected this man might have a few un-Torth-like qualities.

Kessa's voice continued to ring out. She described freedom. Not childish chaos, as many slaves believed, but fertile soil in which new thoughts and ideas could grow.

She informed the city's alien population that they could choose their own destinies. They could drive vehicles and operate other technology if they wished. They could be nurses, or builders, or suppliers, or engineers, or warriors.

Thomas parked his hoverchair and focused on the defiant prisoner.

They were close enough so that their thoughts overlapped. Thomas tuned out the minds of the nussian guards. He had already absorbed their names, their life stories, their hopes and dreams.

The prisoner's mind was full of distant observers who sang warnings.

Do not listen to the Betrayer.

Do not cooperate with the Betrayer.

Remember, he tricked the Upward Governess.

He tricked the Former Commander.

He can offer nothing but (tempting) deceptions.

Thomas remained below the Megacosm, apart from the distant audience. He gazed into the prisoner's artificially deep-blue eyes. *Will you be brave?* he wondered. *Will you take a risk and join Me?*

The Blue Rank recoiled. He closed his eyes, fervently missing his tranquility mesh. He yearned for his relaxing room and a foot massage from his favorite slave.

You are a prisoner. Thomas spoke no words. The language of thought was much faster and easier for both of them. *You will never have a relaxing room again. You will never own slaves again.*

Inside the prisoner's mind, distant orbiters screamed. *Never surrender! Never capitulate!* They urged the prisoner to punish the Betrayer with a pain seizure.

The prisoner shuddered. Guards had warned him, and all prisoners, not to inflict harm.

He was caught between the Torth Majority and the Betrayer. Disobedience toward either one meant death.

The Majority has no power in this liberated city, Thomas pointed out. *This is My city.*

He pictured this man toiling under a hot sun, chained to hundreds of other prisoners. Such prisoners would grow frail and die in silence and in shame, each one alone among many. No one would rescue them. The Majority would cut its losses and let them die.

Or . . .

Join Me, Thomas urged.

He pictured the same man relaxed, at a table, deferential to other species but freely offering information to help them. In this version, the prisoner wore a simple tunic instead of rags and a slave collar. Aliens would scorn him as a former Torth, but he would have a chance to win their trust, if he agreed to—

NO. The prisoner jerked back. He could not get far, held by chains and gigantic nussians.

Thomas sensed deep conflict within the prisoner. He probed further.

The prisoner did not believe that it was possible to escape the Torth Empire. The Torth owned everything.

When Thomas urged the prisoner to question that belief, he was drowned out by an overwhelming cacophony from the Majority.

NEVER! millions of minds screeched.

   Do not listen to the Betrayer!

    Tune him out!

     We do not tolerate traitors!

"Never," the prisoner croaked in a voice that was rusty from lack of use.

For one frustrated microsecond, Thomas wondered if dragging this prisoner out of the Megacosm might help.

Except that was impossible. Thomas *could* force someone out of the Megacosm by twisting their mind, but that would defeat the whole purpose. He needed willing converts. He needed true allies, not helpless victims. Other Torth needed to see reasons to join him, not reasons to flee him.

Even if he could gently guide someone away from their mental audience . . .

Torth carried imaginary orbiters inside their souls. Thomas knew that. It had taken him months to break free from the mind-set of being Yellow Thomas. The imaginary audience was a protection. It gave warning before a Torth could do something fatally stupid: something illegal that defied the Majority.

"N e v e r." Other prisoners whispered throughout the gallery.

Guards shared nervous glances. Few of them had ever heard Torth communicate out loud.

The whispers synced up. "N e v e r r r. N e v v v e r. N e v v v e r."

On the mezzanine, Garrett glanced toward the gallery with a skeptically raised eyebrow. Ariock looked disappointed. Kessa went on with her speech, but Thomas knew that she was not oblivious. She heard.

And she knew that he had failed.

Thomas leaned against his ergonomic headrest, frustrated. If only the Upward Governess would show up. With her capable mind, she would grasp all the implications of joining him. Surely she would want to?

He would, if he were her.

"N e v v v e r."

The dud glared at Thomas. His thoughts sizzled with defiance. *The Upward Governess will never (betray civilization) join you,* he thought. *And neither will I. Go away, BETRAYER!*

So be it.

"This one can go back into the Tunnels," Thomas told Nethroko. "Give him a slave collar. He's beyond redemption."

Guards hauled the prisoner away, and Thomas scanned the remaining thirty-nine. Inwardly, he cataloged every face. He noted the slightest hints of doubt.

All he needed was one brave Torth. Just one top rank should be enough to crack the peer pressure of the Majority. Once one took the risk, others would follow.

"Next," Thomas said.

CHAPTER 11

QUESTION MARK

Help Us.

Rescue Us.

We are (filthy) (wretched) (disgusting) (odious) (miserable) prisoners.

What a bunch of whiners.

Thomas tuned out their mental wails. He was not in the Megacosm, so he did not have to endure the full brunt of the pleas for help, but he did float close to yet another defiant prisoner. He could not help but overhear the low-ranked wretches who filled the Tunnels beneath the conquered city.

While Thomas urged the cruel-looking man in front of him to aid freed slaves instead of the Torth Empire, an ummin courier showed up. The out-of-breath ummin stood on tiptoes and whispered something to the premier Yeresunsa in charge of the local guards.

?

Thomas realized the Crimson-Red prisoner was studying the exchange. Alert. He listened with all his senses while an enormous inner audience peered through his eyes.

Thomas moved out of the range of the stubborn prisoner, precluding any possibility that he might glean sensitive military information. He wondered why he was even bothering to try to convert these top ranks. They were so staunchly loyal to the Torth Majority, they refused to contemplate a single idea offered by the Betrayer. They tuned him out.

The premier Yeresunsa saw Thomas floating toward him and stepped back.

Thomas stopped short. By now, every Alashani had learned what constituted a four-yard range. The premier would probably scream for help if he floated any closer.

"What is it?" Thomas asked politely.

The premier answered after a guarded hesitation. "A fat Torth with blue eyes has showed up. She presents herself as a voluntary slave."

Thomas sat up straighter, as much as his bent and weakened spine would allow.

He tapped the data tablet by his side. Judging by the direction the courier had run from, he could guess which gate the supplicant was at. He accessed a live feed.

It was her.

As Thomas watched, former slaves inspected the Upward Governess. They checked her voluminous robes. They removed small items from her armrest compartment, probably candy. She must have showed up unarmed. Any hint of a threat would have triggered his people to open fire on her.

Alashani warriors stood nearby, ready to attack the Upward Governess if she showed the least sign of malice. No doubt they had already stuck an inhibitor patch to her skin.

"I would like her brought here, please," Thomas said.

"They will bring her," the premier said with a resigned shrug. He knew the rules. "But I warn you, this one is hard to take seriously. She cannot perform slave labor. Her limbs are as weak as yours, and she is very fat. She floats in a hoverchair more ornate than—"

Thomas cut the premier off. "Let her in."

In the corner of his vision, he noted that the prisoners looked alert. The nearest ones must have overheard.

The Upward Governess was the elected leader of the Torth Empire. This news would spread through the Megacosm like wildfire. The instant she switched sides— if she switched sides—the Megacosm would shatter into pieces. A flood of renegades would follow.

Garrett would have said something if this news had already hit.

So the Upward Governess must be avoiding the Megacosm—a definite sign of goodwill. It implied that she was serious about obeying Thomas's laws for mind readers.

Unless . . .

Could this be an elaborate trick?

The Upward Governess had been working on a secret weapon. What if she was concealing a heretofore-unknown type of bomb in her hoverchair? Something deadly that Thomas's people were unable to detect or confiscate?

Or perhaps she intended to serve Thomas loyally for a few minutes—only to double-cross him when it was most convenient for the Torth Empire?

She might have already sent encrypted messages prearranging her own rescue.

Even if this was not a ruse, Thomas had to be prepared for nasty battle tactics. If the Upward Governess joined him, the Torth Majority would become a lot more desperate. And more vicious.

"Ariock," Thomas called.

Ariock lumbered away from his position on the mezzanine, where he had been leaning against a marble support pillar. He gave Thomas a questioning look.

"We might have a tense situation in a bit." Thomas kept his voice low. "I think we might have a high-profile Torth on our side." He hesitated, then voiced his hope out loud. "The Upward Governess."

Ariock's expression went from neutral to cautiously approving. He was close enough for Thomas to overhear his thoughts. As far as Ariock was concerned, any new ally they gained was good news. A supergenius? That was the best news possible.

Ever since Evenjos had joined them, Ariock had felt more secure, confident that someone powerful could back him up if his powers got depleted or if he fell in battle. If Thomas gained his own version of a backup? Well, then. Perhaps they really could take over the galaxy together.

Garrett strolled toward Thomas. The stir of whispers must have alerted him that something was happening.

Vy, too, and Jinishta, and Weptolyso had noticed. And others.

Kessa paused in her speech. She glanced at Thomas.

"We might have a new ally joining us," Thomas admitted, his young voice seeming too loud in the relative silence. He would need to scan the Upward Governess's mind in order to feel reasonably sure.

He would need to let her get close. Within telepathy range.

But that was all right, he told himself. He was going to search her mood, search her thoughts, and get reacquainted with who she really was. Never mind the layers of subterfuge she had adapted in order to survive and thrive as a Torth. Thomas understood how that worked. He had done it himself. If the Upward Governess was an expert at fooling mind readers . . . well, so what?

She might be eager to put her masks aside and allow someone else to see the deepest truths at her core.

Thomas actually wanted to reconnect with her vast mind, that mind that was so unique, so filled with alien knowledge and endless things to learn.

"When she shows up," Thomas said to Ariock, "please protect her."

Ariock nodded. He understood. Garrett looked suspicious, but Ariock grasped the implications right away.

"Should I teleport her to our encampment on Reject-81?" Ariock asked.

"No." Thomas had considered the optics of the situation. He couldn't afford the appearance of kidnapping the Upward Governess. That was a form of coercion. The whole point was to make a show of her willingness to join him, so that other Torth would be brave enough to follow her example.

If, of course, she was actually joining him and not just faking it.

Thomas had to learn that.

"I'm going to need to probe her mind," Thomas said, "before we do anything with her. So you'll need to protect both of us while I do that."

"I don't see the Torth surprise attacking us here," Garrett said dryly. "Their nearest fleet is more than an hour away."

Thomas acknowledged that with a nod. Garrett was likely right. Still . . .

"I'd appreciate it if you keep scanning the Megacosm," he told the old man. "You'll have to alert us if the Torth suddenly figure out how to teleport or if they gain any type of new advantage."

"Got it," Garrett said. For once, he sounded respectful instead of sarcastic. Today's victory had impressed him.

On the promontory, Kessa began to finalize her speech. "You are in charge of your own lives now." Her voice continued to be amplified, probably boosted by Jinishta's power. "You may claim the rooms of your former owners for yourselves and for your friends. If you need a place to sleep, or anything else, please seek out my clerks. You are welcome to volunteer to help us liberate more slaves. But remember, no one owns you. No one has the right to claim you as property or to force you to labor. If anyone tries to force you, please visit one of the peacekeepers or have someone deliver a message to them."

The assembly jostled with excitement. They had seen that the peacekeepers were mostly nussians who wore a black armband or black spinal decorations. Weptolyso and Nethroko had displayed their accoutrements.

Kessa had to raise her voice to recapture attention. "I beg you to show mercy to the Torth prisoners. They will be our slaves."

A great cheer went up.

This was not the cheer of sports fans or theatergoers. This was the release of centuries' worth of pent-up steam. It didn't matter what species the aliens were. From the strangest exotics to the most average of ummins, everyone jumped and screamed with victory.

In the midst of all that, the Upward Governess arrived.

Thomas had already turned his back on the worthless high-ranked prisoners. He floated out of the gallery, where he could see the terrace doors at the far side of the crowded, wraparound mezzanine. While aliens cheered, the doors slid open.

Alashani warriors flanked her extrawide hoverchair. The Upward Governess floated there, slightly disheveled, although her robes gleamed with rich brocade. Shackles squeezed her wrists. What ridiculous symbology. She was as physically weak as Thomas. She couldn't lift a gun or a blaster glove unless it was specially modified, and she had none. The guards had searched her.

Jubilant aliens fell silent as warriors marched the rotund prisoner toward Thomas. People gawked. Some looked offended by her decadence. Some looked stunned.

"She should bow to us," Garrett suggested.

"To Kessa," Thomas corrected. He knew that the Upward Governess needed to show visible subservience. She had to make her allegiance clear. If she joined Thomas, she would be embarking on a long path toward earning the trust of freed aliens.

Murmurs rippled through the freed people. Skeptical glances passed from one to another.

One of the Alashani guards escorting the Upward Governess was none other than Flen.

How had that happened? Flen must have swapped shifts with someone, insistent on being near Kessa's first-of-its-kind speech. Or maybe he had heard that Thomas was silently trying to persuade Torth to go renegade? Maybe he wanted to see it for himself. Or put a stop to it. Most Alashani distrusted *rekvehs*, but Flen seemed to feel especially strongly about it.

"Protect her." Thomas wished he'd had time to brief Ariock on the myriad of possible dangers. Some people in this assembly wore weapons. What if someone got trigger-happy? What if her armed escort turned against her?

Thomas sensed Ariock's focus sharpening. A pressurized air shield blazed around the Upward Governess, visible as colorful waves traversing the surface of a bubble.

Good.

Another air shield solidified around Thomas. He blinked in surprise. This wasn't Ariock.

"She could be dangerous," Garrett said, his voice tight with tension.

Thomas glanced at Garrett and saw confirmation that the old man was invisibly protecting him. It seemed he expected an attack from the Upward Governess.

And he was right to be wary.

In order to get this far, the Upward Governess must have persuaded the entire Torth Majority to allow her to visit the Betrayer in person. She must have fed them a logical reason. Otherwise, a military fleet would have stopped her.

Her mind was too vast for anyone, even Thomas, to fully probe in one sitting. He should be able to determine her true motives . . . but she knew him very well. She knew every second of Thomas's childhood. If anyone in the galaxy was capable of outwitting him, it was her.

She might do anything.

The alertness throughout the forum kept notching up. Kessa remained out-wardly regal, her hands folded casually on the promontory railing, but she was watchful. Ariock maintained that shield, but he would struggle if he had to split his focus. And he was still a novice at using clairvoyance in battle. He might fail if he had to perform a quick relocation.

Thomas focused on the Upward Governess's blue eyes. Her face was serene, as only a Torth face could be. He ignored her lack of expression and focused on her eyes. Nothing else mattered.

Was that desperation? Or trust?

Love?

Thomas saw the mentor who had protected him. She had argued in favor of letting him live when he was a mere primitive without any rights, before he was even a Yellow Rank.

He saw the gulf between them.

He saw that she was on a precipice, pursued by her own orbiters, in danger of falling, yet she was taking the risk anyway, forcing herself to cross a deadly chasm in order to join the one person in the universe who might sincerely respect her.

Thomas knew her better than anyone else. He could offer her that. No one else could.

He lifted his weak hands, although it cost him tremendous effort. He reached out to her.

The moment seemed to stretch.

Everyone watched. The high-ranked prisoners were interested, of course, but even nontelepaths seemed to understand that the future of the galaxy depended on what might happen next.

CHAPTER 12

ON THE TRIGGER

The Swift Killer stretched languorously, allowing spa slaves to massage her calf muscles. So few Torth appreciated professional bodywork.

The spa was empty except for her and the slaves. The entirety of Rare Moonrise MetroHub had emptied out.

What fools.

Fragrant water trickled over red stone baths, glistening beneath skylights. The sky above remained a sunny blue-green. Yet the local population had fled, abandoning their luggage and valuables, as if this might turn into the annihilation of the Torth Homeworld all over again. The Majority seemed to lack common sense. Didn't they realize that the Giant and the Betrayer were sated?

The enemies would surely not leap into battle any time soon. They were celebrating victory. There was not so much as a cloud on the horizon.

Perhaps the Majority was rattled by the nonstop complaints from prisoners?

We are (thirsty)
(hungry)
(miserable) please
(please) please help.
Save Us.

How tiresome.

The Swift Killer avoided that moaning sector of the Megacosm, but each one of the 1,101,641 individual prisoners had their own mental audiences, so their relentless whining ended up leaking into unrelated discussions. They dragged everyone's mood down.

Why did they still have audiences?

Because of dumb curiosity.

Apparently, a lot of Torth wanted to experience imprisonment vicariously, if only for a few seconds at a time. The Majority wondered if raw sewage and close quarters and hunger were really so awful. After all, slaves endured those conditions every day.

Idiots.

The Swift Killer sighed with pleasure as stubby govki hands kneaded her muscles. Sure, technically, she was close to the conquered metropolis. And sure, she was a highly ranked military officer and also a Yeresunsa who was capable of slaughter. But to face the enemies right now would be suicide. Even the Majority understood that.

Torth supergeniuses such as the Upward Governess and the Twins needed to figure out a military strategy. This current crisis was their job. Not hers.

Listen.

Look.

The Swift Killer's inner audience tugged at her attention. Soon the whole lot of them were agitating.

There is something you should see.

The Swift Killer followed excited mental beacons. Her followers implied that this was news she would appreciate. They swirled into orbit around . . .

Ugh.

The Swift Killer began to flit away in disgust. She had no interest in the churning ideas of a supergenius.

Teleportation, her orbiters sang. *You can probably teleport!*

Oh. Wow.

The Swift Killer let herself be reeled in despite her reluctance. It seemed the Death Architect was, indeed, offering lessons on how to teleport.

It works like this. The Death Architect performed an imaginary demonstration. The mental behemoth could not do it herself. She was not clairvoyant. But she had come up with some sort of theory.

Clairvoyant Torth across the empire tested out her theoretical procedure.

Few of them could manage to ghost for more than a few seconds. The vast majority failed to get anywhere.

Others were able to ghost to a targeted location, but they were unable to grasp the mental trick of relocating their core self. They failed, too.

Others lacked enough raw strength to teleport. They followed the instructions, but either their target location was too far away or they simply could not muster enough power. They suffered excruciating headaches. Few of those returned to the Megacosm.

However, there were a handful of successes.

We have another!

Billions of minds celebrated a Servant of All known as the Burning Hilt when he magically appeared in a crowded boulevard full of witnesses. He immediately fell, apparently queasy and suffering from a headache.

But who cared? It had worked!

TORTH RULE!!! the Majority thundered. *MAY THERE BE MANY MORE!*

The Swift Killer signaled for her massage to end. Slaves backed away, bowing, allowing her to concentrate.

She studied every step of the procedure. The Death Architect made it look easy.

It would be so much fun to be able to show up anywhere, unannounced, instantaneously! The Swift Killer did not care who saw her uncouth smile. Let the Betrayer fear her. Let runaways quake in terror at the mere thought of her. She was the stuff of nightmares!

The spa slaves looked terrified.

She grinned wider. This was the chaotic birth of a new era. Once she could teleport, she would be godlike. She would easily be in the same league of power as the Imposter and the Betrayer. And she would be so very unpredictable.

She felt ready for a practice session.

One could not ghost and commune at the same time, so the Swift Killer prepared to drop out of the Megacosm. That was an unfortunate necessity. Like giving a pain seizure, clairvoyance consumed all of one's focus.

Where should she teleport to? A random suite nearby? Maybe she could attempt ghosting and teleporting into a space station?

WAIT (Swift Killer).

The godlike command could not be ignored.

The Swift Killer hesitated. It seemed the Death Architect and her billions of orbiters wanted something from her?

Yes. The harmony was inescapable. *Yes indeed.*

You (Swift Killer) happen to be in proximity to the conquered metropolis, the Death Architect remarked.

The Swift Killer did not like this line of thought.

And, the Death Architect went on, *the Imposter does not yet realize that We (the Torth Empire) have learned how to teleport.*

YES (YES) YES! Prisoners swirled around them both, fast enough to make the Swift Killer feel dizzy.

SAVE US?

SET US FREE?

They were a thunderous chorus. They raved about how brilliant the Death Architect was. They crooned in admiration.

The Swift Killer lost her smile. She had better things to do than risk her superior existence for the sake of a bunch of sniveling low ranks.

Sure, it was tragic to see Torth citizens suffering. But whatever. The imprisoned Torth comprised less than 0.00000001 percent of the galactic Torth population. Even if the enemies murdered all of them, such an insignificant loss would not cripple the mighty empire.

The Death Architect seemed to agree. *Their plight can wait.* Her enormous mind shoved aside the beggars, stomping them into silence. *We have an advantageous situation. The Betrayer (and his minions) are (critically) distracted.*

She directed everyone's attention to a live perceptual feed. A few imprisoned high ranks watched the enemies in a so-called Victory Forum. The prisoners served as eyes for the entirety of the Torth Empire.

There was the Betrayer. He floated in a hoverchair that had been crudely painted black and purple. All the enemies and their minions faced in one direction.

Toward the Upward Governess.

She was immediately recognizable to every Torth in the galaxy. How had she escaped her lair? Why did she dare to enter the Betrayer's territory alone? And unarmed? She floated toward the Betrayer, escorted by hostile guards.

The Upward Governess is going to assassinate the Betrayer, billions of Torth assured each other.

She must have a secret weapon.

She will surprise him.

The other half of the empire disagreed.

She is a traitor! they roared. *We can no longer trust her!*

Kill her, they urged.

KILL HER.

KILL!

KILL HER BEFORE SHE CAN BETRAY OUR SECRETS TO HIM!

The Swift Killer winced from the nearly overwhelming pressure of minds urging her to kill, kill, kill.

Oh, she did want to. She had often fantasized about destroying the eldest supergenius and getting praise for the deed. This was her fondest wish come true.

She hopped off the massage bed. There was no time to get dressed. No time for armor. She grabbed her blaster glove and tugged it on.

Then she hesitated.

The Giant was standing right there.

Teleportation was a very intensive, taxing power. Even if she managed to pull it off and shoot the Betrayer and the Upward Governess . . . well, wouldn't she be crippled by a depletion headache?

And the Giant was right there.

This was a suicide mission.

Time is short, the Death Architect warned.

SHORT ON TIME, the Majority echoed in a screech of urgency.

Aren't you (the Swift Killer) a loyal Torth citizen?

You have a chance to be special.

Don't you want to be a champion for civilization?

The Swift Killer stiffened her back. Most Servants of All would cave in, but she had always been a little bit . . . well . . . unusual, she supposed. A bit too independent.

She was not a disposable weapon. It seemed idiotic to throw away a magnificent Yeresunsa such as herself when there might be other options. *Why should I go on a suicide mission*, the Swift Killer queried her inner audience, *when the Upward Governess wants to prove Her loyalty? Let Her assassinate the Betrayer. She is such a great leader. Surely She deserves this glory?*

The Majority swirled with debates.

Other supergeniuses weighed in. The Twins pointed out that the Upward Governess had earned the trust of the Majority, to the point where they had elected her as an interim commander. Surely that meant that she deserved a fleeting chance?

She probably has a secret scheme, the girl Twin thought.

With the good of the galaxy in mind, the boy Twin finished.

The Death Architect readily agreed with the Twins, the Swift Killer, and the Majority. *You are All correct*, she admitted. *I do not wish to cast aspersions upon My esteemed colleague (the Upward Governess). Let Us trust Her.*

The Torth Majority sang with approval. They liked harmony.

However, the Death Architect thought with lazy aplomb, *at this particular moment in time, the Betrayer is more distracted than usual. Look at him.*

In the conquered city, sure enough, the Betrayer searched the Upward Governess with his yellow gaze. He was clearly not paying attention to much else.

He is probing the mind of the Upward Governess. The Death Architect's mental tone was dry and factual. *The task absorbs all his vast focus. I calculate that this is a (rare) optimal time window in which he is particularly vulnerable to a surprise attack.*

Billions of minds fluttered with excitement. *Oooooh!*

The Betrayer is vulnerable.

Distracted.

Can he be killed?

The Death Architect went on, backed up by a harmonious chorus. *Consider how much harm might be done to the morale of the Empire if the Upward Governess (turns out to be untrustworthy) fails to kill the Betrayer.*

That was inarguably true.

It is only logical, the Death Architect reasoned, *that We double up Our assassination power.*

The Majority sparked and crackled with impatient agreement. They numbered more than a trillion now. The whole galaxy was invested.

Yes.

 Kill the Betrayer.

It turned into a thunderous command. *Kill. KILL.*

KILL HIM!

 SAVE THE EMPIRE!

  KILL HIM!

Yes, the Death Architect thought with approval. *Here is a map.* She projected a blueprint of the conquered city. *Here is his current location.* She highlighted the Victory Forum and zoomed in on a mezzanine. *I will manufacture some rowdiness (distractions) among the prisoners.*

That might help.

The Death Architect went on, merciless. *You (Swift Killer) should take these grenades and destroy the Betrayer.*

Grenades?

What grenades? the Swift Killer wondered.

The Death Architect projected an image of the Rare Moonrise spa, where the Swift Killer stood. She directed everyone's attention toward a terrace of alien lilies.

The Swift Killer didn't believe it.

But her inner audience was insistent. So she traipsed to the lilies and dug into the garden mulch, where the Death Architect directed her to look.

Sure enough . . .

The Swift Killer stared at the egg-shaped devices, covered in dirt. As a Servant of All, she used to train with such gear. Once turned on, a grenade could not be deactivated, except by specialized tools. An activated grenade would detonate within five seconds. Their Velcro-like surfaces enabled them to adhere to cloth or fur.

Ooooooh! Trillions of minds swirled, amazed and impressed by the foresight of the twelve-year-old supergenius.

The Death Architect must have prearranged this. She must have directed someone in Rare Moonrise MetroHub to bury grenades in places that the Swift Killer frequented.

She had urged that helper to keep it a secret.

Then she had waited for an opportune moment before teaching the empire's clairvoyants how to teleport.

None of the clairvoyant Torth could ghost very far. That meant that Torth teleporters had a limited range. They could not leap from planet to planet. At least not yet. However, they might leap from one room to another, or from one city to an adjacent city.

This must be why the Death Architect had sent the Swift Killer to a strategically located city on Umdalkdul.

Had she foreseen the conquest of New GoodLife WaterGarden City?

But how?

I merely acted upon a few hypotheses. The Death Architect reacted to her admirers with serenity, which made her seem humble. *I suspected that the Betrayer might target the city where he spent time as a Yellow Rank (to settle old scores, and perhaps to target his erstwhile mentor). And I suspected that the Swift Killer and other Servants of All might have teleportation talent. So I urged those particular Servants to relocate to strategically advantageous regions. Just in case.*

Other titanic minds listened with silent admiration.

But . . . The Swift Killer hefted a grenade in each hand. *What if the Giant kills Me?*

It was strange. She did not wear anything like a slave collar. She was one of the most powerful people in the known universe. And yet she felt trapped.

The Majority debated her concern for a microsecond. Then they chorused a unanimous vote: *GO.*

And KILL.

The Majority's decision thundered inside the Swift Killer, inescapable. Unavoidable. She knew what would happen if she refused. She would be hunted down. Tortured. The Majority would have her fed, alive, to battlebeasts.

Kill the Betrayer, the Majority urged.

And be remembered for eternity—

—as the champion who saved galactic civilization.

Torth throughout the galaxy mentally cheered for the Swift Killer. They reeled in their comrades and neighbors to share the good news.

She was going to make the Majority proud.

What choice did she have?

The Swift Killer gripped the grenades and sought the clairvoyant trance.

CHAPTER 13

GALACTIC MINDS

Thomas touched the Upward Governess's hand.

She gently brushed his.

Thomas saw layers buried inside her core that he had never seen until now. Beneath the despotic dictator, beneath the spoiled child, beneath the careful scientist . . . a tentative beauty glowed, revealed for the first time ever. A delicate flower bud. A hatchling of a rare species.

This was exactly what he had hoped to see.

They each contained many thousands of lifetimes. She contained millions. They were two children, yet they were also two separate empires. They were two galaxies colliding. They were all the pertinent knowledge in the known universe. They were cloaked in secrets and desires. One was X, one was Y. One was yin, one was yang. They were going to merge, and reemerge, and become . . .

Supreme, she thought.

Dominant, he thought.

Albino warriors scrambled out of their range. Flen and the others distrusted supergenius mind readers. That was fine. Thomas didn't want any interference with this moment.

Joy transformed the Upward Governess into someone who looked entirely human. They held each other's hands, embodying what their minds were already doing.

"I am yours," she whispered in a voice that was raspy from disuse.

This could mean victory. Galactic victory.

They both knew it.

This was far bigger than his first breakthrough with inventing a medical treatment for neuronal apoptosis, or her breakthrough with engineering city infrastructures. For Thomas, this was better than the rush he had felt when he'd tricked Torth leadership into allowing his friends enough time to free the Lady of Sorrow. He was going to force the Torth to evolve.

They were Upward and Thomas, their enormous minds enmeshed and beginning the long process of integration. They were syncing up. They could trust each other.

Full merging would take months or years. But that was all right. Thomas welcomed the process of absorbing everything the Upward Governess had ever known, including her secret research. She felt the same way. So much knowledge would satisfy them both for a long time to come.

Ascend into the Megacosm, Thomas silently told her. *Let All know.*

She did.

Trillions of minds glommed onto hers, orbiting her like stars around a galactic core. Their shock was mind-numbing.

( ) ( ) ( ) ( ) ( )

Discussions began to fill the thunderous, gaping silence.

She's a traitor.

A renegade.

She (abandoned Us) (betrayed Us) joined the enemies.

Her staunchest fans dropped out of the Megacosm, too shocked for polite society. Others were contemplative. If a highly esteemed thought leader actually wanted to join the Betrayer . . . well, the Upward Governess was very smart. Was treachery (*joining him?*) worth serious consideration?

!!!!!!!!??????!!!!!!!??????????!!!!!!!!!??????!!!!!!!!!!??????????!!!!!!!!!!!?!?!?!

SHE IS INSANE, the Majority roared, as a matter of official decree.

TRAITORS TO THE EMPIRE MUST DIE.

ROOT OUT ANY TRAITORS.

SHOOT YOUR NEIGHBORS IF THEY CONSIDER JOINING THE ENEMIES.

KILL THEM NOW. NOW. NOW!

The Upward Governess beamed sublime happiness. *I am out of your reach.* As far as she was concerned, the Majority had become as ineffectual as a bunch of schoolyard bullies hurling rocks at a van while she sat inside, cozy and safe. *You cannot reduce Me. You no longer hold any influence over Me.*

Minds reeled away from hers, unwilling to analyze her message for fear of its toxicity.

KILL HER!

KILL BOTH BETRAYERS!

KILL KILL KILL!!!

The high-ranked prisoners fought their chains and croaked insults. Someone screamed.

Apparently, the prisoners had gone berserk at the behest of the Torth Majority. Flen and other guards drew throwing spears and hurried away, drawn by shouts for help. It seemed there was mayhem happening elsewhere in the city. In the Tunnels?

"I've got this," Garrett said, and he rushed toward the commotion.

The bubble shield around Thomas vanished.

Ariock's bubble shield increased in size, making up for the loss. That should work. Ariock had practiced focus-based multitasking plenty of times. His protection encompassed Thomas and the Upward Governess both.

The Upward Governess was the eye of a colossal mental hurricane. Thomas sensed her addressing a massive inner audience. On distant planets, some Torth cautiously lent her a fraction of their attention, struggling to go unnoticed by their peers.

Your only viable future is escape, the Upward Governess urged her orbiters. *Discard your assumptions. Discard your possessions and come join Us.*

She was the epicenter of a cosmic quake, just as Thomas had been earlier that day—but even more so. She was much more influential.

Together, they would surely gain millions and more on their side. They would—

!!!!!

Terror ripped through the Upward Governess. Thomas, holding her hand, felt it viscerally, as if it was his own.

The Swift Killer materialized and dropped to one knee, disoriented.

She wore a skintight undergarment that matched her blank white eyes. She clutched something in each fist. Judging by her recent memories, she had teleported here from a spa in Rare Moonrise MetroHub.

She should not be able to do that.

And she was not a courteous distance away, as most Torth would be, outside of a private conversation. Instead she showed up within telepathy range.

By teleporting into such close proximity, she had placed herself directly inside the bubble shield that Ariock had encircled them with.

KILL!!!

Thomas was close enough to overhear countless voices shouting inside the Swift Killer's mind. The Majority formed a collective command, urging her to action.

KILL THE TRAITOROUS UPWARD GOVERNESS!

 KILL THE BETRAYER!

They overrode her headache and drove her to her feet.

KILL BOTH TRAITORS IMMEDIATELY—

 —OR ELSE YOU DIE!

The Majority imagined all sorts of painful ways to punish the Swift Killer. They would lock her in a dumpster with carnivorous garbage-eaters. They would command her to swallow her own tongue.

Altogether, it was enough of a goad.

The Swift Killer slapped an egg-shaped device onto Thomas's hoverchair. The thing displayed a glow strip, morphing from blue to green. Then yellow.

A spectrum countdown.

Orange.

The countdown was engineered to be hyperfast. It was sped up to microseconds. And Thomas was too weak to reach the grenade, let alone flick it away. He frantically tried to wick heat out of the device.

Ariock lacked a clear line of sight, but even if he could see the little egg-shaped grenade, he would be unable to react fast enough.

Events after that happened in such quick and overlapping succession, bystanders were unable to process the sequence. But a supergenius could process data faster than a normal mind. To Thomas's overclocked perceptions, everything was alarmingly clear.

The Upward Governess dropped out of the Megacosm in order to attack the Swift Killer with a pain seizure.

!!! The Swift Killer clearly did not expect an instant reaction. She was used to the reflexes of normal minds, not the millisecond-fast thoughts of supergeniuses.

She was unable to somersault away, unable to follow through on her half-formed plan of getting out of range to hurl her second grenade. Instead, pain slammed into her.

Growling with rage, the Swift Killer triggered her second grenade. With its spectrum countdown already shifting from yellow to orange, she had no time to do anything except toss the device. It stuck to the Upward Governess's chest, rolling down but still clinging to her shimmery robe.

Thomas chewed through several protective strategies within microseconds.

One strategy might save him and his new partner, the Upward Governess. He could zombify the Swift Killer. Twist her mind, destroy her free will, then force her to use her superhuman reflexes to tear off the grenades and toss them up high in the air, where they might detonate without causing harm.

Well.

Maybe.

But the whole empire was watching. Judging him. Closeted renegades needed to feel safe and welcome on Thomas's side of the war. How would they react if they saw Thomas violently twist a mind, robbing it of free will?

Thomas's hesitance to zombify the Swift Killer had nothing to do with the fact that she was his biological aunt. It was not mercy. He just did not want to come across as a monster.

He wasn't going to undermine his own goal of gaining Torth allies.

And then the microseconds of grace ended.

Massive pain sheared through Thomas, obliterating his thoughts, as the Swift Killer brutalized him with a pain seizure. She had ignored her attacker, the Upward Governess, in favor of switching her full focus to the Betrayer. Perhaps she had overheard some hint of his thoughts and now considered him to be the most dangerous threat?

A white-hot bar of light slammed into the Swift Killer.

The pain seizure ended abruptly. A concussive sound followed an instant later. Lightning.

Ariock had taken out the Swift Killer, and that was great, except the grenades were shifting from orange to red. The egg-shaped devices were almost in sync, triggered at nearly the same time. Thomas saw the grenade on the Upward Governess's chest shift to red. No doubt the one on his hoverchair had just done the same.

Thomas had almost no physical strength. Nevertheless, he tried his best.

He attempted to hurl himself out of his hoverchair and onto the Upward Governess, to knock that grenade away. It was futile. But maybe the gesture would alert Ariock, or someone, to the emergency. Only one second had passed since the Swift Killer had first appeared, and that might not be enough time for Ariock to register the—

Detonation.

*! * ! * ! * ! * !*

His hoverchair was gone, torn away from him, probably ruined. But somehow, he was alive.

And in the air.

The Upward Governess gazed up at him with her deep-blue eyes.

Thomas's overclocked mind registered every millisecond. He sensed her assurance that failure was okay.

And death?

Death was . . . well, not okay, but it was good to be able to die as a free mind instead of as a Torth. It made the experience more poignant. Almost worthwhile.

A shocking force hurled Thomas away.

He hurtled above the alien crowd. A wet explosion rang out.

For a second, he assumed that the detonation had sent him over the railing of the mezzanine. But he was not falling. Thomas was unharmed, not even singed. He floated like a cloud, suspended in midair.

The telekinetic power that had saved him—probably Ariock—reeled him back over the mezzanine.

Over a gory mess.

All that was left of the Upward Governess was a bloody crater and scattered pieces of hoverchair and meat.

The fried remains of the Swift Killer, too, were plastered across the floor. The only recognizable chunk of her was a piece of scalp, with blond hair still attached.

Bad strategy, Thomas thought numbly.

Whoever had orchestrated this attack could have done a more elegant job. The Swift Killer should have known better than to appear within telepathy range of two supergeniuses. That was stupid.

A smarter way to play it would have been to command the Swift Killer to appear behind Ariock. She could have detonated the Giant, or at least distracted him long enough to destroy his air-bubble shielding. Then, with the bubble shield gone, she could have hurled more grenades at the supergeniuses without risking a pain seizure or any other counterattack.

Then, sure, she would have had to fight Garrett. But she might have been able to vanish, teleporting to safety, while Thomas and the Upward Governess died in the double detonation.

That was how Thomas would have planned it if he were in charge of the Torth side of the war.

His thoughts were reeling, tripping over an aftermath that he did not want to think about. He could still feel the Upward Governess's pudgy hand around his.

They were supposed to change the universe together.

They were going to transform the Torth Empire into something better.

"Are you all right?" Ariock gently caught Thomas, cradling him in the crook of one massive arm.

The question was nonsense. Thomas didn't reply. The sudden obliteration of his partner's towering mental presence seemed like too much to process, even for him. It was as though she had taken a temporary break from existence. As if she would return at any moment.

A coldly logical part of his mind admitted that this attack had been clever.

Maybe more than clever. Someone had laid groundwork for this attack, planting grenades and Servants of All in advantageous locations. Then they'd awaited an opportune time, when Thomas was distracted, high on victory. Then the antagonist had suddenly and viciously trained military Torth on how to teleport. They'd done it covertly, and fast, before Garrett might pick up on it.

A brilliant move. Evil. But brilliant. It had mostly succeeded.

Desperate to recapture the scattered shreds of his collaboration with a fellow supergenius, Thomas ascended into the Megacosm. He would see the Upward Governess there. Celebrities never truly died in the Torth Empire.

Sure enough, Torth shared and reshared various replays of her final moments.

Discussions about the Upward Governess reeled on, varied and endless. Torth swapped memories and impressions of her.

But that data was just a bunch of empty echoes.

The remnants of her hugely majestic mind were as insubstantial as ozone after a thunderstorm. Altogether, Thomas gathered nothing but a fading afterimage of who she had been.

She was gone.

CHAPTER 14

SHOULD HAVE

Although Ariock stood in the Victory Forum, he felt defeated.

He had failed to see the grenades. He hadn't detected the small devices, so he had failed to rip them away or neutralize them. He had been so slow the Swift Killer probably could have murdered both disabled children and then escaped by teleporting away.

But she'd been hit by a pain seizure. Either Thomas or the Upward Governess had attacked her. Good for them.

Would things have turned out differently if Ariock had slammed the Swift Killer with lightning in the very instant he saw her instead of deliberating for one stunned moment of shock? Perhaps his lightning would have vaporized the grenades before they could detonate.

Instead, he had reacted a second too late.

Then, when Thomas had purposely fallen out of his hoverchair, Ariock had guessed there was an additional problem: a bomb. So instead of reestablishing his bubble shield—which would have ended up getting both kids killed as the grenades detonated—he had caught Thomas.

And he'd found himself faced with a terrible choice.

He could either struggle to shield each child individually and likely fail, with his attention split and too many unknown factors. Or he could prioritize Thomas.

All he had known, with utter certainty, was that he could not win this war without Thomas.

So he had downgraded Thomas's request that he protect the Upward Governess. As the explosion began, Ariock had shielded Thomas and yanked him away to safety.

That was his call. He had made that choice. No doubt he would be second-guessing his own judgment for the rest of his life.

If only he'd had more time. With another second or two, Ariock was sure he would have figured out where the grenades were, and he could have saved both kids. That was how it should have gone.

"I failed." Garrett sounded gruff.

Ariock glanced to where his great-grandfather stood. Judging by Garrett's grim expression, the rapid events had taken him by surprise as well.

"I should have been scanning the Megacosm constantly." Garrett sounded angry at himself. "I should have known the Torth would discover teleportation sooner rather than later. And of course one of their supergeniuses waited for an opportune time to disseminate that information!"

Oh. Right. The Torth could teleport now.

Ariock shifted Thomas from one arm to the other, aware that he was still being an idiot. He needed to be on high alert. Once one Torth revealed a secret, the rest of the collective would learn it within minutes.

"Let me take care of it." Garrett sounded grim. "Be right back." He vanished with a suck-pop sound.

Nearby onlookers looked wild-eyed and edgy. No one was used to teleportation.

Ariock glanced at Thomas, but the boy was not in an advice-giving mood.

"Are you all right?" Ariock delved Thomas for injuries. There did not seem to be any, but Ariock held one hand over Thomas's small form anyway and gave him a refresher healing.

Thomas continued to look stunned. He stared at the horrific remains.

Ariock turned around, blocking Thomas's line of sight. He hated failure.

The high-ranked prisoners stood in the other room, still chained up and looking innocent. What deception. During the attack, they had thrown themselves at their guards like mindless beasts, causing mayhem. They had made a mockery of the amnesty Thomas had offered them.

Now, behind their blank expressions, they were probably celebrating along with trillions of their Torth brethren.

Ariock wanted someone to blame. He wanted to take action, to make all future threats go away. He walked closer to the room full of prisoners, his voice was as dark and deep as space. "Whose idea was this?"

"Mine," a defiant Torth said.

Another volunteered, "I thought of it."

Some of the prisoners wore smug expressions, mocking the Giant's ignorance. They all began to speak in croaking imitations of human voices.

"I s e n n n t h e r r r."

"W e A a a a l l s s s s e n t h h h e r."

These captured high ranks had been given a golden opportunity to switch sides. They could have joined Thomas. Instead, they condemned that which was good and they glorified that which was evil. The Upward Governess had dared to be different. That was all. That was enough for these inhuman zealots to metaphorically dance on her corpse.

Even while they celebrated the death of the Upward Governess, they were probably glorifying the Swift Killer. No doubt the Majority in the Megacosm would revere her as some sort of heroic champion.

Like they had celebrated the moment Ariock's father died. The Torth Majority must have cheered when the clone sister of the Swift Killer had rigged that airplane to crash.

They had probably celebrated when each of Ariock's family members had died. Just like they must be cheering right now, relieved that they had one less renegade supergenius to worry about.

They could go back to their snacks and massages.

At least until Ariock invaded their next city.

"Ariock." Vy sounded scared.

Thunder rumbled, close enough to shake the floor. The sky matched his mood, ominously dark, visible through the skylight windows. Clouds rolled overhead, flickering with lightning. And all around Ariock, small objects floated, caught in the excess power he was failing to control.

Throughout the Victory Forum, people were quiet. Some were trying to exit without being noticed. Kessa and others watched Ariock with wary respect.

Ariock slowly let out his breath. He needed to reserve his anger for battle arenas. Vy did not need to see him like this. Ever.

Someone ought to take those prisoners away. Put them in dungeon cells where they belonged.

An old man appeared out of thin air, on one knee, encased in a tattered cloak. A smell of ozone appeared with him. Ariock lashed out with solidified air before he could register that the old man was Garrett. He wasn't taking any chances.

"Sorry to alarm you," Garrett wheezed.

Ariock let go of his great-grandfather, chagrined. At least he was not the only one who had overreacted. Jinishta and several warriors were poised to throw spears. Weptolyso's spikes were popped out.

Garrett used his silvery staff to haul himself to his feet. "I got rid of all the potential teleporters on this planet that I could find."

No wonder Garrett looked battered and exhausted. How many Yeresunsa Torth had he hunted down just now? And . . . well . . . murdered?

"Thank you for doing that." Ariock figured it should have been his job. He sensed Garrett's diminished life spark. His great-grandfather could only teleport four or five times before depletion.

"I'm fine, I'm fine," Garrett grumbled, seeing Ariock's concern. He limped toward a chair and sat down heavily. "You should leave the targeted hunting up to me. I can find so-called Torth champions via the Megacosm. For you, it would be blind lurching around and guesswork."

That was an inelegant way to put it, but Ariock realized that his great-grandfather was right. The only way Ariock could locate Yeresunsa was to assess a lot of life sparks all at once, sifting through them. He could not detect life sparks while ghosting. So he would need to teleport, physically, from place to place, and each time he would have to spread his awareness and encompass millions of people.

That sort of stature required extra gentleness and caution. He wasn't in the right mood for it.

Anyway, how many teleporters existed now, spread over the millions of colonized planets in the galaxy? With an astronomical number of cities throughout the Torth Empire, it could turn into an endless errand.

"The Torth can't do the interstellar thing." Garrett pulled a cigarette out of a pocket in his cloak. "Clairvoyance is a huge power drain, and very few Torth are that powerful. So I honestly don't think we need to worry about them teleporting from planet to planet. Yet." He fumbled a small lighter out of his pocket and lit his cigarette. "I got rid of the ones local to our planet. We should be safe here for a few days."

A few days of relaxation? Ariock hoped that would do everyone some good.

"What about faster-than-light travel?" Vy asked. "Isn't it just, like, a day of travel for them to use a temporal stream and get here?"

Garrett waved his cigarette in a dismissive motion. "Ariock can scan our local solar system. If he detects a space armada or any sort of problem, he'll shove them away."

Fair enough. Ariock nodded. He could do that much. One scan per day should be enough.

"What about linking?" Kessa asked.

They all looked at her. Ariock realized that somehow the rest of them had over-looked that factor. Evenjos had restored Ariock from fatal depletion by linking her raw power with that of Garrett, Thomas, and all the Alashani warriors. The link had enhanced Ariock's nearly dead life spark until he was able to recover. According to Evenjos, linking could boost someone with lesser strength to gain greater strength.

"That could be a problem," Garrett admitted. "But the Torth don't know about linking. With luck, it's not something that will occur to them."

A vague reassurance.

Better than none, Ariock supposed.

"Linking requires emotions, doesn't it?" Vy asked.

Garrett gave her a nod of respect. "It does. Which makes it even more unlikely that any Torth will try it out."

The assembly was beginning to loosen, heading toward the exits. Aliens cast speculative glances toward the death scene, and discussions filled the vast space. They had a lot to talk about.

Kessa stepped up to the promontory. "If you have questions about what hap-pened here today," she said, "I will be here at dusk."

Ariock was glad she had taken charge of offering answers and comfort. He had experienced firsthand how fear could spark wild rumors that mutated and escalated.

Reassurance was important. Hope was important. Without it, people might act on wrong assumptions or misinformation.

And Ariock wasn't in the mood to give a hopeful speech. It would feel like a pretense.

"I'm sorry," Garrett told Thomas. "You were right about her."

Thomas looked as if turning his head was an indescribable effort.

"I never would have expected it," Garrett said with apologetic guilt in his voice. "But conquering this city was a great idea. And we did get her on our side, for a minute!" He pounded his fist into his palm, emphasizing the missed opportunity. "I see what it would have done. It would have broken the will of the Majority."

Thomas looked sad rather than vindicated.

And Ariock realized that Thomas might have invited the Upward Governess to join him for more than one reason. Maybe his original intention was to gain a useful ally. But he had also lost someone he cared about on a personal level.

"I should have acted faster." Ariock wished that he had treated the Upward Governess like a sacred treasure. Why hadn't he?

"No." Thomas sounded small. "This wasn't your fault, Ariock. It was mine."

Ariock couldn't tolerate that.

"I had to put all the risk onto her," Thomas said, forlorn. "If we had abducted her and transported her to some faraway planet under our control, then the Torth Majority would rightly argue that we pressured her to join us. It had to look volun-tary. It had to *be* voluntary."

Garrett nodded, smoking his cigarette. "Brilliant," he remarked.

"I forced her to take a risk." Thomas gazed at the gore-smeared crater. "I wanted to pressure the Torth Majority to join our side."

"Well, I don't think you forced her," Vy said with gentle emphasis. "She came here of her own free will."

"Right," Garrett said. "She was, like, the smartest being in the known universe. I'm sure she calculated all the risks and all the odds, and she chose to join us anyway."

Thomas continued to look guilty. Ariock thought that Thomas rarely made mistakes, but in this case, perhaps, he was taking on too much self-blame.

In fact, as far as Ariock was concerned, Thomas should be proud. He had achieved a miracle. Forty prisoners stared at the carnage, broadcasting everything they had witnessed—and that had included the de facto leader of the Torth Empire peeling herself away from the collective.

A couple of the prisoners did look mournful. They were not all slack-faced or smug.

Thomas had given the Torth Empire something to think about.

"Maybe we can revisit converting other Torth," Ariock said. "The Upward Governess might not have been the only one willing to go renegade."

"Humph." Garrett surveyed the mess. "I'm not sure how many will jump at the opportunity now."

Thomas had a sickened, morose look.

"We'll make sure her remains are treated with respect," Vy said with gentleness. "Do you have any requests?"

"The indoor lake," Thomas said. "The island with the turtles and cranes. That was her favorite place."

Vy gave Ariock a look, and he nodded in confirmation. A funeral would be awkward, with too few mourners. Maybe they would skip doing that. But he could transport her remains with dignity.

"How about if we find a hoverchair for the boy?" Garrett looked around the forum.

"I can handle that." Ariock offered Thomas to Weptolyso. Once his arms were empty, he could safely go into the clairvoyant trance, leaving his body unprotected. He would ghost around the city until he found an empty hoverchair. Then he could item-teleport it.

"Make sure it's child size." Garrett held his hands apart as an indicator. "With a neck rest and adjustable cushioning."

Thomas looked grateful.

"Got it," Ariock said.

"After this, let's all take some time." Garrett offered Thomas a look that was actually sympathetic. "You don't need to stick around if you don't feel like it. We'll talk about important things tomorrow." He aimed a kindly look toward Ariock. "That goes for you, too. Get him a replacement hoverchair and whatever, but then take the rest of the night off."

Thomas settled into Weptolyso's arms.

Vy looked concerned. "Do you want anyone else to be with us at the lake? I could ask, um—"

"No," Thomas said. "I'm fine. I'd rather say my goodbyes alone."

To Ariock, Thomas looked more alone than anyone in the vast forum.

Perhaps he would be better off with sympathy from Cherise? Or maybe his lab assistant, Varktezo, ought to be with him? But they weren't here. And Thomas, being a supergenius, probably knew what was best for himself.

Ariock and Vy could try to be with him, at least.

CHAPTER 15

REWIRED

Cherise swiped a carousel of icons on the data tablet. When she looked up, she no longer sat in a plain antechamber. She appeared to be in the middle of a parched desert full of eroded mesas.

Except for the air-conditioning.

Nothing visual could be trusted in a Torth environment. Cherise had learned that when she was a slave in this city. Doors were often disguised as walls. Windows might offer fantastical views of imaginary vistas.

She swiped again.

Everything changed. Now she sat in a conservatory overlooking a river valley. Sunlight streamed through cathedral-like windows, gleaming on waxy blue leaves and huge white flowers.

She knew the cushioned bench seat was real, since she sat upon it. And she knew that the garden it surrounded was likewise real. Slaves were supposed to tend the plants, no doubt. Someone still needed to do so. Perhaps they would enlist the Torth who used to own this wonderland? Make him or her clean away the rot and replenish the mulch.

"Why are you fooling with Torth trickery?" Flen paced, his voice tight with disapproval. "Councilor Karyum's party is not far. Are you ready to go yet?"

Cherise had heard Flen the first two times he had mentioned the party.

The whole city was intoxicated with freedom. Free aliens sang in the streets or raced each other on hoverbikes. They were gleefully discarding every law the Torth had forced upon them. Some were even making love, since the Torth had forbidden city slaves from any activity that might lead to the establishment of a family.

The Alashani had their own private celebrations. They didn't seem interested in mixing with former slaves, and the feeling was mutual. Many aliens eyed the albino strangers with mistrust, unsure how closely related they were to the Torth.

"Karyum found mushrooms," Flen said, as if to tempt her. "And if you have not yet tried the mushroom mead his family brews—it is famous. You will love it!"

"Sorry, Flen." Cherise continued to fiddle with the data tablet. There must be artistic fine-tuning buried in the interface. It was so incredibly intuitive. "I really want to figure out how this works. Please, just go without me. I'll join you later!"

Someone had designed these tablets with care and creativity. The gadget was far superior to any smartphone on Earth. Cherise supposed that a thousand generations of expert engineering had enabled the Torth to iron out any imperfections or bugs.

The file structure was as moldable as clay. Cherise was just beginning to figure out how to customize everything she saw. She was going to be able to create wonders!

Better yet: she knew that a few ummins had figured out how to pair tablets like these to each other. What marvelous teaching tools!

Cherise could imagine how life would change once they figured out how to pair tablets like these with speaker systems and monitors. Free aliens would be able to create and share their own custom recordings!

She imagined ummins and nussians dancing to their own version of a rave. Or . . . what if they pumped music into the Tunnels, where Torth prisoners would be forced to listen to it? Ha. Smooth jazz. Musicals. The Torth would probably lose their slack expressions and start sneering uncontrollably.

"What is so amusing?" Flen sat next to her.

"If I ever get my hands on some music from Earth, you'll see." Cherise made her smile reassuringly innocent. Flen didn't understand much about her world of origin, and the topic often frustrated him or made him lose interest and tune out.

"Do you really want to just sit in this Torth place all by yourself?" Flen's luminous eyes were full of pity.

As if Cherise was being weird.

"Talk to me, Cherise." Flen's face was so close that she could not ignore him without being cruel.

She met his gaze. Did he think she was Silent Cherise, the girl no one saw or heard?

"I am worried about you." Flen gently gripped her hand. "Can't you set aside the temptations of that *rekveh* gadget? This is a time for being with friends. We are alive. I . . ." He grimaced and seemed to force himself to continue. "I was not certain I would live today."

Cherise put the tablet aside and tried to rid herself of selfish inclinations. Flen and the other warriors had been brave and heroic. They'd helped to liberate slaves.

And while Flen risked his life in battle? Cherise had done little other than chat with alien friends.

Flen had lost his entire family in the destruction of the Torth Homeworld. Was it any wonder that he feared losing what little he still had?

"You're right." Cherise tucked the tablet in her satchel and pushed the bag out of sight. "I want to celebrate with you."

In truth, she did not enjoy boozy Alashani parties. The albinos dealt with each other according to an unspoken hierarchy, based on who was related to whom. The hierarchy excluded Cherise from gossip and inside jokes.

On top of the cultural barrier, Cherise lacked motivation to learn the Alashani native language. She had picked up a few words and phrases, but anyone could guess that the common slave tongue was the language of the future. The language of albino cave dwellers was already beginning to feel niche and obscure.

Still, that was a major vector of exclusion. She did not speak their language.

However, Cherise knew that she owed a lot of gratitude to the Alashani. The whole city owed them. She wanted to assure Flen that she appreciated him and his people.

So she twined her arm around Flen's and said, "Let's go."

As they exited the magnificent garden, Cherise took one last look around. This room was just one of many playgrounds that used to belong to mind readers who considered themselves gods. The Upward Governess, for example, used to enjoy surroundings even grander than this.

Cherise wondered how Thomas had reacted when his former mentor and his biological aunt had canceled each other out.

Perhaps he was unaffected? His emotional armor was thick enough to weather any loss, let alone the loss of two silent Torth who had made themselves his enemies. Cherise doubted he'd had any reaction. She could imagine him telling someone to dump the remains down a garbage chute.

Flen gave her hand a squeeze. His smile came easily, and it was a really attractive smile.

Cherise rejected her urge to ask if Thomas had seemed upset. Flen had volunteered for that duty shift, so he had actually been there. But he would say that *rekvehs* were unworthy of analysis. That was what most Alashani believed, and Flen was the epitome of Alashani.

Plus, he had a suspicious streak.

Cherise reminded herself that Flen cared about her, whereas Thomas . . . well, he had made his lack of caring plain. Hadn't he?

It would be easy for Thomas to reestablish a friendship with Cherise if he wanted to. All he had to do was ask.

Instead, he remained aloof. Torth-like.

If Cherise was honest with herself, she had to admit that Thomas had always been aloof and Torth-like, even on Earth. She thought, now, that the glimmers of emotion she used to see in him were as superficial as sunbeams. She had seen depths only because that was what she'd wanted to see.

It was futile to expect a full range of human emotions from someone who was so Torth.

He would be fine.

She grinned at the jubilant aliens in the boulevard and snuggled closer to Flen.

CHAPTER 16

MONSTROUS WITHIN AND WITHOUT

"I'm fine," Thomas said whenever anybody expressed concern.

It wasn't a lie. He figured it was the rest of the universe that was screwed up, not him.

Not a single person acknowledged the enormous heroism of the Upward Governess. The loss did not even register with most of the newly freed aliens.

As for his friends? They, too, celebrated freedom as if nothing devastating had happened. Their caring questions were all for Thomas.

"I'm fine," Thomas told Vy and Ariock after the sad little farce of a burial. "Enjoy your night off."

He declined a dinner invitation from Varktezo. "No, thanks," he told his ummin lab assistant. "I'm not hungry. Say hi to the science team from me."

Kessa was giving instructions to a group of newly appointed clerks. She interrupted herself when Thomas floated past, asking him if he was getting enough nourishment and sleep.

"I'm fine," Thomas said. "You're doing an amazing job, Kessa."

His friends seemed able to return to business as usual. That was awful—but it was better than the reaction of the Torth Majority.

As far as most Torth were concerned, the Upward Governess was a vile traitor. They cherry-picked memories to replay, showing her as nothing but a spoiled, pathetic monster.

Quite a few Torth dropped out of the Megacosm for an extended period. They offered flimsy excuses to their orbiters. They were tired. They felt sick. They had tasks that required their full focus. Thomas suspected they were actually sick of the propaganda against the Upward Governess, and they must be secretly worried about the path this war might take. Should they entrust their civilization to the twelve-year-old Death Architect? Should they return to an overreliance upon the Former Commander of All Living Things? Would they elect someone else?

Nussian bodyguards protected Thomas as he made his way through gateways and gardens. Thomas waved them away. "Take the rest of the night off. Please."

The nussian captain began to argue.

"You have a communicator," Thomas pointed out. "I'll call for help if I need it." He tried to inject warmth into his tone. "Really. I want you to enjoy the victory celebrations. I'm totally fine."

The nussians obliged and left him alone.

Thomas continued on his way, floating past groups of revelers. Aliens eyed him askance. They whispered to each other, sharing a rumor that Kessa the Wise trusted this puny little mind reader. Then they went back to celebrating their freedom. They danced. They fell into each other's arms, laughing.

Their merriment did not touch Thomas. These liberated people assumed they would keep winning.

They had no idea.

Any possibility of an easy victory over the Torth Empire had died along with the Upward Governess.

Thomas hovered around the shore of the indoor lake. It was dusk, and bioluminescent gas bugs lit the area. It would have been peaceful except for the revelers who splashed and shouted and laughed. Alien birds and amphibians must be hunkered down, frightened by the unfamiliar sounds of joy.

Thomas hovered along a winding pathway to a jetty that was concealed by marsh grass and rocks. The celebratory sounds grew distant. No one was likely to impinge on his private thoughts out here.

He gazed at the darkening water and berated himself.

He could have prearranged a safe haven for the Upward Governess. It would have been difficult to persuade Garrett and the Alashani that it was necessary, and keeping her protected would have entailed ongoing stress. It would have required a lot of diplomacy. But it would have been worth it.

If only he had known who she really was.

He had failed to respect her enough.

The Upward Governess had been his biggest nemesis, and no matter how well they meshed, trust would still have taken time to build. Therefore, Thomas had engineered a situation that required her to shoulder most of the risks.

He had essentially invited her to join him or die.

That was the exact same unfair choice the Torth Empire had once offered him.

What had he learned from that awful experience? Nothing, it seemed. Perhaps he was more calculating and Torth-like than he wanted to admit to himself.

The lake sparkled in an unnatural way.

Water vapor swirled, rising and collecting into the shape of a winged woman with long, flowing hair.

Details sharpened. Evenjos floated above the surface. Her watery reflection shimmered below her.

"Do you mourn that Torth girl?" she asked in a voice that seemed nearly as insubstantial as her misty body.

"You wouldn't understand." Thomas didn't care how rude that sounded.

He floated backward a few paces. Evenjos had coalesced just beyond his telepathy range, and that was too close for comfort. Did she want him to accidentally read her mind? That way, she could tell Ariock and Garrett that she had slain "the little monster" in self-defense.

Not that it mattered. If Evenjos decided to slay him here and now, no one could stop her. Not in time.

"I sense your sorrow," Evenjos said. "It resonates with me."

Well. That was embarrassing.

Thomas gazed at the twilit waters, pointedly ignoring her shimmery presence. He wished he could dismiss Evenjos by telling her, "I'm fine," but she wouldn't believe him.

Nor would she understand why he ached over the loss of a Torth thought leader. No one understood.

"Leave me alone," he suggested.

Evenjos solidified more. She sank knee-deep into the water. Still scrutinizing Thomas, she lifted her gown and waded to the nearest rock. She took a seat, barefoot, and studied him.

Thomas wanted to escape, but Evenjos could snake through air ducts if she wanted to. She could follow him anywhere he chose to go.

A medical timer went off in the background of his mind. He ignored the urgency to take a dose of NAI-12. He had deprogrammed his wristwatch, and he had not asked for the improved version, NAI-13, either.

He didn't want it.

Death breathed down his neck after his months in the Alashani dungeon pit. He supposed he didn't need to mourn the Upward Governess. He was going to join her in death before much longer.

"Do you think you fight for the wrong side?" Evenjos asked.

Ah, there was an ugly accusation.

Thomas was not in the mood for whatever mind games Evenjos wanted to taunt him with. He met her purple gaze with a level stare of his own. "We all failed to protect that girl," he said, making sure to include Evenjos in the failure. "And because of that, the Torth may win this war. Their darkness will last for eternity. Is that not plenty of cause for sorrow?"

Evenjos's skepticism was apparent on her face.

Right. To her, all telepaths were evil. She had probably celebrated the death of the Upward Governess.

A daring impulse seized Thomas. If Evenjos wanted to pick at his wound . . . well, then he would go ahead and pick at one of hers.

"You are misjudging the Upward Governess." Thomas spoke in her long-extinct tongue. "Just as you once misjudged Elome."

That name hit her hard.

She eyed Thomas with a dangerous expression, like a crocodile sizing up its prey. She had never spoken of Elome. At least, not in this era. No one alive should know that name.

"I picked up some of your memories during the one time I was within your range," Thomas explained. "I can absorb quite a lot in just a few seconds."

Murder gleamed in her eyes.

Yet there was also wary respect in her gaze. Perhaps even guilt? The fact that Evenjos had never shared this secret implied shame and embarrassment.

Why? Did she believe that she could have prevented her own imprisonment? Or . . .

Perhaps she blamed herself for the rise of the Torth Empire?

Hm.

"Don't worry." Thomas decided to reassure her. "I didn't tell anyone. If Ariock ever learns about your past, it won't be from me."

Evenjos searched his face. After a moment, she relaxed slightly. "They would have contempt for me if they knew."

Thomas doubted that. But he didn't care enough to say so.

"So." Evenjos studied him with a different kind of suspicion, as if she could not quite believe he was capable of decency. "You kept my secret," she said with cold imperiousness. "In exchange for a favor, I assume. What is your price?"

Thomas blinked at her. He had not expected any sort of exchange.

"I keep secrets all the time," he admitted. "All day, every day." More secrets than any child should be forced to keep. "I don't need anything in return." He switched from her archaic language to the slave tongue. "I promise, I won't blackmail you."

His promise to respect her privacy seemed to surprise her, as much as her clemency surprised him.

Thomas supposed that in her era, telepaths always expected a price for their services. And few people could have hidden secrets from Unyat and his telepathic minions. That was how the Torth were able to take over so completely.

"You are not acting the way I expected," Evenjos admitted.

Thomas looked away from her curiosity. In truth, he thought there were valid reasons to be distrustful of him. Cherise had learned that the hard way.

So had the Upward Governess.

If he had twinned with her mind, would the two of them truly be galactic heroes? Or was he fooling himself? The Upward Governess had plenty of appealing traits. But she also had a few bad ones, didn't she?

As telepathic supergeniuses, they had begun to mirror each other's mentalities. They would have fed off each other's knowledge, boosting each other's inventiveness and ambition. And Thomas had absorbed tantalizing hints about her secret project. The Upward Governess had been testing practical applications with dark energy and stochastic supersymmetry, and that was enough to drive him crazy with unanswered questions. Her experiments implied a superweapon.

Something new. Something dangerous.

"I wish to know more about you." Evenjos sounded decisive. She slipped off the rock and waded toward Thomas.

He glided backward at top speed. "You said you'd kill me."

"Stop." Evenjos stepped onto the jetty, water streaming off her legs and wing tips. "Come back."

Thomas glided to a halt, heart pounding with adrenaline. Was this a murderous trick? Or had Evenjos honestly changed her mind?

Evenjos sat on a rock. She wrapped her arms around her knees, and her colors changed from saturated hues to meek and gentle pastels. Altogether, she looked less threatening.

"I want to try this," Evenjos said. "Please. I promise, I will not harm you unless you assault me."

That sounded promising.

Thomas approached her with wariness. He remained hyperaware, ready to flee at the smallest hint of danger.

When he entered her range, the first thing he became aware of was her godlike potential. Evenjos was as dangerous as Ariock, in her own way. She was as cautious as a sparrow, yet she had hardened her exterior to a diamond-tough shell.

She was ready to kill at the least sign of a threat.

Thomas was careful. He yearned to explore her memories, but he knew better than to dive in without explicit permission. He forced himself to merely float and bask in her presence. He could not help but touch the lapping waves of her emotional state, but he dared not follow anything to its source. He did his best to ignore her stream of consciousness.

Meanwhile, Evenjos gingerly studied the towering storm of godlike knowledge that she perceived as his mind.

Her gaze tightened with wonderment and unease. She had never encountered a mind like his. Unyat might have been a supergenius, but Evenjos had never met Unyat, or any of his clone descendants, in person.

She felt as if she might be meeting a version of Unyat right now.

Overwhelming. She scooted back and leaned out of Thomas's range for a short breather.

Then she leaned in again, determined to explore the dazzling complexity and sheer enormity of his mind.

She seemed to be searching for something.

For friendliness?

Bit by bit, Thomas lowered his mental walls and lessened his guarded mind-set. Instead of exploring her memories, he forced himself to be meditative.

They were both titans. Her raw strength was frightening. But in the realm of thoughts, Thomas was the colossal one. The most she could do was leg around the surface of his personality. She might as well be a bug exploring a mountain.

He let her explore as much as she was able to.

CHAPTER 17

TO KNOW ANOTHER

Thomas could not help but overhear the stream-of-consciousness thoughts running through Evenjos. *There is too much here,* she thought as she crawled across the surface of his mind. *It's as if he is many people, a great collection with more facets than a nation. How can I dig out any truths that are his alone?*

All the while, Thomas was aware that Evenjos could tell he sensed her frustration. She did not like feeling so inept, so out of her depth.

Ask me anything, Thomas invited.

He hoped he would not regret making that offer. But he wanted to set Evenjos at ease and give her some semblance of being in control. This way, she might gain helpful shortcuts to learn whatever it was that she was searching for.

Evenjos cleared her throat. "Why respect my privacy?" she asked. "Why have you refrained from sharing *(my misjudgment of Elome)* the most shameful *(biggest)* mistake I have ever made?"

Thomas replied without sound. *That is not my secret to tell.*

If he were to speak out loud while she was fully focused on his thoughts, she would perceive the communication as excessive and godlike. It would be rude. He wanted to be as considerate as possible. Besides, the language of thoughts was purer and faster than any spoken tongue.

Why do you respect secrets? Evenjos wondered, likewise discarding the friction of spoken words. *Why have you—a telepath—decided that privacy matters?*

That would require more than a simple answer.

Thomas opened up his internal code of honor and displayed it for her. He allowed Evenjos to catch inklings of the secrets he had grown up around.

Children in foster care tended to have dark secrets. They contained silent screams. They were survivors of gross injustices. Thomas had borne silent witness to a thousand crimes, even before he had discovered the existence of the Torth Empire.

He was one of those children.

Secrets were often mental wounds, festering with guilt or shame or self-hatred and buried beneath a scab of lies. Thomas had felt terrorized *(betrayed) (scathed)* when the Torth tore open his old *(wounds)* secrets during his Adulthood Exam. And that was not a pain he wanted to inflict on anyone.

He was not in the business of picking at scabs. Nor was he in the habit of blackmailing people, or bullying them, or taking advantage of other people's ignorance.

Justice mattered. Consideration mattered.

Whether it was a law or not, Thomas would not abuse the advantages he had been born with.

So he only spoke truths. He kept silent about the secrets he absorbed. He was always cognizant of his advantages over nontelepaths—because he knew all too well what it was like to be at a disadvantage.

Evenjos seemed intrigued. *Will you show me your most shameful secret?* she wondered with childlike innocence.

Thomas decided to end his ask-me-anything session. *Nope.* He locked up his innermost self, using so many layers of complex data not even the Upward Governess would have been able to fish out the truth.

Evenjos leaned back on her wings and reassessed him with a judgmental gaze. "But," she said softly, "you were going to reveal all your secrets to that Torth girl. Weren't you?" *Why her and not me?*

Shame rolled through Thomas, as if he'd been caught in a guilty act.

His nascent bond with the Upward Governess was not common knowledge. Evenjos should have no idea about it, unless . . .

"Were you there?" He glared at the Lady of Sorrow. He knew it was dangerous to explore her mind, yet he began to probe, enraged by the idea that she had floated idly while the mayhem unfolded. What an untrustworthy—

"No!" Evenjos stood and floated backward a pace, out of his range.

Thomas braced himself. He had crossed a line. She might attack him.

"I was not there," Evenjos said. "I was healing people."

That was plausible. Thomas had picked up rumors from liberated slaves, and they already revered Evenjos as a magical healer of illnesses and injuries. She was making her powers known.

"Then . . . ?" Thomas did not want to confirm her guesswork.

"It was a guess," Evenjos admitted. "But not a big leap, I should think. I feel your sorrow. You wanted her on our side for personal reasons, not just for strategic reasons."

It was true. But Thomas didn't want to be judged. So what if he had yearned for a friendship of equals. Was that so wrong?

"The Upward Governess knew me well already," he said, struggling to offer an acceptable explanation. "And I wanted to gain access to whatever weapons she was developing. It made sense for us to get to know each other better."

He felt cornered. Somehow, Evenjos had needled her way into his wounded heart without reading his mind.

"I used to have a best friend," he went on, "when I lived on Earth." Cherise. He still missed being around her mind. "But she couldn't comprehend the entirety of who I am."

He used to share a lot of himself with Cherise. Perhaps he had made attempts to balance the uneven scales of their friendship by sharing harmless, meager secrets with her. Cherise had been unable to stop Thomas from soaking up every detail of her life. He had wanted to offer some recompense.

"I absorb the deepest secrets and the dearest hopes and dreams of my friends," Thomas admitted. "But they can never know me that well."

Only another supergenius could be his equal.

That was a shameful thought, in and of itself. Thomas dared not say it out loud. But Evenjos came closer, and she guessed what he had left unspoken.

Only another supergenius can be your equal? she thought with a flash of insight. *That is why you cared for that Torth girl? She was your potential equal?*

Resigned and ashamed, Thomas acknowledged that she was correct.

Evenjos emanated sympathy. *I am sorry that she is lost to you.*

They both listened to the sounds of merriment from the distant shore.

The loss is not only mine, Thomas thought. *The Upward Governess had no friends, and nobody cared for her (except for me), but she could have changed the universe for the better.*

He was unlikely to ever meet another supergenius like the Upward Governess. She had risked her life repeatedly—and ultimately died—in pursuit of a relationship that was forbidden in Torth society. She had longed for love. Not just love, but an equally balanced love, between two individuals who complemented each other in terms of scope and power and knowledge.

What other supergenius would care that much?

The Twins had each other, but their mirrored minds were likely a form of codependence rather than the mutual love and respect of a healthy relationship.

As for the Death Architect, the Geodesic Flux, the Rind Topographer, the Spin Overture, and the Stalled Proofer . . . they were undistinguished scientists. They exhibited no glimmers of hidden emotions or intriguing quirks.

The Mechanized Meeter, the Stemmer Linguist, the Neurobioticist, and the Climbing Storm were a good deal younger. Due to their constant immersion in the Megacosm, they contained more trivial facts than Thomas, but their minds were immature. By the time they ripened into mature supergeniuses, Thomas would be dead from his neuromuscular disease.

As for the rest? They were toddlers and babies. Some had been awarded titles by overeager fans of supergeniuses, but their personalities were still in the early stages of development. Thomas would be long dead by the time they achieved sentience, sapience, and enough mental maturity to function as individuals.

He had torpedoed his one and only chance to befriend an intellectual equal.

An equal. Evenjos examined the concept. *Perhaps there is value in equality on a personal level. I yearn for someone (Ariock) who naturally comprehends the burdens and responsibilities of cosmic power (like mine). I want someone (Ariock) who complements me, who will never leech off me. I have had enough experience with helpless types.*

Thomas had not expected so much understanding from Evenjos.

She really did understand. Power like hers was a rarity. It was no wonder she yearned for Ariock.

Or for someone powerful. Someone like Garrett, or Jinishta, or perhaps even . . .

They gazed at each other.

Thomas looked away. They were equals in some ways, yet not equals at all. Evenjos was almost indestructible. She could absorb nuclear bombs without damage, while Thomas . . . ? Thomas was as fragile as it was possible to be.

I have no interest in fragile lovers, Evenjos admitted. *If I were to welcome the advances of an average Alashani or nussian (or even you), then I would worry about hurting them.* She seemed excited to be so well understood. *I want Ariock.* In a burst of jealousy, she added, *Isn't Ariock in a constant state of worry for his flimsy, mundane girlfriend? Doesn't he realize that he can do better?*

Thomas gave no hint of his opinion on the matter. He felt loyalty to his foster sister and caretaker, Vy.

An unequal relationship is a point of vulnerability, Evenjos silently added. *If I were to take a weaker lover, then I would worry about them being abducted by the Torth, to be used as bait against me.*

Thomas acknowledged that as a valid concern. Deep down, he supposed that he agreed.

Equality was more than a matter of shared understanding. If Thomas were to make a habit of revealing his personal weaknesses to nontelepaths—to Cherise, to Ariock, to Varktezo or Kessa—then it would only be a matter of time before his enemies fished out his secret vulnerabilities.

So he never got close with anyone.

Cherise had outer beauty and a lovely mind . . . but rationally, Thomas knew that she could not safeguard his schemes from the Torth Empire. Only another telepathic supergenius could be entrusted with his darkest fears and deepest desires.

He wanted the Upward Governess.

You truly are not Audavian. Evenjos studied him with fresh eyes. *Or Unyat.* She was rolling back all her assumptions about him. The monsters she had known had only wanted to dominate people, not form alliances or partnerships. *Perhaps you are not such a monster as they were.*

Thomas could not help but probe her mind a little tiny bit, then. He didn't trust anyone who came to him like this, seeking friendship. Nobody sane would want to befriend a telepath who could twist minds. Did she have an ulterior motive?

She sensed his distrust. *Allow me to explain.*

Thomas forced himself to wait patiently.

I dislike being alone, Evenjos admitted.

Indeed, Thomas sensed her relief at being able to converse with ease. The slave tongue was like wading through muck to her. Telepathy came naturally.

On top of that, she felt desperate for a friend. As a former goddess-empress, she yearned for someone she could actually respect.

She wanted that person to be Ariock.

But if she could not entice Ariock, well, she found Thomas to be powerful and extraordinary in his own way. He was enough like her to be interesting.

And she did not have to dance around secrets with Thomas. She did not feel a constant pressure to hide her true feelings, or to be brave and stoic the way the Dovanacks were. Thomas accepted her even with her flaws and her grievous past errors.

She felt like she could discuss anything with him.

She liked that.

I am tired of fear, she added. *You can brainwash me with a thought. You are a monster to me. Well, okay. I can murder you with a thought. I am a monster to you.*

Thomas silently acknowledged the equality of their mutually assured destruction.

So, Evenjos went on in the language of thought, *perhaps we can speak to each other, not as victims or targeted prey, but as equals?*

Thomas gazed at Evenjos, marveling that she was willing to . . . well, befriend him.

He sensed that she was reevaluating everything she believed about telepaths. She was scrapping all her assumptions about him and starting fresh.

That required guts. That required intellectual honesty and integrity—a scientific approach.

I think I have misjudged you as well, he acknowledged.

Her smile was gentle and radiant.

They did not share their deepest secrets. Thomas would not share his innermost self with anyone whose mind could be probed. But respectfully, cautiously, they began to explore each other's memories.

They began to know each other.

PART FOUR

Supergeniuses make useful tools, but they grow more dangerous the longer they live. Anyone who trusts the successful ones is a fool.

—Former Commander of All Living Things

POSTMORTEM

The war room was diverse, with more than one hundred people of various species taking seats around an oblong table.

Normal-size people sat in elegant chairs that floated like delicate tulips. Stately Alashani councilors looked uncomfortable next to ummins and govki. Nussians took up space between chairs, since that species crouched, and they were not the only sapients who did not use furniture. The so-called exotic species each had a representative.

Competition for the limited number of seats must have been fierce.

Ariock had agreed with Garrett that the war council ought to be a private, focused discussion. They did not want side galleries full of onlookers, innocent people who might later walk within range of Torth prisoners and unintentionally leak strategic information to the empire. So Garrett had set up this private room. Soothing colors played along the walls and ceiling.

"Are you sure I belong here?" Vy asked in a small voice.

"Of course." Ariock turned to look at her. "Someone needs to represent humankind."

"That isn't funny," she said. But her tone was teasing, and Ariock knew she had taken his comment as a joke.

Good. He wasn't joking, but he did want her to feel comfortable on the war council. When a dignified ummin ushered Vy to a seat reserved for her, she looked honored rather than terrified.

The massive throne-like chair at the head of the table must be reserved for Ariock. He walked past alien dignitaries who he assumed must be war heroes, councilors, major battle captains, and city elders.

He wasn't sure he wanted to learn the details of how each of these dignitaries had won their seats. Through fair elections? Or through threats of violence, with gang support? Perhaps a high-stakes lottery?

He supposed it didn't really matter.

They were here because they wanted to uphold freedom and destroy the Torth Empire. No matter how they had been chosen, each representative must feel intense pressure to meet the frenetic expectations of their people. They could be trusted to voice concerns and raise pertinent questions.

If anyone was overrepresented, it was the Alashani. There was no way to avoid that. This was a war. Although albinos were scarce throughout the city's general population, Ariock had agreed with Garrett that all fourteen premier warriors—thirteen plus Jinishta, the premier of premiers—ought to be included. Yeresunsa would be vital to any military strategy.

Ariock took his seat. Expectant faces watched him.

He was uncomfortably aware that he was the youngest person at this council, except for Thomas, who hadn't shown up yet. He did not think he belonged at the head of the table, right next to Kessa, who was boosted in a petite hoverchair.

Garrett had seated himself next to Kessa on her other side. He looked positioned to take charge.

The room grew hushed as dust swirled overhead.

At the same time, Thomas entered, floating in his replaced hoverchair. People eyed him nervously as he passed, no doubt struggling to hide their secrets. They scooted closer to the table to give him more room.

These councilors must have seen the hordes of defeated Torth in the bowels of the city, filthy and begging. Even so, Ariock guessed it would take more than a few days—perhaps more than a few years—for their fear and hatred of mind readers to fade.

Thomas ignored the distrust aimed his way and floated to his reserved spot. He was between Ariock and Vy.

Evenjos took shape. She occupied a seat between Garrett and Jinishta, wings folded and framing her stormy mass of purple hair. The plunging V-shaped neckline of her shimmery violet dress exposed the inner slopes of her breasts.

Fake breasts, Ariock reminded himself. Everything about Evenjos was artifice.

He pretended not to see the sultry look she aimed his way. Why did she keep trying to seduce him? Would she ever quit?

Once everyone was seated, Garrett slid off his chair and cleared his throat for attention. "We need to discuss our next moves against the Torth."

The council fell silent. They eagerly awaited more.

"We won a great victory here," Garrett acknowledged, slapping the table for emphasis. "But if we sit back and rest, the Torth will take advantage of the time we give them." He looked toward Thomas. "Would you agree?"

Thomas nodded, grim-faced. "Yep. We need to make plans."

Ariock leaned back in the chair, grateful that he'd had a full night's sleep. Vy had slept on his chest. She had not invited greater intimacy. He would have appreciated a friskier night, but . . . well, he wasn't going to get pushy.

Garrett went on. "We know the Upward Governess was working on an invention that could be weaponized against us."

That was news to Ariock.

Judging by the concerned looks around the room, it was news to everyone who couldn't read minds.

"Unfortunately," Garrett said, "we don't have details or any of her notes. I suspect the Torth supergeniuses regularly exchanged notes via encrypted messages and secret couriers. We need to assume they have her latest research. And we don't."

Thomas gave a reluctant nod of confirmation.

"I can't get any hints out of the Megacosm." Garrett focused on Thomas, intense. "Is there any chance you gleaned what she was working on?"

If anyone could soak up secrets at a rapid pace, it was Thomas. Ariock turned to him with hope. Everyone's attention shifted his way.

But Thomas's reply was disappointing. "She died too soon."

There was unspoken grief in that statement. Now that Ariock studied Thomas, he saw a burden weighing down his thin shoulders and a tightness around his eyes.

Garrett waved as if clearing away a pest. "Well, that's too bad. We could scour this planet in search of her underground lab, but it's likely the Torth already destroyed it in order to prevent us from rooting out her secrets."

Thomas nodded.

Ariock wondered how dangerous a hypothetical prototype weapon could be, anyway. Shouldn't he be more worried about Torth teleporters?

"The teleporters are taken care of." Garrett looked past Kessa, who floated between them, and focused on Ariock. "I've killed all the ones within a three-day range of travel. And I'm keeping tabs on the rest."

Garrett had said that none of the Torth could ghost from planet to planet, which meant they could not teleport across the galaxy. Ariock hoped that would not change.

"How many teleporters do they have?" Ariock asked.

Garrett shrugged, like it was unimportant. "Unknown. The Rosy Recruits are experimenting with their newfound powers, so I expect their numbers will go up, but they will eventually plateau."

"More than a thousand," Thomas clarified. "Less than ten thousand. So far."

Ariock tried not to show his worries.

"We're safe here," Garrett assured everyone. "I can tell you what planets the teleporters are on, and if they make any moves closer, I will find them and kill them."

That would work for a while. But Ariock suspected the Torth supergeniuses would think of deadly ways to use their teleportation forces.

"Now," Garrett said with impatience, "I think we should discuss our next target of acquisition."

He had a portable workstation on the table, small and flat. He tapped it, and a holograph glowed into existence above the table, projected on a cone-like beam of light.

"We could annex Rare Moonrise MetroHub and its surrounding canyon lands," Garrett said, pointing to a spot on the transparent globe. "The Torth have already largely abandoned this territory. Strategically, though?" He pointed to a spot on the far side of the globe. "Happenstance City is a better choice. The more sprawled out we are on Umdalkdul, the less chance the Torth have of regaining ground or setting up a military base. Or . . ." He tapped the workstation, and the holograph changed to a galactic spiral. "We could discuss a leap to another hub planet. Nuss could give us some strong allies." He aimed a respectful look at Thomas, hands flat on the table. "What do you recommend?"

This was the first time Garrett had publicly regarded Thomas with respect.

But the assembled aliens did not know that. Most of them, especially the nussians, looked uneasy about two mind readers dominating and leading the discussion.

Thomas folded his thin hands. "We can only expand so far without Torth allies. In our current state, we cannot expect to hold territory on a hub planet." He sounded dejected. "I took a gamble here. And lost. We're going to need to take a longer-term approach."

Garrett's brow furrowed. "But we won. With zero casualties."

Ariock understood what loss Thomas was referring to. The Upward Governess would have furnished their side with a superweapon or two and perhaps with hundreds or even millions of willing Torth converts.

Instead? All they had gained, really, was a larger population to defend.

They had a city in the desert, cut off from supply lines. Their resources were going to be stretched thin. Meanwhile, the Torth still owned the entire galaxy, including a lot more Yeresunsa and supergeniuses. Ariock glanced at Garrett. Didn't he realize that?

"I suggest we work on converting the Torth prisoners to our side," Thomas was saying. "We should set up a secure base of operations that is not within easy reach of any Torth military force. My top choice would be Reject-20. It's seven days from any temporal stream, which should give us plenty of warning if the Torth send an armada in that direction."

"Really?" Garrett slumped with disappointment. "Look, I agree that her death was a setback." He meted out his words. "But we won! Now is not the time to back off and allow the Torth Empire to reclaim territory. We should hammer them while we have a million prisoners under our—"

Thomas cut in. "The way the Upward Governess died—supposedly under our protection, in our territory, under our amnesty—makes us look like untrustworthy liars." His voice was pained, as if he was trying to teach a difficult lesson. "That will make it ten thousand times harder for us to win."

The assembly was shocked.

Dignitaries exchanged glances, worried or dark. Perhaps they weren't sure they could trust the *rekvehs* at the head of the table. Even if they did trust Thomas, they didn't like the implications of his words.

Ariock half wished that Thomas had not spoken. Couldn't he have been more tactful? It was all too easy for lifelong slaves to fall back into the habit of despair and giving up. Nobody wanted to hear that they were at a disadvantage, or that winning this war might be an out-of-reach goal.

One of the councilors looked furious. She was a forbidding-looking nussian with pebbly, scarlet-colored skin, and she leaned on the table to glare at Thomas. "I hear that you are supernaturally clever. They say you meticulously planned every part of our liberation. Well, then, why did you fail to prevent this setback?"

All gazes turned toward Thomas.

Ariock understood the pressure of expectation. He inwardly considered ways to rescue Thomas from harsh scrutiny.

"I . . ." Thomas hesitated, and Ariock prepared to intervene.

But then Thomas did answer, his face pink from humiliation. "I got outsmarted by another supergenius."

No one expected that answer.

The room went quiet. Ariock, too, felt shocked. He had assumed that the Swift Killer had acted alone, goaded by her inner audience. It had not occurred to him that another supergenius might be involved.

"Who is this other supergenius?" Kessa asked.

Thomas's gaze intensified as he used his powers to conjure a holograph that glowed above the polished tabletop.

A little girl floated there, three-dimensional. She sat in a hoverchair, her limbs withered from a neuromuscular disease, and her hair was tied up in pigtails with ribbons. Her cheeks had dimples. Her innocent eyes were a bright turquoise blue.

Thomas rotated the holograph for everyone to see. "The Death Architect."

CHAPTER 2

DEADLY CHILDREN

The war council studied the projected holograph of the little girl with varied reactions. Some narrowed their eyes, as if acquiring a target. Others looked ashamed and uneasy, the way Ariock felt.

The very idea of hurting an adorable, disabled child seemed wrong. No matter what the Death Architect had done, no matter what she planned to do . . . surely she could not be entirely at fault? She was just a child.

"I know she looks harmless," Thomas said. "But do not underestimate her."

"Definitely do not underestimate her." Garrett echoed that statement as if to underscore it.

"How old is she?" Vy sounded pained.

"Twelve," Garrett said with callous indifference.

"She's a child." Vy pleaded for sympathy, as if she wanted to cradle the Death Architect in a protective embrace.

"Yeah, she's twelve going on one million." Garrett flung a hand in disgust. "She's a Torth! You can't trust what you see with your eyes. She has personally tortured hundreds of slaves to death."

Ariock studied the holograph anew. It was hard to believe that a little girl could be a mass murderer.

But, well, he supposed he could imagine it. He had watched a lot of movies and TV shows.

"Can we not hunt her down?" one of the Alashani councilors demanded. "And kill her?"

"I wish." Garrett snorted. "No. The enemy supergeniuses are in hiding, isolating themselves as much as possible. They know that if they slip up and reveal their secret locations in the Megacosm, I'll be able to find them. And kill them."

Ariock stared at his great-grandfather. Did he have to be so cavalier about the concept of murdering disabled children? Was the Death Architect truly more of a threat than, say, a space armada full of clairvoyant, teleporting Servants of All?

"They're protecting their fifteen remaining supergeniuses like national treasures," Garrett said.

"Fourteen," Thomas corrected. "I soaked up some news, by proxy, from prisoners. The Colossal Failure committed suicide last week."

"Oh yeah, I forgot," Garrett said. "What an apt name-title. The Failure never graduated off a baby farm, but he was actually one of the elder ones. Wasn't he?"

Ariock wanted to believe that Garrett's roughness was an act.

"And the baby supergeniuses aren't a threat," Garrett said. "Right?"

He actually sounded uncertain.

"Right," Thomas said. "Babies grow up, but yeah, for now, they lack self-awareness. I'm not worried about the young ones. Overall," he said to the room, "we have seven to worry about. I'm particularly concerned about the threat posed by the eldest three. They're in the same league as the Upward Governess."

Ariock wondered if he could steer the war council onto another topic. He really didn't want his worst enemies to be disabled children.

"Who are the eldest three?" Weptolyso asked.

"The Death Architect," Thomas said, "and the Twins."

He concentrated, and a second hologram appeared next to the first one. Two ghostly children floated in hoverchairs, side by side.

The boy Twin was pudgy, with sharp features and hair swept to one side. The muted colors of the holograph implied that he was very dark-skinned.

The girl Twin looked vaguely like a pallid earthworm, with a bulbous nose that took up half her face. One side of her head was slightly misaligned. She looked like a science experiment gone awry.

"They don't look alike." Vy sounded surprised.

"They're not genetically related," Garrett explained. "The Torth consider them to be twins because they constantly siphon information from each other. Since they can't forget any detail, no matter how small, the end result is that their minds are duplicates. In the Megacosm, they appear to be identical. Their minds are exact mirror images, with only the slightest of variations."

Ariock tried to guess their ages, but it was a painful exercise.

"The boy Twin is twelve," Thomas said. "The girl Twin is nearly fourteen—one month older than I am. That makes her the eldest supergenius now. I'm guessing the Torth Majority will put her under intense pressure to be a leader and invent new weapons."

"They already have," Garrett said. "I scanned the Megacosm earlier today. The Majority is clamoring for the supergeniuses to save civilization and yada yada yada, and of course, they're really spotlighting the Twins."

Kessa studied Thomas with her piercing gray eyes. "Do you think these Twins are dangerous?"

"Very," Thomas said.

"One thing about supergeniuses," Garrett said, "is that they're good at hiding secrets. Their minds are like cosmic storms. So who knows what they're working on?"

"There's more to it," Thomas said. "Consider their ages. And consider the fact that they have been cruising the Megacosm since they were babies, unable to forget a single thing they've soaked up."

Ariock tried to figure out the implications.

Garrett said, "A supergenius absorbs one whole lifetime, on average, every eighteen seconds or so. I think that's the statistic?" He looked at Thomas for confirmation.

Thomas nodded. "In the Megacosm, yes. While they're awake. So the Death Architect, for instance, contains about thirteen million lifetimes' worth of knowledge."

Ariock avoided looking at Thomas. He had never put a number to his friend's ability, but Thomas was nearly fourteen years old. He had been around longer than the Death Architect.

"The Twins contain a good deal more than that," Thomas said. "Since they siphon off each other, and they're older. My point is, I'm nowhere near that league." He looked embarrassed. "I was only immersed in the Megacosm for a few months. So . . ." His voice lowered in shame. "I'm developmentally delayed."

Ariock doubted that. Thomas was many things, but he was not a mental shrimp.

"I'm not sure mental size comparisons are all that useful," Garrett said.

"It matters." Thomas sounded definite.

"How many lifetimes of knowledge do you contain?" Kessa asked, curious.

"Two hundred ninety-two thousand," Thomas said. "Give or take."

He did not say that he was unable to compete. But everyone in the room heard the unspoken implication.

Thomas sounded broken. "This is why we could have used the Upward Governess on our side."

"You underestimate yourself," Garrett said.

"Not really." Thomas let the holographs fade.

Ariock half wished he could forget the childish faces and malformed bodies. He felt unconvinced that they were true enemies. The Upward Governess had been willing to come over to his side of the war. Maybe there would be others?

"Can we lure the Torth supergeniuses out of hiding?" Weptolyso suggested.

"I doubt those kids will fall for a trick." Garrett turned to Thomas. "Do you have any ideas?"

Thomas gave him a flat look.

Kessa spoke, her tone inquisitive. "Slaves serve those supergeniuses even while they are in hiding. Correct?"

"Yes." Thomas gave her a respectful frown. He seemed to guess her line of thought, but he allowed her to continue.

"Why don't we circulate rumors among the slave populations of every city?" Kessa asked. "We will tell them who to look for. And we can distribute radio communicators."

Ariock gawked at Kessa with respect. He understood the gist of her idea. Although the Torth supergeniuses were isolated, cut off from contact with most Torth, they were physically disabled. Someone had to feed them, dress them, bathe them, and clean their laboratories.

They must be served by contingents of slaves.

And slaves spoke with each other. Never in the presence of Torth, but they had slave quarters where they met and mingled.

"Perhaps we can distribute holographic images as well?" Kessa said. "Or sketches of the supergeniuses?"

If rumors and sketches spread throughout slave populations across the galaxy . . . sooner or later someone would recognize the supergeniuses. And if any of those slaves had secret access to a radio communicator? Then the whereabouts of the supergenius would spread fast. It would only be a matter of time before the rumor reached someone on Ariock's side of the war.

"That's a brilliant idea," Ariock said.

"I like it," Garrett chimed in.

But Thomas looked dismayed. "It's brilliant," he said reluctantly. "But it's too much to ask of slaves. The Torth Empire will figure out what we're doing, and they'll hunt down any subversive agent. They'll murder them in awful ways."

"Of course they will." Kessa nodded serenely. "So we must make sure the slaves in charge of distributing this information understand the dangers."

Thomas shook his head, as if she didn't understand. "They're likely to die."

Kessa rotated her hoverchair, speaking past Ariock to Thomas. "You say that we are free. Well. Is freedom not the ability to make meaningful choices?"

Thomas looked like he wanted to voice objections. Then his resolve seemed to wither. He gave a tight nod.

"These volunteers will be brave," Kessa said. "I already know more than a few who will risk death—even a terrible death—if it gives the rest of us a better chance to destroy the Torth Empire forever."

All around the table, elders and councilors and warriors signaled approval. They nodded toward Kessa with respect.

"We will let people decide for themselves what risks to take," Kessa said. "I will need copies of those holographs."

"I'll make sure you get everything you need," Thomas said. It seemed he trusted Kessa's judgment on the matter.

Ariock imagined slaves throughout the galaxy whispering news to each other. A secret network would undermine everything the Torth Empire taught about slavery. People would begin to think freely, even while they were still slaves.

After that, Garrett invited each representative to bring up their own topics. He guided the discussion around the table, and the war council hammered out details concerning neighborhood subdivisions, sensor drones, and day-to-day logistical concerns.

Ariock was grateful to sit back in his huge chair and feel extraneous. He didn't need to think about battles right now. He merely listened as one elder volunteered to oversee the Torth prisoners and another promised to work with Cherise on expanding the school. Thomas explained that he was building something like a telecommunications network.

"You need to invent an anti-inhibitor, boy," Garrett said.

"Yes." Evenjos stirred at the mention of that. "Please."

Thomas looked like he was suppressing irritation. "It's on my to-do list. But it won't be any time soon. Developments like that can take a long time."

Ariock wondered how much faster it would have gotten done if the Upward Governess was with them.

Garrett guided the war council back toward the subject of future plans. They agreed to meet tomorrow to discuss what city to conquer next.

"Is Earth in danger?" Vy asked.

Garrett hesitated. "No."

"I'm sure the Torth will try to use Earth," Thomas said. "Either as bait for us, or to use humans as fodder for experiments."

Vy looked horrified.

"But they've postponed the invasion of Earth," Garrett told her in a reassuring tone.

"At least for now," Thomas said. "One more thing." He shifted his focus to Kessa. "It would be wise to segregate any Torth with Yeresunsa powers from the general population. You don't need to treat them any differently, but we should know who they are."

Kessa gave a hesitant nod.

"You mean you haven't killed them?" Garrett glared from Thomas to Weptolyso. "We can't afford to keep them alive."

Ariock silently agreed. The last thing he wanted to deal with was enslaved Torth figuring out ways around their inhibitor patches. One superpowered Torth could slaughter a lot of innocent people and cause mayhem.

Thomas looked as if he was containing an angry retort.

"We don't want them ghosting around, either," Garrett added. "We can't be taking risks with them."

Thomas spoke with forced patience. "Torth Yeresunsa would be useful allies."

"Allies?" Garrett threw up his hands in disgust. "You're dreaming. You had the Upward Governess, maybe, but I think everyone can agree she was an exception. We're not going to get any others."

The same old argument.

Ariock prepared to separate his telepath friends. But he didn't need to. Thomas backed away from the table.

"I'm done here." Thomas glided toward the doorway.

Dignitaries watched him go. A few looked uneasy about his mood, but none dared to stop him.

"We don't need willing Torth allies." Garrett addressed the whole council. "Really. We have a million prisoners, and we have a boy who can—"

"No." Thomas glared from across the room.

Garrett glared back.

Ariock tensed up, certain the two of them were going to explode into a fight.

But Thomas left without another word. Within seconds, he rounded the corner and was gone.

The air felt tense. Kessa looked toward the doorway where Thomas had disappeared, her gray eyes full of concern.

Ariock knew that Thomas didn't want to zombify anyone, but he seemed touchier than usual. Perhaps it was because he had lost a . . .

Well, not a friend.

The Upward Governess had been inhuman and his nemesis. She couldn't have been friendly. But she had meant something to Thomas. A cherished hope? A dream?

"I'll talk to him," Ariock said. "I'll be right back." That was for Vy.

He hurried across the room. He passed Evenjos, who had risen out of her chair with a look of sympathy. For Thomas? That was impossible to believe.

Ariock ducked under the doorway. With his long legs, he could cross distance faster than most people.

"Thomas."

The hoverchair stopped. Thomas's thin shoulders were more hunched than usual.

Ariock caught up and knelt so they could talk face-to-face. "Garrett is being a jerk, as usual. He doesn't have the right to pressure you. I'll talk to him. All right? I'll make sure he doesn't force you to do anything you're not comfortable with."

Thomas seemed to crumble. "Thank you."

He looked incredibly vulnerable, like a child.

"I promise." Ariock wanted his assurance to be meaningful. "And," he added, "I can see the Upward Governess was more than your nemesis. I'm sorry she's gone."

Thomas's guarded look returned. "That was a loss for all of us."

"I know." Ariock searched for something else to say. He didn't know how to reassure Thomas that it was okay to have human emotions, or that it was okay to be sad. Anything like that would sound condescending.

"Thanks for your concern, Ariock." Thomas's tone was stiff. "I'm all right."

He hovered away.

Ariock straightened, watching the lone hoverchair float down the boulevard. His instincts told him that Thomas wasn't all right.

But it would be wrong to chase after him, to disrespect his personal space. Thomas didn't open up to anyone. That was just the way things were.

Ariock ducked back into the war room. The meeting was over, and people stood in knots of conversation. He passed councilors, who ought to be kinder to Thomas, and he passed a cloud of dust as Evenjos plumed away. She really ought to get over her reflexive fear of Thomas.

At least Vy was reasonable. And she was waiting for him.

CHAPTER 3

RECOMPENSE

Ariock could not enjoy the multispecies theater performance.

He tried to appreciate the unearthly choir of kemkorcan serpent people, their fluted snouts producing a range of vocalization that no human choir could match. They stirred feelings of epic adventure. And there were govki and albino trapeze artists. The production had a loose narrative, clearly meant to honor the feats of Kessa the Wise and the Bringer of Hope.

Audience members glanced at him all too often. They were anxious for his approval, Ariock knew, but their attention was distracting.

Almost as distracting as Vy.

She sat by his side, decked out in a gorgeous outfit with a metallic bodice. Someone had coiled her shining braids on top of her head. With her jointed leg prosthetic and eye makeup, she looked like a steampunk princess.

Every time she glanced at Ariock and smiled, his body felt tight. He wondered if he was living in a dream. At least his sturdy wool-and-leather outfit hid his reactions to her smiles.

"Wasn't that incredible?" Vy asked later, after the thunderous applause following the grand finale.

Ariock nodded. He didn't trust himself to make any respectable or intelligent comment.

"I mean, less than half of those performers were Alashani," Vy said. "The rest were liberated slaves. Isn't it amazing how much talent they kept hidden?" She twirled in the middle of the crowded boulevard, uncaring about the amused stares she attracted. "There's going to be a renaissance!"

They walked into the quiet garden neighborhood reserved for Kessa, Ariock, and their friends. On impulse, Ariock passed the door to Vy's suite, continuing onward. His door was at the end of the cul-de-sac.

He glanced back.

Instead of saying a chaste "Good night," Vy's cheeks turned pink. "Ooh, are you inviting me to your place for a drink?"

Ariock tried to look innocent. "Maybe."

Vy smoothed her skirt. "All right. Just for a little while."

They passed nussians, who offered Ariock respectful snorts and eye swivels. The nussians had volunteered to guard the hero's quarters.

Not that Ariock expected threats in a city he had conquered. But this way he was hidden from mobs who sought the Bringer of Hope. It was nice that he could count on undisturbed peace.

With Vy.

She giggled and hopped up onto his massive bed. "Everything here is sized for you."

The bedchamber did look that way, although they both knew that palatial, ornate furniture was typical for Torth, even low-ranked ones. The Torth standard of living was just very high. Ariock still had to duck his head when passing through doorways. Not everything was sized for him.

"If you'd like to take off that metal bodice . . ." Ariock tried not to stare. "You can make yourself more comfortable, if you'd like. But, um, you don't have to." He cleared his throat. "You look amazing."

"I might need some help." Vy wriggled.

Ariock sat next to her. He gently reached around her back. His fingers were too big for the delicate little clasps.

That was all right. He had Yeresunsa powers.

One by one, he undid her clasps with his powers while pretending to use his hands. It was an excuse to caress her back. Her waist.

Her sparkling eyes hinted that she expected wonder and magic.

Soon her restrictive bodice was gone. Her low-cut silk tunic looked loose and easy to slip out of.

Vy cuddled onto his lap before he could peel off her clothes. She met his lips with her soft mouth.

Ariock pulled her closer. He gently, reverently kissed her neck. Her collarbone.

He needed to get out of his low-key armor, which felt too restrictive, even though it was all wool and leather. He used his powers to unclasp his Yeresunsa mantle. It fell away.

"Oh no." Vy laughed softly. "I'm getting you worked up."

"Mmm." Ariock enfolded her in his arms so she couldn't easily slip away.

Their kisses gained heat. Vy pressed close, and Ariock began to wonder if maybe, just maybe, he could persuade her into a night of exploring each other. No one would interrupt. There were no chambermaids here.

Maybe he could stimulate her with his powers? Nah. That might be creepy. Ariock tucked that idea away for later consideration. Instead, he used his powers to remove his armor while still kissing and holding Vy on his lap.

"Um." Vy pulled back slightly.

Ariock was dimly aware that the recessed lights around his bedchamber seemed brighter. Maybe that was his imagination? He was busy reaching under Vy's tunic, feeling her breasts with his hand. Together, her breasts were a pleasant handful, soft and round.

"No." Vy sounded scared. "Ariock. Stop."

Her tone made him quit what he was doing.

That was when he saw items bobbing in midair throughout the bedchamber.

Orb lamps and throw pillows levitated amid sparkling dust motes. His awareness had swelled along with another part of him.

Vy giggled nervously. "I feel like something's floating inside me."

She was trying to make the situation less tense and serious. Maybe she was trying to downplay her fear?

It wasn't funny.

As Ariock tried to figure out how to apologize—and how to set down all the stuff he'd accidentally picked up, and how both of them might regain their dignity—a sultry female voice spoke out of nowhere.

"Ariock Dovanack."

That voice did not belong to Vy.

The interruption sliced between the two of them. It destroyed Ariock's focus, and levitating objects crashed to the floor. Data marbles dropped and rolled. A ceramic vase shattered.

Vy jumped off Ariock and hastened to adjust her tunic. One of her braids had slid out of its artful coil, and the end of it spilled down her back.

Ariock searched for the intruder. He recognized that throaty voice.

Sure enough, Evenjos lounged against a stone pillar. She wore a clingy dress, one rounded hip jutting out.

Did she actually believe she was sexy?

Well, maybe she was, but that could not overcome a terribly rude, overly entitled, ugly personality.

"Get out," Ariock told her.

Anyone else, faced with that tone from Ariock, would have fled. Evenjos pouted. "I have an important matter that I wish to discuss with you."

Ariock considered using his powers to supercompress Evenjos into a ball of dust, then item-teleport her into the cold void of outer space. It wouldn't kill her. It might keep her occupied for a few minutes, long enough for Ariock to apologize profusely to Vy.

Then again, it might start a battle with the former goddess-empress. An apocalyptic battle.

"Make an appointment," Ariock said coldly.

Evenjos looked hurt, as if she could not comprehend why she was unwelcome in Ariock's personal, private life.

"Leave." Ariock sat rigidly straight. The lights glowed brighter, and he fought to keep his awareness tightly reined in.

He wasn't going to lose his temper. Not in front of Vy. And there was no way he was going to start a fight with Evenjos.

"You don't get to show up here unannounced," Ariock tried to explain in a patient tone. "I have guards posted at the door. There's a reason for that. You need to respect my personal space."

Evenjos assessed Ariock's undressed chest, her eyes flicking up and down like he was a treat on display. "Humph." She made a subtle movement, and her dress revealed even more cleavage. "In my era, we did not consider sexuality to be something to hide."

Ariock began to spread his awareness, despite his resolve. He would sweep her away like trash if he had to.

Evenjos spoke quickly. "The matter I wish to discuss has to do with Thomas."

Vy paused in the middle of fitting into her bodice. "Is he okay?"

Ariock felt torn between demanding that Evenjos scram, and the question her words raised. Evenjos usually referred to Thomas as a monster. She never used his name. There was always an unspoken threat that she wanted to kill him.

"I am ashamed," Evenjos said. "Ashamed, because I have misjudged him. You were both correct about Thomas. He is not the monster I feared him to be."

Ariock suspected Evenjos was too proud to ever admit she was wrong. He studied her, trying to discern her motive. Was this an elaborate trick? She was close enough to read his mind, to mess with him.

"I can admit when I have made a mistake," Evenjos said defensively. "I am not the monster you think I am, either." She saw Ariock's impatience and quickly went on. "In my time, anyone who was wronged by a Yeresunsa had the right to reparations. Even peasant commoners had that right. The Yeresunsa who committed the wrong was supposed to offer recompense to the victim."

Was she hinting that she wanted suggestions for an apology gift?

The lights in the room dimmed to their normal glow as Ariock withdrew his awareness, losing some of his defensiveness. "If you're looking for gift recommendations," he said pointedly, "how about some privacy?"

"You should ask Varktezo," Vy said. "I think Thomas wants a mini particle accelerator, but I don't even know what those look like."

"I have a reparation in mind." Evenjos trailed her hand across the pillar, as if teasing it. "But I need your help, Ariock. That is why I came to you. I wish to see if you are interested in adding your power to mine to give Thomas that which he most fervently desires and needs."

Ariock felt ready to explode with impatience. "What are you talking about?"

"A healthy body," Evenjos said.

Ariock stared at her. Thomas's body was so far outside the definition of health, this could only be a cruel joke.

"It is a special kind of healing," Evenjos said. "I am a sixth-magnitude healer." She held up one slender hand, and the fingers became particles, then hardened into digits. "In my time, regeneration was used to restore sight to the blind and to rejuvenate the elderly. In theory, it should be able to correct the gene-level errors that are the root cause of his congenital illness."

Ariock could hardly believe what Evenjos was suggesting. Did she actually believe she could heal . . . or replace . . . Thomas's body?

Without harming his mind?

"But it is a very laborious, costly process," Evenjos went on, oblivious to his reaction. "If this was merely a scar, then I could correct the problem myself. But—as I am sure you are aware—Thomas's deadly affliction is endemic to every cell of his body. My power will be insufficient."

The implication was clear. She would need a boost of strength.

Vy straightened. "Are you saying you can give Thomas a future?" She studied Evenjos with incredulity. "You can do that?"

Ariock remained on the bed, unwilling to tower over everyone, but he wanted to bounce to his feet with excitement. "Count me in. Let's heal him!"

Evenjos smiled, but it was a terse smile, like she had caveats.

"I have considered this regeneration from every angle," Evenjos said. "And my conclusion is that it requires more than double my strength. This healing will likely entail three days of nonstop work. I cannot focus for that long at such a high level. I will need at least two assistants, and they must also be high magnitude—at least fourth-level healers. They must be able to follow my instructions exactly. They will need to subdivide their attention in extremely complex ways. We would work in shifts, with only minimal breaks. It will be extremely draining and taxing."

"But it's doable?" Ariock wanted to make sure.

"Doable," Evenjos affirmed. "I wanted to ask you and Garrett before I bring this possibility to Thomas's attention. As far as I know, there are no other fourth-magnitude healers in this era. I need both of you. If either of you refuse, then I would rather not dangle an impossibility before Thomas. To do so would be cruel."

Tonight seemed full of miracles. First Vy, offering intimacy. And now Evenjos, despite her rudeness, offering a future for Thomas. That meant a better future for the whole galaxy, as far as Ariock was concerned.

Vy scrutinized Evenjos. "What about Orla? She healed my leg after it was amputated."

"The albino maiden?" Evenjos looked distasteful. "I suppose she may be third or fourth magnitude. But if she is fourth, she lacks the raw strength. She would need a power boost. And the only people who can boost her that much are us, and we will be focused on the regeneration procedure, so we cannot do it."

Vy looked disappointed. "Ah. I see."

"Have you done this kind of healing before?" Ariock asked.

"You must understand," Evenjos said, "in my era, people with severe disabilities did not exist."

That confused Ariock for a moment. Then he remembered that her world had been "backward." Perhaps they hadn't had anything like motorized wheelchairs? Or hospitals?

"People with severe disabilities could not be cared for," Evenjos confirmed. "But monarchs and elite Yeresunsa would get rejuvenated from time to time. They would get facial reconstruction, or the effects of aging peeled back."

So the golden era had been golden only for Evenjos and her royal Yeresunsa friends.

"I did participate in those healings," Evenjos said with pride. "I led some of them. But the regeneration I am suggesting now, for Thomas, is going to be much more intensive. We cannot risk being interrupted during this procedure."

She seemed oblivious to the fact that she was the queen of interruptions.

Ariock glanced at Vy, trying to gauge what she thought. Did she trust the former goddess-empress to save the life of her foster brother?

Vy looked at him, and he saw his own hopes reflected there. She gave him a nod. She might not trust the winged woman, but she would take any chance to save Thomas's life.

Anyway, she clearly wasn't going to sit on Ariock's lap again. Not anytime soon.

Ariock put aside his sexual frustration. He was ready to plan a future for Thomas. If the healing required three days of uninterrupted work, he would need to postpone battles and war councils.

Maybe a few days would solve his fumbling mistake with Vy, as well. She might forgive him after he saved her foster brother.

"When can we get started?" Ariock stood.

"We ought to start as soon as possible." Evenjos seemed pleased. "Since you are willing, let us ask Garrett."

CHAPTER 4

CONDITIONAL SALVATION

People waved or whooped in delight upon seeing Ariock. He offered smiles and inwardly wished he was less noticeable. That way, he could breeze through crowds like Vy and Evenjos.

"We could fly." Evenjos's low voice was full of hints.

"We could," Ariock agreed in a tone that made it clear that he would not put Vy through the indignity of being carried. If she wanted to be picked up, then she would make the suggestion.

Vy smiled at Ariock.

That was a smile he could get used to seeing every day. He smiled back.

"Are you sure you know where Garrett is?" Evenjos said, annoyed. "I can scan minds to learn—"

"We're heading in the right direction," Ariock broke in.

Two particular life sparks glowed with nuclear intensity whenever Ariock stretched out his awareness. The city had plenty of Yeresunsa, but only Garrett and Evenjos stood out, apart from all others. Their raw power made them blazing beacons to Ariock's senses.

He might guess which of the other life sparks was Thomas, but only because the Rosy Recruits in the prison cells were shot full of inhibitor. If their powers had been active? Then Ariock would be unable to distinguish the Rosies from Thomas. As it was, he could sense blazing sparks that must be Alashani warriors, such as Jinishta, Orla, Flen, and hundreds of others. Thomas blazed slightly brighter than those, but only slightly.

Ariock led Vy and Evenjos through forums with mirrored floors that reflected incomprehensible luxury. Aliens amused themselves with Torth gadgets and vehicles. Unlike their former owners, these people chatted and laughed out loud, and they gave him friendly shouts or waves.

Ariock's senses led him to a district full of tabletop games. Tough-looking aliens moved stone pawns on makeshift casino tables. Every so often, a raucous chorus of shouts indicated that someone had won or lost a game.

Perhaps Ariock should have expected to find his great-grandfather gaming.

Even so, it was strange to see Garrett with a bunch of unfamiliar aliens, smoking a cigar and laughing at something a govki had said. He looked comfortable as he moved a turquoise pawn that was carved to look like a spherical Torth.

One of the gamers on the opposite end of that table, a hammerheaded mer nerctan, saw Ariock approaching.

Soon everyone in the vicinity quieted. Garrett must have sensed the change in mood, because he rotated his ergonomic chair to face Ariock. When he saw Evenjos and Vy, he stood.

"Yes?" Garrett's expression was still jovial. "What is it?"

Evenjos smoothed her gown and stepped closer.

Garrett's expression went from open to guarded to forbidding within seconds. He must be absorbing Evenjos's explanation.

He took the cigar out of his mouth. "No."

Maybe Evenjos hadn't presented the idea well enough? Ariock began to explain it out loud.

Garrett forestalled him. "Now would be a terrible time to drop everything we're doing and go on a retreat just to heal the boy. Let's revisit this in a month or two."

As if Thomas had plenty of time.

"He's dying," Ariock pointed out.

"He's always dying," Garrett said.

"It would be unwise to wait," Evenjos said. "I spent numerous hours in his presence yesterday, and I have assessed his health. His condition is critical. His internal organs are in a state of rapid deterioration, and he may not survive the process if we wait until he is on the brink of death. Truly, he may die at any minute. He needs regenerative healing now."

Garrett took a puff on his cigar. "My answer is no."

Ariock stared at his great-grandfather, stunned. What was wrong with him? Why did he hate Thomas so much?

"I don't hate him," Garrett said. "But let's be realistic. You saw the prophetic paintings. The boy isn't slated to die any time soon. Now isn't the right time."

Ariock had glimpsed a few ancient, moldering murals. He barely remembered what he had seen. Had there been an image of a boy who looked like Thomas, standing up?

"If that is the future," Evenjos said, "how do you think it comes to pass?"

"We have to make it happen!" Ariock said.

"Exactly," Evenjos said. "Ah Jun was an oracle. She painted the future she wanted. It is a guide for us, but we must be wise enough to follow it."

"You need Thomas if you want to win this war," Vy said.

Garrett inclined his head to each statement. Ariock figured they must have persuaded him with such reasonable arguments.

"My final answer," Garrett said, puffing on his cigar, "is no."

Ariock studied his great-grandfather, trying to figure out what was wrong with him.

It was easy to forget that Garrett wasn't human. He acted human. He looked human. He had passed as a human long enough to raise a family amid reserved New Englanders. But clearly, he was equally comfy playing dice games with gangster aliens—and he could cruise the Megacosm without raising suspicions.

Garrett blended in everywhere.

Perhaps his true nature was cold, empty, and heartless. He was, after all, half Torth.

Garrett took Ariock by the arm. "Every concern you have about me should go triple for the boy. He's also half Torth. He's very dangerous. Giving him perfect health is likely to cause more problems than it solves. Do you want another Unyat? Because this is how you get Unyat."

Ariock removed Garrett's hand from his arm. The old man's fatherly tone was maddening.

The gamers began to leave in a hurry. The chandeliers seemed too bright, and game pieces floated, caught in furious waves of spillover energy.

Ariock forced himself to retract his awareness. The game pieces dropped. He was not a mindless brute. He would not cause a storm.

Yet . . .

How could any of them sleep at night if Garrett was willing to let Thomas die? That was criminal negligence. It directly undermined the cause they were all fighting for. Ariock didn't even want to be associated with this Torth hybrid who had failed to protect most of his family. Garrett could pretend to be human—but so what? That wasn't good enough.

Either Garrett would cooperate, or he could no longer be considered an ally or a friend. Ariock would banish him.

"There is a way I would agree." Garrett stood still, watching Ariock the way a prey animal might watch a predator.

"Yes?" Ariock prompted. He didn't like the old man's crafty, calculating look. This had better not be a trick.

"Yeah." Garrett poked the cigar back into his mouth. "I'll heal him if he agrees to my condition."

Ariock braced himself for something infuriating.

"What is your condition?" Evenjos asked.

"That's between him and me." Garrett strode toward the thoroughfare, leading the way. "Let's let him decide."

Ariock kept glancing at his great-grandfather as they walked, trying to catch some hint of the stipulation. "You can't coerce him into zombifying prisoners. I won't let you."

"This isn't your decision," Garrett said.

Ariock felt ready to banish the old man from their side of the war. He began to say so, but Garrett spoke again.

"That's not what I'm going to ask." Garrett turned a corner, leading the way down another boulevard. "Calm down. I think he'll be okay with my stipulation. We're all on the same side here. The boy shares my goals."

Ariock wished he could dive into Garrett's mind. He could demand to know what Garrett was planning to spring on Thomas . . . but any heated argument between the two of them might cause damage. Ariock and Garrett were both storm-bringers. They might frighten the newly liberated people. Wasn't it better to avoid a fight if possible?

Maybe the stipulation was something stupid and inferior, like Garrett himself. The old man was probably too embarrassed to admit that he'd been wrong, and now he was trying to save face. He would probably just reiterate his demand for an antidote to the inhibitor. What a petty man.

Anyway, Thomas never let anyone take advantage of him. He was smart enough to sidestep traps.

Most likely, Thomas would figure out Garrett's craven stipulation within a microsecond, then engineer a bunch of ways to force the old man to back down.

It would be fine.

They found Thomas teaching science to a group of studious-looking aliens. He floated in a secluded lounge, avoiding the gigantic rays of artificial sunlight that streamed through ornate windows. One of his complex-looking wireframe holographs glowed in the shadows.

"If you extrapolate the hyperspace equation across the local m-brane . . ." Thomas followed the attention of one of his distracted students and trailed off. His vapor-projected holograph vanished.

The students jumped up and hurried away, leaving their seat cushions and retreating into an alcove where they could watch from an unobtrusive distance.

"What's wrong?" Thomas asked with weary expectation.

His physical weakness was blatantly obvious. His limbs were malformed and twiglike, contorted from years of atrophied muscles, with stunted tendons and bones. He was so underdeveloped, his shoulders looked impossibly narrow and bony in contrast to his head.

Ariock remembered when Thomas had been able to nod or shake his head, or shrug. Now? He had to rotate his chair in order to face them. A neck pillow cradled his head.

"I come to offer you a gift." Evenjos stepped into Thomas's range of telepathy.

Ariock watched Thomas with apprehension. He suddenly feared that Evenjos was being presumptuous. What if she merely assumed that Thomas would be grateful?

Raw emotions flitted over Thomas's face in rapid succession. Shock. Delight. Wonder and amazement. Gratitude.

"You would do that?" he asked softly. "For me?"

Thomas rarely showed emotions, let alone so much intensity of emotion. Ariock relaxed. This was the right thing to do.

"It is common sense," Evenjos said. "This war needs you. And it is recompense. I have treated you poorly, and I misjudged your character. That was wrong."

Thomas's gaze shifted to Garrett. "What's the condition?"

Ariock assured himself that Garrett would not be too cruel or unreasonable. The book of prophecies featured Thomas as one of the four main heroes, vital to victory over the Torth Empire. Garrett should know better than to turn Thomas into an enemy.

Garrett took a puff of his cigar. "I want you to become a slave," he said. "My slave."

CHAPTER 5

IN EXCHANGE

"No." Ariock expanded his awareness, ready for a fight. "You're not enslaving him."

Garrett seemed to realize that he could not simply shrug off Ariock's judgment. He sighed with annoyance, but he beckoned for Ariock to follow him a distance away so they could talk in relative privacy.

Ariock followed with deep misgivings.

"You see an innocent boy," Garrett said in a low voice as soon as they were out of Thomas's earshot. "I see a monster. If you could read minds, you would see what I see."

Ariock doubted that.

"That kid is no child," Garrett said. "He's thousands of years old, mentally. You want to gift him with a lifetime of health? Then you need to understand the Pandora's box that opens up. There is a reason why supergeniuses are bioengineered to expire before adulthood."

Garrett must have absorbed too much propaganda from the Megacosm. Ariock began to argue.

"They've always died young," Garrett whispered fiercely. "Unyat baked it into the Torth genetic code, to prevent his own offspring from running amok and taking control of the galaxy. That was the smart thing to do!"

"It's wrong," Ariock said, but his great-grandfather kept talking, fervent and insistent.

"Anyone with half a brain should fear those mutants. You want to give the boy a healthy body? Then you need to understand how he can leverage that. We'd be granting him a *future*. That means *time*. With time like that, a supergenius can invent anything. Understand? He can do *anything*."

As if unlimited power was something to be feared. Ariock rolled his eyes. For someone who had been born overpowered, his great-grandfather was ridiculously insecure. Couldn't he see that they needed more friends with power? Didn't he understand that Thomas was on their side?

"You don't get to treat Thomas like he's our enemy." Ariock made his voice implacable. "You need to withdraw your ultimatum."

"But we absolutely need a way to control him!" Garrett pleaded, like he was talking about a berserk battlebeast. "If we're going to give him an unlimited future, like you want, then we need insurance that he won't seize control of our minds."

"Will you listen to yourself?" Ariock braced himself for a serious fight. "You don't trust him as a person—but you'll trust him to be your slave? That doesn't even make sense!"

"It's better than nothing!" Garrett snapped. "We know the boy doesn't lie! If he swears to obey me, then at least I can sleep at night. I'll be able to assure myself that he's trustworthy, even if the prophecies hint—"

Thomas's quiet voice interrupted. "I accept."

Garrett went still. He looked surprised.

Ariock stared at Thomas in disbelief. This was insane. Surely he had misheard his friend, or misunderstood?

"Within reasonable limits." Thomas focused on Garrett. "I won't obey an order that will end up harming my friends."

"Naturally." Garrett spread his hands, as if to sweep aside any doubts. "We're on the same side."

Thomas's yellow gaze seemed to drill into Garrett. "And I won't obey an order to kill myself. You won't put me in a situation that unnecessarily jeopardizes my life. The whole point of this is to give me a future."

Garrett looked sour. "All right."

Ariock stared from Thomas to Garrett, horrified. This whole slavery proposition had to be a joke. "You're not actually considering this."

They ignored him.

"You need to take my health into account when you give me orders," Thomas said. "You won't force me to deplete myself to the point of death. If I tell you I can't do something, you will respect my limits."

"Yeah, yeah." Garrett took a puff on his cigar. "Enough with your limits. By agreeing to be my slave, you are agreeing to never lie. You won't deceive me in any way. In front of witnesses, right here, you are swearing to obey my commands, starting from the moment that you are healed."

"Agreed," Thomas said smoothly.

As if he had no reservations whatsoever.

Ariock gawked. Couldn't Thomas guess what sort of things he would be ordered to do?

Brainwashing.

Zombification.

"No." Ariock strode in front of Garrett, separating the mind readers. "I won't let this happen."

"It's not your choice," Garrett said.

Ariock glared. Didn't the old man understand the ramifications of slavery? Thomas was an individual, with dignity and self-respect. Take away those things, and what would Thomas become?

Their friendship would wither. Resentment would build up. Thomas would lose respect for Garrett and, by extension, Ariock. He would lose trust in them. Why should a slave side with his oppressive owner?

It was a recipe for disaster.

"I am not okay with this," Ariock said.

"It's worth it," Thomas said.

"No, it isn't!" Ariock's voice came out too loud, causing chandeliers to sway and distant people to look alarmed. He had accidentally connected with the environment. He tried to lower his tone. "You can have the healing without conditions."

He would force Garrett to agree. He would figure out a way.

Thomas scrutinized him. So did Garrett. They were probably both scanning Ariock's mind, absorbing his thoughts, but so what? He wasn't going to budge.

"Ariock," Thomas said. "Can I speak with you in private?"

Ariock could not imagine any argument that would convince him to allow one friend to enslave another. Nevertheless, he followed Thomas past walls of ivy and trickling waterfalls. Maybe Garrett would reconsider his inhuman cruelty if given a few moments to think about it? And meanwhile, Ariock would try to convince Thomas to value his own autonomy a little bit more.

They rounded a corner. Thomas used his data tablet to make vapor falls appear, so they were enclosed within sound-dampening veils of mist. The ambient garden noises and whispering aliens became inaudible.

Thomas said, "The regenerative healing Evenjos offered won't work unless both you and Garrett participate. I need his willing help."

Ariock began to say that Garrett had no right to demand such a steep price.

"He won't change his mind," Thomas said. "There's nothing you can say to persuade him."

Ariock began to argue.

"People fear me," Thomas said.

Ariock knelt, facing Thomas directly. Was this why his friend was willing to be a slave? Did he care so much about what Garrett thought of him?

"Not just Garrett," Thomas said. "He's outspoken, but just about every Alashani thinks the same things. And they're not the only ones," Thomas quickly went on, forestalling arguments. "Everyone knows what I used to be. Garrett acts human. He reminds people, every chance he gets, that he's an Alashani and not a Torth. He pretends he can't read minds."

Ariock opened his mouth, wanting to say that none of that mattered.

"I'm unwilling to hide what I can do." Thomas sounded like he was choosing his words with care. "I'm a mind reader. My mother was a Torth."

Ariock glanced behind them, hoping no passersby were eavesdropping. Thomas should know better than to state that heritage out loud. It wasn't something to be proudly blurted out. It was something that should be whispered and downplayed.

"I'm willing to experience slavery," Thomas said. "After all, I'm asking Torth to convert to my side as slaves. Why not lead by example?"

Ariock had so many arguments, he didn't know where to begin. For one thing—did it count as slavery if there were caveats? Real slaves did not get to lay ground rules.

"Right," Thomas said. "This is a mild version of slavery. And it won't last my whole life."

The way he caressed that last word . . .

Ariock reassessed Thomas and saw a fierce determination that had not been there before.

Thomas had grown up struggling to live to adulthood. He had given up on that ambition. But now that the possibility was suddenly handed to him . . . it seemed his ambition was rekindled. He wanted life.

A healthy version of Thomas would almost surely outlive Garrett.

One of the faded murals in that hall of prophecies had shown a decapitated old man. Ariock remembered that depiction of Garrett's death.

"Exactly," Thomas said softly.

Ariock shook his head, dismissing Thomas's justifications. Could Garrett even be trusted with owning a person? He wasn't a paragon of virtue.

It was one thing for former slaves to claim ownership of their former owners. But Garrett used to be a slave owner. He had not earned this. He didn't deserve it!

"Maybe somebody will enslave Garrett at some point," Thomas said. "Maybe someone will pressure him to transfer his ownership of me to someone else. I wouldn't object if that's what happens."

As if slavery was a casual game. No big deal.

Ariock tightened his jaw. Perhaps Thomas envisioned this as a fun new experience, like role-playing, but he was glossing over endless downsides.

And considering how much power he wielded . . . how much power Garrett and Thomas could wield, combined . . . Ariock imagined many ways this could go wrong.

"I want this," Thomas said, "precisely because I am powerful."

He was serious. Honesty blazed from his yellow eyes.

"I need people to trust me," Thomas said. "If I'm constrained by a set of obvious rules and laws? I'll be less intimidating. Garrett is not the only person who needs convincing. Most of our population needs the same persuasion." He gave Ariock a beseeching look, as if begging him to understand. "Garrett is terrified of me. Once he thinks he's in control of me? All that friction will end. We'll be able to work together, without animosity. He'll stop being afraid."

"But—" Ariock struggled, wanting to list all the awful things Garrett could command.

"Garrett isn't actually in control," Thomas cut in.

Ariock felt lost. "What?"

"Garrett isn't the leader," Thomas said. "He doesn't command anyone. And he won't, except for me."

A new understanding began to dawn on Ariock.

"You made me a promise." Thomas's gaze was intense.

Of course. Ariock remembered. He had stopped Thomas in the hallway the other day and promised to prevent Garrett from forcing Thomas into doing anything he didn't want to do.

That had been a solemn promise. Ariock meant it.

"You can overrule Garrett at any time," Thomas said. "On any matter."

Ariock's mouth worked. He struggled to think of a way to explain how unfair this was. If Ariock had to be the one to overrule Garrett . . . if he had to argue every time the old man came up with a harebrained scheme, or a bad idea, or a stupid command for Thomas to follow . . .

"That means I'll be arguing with Garrett," Ariock said. "Instead of you doing it."

"Yup." Thomas seemed pleased.

"But Thomas—" Ariock needed to explain that he was a clumsy, uneducated screwup. The galaxy couldn't afford to have a failure in charge. He wasn't cut out for leadership.

"You're the leader this war needs." Thomas looked earnest. "Our people would die for you. They won't die for anyone else."

Ariock began to dismiss that as a fluke. It was just happenstance, because he happened to fit a messiah prophecy.

"You've earned people's respect," Thomas said. "You don't realize it. But you're a moral compass. Everyone respects your decisions. Including me."

Ariock couldn't think of any response to that. Thomas sounded serious.

Shouldn't the supergenius be in charge?

"You'll have my advice whenever you need it," Thomas said with fondness. "Always."

At last, Ariock understood. Thomas wanted to be a consultant, not a decision-maker.

Because Thomas didn't trust himself with power.

He didn't even trust himself with freedom.

"As soon as I go through the regeneration healing," Thomas said with contentment, "all the important decisions will be yours, big guy."

Thomas had been morose ever since the loss of the Upward Governess. Now he seemed lighter in spirit. Without the freedom to make his own choices, perhaps he believed he would gain a different sort of freedom?

And perhaps he was right. If Thomas caused harm while he was an alleged slave, he would be able to shrug it off as not his fault.

It seemed he was ready to wash his hands and absolve himself of guilt. He would shift his burdens of care, shame, and guilt onto someone else's shoulders.

Someone with broad shoulders.

Ariock supposed he could take on Thomas's share of leadership, if that was truly the wise choice. But he had doubts.

Perhaps no one was fit to wield absolute authority. In truth, Ariock wasn't sure anyone existed who could be trusted with his tremendous level of power.

"You'll do fine." Thomas gave him a grateful, confident smile.

CHAPTER 6

AT A LOSS

The Former Commander stood in utter, silent desolation.

She wore a spacesuit, allowing her to stand on the barren surface of an asteroid in the Araya Moon Belt. Above her awareness, she knew the Megacosm roiled. A million prisoners begged for help. Everyone in the galaxy was afraid.

But she stood apart from that chaos.

She had made a pilgrimage.

She was seeking the little girl known as the Death Architect for a personal consultation. She wanted guidance. Deep down, the Former Commander wondered if she might be able to reclaim some semblance of authority so she could help stop the monstrous enemies of civilization.

She consulted her data tablet again.

The encrypted packet had passed every verification check. She'd picked it up in Permafrost City and plugged that high-clearance data into a private jumper shuttle. She had arrived at what should be the correct coordinates on the correct asteroid.

The distant sun offered just enough light to show her that there was no hint of civilization. There was certainly no sign of a fortress.

Her space boots had grippy soles, but that would not stop her from floating away if she accidentally walked with too brisk a stride. The weak gravity made her as light as parchment.

With a sigh of resignation, the Former Commander ascended into the Megacosm.

SAVE US.

HELP US.

She ignored the collective moans and instead followed opinion threads, seeking the cavernous mind of a particular supergenius. She just had to hope that the Death Architect was taking a social break instead of deeply absorbed in work.

Navigating the Megacosm was not as fun as it used to be. Fear and uncertainty tainted most discussions. Between the worries . . . there were gaps.

The Megacosm felt rotten, like parts were missing.

The Former Commander could guess why. Supergenius minds were like pillars of pure data, collated and stacked into narratives that normal-minded scientists and historians could easily access. Supergeniuses shepherded and nurtured a lot of esoteric speculations and obscure facts.

With the Upward Governess and the Colossal Failure gone, and with other supergeniuses too busy to pursue their own meandering interests . . . ? The whole Megacosm felt slightly unstable. It was full of holes.

There is nothing to fear. That reassurance radiated from the oceanic mind of the Death Architect.

Billions of minds orbited the Death Architect, eager for any hint of her next move against the enemies. Would she invent a deadly serum? A bomb even more explosive than a comet-class warhead? A new method of torture?

The Death Architect ignored all questions while hard-core fanatics of her mind disseminated her position for her.

She (the Death Architect) shall reveal Her magnum opus when She judges the time to be right.

She is a master of timing.

She is wise enough to withhold military secrets from the public.

Just in case the Imposter listens in.

That was commendable. Yet the Former Commander felt uneasy, and she sensed that she was not the only high rank with concerns about allowing super-geniuses to lead the war.

Let Us continue to build up Our military, the Death Architect urged her billions of orbiters. *We need more swarmships, more inhibitor microdarts, more Rosy Recruits.*

She might as well be a galactic commander instead of a disabled prepubescent child. The Majority backed up every thought she had. *Yes (yes) yes.* After all, this little girl had saved civilization. She had handily destroyed the traitorous Upward Governess.

Where are You? the Former Commander wondered, trying to stand out amid all the other minds. *I am (here) at Your—*

The Death Architect focused on her for a split second. *Get out of the Megacosm and find Me.*

Then she returned to placating the masses.

In response to a common worry, the Death Architect thought, *Let Us remember: the Betrayer is not taking NAI-13. Judging from eyewitnesses, his health is poor. He is dying.*

The Majority liked that. They swirled with relief.

Also, the Death Architect went on, *the Betrayer is mentally handicapped compared to Me (and those like Me). He does cast a long shadow, but that is solely due to his helpers (friends) (minions). We shall see how well he does once I begin to sever him from his help.*

Her logic smoothed the spikes of emotion in the Megacosm.

Even the Former Commander felt heartened. The Betrayer was, indeed, in ill health. His upcoming death would cause the whole war to fizzle. The galaxy must soon become safe again.

Maybe people would quit blaming her for failing to kill the Betrayer back when he was nothing but a feral animal from Earth. Sure, if she had made such a bold move, the Majority would have then executed her for going rogue. But the Majority was never wrong. If she had gone rogue in order to save civilization . . . well, at least she could have gotten executed with some of her inner dignity intact.

Instead? She had allowed a mistake to live.

She survived in ignominy, stripped of her mantle of office. The entirety of the Torth Empire—including all future generations, for eternity—knew that she had made a terrible mistake.

Why are you (Former Commander) lingering in My audience? The Death Architect spared a fraction of her attention. *Get out. Use that poor excuse for a brain inside your skull.*

The Former Commander tried to let the insult pass.

She dropped out of the Megacosm as commanded. But she inwardly resolved to teach the little girl a lesson. Once they met face-to-face . . . well. She would twist the girl's underdeveloped limbs until her twiglike bones cracked. No permanent damage, but the Death Architect would have to suffer a painful reminder that she was weak. Technically, she ought to be subordinate to someone with a military career and powers.

This asteroid was just icy rocks and layers of dust.

The Former Commander huffed, the sound too loud inside her helmet.

She took careful steps. She had already explored these rocks with her Yeresunsa awareness, but she tried it yet again. Maybe she ought to delve lower? Underground?

Weird.

Was that a crisscross pattern? It confused her awareness, leading her this way and that, ultimately nowhere.

Frustrated, the Former Commander withdrew to her focus. Maybe there was a hidden lair beneath the airless surface, but then again, maybe the little girl was toying with her, making her look like a fool. Maybe the Death Architect thought it was amusing to send supplicants on fruitless quests. What a nasty little . . .

A section of the rocky ground sank.

The Former Commander stared in disbelief. A ramp led down into glossy darkness.

There actually was a subterranean facility here.

How had her extended awareness missed it? She really wanted to know.

She suppressed her urge to ascend into the Megacosm and make inquiries. That would be illegal. Visitors to this hidden lair were not permitted to share anything about the visit. Once the Former Commander returned to civilization, no one would dare probe her mind about this visit, lest they be branded a traitor to the empire.

The Former Commander walked down the ramp into a mirror-coated labyrinth. Every surface was reflective chrome.

She stepped over a gravity warning and felt the artificial gravity take hold of her. A gravity mesh must be hidden beneath the chrome-plated floor.

The airlock sealed behind her.

The Former Commander walked down empty hallways, accompanied only by the multitudes of her own blurry reflections. She used her spacesuit to test the air quality. Satisfied that the air was breathable, she caused her helmet to retract into her collar armor.

Now, where might she find the smug little supergenius?

Every chrome hallway intersected another. There were not enough lights. The Former Commander rounded corner after corner, encountering only her own dim reflections.

Shouldn't she have encountered a slave by now, at least?

The place smelled, very faintly, of excrement and blood.

The Former Commander sighed with annoyance. She had better things to do than wander, lost, through a labyrinth that needed a thorough cleaning.

Just as she began to expand her awareness, to search for life, the Death Architect floated out of the darkness ahead.

The little girl lacked a life spark.

The Former Commander stared, studying what could only be a perfectly realistic holograph. Projected images were ubiquitous in most cities, but they tended to glow, and they were not easy to mobilize. This one somehow—how?—was indistinguishable from reality.

Like all color ranks, the girl's eyes were iridescent. The turquoise color glowed balefully out of the darkness. Her hair was fluffed up and tied with ribbons. Other than that, the girl wore strictly utilitarian clothes.

Where are you, really? the Former Commander wondered.

Why did she have so many misgivings? Everything the Death Architect had done was laudable. Logical. But the Former Commander mistrusted supergeniuses. Only she seemed to remember that not one, not two, but three ripe supergeniuses had gone renegade in recent times. The Betrayer. The Upward Governess. And the Colossal Failure. If anyone could mislead the masses, it was one of those freakish children.

She stretched her awareness farther . . .

. . . and jumped when a cage slammed down around her.

Something stung her neck.

The Former Commander lost her expanded awareness. She tried to expand again, but her powers were gone. She had been shot with a microdart of the inhibitor serum.

She seized the bars of the cage. No good. Her enhanced strength was no match for thick tungsten polymer.

Someone was toying with her, treating her like an animal or a slave. This was unacceptable.

An enormous mind entered her local awareness. It crackled with offshoots and curlicues of irreverent knowledge, without any hint of smugness or remorse. No emotions whatsoever.

The Former Commander whirled around to confront the Death Architect, who was backed up by four battlebeasts.

Ropes of drool swung from the enormous jaws of the monsters. Battlebeasts and nussians were roughly the same size, and they served the same purpose. But unlike nussians, battlebeasts were pure carnivores. They enjoyed killing, and they were bred for savagery. Also, since they lacked the sapience level of nussians, they tended to adore their Torth masters.

Their lesser sapience was also a detriment. Battlebeasts could not handle complex instructions. Drudge work and sentry duty were beyond their capabilities. They were hard to train, and their naked, mottled-green skin gave them a certain vulnerability.

You (Former Commander) compromised My security, the Death Architect thought without any hint of resentment or rancor. *You ascended into the Megacosm when you should not have. So I am handling you with similar disdain. I failed to deactivate My security system. Oops.*

The Former Commander struggled to suppress her own rancor. The little girl had shot her with the inhibitor, which disabled her powers for three days, at least. That was inexcusable. They were not equals!

How dare you, she thought.

The Death Architect poked at the data tablet balanced on her bony lap. *Nevertheless*, she thought, uncaring, *your arrival (at My lair) is fortuitous.*

The cage bars lifted, retracting into the ceiling.

The Former Commander became aware that this subterranean labyrinth was riddled with traps. There were misleading holographic illusions, cages, and microdart launchers embedded in walls.

And other pitfalls, the Death Architect affirmed. *I am experimenting with the binding effects of mirrored surfaces upon ghosting clairvoyants. Unfortunately, most of My test subjects have died. I want more Yeresunsa for My experiments.*

The Former Commander considered tormenting the child with a pain seizure. Someone ought to remind her that she was just a Turquoise-Blue Rank, not even Indigo-Blue. Nor was she the eldest supergenius. That honor went to the girl Twin. The Death Architect needed to serve her betters, instead of—

!!!!

All four battlebeasts lunged at the Former Commander as if they did not recognize her as a superior being. They raced toward her on their spindly legs.

The Former Commander signaled them to stop. Every slave, even battlebeasts, knew the universal hand signals given by Torth masters.

But these monsters paid no attention. They crunched her limbs in their huge jaws.

The Former Commander screamed in pain.

The battlebeasts slammed her against the wall, and she sensed that they were conditioned to obey only their child mistress, no one else.

Someone needed to accuse the Death Architect of illegal battlebeast training and reckless behaviors. The Former Commander began to ascend into the Megacosm, ready to call for help, and to identify and accuse her attacker.

I wonder which one of Us the Majority will side with? The Death Architect remained tranquil. *Hm.*

The Former Commander had never felt so helpless in her life.

She did not ascend. The problem, she knew, was that she had already eroded much of the sympathy and goodwill she had amassed over her long life. The Torth Majority did not forgive incompetence.

The Death Architect had scored trust by figuring out a way to swiftly destroy the traitorous Upward Governess.

The Former Commander, in contrast, had made too many blunders.

Why are You hurting Me? The Former Commander resumed her struggles, desperate to break free. Why hadn't she been more cautious?

The Death Architect signaled the battlebeasts, and they halted their attack.

They did not let the Former Commander go. They held her against the wall, and monster drool soaked down into her collar, sour and sticky. Their breath smelled offensive.

I had no intention of harming you. The Death Architect radiated sincerity. *I merely wish to teach you a lesson. Have you learned?*

Humiliating tears leaked from the Former Commander's superior white eyes. She supposed she had learned something. She needed to tread carefully here. She was disadvantaged.

I knew you would visit Me. The Death Architect made a gesture, and a quivering govki slave cringed out of the darkness. *I prepared a gift for you.*

The slave offered a cushioned tray. Atop the tray lay a curved sword. It was a scimitar of the type that humans used to fight with.

This blade is ionic bone-slicing polymer, the Death Architect informed her.

The Former Commander tried to summon a response. But as she hung in the jaws of the battlebeasts, all she had were questions.

Wasn't this proffered weapon made for primitive combat? No matter how sharp its blade, it was surely useless against enemies that mattered. Wouldn't a blaster cannon be more effective? Or something new?

I designed this scimitar, the Death Architect thought, *especially for those who can teleport.*

The Former Commander was unused to feeling obtuse. She stared at the Death Architect, daring her to clarify what she meant.

You answered My call for champions. The Death Architect pictured an armored Servant of All who blinked in and out of existence, wielding the scimitar and beheading Alashani warriors right and left. *Either you will become an agent of death yourself, or you will find someone who is worthy of this blade.*

Then the Former Commander understood.

A primitive blade could become a weapon of massacre if it was wielded by a masterful teleporter. The Torth Empire needed someone who could match the Imposter.

Correct. The Death Architect stared into the blank gaze of the Former Commander. *This needs to be a priority. Find Torth who have exceptional power. Find those who can teleport across the galaxy. Most of all, find those who can brainwash. Find them. And introduce them to Me.*

The Former Commander forced her breathing to slow, reminding herself that she used to rule all living beings. She had lived one hundred and eighty-six years, whereas this little girl was twelve. The Death Architect had never worn the horned mantle of the highest office in existence. She was inferior, just a dying child, no matter how much she—

You will serve Me. The Death Architect appraised her, ignoring the slathering battlebeasts.

The Former Commander struggled to probe the little girl's voluminous mind, searching for any hint of leeway.

She realized that the girl was taking a calculated risk. If the public learned that she was threatening a Servant of All, they might gang up against her. After all, they had not elected the Death Architect to leadership. They had not technically elected anyone.

The Majority has enough to deal with, the Death Architect thought, *without petty squabbles about who should wear the mantle of office.*

That was true. The Majority did not want extra stress. They yearned for easy answers, preferably from someone who would take responsibility for fixing galactic problems.

Should they be forced to vote? The Death Architect folded her small hands on her data tablet. *They would not thank the one who forced the issue.*

That was also true.

We do not need to be at odds, you and I, the Death Architect thought. *You (Former Commander) are trained to keep secrets. I am good at keeping secrets. Let this be a private matter.*

There was no mistaking her silent threat.

Yeresunsa powers had become commonplace. The Former Commander wanted to feel special and irreplaceable, but there were now many millions of Rosy Recruits, in addition to many thousands of Servants of All. Plenty of fanatical military ranks would serve this supergenius without question. If the Former Commander refused to obey, then the Death Architect would feed her to the battlebeasts. She could find other, more obedient, champions.

You finally get it. The Death Architect illustrated her thoughts with vivid imaginings. *In public, in the Megacosm, I will act deferential to you. I prefer it that way. But (in secret) (in private) you are under My command.*

It seemed perverse. But the Former Commander dared not argue.

Once you recover your powers, the Death Architect thought, *you will fetch and deliver a year's worth of NAI-13 to Me (in secret, of course). Deliver it within two weeks. Otherwise I will have you replaced.*

The Former Commander bowed her head. The Torth Empire was in dire straits if this child was truly in charge.

The Death Architect rotated her hoverchair and floated away without a concern. *For now*, she thought, *although your powers are disabled, you are not entirely useless. I will collect samples of your flesh for My experiments. Come.*

She signaled the battlebeasts, and they released the Former Commander in a cascade of slobber.

CHAPTER 7

THE BRAIN

Thomas sat on a stone slab, supported by attendants. Evenjos called the slab a healing altar.

Dozens of volunteers stood ready to fetch anything the healers might want. An army guarded this pristine beach, ready to fend off anything unexpected.

Everyone was prepared.

Everyone except for Thomas. He did not feel quite as mentally prepared as he should be.

"Lay him down," Evenjos commanded.

Vy and Orla gently eased Thomas onto his back on the altar of rough-hewn granite. The position was painful and unfamiliar to his fragile body. Thirteen years of atrophy had pulled his limbs into permanently bent shapes and contorted his spine. He was not supple.

"Shouldn't he have cushions?" Vy asked.

"No," Evenjos said. "The fibers of garments are too easy for a healer to confuse with keratin structures such as skin and hair. Please remove his clothing."

Vy took care of that task.

Soon Thomas shivered in the ocean breeze, naked, his underdeveloped body on display for all to see.

The reek of pity should not bother him. He sensed it in the minds of nearby attendants such as Orla. He could not help but see himself through their eyes: grotesque. He was stunted and malformed, like a starved child. Years of enfeeblement had warped and twisted his limbs so they were permanently disfigured, frozen in horrific postures. He was painful to look at.

Thomas was glad when the attendants retreated out of his telepathy range.

The process should go smoothly on this planet, Reject-20. The hub planet of Umdalkdul was too close to a temporal stream for security. It was vulnerable to surprise attacks.

So Thomas had chosen a pristine world.

Any space vessel would require seven days of slow travel to arrive at Reject-20. Thus far, the Torth Empire had yet to even figure out where their enemies had mass-teleported away to. Reject-20 was among the most remote habitable planets in the galaxy, ideal for a rebel stronghold.

It had nice beaches, too.

A salty breeze kept bugs at bay. Nearby torches were infused with a natural floral insect repellent. This planet had a lot of wildlife, and the three healers could not afford to be interrupted, even by something as minor as a buzzing gnat.

The healing altar was enclosed by stone pillars, draped with a gauzy canopy. That would conceal Thomas and his healers from flying sky crocodiles.

At least Thomas didn't need protection from sunburns here. Reject-20 had a spectacularly unique sky, filled by a gas giant. Colors gradated across the daytime overhead, obscured only by wisps of clouds.

Evenjos gave him a concerned look. "You should understand," she said, "this healing will not cure all your problems. Think of it as a forest fire. It will cleanse away the dead wood that is strangling your future in order to open up possibilities for new growth."

Thomas expected that. Regeneration healing would not magically give him extra muscle mass. Evenjos could not transform him into a giant, or an ummin, or anything new. She could not bulk him up.

What she could do was replace his erroneous DNA with healthy copies.

"Correct," Evenjos said, listening to his thoughts. "If you have never walked—"

"I did walk," Thomas interrupted, "when I was very young." He had dim memories of tottering around as a two-year-old, supporting himself on furniture and falling a lot.

"If you have never walked well," Evenjos went on in a gentle tone, "it will take time for you to relearn how. You will need time for your core muscles to develop. It may take months or even years. You will need to be patient with yourself. At first, you will be as weak as you ever were."

Thomas expected that, as well.

Muscle memory was different from experiential memories. Although he knew how it felt to be a kung fu master, and a ballerina . . . although he had absorbed the lived experience of thousands of athletes . . . well, his body would learn at its own pace. Physical prowess could only be achieved through practice.

Before he could walk, he would first need to learn how it felt to stand up, to have a sense of balance.

"Understood," he said.

Vy's eyes shone with the excitement of a foster sister. Thomas tried not to scan for Cherise. She must be in the bustling encampment city. She was probably arm in arm with Flen, trying to forget all the times she had helped Thomas open his laptop or get food.

She used to sit near Thomas while he worked toward inventing NAI-12.

She had supported him, even when he'd given up.

He missed Cherise. He tried not to, but he wished she were here.

"How do you feel?" Evenjos turned to Garrett and Ariock. "Are you at full strength?"

The two Dovanacks had been waiting near the pillars. Now they ambled over.

"Yup. I'm ready." Ariock gave the canopy a look of annoyance. It hung a scant inch above his head. "Maybe we can remove the canopy at night?" he suggested.

"Nah." Garrett tossed away the stub of his cigarette. "I saw one of those house-size predators flapping along the coast. They eat animals that are approximately our size. I'd rather us not look like standing targets."

"I worry about anyone out in the open," Orla said from the far corner.

"Make sure they carry torches," Garrett said. "Fire scares the beasts."

The indigenous wildlife of Reject-20 had a size range equivalent to that of Earth's Cretaceous period. There were tiny critters, akin to snakes and lizards, and those were mostly harmless. But there were also thirty-ton herbivores. The apex predators would rival a Tyrannosaurus—and some of those could fly.

That was why Thomas had asked Ariock to carve the seaside cliffs into buildings.

Thomas had designed the city's layout, including water pipes and other infrastructural elements. He'd projected his designs for Ariock, and then Ariock had spent a day raising bedrock and hollowing cliffs in order to create fortresses.

Ariock had single-handedly created a full-size metropolis. It even had a downtown. In Encampment City on Reject-20—or Freedomland, as people were beginning to call it—all the entrances and roadways were built narrow, designed to discourage unwanted wildlife.

The steep, narrow alleys should also stymie Torth transports. Not that Thomas expected enemy Torth to show up here.

An underground prison facility held all their "unprocessed" captives. Those mind readers were kept in the dark, both literally and figuratively. Their pleas for help in the Megacosm went unanswered—no one in the Megacosm could figure out their location.

"Are you sufficiently well rested?" Evenjos sized up Ariock. "After building that huge city? And mass-teleporting everyone to this planet? Are you sure?"

It was a frightening amount of work by anyone's standards. Ariock had transported millions: the twelve million refugees, plus seven million liberated slaves from Umdalkdul, plus the million Torth prisoners, and enough supplies to keep everyone fed and clothed for more than a week.

He had moved them all across the galaxy.

He had erected enough buildings to house them all.

Then he had rested for two days, all the while arguing that he felt fine and he could do more. Ariock wanted to import Torth hovercarts and transports and even streamships. He wanted the denizens of his city to have a spaceport. He also wanted to refine the crude stonework of his buildings. Oh, and he wanted to set up a satellite telecommunications and defense network.

Thomas, Vy, Garrett, Evenjos, Jinishta, Kessa, and others had talked Ariock into using some common sense for a couple of days. They made sure he rested. But it hadn't been easy.

Now, as Ariock loomed over Thomas, he radiated power.

"I'm fine," he said.

And he was.

Thomas sensed that Ariock had tested the scope of his strength a few minutes ago by stretching his awareness across the entire solar system. When Ariock was drained, he would have trouble stretching around a city. But right now? The raw power Ariock could wield was unquestionable. He was stronger than anyone else here, by far. He could destroy this planet if he wanted to.

And he was going to use all his prodigious strength to rebuild every eukaryotic cell of Thomas's body.

The power to build colony starships. To raise cities. All of it was going to go into Thomas's body.

Thomas swallowed. He assured himself that his friends were gentle and knowledgeable. Ariock was good at focused tasks.

Besides, Ariock would have Garrett reading his mind nearby, to guide him. And Evenjos. She would make sure there were no irreversible mistakes.

"I will take the first shift." Evenjos ran her slim fingers down Thomas's naked torso. "My first goal is to rebuild his spinal column. This will necessitate breaking every bone and stitching them back together. It will be excruciating for him. Unfortunately, we cannot give him painkillers during any part of the regeneration healing."

"Why not?" Ariock looked alarmed.

"A drug would alter his neurochemistry." Evenjos smoothed Thomas's hair in a strangely motherly gesture. She had no children, and Thomas sensed that a part of her yearned for them. "We must work with him in his natural state. We will rebuild every cell of his body, and it is crucial that we work from the correct baseline."

"But we're not touching his brain," Garrett said. "Right?"

Thomas knew what Evenjos would say.

He answered before she could, uncaring that he was lying naked on a stone slab. "You have to rebuild my cerebellum, if not my whole brain. This is a *neuromuscular*"—he emphasized the prefix—"illness. It originates in my brain."

As Thomas spoke, he realized that his feeling of apprehension was not just a dread of pain. Nor was he merely worried about permanent damage from a mistake. His fears were based on something more.

He was about to lose a part of his identity.

He was going to change. Not only in body, but in mind.

Thomas was at peace with his physical disability. That was his daily life. It had always been his daily life. He was too weak to stand, unable to do anything physical for himself. He had grown so familiar with thinking of his mind as all-important, and his body as a messy secondary appendage, that he rarely imagined any other mode of existence for himself.

How would he cope with such an enormous change?

After this healing, he was unsure if he would really be the same Thomas. In a way, he was going to die and be reborn. Perhaps the new version of Thomas would be someone completely different. Someone unrecognizable.

"Yes," Evenjos was saying. "We must replace parts of his brain. His motor cortex. His hypothalamus. His hippocampus." She plucked each word from Thomas as he silently offered translations from her language of antiquity. "We must correct the misfires and mistakes in his neurotransmissions." She caressed his head. "Please understand, once this healing is begun, we dare not stop until it is finished. And we must save his brain for last. We will be exhausted by that point, but it is an unfortunate necessity."

Garrett stared at Evenjos as if she had just announced that she was joining the Torth Empire. He looked horrified.

Evenjos answered one of his unarticulated questions. "Because rebuilding a brain is the most delicate, intensive work. The rest of his body should be whole and healthy in order to withstand what we are going to do to his brain."

Orla was wide-eyed. She had not guessed that Thomas's illness was so deeply intertwined with his brain functionality. The idea negated her primitive understanding of anatomy. She had assumed that his brain was the one and only part of him that was very healthy.

Garrett looked pugnacious. "What are the chances that this will cause him brain damage?"

"I will take charge for that part of the healing," Evenjos said in a soothing tone.

"But this won't change his intelligence," Garrett said. "Right?"

Evenjos hesitated.

Thomas deduced her answer, and he suppressed a soft laugh. He didn't care. If he lost a bit of memory or processing speed . . . so what? He had plenty to spare. He could stand to lose some.

"Memory loss can happen with brain alterations," Evenjos admitted. "Personality changes have been reported, in some cases. Naturally, since he is a supergenius, I will be extra, extra careful. I will leave as much of his brain untouched as possible."

Garrett's glare bored into Evenjos. His thoughts were seething.

"Now." Evenjos cleared her throat. "Let us discuss the order of healing. Once I finish with his spine, Ariock should take over his heart and digestive tract. I will guide Ariock. Garrett, you ought to take over his lungs once Ariock finishes—"

"Hold on," Garrett snapped. "You never mentioned brain damage as a possibility."

Evenjos's wings drooped. Thomas felt her dismay, very similar to his own.

"This is unacceptable," Garrett snarled. "We need his brain untouched!"

"It's the only way." Thomas strained to tilt his head, wishing he could sit up and face the old man directly. "My illness is a problem of neurotransmitters and misfires in my limbic system. You have to rebuild my cerebellum. It's the only way to give me a future."

Ariock gave a hesitant nod of support.

"His mental changes may be very minor," Evenjos said in a hopeful tone. "His intelligence will likely remain intact. I cannot imagine that we would cause devastation. I will be very careful."

The sky began to cloud up. Thomas sensed offended rage churning through Garrett, and he braced himself for a storm.

Well. So what if the old man threw a temper tantrum? Thomas reminded himself that he had survived all kinds of hatred aimed his way. A rejection from Garrett would not be any worse, really, than suffering in a sensory deprivation pit.

Except . . .

What if his friends decided to roll with what Garrett wanted?

Thomas tried to assure himself that he could handle anything. He had spent most of his life dying. He could accept an early death if that was really what everyone agreed on. He could take it.

"What is the point of having a brain-damaged supergenius?" Garrett demanded.

Evenjos began to answer.

"Forget it!" Garrett snapped. "I'm not doing this."

He stomped away.

None of Thomas's mental preparations softened the blow. He whimpered, helpless tears leaking from his eyes. He felt as if he had been flung about by an earthquake and skewered by lightning.

He was no one. He was nothing. He was worthless except for his brain. And apparently that was just an expendable tool to Garrett Dovanack.

"Give me a second," Ariock said. He ducked under the edge of the canopy and caught up to Garrett on the beach.

The two Dovanacks argued in low rumbles. The crash of waves, and the wind, and the distance, drowned out their words, but Thomas could guess at the arguments each must be making.

Ariock would say, *"You made a promise."*

To Ariock, integrity was everything. He would not tolerate someone who broke his word to a dying child.

Then Garrett would say, *"That boy is nothing but a brain! To us, occasional forgetfulness is no big deal, but you have to realize, even the smallest memory problem will cripple his ability to compete with the other supergeniuses. And then the Torth Empire will win!"*

Garrett was right.

That was the worst thing. Thomas yearned to be able to side with Ariock, and to despise Garrett without reservations, but he could not lie. Not even to himself. He had wasted his time as a Torth lying to himself every minute of every day. He would never sink that low again. He had to be intellectually honest, or else he might as well quit fighting the Torth and join them.

So he inwardly admitted that he needed to remain sharp. With enemies such as the Twins and the Death Architect, he could not afford to be mentally crippled. His own future was nothing compared to what was at stake in this war. His emotions and goals did not really matter. His personality did not matter. His mutant brain was the only thing of value he had to offer.

On the other hand, if he died from his illness . . . he would never get the chance to prove otherwise.

Ariock and Garrett returned, taking their places on either side of the healing altar. Garrett looked chagrined. Ariock was triumphant.

Thomas dived into their minds, trying to understand what had happened.

Aha. Ariock had pinpointed Garrett's fears. *"You're giving him a valid reason to leave us,"* Ariock had said. *"Why should he work for people who offered him a future and then snatched it away? That's sadistic. It's something a Torth would do. Why would he stay loyal to us?"*

That argument had worked. But it filled Thomas with mixed feelings.

Shame, mostly. Did his friends really believe that he was capable of abandoning the fight? Did they think Thomas would flee to the Torth Majority just so he could receive empty praise, pats on the back, and nectar drinks? Did they really believe he was that sort of monster?

No.

Thomas sensed that for Ariock, the argument was hypothetical. He knew Thomas well enough to trust him. He had hinted at betrayal only because he intuited that it would prickle Garrett's paranoia.

As for Garrett . . .

The old man fixed Thomas with a dangerous stare. His opinions were his own, yet Thomas glimpsed a secret truth: a painting.

The book of prophecies depicted Thomas—a healthy version, who could walk—leading an army of empty-eyed zombies.

Thomas recalled a similar foretelling from Migyatel.

He had never told anyone about her final precognitive vision, which he had absorbed from her as she fell dead from a stroke. The holy prophet of the Alashani had foreseen a healthy version of Thomas. That future Thomas commanded legions of Torth minions who left fire and devastation in their wake.

Migyatel had considered that future so shocking and horrific it had killed her.

Garrett watched Thomas with wary distrust. He knew.

You had better be an obedient slave to me, Garrett thought.

Thomas offered a meek smile. Was it possible for prophecies to be wrong? Could both Migyatel and Ah Jun have misinterpreted what they foresaw?

This was why he needed the constraints of enslavement. If he was destined to be a tyrant . . . well, that would never be his choice. Wasn't that obvious? He had no desire to become a leader, let alone some kind of ultrasadistic Commander of All Living Things. He was much more at home in a science lab. Battlefields were not his forte.

One thing Thomas was absolutely certain of: he would never join the oppressors who had tortured his mother to death. He was not going to join the people who had murdered the Upward Governess and who had forced him to torment Cherise. He would never stop fighting the Torth Empire.

If he had to resort to zombifying hordes of militant Torth in order to liberate all the slaves in the galaxy . . . ?

That was the future. He would twist that mind when he came to it.

"All right." Garrett continued to look troubled, but Thomas sensed him pushing down his private misgivings. "I suppose we need the boy."

Ariock emanated approval. "Right."

Evenjos pulled her waves of purple hair into a thick ponytail. "Are you ready?" she asked Garrett, on her left, and Ariock, on her right.

"Yes," Ariock said.

"Yes." Garrett sounded reluctant, yet determined to get it done.

Evenjos raised her hands in the healing pose.

She remembered Vy and the other attendants at the last moment and glanced their way. "Remember," she said, "once we begin, we cannot be interrupted. Thomas will scream. He will be in pain, but you may not interrupt our work."

Orla gave an eager nod.

Vy was less worshipful, but she said, "I understand." No doubt she felt a little insulted by the way Evenjos treated her.

Thomas nearly mentioned his theory that humans, such as Vy, might be able to augment the powers of Yeresunsa. If he was correct, then Vy might lend him extra strength during the process.

But as Thomas assessed the team of ultrapowerful healers, he decided to keep his speculation to himself for now. They had plenty of power. An unexpected surge of excess power would complicate an already-complex process.

Evenjos peered down at Thomas. "Are you ready?"

She stood behind his head, so she appeared upside down. With her hair gathered behind her, she looked less royal and more casual. Her violet eyes were full of concern and goodwill. "This will be worse than any pain you have ever suffered in your life."

"I understand." Thomas refused to think about the upcoming agony. Pain was part of life.

It was worth it.

"The agony will last for three days," Evenjos warned. "Afterward, we shall all need recovery time. You, in particular, should rest. And—"

"I know." Thomas could not take much more anticipation. "I understand that everything will be different after you regenerate my body. I understand that you will rebuild parts of my brain and that I will be irrevocably changed, forever. I know that I need to be gentle with myself. That I will need hearty food, and rest, and friends who will evaluate me as I recover. I get that. I will risk losing parts of my mind. This will hurt. I will be reborn. I know and accept every risk and potential consequence. I've thought it all through. Just get on with it!"

Evenjos raised her hands. The canopy overhead rippled in a breeze, caught in an eddy of her power.

The agony began.

CHAPTER 8

REBORN

Helplessness was the worst feeling.

Vy walked along the beach, carrying a torch and a blaster glove as protection against beasts. She limped because her prosthetic leg could trip on bumps and depressions in the sand.

Regeneration healing altered existing cells and DNA, but it could not conjure new flesh or matter. Vy might wish for a regrown leg, but that was beyond anyone's ability to give her. And even if it was somehow possible . . .

Vy wasn't sure she wanted to suffer multiple days of agonizing pain.

Thomas had gone quiet intermittently during the first day and into the first night, and on into the second day, and through the second night, and throughout the third day. But he'd also screamed like a torture victim.

Vy had needed to get away from the hoarse, nearly voiceless screams of her foster brother. So she'd made her way past the cots and hammocks that dotted the beach. Attendants and guards took turns sleeping in shifts, protected by torches and netting to ward off critters.

The city loomed in the near distance. Huge buildings, carved from cliffs, spilled over the verdant mountains. People were calling it Freedomland, or even Ariock's City.

And it was unlike any city Vy had ever visited.

There were all-night taverns, places where aliens exchanged practical theories and philosophy with each other, or where they learned about freedom from Alashani refugees. Kessa was in command up there, making sure people stayed happy and busy. Lamps glowed on the rickshaws that transited the winding roads. Streets bustled with activity even in the predawn hours.

Vy had scouted this site with Ariock and Thomas, so she remembered the natural cliffs before Ariock had extruded buildings out of bedrock. This place had been untouched by civilization ten days ago. It was primordial. A dormant volcano dominated the landward horizon, and a banded gas-giant planet dominated the sky.

Then Ariock had simply conjured the entire metropolis into existence.

He had pulled immense buildings out of the rugged landscape. He had given them windows and stairways and rooms with the expertise of a maestro conducting an orchestra. The completed city appeared to be as ancient as the rock it was carved from.

Few people even commented on the miracle. The citizenry took superpowers for granted.

Vy supposed that if Ariock were to collapse from depletion, the denizens of Freedomland would accept despair as easily as they accepted miracles. If a Torth armada showed up right now and bombed the free metropolis into oblivion, the survivors would merely shrug and get on with their lives.

Because ordinary people did not make things happen.

Ordinary people were powerless.

Vy turned to the shimmering sea, where flying fish played in the surf. A spout of water in the distance indicated an alien whale. If those fish got eaten by monsters? They would remain oblivious right up until a greater power swallowed them.

She understood why Unyat's Formula had been so tempting for the peasants of ancient times.

Those women and men must have felt powerless, at the mercy of people like Evenjos. Their stories went untold. They were utterly forgotten. No one cared about mundane peasants.

But their desperation to grow, and to change, and to give their children a better life . . . that was felt throughout the known universe.

Their discontentment affected the lives of every sapient being across a thousand generations.

Their children had transformed into the Torth Empire.

They had knocked Evenjos off her pedestal.

Vy figured that she would have sought Unyat's Formula, too, if she had been born in that era. She would have given birth to Torth. And she would have been proud to do so.

It was strange to feel sympathy for Torth.

Perhaps she was giving them too much credit. Their originators had had cause for complaint, but modern Torth were a problem.

Vy turned away from the ocean and trudged down the beach, toward the healing altar. A purple blush on the horizon hinted that the gas giant would soon shrug out of the ocean. It would obliterate the stars and blaze across the sky.

The third night had finally drawn to a close.

It was well after daybreak by the time Vy arrived. Bleary-eyed shani warriors allowed her to pass a makeshift blockade. They wore wide-brimmed hats to shade their pale faces, and their eyes glowed like those of nocturnal animals.

Ariock and Garrett each slept in a secluded cabana. They were not to be disturbed.

Evenjos was nowhere to be seen. Perhaps she was in that urn, in the shade of a broad, palmlike tree? After three days of intensive work, she must have collapsed into dust.

Thomas slept alone on the altar.

Vy made her way toward him, nodding in gratitude to various sentries and attendants. A few of the Alashani looked resentful. Vy overheard their mutterings, so she understood that they wondered why the young *rekveh* deserved such a fancy healing. They believed that surely there must be other, more deserving, people.

Well. They didn't know Thomas.

When Vy drew closer to Thomas, she blinked in shock. The boy who slept on the altar did not look at all familiar.

His face was the same, she thought. As for the rest . . .

His limbs were straight.

An attendant had been kind enough to drape a woolen blanket over his lower body. Even so, it was obvious that he was now straight and symmetrical, not at all lopsided. His joints connected in natural ways. He looked painfully elongated and starved—but then Vy realized that was only because he lacked even a bare minimum of muscle tone.

His skeletal structure was that of a typical thirteen-year-old boy.

He was no longer underdeveloped for his age. But he was clearly very, very weak. His slight mass had been reconfigured, making him approximately five feet tall and toothpick thin.

Even his neck was too thin. He lacked enough muscle tone to raise his own head.

"Holy hell," Vy whispered.

She hoisted herself onto the altar, wanting to examine his health status. She needed time to get used to these major changes.

Thomas did not exactly look like a victim of torment, despite his lack of muscle or fat. His skin was clean and looked as smooth and fresh as that of a baby. The sea breeze ruffled his sand-colored hair. His breathing sounded natural and easy.

Vy simply sat for a while. She gazed at the cabanas and hammocks. Then up the beach, toward the city.

Someone besides her ought to be here for Thomas. This must be the most meaningful change of his life. Where were his friends?

Did he have friends?

Cherise never asked about Thomas anymore. Right about now, Cherise was probably waking up in a bed with Flen, in the so-called war palace. She filled her days with teaching. Aliens had founded a school in one of the cliffside buildings.

"I guess you only have me," Vy said, unsure if her words reached the sleeping boy.

She hopped off the altar. Maybe she would put together a meal, since Thomas would likely be hungry once he woke up.

"Vy?" a voice called from the distance.

She looked up and saw an ummin making his way down the beach, carrying a large picnic basket.

"Varktezo!" Vy hurried to meet him. She offered to carry the basket.

"It was difficult for me to get away from the lab," Varktezo said, puffing from exertion. "I told Gosmaga to take over the particle collider experiments, and getting her set up with the differences between qubit states and eigenstates took longer than I thought it would. Sorry if I'm late! He hasn't woken up yet, has he?"

Varktezo chattered on, speaking of experiments and projects, leaping from topic to topic so fast that Vy could not keep up with his train of thought. She was just glad that he had thought to visit.

"And we only have five capacitors that can— Oh my." Varktezo interrupted his own monologue and stopped short. He gawked at Thomas's sleeping form.

"Yeah." Vy still had not processed the changes herself.

Varktezo hopped onto a step stool so he could study the sleeping boy with fascination. "He looks completely different."

Vy brushed a lock of hair off Thomas's forehead.

Thomas stirred. His eyes fluttered open.

"Welcome back," Vy said.

Then she froze, because she feared there was something wrong with his eyes. Was he blind? His gaze was the wrong color.

Or the right color!

Vy laughed in relief. He had purple eyes, like any Yeresunsa. Perhaps his had more of a red tint than most? But it didn't matter! His eyes had reverted to their natural state, and that made him look a lot less like a Torth and more like her foster brother.

Thomas lifted one hand, then the other. He stared up at his own hands in wonderment.

He had never been able to lift his hands that high before.

Soon his hands fell, limp. Thomas twitched his hands, lifting them again. He moved his fingers. He had a sublime look of joy, and Vy could only imagine how amazing this experience must be for him.

"Do you feel all right?" she asked.

Thomas moved. After a moment, Vy understood that he was trying, and failing, to raise his head.

"I'll get a pillow for you," Vy said.

The sandy floor was strewn with cushions and pillows, where attendants had sat. Vy chose a couple of thick pillows, then carefully lifted Thomas's upper body. Soon she had propped him up.

"Are you okay, Teacher?" Varktezo asked.

Thomas wore a grin so wide, he looked like the kid he was. He smiled at the canopy and the striated sky beyond it. A sky croc flapped lazily in the morning breeze.

He smiled at the granite pillars. The jungle, with its cabanas and sentries. The woolen blanket that covered his lower body. He smiled at Vy and at Varktezo.

"I feel amazing," he said.

Vy and Varktezo grinned.

"There's no problems?" Vy asked. "Are you thirsty? Or hungry?" She swallowed, not quite nervy enough to ask if he had any personality changes.

"I feel incredible." Thomas laughed softly, as if he could not quite believe it. "Yeah, I'm hungry. Thanks for bringing my favorite spiced puffs, Varktezo!"

Varktezo happily opened the picnic basket and pulled out various containers. He placed flatbread and chutney and more food on the altar, within Thomas's reach.

Thomas attempted to hold the food for himself, but he was clumsy and weak, his hands unused to gripping and lifting.

"Let me feed you," Vy said.

Thomas gave in, yet he still kept trying to hold the food, or guide it. And Vy was surprised by how much of it he ate. Sure, he hadn't eaten in three days—but even when ravenous, Thomas used to have trouble chewing. Eating required as much energy and strength as he typically had.

Now? He savored each bite. He still had trouble chewing, but he did not run out of energy. He kept at it.

Vy and Varktezo enjoyed some of the meal themselves.

"That was delicious," Thomas said.

Varktezo beamed.

"I need to get dressed." Thomas nodded toward a chair, where a pile of plain woolens were neatly folded. "An attendant brought clothes that should fit the new me."

"Sure," Vy said.

As she tugged the clothes onto Thomas, he said, "I want to try to stand."

Vy ignored that. Thomas must be joking. Anyone could see his utter lack of muscles and the fact that he couldn't even support his own head. He would flop right over.

"Seriously!" Thomas said. "I just want to test how it feels. You can brace me. Just for a few seconds? Please?"

His pleading purple eyes fixed on her gaze.

Vy glanced at Varktezo and saw that he was willing to help.

"All right," she said.

Together, they braced Thomas, giving the illusion that he was standing. Thomas laughed with delight.

His laugh was so childlike, so carefree, that a shiver ran down Vy's spine. She wanted to be happy for his happiness. Instead . . . Well, when had he ever laughed like that?

The answer was never.

Thomas was supposed to have a cynical laugh, when he laughed at all. He didn't sound like himself. Or look like himself.

"That was amazing!" Thomas said while Vy lifted him back onto the healing altar. "Can you put me in my hoverchair, please?"

Vy hesitated. Evenjos had instructed Thomas should rest and recover.

"Come on, please, Vy?" Thomas swung his legs, albeit weakly.

"Okay." Vy carried Thomas to where his hoverchair was parked. She marveled at how long and straight his body had become. If he filled out a bit, he would be hard to carry. "But I think we should find a cot or a hammock for you so you can rest."

Thomas settled into his hoverchair seat, chuckling as he had never chuckled before. He adjusted his arm positions. He waggled and stretched his fingers, no doubt enjoying his new range of motion, which was noticeably greater than before.

"Let's go into the city!" Thomas grinned at Vy and Varktezo.

Vy had been hoping for a quiet, restful day.

"Uh . . ." Varktezo frowned at Thomas. "Teacher? Perhaps you should get rest, as Vy recommends."

"Nonsense!" Thomas said. "I feel great. Let me enjoy my freedom before my master wakes up!"

His head looked ridiculously top-heavy atop his toothpick-thin neck and body. He had to use the headrest. His legs dangled in a way they never had before.

He suddenly seemed to notice the blocky briefcase tucked next to him. Still smiling, he tried to lift it.

"I guess you don't need that anymore." Vy stepped forward and reached for it. "Do you want me to get that out of your way?"

The battered briefcase was a relic from Earth, covered with faded stickers and drawings by Cherise. Vy didn't want to simply get rid of it. Perhaps NAI-12 could be repurposed for some experiments in the burgeoning science laboratories of the Freedomland Academy? Or maybe she could return it to Rasa Biotech if she ever went back to Earth.

"Ha!" Thomas said.

The NAI-12 briefcase arced high above the beach, propelled by a conflagration. The fireball burned orange, then white-hot.

Thomas laughed with savage glee as the medicine he once needed disappeared in wildfire. The remains dropped into the ocean, unidentifiable as charred lumps.

Vy folded her hands and tried to suppress her mix of concern, worry, regret, and chagrin. She wasn't going to judge Thomas for that outburst. She wasn't the one who had relied on NAI-12 to survive. She wasn't the one who had invented it. She had not spent years—the bulk of her life—striving to avoid an early death.

She supposed Thomas's life used to revolve around that medicine. It had dominated his schedule, with a wristwatch timer that beeped every six hours. He had survived in the Torth Empire because the Upward Governess had valued that medicine.

Other Torth supergeniuses probably wanted it, too. The Twins and the Death Architect and others.

Could they have been bribed into switching sides?

It was too late for that. The thing that had symbolized Thomas's old life was now less than nothing. It was worthless trash.

Thomas turned his hoverchair and glided toward the city. "It's party time!" he whooped.

Vy exchanged a look of concern with Varktezo.

They both packed up and hurried after the speeding hoverchair.

CHAPTER 9

WINNING

Vy found it frustratingly difficult to keep up with Thomas. He stopped at a beverage stand and asked for a drink that came in a fruit that looked like a hollowed-out pineapple. The nervous vendor, a govki, began to refuse.

"Go to the pan-fry stand this evening," Thomas said. "Yoush will be in the weaver's booth next to it. She wants to speak with you."

That must have meant something to the vendor. He slid the drink to Thomas, and Thomas recklessly lifted it in both hands, spilling some juice.

Vy helped him sip. Then she fit the drink in the cupholder on the hoverchair's armrest. "Is this alcoholic?"

"It's no big deal," Thomas said.

The only reason he had survived three days of regeneration healing was because he was a Yeresunsa. That ordeal would have killed anyone else. Vy started to tell him that he really needed to avoid anything toxic, such as alcoholic drinks.

"Did you know that you can entice Ariock if you wear plumeria oil?" Thomas said. "It's the indigenous plant behind the cot you slept in."

"Errr . . ." Vy hesitated. Thomas rarely offered personal advice. It seemed like an uncharacteristically clumsy attempt to lead her attention elsewhere.

"I know that was manipulative to say," Thomas admitted. "But I'm just trying to help out and have fun!"

He floated down a beach pathway, swinging his legs and greeting every startled person who saw him. Vy and Varktezo had to race to catch up.

Thomas paused in a clearing where musicians practiced. Kemkorcans intertwined their sinuous bodies, singing a melody with voices like flutes. A pair of nussians slapped makeshift drums. Vy had not expected to hear music, let alone such original, complex music. She leaned against a palm tree and listened, agape.

Until Varktezo tugged her sleeve. Thomas was gone.

They tracked his hoverchair through a group of children who were herding alien lizards. They passed a street performance, where sapients reenacted Ariock's deeds. After stopping there for a few minutes, Thomas wove through a bazaar full of alien merchandise. Every time Vy thought he had stopped, he moved on.

He sampled street foods. He sampled beverages. He admired garments undergoing dye treatments. He exclaimed at the craftwork of wood-carvers who made whistles. He watched nussians chip at rocks, experimenting with sculpture.

"You should rest," Vy said when she'd caught up with him for the umpteenth time. She was weary from trekking across the city's outskirts.

"No way," Thomas replied. "You can take the day off, but I'm having a good time!"

Even Varktezo looked like he wanted to retire for the rest of the day. He muttered about important work that needed to be done. But he gritted his beak and kept up, jogging alongside Vy.

"Hey, Pung!" Thomas called.

Vy was unsurprised that Thomas had randomly found Pung playing tabletop games. Thomas's path looked meandering, yet he had an unfailing knack for coming across notable or unique events, even when they were spontaneous. He must have collated a mental map from the minds of passersby.

A few dozen former slaves sat around makeshift tables cobbled together from supply crates. They gawked as Thomas approached, entering the shade beneath canopies strung across jungle trees.

"Thomas?" Pung spoke with disbelief. His gaze roved over Thomas's lanky, toothpick-thin frame, his straightened limbs, and his purple eyes. "That can't be you. Can it?"

"Yup!" Thomas beamed. "Oh, hello, Nror." He addressed a yellow govki with golden eyes. "How have you been?"

The govki looked fearful and uncertain. "Uh . . ."

"Of course I know your name," Thomas said fondly. He parked his hoverchair between the gamers. "I know practically everything about you, since you were my personal slave."

That brought every conversation in the gamer bar to a screeching halt.

People stared at the mind reader in their midst, the former Torth who exhibited no hint of shame. He had simply blurted out the fact that he used to own one of them. Like there was nothing wrong with that.

Thomas! Vy thought, frantic. Had he lost all sense of propriety? Was he trying to provoke a fight?

"Thanks for taking care of me," Thomas said to Nror and Pung. "I'm sorry for every time I mistreated you. I really owe you both a lot."

They looked uncomfortable.

"How about a game of Blast Three?" Thomas gestured to the geometric pawns. Some had six pegs, some were rectangles, but all were crude approximations of common sapient species. "It's pure luck, so I can't cheat."

Nearby people scooted away. They wanted nothing to do with the mind reader. The govki Nror looked annoyed. He clearly wanted Thomas to leave.

"No, thank you," Pung said politely.

"Anyone can play," Thomas said. "If you lose, then I get a cup of that wine you're drinking."

They looked unpersuaded.

"And if someone wins against me?" Thomas said happily. "They can ask any favor. If it's within my abilities, I'll grant it, with no restrictions!"

All the whispers stopped. Suddenly, everyone in the bar looked intensely interested.

"That's an offer for anyone present," Thomas reiterated.

Vy gripped the backrest of his hoverchair. "Thomas," she hissed, trying to bring him to his senses. This was the dumbest, most unfairly lopsided farce of a game that she had ever heard of.

Pung scooped up three pawns. "I'll play," he said.

Vy wanted to ask Pung to stop this madness, but he did not revere her the way the Alashani did. Pung remembered that Vy was just a former slave. He didn't think she was an angel.

And, of course, he didn't revere Thomas, either. Pung did not believe in gods or messiahs. He worshipped no one.

Vy took a seat on one of the vacated stools and hoped Ariock would wake up before nightfall. Thomas needed someone powerful to rein him in.

Pung tossed the pawns between two parallel lines demarcated on the table. Some of them landed inside the channel, some outside. Vy had a sketchy idea that the channel flipped the value of each piece, from negative to positive or vice versa.

"I won!" Pung crowed.

"What would you like?" Thomas asked pleasantly.

Pung stood in thought. He took such a long time, onlookers began to shout suggestions.

"Ask the *rekveh* to spy on that devious merchant! You know, the one you think is lying all the time!"

"No! Tell him to concoct the best meal anyone has ever eaten."

"He should free a thousand slaves!" someone else shouted.

"Make him enslave a Torth, just for you!"

"Tell him to ask the messiah to build a city in your name!"

Meanwhile, other aliens grappled for pawns. They shouted at each other for a chance to play.

Pung sat on a stool with a look of frustration. "I need to think about this," he told Thomas. "Is that all right?"

"Take as much time as you'd like," Thomas said.

A big, fluffy govki tossed down three pawns. "I won!"

Thomas didn't even pretend to want a fair chance at winning, himself. He didn't even ask to play. Instead, he spoke like a classy waiter taking an order from a customer. "Great. What would you like?"

The fluffy govki smoothed his tan fur while other people fought for space to play the game. He faced Thomas with a challenging glare. "I want my family," he said. "The family your people—the Torth—stole."

Vy winced. City slaves never got to see their families once they were ripped away from their slave farms. They were not allowed to mate, or have children, either. City slaves died as orphans.

Thomas did not hesitate. "Your sibling Sree," he said, "was enslaved in the same city you were, but in a distant neighborhood. She identifies as female. You'll find her if you go past the lantern shop up that street"—he pointed—"and enter the fifth barracks. Ask for Ausgar, the red govki. He can reunite you."

The tan govki looked stunned.

"Your secondary parent," Thomas went on, "still resides in the slave farm known as Ov Hill. Unfortunately, your primary parent is deceased, but you're likely to reunite with your secondary parent if we liberate the planet Umdalkdul. Unfortunately, individual slave farms have to be low priority for us. Liberating them is unlikely to harm the Torth Empire in any substantial way."

The govki blinked in surprise.

"Two of your other siblings," Thomas went on, "are slaves in a city known as Rare Moonrise MetroHub. I don't know if Swa and Kerr are alive, or anything about their current status. I'm sorry. But if—or when—we liberate Rare Moonrise, I'll remember to send you a personal update about them."

The govki gawked in shock.

"Of course I'll be able to send you a message, Fru," Thomas told the govki. "Information is my specialty. I'm a Torth."

That was definitely brash to admit out loud. People looked shocked. The govki, Fru, backed away, half in awe and half fearful.

"I'm sorry for what you suffered," Thomas said.

Another govki won the game, as well as a mer nerctan. They shoved their way closer.

"Show me a picture of the Torth who murdered my mate!" one demanded. "And tell me where I can find that murderer."

"Where can I find my children?" the other pleaded.

Vy prepared to intervene. What mischief was Thomas getting himself into?

He answered each question as if this was perfectly normal. He described a monstrous Torth who needed to be killed, and he explained the fate of every lost child.

"How about if Thomas gets a chance to play?" Vy asked.

No one listened to her. Not even Thomas.

The gamers were getting unruly. Winners began to form a mob, so eager to receive a favor, some of them shoved each other. Losers demanded a chance to play again.

"You lost your toss," Thomas gently told one supplicant. "I'll give you what you want, but would you mind bringing me a cup of that wine you've been drinking?"

So it went.

Throughout it all, Thomas did not grow bored or resentful. He kept at it. He delved into repressed memories so he could tell winners whom their true families were and where they might be found. He answered questions about where a particular person might find love or what crucial ingredient they needed in order to enjoy success in their new freedom. He told every former slave exactly where they could find their missing loved ones.

Thomas accepted another cup of wine. Vy disapproved, especially since this was his third alcoholic beverage of the day, but Thomas surely knew the dangers of getting drunk. She wasn't going to cut through a desperate mob of answer-seekers just to lecture the supergenius about a very basic fact of biology.

Thomas drew a line at mind control. When a plucky ummin asked him to adjust the mood of her chronically depressed mate, Thomas said, "I cannot do that without destroying your mate's mind. I'll grant any favor, but not if it robs someone else of freedom. Please ask something else. You can take your time and cut in line once you know what you want."

The mob grew even more fervent.

Word must be spreading throughout the city, because the beach bar became intolerably overcrowded. Canopies tore and branches broke as people tried to sit overhead.

Vy feared that she and Varktezo and Thomas would all be crushed or trampled. But the crowd loosened a little bit when nussian patrols showed up to impose order.

"That's a great request," Thomas answered one winner, his tone apologetic. "Curing every fatal disease in the known universe is on my to-do list. But I'm going to be the slave of Garrett, so I won't necessarily have the freedom to make it my top priority. Plus, I've been prioritizing the destruction of the Torth Empire. However, I sense that you have a mind that will make you perfect for my molecular biology team. If you would like to work on cures, please go to my lab. It's uptown." He pointed. "Look for the cliffside annex of the academy and ask for Naglitay. She's an ummin."

The demands went on. As Thomas answered, he finished a cup of berry wine. Someone replaced it with a cup of ale.

Vy folded her arms. She had never seen Thomas do anything with gusto before today. He had ten times more energy than usual.

Pung got in line. When it was finally his turn, he said, "Tell me how I can be most effective against the Torth Empire."

Thomas didn't hesitate. "Become a pilot. We're going to build an armada. When you're in control of a jumper shuttle or a swarmshuttle, you'll be more powerful than an Alashani Yeresunsa."

Pung looked thoughtful.

"I'll arrange for private lessons," Thomas said. "We will need capable pilots."

A number of sapients looked happy about that, including Varktezo.

Vy wondered if she dared volunteer as an aerial combatant. Battle action might boost her confidence with handling danger and maybe erase some of her hang-ups about getting intimate with Ariock.

Then again, constant anxiety about getting killed might just exacerbate her fears. After a vicious space battle, she could imagine yearning for comfort and familiarity. Cuddling. Not sex.

Plus, Vy had a feeling that Ariock would disapprove of her going into dangerous situations. Her scream of pain had distracted him once. That had led to his defeat and her losing her leg. Would he let her near a war zone again?

Well. Maybe she would take piloting lessons anyway. An air force would need support vessels, for cargo and medical teams.

"You don't need to describe your missing mother," Thomas told the latest winner. "I can see her in your mind."

Each winner left with fresh purpose, eager to seek a long-lost relative or to pursue a career that would better their lives. They wanted to raise children who could enjoy freedom without having to fight so hard for it. Some of them learned which city, exactly, they wanted to infiltrate, so they could liberate siblings or mates they had lost contact with.

Vy feared that Thomas was overpromising. How many missing relatives had he agreed to find already? It must be hundreds. Yet he laughed at good-natured jokes and shrugged off skepticism, as if each favor was something meager.

Nror won the game after several tosses. When he faced Thomas, he shyly asked where his siblings could be found. Thomas gave him the name of a city and added, "I owe you a lot more than just one favor, Nror. Ask me anything."

Another cheerful govki placed yet another fresh cup of ale in front of Thomas.

Vy drummed her fingers on a tabletop, frustrated. The colorful sky was darkening. Was Thomas going to be reckless all night? She didn't want to ruin his beneficent mood, but wasn't he supposed to be more practical than Ariock?

The crowds quieted and made way for a small, wizened figure.

"Kessa!" Vy sagged with relief. "Thank goodness." If anyone could rein in the wayward supergenius, it was her elder friend.

Kessa smiled. "My informants told me what was happening here."

"Kessa!" Thomas shouted happily, spotting her from a distance. "Did you come to ask a favor? Well, come here!"

He definitely sounded drunk.

People made way, and Kessa approached Thomas with a serious look of amazement. "Thomas." Her tone was polite. "You are so different."

"I know!" he said.

"How do you feel?" Kessa sounded concerned.

"Better than ever!" Thomas drank, accidentally spilling ale. "I owe you more than most people here. I owe you so much. Tell me what you want!"

Kessa smiled.

Vy expected her to be motherly and remind Thomas that he needed rest. Surely Kessa would figure out some clever way to induce him to quit making outlandish promises?

"I would like you to truthfully answer any question I ask," Kessa said. "Any time. Without limit."

The crowd quieted.

Thomas grew serious. At last, he seemed to have a dawning awareness that his antics were landing him in trouble.

Vy took a sip of wine from a cup she had swiped from Thomas's armrest. She should have guessed that Kessa's curiosity would override her motherly concern. When they had been slaves together, Kessa had confided that she yearned to possess the knowledge of a Torth.

Well. Vy figured that Thomas would say that no one was allowed to wish for more wishes. It had to be one per customer.

"That's a dangerous request," Thomas said. "Are you sure you want to enter the realm of secrets and make noise there?"

"Yes." There was no mistaking Kessa's certainty. "I have lived a lifetime with insufficient knowledge. This is what I want."

She held his gaze.

Thomas seemed to be considering unspoken details or potential limitations to the agreement. No doubt he was evaluating Kessa's mind.

"All right," Thomas said.

As if indenturing himself was no big deal.

Vy gaped. Thomas had valid reasons to back away from such an enormous, ongoing obligation. He would be enslaving himself, in essence, to Kessa. But he was already enslaved to Garrett!

"With a caveat," Thomas said. "You must ask me in private. Some answers may have unintended consequences, and I don't want anyone endangered by accident, from overhearing."

Kessa nodded. "I accept."

A few bystanders, including Pung, looked chagrined. Their requests had been too meager and had aimed too low.

Vy, too, felt chagrin. Thomas had effectively won the trust of a lot of former slaves, even while being open about the fact that he used to be a Torth. Instead of downplaying his telepathy, the way Garrett would do, he was playing it up. He had swatted away suspicions as easily as an adult would teach a toddler.

"Let's go onto the beach," Thomas invited Kessa. "You can ask me anything there."

When the mob saw Thomas leaving with Kessa, they began to disperse. They marveled about what Kessa the Wise had gained, and they speculated that something new had been achieved—a former slave had claimed the knowledge of gods. A former Torth had chosen to entrust an ummin with secrets.

The favor session was at an end.

CHAPTER 10

SECRETS IN THE SURF

Thomas swung his legs, uncaring that it cost him effort. He was tired. But he was nowhere near a state of collapse—which used to be his constant state. Whenever he moved parts of his body, instead of feeling defeated, he felt a marvelous sense of potential.

He felt unstoppable. His face hurt from the sheer amount of grinning he had done today.

Kessa studied Thomas with owlish eyes. He sensed a long list of questions queuing up in her mind. The crash of the surf was loud enough to drown out voices from the beachside bar and other makeshift establishments, and her bodyguards followed at a respectful distance, out of earshot. Kessa's torch should warn flying predators to stay away.

"What would you like to know?" Thomas prompted.

Kessa considered her list. She knew that she must avoid information that could be weaponized. She wasn't going to ask for tactical specifics, which Torth prisoners might be able to soak up. But generalities . . . ?

"Tell me," she said, "what is the actual likelihood that we will defeat the Torth Empire?"

A tough question. Thomas leaned back in his hoverchair and wrapped his arms around himself, chilled by the ocean air. "Different people would give you different answers to that. I calculate our chances of victory to be around three or four percent."

She raised her brow ridges. "That little?"

"Given the knowledge I have now," Thomas replied. "Yes. But I would have said it was zero percent if you'd asked me when I was a Yellow Rank. Things change. It depends on what happens."

"What if we follow the prophecies?" Kessa asked.

"I'm not allowed to look at the prophecies," Thomas reminded her. "So as far as I'm concerned, they're not helpful."

He tried to suppress his bitterness. He needed to mentally adjust to obeying Garrett's whims. Perhaps if he was lucky, the old man would let down his guard enough to share a few secrets.

"Anyway," Thomas said, "according to Evenjos, the prophecies are no guarantee. At best, they're a sketchy guidebook."

"So you believe the Torth have us outmatched?" Kessa said.

"Undoubtedly," Thomas replied.

"But they do not have an Ariock," Kessa pointed out. "Or an Evenjos."

Thomas hesitated. It felt strange to divulge the concerns he would normally not share with anyone. Why share a problem he had yet to solve? All that would do was spread worry around.

But he had promised to answer Kessa's questions.

"You do not believe that Ariock and Evenjos can win this war for us?" Kessa peered at him. "Why not?"

"As individuals," Thomas said, "they each wield great power. But individuals have specific points of failure that can be exploited." He floated farther down the beach, with Kessa strolling alongside his hoverchair. "On Earth, there is a myth about a superpowerful man named Achilles. His body was impervious to danger. Except for one spot: his heel."

Kessa was familiar with all sorts of myths and legends. Whenever ordinary slaves dealt with gods or monsters, the supernatural deity often had a fatal flaw. How else could they be tamed or defeated?

"You are saying that Ariock and Evenjos have a fatal flaw?" she asked.

"They each do," Thomas acknowledged.

He sensed Kessa wondering how far she dared to take this line of questioning.

"It's a loosely held secret," Thomas said. "They know their own flaws, and Garrett and I know, as well. And I'm sure the Torth supergeniuses will guess how to defeat them, if they haven't already. But I don't think it should become common knowledge."

"That is fair." Kessa inwardly made her choice. "I will be careful. Please tell me."

Thomas knew that Kessa would stay out of range of the Torth prisoners. In any case, after a few more battles, enemy Torth would be able to start making insightful guesses.

"For Evenjos," Thomas said, "sleep or power depletion means certain death."

Kessa was startled. "I did not know."

"That's why she is terrified of the inhibitor serum," Thomas explained. "For any other Yeresunsa, the inhibitor entails powerlessness and defeat, but for her, it is the end. She won't go into up-close combat."

"That makes sense." Kessa was thoughtful, and Thomas sensed her inwardly revising her opinions about the Lady of Sorrow.

"Ariock's flaw," Thomas said, "is that he's too human. He has literally more power than a person can safely wield. He's good at wielding it. But he will always be prone to getting distracted, or losing his temper. Or getting overconfident, or underconfident. His human mind is one of his strengths. But it's also his weakness."

Kessa could not deny that.

"And," Thomas said, "like any mortal being, Ariock cannot survive without periods of sleep and other survival basics. He's mortal. He has mortal vulnerabilities."

Kessa nodded her understanding. "The Torth Megacosm does not have needs like that."

"Right," Thomas said. "I can think of ways to exploit the flaws of Ariock and Evenjos. That means the Torth supergeniuses definitely can. And I can't compete with the Torth in terms of sheer knowledge resources. I don't have constant access to the Megacosm. I haven't soaked up as many basic facts about the universe as a three-year-old Torth supergenius. So, in conclusion, we are badly outmatched."

"I see." Kessa did not volunteer her reaction, and Thomas didn't pry.

After a moment, Kessa asked, "How can we win?"

The answer was not a secret. "We need Torth on our side." Thomas had explained that during their first war council, and he had reiterated the idea several times.

"That is the only way?" Kessa radiated disbelief. The notion must sound unthinkable.

Unfortunately, it sounded unthinkable to everybody.

"Yes," Thomas confirmed. "As far as I can see."

"I have put many of our Torth prisoners to work," Kessa said, and Thomas glimpsed chain gangs of prisoners in her mind. Her lieutenants forced Torth to dig latrines, pave roads, finish apartment buildings, and perform other unpleasant labor.

"They are not happy about it." Kessa's tone was ironic. "I would not put weapons in their hands."

That was an understatement. Overseers with blaster rifles watched the prison work crews. The overseers kept their distance. No one dared allow the prisoners to read their minds, just in case that gave the Torth a chance to attack or escape.

"I know." Thomas slumped. "It could have been easy if I'd thrown all my trust in the Upward Governess without reservations. Then I would have had Ariock whisk her away somewhere safe, and she'd be on our side, and a lot of her orbiters would have followed where she led. We could have gained a flood of allies."

"I am sorry." Kessa gave him a look of commiseration. "But you did not fully trust her. Is that right?"

Thomas gave a nod of acknowledgment. "I didn't fully know her. Torth do a lot of self-deception to survive. It's a way of life for them. So I couldn't know if she was trustworthy until . . . well, until it was too late."

Kessa was silent for a moment. Thomas sensed her thoughts at work, reprioritizing questions.

"How do you believe we can convert Torth into friends on our side?" she asked.

It was an excellent question.

Thomas wished he could offer a brilliant answer. Without his former mentor, it seemed hopeless.

"I've soaked up two hundred and ninety thousand lifetimes of knowledge," he said, "and I can't think of a way. I pinned all my hopes on a high-profile Torth joining us and illuminating the way for others. But . . ." He shrugged in defeat. "It didn't work out."

"Can you not manipulate public opinion in the Megacosm?" Kessa asked. "Show the other supergeniuses that you are healthy and happy. Offer them the same."

Thomas chuckled. "I've done that today, for a few seconds here and there, off and on. It's already having an effect." He had enjoyed the seething, barely hidden envy of his supergenius peers. "But unfortunately, the Torth Majority is now on guard for defectors. They won't let their supergeniuses go rogue. If any high-value military asset shows the least sign of wanting to switch sides, the Majority will have them killed rather than take the risk that they might join me."

Kessa clicked her beak in frustration. "And we cannot save them?"

"We don't know their locations," Thomas said. "They likely aren't privy to their own location information. And they're under guard. There will be guns aimed their way. If they cry out in the Megacosm, begging for rescue—even if they send us an accurate map, even if one of us is paying attention in that exact moment—we won't be quick enough. Ariock needs time to learn a new galactic route. He can't teleport instantaneously to any random place in the universe."

"I see." Kessa looked defeated. Then a new idea occurred to her, and she perked up. "What about—"

"There will be Torth separatist movements." Thomas answered her question before she could finish asking it out loud. "I don't see them yet, but I do expect the empire to start breaking apart if we keep hammering at it. That will weaken them. But even so, any large faction will still be stronger than we are right now. And factions tend to team up against a common enemy." He indicated himself. "A broken empire isn't enough. That could be temporary. We absolutely need strong Torth allies on our side."

Kessa tapped her beak. "Hmm. Are you certain it is possible to gain friendly Torth? Even though you cannot think of a way?"

Thomas had trouble justifying his certainty, yet he could not shake it. The Torth were the descendants of ordinary, downtrodden commoners. Not monsters. They had become monsters. But they had not started out that way.

His mother had sacrificed everything to give him a chance at life. And she had been a clone sister of the Swift Killer.

There was humanity buried in many Torth. He felt sure of it.

"Yes," he said.

Kessa gave him a skeptical look.

"I'm just not the right person to figure this out," Thomas explained. "That doesn't mean it's unsolvable. Most of my knowledge comes from the months I spent immersed in the Megacosm. That's a lot of facts about the universe, but not a whole lot about friendships or emotions."

Kessa found that interesting. "So your emotional intelligence is not on the same level as the rest of your intelligence?"

"That's a good way to put it," Thomas said. "Exactly."

"All right," Kessa mused. "Well, then. Who would you go to for advice of this nature?"

In the past, Thomas would have recommended Cherise without hesitation. She used to have insights about him.

But now?

Even if Cherise suspected that Torth could be turned into allies, even if she secretly trusted Thomas, she would never say so out loud. Not in front of her Alashani boyfriend. Anyway, Thomas could no longer presume to know what was going on inside her mind.

"You," Thomas told Kessa. "If anyone can figure it out, it's you."

Kessa gave him a worried frown of doubt. He sensed her curiosity, her quest for more answers.

"I'm sorry," Thomas said. "Ask me scientific facts. Ask me for secrets of the universe. I can tell you quite a lot. But some things are mysteries even to me."

CHAPTER 11

VOLITION

Kessa asked about the infrastructure of the Torth Empire, in the context of conquest. She wanted to understand supply lines. Baby farms and pedigrees. Munitions factories. Slave-breeding programs. Her questions were nonstop and relentless. Clearly, her main focus was on sizing up the enemy.

Thomas answered everything. As Kessa herself had said, she had waited a long time for answers. She deserved them.

Besides, she was a leader. She ought to be included, whether or not the rest of the war council respected her.

Thomas sipped wine as they talked. He forced himself to slow down, though, because he wanted to stay somewhat alert. Power was new to Kessa. It might take her a while to get comfortable wielding it. They fought for the same overarching goal, but within that, her interests might not always align with his.

He just hoped Kessa would remain tactful and stay away from questions of a personal nature.

"I have a team setting up a preliminary neuroscience lab," Thomas said in response to her latest question. "We need to experiment with neurotransmitters if we're ever going to figure out a way to block the inhibitor. But we're starting from scratch there. It's a long shot. In contrast, our communications team is working with existing knowledge. Setting up a global communications network is more a matter of labor than research. And that's a superhigh priority, because we absolutely need to catch up to the level of tech that the Torth can wield. If we can't even—"

"Thomas!"

He rotated his hoverchair and saw Evenjos, aglow with an unearthly light. Her gown and hair flowed in the breeze. She was beautiful in a more wholesome way than usual.

Thomas could see why people used to worship her. He felt a worshipful urge, given what she had done for him.

Her soft glow reflected on Ariock's leatherwork outfit. Since Ariock was much taller, his upper body and face were lost in darkness.

And there was Garrett, struggling to keep up behind Evenjos and Ariock. He must still feel weak, or he would have imbued his elderly body with youthful vigor and agility. Instead, he hobbled through the sand, leaning on his staff.

"Thomas, are you well?" Evenjos rushed to him. "How do you feel?"

She leaned close, examining his body, then his mind. Thomas sensed her concerns. Although she had done regeneration healing before, she had never worked on a patient with so many entrenched genetic factors, or anyone with a severe neuromuscular disease. She worried that the pain might have permanently scarred his psyche.

"I'm all right." Thomas had compartmentalized the agony. To him, the memory of pain was reduced to meaningless data, like a nightmare. He didn't plan on dredging it up ever again.

Evenjos continued to examine him, looking for any hint of an error or unforeseen consequences.

Thomas gathered all his bodily strength and wrapped his arms around her in a fierce hug. Evenjos squeaked in surprise.

"Thank you," Thomas said.

Mere words were inadequate. Evenjos had gifted him with physicality, a whole new way to express emotion. A brand-new future stretched out before him, with infinite possibilities. He would grow stronger instead of weaker. Everything he did from now on would be owed, at least in part, to the regeneration healing she had given him.

Thomas trembled and sweated from the effort of the hug. He had to slump, exhausted. But it had been worth it.

Evenjos gently embraced him. "You gave me a future, too." Her smile was tender. "We saved each other."

So they had.

Thomas recalled the painting from the book of prophecies, in which Evenjos had stood triumphant over him, her hair in a ponytail. "*The Transformation of Wisdom.*" Garrett had announced that painting's title with a smug sense of irony.

Garrett had misinterpreted it.

And so had Thomas. They had both assumed, wrongly, that Evenjos intended to torture Thomas, or harm him in some way. Instead, she had literally transformed him.

"Thank you." Thomas included Ariock and Garrett in his gaze as well as Evenjos.

Ariock bent to study Thomas. He tried to look pleased, but Thomas detected a mountain of concern. Ariock thought Thomas still looked like a sufferer, painful to look at, with his bones elongated and a lack of muscle tone and fat.

Also, Ariock had overheard people exclaiming about the *rekveh* handing out favors willy-nilly. He was afraid that he might have done permanent damage to his friend.

"You're very skinny," Ariock said worriedly.

Thomas sipped wine. "Don't worry. I'll put on weight quickly if I eat a quarter as much as you do."

That amused Ariock. He straightened, thinking Thomas must be joking about having a healthy appetite.

"What are you drinking, boy?" Garrett snatched the cup out of Thomas's grasp. He took a swig of the wine and made a face, as if it was unexpected. "I'm going to set some ground rules."

Thomas sighed.

"You will not use toxic substances." Garrett emptied the cup and tossed it aside. "You will not do anything that impairs your ability to think."

Thomas had gotten drunk specifically in anticipation of this rule, because he wanted to experience a buzz just once. Still, he felt a little bit nettled. He had hoped that Garrett would be lax about vices, since the old codger had so many of his own.

"What if I'm in a situation where a painkiller will help me think better?" Thomas asked.

Garrett glared. After a moment, he relented. "All right. But only in situations where it is absolutely necessary."

Thomas reminded himself that limits were part of being a slave. He needed limits. That was the whole point.

"Another ground rule," Garrett said. "A big one. You will not harm me, or kill me, or scheme against me. You will not plot ways to escape your slavery."

Ariock gave Garrett a look of consternation.

"Yup," Thomas agreed.

"You will not harm anyone here," Garrett said.

Thomas rolled his eyes. "Jeez, what do you think I am? Of course I won't."

"You will not brainwash any of us," Garrett commanded. "You will not zombify me, or any one of our allies."

Thomas gave him a withering look. He wasn't the Death Architect.

"I need an answer," Garrett said.

"Yes, Master." Thomas made his tone just as grating and pedantic as Garrett's. "I will not destroy the minds of anyone we care about. I promise. I'm on your side."

"Mmm-hmm. Okay." Garrett dared to limp one step closer. "Another ground rule: if you happen to learn anything personal about me, you will not share it. Not with anyone."

Thomas hesitated.

Kessa clicked her fingertips together.

Ariock saved them. "That's too controlling," he told Garrett. "I want to be able to trust Thomas. That won't work if you force him to withhold information."

No doubt Ariock was thinking of the book of prophecies. He wanted access to that book as much as Thomas did.

"I am certain that Thomas will be respectful of your privacy," Evenjos assured Garrett. "As he is for all of us."

"Yes." Thomas inwardly reminded himself that everyone would feel more at ease once they saw him being respectful and obedient. They would see him as a meek prisoner, seeking atonement, instead of as a manipulative, powerful *rekveh*.

Any use of force should be Ariock's domain. He was in charge. The decisions were his.

Garrett looked cranky, but he glanced at Ariock and seemed to decide the argument was not worth forcing. "Fine." He turned to Thomas. "Then you will not probe my mind."

Thomas rolled his eyes, but he supposed that limit was semireasonable. "Yes, Master."

Evenjos tried to interrupt. "Thomas needs rest. As do we all."

"I'm not done." Garrett leaned on his staff and scrutinized Thomas. "How's your mental health, boy?"

Thomas resisted his urge to plunge into Garrett's mind and yank out his intentions. "What do you mean?" He had a guess, but he remained calm and pleasant.

"Are you brain damaged?"

"Hm." Thomas swung his legs, enjoying the power of being able to set his own limbs in motion. "I don't think so. I doubt it."

Garrett's gaze sharpened. Even Ariock, Evenjos, and Kessa looked newly concerned.

"What does that mean?" Garrett asked with suspicion. "It's a simple question. Are you brain damaged? Yes or no?"

"It's not a simple question for me," Thomas said. "I don't detect any problems upon running a cursory self-examination. But I have a lot of memory." That was an understatement. "A cursory analysis excludes checksums and hash functions to test data integrity. In theory, it's possible for me to forget entire lifetimes, or whole talents, without being aware of the loss until I try to call upon it."

Garrett stroked his short beard. "It sounds like you would need to do a scan for the probability of errors, I guess?"

"Pretty much," Thomas said. "And then I'd have to compare it against the statistical probabilities from before."

"How long would that analysis take?" Garrett asked.

Thomas internally began some calculations and estimates.

"Oh, come on," Ariock said. Clearly, he thought this was a pointless waste of time. He was mistaken.

Garrett, at least, was not underestimating the enemy supergeniuses. Garrett was likely to make other mistakes, but he seemed to have a realistic assessment of the dangers posed by the Torth Empire.

"Forty-nine days," Thomas said. "Give or take eighteen hours. That's assuming I perform normal functions and duties at the same time. If I prioritize this diagnostic check and deprioritize everything else, I can speed through it in less than two weeks."

Garrett waved that away. "Nah." At least his priorities were in the right place. "Will this diagnostic process impair your normal mental performance? I mean, will it entail lag time in your processing speed?"

"On the order of nanoseconds," Thomas replied. "Not much."

"All right." Garrett made an imperious gesture. "Get it started."

Thomas began to painstakingly filter his memories. He compared similar encounters, as well as similar subject matter and similar webs of acquaintances. Once he'd smoothed out the kinks in the process, he reduced it to background automation, equivalent to having a song stuck in his head. A mental alert would blare if his algorithms stumbled across any hint of a hole in the data stream.

"Tell me as soon as you have the results," Garrett said.

"Will do," Thomas said.

Ariock hooked his hands on his belt, shaking his head in disbelief. "Do you really think this is necessary?"

"We have enemy supergeniuses to compete against," Garrett replied.

Thomas resisted an urge to mediate between Garrett and Ariock. The Torth supergeniuses outmatched Thomas whether or not he was missing a few neurons. This diagnostic would simply reveal how badly outmatched he was.

Garrett made a cigarette appear. He cupped his hand to shield it from the wind while he lit it, then began to puff away.

"Now that the ground rules are set," Garrett said, "let's get down to business."

Ariock groaned. "You've got to be kidding."

Garrett turned to give his great-grandson a tolerant look. "You are welcome to go off and do your own thing."

"We need rest," Ariock said, insistent. "Especially you. And especially Thomas! Your commands can wait until tomorrow."

Ariock was right. However, Thomas could guess what Garrett was angling toward, and a part of him approved. The Torth Empire never slept. Every hour that Thomas's side put off their own plans, the Torth gained an hour for their schemes.

Thomas wanted to enjoy his new life. But he also wanted to deal with any new, painful commands while Ariock was watching and could intervene, if necessary. He would sleep much easier if he knew what to expect from Garrett.

"I think you can guess what I am going to ask from you, boy," Garrett said.

Ariock and Evenjos were watchful, like protective older siblings. Thomas swallowed a lump of gratitude in his throat. He didn't deserve to have friends like them.

"Yes," Thomas admitted. "I know what you want."

Garrett raised one bushy white eyebrow. "Without a quibble?"

"I have arguments," Thomas said dryly. "And misgivings. But I'm your slave. I will do what you command."

"Excellent." Garrett rubbed his hands together, pleased, as if he had just navigated through an asteroid belt and now expected a much easier journey. "Starting tomorrow, we're going to zombify some of our captive Servants of All."

A vision of bloody carnage surfaced in Thomas's mind. Zombified Torth, imprisoned inside their own minds, dying as flesh shields in service to Thomas's warriors and soldiers. The prophet Migyatel had foreseen a holocaust before she had died.

Thomas was the evil stuff of nightmares. He was the monster that could remove free will and turn people into automatons.

He said nothing.

"No." Ariock sounded firm. "He doesn't want to do that."

Garrett glared up at his great-grandson. "He gave up his volition. Remember?"

"I remember," Ariock said. "I don't care. That's a dangerous path. We're not going down it."

"We have over twenty million people to protect." Garrett gestured to the city. "And a limited number of warriors with powers. We can literally count the Yeresunsa on our side. There are less than twelve hundred."

Ariock's defiance became strained. He knew very well that Garrett had a valid point. As a warrior himself, Ariock felt every battle as a personal risk and every loss of life as a personal devastation. His warriors were a finite resource. They were not replaceable.

"The Torth have at least ten thousand times more Yeresunsa than we have," Garrett said. "And that's not counting all the other advantages they have over us."

"I get that," Ariock grudgingly admitted. "We could use Torth allies on our side. But forcing them—"

"Is our only path to victory," Garrett cut in.

Ariock looked toward Thomas, hopeful. He wanted a solution that did not entail the brutal enslavement of minds. He expected a brilliant plan.

He deserved one.

Thomas looked away, full of guilt and shame and a host of undefined feelings. The Upward Governess could have solved this problem for them.

He realized that he had been idealistic.

He had assumed that tearing a bunch of Torth away from the Majority would restore their buried humanity. He had assumed they would feel safe enough to go renegade once they were out of reach from Torth military ranks and armadas. That should have been enough.

But it wasn't. They still cried for help in the Megacosm.

He did not have the faintest clue how to turn them into trustworthy allies. Unless or until someone figured that out, the Torth prisoners were just baggage.

Or slave labor.

Or minions.

"We'll give it time." Ariock sounded firm, but Thomas sensed his buried uncertainties, and he knew that Garrett must sense that, as well. "We're not going to enslave minds—even Torth minds—unless we have no other choice."

CHAPTER 12

A SLICE OF EMPIRE

There were no more enemies in Skylit Mesa City to kill.

Ariock was an avalanche of violence, but he had destroyed all the Servants of All and Rosies who wanted to challenge his people. It was over. He was done.

For now.

When he let go of his extended awareness, his rage ebbed. He remembered who he was and what was important.

The double-headed battle-ax in his hands vanished. It was forged from pure energy, and when Ariock stopped killing, the weapon ceased to matter. All that was left of it was a smell of ozone. The room was dimmer without its electric glow.

Ariock ducked through the shattered remnants of a stone wall. He had smashed his way through this plaza. A Torth corpse hung, skewered, on a decorative obelisk. White armor signified that it had been a Servant of All. That had been a worthwhile kill.

He backtracked through the wreckage, past more Torth corpses. Most of these were pink-eyed Rosies, the Torth who dressed like civilians yet wielded deadly powers. Rosies could hurl fireballs and tear stone apart.

They were no match for Ariock. Not when he was in battle mode.

Soon he was in the undamaged neighborhoods of the indoor city. Decorative holographs glowed in neon hues, some still showing Torth propaganda. He made his way to the prearranged meeting forum where Kessa would appoint a military mayor for this city.

Conversations quieted when Ariock arrived. People skittered away.

Ariock remembered that he was a monstrous giant, splattered with blood from the Torth combatants he had killed. Black armor helped to hide stains, but it was no disguise. It only emphasized what he was. He had grooved his armor specifically for the purpose of letting blood and gore slide off him.

Garrett seemed to be the only person who had no fear. He made his way through the unsettled crowd and clapped Ariock on the back. "Stellar job!"

Of course, Garrett was used to uneasy reactions himself. He might not look imposing, but he did look like a Torth.

"You get more masterful with every fight," Garrett said proudly. "I wish you could see yourself in the Megacosm. There are Torth who crap themselves at the mere thought of meeting you in battle."

That sounded like hyperbole. Garrett tended to exaggerate.

"Well, maybe only one or two of them," Garrett admitted. "But they're all scared. You move like liquid, anticipating everything, and you're not even a mind reader." He chuckled, apparently in a good mood after winning. "Magnificent."

Ariock used his powers to wipe excess Torth blood off his armor. He gathered the sticky matter into balls and sent them overhead, out one of the open-air windows. He didn't understand how Garrett took joy from such tenuous victories.

"We've won Skylit Mesa City." Ariock lowered his voice, so the mayoral candidates and others could not overhear. "Now how are we supposed to hold on to it?"

Garrett waved as if that concern was inconsequential. "Eh, we'll figure it out."

Ariock surveyed the crowd. This forum was designated as a safe zone for Torth who wanted to surrender willingly. Thomas and Garrett made frequent announcements in the Megacosm: if any Torth wanted to switch sides, they should beg to come to a designated safe zone and kneel before Kessa.

Former slaves chatted with each other, excited about the future. But there were no Torth.

Ariock was especially keen to gain friendly Rosies and Servants. Despite how he slaughtered them, Thomas insisted that it could—it would—happen. Sure, the Alashani warriors might not be thrilled to join forces with *rekvehs*, but how else could they hope to conquer a galactic empire with millions of metropolises and an immense military force?

It had to happen.

But the Torth had to be willing.

Friendly Torth needed to prove their willingness by taking a risk. They had to sneak away from their own kind, sacrifice their status forever, lay down their weapons, forsake the Megacosm, and present themselves as allies.

"That flood of renegades is never going to happen," Garrett said.

Ariock thought of the Upward Governess. It had happened.

But only once.

It was possible that a flood of closeted Torth with emotions secretly hid among the defeated captives, too afraid to risk breaking away. Why couldn't they realize that Ariock's failure to protect the Upward Governess had been a onetime situation? He hadn't known that Torth could teleport. So the conniving Death Architect had taken advantage of his ignorance and engineered a surprise attack. Once.

How often could something like that happen?

The Torth were leaving this planet in droves, taking their personal slaves and luggage. They had prioritized the evacuation of baby farms. It seemed they did not want their enemies to gain Torth children. But they left their technology and many slaves behind—so with every city Ariock conquered, he acquired gadgets, vehicles, spaceships, weapons, and millions of fresh recruits for his armies.

Lone Torth were welcome to show up and surrender.

The Torth Empire might reconquer Umdalkdul in the future, but Freedomland was untouchable. Ariock's main stronghold was located on the isolated planet known as Reject-20, a full seven days of space travel from the nearest temporal stream. He used his powers to check the local solar system every so often. His people used telescopes and other instruments to keep watch. An alert would go out if anything like a Torth armada approached.

So far, Torth could not teleport across the galaxy like the Dovanacks.

So the Torth Empire was entirely unable to sneak up and attack Freedomland. Any lone Torth was welcome to show up at the Freedomland spaceport and willingly surrender to Thomas or Kessa.

Garrett made a pipe appear. "Do you know what happens whenever some random Torth dares to think that maybe, just maybe, they would like to try having emotions and being a slave?"

Ariock looked at Garrett, uncertain where this was going.

"The Majority replays footage of the Upward Governess," Garrett said. "Exploding in gore."

Ariock did not know why Torth cruelty still had the power to shock him. They really weren't human.

"The message is inescapable," Garrett said. "'Try to leave the Torth, and this will be your fate.'"

"It's psychological terrorism," Ariock said.

"Yup," Garrett said agreeably. "Anyway." He stuck the pipe in his mouth and puffed fragrant smoke. "We're not doing too badly. We've won every battle."

Yes. Thanks to Thomas's battle planning and tactics, they had won another slice of the Torth Empire.

They had won another tiny, minuscule, barely discernible piece of a galactic map.

Ariock now protected—or ruled—five major metropolitan areas on Umdalkdul. On top of that, he technically ruled the planet Reject-20. Altogether, he had more territory to watch over than existed on Earth.

He used to assume it must be hubris to be a conqueror, to gobble up nations and claim vast tracts of territory without ever visiting the people there. But now he wondered if most emperors felt inadequate all the time, the way he did. Perhaps many of them spent more time on battlefields than in palaces.

Ariock was not aiming for a throne. He went into battle every day. Multiple times per day.

He did it because he refused to allow the Torth to reclaim any of the people and lands he had taken. He refused to let the Torth reenslave and punish everyone. He had to win, but it was only because failure was unacceptable.

"The boy is making good progress on his superluminal research," Garrett said, in a tone of offering good news. "Soon we'll have a dispatch service, and our cities won't be so isolated from each other."

Ariock couldn't help but snort at that good news. Perhaps the average citizen would enjoy being able to call up their loved ones on other planets. As for the warriors, and Ariock . . .

"So I'm going to be on call?" Ariock said, putting the ridiculousness into words.

"You already are." Garrett pointed to the small speaker embedded inside his neck shield.

"From anywhere in the galaxy?" Ariock clarified. He wondered if Thomas and Garrett had considered the fact that Ariock was only one person. He could not visit every city at once. If the Torth attacked multiple targets, what would he do?

"Well . . ." Garrett paused. "You need to make it mandatory for warriors to wear those things. It's hard when only the premiers are reachable. And half of them aren't reliable about it."

Ariock sighed. That would be a different sort of fight. The Alashani resisted change. He had had a hell of a time persuading Jinishta that long-distance communication was vital.

The Alashani refused to ride in transports or hovercarts. They refused to wear blaster gloves. Ariock was struggling to be respectful of their religious beliefs, but he was unwilling to lose the war because they avoided "evil" Torth technology.

"Superluminal communications will erase one of the biggest advantages the Torth have over us," Garrett said. "We'll have a news network. A real one. Like, galaxywide radio broadcasts."

Ariock could embrace that as an advantage. He had no idea what was happening on Reject-20 right now. Or Earth, for that matter. It would be nice to be informed without needing to go into a clairvoyant trance and ghost across the universe.

Ghosting was a drain on raw power. Only Ariock could afford to do it frequently.

He had already scanned the solar system outside Umdalkdul a few hours ago, to make sure there were no comet-class warheads or other dangers heading his way. Space scans were becoming part of Ariock's daily routine. He shoved away Torth space armadas whenever he encountered them—and he had taught the Torth Empire a lesson, in that regard. The Torth had ceased trying to approach Umdalkdul or Earth with dreadnoughts or swarmships. But they owned overwhelming forces. They kept raiding the cities Ariock held.

"What about Evenjos?" Ariock strolled toward an outdoor balcony so he could gaze at the limestone buildings shining white under the desert sun. "Is she going to wear a com and finally go into battles, like the rest of us?"

Garrett must have picked up on his bitterness. "You're not being fair to her." He followed Ariock onto the balcony. "The inhibitor can kill her in a much more instantaneous way than it can kill you or me."

"So she's afraid to die," Ariock said dryly. "That makes her different or special—how?" He planted his armored hands on the limestone balustrade, leaning on it so he could gaze at the newly liberated city. "I'm afraid to die in battle. So is every warrior. We don't let that stop us."

Ariock suspected that the former goddess-empress just didn't want to get bloodstains on her immaculate wings. She could be a military powerhouse if only she would dare to take risks.

"Evenjos was tortured," Garrett said in a strained tone. "Can you blame her if she doesn't want to jump right into the brutality of war? She's in the prophecies of Ah Jun, and that didn't go so well for her last time. If you were a mind reader, you would see . . ." He stopped himself and took a deep breath. "She has suffered more than any living being has ever suffered, Ariock. Cut her some slack."

Ariock supposed Garrett was right. Evenjos was still acclimating to the modern era. Perhaps she would get over her fear and decide to fight in battles?

Eventually.

"Be kind to her," Garrett urged. "She is not our enemy."

"I know." Ariock slumped, remembering that Evenjos had led the regeneration healing to save Thomas's life. She was definitely an ally.

He just felt so frustrated and tired all the time.

"We're stretched thin." Ariock gazed at aliens on a distant plaza. They were partying, celebrating freedom, in the terraced gardens. He wondered what their names were, what their stories were. "The Torth still rule most of Umdalkdul. I don't see how we can conquer another city without losing one we already have."

Garrett gave Ariock a knowing look. That was enough to summarize an argument that they kept having.

"No," Ariock said.

"You know I'm right," Garrett said. "The boy knows it, too."

Ariock observed shackled Torth prisoners in the distance, trudging toward a holding pen. Later, he would export those conquered prisoners from this city to a slum outside Freedomland on Reject-20. Former slaves would then oversee them.

The former Torth hoed dirt. They washed laundry. They sowed fields.

People called them "penitents" instead of Torth, because they looked too pathetic to be gods. They were bedraggled and clumsy. Children threw stones at them.

But even that existence was better than zombification and the total loss of independence.

At least a penitent Torth had a hope of working his or her way toward redemption. They still had free will.

"We can have disposable armies," Garrett said, as if to entice Ariock. "We don't have to risk our warriors in every battle."

"No," Ariock said.

Yet . . . how nice would it be, to tell Jinishta and her overworked warriors that they could have a day off? Fewer than twelve hundred warriors and a few thousand soldiers could not protect countless cities. Every one of them was working double and triple shifts.

They could not protect the entire galaxy.

"How about those prophecies?" Ariock asked. "Is there any hint of how we're supposed to win?"

"Zombies." Garrett stated it like a fact.

"Are you saying they're in the book of prophecies?" Ariock wished he could see the next major painting. He longed for hints about the best course of action.

"They're there." Garrett puffed furiously on his pipe. "But sometimes it's best to work without a deluge of easily misinterpreted clues. Trust me. Just like some things are better left unsaid, some knowledge is best left unknown."

That was easy for a know-it-all mind reader to say.

Ariock assessed his great-grandfather, wondering if there was any reasonable way to pressure him to share the book.

"If I knew anything helpful," Garrett said, "I would tell you. I promise. But the book doesn't reveal much about our next step. There are small panels showing zombified hordes, so I sincerely think that has to happen."

Maybe he was telling the truth.

Maybe.

Ariock was tired of prying information out of his mind-reader friends. It wasn't just Garrett. Thomas, too, had nothing new to say. Whenever Ariock asked him about Torth allies, Thomas hunched his shoulders and looked hounded. His shame was obvious.

According to reports, one penitent Torth had strangled a child to death.

The victim was one of those who pelted mind readers with stones. Apparently, the overseers had been distracted, and a child had made the mistake of straying too close to a chained crew of penitent laborers.

There were no miraculously friendly Torth.

Incidents like a penitent murdering a child sparked anger. If incidents like that happened more frequently—and they would, if the populations kept growing—there could be murderous mobs.

Ariock lifted his gaze to the sky. The moons of Umdalkdul hung visible in the daylight, their surfaces scarred with factories and other signs of industrialization. No doubt they were overcrowded with slaves and oppressive Torth masters.

And Ariock dared not liberate them yet. He did not have enough of a military.

His communicator crackled.

The tinny voice of a dispatcher came through the speaker. "Rare Moonrise MetroHub," the voice said. "Torth raiders on approach! Northwest quadrant. Premier Chaizatel in charge."

Ariock checked to see if Garrett had heard the same alert.

Garrett gave a nod, never perturbed by the idea of killing Torth. He had killed dozens today, yet he looked eager for more violence.

"I knew I couldn't have an afternoon off," Ariock said.

"I'll take care of it," Garrett offered. "I have enough strength left."

Garrett could only teleport five times per day or so. If he fought in too many places, he ran the risk of depletion.

Ariock could not afford to lose him. In battle, Garrett was almost as effective as Ariock himself.

"You stay here," Ariock said. "Protect Kessa and make sure everything goes smoothly for the new mayor."

"Stay in touch." Garrett gave him a look of concern.

Ariock went still and prepared to teleport. First, he had to clear his mind of troubled thoughts. Evenjos. Superluminal communications. Thomas's foolproof battle strategies, with no long-term plan. Even if they kept winning, Ariock felt as if their territories hung by a thread.

All the Torth had to do was push slightly. Threaten Earth. Learn interstellar teleportation. Invent a new superweapon.

Whatever they did, it would knock Ariock and his forces over like a row of dominoes. And no one else seemed worried enough.

CHAPTER 13

ROSY DEFIANCE

A Rosy Recruit known as the Diplegic Settler rode in a military transport, leaning her head against the window. She grimaced from familiar pain. Medicines never quite dampened her bone-deep aches when she was having a flare-up. It was in her hips and knees. Her elbows and hands ached as well.

For combat, she wanted to stay sharp. So she had taken a lower-than-usual dose of her favorite painkiller.

The Giant must be asleep!

We (the Majority) have calculated the perfect time for this raid!

Hundreds of military transports flew into cities the enemies had stolen. The Giant and his powerful cohorts were hundreds of light-years away, safe on that isolated reject planet. It was late night there. If the Giant was going to teleport to the rescue, he would need time to wake up and get dressed.

That time would be lethal to his subjects on Umdalkdul.

The Diplegic Settler felt more alive right now, in this stinky, overcrowded, utilitarian transport, without a single slave to serve her, than she had felt during the rest of her twenty years of life.

She was tired of lounging around. All she had ever done—before learning that she had powers—was sleep, bathe, snack, undergo massages and physical therapy, and shop for cosmetic products. She had shown off her acquisitions to a circle of admirers. And she had passively absorbed a lot of other people's opinions, just like everyone else in the Megacosm.

Now she had a chance to fight for fundamental freedoms.

She might literally save civilization.

Of course she wasn't going to stay home, no matter what her favorite orbiters advised. She was a superpowered Yeresunsa. She could melt or freeze a walkway so fast, anyone on it would die. She wasn't going to sit around and passively wait for the enemies to conquer a city on her own home planet.

And so what if she had to lean on hovercrutches? So what if she was unable to run?

She was one of the elite. Other Rosy Recruits deferred to her. Even Servants of All had to respect her superiority in raw power. Unlike most of them, the Diplegic Settler could put herself into a clairvoyant trance in less than a second. She could ghost to a new location and then yank her body to that place.

As long as she wasn't having a flare-up.

You're too valuable to take risks, her orbiters sang in the back of her mind. *Teleporters should not be wasted on random raids. You (Diplegic Settler) ought to wait for one of the supergeniuses to devise a more effective strategy.*

No. The selfish Betrayer needed to be shown that his aggressive greed was unacceptable. The enemies could not expect to keep every piece of property they had stolen. They could not keep taking and taking.

The goal, as decided by the Torth Majority, was to exhibit strength.

If the city was bombed into oblivion? That was acceptable. Slaves would be forced to rebuild and repair damaged cities after the Torth Empire won.

The runaways are softened up. Her local sector of the Megacosm shared images of terror. Grenades exploded. Runaway slaves—or "liberated people," as they wrongly thought of themselves—struggled in rubble or screamed from injuries. They were, indeed, softened up.

Attack! the Majority commanded.

The remaining transports docked at roofs and balconies. Red Ranks spilled out, armored and eager to wreak havoc.

Remember Our objective, Torth silently chorused to each other.

Grab runaways.

Load them into cargo transports.

Get out fast—

—before the Giant can show up!

The Diplegic Settler followed her fellow raiders out of the transport and onto a terrace. She savored the sensation of warm wind. The evening had a dry mineral smell, unlike the swampiness of her home city.

An enormous audience began to pile into her mind. A lot of distant Torth wanted to experience this raid from her point of view.

She tucked hovercrutches under her armpits, with a couple more strapped to her forearms, for balance. That helped her to walk.

She didn't need to be agile or graceful. Let the Red Ranks grab runaways and chain them up. Her job was to seek and kill more dangerous foes.

Treat all albinos as dangerous combatants, the Majority reminded the raiders.

The Betrayer would not be so foolish as to risk the Shapeshifter or the Imposter. No doubt those powerful enemies were far away, protected from surprise attacks. Every one of the conquered cities was garrisoned with nothing more than albino menaces.

The Majority reminded everyone, *It is impossible for Us to quickly identify which albinos have powers—*

—and which do not.

So kill their kind on sight.

Many Torth were disappointed because they wanted albino slaves. The Diplegic Settler quashed her own dismay. She had hoped to acquire a pair of the harmless variety of albinos to add to her growing collection of exotics. They looked like silly, delicate imitations of Torth. So cute.

But if she had to kill them instead? Oh well. That was why she was here.

Her inner audience provided her with a city map. They pointed out a target: one of the female albinos, armored in black and crackling with electric energy.

The Diplegic Settler looked for a hovercart. She flared with fire, chasing off a few runaways, and appropriated the vehicle. Soon she was speeding down a boulevard.

It was one thing to see hordes of runaways in news feeds. It was another thing to see them in person.

The ummins wore tunics and pants that were custom-tailored to fit their alien bodies. Belts. Sashes. Head covers worked with embroidery or beads.

Weird. They almost looked like people.

The armored skin of nussians was too rough for most types of cloth. Their overlapped plates hid their genitalia, and as a people, they had never worn clothes. Yet these runaway nussians adorned themselves with cuffs or medallions. They wore beads on their spikes. They looked outlandish.

There were so many of them. Runaways leaped out of the way of her hovercart, but despite their panicky terror, it was clear that they had been interrupted in the midst of running bazaars and . . . well . . . operating the city.

They had been acting like people.

It was unnatural.

Not for the first time, the Diplegic Settler secretly wondered if the Betrayer had some valid ideas about rethinking the way civilization worked.

She had to drop out of the Megacosm to consider such thoughts. Fortunately, she was valuable enough so that no one would judge her harshly for taking a minute of private time. Power meant getting away with stuff.

She knew the Betrayer was bad, of course. Everyone knew that.

The Betrayer had directed his minions to enslave innocent Torth citizens. Everyone heard those prisoners crying for help in the background of the Megacosm, a constant song of misery that no one sane wanted to tune in to.

The prisoners had to fetch and carry like slaves. They were treated exactly like slaves, sleeping in leaky barracks, mistreated and abused. What had they done to be punished like that? It seemed they were targeted simply for being Torth.

Did the Betrayer think he could enslave every Torth in the universe?

That was impossible. It was madness. Surely as a supergenius he knew that?

And yet he persisted. Every day, the Betrayer entered the Megacosm. Sometimes he showed up for a mere second. Sometimes it was minutes. But no matter how brief his appearance, it always sent shock waves throughout the empire.

Join Me. That was his message.

It sent shivers through the Diplegic Settler. It was impossible for her to ignore the Betrayer, because he was no longer physically disabled. His minions had *(worked a miracle)* done something to erase the symptoms of his neuromuscular disease. Without medicine, without technology, they had proved that something impossible was, in fact, possible.

And that begged the question, what other miracles were possible?

What else was the Betrayer capable of achieving?

He had burned his medicine in a fireball. He was lifting weights. Each weight was hardly that of a cup, but even so, the very fact that he could lift things proved that his degenerative disease was gone.

Join Me if you want a future, the Betrayer whispered inside everybody's mind on a regular basis. *If you are weak? If you are sick? If you are afraid? Come to Me.*

What a terrifying, perplexing, and weirdly enticing message.

The Diplegic Settler reminded herself that the Betrayer just wanted to enslave people like herself. He could not be trusted. Everyone knew how he had earned the title of Betrayer. His message was misleading—a means to an end.

He had no idea that the Diplegic Settler used to feel purposeless and unexceptional. She was mentally suited for the action-oriented Browns and Reds, but her fibromyalgia had guaranteed that she would never be granted even that much of a promotion. So she had been stuck as a Yellow Rank—until her dormant powers were awakened.

The Betrayer's insidious message really could have gotten to her, back when she was a Yellow Rank. Might she have traded away her freedom for the hope of physical prowess? Certainly there were Yellow Ranks who would.

She was fortunate, because her life was now imbued with meaning and purpose. She was a Rosy Recruit.

She would not allow the Betrayer to destroy civilization with his whispered promises. She, of all people, understood how dangerous that *"Join Me"* message was. It had nothing to do with altruism. It was merely a way for him to lure Torth so he could imprison more of them and abuse them as slaves.

It was monstrous.

Also, the fact that the Betrayer was cured should be taken as a dire warning, not as a miracle. An adult supergenius was an obvious threat to civilization. The Betrayer had figured out how to annihilate the Torth Homeworld and start a galactic war and enslave gods—and he had yet to go through puberty. His future was terrifying.

If the Diplegic Settler could possibly kill the Betrayer, she would. That was her civic duty.

For now, the best thing she might do was freeze a random albino warrior to death.

The warrior was nimble and fast, almost too fast for her hovercart. The Diplegic Settler gave up on trying to run the combatant over. She coasted and threw her focus into leeching away the albino's body heat.

The albino must have sensed what was happening. Without breaking stride, she threw a lightning bolt.

The Diplegic Settler reacted just in time. She ducked and then found herself shaking with illegal laughter. What a close call! She had nearly died!

Her hovercart spun, and she realized that the albino warrior had shoved her vehicle with a shock wave of telekinesis.

This was a battle. An actual one-on-one battle!

The Diplegic Settler flared thermal currents before she could spill over a balcony. When she rose into the Megacosm, just to get her bearings, a massive audience piled into her mind.

She was more popular than she had ever been! A lot of Torth wanted to see this battle.

The warrior was running away. Either she was baiting the Diplegic Settler, trying to lead her into a trap, or she considered the Diplegic Settler to not be worth her time. Unacceptable.

The Diplegic Settler leaned on the hovercart controls and pursued the combatant down a boulevard. She threw a fireball. The warrior threw lightning back.

They went on like that, exchanging snaps of wildfire or lightning, dodging around pillars or wreckage.

It was clear that the albino warrior was getting tired. She was on foot, after all. She could not run forever.

The Diplegic Settler threw her awareness into a chandelier hanging from the ceiling by a single chain. She leeched ambient warmth out of its chain until it froze and snapped.

The chandelier crashed to the floor directly in front of the albino, who was forced to leap aside and backpedal.

That gave the Diplegic Settler enough time to gather her focus without needing to dodge obstacles or shield herself. She manifested a fireball and aimed a killing blow . . .

Something slammed into her from behind.

It had no weight or warmth, so the Diplegic Settler knew right away that a Yeresunsa had shoved her against the control panel.

She had drilled enough with other recruits to know how to counter this attack. She used her extended awareness to pinpoint the direction the force was coming from. Then she leveraged heat currents into a personal shield and pried the telekinetic force off her body.

As soon as she was able to move freely, she regained her balance, breathing hard. She stared around until she located the second albino. He stood on a balcony overhead.

Two combatants.

Well, all right. The Diplegic Settler felt as if fighting was what she was born to do.

She ripped heat out of the air around the female albino, freezing her in place. At the same time, she redirected all that heat upward in a burst of force. Very few people could channel that much thermodynamic energy so expertly, so quickly. She was a maven.

Although she couldn't afford the distraction of the Megacosm right now, she would replay this moment for her inner audience as soon as she killed the foes. It would be awesome. Millions would cheer for her!

The male albino somersaulted in the air just as her massive fiery blast exploded where he had stood.

Her blast destroyed a decorative sculpture. The Diplegic Settler shielded herself from a lightning bolt. Her eardrums shuddered from the thunder, and the soreness of her joints worsened. How she hated loud sounds.

She sent her awareness into the mirrored floor just as the male albino landed on his feet. She froze that floor so fast it turned white and cracked, emitting a fog of cold vapor.

If this didn't kill him, she might have to put herself into a clairvoyant trance and teleport behind him. That would be incredibly risky. Teleportation would deplete most of her power.

But it would surprise him. Let these albinos try to—

Something tiny pricked the back of her hand.

Her extended awareness evaporated.

!!!

The Diplegic Settler instinctively rose into the Megacosm, sharing her shock. Her orbiters shuddered with dismay.

!!!!!!!!!!!!

She scanned the vicinity, searching for an explanation.

"No." The female albino was unfrozen. "We preserve them, remember?" She seized a spear out of the male's grasp. He had been aiming that spear at the Diplegic Settler with murderous intent in his purple gaze.

The Diplegic Settler desperately tried to expand her awareness. Nothing. She felt trapped.

"Thank you," the female albino said. She was speaking across the room, to an ummin.

An ummin who wore a blaster glove.

He inspected the glove, as if amazed by what it could do. Perhaps the glove used to belong to a Torth child, but it had been altered, customized to fit his three-fingered hand.

This ummin had shot the Diplegic Settler with an inhibitor microdart!

"What is your name?" the female albino called.

"Nainzong," the ummin replied.

"Nainzong, you saved our lives," the albino said.

The Diplegic Settler turned to the controls of her hovercart, but she wasn't quite fast enough. A nussian seized the vehicle and blocked it. Before she could throw it into reverse, the nussian casually shoved her hand away and powered down the hovercart.

The nussian knew how to operate vehicles. Great.

After that, there was nothing she could do. She tried to whack her captors. She fought as they snapped a collar around her neck. She spit at one of them as they stole her arm braces and removed her hovercrutches.

Her frail strength was nothing against a one-ton nussian. He half carried, half dragged her onto a cargo hovercart.

"That one really is a fighter," the male albino remarked as the nussian dumped her into a cell with a couple of other captive Rosy Recruits.

The prisoners were chained too far apart to help each other. The Diplegic Settler leaned against the filthy wall, disbelieving what had happened. She hated how vulnerable she felt.

Maybe she was valuable enough to get rescued?

News in the Megacosm showed that the multicity raid was over. A few Torth had successfully grabbed a few dozen runaways and flown off with them in transports. Not bad. It wasn't a victory, but at least it wasn't a total loss.

The Giant and his cohorts failed to stop Us, her inner audience sang.

We lost a few assets (such as the Diplegic Settler, unfortunately)—

—but

—the enemies will be more fearful.

The Diplegic Settler was nothing but a lost asset. It was as if she no longer existed.

Much of her inner audience leaked away, seeking more entertaining and more relevant hosts. They left her alone. Her mind felt empty. Worthless.

The Diplegic Settler reminded herself that she was not dead.

She was not lost. Not really. That tiny little drop of inhibitor serum rendered her helpless, but that was temporary, wasn't it?

The enemies might force her to perform slave labor tasks. They might attempt to humiliate her. They might even murder her.

But no matter what, she would not forget her purpose.

The Betrayer thought he could take everything. But he could not take away who she was.

He would not have that.

She analyzed the two albinos who stood guard outside her holding cell, deconstructing every little shift in their stances, memorizing their facial expressions.

Her relentless stare made the guards uneasy. That was plain, judging by the way they avoided looking at her.

Don't stare! other prisoners silently warned her.

Don't antagonize the enemies.

One of the guards used powers to send a strip of cloth, like a dirty bandage, toward her face. The bandage wound itself around her eyes.

In total darkness, with only moaning prisoners for company, the Diplegic Settler did begin to feel truly lost.

CHAPTER 14

FREEDOMLAND

The war council was angrier than usual, full of shouts and squabbling.

"They've carried off good people!" a govki elder said, having reared up in order to be seen.

"How are we supposed to protect multiple cities?" a nussian captain rumbled. "There are Torth who can actually teleport. How do we predict that? Or effectively counter it?"

"We need a genius plan." That sarcastic remark came from a premier warrior. She glared hatefully toward Thomas.

People grumbled. More than a few slid their gazes to a corner next to the dais, where Thomas floated, trying to look insignificant and unobtrusive. He was nowhere near the huge meteorite chair that Ariock had carved for himself.

If only he could be invisible. Evenjos was lucky, the way she lurked in the air overhead, unseen and unheard. Thomas and Garrett were the only people who had any clue that she was present.

Thomas wore plain woolens, a humble outfit when compared with the typical council armor and brocades. He had asked his caretakers to stay away, so no one wiped the sweat off his brow or served him refreshments. He tried not to look Torth-like.

Really, he didn't even want to be here. He would much rather be working with Varktezo and other lab technicians, upgrading the communications system.

But Garrett had commanded Thomas to attend the war council every time it met. No doubt the old man was afraid to be the sole mind reader present. He wanted another *rekveh* in sight, handy to blame if things went wrong.

"We hear you," Garrett said. "Believe me, we are well aware that it's hard to defend every city we've conquered."

Garrett had his own junior chair next to Ariock, but he rarely sat in it. Instead, he paced, his staff clacking on the rough-hewn stone floor. He probably believed that he was serving as a buffer between his great-grandson and the angry councilors.

"But it's not all bad news," Garrett went on. "We did capture some high-value Torth. We now have—"

There were derisive cries.

"So what?" an Alashani councilor snapped.

"More useless mouths to feed!"

"The Torth will just send an armada the minute the messiah turns his back!"

Jinishta stood. "With respect," she said to Ariock, "perhaps it is time to abandon the cities we have liberated?"

Albinos frothed with enthusiasm. Some of them had been treated for severe sunburns after standing outdoors in the Mesev Desert for five minutes. They detested the harsh sunlight of Umdalkdul.

"That's right!"

"Let's retreat!"

"Let the Torth have Umdalkdul!"

"Slaves should fend for themselves!"

If the war council was tense, this triggered an eruption. Councilors jumped up, shouting and gesticulating, each one trying to be heard over the others. Former slaves yelled at albinos and vice versa.

"Who are you calling slaves?" a nussian captain roared over the hubbub.

One of the more vocal albino warriors puffed up. "My people do not need to be liberated."

"Your people," the nussian sneered back, "are whiny Torth rejects!"

Garrett tightened his jaw. Behind him, Ariock rested his forehead in one massive hand, his dismay apparent. He had probably stayed awake half the night, struggling to protect various cities on Umdalkdul.

Thomas was tempted to escape into the Megacosm.

He gazed beyond the assembly, beyond the rough-hewn stone pillars that framed the open-air veranda.

Stone buildings lined the verdant hills. Hovercarts and hoverchairs zipped along crisscrossing streets, carrying passengers of various sapient species. The ocean sparkled in the distance.

There were factories and bazaars. There was the albino quarter, where Alashani could drink mushroom ale and reminisce about their cave cities. A construction project dominated one of the cliffside districts—the nussians were building a memorial edifice, dedicated to freedom fighters who had lost their lives.

Much farther away, jumper shuttles and transports were open for anyone to explore. The city lacked a proper spaceport, but Ariock had imported a few dozen launchpads so pilots in training could log some practice hours.

Freedomland was peaceable. Mostly.

Garrett thumped his staff on the floor, trying to regain control of the meeting. "Please. Can we stay focused on the Torth threat instead of attacking one another?"

The councilors quieted a bit.

"The boy is training a fleet of pilots," Garrett said. "Soon, we'll have—"

"Oh, is that what your little *rekveh* does all day?" an Alashani premier demanded. "While we stand guard on that planet with a scorching sky, he plays with transports?"

Shouts of agreement.

Thomas had been flexing his fingers and toes, working on strength. He stopped, aware of the hostile attention aimed his way.

"Let's not waste time teaching slaves how to play with evil Torth gadgets," another albino yelled. "The Torth will always have more gadgets than we ever will!"

Garrett tried to interrupt, but he had completely lost control of the war council.

"You want *rekvehs* to run this war!" one of the albinos shouted. "You will turn former slaves into your lackeys! Just admit it!"

It was like ripping open a valve on a pressure tank. Everyone leaped out of their chairs, bristling or red-faced and shouting. Thomas half feared that one of the outraged nussians might squash an albino or an ummin elder.

Ariock stood. The padded armor he wore was not spiked, but hints of stars glinted in the polished blackness. Cherise had designed the galactic arms on his chest and back. There was no escaping the fact that Ariock looked formidable.

"Quiet."

Ariock used his powers to amplify his deep voice. He simultaneously sent a breeze through the atrium, causing mantles and head covers to flutter.

Everyone went respectfully silent.

"We are doing our best," Ariock said, his immense voice filling the silence. "If anyone is running this war, as you put it, I am."

No one quite dared to argue with that.

Thomas was thankful. The last thing he needed was people blaming him for every loss of life, or every skirmish that went even slightly wrong.

"I realize I have been asking a lot of you," Ariock acknowledged, sweeping everyone with his gaze. "Everyone here is working hard to improve our situation. That includes Thomas." He nodded to the corner where Thomas was parked. "If you have something to say," he told the assembly, "then ask first."

Most of the councilors bashfully took their seats.

One of them, a thin Alashani councilor named Yarl, remained standing, with several of his fellow councilors patting him on the back and urging him on.

"May I speak?" Yarl asked.

"Go ahead." Ariock eased back down into his own huge chair, polished and glittering.

Yarl stepped forward, allowing the whole assembly to see him. "We have heard a lot of promises. For instance, we have been told that there will be an antidote to the inhibitor serum."

"That's in progress," Garrett said with smooth assurance.

Yarl stared at Thomas. Every gaze was dragged in that direction.

"We have been told," Yarl went on, "that we will be able to, uh, 'call up' our friends on other planets?"

"That will happen." Garrett sounded definite.

Thomas was able to nod in affirmation. He had figured out how many interstellar repeaters were necessary, and where they should be placed. He had worked out a scalable system of personal identification. At this point, establishing superluminal communications was just a matter of manufacturing and logistics. His technicians were hard at work.

"We have been told," Yarl said, "that we will have a space armada. And nuclear warheads. And an ever-increasing arsenal of weapons with which to defeat the Torth."

Thomas rolled his eyes. He had not made such outlandish promises. That was all Garrett.

"We will," Garrett said soothingly. "In time."

"And," Yarl said, "we were told that the little *rekveh*, in that hoverchair, will twist the minds of Torth? You say that he can make them obey us? That he can turn them into slaves and weapons for us?"

Silence.

Many of the people on this war council remembered the two captive Torth in a cage on the planet Reject-81. The captives had killed themselves before anyone could do anything to them, but the incident had sparked a lot of rumors about Thomas.

The rumors had grown greatly exaggerated in some quarters. There were Alashani who believed that Thomas could whisper commands to rats and snakes.

They believed he could puppeteer animals from afar and use them as a personal spy network.

"I wasn't lying about that." Garrett sounded frustrated. "Why do you think I asked you to collect and hold Torth who have Yeresunsa powers?"

Garrett could have said that more tactfully. The Alashani on the war council stirred and aimed resentment his way.

"We don't need to resort to that," Ariock said. His gaze settled on Kessa, near one end of the horseshoe arrangement of chairs. "Kessa. Can you please report your progress with the penitents?"

That was an optimistic request. If Kessa had had anything new to report, she would have sent a message to Ariock or Garrett before the war council assembled.

Nevertheless, she stood.

All eyes turned to her. Everyone had an interest in the penitent Torth, even if it was only for the purpose of an indefinite supply of slave labor.

The penitents were not allowed to touch a weapon. They had to obey commands from overseers, and they could not harm or threaten anyone. Nor could they be caught leaking information into the Megacosm or aiding the Torth Empire. If they broke any of those rules? They faced immediate execution.

There were no trials. Justice for penitents was swift and merciless. If it was not always accurate . . . well, that was a form of justice in and of itself, as far as many former slaves were concerned. Slaves in the Torth Empire had never been able to count on justice. Few had even believed in it.

"I am sorry." Kessa bowed her head to Ariock, regretful. "I have put out word that any penitent showing any signs of emotions should be brought to my attention. But . . ." She trailed off.

Ariock studied her. "I guess there are none?"

Kessa paused for so long, Thomas looked at her and dared to hope. Had she encountered a penitent with emotions?

"There are rumors," Kessa said, hesitant. "But when I go to verify them, I find nothing encouraging."

"You're doing well." Ariock's shoulders slumped. "We all appreciate it."

"I am sorry," Kessa said. "So far, I have not seen a Torth with credible emotions."

She took her seat amid angry grumblings.

"Not only that." An ummin elder stood on his chair, trying to be heard over the general sourness in the atrium. "Did you know we had eight penitents break free last night?"

People hushed each other.

"No!"

"What happened?"

The elder realized that he had grabbed a lot of attention. He looked flustered. "Well, we killed them, of course. We shot them with long-range blaster rifles. Otherwise who knows what they would have done?"

Thomas had absorbed that particular incident from the Megacosm. One muscle-bound penitent, a former Red Rank, had battered open the door of his barracks. Eight of the ten penitents on his work crew had dared to shamble outside with him, hobbled by leg shackles. Their inner audiences had urged them to be sneaky. They were supposed to surprise a sleeping guard, steal the guard's blaster rifle, and set themselves free. Then they would endeavor to cause as much murder and mayhem as possible before the forces of Freedomland descended upon them.

Luckily for Thomas's side of the war, the nussian sentry on duty that night had been vigilant and smart. She had seen the escaped prisoners approaching, and she had pretended to be asleep. When the escaped mind readers crept close, the nussian had sprung into action. She had used her blaster rifle to shoot the first few attackers. The ruckus caused two more sentries to come running, and they blasted the defiant prisoners to death.

Thomas figured that sentry deserved a reward or a promotion. He had sent Weptolyso a message about it.

"Why are we even keeping penitents around?" someone shouted.

"Let's just kill the filthy *rekvehs*!"

"If Torth with emotions actually existed, Kessa would have found them by now!"

"They have a point." Garrett turned to Ariock, and his placating demeanor vanished. He gave his great-grandson a hard look. "We need to start zombifying the prisoners."

Ariock's face might as well have been carved from stone. "No."

The war council quieted, as councilors strained to hear what the Dovanacks were saying to each other.

"The time for choice is passing us by," Garrett told Ariock. "Either you want to win or you don't."

"We'll figure something else out," Ariock said. "We'll retreat. I can teleport the population of Umdalkdul to here. I'll teleport the population of Earth here, if I have to."

"That's very impractical," Garrett said, and Thomas inwardly agreed.

Reject-20 was safe . . . for now. But that would not last forever. Once the Torth figured out how to teleport across the galaxy? Or if Ariock's vigilance lapsed for more than a week? Then nowhere, not even Freedomland, would be safe.

Garrett had paced into Thomas's telepathy range. *You know what needs to be done, boy*, he silently prodded.

Thomas gazed at his hands.

He had healthy adolescent hands, with straight fingers, and enough strength to lift things. He could almost take care of himself without needing a caretaker.

He remembered how it felt to be dying instead of living.

He had wanted a future for a reason: to win. Garrett wanted the same thing. They shared that goal. Deep down, Thomas knew that he had run out of excuses for avoiding what really needed to be done.

Are you willing, boy? Garrett asked without words.

If Torth allies did exist in great numbers, they were afraid to reveal themselves. If good penitents truly existed, then they must be secretly terrified. They probably felt trapped in a nightmare.

But Thomas had done everything possible to help them.

He had carried more than a million Torth to a metaphorical door of redemption. He had opened it for them. All they had to do was step through it and embrace their long-suppressed, emotional, human nature.

Instead . . .

Betrayer! The Majority screamed silent invectives every time Thomas showed up in the Megacosm. *Greedy tyrant! We will never be your slaves!*

Thomas had assumed that gaining Torth allies would be easy, just a matter of winning over a key Torth or two. But if they were too cowardly . . . if they still refused . . .

Well. He supposed he might need to prod them with an *or else.*

"The boy is willing," Garrett said. "He knows what we need to do."

Thomas stared at his hands.

Perhaps he would not mind brainwashing the most offensive prisoners—the ones who gleefully replayed the Upward Governess's death over and over, with triumphant repetition. Thomas should not allow the Torth Empire to reclaim territory his people had won with their sweat and blood.

He didn't want the smug Majority to believe they were winning, even for a second. They did not deserve victory.

He would not zombify a lot of them. Just a few.

Just enough to send a message that would reverberate throughout the Megacosm and make every Rosy Rank and Servant of All tremble at the thought of going into battle.

Just the ones who deserved to lose all their freedom.

He nodded.

CHAPTER 15

WHEN STONES WEEP

"Oh, Bringer of Hope! And advisers." A nervous ummin clerk greeted Ariock, clicking his fingertips together. "Thank you for being on time. Will you please wait here? We will bring you the prisoners you requested. They are being brought right now."

Ariock sat on a stone bench cut into the wall. Everything in the prison was large enough for him, since he had carved this entire facility out of bedrock. But it seemed rude to loom over an ummin who was the same size and height as his shin.

Thomas floated nearby, ensconced in a semitranslucent gray hoverchair. Its smoky color suited the dark lobby. Garrett took a seat next to Ariock.

"What's your name?" Ariock asked the clerk, trying to set him at ease with small talk.

The clerk introduced himself. Ariock asked how he had ended up working in the prison.

"Oh, I like it here!" The clerk went on to explain that some people likened the underground dungeons to slave tunnels, whereas others, like himself, saw Ariock's strength here. It made them feel safe.

The so-called Mirror Prison was stronger than any fortress. Every cell was pressure-sealed and walled in reflective chrome plates, to block potential teleporters. Shafts for sewage and ventilation had multiple razor-lined choke points. Sentries squatted in hidden alcoves, armed with blaster gloves or rifles. A huge ramp—well lit and well guarded—was the only point of entry and egress.

No one was going to rescue these Torth.

Ariock wished he could feel proud of his handiwork rather than ashamed. If only the Mirror Prison was unnecessary.

Maybe, someday, it would be.

Alashani warriors approached, their black garb blending with shadows.

"So the rumors are true." Flen looked Thomas up and down. "The *rekveh* does look different."

That was such an understatement, it was almost a jest. Thomas resembled a wraith. He had begun to add muscle mass, but that was only apparent to Ariock and other people who hung out with him on a regular basis.

"Very different," one of the warriors agreed.

Flen smiled. His tight white curls gave him the smug primness of a British judge. "It looks like the *rekveh* still cannot walk, though."

"The *rekveh* is working on it," Thomas said, his tone strained with the effort of politeness.

Ariock had imported gym equipment at Thomas's behest. He had actually seen Thomas stand up a few times, with help. Thomas could now shuffle a few steps, leaning on people for support, like an old man. He made progress every day.

"Ooh." The ummin clerk peered into a distant darkness, barely lit by hovering orb lamps. "Here they come."

Nussians hauled ten prisoners who were shackled together. Despite their former status in the Torth Empire, these mind readers lacked armor, and they smelled awful.

"They are on the inhibitor, of course," the clerk said. A second later, the clerk seemed to recall that his famous guests probably detested the inhibitor serum. He hurried to downplay his statement. "I mean, we keep them dosed, but the doses are probably about to wear off." The clerk smiled with nervous shame. "Whatever you prefer! We will dose them or not, as you desire. I hope that's okay?"

Ariock spoke in a reassuring tone. "It's fine."

Thomas looked like he was preparing to swim through raw sewage.

"Boy." Garrett stood. "Are you ready?"

One of the prisoners flung herself prostrate. "Please." She gazed from Thomas to Ariock with beseeching pink eyes. "I can be obedient. Do not twist my mind?"

Ariock wanted to distance himself from the former Rosy Rank who looked and acted exactly like a pleading teenager. She looked barely older than his twenty-three years. How different was she from a human, really?

"I can be your slave," the teenage Torth pleaded. "Just give me a chance."

Ariock wanted to believe her.

Garrett rolled his eyes. "Oh, wonderful. Here they go, trying to play on your human sympathy."

"I can learn to be good," another prisoner said.

Soon all ten prisoners spoke to Ariock and Thomas, begging. "L e t u s s s l e a r r r n."

"L e t u s s s b e e e s s s s l a a a v e s s s s."

They reached feebly for Ariock's armored boots. Ariock moved his feet under the bench. They sounded just like terrified women and men.

Instead of enjoying the advantages Ariock had grown up with—such as a loving mother—their lives were devoid of anything like that. Was that a crime? Should Torth be punished for having been raised on baby farms?

"I think we should hold off," Ariock said.

"They're lying," Garrett said. "Even mosquitoes and leeches have a survival instinct. They know you'll feel sympathy, and they're just appealing to your better nature—because you *have* a better nature. Unlike them."

Ariock wondered if his great-grandfather ever questioned his own convictions. How could a mind reader be so consistently judgmental?

"They feel no joy, no love, no pain," Garrett said. "No nothing."

Jinishta looked somber, as usual, but she nodded in solidarity. "We can never trust them. They are better off protecting us as zombies."

Ariock had never seen Torth express so much raw emotion. He felt like a monster. A glance at Thomas confirmed that he was not the only one with doubts.

"Listen, Ariock," Garrett said in a grandfatherly tone. "You have a lot of sympathy in you. They know that. Don't let them fool you!"

"P l e e e e a s e."

"W e e e c a n b e e e o o o o b e e e e d i e n n n t."

"H h h a v e m e r r r c c c y?"

Ariock shut his eyes. If only he could shut down his doubts.

The dungeons were full of edge cases. Penitents who disobeyed orders would be executed, of course. But sometimes there was nowhere better to put an ill or injured penitent. Those who were ill-suited for manual labor ended up here in the Mirror Prison.

"The problem with Torth is that they're parasites." Garrett's tone became hard. "They live to survive and multiply, and that's all they do, without contributing another thing to this universe. They leech off everyone. What happens when there's nothing left to leech off?"

Sometimes Ariock wondered what was wrong with Garrett. He behaved like a hotheaded Alashani or a jerk of a human, yet he seemed unaware that he also had more than a touch of calculating Torth coldness. Had he gotten dropped on his head too many times as an infant?

Or what if it was genetic?

Garrett never spoke about his father—a nameless Servant of All. He never brought up his twenty years spent masquerading as a Torth Blue Rank. He insisted that he was perfectly fine.

But there was pain and anger in him that seemed to have deep roots. Garrett's hatred for mind readers was even more acute than the typical Alashani hatred for *rekvehs*. He enjoyed slaying Torth more than anything. Every time he triumphed over a mind reader, he seemed to be triumphing over his inner demons.

Perhaps he was killing his long-dead father again and again.

"I've killed a lot of Torth," Ariock said pointedly. "I've seen them run. But I've never seen them beg for mercy like this."

Garrett lit a cigarette. That was a sign that his nerves needed calming. "Earth is their next target."

Ariock grimaced. Maybe he was being naive, to show mercy to Torth prisoners. But, well, couldn't he hold high-value prisoners as hostages instead of asking Thomas to twist their minds? Could he negotiate with the Torth Empire?

Could he strong-arm the Majority into liberating all their slaves?

"That's why we have to do this," Thomas said in a quiet voice.

Ariock searched his gaze.

"The most powerful Torth won't fear us," Thomas said, "unless we prove that we're serious." He gestured toward the miserable prisoners. "Death in battle is honorable. It adds to status. But to lose free will? That's the opposite of status. It erases a person. It's a fate worse than death."

That did not make Ariock feel righteous. He only felt more monstrous.

"When I twist their minds," Thomas said, "they lose everything. Not only the Megacosm. Not only their personhood. Without free will, they are the equivalent of garbage."

"Right," Garrett put in. "They're basically reject fetuses from a baby farm. Without potential, they can only have value as an organ donor."

"Torth don't have family or friends," Thomas went on. "Volition and status are literally the only things that matter to them. Once I remove those things . . . that means we're forcing them to betray everything they've ever valued in order to obey us as worthless drones."

Garrett smoked. "It's like accruing negative status. It turns them into stooges."

"No Servants or Rosies will want to risk that," Thomas said. "It will cause them to stop fighting us."

For now.

For a while.

Ariock folded his massive arms, trying to contain his sympathy and mercy. Tears rolled down the cheeks of Torth prisoners. They feared an existential end. They would be erased.

That was not honorable or noble.

Ariock remembered when he had been powerless, fighting in an arena, surrounded by silent Torth. Any fight could have been his last. Fear had made him reckless.

But this was not a warrior's death. This was worse.

"Are you sure?" Ariock studied Thomas.

Everyone else had backed away, giving Thomas plenty of room.

"It has to be done," Thomas said. "We're at an impasse otherwise. This allows us to make progress. It will stop their elite ranks in a way that our Alashani patrols can't accomplish." He offered Jinishta an apologetic look. "No offense."

She gave him a respectful nod. "I agree with you completely." She turned to Ariock. "Fear makes a difference."

Thomas floated toward the prisoners. The nearest one mewled like a cornered animal. "No," he whimpered in a voice that was creaky from disuse. "No. No. Please kill m—"

His head sagged to one side.

His empty eyes looked even emptier. A dribble of saliva came out of his mouth. A tear leaked from his eye and rolled down his cheek.

"It worked?" Ariock asked, wary. He fervently hoped that Thomas wouldn't need to do this often. A few zombified prisoners should be enough to scare the Torth Empire for years to come.

He hoped.

When Thomas looked toward Ariock, the freshly zombified prisoner looked in the same direction, perfectly in sync.

The remaining prisoners rocked violently, as if they could wrench free. It was no use. They were shackled together, and heavy nussians pulled the chains taut. Their rusty whispers filled the lobby, in sync as only mind readers could be.

"P l e e e e a s s s s e."

"H h h h a v e m m m e r r r r c y y y."

"It is fouling itself," Flen said with distaste.

Urine dripped out of the newly zombified prisoner's pants.

"That's a normal reaction," Thomas said, "to colossal brain damage."

"How useful," Flen said sarcastically.

Jinishta shot Flen an annoyed look. "This creature might save your life in battle." She gave Thomas an uneasy look of respect. "Will it obey us? How do you prevent it from obeying Torth instead?"

"I'm giving it a list of priorities," Thomas explained, focusing on the zombified prisoner. "Telepathic speech is a lot faster than spoken commands. From now on, it will obey Alashani warriors above all others. And it will kill itself if any Torth tries to take control of it."

Garrett used his powers to unlock the zombie from its shackles. The released zombie did not try to run away. He—it—trudged toward Flen and his friends, then stopped, head down, as if waiting.

The warriors looked fascinated.

"Turn around," Flen told it.

The zombie turned in a circle, over and over, until Flen told it, "Stop."

The zombie stopped in an off-balance position. It held that position, struggling to stay upright, until Flen said, "You can catch your balance."

The zombie obeyed. As far as Ariock could tell, it did not blink enough. Its blank stare made it look insane.

"If we bring them to battles," another warrior said, skeptical, "won't their Torth kin try to rescue them?"

"Not a chance," Garrett said with satisfaction.

"They don't count as Torth anymore," Thomas said. "They're disposable weapons. Think of them as spears."

The warriors seemed pleased. The guards and the clerks seemed pleased. Garrett was clearly pleased.

Ariock gave Thomas a searching look, full of inner conflict.

When he crushed enemies in battle, at least they died as self-aware people. They chose that fate. This seemed immeasurably worse. He wanted Thomas to at least acknowledge that.

Thomas gave him a slight nod. He was beyond telepathy range, but he seemed to hear all the unspoken doubts in Ariock's mind.

"It is awful," Jinishta said.

Ariock caught her gaze.

"I know that," Jinishta admitted. "But we must not forget how Torth treat their slaves. They have sown injustice. Perhaps this is wrong, but I do not think it is entirely undeserved."

She had a point, Ariock supposed.

"If you want to keep Torth away from the people and places you care about," Thomas said, "this is the way."

Ariock supposed that he, too, would avoid battles if there was any chance that an enemy could seize control of his mind and turn him into a weapon against his friends.

That was a nightmare scenario he never wanted to consider.

Garrett had spent decades studying the book of prophecies. Perhaps this was all preordained? Every city Ariock conquered entailed more people to protect, while the Torth had fewer. There was no denying that he needed to reverse that trend.

Ten zombies. That wasn't many.

Ten zombified prisoners would scare the Torth military forces and thereby save countless millions of lives. Ariock had to acknowledge that his friends—and his telepathic advisers—were right.

His shoulders slumped. "Right."

He got up and walked away, giving Thomas room to destroy the minds of the weeping, pleading prisoners.

EPILOGUE

Kessa stood in a supply yard, beneath an oiled canopy that shielded her from the rain. Perhaps her owner used to feel comfy and secure like this?

Her former owner was now one of the penitents.

They worked in frosty silence, laying cobblestones with a rapidity that looked choreographed. Slave collars encircled their necks. Mud slicked their formerly shiny robes.

Kessa figured the penitents peered through each other's perceptions, and that probably spurred their cooperation. Whenever a comrade laid down a cobblestone, the next in line must feel a subconscious prompt.

"They are creepy," the overseer said. "Aren't they?"

Kessa made a noncommittal sound. Inwardly, she admitted that it was true. City slaves endured silent misery, yet these penitents could gossip and complain without their overseers being able to eavesdrop.

Companionship would make dull work seem less burdensome.

And they could scheme in secret.

Filthy and wretched, they still had the power to read minds. That was why Kessa made sure they were separated into crews and hobbled with chains. No one wanted the former Torth to be able to run and attack. No one wanted them within telepathy range.

"I imagine they are calling for help nonstop in their mind language," the overseer said with a chuckle.

This overseer was named Dlaydlum. Although he was a delicate alien, with a spindly, compact body, he used to be a gang boss.

Most sapients found mer nerctans to be intimidating. Dlaydlum had an enormous bony head, dominated by a sharp, sickle-shaped beak. Even a small mer nerctan towered over any ummin, govki, or albino. If Dlaydlum extended his triple-jointed neck to full length, he would be at eye level with most nussians. He should be able to frighten a penitent Torth.

If the mind readers could feel anything like fear.

"We are safe here," Dlaydlum said. "Aren't we?"

"We are." Kessa tried not to think about how precarious their freedom was.

People like Dlaydlum took safety for granted. They had never met Ariock. They had not known the Bringer of Hope when he was crucified, or when he was hiding in an ummin cave, or when he had fallen in battle and nearly been torn apart by cannibalistic apes.

As far as most free people were concerned, Ariock was as eternal and unshakable as the granite cliffs around Freedomland.

People were hardly even aware of the existence of Evenjos, Garrett, or Thomas. There were rumors about *rekvehs*—mind readers—who secretly aided Ariock, but people did not like to speculate about friendly mind readers. The very idea had scurrilous implications.

So perhaps the penitents had good reasons for their silent pretense of obedience.

They tolerated manual labor as if it was just a temporary setback. They worked with dignified expressions, like they expected to be rescued and restored to godhood at any minute.

Maybe they were right.

"Which penitent is the one your friend reported?" Kessa asked.

"That one." Dlaydlum pointed with a spindly finger.

Kessa identified a chubby female penitent with her hair tied back by a rain-soaked rag. She seemed slightly out of sync with the others, missing her turn to place a cobblestone.

"She protected an Alashani child from being beaten by her father?" Kessa asked.

"That is what my friend said." Dlaydlum sounded disparaging, as if anyone who believed such tripe was a fool. "I have doubts. No one else saw what happened, and the girl and her father will not come forward. If they exist."

Kessa studied the idiosyncratic woman on the work crew. This was the fifth report she had investigated, after five weeks of studying Torth penitents.

So far, the reports amounted to nothing. Hearsay. Rumors. No one could verify anything. The penitents would not admit to anything.

But Kessa remembered rumors of Torth with emotions even in her youth. Almost every slave had heard such rumors.

Kessa had witnessed many things that were supposed to be impossible. She used to believe that freedom was a myth.

Anyway, the most knowledgeable person she knew—Thomas—believed the Torth could be redeemed.

"Wait here." Kessa picked up her umbrella and walked toward the penitents.

"What are you doing?" Dlaydlum hissed, extending his neck to follow her for a few steps. "Are you insane? Those are Torth, no matter how chained up they are! Please. Do not go near them!"

Are you insane? Kessa had heard that before.

Her bunkmates in the slave Tunnels had called her insane when she had cautiously approached the enslaved humans. Kessa had ignored the jeers, and in doing so, she had befriended Cherise, Delia, and Vy.

Nevertheless, she stopped well beyond the range of the enslaved mind readers. One did not survive to become an elder by taking foolish risks. Torth could lunge, and Kessa was the face and the voice of the revolution. Any penitent who managed to torture her with a pain seizure—or kill her—would be rewarded with a big audience in the Megacosm. Torth seemed to love feeling important.

"Go!" Dlaydlum was urging the sentries. "Get closer. Guard her! That is Kessa the Wise!"

The sentries moved closer. They thumbed their blaster rifles into a deadly mode, prepared to defend Kessa against any threatening moves.

Kessa held up a hand, signaling them to stay back.

The penitents continued to work as if unaware of the byplay. They did not look up. Even with their hair dampened by sweat and rain, they showed no signs of humility.

"You." Kessa pointed to the chubby woman. "Tell me your name."

The woman glanced at Kessa, her iridescent-yellow eyes shy and furtive.

There were a few penitents with other eye colors, but most of them had yellow eyes. The military ranks—Red, Rosy, and white-eyed Servants—were mostly killed in battles, defiant until the end. Most of the military ranks who survived ended up in the Mirror Prison.

"Your name?" Kessa repeated. She had laid out very clear rules for penitents. They must obey any direct command from a free person.

The woman lowered her face. Her voice was a quavery whisper. "I was Cloud Fashionista."

The penitents did not seem to grasp why individual names mattered, or why simplistic titles did not translate well into spoken language. "Cloud Fashionista" probably included all sorts of personalized identifiers and extra data in the language of imagination. But in the slave tongue? It sounded impersonal, more like a description than a name.

"All right." Kessa sighed. "Cloud Fashionista, did you save a girl from being beaten?"

The penitent grabbed a cobblestone and laid it down, completing a row. She picked up another stone. "Yes."

"Stop working while you speak to me," Kessa said. "Stand up and face me."

The penitent paused, one mud-streaked hand still clutching a cobblestone. She set it down. Then she rose to her feet, hands clasped meekly in front of her. Rain kept her hair plastered to her head.

Kessa felt awkward, sheltering beneath an umbrella while this sapient stood in the rain.

But the sapient was a Torth.

Cloud Fashionista exhibited no shame or guilt, or any emotion. She had likely tortured her slaves with pain seizures whenever they failed to serve her fast enough.

"Tell me how and why you protected that girl," Kessa commanded.

The penitent answered in an emotionless monotone. "I was harvesting grains. I heard a girl pleading. She made loud, rude sounds. The girl's father was whipping her with a belt. I stepped in front of the girl. The girl's father stopped."

Kessa waited, hoping for further explanation.

Cloud Fashionista seemed to consider the chore of speech finished. She closed her mouth.

Kessa imagined the scene. The father, an Alashani man, must have been shocked by the sudden proximity of a *rekveh*. He would have feared a pain seizure or some other evil Torth magic.

No wonder he had stopped beating his daughter. He had probably fled in terror.

"Why did you intervene?" Kessa asked, studying the penitent's impassive face.

Cloud Fashionista shrugged.

Penitents were required to answer questions if asked. But sometimes they avoided speech by pretending to be perplexed.

"You don't know?" Kessa prompted.

"I dislike noise," Cloud Fashionista said in a cold tone.

This seemed to be yet another dead end. There were so many penitents, it was inevitable that some might perform accidental kindnesses, just as there were some penitents who were sneaky or cruel.

Kessa had heard reports of penitents who directed venomous lizards or snakes toward unsuspecting free people. She had heard reports of work crews silently working in concert to attack their overseers.

Had she expected anything better than a Torth response? She began to leave. Yet . . .

Kessa had an uneasy feeling, as if she might be abandoning a hatchling. She glanced back.

Penitents were not allowed to approach free people without permission. Either this incident was a false report, or the overseer on duty at the time must have allowed the incident to play out.

That was plausible. Kessa could imagine a govki or mer nerctan overseer watching a penitent sneak close to a couple of albinos without doing anything to stop it. Not everyone loved the smug, supercilious Alashani people.

But . . . had this penitent really put herself in mortal peril just because she disliked noise?

"Cloud Fashionista," Kessa said. "How did the shani girl react when you intervened?"

The penitent seemed to be searching for a correct answer.

"Did she speak to you?" Kessa prompted. "Did she run away?"

"She ran," came the emotionless reply.

It was possible that this penitent had a whispery audience inside her mind, coaching her on exactly what to say to Kessa the Wise. Perhaps a faraway super-genius was guiding her.

Or perhaps not. Maybe she was telling the truth.

Kessa took a step back, conflicted. No one else seemed to think about these things. No one else seemed consumed by curiosity, wondering whether a penitent Torth had rescued a child, and why. Most people assumed it was a false report.

"Resume your work," Kessa said, and she swept back toward the canopy in the supply yard.

She would have Cloud Fashionista transferred to a new overseer, one who was specifically chosen for empathy.

Kessa had secretly selected volunteers who were willing to look for kindness in Torth penitents. Those overseers, Kessa's lieutenants, would nurture the compassion of their charges, if at all possible. They would treat them like individuals. They would speak with them. And they were instructed to keep audio journals, to record progress.

Kessa suspected that drastic personality changes would take time. Torth would not become humans overnight.

In the meantime, she wanted any potentially emotional penitent to be protected from cruel overseers and the dangers posed by other penitents.

"Yanyashta?" Kessa called to her liaison clerk.

The clerk came running. She was a pink-cheeked adolescent albino, raised in the cave cities, yet she was also a student of philosophy at the academy. Kessa had chosen Yanyashta not for her clerical skills—many people were better with lists and logistics—but because Yanyashta bridged the gap between one type of free people and the other type.

Smug Alashani, who disdained former slaves, would talk to Yanyashta. And since Yanyashta embraced education and admired Kessa the Wise, former slaves saw her as a rare approachable albino. She was perfect for setting up meetings.

"Please arrange a meeting with Thomas," Kessa said.

Yanyashta gawked.

Nearby, Dlaydlum looked incredulous. "The *rekveh*?"

"Yes."

"But why?" Dlaydlum probably could not imagine any possible reason for dealing with a mind reader as an equal.

When Thomas had nominated Kessa for the task of converting Torth into friends, she had assumed that such a task would be far too daunting and challenging for one elderly ummin. She still felt that way.

But she had the perfect consultant: a mind reader who was obligated to answer any questions she asked.

"Um . . ." Yanyashta pulled out her data tablet and glanced through the calendar. "Who else should be there?" The liaison clerk looked pained. She was accepting of all people, but she probably drew the line at free mind readers. "I recommend at least four warriors. Please give me a day to see who is available, and—"

"No." Kessa touched Yanyashta, interrupting her. "I don't need an entourage for this. That really is not necessary."

She wanted a relaxed conversation with Thomas. She wanted to feel comfortable asking him any question she wanted to ask, without external pressures or expectations or listeners.

"You want to see him alone?" Yanyashta stared at Kessa with disbelief. "You know what he can do, right?"

"I know." Kessa touched the ring of scar tissue around her neck.

Perhaps she ought to fear Thomas, the way everyone else did. But Thomas had removed her slave collar.

Anyhow, knowledge was worth a few risks.

Thomas was always working toward some goal. He directed Ariock in battles. He directed Varktezo in science laboratories. Thomas gave people objectives—he did that with Kessa, as well—but that was not a relationship of equals. He treated people like cogs in the machinery of his plans.

Kessa realized that she wanted to find out if Thomas could still grow some more, as a person.

Was it possible for them to respect each other as equals?

"I want you to clear my schedule for an evening this week," Kessa said.

"I don't understand." Yanyashta hurried after Kessa, following her to the waiting hovercart. "Surely you are not going to visit that *rekveh* alone?"

Sentries stared at Kessa as if she had sprouted wings. As far as they were concerned, mind readers were dangerous, even when shackled and exhausted from manual labor. A mind reader could prey upon the deepest secrets of the soul. A mind reader could hurt someone with words and twist secrets to serve their own ends.

And Thomas was even more dangerous than that.

Rumors would ensue. Some people whispered that Kessa was a puppet ruler. If she spent time with Thomas, people would speculate that she remained a slave, despite her fancy clothes. Nobody could be friends with a *rekveh*.

But someone had to stop being afraid.

Someone had to try a new way of approaching former Torth.

Kessa stepped onto the hoverplatform. "Sure," she said. "I am going to invite Thomas to dinner."

AFTERWORD

Thank you so much for reading *Megacosmic Rift*. Your support is like regenerative healing for me!

In the next book, *Greater Than All*, Thomas and Ariock conquer cities and planets, bringing freedom to the galaxy. But can they transform their most hated enemies into friends? If they fail to win over Torth rogues and renegades, then freedom might just be a blip in galactic history.

I'm an indie author. Please recommend this series to anyone who might like it. And please leave an honest review wherever you bought this book. Your feedback will ripple across the internet and make me feel as if I have an inner audience, and I will love it.

If you would like to hang out in the Megacosm, join the Torth Discord server at: https://discord.gg/gDYVXdS2qz, or subscribe to Abby Updates at: https://abbygoldsmith.com/subscribe.

The Torth series:
Torth Book 1: *Majority*
Torth Book 2: *Colossus Rising*
Torth Book 3: *World of Wreckage*
Torth Book 4: *Megacosmic Rift*
Torth Book 5: *Greater Than All*
Torth Book 6: *Empire Ender*

ACKNOWLEDGMENTS

Special thanks to my subscribers and former subscribers on Patreon: Nyroe, Wrath, Godlyskeleton, ryan ukeiley, volpol, NoteOfE, G O L I X T H, KarenSampson, John O'Connor, Adil Riggs, Bunny Waffles, Zak Pr, Josh Cothran, Aqua, Pokey Equation, Xavier Lamphere, Ceagle, The Dargon, JC, Tyler Smith, Sparkie, A. Brown, Pietro Simone, JJBlack, Certa, Jason Gross, Isaac Boyles, faisal, Mitchell, Gres, Grosbilljunior, Orion Mitchell, LiraGuitar-, luke, MrNobody, John Hurley, Chikkane, Jonathan Williams, mythic, TurtleOfRainbow, Andrew Webb, Dave The Technician, Gavin Olsen, Scott Southworth, E, Alexandre Ablon, Conor lennon, Adam Moore, bensorme, Naorke, Sherriff kadir, Corella, Dvn, George Waller, Jack, Jackson Ragland, Derrick McDowell, Philldoran, Alric Good, Joel Wells, Jerry, Notlimah, Timecrafter, Ithri Benamara, F M, Frightful6_7, Jason Denzel, Теодор Жечев, Aph, and Michael Goldsmith. Your support means a lot, and it's hugely helpful to my writer lifestyle. You help me feel legit!

Huge thanks to my readers on Royal Road and Wattpad. I only know you by your usernames, but I've learned to recognize those names. Especially commenters: Cjenx, General Peaceful, Shadow of Marethyu, Zombie Unicorne, Miss Nomer, Smoarville, dishtv, EatMoreVegetables, The Lord of The Cookies, Ghosti, sid_cypher, UpsilionEnlightened, Omni-Origin Perfect-Inheritor, Banarok Lionrage, Raszhivyk, Ars404, Mofy, Megapooz, MicahLM2, playr543, Ceilingfanenvy, Whiplash246, V6ct9r, micpanda, IcefireStarfire, biravincent, _mehatepizza_, ShaunKZ, Rhandyabao5, Joey-Jay_Spooner, Marysiak14, SubZero_005, Kafui27, MelissaKimFernandes, AGENT_88, Art3miss777, DeSmiley, ko0025, lisadavis910, and a whole lot more. I appreciate you very much!

I'm very grateful for consultants. Carl Frederick, physicist and author, helped me with world-building issues. Rebecca Roland, physical therapist and author, helped me to get a handle on caretaking for Thomas. I also learned about spinal muscular atrophy from Shane Burcaw's videos and books.

And beta readers! These wonderful writers and friends offered constructive advice on the first draft of this novel: Ellen Van Hensbergen, Leigh Berggren, Brian Rappatta, Sarah Kelderman, Rebecca Shelley, Susan Shell Winston, Marc Geddes, Jose Gustavo Costa Jr., Ethan Reid, Mike McCauley, Marissa Engel, Colleen Robbins, and also my mom, Judith C. Goldsmith. Thank you so much!

Last but not least, my alpha-reader husband, Adam Robert Thompson, really helped me shape this story. He's the reason the Torth series goes noblebright instead of spiraling into grimdarkness.

ABOUT THE AUTHOR

Abby Goldsmith is the author of the Torth series, originally released on Wattpad and Royal Road. She continues to write novels and has sold short works to Escape Pod and Writer's Digest Books, having attended the Odyssey Fantasy Writing Workshop. Goldsmith is a 2-D and 3-D game animator, has lived on all three coasts of the United States, and is married to her alpha reader.

Website: AbbyGoldsmith.com
Twitter: @Abbyland
Facebook: facebook.com/TheTorth

9 781039 442900